HOUSE
OF
OPEN
WOUNDS

ALSO BY ADRIAN TCHAIKOVSKY

HOUSE OF OPEN WOUNDS

ADRIAN TCHAIKOVSKY

An Ad Astra Book

First published in the United Kingdom in 2023 by Head of Zeus,
part of Bloomsbury Publishing Plc.

9 7 5 3 1 2 4 6 8

A catalogue record for this book is available from the British Library.

ISBN (HB): 9781035901388
ISBN (XTPB): 9781035901371
ISBN (E): 9781035901418

Printed and bound in Great Britain by
CPI Group (UK) Ltd, Croydon CRO 4YY

MIX
Paper | Supporting
responsible forestry
FSC
www.fsc.org
FSC® C171272

Head of Zeus Ltd
First Floor East
5–8 Hardwick Street
London ECIR 4RG

WWW.HEADOFZEUS.COM

I'm dedicating this book to everyone on the
Friday night creatives' Zoom that helps keep me sane.

About the Author

ADRIAN TCHAIKOVSKY was born in Lincolnshire before heading off to Reading to study psychology and zoology. He subsequently ended up in law and has worked as a legal executive in both Reading and Leeds, where he now lives. Married, he is a keen live role-player and occasional amateur actor and has trained in stage-fighting. He's the author of *Children of Time*, the winner of the 30th Anniversary Arthur C. Clarke Award, and the *Sunday Times* bestseller *Shards of Earth*.

Contents

An incomplete list of nations involved in the Palleseen wars of perfection

Allor – conquered, a haunt of conjurers
Bracinta – a protectorate split between Pallesand and Lor
The Divine City – unconquered, a city of powerful magicians
Galletes – conquered, a mobile, island-dwelling people
Jarokir – conquered, formerly a land of many temples
Lor – unconquered, currently at war with Pallesand
Oloumann – conquered, formerly a land of many gods
Pallesand – heart of the Palleseen Sway
Telmark – conquered, a land of proud traditions, including the
city of Ilmar

Elements of the Palleseen Sway

Temporary Commission of Ends and Means – the ruling body
of Pallesand
School of Correct Erudition (Archivists) – responsible for
learning and magic
School of Correct Appreciation (Invigilators) – responsible
for art and law
School of Correct Exchange (Brokers) – responsible for trade
School of Correct Conduct (Monitors) – responsible for
military and enforcement
School of Correct Speech (Inquirers) – responsible for religion,
language and espionage

Regulars (Troopers and Statloi) – the soldiers of the Palleseen army

Accessories – conscripted foreign troops, also known as Turncoats and Whitebellies

From L–R: Trooper Lidlet, Former Cohort-Broker Banders,
Cohort-Monitor Cosserby, Guest-Adjutant Alv, Chief Accessory
'Butcher' Ollery, Accessory Masty, Accessory Tallifer, Accessory 'Maric'
Jack (bottom), Accessory Lochiver (top), Fellow-Inquirer Prassel
Thaumagraph © Adrian Czajkowski

In Forthright Battalion
(Palleseen unless noted)

Caeleen – Maserley's demon companion
Cohort-Monitor Fosby – quartermaster
Trooper Foley – regular soldier
Companion-Monitor Goughry – officer
Trooper Klimmel – regular soldier
Trooper Lidlet – regular soldier
Fellow-Invigilator Maserley – Conjurer
Trooper Paucelry – regular soldier
Statlos Peppel – Watch officer
Sage-Monitor 'Uncle' Runkel – Commanding officer,
    Forthright Battalion
Mother Semprellaime – Allorwen bawd
Fellow-Inquirer Sherm – administrative officer
Fellow-Archivist Thurrel – Decanter

In Landwards Battalion
(Palleseen unless noted)

Companion-Archivist Callow – scholar of sympathetic magic
Cohort-Monitor Festle – Necromantic Unnatural
Cohort-Archivist Hobbers – scholar of sympathetic magic
Fellow-Inquirer Killingly – necromancer
Cohort-Inquirer Megget – Watch officer
Accessory Pirisytes – Oloumanni conscript
Professor-Invigilator 'Old Eyeball' Scaffesty – Commanding
officer, Landwards Battalion
Cohort-Archivist Skilby – scholar of sympathetic magic
Sage-Archivist Stiverton – senior necromancer
Cohort-Monitor Tunly – Watch officer
Zenotheus, the divine scorpionfly – a divine being

Others

The Dread Lord Ghastron – Varinecthes's demonic familiar
General Halseder – Bracite loyalist
Kosha – former priest of God in Ilmar
Varinecthes 'Varney' – ancient sorcerer of uncertain provenance

Hell – The Butcher

He does look a bit like a butcher. Not the murderer sort but the jolly figure serving up paper-wrapped parcels of sausages and ham. A family butcher, so to speak. The sort of man – ruddy-faced, rotund, moustached – who always has a disarming joke at his own expense. A pillar of the community. And that last is true. For a given value of pillar. For his own definition of community.

It is a vision of hell.

The air is made of screaming. Like a picture where the gap between two objects is revealed, after a squint, to be just more of the same, here the gap between throat-stripping shrieks is just less-insistent sounds of men and women in agony. A hierarchy of torment so constant and yet so varied it becomes something close to a choir.

Here, then, is the choirmaster. A great weight of a man who nonetheless passes through the bloody clutter of the space with an appalling deftness. Like the thing in your dream, that cannot possibly follow you into the small spaces, and yet does so in defiance of reason. His bulk is gravity, demanding the attention of everything around him. It's a wonder the rivulets of spilled blood don't orbit him in a wheeling astronomy of gore.

Behind him his minions, his attendant devils, are hard at work. Time enough for them when you've escaped the pull of this man, this bloody-handed emperor, even now stomping to look over the new arrivals thrown to his mercy.

His face is a thing of parts. It can clench like a fist, open like a flower. In other moments, with the rigour of his profession lifted from him, it's a good face. A friendly thing to see. A broad smile, such as might be used to persuade you to open your door to him at night. His moustache, which right now is crusted with red, can make him seem clownish and harmless. The mass of him, which can drive a cleaver through a limb or give bite to the teeth of a saw, becomes the ungainly comedy of a dancing bear. When he wants it to. Right now, though, he's working. The worst kind of torturer, who preys only on those already in agony. No fit and healthy victims come to his dungeon to be broken. He takes the leavings, and his people make them squeal.

Spilling into his tent now: a flurry of men and women, some in full uniform, others stripped to their shirtsleeves. They are whole as yet. They aren't *his*. And those that are his, well, their uniforms are already ragged, holed, sodden, scorched. The fit set down the stretchers of the infirm and retreat. Nobody wants to spend time in the Butcher's company when he's working. Most especially not the howling victims set at his feet.

One figure remains. Uniform jacket open, slovenly, hanging improbably from her shoulders as though it'll slough off any moment, save it never does. She's been outside with the bearers, taking details, and she bends to the Butcher's ear.

"Taking the wall. Caught a bonecutter, then counterattack." The words almost stripped of their regular meaning, a code between her and the Butcher to give him context.

He casts a look over the array of the agonised, a workman inspecting the damage; a clerk, today's agenda for the meeting. Nearest to him a man whimpers with his leg laid open. *Sword-stroke.* Next, the woman without a hand, screaming at the stump. Then three silent ones. He sees where their uniforms are shredded, the ripped edges presented outwards where the shards of shattered bone erupted from *within.* Then the next, and the next. The pucker-and-scorch of baton-shot. The man whose head is laid open so that the jigsaw of his skull is present

2

for any budding puzzlesmith to piece together. The woman – the loudest screamer in the place, whose leg was splinted by some cack-handed amateur who doesn't understand how bones go.

The Butcher works his first magic. The silent man whose ribs were shattered on one side can still be saved for future torments. Blunt-fingered hands signal and that stretcher is hauled deeper into hell where the devils can get to work with saw and tongs. The woman with the shattered arm, she can be saved. She goes to the foreigner with the shimmer skin, staring up with eyes pulled so taut it's a wonder her lids will ever close again. The gutshot man can be saved. He's placed in the far corner for a scouring and a working over, back where a weird old man plays a weird old pipe, skirling and squalling on it as though mocking the screams of the afflicted. It's all a part of the service. A necessary component of this precise and exacting hell the Butcher built.

Those are the highest priority, where a little delay means the difference between live victim and corpse. Now it's time for the Butcher's second magic. His apron is not that of a friendly family butcher. There are twenty pockets in the leather, each with a flap to keep the worst of the ambient weather out, though most have an inch of red at the bottom of them by now. He goes down the line of the brutalised, his blunt fingers finding phials and bottles by long habit, feeling for the nicks he cuts in the corks, to tell him concentrations and active ingredients. A personal love-language of agony and alchemy. The woman without a hand has had the stump cauterised – not battlefield medicine but the side effects of a point-blank baton discharge. She'll keep. He forces the lip of a glass phial to her lips. She chokes, swallows. Her screams fall inwards until their scrabbling fingertips can't reach her lips any more and she's silent. He goes down the line, a bespoke service for each, this philtre or that, based on wound, on whim, on the individual predilections of his busy hands that seem to act on their own recognizance. Sometimes he salts the wounds with powder, stuff that burns and eats away necrotised flesh, undoes the work of energies and corruption or at least staves it off for long enough.

For a couple, the man whose skull is a puzzle with too few pieces, the woman whose innards are not only no longer *in* but entirely absent, he gives a double dose from the black flask. It's not to quiet them. Or it's not only to quiet them. And the noise doesn't get to the Butcher any more. He's been doing this for years.

The man whose spine and pelvis have shrapnelled out through his skin gets a triple dose. He doesn't need quieting. He's wide awake, obviously feeling every shard and chip and razor-edged piece of himself that cuts a little more with each breath, but the screaming has gone out of him. He's already passed into a silence so greedy that not even the gravity of the Butcher can pull a whimper from him.

Last he comes to the woman with the badly set leg. It's a mess. Someone thought they were helping, is the Butcher's guess. Some infantry regular with pretensions of erudition. It's not just that they clamped the leg straight with the jagged ends side by side, like they were trying to use the leg bones to splint each other. It's that the backwash of necromancy from the munition has already fused the broken stumps into a needle-spined fist of conjoined bone. Leave it like that, she'll need more than a cane.

The Butcher looks back along the line. It's under control, at least until the next consignment of stretchers comes in. Behind him, in the bowels of hell, his devils are at work. Cutting, flaying, rending; stitching, severing, scouring; decanting, disenchanting, decontaminating. Practising each their own particular arts, a collection of miscreants and misfits not otherwise seen this side of the army paymaster's rolls. And they know what they're doing. He doesn't need to micromanage them, nor would he even know how in most cases. But this: this he knows.

One heavy hand comes up with a blade: what's a butcher without a knife, after all? He slits away the splint. Beneath it, the breeches are already a sopping ruin. He scowls, the fist of his face tightening further. A jagged gash up the inner thigh that he hadn't even seen, because the professional insult of the badly set leg had demanded his attention. She's been bleeding out all this time.

He looks around quickly. Somehow Alv always knows when he's after her. She's just finished up with someone. Her arm is a mangled mess. One of her assistants is putting it in a sling and her face goes tight every time he jostles her. No screams from Alv. No loss of control, not now, not ever, not her. Just that tightness, like an ambassador who's been served the wrong kind of canapes but won't make a fuss. The ragged ends of her arm grind as the man fumbles the sling. Another tautening of Alv's glitter-skin features. The shout of her foreignness here in a room where most everyone is of one nation.

She comes over, trailing attendants. They're all bloodied. They've been in the wars, if not first-hand then vicariously. He shows her the woman's wound. Alv's tight face tightens a whole extra notch. She's not got much left to give. She nods. Alv is like a goddess personifying grudging adherence to duty. Although perhaps not *that* much like, given that there are at least two actual deities currently in the tent and assisting with proceedings.

The Butcher is a good Palleseen soldier. He has no religion. But he'll use it, if it works for him. Just as he'll use Alv and her particular brand of magical fuckery. He only needs results, not five pages of theory with diagrams showing him how it all works.

Alv kneels haltingly by the woman, trying not to jolt her own ruined arm. She places her good hand almost on the wound. There is barely any blood on Alv. Her pale uniform is almost spotless, and this surely is a miracle far greater than the act she's about to perform.

The Butcher actually braces himself, despite the fact that, of all the actors in this little drama, he's the only one not in appalling physical pain. Alv is doing something to the universe.

5

Some singular trick of her people. Her attendants, who have learned a little of it, look on and try to learn, using some sense they've developed that the Butcher can't guess at. He feels the tilt point. That's the only way he can think of it. Like a cart he was on once, that was going too fast down a mountain track. Rocking side to side. The moment when he understood that the whole out-of-control contraption wouldn't be righting itself to swing the other way again. That nothing was left but the falling. Like that, but with reality. And the wound in the woman's broken leg closes, leaving behind a wealth of wasted blood suddenly robbed of its cause, a crime scene without the murder. And Alv's face pulls like the drawstrings of a bag as the pain hits her. She goes from kneeling to sitting as her own leg opens beneath the cloth of her breeches. Her attendants are already tying the suddenly sodden cloth off. And Alv's done. Has no more to give. They get her out of the way, off to the side, sitting by those who've already been ministered to by the devils and are waiting to be stretchered right back out of the tent again.

That leaves the broken leg, that clasp of prematurely merged bone. The Butcher rolls his shoulders speculatively. He places his hands on the leg, locks eyes with its owner. She's had a nip from his flask by now but she's still very awake and aware of what's about to happen. There's a lot of begging in that face, and it's something the Butcher is very used to. He's very used to not feeling it, not caring. Taking joy in it, almost. The sign that he's doing his job properly, if people are begging him for mercy.

Three tents along, there are torturers. Actual torturers. The scions of the School of Correct Speech ply their trade on captured spies and enemy soldiers, to scour them of useful information. Delicate morsels to be chewed over by the gourmands of military intelligence. People beg those torturers for mercy, too. And here is the chief difference between the Inquirers of Correct Speech and the Butcher: sometimes they are merciful. When they get what they want, they withhold the thumbscrews and the irons and the sparking wires. But the Butcher knows no mercy. His job is to take the injured and hurt them worse until they're better.

He feels out the precise topology of the bones, where they've prematurely merged, the necrosis already seeping into the flesh. Act now, without mercy, perhaps the leg can be saved.

He leans on it thoughtfully, like a carpenter testing a joist. The woman whimpers despite what was in the flask. She has the curse of a good imagination, and the Butcher's philtre can keep her mind from the pain of the body, but not from the pain the mind itself can create.

He rebreaks her leg. A single movement, the fullness of his weight, the brute ape strength of his hands. Part-healed bone shearing from bone, the ragged flesh wrung and torsioned. And then the orderlies – the woman who'd given him the brief, plus the olive-skinned man with the weak beard who somehow always manifests just when he's needed and only then – are hauling her onto the Butcher's table. Fresh meat on display for discerning customers. A kit is unrolled for him, the little blades and the large ones. Clamps and grippers and probes and, honestly, if some prankster had switched the tools of his trade with those of the torturers three tents over, would anybody actually spot the difference? But now that his particular gift for triage is no longer needed, he can't just sit idle. It's all go, here in hell. Even the supervising fiend gets bloody to the elbows in the exercise of prolonging pain.

If you prolong pain enough, after all, then wounds heal and your victims live. Some of them may even thank you. And can the torturers say *that*, with all their mercy? He thinks not.

He does what he can with the leg. He has salts to nullify the lingering taint of necromancy about the wounds, that otherwise would only decay even though he keeps a clean tent of butchery here. He has the old man's incessant, ear-offending pipe, which everybody fucking *hates*, even or especially the old man himself, but which is an absolute godsend. A literal God-send, tolerated here in the heart of the Pal army because the Butcher says so; because it works. He has a box of hungry, hungry beetles that devour dead flesh, that eat the withered fringes of the wound once the necromancy has been scoured away. He has a curved needle and gut thread the colour of snake venom. He has big, thick-fingered hands that are nonetheless nimble as any butcher's when working with meat. And he sets the bones properly, with a little grinding and wrenching. With a certain targeted application of muscular force, pressure of thumbs, clench of his monstrous crusher's hands. He aligns them with the fastidious perfectionism of a clerk lining up his papers with the edge of his desk. He smooths the ragged edges of flesh together and sets two inscribed bone buttons to fasten them together, that will be digested by the woman's blood over a week, and help the muscles knit. He stitches the skin with his poison-coloured thread. No magic there, just a tailor's work combined with the Butcher's utter lack of squeam. He is a man who knows how the sausage is made, in respect of all the many working parts of the human body. His attitude to it all is, he likes to say, entirely sanguine. He enjoys watching people's faces as they try to parse which sense of the word he means.

Then there are the others. The ones who got two, sometimes three, doses from the black flask. It's their time, now. Not because he says so, but because someone new has stepped into the tent, who outranks him and everyone else there.

The grey-faced woman. Not actually grey, although pallid even for a Palleseen. Certainly far paler than the blotchy ruddiness of the Butcher's face even before today's consignment of sprayed blood. Grey in her soul, though. Everyone gets the same impression about her. The Fellow-Inquirer from Correct Speech, come to take her due.

She meets his gaze. Her eyes really are grey, against his brown-nearly-black. They are cold, but he's used to them by now. He's a big man. It takes a lot to send a shiver through him.

He indicates the remaining casualties, the black flask brigade.

Her rightful due. On the forehead of each he has marked a cross in black grease, a sacrament from the lowest and rightmost of his pockets. The Sign of the Forlorn Hope. She nods. She's here because there's a need, and he's only glad that the precise mathematics of how great that need is and how many he had to administer the black flask to have balanced out again. Because some day that need will outweigh his means, and then what will he do?

The grey-faced woman, the Fellow-Inquirer, takes off her black leather gloves. Human skin, some say. Demon hide, claim others. But they're just kid leather, dyed black. And anybody who knows anything about the magical sciences will tell you demons and necromancy don't mix. Opposing poles of the distasteful-but-necessary.

There is a string of tablethi at the grey woman's belt. Golden lozenges the size of a finger joint, inscribed with a word. She mints her own, the Butcher's heard. Uses commands unique to her. Tongue-twisters she practices every night, that nobody else can even say. Not for any particularly eldritch reason but because tablethi are in limited supply and people kept running off with hers and leaving her short.

She speaks the words, bare hands twisting through gestures that aren't strictly necessary but do focus the mind. She is a scientist, after all, and the Pal philosophy prefers to strip away the trappings of ritual from its magical practices. But sometimes a good dramatic gesture, fingers crooked upwards, hands lifting, does wonders for your concentration.

Arise say her hands, even as her mouth says something twisted and harsh.

They get up, those lost bodies. The black flask brigade with the crosses on their foreheads. A symbol known and loathed throughout the army as meaning *Property of the Necromancers.* It shouldn't be possible to slouch *upwards* but they manage it. They stand on shattered legs, stare with closed eyes, with ruined sockets, without faces, some of them. The man with the shattered skull tilts his head as though listening and a motley of fluids runs down the side of his raw face.

The grey woman nods to the Butcher, accepting her due. Those who cannot be saved can yet serve. Once more into the breach – just the once, because repeat necromancy suffers from dramatically diminishing returns.

When she leaves the tent with her new re-recruits, there is a rumble from far away. Not dramatic thunder, but the last flourish of today's allotment of war. And there will be new casualties – there's a whole string of stretchers heading back from the front. Hell will keep working its devils for hours yet, long into the night. But the actual fighting's reached some sort of stalemate or equilibrium, and so hell's work has become finite. An end is in sight, and the Butcher will be able to pack away his knives and potions and clean the blood from his moustache and try to decide if it was worth it, the thing that got him sent to hell.

The Price of Tea

A grey woman. Nothing wrong with that. It was de rigueur for the orderly and rulebound Palleseen after all. An excess of character was in itself a character flaw. So she made herself neat and cleanly, kept her uniform immaculate and had down, by muscle memory, every little tic of decorum. Only her gloves, her aversion to skin against skin, marked her out. And who would want to shake hands with a necromancer?

Fellow-Inquirer Prassel had a tendency to enumerate. Honestly she sometimes thought she should have ended up in Correct Exchange, counting beans and embezzling. It had always seemed the most pedestrian branch of Correct Thought to end up in. Now she could count at least three classmates who were doing *very* well for themselves, *thank* you very much, and hadn't even had to leave the Palleseen Archipelago. Hadn't had to go to war. Hadn't had to learn *magical techniques.* And magic was just a part of the world, to be mastered and understood. No more inherently controversial than double entry book-keeping. Except, because so much of the current understanding had been borrowed from more primitive and less sound cultures, a certain touch of the barbarous clung to it nonetheless.

And, honestly, *necromancy.*

Last time she'd been home on leave – three years ago now – she'd spoken about the subject at her old phalanstery, before the eyes of her former lecturers. She'd painted the whole discipline as admirably clean and antiseptic; exacting, scientific. You applied the energies to animate the dead flesh. You manipulated them *thus* to create fields that could trap or exclude a ghost. All well understood, *thank* you very much. And been aware, as she spoke, of their eyes on her. The faint but cutting disapproval of her teachers, the eager horror of the students. No, no, she'd tried to make them see. It wasn't anything like *that*. It wasn't ghost stories and vengeful spectres. It wasn't... superstition and dirty things.

Except it was, she had to admit to herself, here in her tent with dawn threatening outside. It was a *filthy* discipline and it meant she had to work twice as hard and show some really outstanding results if she wanted to look even half as good as the bean-counters. And that was a problem.

She added it to the head of the list she was making. Problem Number One: necromancy is horrible.

Her current aide made a game try of putting her teacup down without spilling. His hand shook, and precious drops spattered her tiny fold-out desk. She winced. There were only three intact cups from the service she'd brought from home. The man was scarred, limping, no longer battlefield material but still serving.

"You've not been taking your medicine," she reprimanded him. "Go to Ollery and get him to mix you up a new batch." And when his lack of expression displayed no recognition. "The Butcher. Go to the Butcher and have him resupply you. You're a reflection on *me*, man."

He mumbled something and left her little tent. She sipped the tea.

It was the very best tea. Not the insipid stuff they grew on the Archipelago, not the decent Maric blend, but from the plantations in the Oloumanni territories. Good enough that, they said, it was the chief reason Oloumann had been added to the Palleseen Sway. So good it was a problem, because Prassel was down to one small packet and her requests to get more added to the supply shipments had been ignored for the best part of six months. And so soon, within days, she'd have to find some inferior blend, and it wouldn't be the same. One more small pleasure ironed out of her life by the relentless Palleseen military machine. Which would rather have tablethi and batons or new boots for the soldiers, than decent tea for a poor Fellow-Inquirer.

She looked mournfully at the spilled drops and pictured how it would look if someone came in while she was sucking them up from the desktop. Not good. Maybe she could claim it was a necromantic ritual.

Problem Number Two was an insufficient quantity of acceptable tea, therefore. She wondered if the Loruthi had good tea, and whether any might be captured when the much-fabled Great Advance happened. Which Advance was at least partially dependent on her being able to provide necromantic support, which right now wasn't at all certain given various other shortages she was labouring under.

She drained the cup a sip at a time, considering logistics. Slotting numbers back and forth in the invisible spaces within her imagination. It was something she was good at. She seldom committed calculations to paper. She'd always been reprimanded for not showing her working, at the phalanstery, even though she always hit the right answers. Another reason she should probably have been counting beans rather than bodies.

When she ventured outside, tugging on her gloves, she met a local weather phenomenon partaking equally of fog and drizzle. Her uniform coat glittered with droplets almost immediately. Every sentry she passed looked thoroughly miserable to have been given the dawn slot. A discontented grumble reverberated from the mess tents, punctuated by the clatter of cutlery. The tea the regular soldiers got was, she was reliably informed, worse even than the rank dregs they'd served at the phalanstery. Probably she'd have personal experience of it soon enough.

She marched herself to the southern perimeter of the camp, her feet finding the way through the perpendicular plan of tents and open spaces. Every one the same, no matter the terrain, no matter the war. Drop a Pal soldier into any encampment in any theatre in the world and they'd be able to find the muster squares and the mess and the privies. The Loruthi didn't have the same exacting standards, she'd heard. It had given the Palleseen some early victories, night attacks against camps full of soldiers who didn't know where the guy ropes were. Although the extrapolated predictions of a swift and complete victory had then failed to materialise.

The assault on the Loruthi lines that had just finished, that had seen such a brisk trade at the Butcher's tent, had been a qualified success. The Loruthi had pulled back, ceded another few miles of ground. Except, in this case, 'ceded' meant 'filled with all manner of nasty surprises' so the Palleseen couldn't just march triumphantly in to fill the vacuum. This was Problem Number Three. The Loruthi fought smart. Palleseen expansion generally involved the ironclad armies of reason clashing with opponents who were zealots, idealists, berserkers, any or all of the above. Marics with bird flags willing to die for their nation, Allorwen conjurer-lords on demon steeds, Oloumanni cult votaries with sacred disembowelling sickles, all that. And those were opponents that the inexorable might of the Palleseen army was very good at dealing with. A measured advance, a clear-eyed strategy and an iron re-education.

The Loruthi, on the other hand, didn't really believe in anything much except profiting from other people, and their soldiers were either conscripts from their own overseas territories, or mercenaries, neither of whom would obligingly throw themselves into massed baton-fire until they broke. So, fighting the Loruthi, even winning against the Loruthi, was a series of careful, tentative steps because they would happily retreat in good order to fight another day, and make every lost step of ground a gift-wrapped present that you had to open *very* carefully indeed.

Needless to say, they'd be waiting for the Palleseen to over-extend themselves, fall foul of the bonecutters and ghost-grenados and the rest, before launching their own precisely calibrated counterattack.

She took the watchtower stairs at a decent clip. The whole edifice rattled, suggesting it hadn't been put up with regulation precision. She decided it wasn't her job to raise a complaint. She had more than enough paperwork from actual necromancy business without poking logistics in the eye. They'd be taking it down and moving it all three miles south soon enough, if she did her job properly.

At the top, the arcanolite sat on its tripod like a telescope wearing an extra pair of spectacles. The soldiers who'd set it up stepped back smartly, trying to make it look like respect rather than discomfiture. And yes, everyone was a bit twitchy around Correct Speech, but at least with the regular Inquirers – the interrogators and torturers and guardians of orthodox thought – it was the honest fear of a purge. With her it was the other thing, the dirty thing. The death thing.

And here she went, doing the death thing. She stripped her gloves off and flexed her bared fingers, trying to ignore the uncomfortable shuffle of the soldiers. She put her eye to the lens of the arcanolite and mustered the proper regimen of thought, the precise series of exercises that unlocked what primitive magickers called the Dead Eye. She saw into the interstitial space between the material world and the Eroding Abyss where ghosts got caught and certain classes of magical working existed.

Under the lidless scrutiny of the Dead Eye, it was evident that the ground between their camp and the Loruthi lines was mined to fuck. The retreating enemy had conscientiously left behind a whole constellation of magical caltrops for the triumphant boots of the aggressors. If they advanced into *that*, they'd lose more people than in the actual battle.

She put her gloves back on. The black leather gloves that, when they came off, you knew the dark magic was about to happen. Terrifying to underlings, intimidating to rivals, a symbol of her status as the worst kind of psychopomp, the woman who could send you out to fight for your country even after you were dead. Especially after you were dead. And nobody guessed that she'd taken to wearing them because she had a horror of touching filthy things. Like corpses. Her Dead Eye meant she could see the rot in them, burgeoning beneath the skin of every corpse. She could see the incipient decay even in the living. Every exercise of her trade made her want to scrub her skin from the inside out. The gloves were the absolute bare minimum of a barrier between her and the world. And, because they were such a symbolic protection between her and the filth, she couldn't do her job with them on, because her job was in itself filthy. See Problem Number One: necromancy was horrible and she didn't actually like it very much.

Which segued neatly into Problem Number Four because Fellow-Inquirer Prassel was very keen to be recognised, ideally in a way that got her promoted to some position involving less corpses. At some point there would be a battalion Sage's credentials handed out, no doubt, along with a position appropriately rewarding and supplied with good tea. She was just the sort of resourceful young Fellow with a good war record. Unfortunately, so were several others of her acquaintance. They had their own stigmas, it was true, but there was no getting away from the fact that she was the one who pushed dead bodies around for a living. All a bit unsound. A science still half-mired in irrational beliefs.

By the time her feet had taken her to the Butcher's domain, she'd got the numbers straight in her head. What it would take to clear a path through the mines, how she could best go about it, what resources she needed. And there was one resource that shouldn't have been in short supply in a war zone, of all places. But here she was, cap in hand. Not literally. She kept her peaked cap jammed down about her ears. The air around the Butcher's domain reeked of unorthodoxy and she didn't want to get it in her hair.

The menagerie of misfits masquerading as a field hospital generally ate together in the evenings, but the Butcher took his morning tea alone. Or, at least, only accompanied by his son. The child was sitting at his feet now, a boy of maybe ten, though Prassel claimed no particular expertise. She stopped, choosing her approach. The big man looked up at her with an avuncular twinkle, straining tea through his moustache from a regulation tin cup. Just a jovial fat man ready to serve up half a pound of sausages, although perhaps the sort who got a visit from Correct Exchange for shorting the weights and measures.

He was sitting on a crate marked 'receptacles, amber-clay, 2 doz' with the size of said receptacles obscured by the breadth of his calf muscle, prominent and massy as a weightlifter's. At the slightest nod the boy scrambled forwards on hands and knees to pull a similar box out, marked 'fish extract, bottled, 4 doz, 16dr'. She chose not to see it as some sort of fantastically elaborate insult.

"Spoilage," she said, sitting down.

His eyes, small and secret in his big face, looked left and right as though trying to spot what she was referring to. "Good morning to you, magister," he said.

"I have fields need clearing," she told him.

The Butcher sipped at his tea, making a big show of excluding absolutely everything from his world bar savouring the taste. "Use sheep," he said.

"We don't have any sheep," Prassel said. "Also, never again. Not after last time. The mess." Exploded sheep, possessed sheep, still-living sheep turned into woolly pincushions of their own bones. Better than living Pal soldiers, obviously, but it hadn't done much for morale. And nobody would touch the meat. A waste. Which was why they wanted a necromantic solution. Necromancy was an inherently efficient use of resources. "Spoilage, Ollery." And, when he affected not to hear her, "Chief *Accessory* Ollery, report." His rank, his shame. A man ten years her senior but so very far below her in station. A Pal, sporting a rank usually reserved for turncoat foreigners. A man under her jurisdiction, because some clerk attached to Higher Orders had doubtless been amused to place the experimental field hospital as a sub-department of Necromancy.

"My people," he said, "have excelled themselves. Other than those you took delivery of during the battle, our charges are all clinging to life. Many will be back in active service soon, the poor bastards. There is no spoilage, magister."

"I'm sure there are some who will not pull through," Prassel told him tightly.

"My people endeavour to ensure that is not the case."

"Your people could stand to be less good at their job." And it was ridiculous, obviously. They both knew it. This whole circus of a field hospital was a tenuous experiment. A word from Higher Orders could have Ollery and his quacks returned to whatever fates they'd been plucked from. The only reason the business was still, as the Butcher said, 'clinging to life' was that they kept soldiers alive where regular Pal medicine wouldn't suffice. But that in itself was an intrusion into the army's carefully-balanced economy. A greater supply of recovered soldiers meant a decreased supply of dead bodies.

"I can't believe we're sitting here," Ollery said, "after a massed battle, and you're short of corpses."

"The Loruthi have learned to take their dead with them," Prassel said grimly. And it wasn't out of respect for their fallen comrades. The enemy had their own necromantic practices, the filthy heathens. Almost as bad as Prassel's own.

The boy was at her shoulder then, mutely shoving a tin cup at her. She took it absently.

"I heard west, along the line, whole camp got overrun at night. Some detachment of Loruthi fighting back towards their own," Ollery observed. "Maybe they didn't get the chance to pack all their luggage on the way out."

"And you heard this from?" Prassel didn't believe it. It was just something he'd made up to send her somewhere else for a bit.

"Banders said," Ollery told her, shrugging his rounded shoulders like an earthquake. And his orderly, Banders, heard a lot, and some of it was true, but it still sounded like a necromantic goose chase. She sipped the tea and froze.

"Where," she said, with a slight quiver in her voice she was ashamed of, "did you get this?"

He had been watching her, waiting for it. His face creased with triumphant humour. "Good, isn't it?"

"This is pure Oloumanni-Alta blend."

"Ah, well, I bow to your superior taste. All I know is it's good. Banders found it."

Banders, the aforementioned orderly, found a great many things.

She sipped at the tea, which tasted like Heaven. And a good Pal scholar-soldier did not of course believe in Heaven, but the Oloumanni did and you surely could taste it in their tea. And Higher Orders expected her to clear the field still, for which she needed some conveniently dead bodies she could send shambling through to set off all the nasty traps. And maybe there were some spare dead lads piled up west, and maybe not, but...

"I can have a packet sent to your tent if you like," Ollery said casually. "I have two. I'm a open-handed man. I can share."

She weighed it up. On the one gloved hand, the necessity of actually doing her job. On the other, the transgressive bliss of sitting down tomorrow morning with some really good tea.

Butcher Ollery's expression was amused, sympathetic, diabolic. *Yes, I tempt*, that look said. *But why not?* The crooked meat vendor slipping a bribe to the inspector to dodge a fine.

Although in this case it would be a fine of the most grievously wounded of the hospital's living patients.

"West, you say," she noted.

"Banders said." Another monumental shrug, disavowing any faith in Banders's veracity.

"Well, thank you for the tip," said Prassel. "And the tea." And, despite the urgency in her orders, she sat there a while longer, refusing to hurry the cup.

There was one more problem to deal with, she discovered, as she strode back to her tent to write her requisitions. A half-dozen soldiers were there, buttoned-up uniforms and batons and everything, far more parade-ground neat than most of the active-duty mob. For a moment her gut lurched. *What did I do? What didn't I do?* What act or omission had attracted sufficient censure from higher up that she was going to be marched out through the camp? Inquirers of Correct Speech didn't fall often but, when they did, everyone enjoyed the meaty splat at the end of it.

She couldn't think of a thing, but that meant nothing. Plenty of ways you could step in something and not realise until someone was using a thumbscrew to ask what the smell was. You might even get taken up for something you hadn't done at all, but that some sly joker had put your fingerprints all over. And it wasn't as though she didn't have rivals for that fabled promotion who wouldn't do just that if they could get away with it...

But no. She saw they were an escort already supplied with a prisoner, rather than hoping to acquire one. A skinny little man fenced into their midst, wearing what looked like three separate threadbare coats, with a wooden box on his back, pierced with holes like a birdhouse. He didn't look like someone it took six burly soldiers to secure. Half of one would probably suffice.

"Wrong tent," she called as she approached.

The Statlos in charge of the squad glanced at a piece of paper in his hand. "Fellow-Inquirer Prassel?"

"Yes, but I don't do interrogations. I'm Necromancy." That was usually enough to get rid of people. "You want Loyalty and Oversight, if they want to put the screws on him." And technically she *did* do interrogations, but only on an overflow basis, not for preference.

The Statlos checked his paper again. "Says your name right here, magister," he said, with that particular deference that made plain he'd be as obstructive as possible because that was how he got his jollies with superior officers.

She scanned the close-lettered script of his writ, feeling her gut sink. *Another one for the Butcher's circus.* Some business about healing hands. "A priest." Spoken with a good Pal's distaste for the trade.

The Statlos shrugged. His entire encyclopaedia of knowledge on his prisoner was contained within the paper she held and, as it was her who was holding it, he considered himself well rid of the problem.

She looked over the list of crimes set down, automatically setting aside the usual ones that just got added by rote to any criminal involved in the occult. An actual priest, though, which would usually mean decanting and correction. A revolutionary, which would usually mean execution, so probably just a sympathiser. Certainly the man – young, thinning hair, hands clasping one another nervously – didn't look like he would be lighting the fires of resistance any time soon. And a...

She frowned. "What in reason," she asked, "is a 'god smuggler'?"

The Statlos didn't dignify the question with a shrug. The man himself – she had to crane awkwardly past the Statlos's shoulder and then he wouldn't actually meet her gaze – seemed embarrassed. As though someone having to invent an entirely new crime for him was far too much, and people really shouldn't have gone to the bother.

He's mine, Prassel thought. *They've given him to me. Some pointless Maric charlatan, fool enough to get caught doing something unnatural. More useful as a corpse, surely. He could be first into the breach on the mine-clearing venture. The Butcher doesn't even have to know.*

It was the tea, in the end. The very good tea. Some residual sense that she owed the man. Later, after it all happened, all the unlucky events and bad decisions, she'd think back on that moment, when she could have just done away with the man. She'd weigh it up and decide that, yes, cutting his throat and sending his reanimated cadaver to clear mines would definitely have been the right decision. In retrospect, it really did turn out to be powerfully expensive tea.

Fresh Meat

By her own estimation, Banders was the most promoted soldier in the entire battalion, possibly in the history of the Palleseen military. She'd lost count of the number of times a superior officer had given her a certificate of rank. She kept them all in her lockbox, treasured each one. That they were all for the same rank was something she was almost as proud of. It took great effort to be simultaneously so useful and so innately imperfect as to get disciplined out of even a lowly rank every time, and then reacquire it. Currently the wheel of her fortune was hauling her through the low arc of its swing, but it would only be a matter of time.

"**O**i, Banders!"

She pointedly ignored the ungracious hail, sitting out in the slanted morning sun with her folding desk, working on her triple-entry accounting. The first entry to calculate, the second to check the calculations and the third, on a separate piece of paper, to include all the errant entries that she wouldn't be reporting to anyone but still felt the obscure need to keep track of.

"Oi!" came the abrasive voice of Statlos Peppel again. "Banders." And then, when he was too close and too loud to convincingly ignore, "Cohort-Broker Banders, got a job for you."

She folded her papers into their wallet, slid the pen home into its loop and stood. "That's *Former* Cohort-Broker Banders to you, Statlos," she said, as though it outranked sages and generals.

Peppel was a Watch Statlos, meaning his job was simultaneously very tedious and catastrophic if he dropped the ball. Just like every other Watch officer, that meant he took lording it over anyone below him very seriously. Technically a Former Cohort-Broker was below just about everything, but as Banders was possibly the only one there had ever been, and Peppel was a man of limited imagination, he didn't know quite where he stood with her.

She was taller than him, too, which helped. He was broad and squat; she, lanky and angular. Somehow, the more formally she wore the uniform, the more of an offence to it she seemed. If anyone got her into full parade-ground dress she'd probably strike Higher Orders dead of apoplexy. Right now she had her jacket hanging open and her shirt unbuttoned to a risqué degree, because it was shaping up to be a warm morning. Her cap had found its customary station perched improbably on the back of her head.

"New recruit for the zoo," Peppel said. There was indeed a thin, lost-looking man in robes behind him, guarded by an unlikely number of soldiers. Banders took the documents Peppel held out and her eyebrows went up a little.

"Fancy," she said. "Never had one of them before."

"Sign off," Peppel told her.

"You might have told me I'd have to sign something before I put my pen away." She made a great show of rummaging in her satchel for the wallet until Peppel sighed and slipped his own from an inside pocket. She made an equally great and laborious show of signing off the prisoner docket, *Former Cohort-Broker Banders*. Doing the capitals with big loops and adding all the optional diacritics and underlinings as though she was still in juvenile phal. She took long enough for Peppel's patience to completely expire so that he and his men just took off the moment she'd given him the paper back. She wondered how long it would be before he realised she'd kept his pen.

"You dangerous?" she asked the robed man. He had a wooden house on his back, the size of her lockbox. It looked like you might keep rats in it. Quite a lot of rats. It looked quite heavy, too, and he looked quite weedy. The sort of lean you got from not eating well most of your life. Not bad-looking, overall. Fair hair shying back from a high forehead, a rather startled expression by nature, now augmented by actual startlement.

"What?" he said. "No."

"Only, the escort." She nodded at Peppel's retreating squad. And the docket hadn't said anything about violence, but on the other hand, priests... People did all kinds of crazy in the name of religion. It was one reason why there was no room for it within Palleseen perfection. You killed priests, or you re-educated them, or in some recent additions to the Sway you tolerated them while giving them sufficient rope to weave enough nooses for the whole congregation. Or you sent them to Forthright Battalion for medical experimentation.

She considered that wording, wondering whether someone was signing off on these dockets because they envisaged a convocation of Inquirer-surgeons vivisecting the incurably religious to find out which organ the faith was kept in. It seemed entirely plausible. Banders had met an endless succession of high-ranking officers who only read the headings and not the details. She had exploited the tendency for her own benefit on multiple occasions, as evidenced by some of her subsequent demotions.

"You mad?" she asked the man.

"What?" he said again. "No. Oh, or. Maybe?"

"You worship gods?" Banders asked him. "Priest stuff. Rituals, sacrifices, prayers, all that?" She had to say it again because she spoke at twice the pace of most people when she wasn't careful, and he was obviously struggling with a second language.

"Am I allowed to say no?" he asked her.

"I don't know. Are you?" She was no expert in what gods permitted their faithful to do.

"No, I mean. I know it was written down. But I don't want to get… hurt or locked up or decanted or something. So if I said no…?" His eyes swivelled. He had, she judged, never been in the middle of a military camp before.

"I mean you say what you want to say, friend," Banders said easily. "If you're a priest then you're my problem. Healing priest?"

"Well. No. Maybe. Sometimes."

"Then you're my problem. If you're not a priest then it said revolutionary on that docket as well, and they just get executed. But don't let me make the choice for you. Some people prefer that."

"Ah, no," said the priest. "Let's not do that. I did that once. I didn't like it."

That suggested a story she'd have fun winkling out of him later. "Right then." Banders folded her desk with a snap – the man jumped – and handed it to him. "Quartermaster's, first off. What do I call you?"

Between her turning away and him fumbling the desk and his accent, she didn't actually catch the name. He pattered after her readily enough, though, and she wondered just what he'd done to warrant a demi-squad escort, that wasn't enough to have him actually executed. The thought had her smiling into the gathering sunlight because this Maric was a nice fresh piece of fruit and she'd have fun peeling his layers over however long he lasted.

Cohort-Monitor Fosby was on duty at the quartermaster's shack, and he had a good line on spiced salt, liquorice and valgaric oil, the latter of which the Butcher had asked her to acquire and the former two she had some potential buyers lined up for. She was somewhat distracted when she filled out the papers for their new recruit, therefore, and most of the writing was just that scrawl she did when she wanted to look like she was jotting something down. She signed the card, though, and anointed it in red ink with Fosby's little rubber stamp. These were a new innovation, the rubber imported from Oloumann, where the good tea came from, and Banders loved the springy feel when she used them. The first time, they'd had to pry the thing from her fingers after a requisition form had ended up peppered with authorisations.

"Keep this with you," she said to the Maric, handing him the incomprehensible card. "This says who you are and that you're allowed to be here." The first was manifestly untrue although the stamp and her signature just about squeaked the second. "You are now Accessory…" And she still couldn't remember his name. "You, you are an Accessory in the Palleseen Army."

"Is that like a…" He fought with a Maric word she didn't know, and then constructed it piecemeal for her. "Turncoat?"

She judged it was a term for Marics who'd signed up to serve alongside their liberators, and not a complimentary one at that. "Sure," she said. "Why not? Is that a problem?"

"I mean I'm here, aren't I?" He looked around as though justifying himself to a larger audience than Banders and Fosby. Fosby took the distraction to slip her a folded paper with the details of where the liquorice and oil was.

"Fine," Banders said, satisfied on all counts. "Let's get you out of that clown's outfit."

She took him round the back, where the uniform stock was. "You must be sweltering in that nonsense," she said. "Get it off. Strip to your smalls, soldier."

He didn't understand the Pel phrase, because although Pel was a language designed explicitly to preclude slang, Banders was very determined and the words broke before she did. He looked satisfyingly horrified when she mimed it out for him, and she nobly turned her back to hoik out some clothes of the right size. Then had to turn right around and hoik out some smaller ones because he was even skinnier than she'd thought, under all those layers. His smalls were also larger than expected, not because of any heroic proportions but because Maric winters were bitter, and so the underwear went down to their knees and had a built-in vest. Honestly, the way he'd been carrying on she'd expected a full-frontal show. Add Marics to the list of nationalities who hadn't grown up with en masse unisex washing facilities, she supposed. On the Archipelago you didn't get a bath to yourself until at least Companion rank, most of the time.

Ah, ambition. Having handed him the clothes she let herself drift into reverie. *Work hard, apply yourself and maybe you could make Former* Companion-*Broker, Banders. Think of the extra cachet you'd have, being kicked out from such elevated company!*

He didn't know what to do with the buttons, so she had to show him. The shirt: cuffs and collar and halfway down to navel. The jacket: cuffs and then secured at the right breast – "No, the buttons down the left are just decoration, *don't* try and secure them to anything. Stockings up, then the breeches here, at the knee and… look, you can do your own codpiece flap. I'm not going there…" And there he was, a little Maric priest in an Accessory's pale grey. Looking as horribly uncomfortable as she could wish, half strangled and as though he'd lost all circulation in his hands and lower legs.

"I can't help noticing," he said, "that you yourself are not wearing your clothes like this." Indicating her loose cuffs, open shirt and the way her jacket was buttoned back open using those forbidden left-hand buttons.

She grinned at him. She'd been told she didn't have a nice smile, mostly by people who had found themselves getting into trouble after being exposed to it, but at least partly because someone had punched her front teeth crooked once. "Oh you'll fit right in. So long as you learn which ranks and officers you *do* need to get the buttons right for. Now, you need this…" She handed him another card, also illegible save for the signature. "This gets you ammies at the mess come midday."

He was frowning at the new and context-free additions to his vocabulary, but he'd pick it up soon enough, or starve. "Breakfast you sort for yourself. Evening meal you eat with your department."

"What if I don't have a department?" he asked, fighting to get his collar undone.

"I'm about to take you to your department," Banders told him. "Docket said you're a healer. A religious healer. You're seconded to the field hospital. They'll love you there. Crawling with your sort." She took pity on him and helped him with his collar. And stopped. He had flinched from the contact of her fingers with his throat. There was a scar there, a weal, as of a rope. *Fuck, maybe they did try to execute him.* That wasn't what had stopped her, though. Over his shoulder she could see the top of his weird backpack, that he'd shrugged right back into the moment she'd finished dressing him up. She could see into the little round holes in it. It was dark inside, but she swore she'd seen something move in there. Something nasty. Something weirdly familiar. She froze up, feeling her fingers on the throat of the priest and knowing it to be sacrilege. Knowing herself to be judged.

"Oh! Oh, I'm sorry." And he turned, jolting the wooden backpack quite viciously as though there really was something there and he was physically shaking it out of sight. Except there hadn't been anything, obviously. Just a... something. And her fingers were caught in the buttonhole of his collar and he had to free her, a weird reversal of her helping him.

"I'm sorry," he said again, though by unspoken and mutual consent he didn't elaborate on just what he might be sorry for. And she sat down on a crate full of boots and pulled out her non-regulation flask and had a nip. Offered it to the Maric, too.

"I'm not supposed to," he said, and then did anyway. His eyes watered just like any reasonable human being's, and that brought him back into the realms of the secular and the comprehensible.

And he really did look apologetic and small and meek, not a threat to anyone.

She grinned at him experimentally. Nothing bad happened. The nine-tenths of her that was world-weary and pragmatic, and navigated the Palleseen army to her personal profit, reclaimed its upbeat nature and resumed its opportunistic plotting. The one-tenth that had crept down to the caves below the orphanage, and come back bloody and terrified, shook and wept in a far corner of her mind, but she'd learned to ignore that a long time ago.

Quartermasters got a shed but the field hospital was a cluster of conjoined tents circumscribed by drainage ditches. When they were at work the canvas walls would all be down, so that those waiting to have terrible, necessary things done to them, or those who'd had such things done already, couldn't see the ongoing terrible things happening to their comrades. Right now, with all but the most critical casualties sent north to the recupery stations, the medicos had rolled up half the walls to let a bit of air in, and the stench of pain and old blood out.

"Oi oi!" she hailed them, hoping an instant later that the Maric didn't take that as a regulation military utterance which it absolutely wasn't.

"In here," the Butcher's voice rolled out like rocks down a slope. "Did you get my oil?"

"I've got a line on it," Banders confirmed, and tugged at the Maric's arm. The Butcher was sitting in the shadow of a slant of canvas, his son just serving up a plateful of chopped eggs and red. It would be to his own recipe, for which Banders had been at him for over a year.

You had to be bold, to enquire after the Butcher's recipes. You had to be bold to eat at his table. Senior officers had proved too white in the liver to accept his invitation. But the hospital staff had all got used to it, and for that they ate well whenever he was moved to cook for them. And Banders was nothing if not bold.

"Got a live one for you," she told him. "Chief, this is... a priest. Healy priest fresh from – where was it, priest?"

"Ilmar," said the Maric.

The Butcher took a mouthful of eggs and then a quick swig of water, which showed the boy had done the red part right. "That's the place up north with the wood?" he asked. He was doing his jolly favourite uncle twinkle, that could turn into a slap very quickly.

"Yes." The Maric caught himself. "Magister? Sir? I'm sorry I've not been in an army before."

"This is Chief Accessory Ollery," Banders explained proudly, as though it was her personal achievement. "He's in charge of you now. You report to him and do what he says. And you call him 'Chief'. On account of how he doesn't warrant a 'Magister'."

Ollery, the Butcher, looked the skinny little slice of Maric up and down as though wondering what recipes he had for this particular ingredient. "You any good?"

"No, Chief," said the Maric promptly. "Not really at anything. Sorry." Wincing at Banders's cackle of a laugh.

"Oh they love us," Ollery said, ostensibly to his son who'd sat on the ground with his own little tin plate of eggs. "Look what they send us, boy. They're just desperate for us to fail. This is how the Fellow-Inquirer will get her ration of corpses. Good soldiers or bad doctors, who kills more in this man's army, eh?" He ate some eggs philosophically. Not the easiest thing to do philosophically, by Banders's estimation, but he managed it. "You'd better show him about," he added, after swallowing. "Most everyone's up already. And make sure Masty's done the rounds of the criticals."

Masty would have done the rounds. Masty, the other orderly, was twice as conscientious about his duties as Banders, which was just as well given her general lack of the quality. Asking

Masty if he'd done the rounds was just about the level of responsibility she felt she could handle.

"Alv up, Chief?"

Ollery cocked an eyebrow. "Alv never sleeps, as far as I can make out. What do you think? And why?"

"Want to see Maric's reaction, is all." She fished another grin from her inexhaustible supply. Taking the priest by the arm she tugged him towards the main tent, eyes hunting through the shadows for her target. "Now, you've got a real good memory for names and faces, obviously?"

"Not really, no," he said.

"Ah well, that's a shame, 'cos you're about to meet about a hundred different people wearing the uniform and they'll all expect you to remember them intimately and not get them mixed up, on pain of hating you forever if you make the slightest mistake. That all right?"

"I, what? I mean, no?" He tripped over a guy rope on the way into the tent. He'd looked the type that would do that. Used to the sort of town where all the houses didn't fold down and go on a baggage train every week or so. "And do I call *you* Magister or Chief or...?"

She stopped at that. "I reckon calling me Magister is probably a court martial offence," she considered. "Disrespect to the uniform, probably. You just call me Banders like everyone else, Maric, and we're fine." And then, just to avoid any confusion, "On account of it's my name."

Then they'd ducked past the drape of the porch into the cool beneath the main canvas, the big space that was common room until the shit came down, whereupon it became waiting room and operating theatre, alchemy lab and necromancer's playground, more commonly known by its tenders as Hell. Through a flap to her left was the ward, where the criticals were kept – those still clinging to life who couldn't be safely shipped out to the recupery stations. To the right was a nest of partitioned spaces where the actual sleeping and living went on, for those consigned to Hell for the duration.

A few of the staff were abroad. A couple of junior sympaticos from Alv's students, washing the bloody clothes from yesterday's fun and games. Bearded, saturnine Masty at the back, cleaning the saws and catling knives. Alv, doing her exercises.

Alv was the most beautiful woman in the world, as far as Banders was concerned. And Banders didn't even like women that way. She was lean, compact, not a spare ounce on her. In uniform breeches and shirtsleeves she was moving through a series of passes, so small and controlled that it was as though she had invisible walls penning her on all sides. Nothing so ungainly as the stretches and exertions regular soldiers got put through at training camp. Nothing that really looked like exercise at all, until you saw that every single muscle was under her strict control, restrained and released only on her mind's express say-so, nothing left to instinct or body memory. She kept one arm close to her side. A little tender, that care said. Not that it had patently been broken so short a time ago. The expression on her face was infinitely serene, and the face itself was weirdly perfect in a way independent of anybody's personal standards. The beauty of self-possession. Plus, there was enough light coming in from outside to make her skin glitter and shine like butterfly scales.

"This is Guest-Adjutant Alv. She's in charge if you can't find the Butcher." Banders stole a glance at the Maric to see how he was taking the sight. With more equanimity than she'd hoped, honestly. "And I want to you to know that familiarities between members of the battalion is absolutely a breach of military discipline," garnished with the most enormous wink.

"Right," said the Maric, and then caught up. "Oh, no. I mean, it's forbidden anyway."

"That's what I said." Banders tried the wink again, but it just bounced off, and presumably the forbiddance he meant was religious, and he was going to be less interesting than she'd thought.

Alv finished her pass, a kind of circling step with the feet and a bringing together of the hands, all within the sort of space you'd need for a broom closet, then looked sharply at Banders and the Maric.

"Fresh meat," Banders announced, to the world at large. "This is... Maric. He's a priest." And the Maric actually said his name in correction but she'd spoken over it so she'd missed it again.

Alv regarded the man dubiously, and Banders was about to drag him off to inflict him on Masty and the rest of them, but then there was a commotion from outside. Shouts to clear the way, curses from surprised soldiers halfway back from fetching their breakfast, then a dozen stretcher bearers thundering down on the hospital tent like bad weather from a clear sky.

Hell – Like a Hole in the Head

Hell arrives like this. Every free hand working at the sides of the tent, bringing the canvas down. The end of one show, the beginning of a private performance. The porch outside becomes a tessellation of stretchers as the bearers drop their burdens. An early harvest clamouring for attention.

Some of them – the luckiest – are screaming. Others are silent because the agonies have already wrestled them to the rail and thrown them over. Or they're already dead. It's not the stretcher bearers' job to check. One just makes a sound, a horrible sound, like nothing anyone ever heard. And then there's the yap of the political officer, the most pointless instrument in the impromptu orchestra, that nobody wants to listen to but that won't shut up.

In the midst of all of this, the Maric, just standing there. A skinny man in the unfamiliar constraints of a uniform. People keep jostling the box he has on his back, but he doesn't know where anything is or how anything works and so he's useless, quite useless. Though everyone is shouting at him or at each other or just howling their pain to the universe, he looks as though he's listening to other voices entirely, an argument going on behind the nape of his neck.

One of Alv's people barks an elbow on the box, spinning the Maric round. He gets the message and unshoulders his burden, stowing it underneath the table they've set up. The injured are coming in.

The Butcher strides in, his boy stumbling after him like someone flying an over-energetic kite as he ties his master's apron strings. "What have we got? Burns?"

The soldiers stretchered in have indeed been burned. The Maric's never seen anything like it, not after a year of sporadic fighting across the streets of Ilmar. Burned, blistered, the fabric of their uniforms melted to charcoal skins. A man with half a face blackened down to his skull, a woman whose arm is charred kindling from just past the shoulder. He can't imagine what has happened to them. If he was a more religious man – even though he's a priest and on familiar terms with a god, he doesn't consider himself that any more – he'd take it as divine wrath.

He puts himself at Ollery's elbow, because he's supposed to be *doing* something. Because people are hurt beyond the knife wounds, baton-shot and industrial accidents he's used to, and he cares. He cares about the pain of other human beings, and would lessen it if he could. It's not the most useful qualification for being on this team but it's one some of his newfound comrades lack.

The Butcher glowers at him, all the avuncular twinkle gone. "Can you take away pain, Maric? Magic powers? God-stuff? Can you stave off death?"

And he wants to say yes, but that would be false advertising, laden with so many conditions it would take a lawyer to go through them, and by then the patients would have died. He just shakes his head.

"Can you get a potion past someone's lips?" The Butcher, to a chorus of begging and screams, is remarkably patient and controlled.

"That I can do," the Maric agrees, and the Butcher gives him a little wooden rack of phials.

"One each. Quick as you like. And this, on the wounds."

The Maric understands it's nothing, it's a sop. Some concoction to take the edge off while hard decisions are made and the real work done. But it's something he can do, and so he does it. Each of the dozen horribly burned victims, he kneels by them, he puts a hand to some part of them not bubbled by the heat, speaks to them in Maric, which does nothing; in soothing tones, which maybe helps a little. Gets the glass to their lips where there are lips, finds somewhere to pour where there aren't. Sprinkles the grey crystals across the volcanic landscapes the heat made of flesh and skin. Doesn't flinch from it, and the screams don't faze him. Doesn't realise how this removes an invisible barrier that would otherwise have stood forever between him and the rest of the hospital squad. He is noted, in that moment. Alv and the Butcher and others, weighing him and seeing that he might be one of them in time.

While he's making a brisk yet patient progress down the line of stretchers, over his head Ollery is arguing with someone.

"Forget them." A sharp, nasal voice. "This man. This is the one. Save him."

Ollery's deep growl. "I can't save him. Look at him."

And, underscoring them both, that sound – barely plausible that it could come from a human throat. That long, drawn-out wail that echoes, somehow, even though there's nothing for it to echo back from. That doesn't even stop for breath but just goes on and on and...

"Save him. This man is valuable," says nasal voice. Then, perhaps perceiving how this sounds to everyone else, adds, "He has information. It's vital he's able to communicate it to Higher Orders. Vital for the advance."

"Look at him," Ollery repeats. "He's – I don't even know what he is. Your spy."

"This is what you're *for*," nasal voice insists. "This is what *they* were burned for, getting *him* out. He dies, they took the hit for nothing."

"Piss on you." But the Butcher is kneeling by the man, even as his nasal interlocutor is spitting feathers at the insubordination. Heavy hands fish ingredients from the pockets of his apron, and then he's sending his boy running out of the tent to get more exotic reagents.

The Maric drifts to his elbow again and sees.

It's hard to focus on the injured spy. The eyes don't like it. He's discoloured, like lichen's grown on him. He's not all there. There's a hole in him, around the juncture of shoulder and neck, but it's not a physical hole. It spirals away into some place completely *elsewhere* and the spy is being dragged into it. That sound comes from the hole, as much as from him. He's not in any position to tell Loruthi secrets to the battalion's Higher Orders.

Ollery registers his presence. "Can you help him?" he demands.

The Maric shakes his head. And that isn't entirely one hundred per cent true, but it's an honest answer nonetheless.

"Get him to the table."

And there are four tables now, where there was just the one before the canvas walls came down. Because Hell wouldn't be Hell if only one person could suffer there at a time. Burned men and women are already on three, shirtsleeved people bending over to them and making them scream despite the potions. The Maric takes the spy's stretcher at one end, and a thin foreigner – meaning non-Palleseen, just as the Maric is – with a pointed beard and an aquiline nose takes the other, and they get the horribly eaten-away man onto the slab with only a little more of him going down the hole. His eye – the one that isn't impossibly smeared away into infinity – locks with the Maric's gaze, pleading.

"I'm sorry," the priest says. "I can't. I'm sorry." And then, "He won't."

Someone's shoving past him then, businesslike and secure in a superior rank. A woman whose uniform – alone of everyone there – is immaculately buttoned up on every front, hands covered with black kid leather gloves. She has a bag with her, also black leather with a folding brass mouth, and she sets up with brisk movements. Copper flasks, catgut tubes, a little bellows pump that Banders gets assigned to. A surgeon of some peculiar specialisation, then. And in that assumption, the Maric is almost correct save for some key detail. Then the woman notices his scrutiny, stares at him, recognises him even as he recognises her. She's the officer who sent him off to his appointment with Banders. He hadn't realised she was the medical type.

The Butcher is at his elbow before the Maric can annoy the woman who has power of life or death over the entire field hospital, and power of death over just about everyone else.

"Go help," and he shoves the priest at the next table.

There's a woman there. Quite old, another foreigner. In fact at least half the people the Maric sees bending over the wounded aren't Pals – and the senior half at that. It's only the gloved officer and the Butcher who have that honour, out of all the medical staff fit to give orders.

The old woman glowers up at him as though he's been sent by divine agency just to complicate her life. She is about an act of comprehensible medical cartography. Drawing a hard border between salvageable living skin and the fire-touched that must be cut away. It's the woman burn-victim whose arm is mostly gone, and the old surgeon is going to turn that 'most' into 'entirely'.

The Maric composes his face into what he hopes is 'eager to help'. It's hard work because Hell isn't conducive to positive expressions. The old woman's certainly hasn't seen this side of a scowl since everything kicked off. Her face is hawkish, hollow-cheeked, deeply lined. Her tied-back hair has a slash of red in the white and the Maric recognises that as a symbol of devotion the Pals don't know to scrub out. It helps that there's a god at her elbow. A small god – but they all are, in the Palleseen shadow. A little burning thing in the shape of a lizard. When the woman sets down her knives and needles, it licks at them in a faintly disappointed way. The Maric hears its voice like a whisper undercutting the cacophony of the injured and the nasal barking of the political officer. He can't catch the words but, from long experience, he can imagine. *They used to offer their first born to my braziers and now this.*

There is an old man in one corner of Hell and he's playing a flute. He has a jar at his feet that's half full of something cloudy and greenish-yellow, like the very worst cider ever brewed, and he shuffles from foot to bare foot, and keeps up something that's simultaneously a skirling wail and a dirge. It's so out-of-place that the Maric isn't entirely sure if anybody else can see or hear it.

The woman snaps her fingers against the bridge of his nose, briefly the most painful thing in the world despite people literally dying right behind him.

"Make yourself useful," she says. "What can you do?" And, when theology gets in the way of a concise answer, "Can you at least hold her down?"

That he can do, and he does. He's a skinny little streak of Ilmar but he's done this before and pins the patient to the table – her ankles and other wrist are strapped but damn she can buck! – while the surgeon with the red streak in her hair wields the saw. Its teeth glow with heat from the salamander god's tongue and it sears through the good flesh down the boundary the old woman drew until there's no burn left and no arm either. The patient weeps, mostly pain but some grief and even a little relief that the worst is over.

"Can you stitch?" the surgeon asks him, and he can do that as well. He's had a remarkable amount of practise because Ilmar hasn't been a quiet city since the big street fight a year ago. She gives him a curved needle that's still hot to the touch, and a length of gut thread that steams slightly, and he gets to work even as she goes to the next table to survey the damage. The woman weeps silently, face locked, and he wishes he could do more for her than just give her someone else's potion and finish someone else's butchery. He makes sure his seams are neat, tucking away the flap of skin like he was taught. He tells her he's sorry, and that better things will come, and that people care even if gods don't. He tells her it in Maric so she doesn't understand a word, but the tone helps. And then he hears the objections. Because he can always hear *Him*. It's a part of the compact he made that he hadn't seen in the small print, that even sticking his fingers in his ears and shouting won't keep out God's complaints. The screams of the dying have no chance. God is telling him the gods *do* care. The voice from his wooden box, from his *shrine* that the Pals would absolutely have confiscated and used for kindling if they'd only known. Gods *do* care and how dare he show such disrespect. *Don't you know who I am?* And the Maric does. Most regrettably he does. He only wishes he didn't. And apparently God cares, but that won't extend to actually helping. Not even as much as the fire god, lethargically licking sawblades at the old woman's elbow.

The old woman nods at his stitching, then follows his gaze. Sees him seeing her god. Her eyes widen in alarm, and he understands he isn't supposed to see it, and that nobody else can. He tries to apologise but he's still speaking Maric and she might not be a Pal but she's no Ilmari either. And then the man with the flute has gone into fresh amusical rhapsodies right in his ear and he says, "Is that really necessary? Does he have to do that?"

The surgeon looks at him, deadpan, and says, "Oh, so you're an expert on modern medicine now, are you?" But then adds, "Lochiver, could you be a bit, you know, *less*. Only it's burns. It's not like we really need your all for burns."

The old man with the flute sends her a look that wishes it could kill, but gives it less on the flute, making up for it with some arthritic kicks and capers that flap the unbuttoned ends of his uniform breeches about his thin legs. His arms are thin, too, as is his scrawny bird's neck. All the weight has fled to his gut, which strains all the buttons of his jacket as it shudders back and forth. He has a god, too. It's part-man, part-unspeakable-slug-thing, and it's dancing slightly out of time with the music.

"Go help Alv," says the woman with the red streak, shoving him towards the next table.

"What is going on up there?" demands the cranky voice from the box. It's still under the first table of course, the one with the spy on it. The gloved woman has taken those gloves off now, and she's just destroyed a copper flask somehow – it's cracked right across in her hands and she's staring at it with exasperation. The nasal political officer is at her shoulder, shouting at her.

"Try again!" he snaps. "It's absolutely essential that his knowledge is preserved!"

She shows him the broken flash. "Look at it. Whatever they've done to him, I can't separate his ghost out. It's being dragged away. We can't hold it."

"Higher Orders don't want your *excuses*," the man snaps, voice shrill.

"Higher Orders can't change what *is*, *Companion*-Inquirer," she tells him, wielding their disparity in ranks like a stick with nails in it. "We can't hold onto him."

Then the Maric's beside Alv, who's treating one of the less burned soldiers. Less, here, meaning a great charred weal from cheekbone to sternum, struggling to breathe, teeth visible where the cheek itself has shrivelled away. But alive and not immediately about to die.

Alv's look says *What can you do?* and he just shrugs, helplessly apologetic. And Alv is... singed, somehow. Her dark hair has withered back across her scalp and one of her hands is crooked, baked into a claw. The young Pal next to her is being helped away, limping, jaw clenched.

Alv, the most beautiful woman in Forthright Battalion, looks the Maric full in the eye and melts her own face off. He screams a little. He can't help it. It crisps and chars, the skin puckering and turning black, flaking like burned paper. Her cheek withers and splits, raw redness underneath and then even that parching to black. He sees her molars crack across with a remembered heat that happened to someone else. Her eyes speak mute agony to his.

She lets out a breath. The woman on the slab is whole, barely a faint shininess to the skin where the burns were. Alv props herself up on the table. One of her people turns up but the Maric has her elbow already, giving support where it won't encroach on the injury, helping her away.

"I'm done," Alv calls. "Carry on." And she steers his support through the right-hand tent flap to where three Pals sit or lie, each of them scorched and disfigured, all to lesser degrees than her.

"Divinati magic," the Maric says, because there was an expat Divinati community in Ilmar and he's heard the stories, though he never saw anything like this. He didn't think they were allowed to work these wonders, outside the Divine City.

Alv sits back against a tent pole. "Can you apply ointment?" she asks him. Her accent is still very Divinati, Pel words twisted by it, and by the pain, until he wouldn't have understood without her gesturing to the pot. He can, though. It's one more mundane but useful thing he can do, that doesn't involve gods. As something of an expert on the subject he feels that things are always better if you don't have to involve gods.

He salves her wounds. It's a weirdly non-intimate thing, the strangeness and the brutality and the screaming from next door serving to obviate any awkwardness.

Then the moment of calm is gone because the salve is applied and it's back into Hell for the Maric.

As he enters, the woman without gloves yells and another of her copper flasks explodes. A piece of it actually whickers past the Maric's head and nearly cuts him a new tonsure. From the box underneath that table that sour voice snickers and comments on filthy necromancy and how it serves her right. The spy continues to make that dreadful drowning noise, voice issuing as from a great depth and distance.

I shall go mad, the Maric realises. And the world around him is clearly already there – the piper and the self-mutilating Divinati woman and the political officer's ridiculous insistences.

43

If the priest went instantly and irrevocably insane right now then all he'd be doing would be catching up.

The bearded foreign orderly has his elbow, guiding him to a stretcher. It's the woman without an arm, who's just staring at the slope of the tent above her, gaze hollow as a tomb. They've strapped her remaining wrist down to stop her picking at the stitches. At the bearded man's miming, the Maric helps bring the stretcher out through the front of the tent. Out of Hell and into what happens when even Hell can't help. Four dead soldiers here, people to whom he had administered the Butcher's potion, but whose wounds were enough that no amount of surgery or Divinati sleight of hand could help. And so, their last moments were eased, but nobody helped them because nobody could.

The woman with one arm gives a single sob at seeing them, her comrades, her squad-mates. Then there's a neat, slightly portly Pal there, with his own bag of tools and an apron smeared with a darkness that seems too greasy to be blood. He gives the bearded man and the Maric a vague nod, even a clipped little smile. He has round eyeglasses on, one of which has a set of extra lenses that can be hinged down. Having experienced Hell, the Maric can't imagine that seeing things more clearly will be desirable ever again. Nonetheless the man fiddles with his lenses and takes measurements of the woman's shoulder stump with callipers and tape, like a tailor. He makes notes in a little book and rubs at his receding hairline.

"Arm," he says, as though he's the officer in charge of identifying absences. "What else?"

"Hand," the bearded man tells him. "Jaw."

"Jaw." Spectacles tuts. "Tricky. Bring them out then. Let's take a look." Banders and another man in a bloody apron are already stretchering someone out whose hand, or the ruin of it, has been cut away. The aproned man stares at Spectacles as though he's a grave robber come early, and Spectacles doesn't meet his gaze. Some subtlety of status that the Maric can't figure out. Then it's him and the beard heading inside to get the woman whose jaw is half gone. Because moving things from place to place is also something the Maric can do.

When he goes inside again, the necromancer is waving her gloves in the face of the political officer, the two of them having a full-on rank-off right there in the midst of all the carnage. The screaming is mostly gone, though, either because the screamers have been operated on and taken away, or sedated, or have died. It's just the spy left, slowly vanishing into the abyss that's been stabbed into his body, a pull so great that apparently not even his ghost can escape it.

And there, on the table next to him, is God.

God god. The God that the Maric was once a proper priest of, before they had a falling out. The God he's still a nominal worshipper of. Not any of the other gods of Yasnic's acquaintance, of whom there have been far too many, but actually God. God, in His divine form as a scrawny, dirty man with a long beard and a sharp nose, wearing a ragged sheet for a robe and overall the size of a small yappy dog. And about as welcome, in most circumstances. He, the divine He, is standing on the table, having clambered out of the box He currently shares with a couple of co-tenants whom He loathes but can't evict. He is peering with some interest down the horrible, impossible hole in the spy. It isn't every day that a divinity as old as the roots of the world sees something new.

"No," the Maric says, and God – who can always hear His former priest, as their relationship is mutually cursed – looks up. His expression is a bit of a sneer, a bit of contempt for the Maric and all of it, and a great deal of mean-spirited mischief. And God used to be so very strict in how He dealt with the world, but ever since His one sole priest started bending the rules, so He began to do the same to get His own back. God and His last and most worthless worshipper, codependent and co-abusive and unable to be rid of each other.

"You wouldn't," the Maric whispers and God lifts an eyebrow

45

because the one thing every man of faith should know is that you *don't* tempt the divine.

The horrible sound stops, and that's a surprise to nobody. A wonder, only, that the spy held out so long against dissolution. Except that, when the political officer and the necromancer look down, the hole is gone, the man is whole.

"That's cheating," the Maric says. "You're not *allowed*. Your own rules. You can't go against your own rules."

God looks nonchalant. "Yasnic," He names His solitary yet still least loved servant, "he agreed. Ignorant Pal bastard. Turns out even they believe in gods when oblivion's staring them in the face. Didn't know what it was to, but he said *Yes*." God's nasty old face goes hard and mean, "And now he gets to pay the price, the credulous goon."

Fresh Meat, Slightly Off

The conquest of Jarokir is celebrated by the Pals as one of their greatest achievements. The wicked, god-ridden Jarokiri, aggressively proselytising their religions out of every ship and land route. The Palleseen mission to perfect the rest of the world received a considerable boost from the gold and the magic they bled out of Jarokir when they finally subdued the place. Even subdued, the old ways didn't die easy. Rogue priests, renegade templars and votaries turned anarchists plagued the occupation for a decade at least after nominal control was assumed.

"I heard Alv and the Butcher talking," said Lochiver, impromptu medical flautist. "They're saying he might be another Erinael."

Tallifer was at the back of their shared tent, setting up for her devotions. That were, of course, utterly forbidden in any Pal army. Catch you worshipping gods or making votive offerings, they'd have you on a charge quicker than kindling catching. They'd have you in chains. They'd have you shot. Though not before they'd given you to the Decanters just in case you did actually have something of the divine about you.

Tallifer had something of the divine about her. A little fiery lizard only she could see, that was the least guttering light of Mazdek, the Chastising Flame. All that was left. And yet here she was at the heart of the Pal military machine, warming up a tin plate over a candle so she could burn a little incense and propitiate her tiny sliver of god.

And here was Lochiver, the horrible old man with his horrible old faith, her ancient enemy, the god that hers had repeatedly cast down. Here he was, in fact, sitting down on his bundled-up bedroll and removing his horrible old boots so that he could pick at the flaking skin of his horrible old feet.

And she was a horrible old woman and her feet weren't much better, and at least he was Jarokiri, and in this army it was him and her and none of their countryfolk within a hundred miles.

"Who," she asked patiently, "would be another Erinael?" Because Lochiver never started a story at the beginning if he could possibly help it. When he was younger it had stemmed from his contrary nature but now it was probably senility.

Lochiver watched the plate heat and the little waxy cone of incense begin to melt into the fragrance of sandalwood and lemon. The lemon scent was sacred to Mazdek, but half the temples in Jarokir had loved sandalwood, it seemed to be particularly godly. There had been sacred groves. The Pals had burned them, of course. One final and extravagant offering to no god at all.

"The new boy," Lochiver grunted, straining over his gut to get to his horrible toes. "That trick he did. Impressive, don't you think?"

"He'd better hope he's not the new Erinael," Tallifer decided darkly. "Because of what happened to the old Erinael."

They both gave that a little time for thought. And Erinael was old news now, forgotten by most, never even known by some of the newer recruits. But she hadn't deserved what they'd done to her, and at the same time it had been utterly inevitable. She'd been a testament to what gave, when the iron Pal drive for rationalism met an infinite capacity for help and healing. Suffice to say the Pals were still driving on, and where was Erinael now?

"He's still going on at anyone who'll listen." Lochiver had

fished his filthy clippers out of his pocket, and that was too much in Tallifer's opinion.

"I am trying," she said, "to hold a sacred devotion here." She nodded at the tin plate, where the sinuous form of Mazdek was coiling about the melting pool of fragrant wax, trying to pretend it was the grand and ever-burning fire of the High Fane. Lochiver, of course, only saw the wax, filthy apostate that he was. On the other hand she couldn't see *his* god either, and for that she was profoundly grateful. They had never made statues of Lochiver's god. Not because of any dissatisfaction with graven images, but because it wasn't very nice to look at.

Lochiver gave her a look along his nose. "This is also a devotion," he said, the words positively larded with hierophantic dignity. "The High Priest of the Unclean Sacristy cannot be seen with ragged nails."

And he had never officially been the high priest of anything, and the Unclean Sacristy had been torn up for spare magic during the conquest, and furthermore that was a rule he'd just made up purely to annoy her. And now that they all had to wear military issue boots and not sandals it wasn't as if anybody was supposed to be seeing his toes, and that was most definitely a boon to the rest of the world. But he was going to bloody well clip his nails in their tent whatever she said, and that was the sort of shrapnel hazard that put whole companies in the infirmary. She took the tin plate – god, wax and all, and left the tent with it. And if the plate was hot enough to blister skin by then, and she took it by finger and thumb without a thought, well, being a priest of Mazdek had some advantages.

Outside, the new boy was tagging along after Ollery, obviously very agitated about something.

"You don't understand," he told the Butcher's broad back.

"I don't want to," the man cast over his shoulder. He was carrying a clinking crate to his tent, some reagent Banders had dropped off.

"I need to talk to him," the Maric said, actually plucking at Ollery's apron strings. "The man. The spy. I have to warn him."

Ollery set down the crate at the mouth of his tent, the big tent where he had three or four cauldrons bubbling all the time, brewing up his various specialties. Four tin chimneys had been sewn into the canvas to let out the fumes, and if you ever got lost in the vast camp of Forthright Battalion, all you had to do was cast about for that weird leaden fug of cloud and it would show you the way back to the hospital.

"Man's a spy," the Butcher said, turning and sitting on the crate squinting up at the Maric. Though not so far up, because Ollery was a big man, and the Maric was a thin stick bent under the weight of that box he had. "It's *his* job to warn *us*."

Tallifer had a bad feeling about that box. Her eyes didn't like resting on it, yet she couldn't ignore it. Eyes closed and facing away she still felt she knew exactly where it was. *So what's your deal, new boy?*

"No, but look—" the Maric started, and Ollery cut him off.

"You did good. Whatever you did. Higher Orders are happy with us, for once. They get their spy. They get their information. They get to plan their next attack or whatever it was all for."

"But that's the thing, what was it for? I have to know!"

Ollery shook his head. "You don't. None of us do. We just patch them up or bury them."

"But I need to know he won't do any harm!"

Oh, thought Tallifer, because *that* had a weird ring of familiarity.

Ollery, the Butcher, found it hilarious. He hailed his boy out from minding the cauldrons. "What does this uniform mean?" he asked the child. "This thing we all wear."

"Means we're soldiers!" the boy shouted, standing to attention to demonstrate.

"Means we're soldiers," Ollery echoed. "He's – what are you, ten, twelve now? And he knows. And you'd better learn. There's nobody in this camp that does no harm. Doing harm is what an army's for. Us, the Loruthi, your Maric lads before you got smashed down four years back. It's a world of harm."

"But he can't," the Maric said. "I've got to warn him. Any harm. The moment he—"

Ollery stood suddenly, the motion quick and brutal enough to shut the little man up. Because Ollery was a great lumbering weight of a man and that could fool you into thinking he was slow.

"Tell you what," he said. "Off you go. Go tell him. Good luck to you and your mission, magister."

The Maric froze for a moment. "Right. Fine. Thank you." And a pause. "Where did they take him?" Looking past the tents of the hospital to the entire Forthright Battalion camp in all its chaos and order. A city of soldiers, busy as ants about their business.

Ollery gave him a look that clearly said, *Oh, I'm sorry, I'd forgotten you were new here*, and then grunted, heading inside to see what was boiling over. The boy gave the Maric a disrespectful look learned from his father, and followed.

That, unfortunately, meant Tallifer was the next recipient of the man's urgent, pleading looks, which were a gift she'd rather return unopened. He came over, though, faster than her old legs could have tottered her away, and his mouth open to beg for directions or assistance or – she didn't find out what because he stopped and stared at her plate.

For a moment she thought he'd inexplicably turn out to be a Pal rationalist hardliner and howl at her for doing something even tangentially religious. "What?" she tried. "You never saw anyone wax a plate before?" Not her top-of-the-line repartee but she was tired. The unexpected emergency had taken it out of her, and burn wounds brought back bad memories. An awkward aversion to have, for someone in her spiritual position.

Mazdek slithered about the plate, his belly drawing patterns in the wax. The Maric's eyes followed the motion. She saw it very clearly. And when the little eft-shape of her god crawled to the plate's rim and pushed himself up with his tiny salamander forelimbs, lifting his blunt ember of a head into the air, the man's eyes tracked it. Making eye contact. With her god.

"Ehm," she said, a noncommittal sound to fill the sudden gap in the conversation. It had been almost thirty years since anyone else had been a witness to the radiant glory of the Chastising Flame, and that someone had been her superior at the High Fane, who had fallen on the swords of the invaders trying to stop them defiling the inner chambers of the temple. Which had subsequently been definitively defiled, because the Pals were nothing if not thorough.

"I…" The Maric stared at Mazdek. And Mazdek, who seldom exhibited more intellect than an actual regular salamander, looked right back with unnerving acuity.

Nothing moved within the box on the Maric's back. Nothing happened whatsoever in it. And yet Tallifer's attention was absolutely drawn to it, beyond all reason. And when she looked back to the Maric his eyes were filled with a terrible hope.

"Do you see?" he asked.

"No," she told him flatly. More emphatically than strictly necessary because she didn't want the answer to become *Yes* any time soon. "Look, yes, it's all new. Yes, they do things different, where you come from. But learn this, Jack. This is the Pal army now. Here we speak Pel and we follow orders and everything's by their book. And those who don't learn, get taught it the hard way. Which includes any little things you might *believe* are the case, that *they* don't see eye to eye on. You keep your *believing* behind closed doors, right, Jack?"

The Maric's eyes strayed to Mazdek again. "But…"

"Nothing to see, Jack," she told him.

His lip stuck out. For a moment she thought he was going to argue. He shrugged, though, and she tried not to think about things sliding about inside the box. There was nothing inside the box. Certainly not more than one of anything, jostled about and complaining.

"Please," he said. "Okay, forget belief. Forget all of that. But I need to speak to the man who was healed."

"The man you healed."

"No, I... Yes, but I... If you like. That man."

"Then you're crap out of luck," she said, not without sympathy. "We are the last appendix of the body military. We are an afterthought. A little game they play until it's not fun any more."

He frowned. "But we're healers."

She shrugged. "We're an experiment. You think the Pals don't have their own doctors? All that reason and logic can't throw up the occasional medico? Of course they do. But some bright spark who'd seen too many cut-open uniforms had the idea that all these barbarians they were conquering might have some use to them, other than decanting. We're an experiment in unorthodox use of tainted resources, Jack. And the moment we make a wave big enough to slop over the bucket, they'll do away with us and just have a few more of their own die instead, and consider themselves more perfect for it."

"But that's..." He wrestled with it, didn't understand it, hated it anyway – all on his face for her to see. "Why do you keep calling me Jack?"

"Banders said that's what you're called," Tallifer said. "On account of you don't do anything well."

"What?"

"Sorry, that's how it comes out in Pel. You do everything a bit, do it all right. Stitch, carry, clean, dispense. Jack of all trades. Maric Jack, she said you were. Seems a safer thing to name you after than... other things."

"I... have an actual name," said Maric Jack.

"Oh sure, but it's one of those weird Maric ones. Can't be doing with them." On the plate the fragrant wax had cooled and set, and Mazdek abandoned it to slither into her sleeve, drawing a hot trail up her inner arm. "I'm Tallifer. The filthy beast coming out of the tent there, with bare feet and his boots in his hand, that's Lochiver."

"The man with the flute." Maric Jack was staring at the old man.

"Don't ask about the flute," she advised. Not because it was forbidden but because Lochiver was a terrible storyteller, especially of the old sacred stories that it had once been his job to tell.

She wondered queasily what Jack saw when he looked at Lochiver. Whether he could spot the extra *presence*, that Tallifer herself could only infer. *What the hell are you, Maric?*

A jolt went through him then, that had nothing to do with gods or their conversation. The hospital had a new visitor: Fellow-Inquirer Prassel. The boss of them all, the Pal officer currently responsible for the hospital experiment. The necromancer.

And straight away, Maric Jack was off on an intercept course, even waving at her like he wasn't a mere Accessory and she a high-ranking Pal officer. Tallifer lunged for him to haul him back, and she'd have managed it, too. Except the bit of him she could have hooked her fingers into was the box, with its sinister little pigeonholes. And she shied away, and the moment was lost.

An Enemy of Peace

There was, of course, a tradition of Palleseen literature. Printed books of appropriately instructional stories were part of a marching army's standard supply. The problem was that, as a society obsessed with perfection, the Pals had perfected the form of the story to the extent that each one followed a prescribed and exacting format, the protagonist's symbolic path slavishly adhered to until any incident of interest was ironed away. There were also collected stories from other cultures that had been brought into the benevolent Palleseen Sway. Whatever flourish and character they might have offered a reader did not survive translation into Pel. The language the Palleseen had created from scratch when they set about perfecting themselves, finding their original native tongue too full of vagaries and mystical reference.

For anyone in Forthright Battalion who sought to while away their time in reading, options were limited.

Chief Accessory Ollery, more commonly known as the Butcher, turned a page with great care. His broad fingers did not play well with the tissue-thin paper – the grade that the Palleseen administration used for mass-distributed forms, circulars and notices, and the Loruthi used for books. He was not supposed to have a Loruthi book, of course. He was most certainly not supposed to have a book printed by the Loruthi in Pel, which was a thing they were doing now. Pel books, but using the language in unexpected ways, like an acrobat escaping a straitjacket. It was, he understood, part of the war effort. Loruthi intellectuals doing their bit to fend off the invaders by sneaking morally corrupting literature where sticky-fingered types like Banders could pick it up and distribute it for coins and favours. For Ollery's part, he thanked them for it. In the rare moments he wasn't up to his elbows in blood or alchemy, he liked a good read, and this current work was a remarkably perverse piece of smut that fair got his juices going.

Speaking of alchemy, though... Something was troubling his nose, a most sensitive organ. "Boy!" he hollered. He was currently reclining on his bedroll in the curtained off nook of his tent, and there had been a suspicious lack of human activity to be heard from the main space. "Boy, what colour? Have you stirred the distillate?"

The silence that greeted this hail signified a world of guilt. Ollery threw the book down and stormed through. Sure enough, the distillate was already discoloured, and probably that was it and he'd need to start the batch again.

The boy was standing there all duty *now*, the big spoon in his hands, but Ollery wasn't fooled for a moment and cuffed him across the ear.

"When it begins to sublimate, you stir. You stir to hold it off, so that the argamesh has time to dissolve properly, without which it won't catalyse the reaction and the whole thing can't enter the third house."

The boy stared at him as though he'd suddenly started speaking fluent Loruthi. "Red," Ollery snapped. "When it starts to go red, stir." Another cuff. They'd been here often enough that there was a kind of ballet to it, the boy's flinch and duck perfectly timed to his swing so that he connected just enough to know he'd done it, while achieving no real impact. "Idiot child." He lumbered over to the tent wall his ingredient racks hung from, and found the henq salts. "These," he said, shoving the little clear vial in the boy's face. "Blue crystals, see? Very pale blue. Not the darker ones, they'll curdle it. One capful, sifted finely across the surface of the mixture, got me?"

The boy had his intent *I'm concentrating* look on, which had no real connection to any actual inner concentration that might be going on. Ollery suited action to words, demonstrating how to apply the salts, that would slow the sublimation and just maybe allow something to be salvaged of the mess.

"If we have to start again because you're too damn idle to watch a pot, I will take it out of your hide," he told the boy. "And I'll send *you* to Fellow-Archivist Plussly to explain why his medicine isn't ready, *and* the others. And they'll each of them be a might less pleased than I am right now, you got me?"

The *I'm concentrating* intensified until the child looked positively constipated with sagacity, at which point Ollery knew the kid wasn't listening any more. He grabbed the boy's ear and hauled him onto his tiptoes.

"This is why we exist," he growled. "This is what keeps us alive, and the hospital open. Not that we save lives, but that some son of a bitch in Higher Orders can get my unguents for his boils, or a noseful of powdered clappa to take his mind off the fact that he's just sent five hundred poor bastards to their deaths. And for that, they tolerate all sorts of shit from us that nobody else gets away with. Like your stupidity or all the god-fondling that goes on behind my back or Banders basically existing at all. You get me?"

And the boy didn't get him. And it wasn't exactly like Ollery was intending to retire any time soon and give the alchemical farm over to the kid as inheritance. But when you knew something useful and were trying to teach it, it was galling when your sole student was so damn slow.

"You are a cursed imbecile," he told the boy. "But it looks like this time you've not screwed up so bad that the batch can't be saved." True enough the redness of the mixture was receding. "Right. Now we add the...?" But that was asking too much. "The Firesian bile, which is the...?" Still, apparently, too much.

"The yellow muck in that pot. No, the other yellow. No, fat-yellow, it's not a fucking custard. And we add how much? Show me with the spoons."

The boy went for the wooden measuring spoons but then – wonder of wonders! – actually diverted and went to the metal ones, because Firesian bile ate away wood like a termite's dream. He got the wrong size, but only by a couple. So either he genuinely had been listening or he was lucky today.

"You do it. One spoon, levelled off, pour off into the near side of the cauldron, then the big spoon for stirring. You got me? And now maybe I can get back to my book." *We were just getting to the good bit with the countess and the conjurer...*

Back on his bedroll, he tried to find his page again. It sounded as though peace and quiet were commodities in as short supply as good tea and well-fit boots today because someone had started shouting right outside. The Butcher gathered in a lungful to bellow the interloper into silence, then stopped because it was the new man, what was his name? Maric Jack, Banders said. He'd not been here a day and already he was off on one, apparently.

"It's vitally important I go see the man, the spy," the man declared, Maric accent making his Pel sound like he had a cold and was doing a funny voice at the same time. And, at whatever brush-off he received, "No, listen. Nobody listens around here. I know you think it's all roses because he's back on his feet, but the moment he opens his mouth he's going to die. It'll all come back. It won't last. Unless he swears not to do – no, don't walk away from me! Why does everyone just walk away from me around here?"

Because you're a madman shouting in the street, Ollery thought uncharitably. *You carry on like this back wherever you come from, see how people react.*

The man barked out something in Maric, a language apparently designed for people to use while being strangled – probably it was some colourfully religious oath that simply didn't exist in Pel, on account of it expressing sentiments unnecessary in a perfected society. Except it was weird how, even after they'd been with the army for years and lost every other word of their native tongue, people always seemed to hang on to the oaths.

"I need to save him!" Maric Jack yelled. "I need you to take me to him now, please! He has to be warned, or else he'll die. It's not a blessing you see! It's a curse!"

Ollery had seen the man that Jack had healed. The spy had looked a long way off dying to the Butcher's experienced eye. The eldritch sucking wound was gone, the man hale and hearty, not a cough or a fever or a stubbed toe. From death's door to the healthiest man in Forthright Battalion. *If I could bottle a curse like that I'd be a wealthy man.*

But enough was enough, and Ollery wasn't going to find out what the countess was going to do to the conjurer with all this going on just a canvas wall away. He hid the book in the concealed pocket of the sock-stuffed knapsack that served as his pillow and shambled back out. The boy was at least putting on a reasonable impersonation of someone watching the cauldrons, and nothing was on fire, so he judged he was free to go slap some quiet into Maric Jack as a welcome to the hospital department.

Except it turned out to be a lot worse than he'd thought, because Jack wasn't just ranting at all comers. Instead he was going full force at none other than Fellow-Inquirer Prassel herself.

Ollery's relationship with Prassel was a complicated thing. Prassel was a woman of many aspects. On the one hand she was exactly one of those ambitious mid-ranking officers that the army was overly supplied with, determined that her future was going to have considerably more badges, medals and certificates of commendation than her present. On the other hand she was the officer in charge of the field hospital, Ollery's direct superior, the bottleneck through which the medicos communicated with the rest of the army. And the thing that Maric Jack had yet to learn is that neither of these hands was the charitable giving sort. And that was even without bringing up Prassel's specialism, because necromancy seldom bred kindness. Arrogance, yes. A heedless disregard for human life. And on occasion an academic over-enthusiasm that led to the sort of experimentation that got Correct Speech called in with the correctional thumbscrews. Except Prassel *was* Correct Speech as well, and that was a whole extra hand poised to slap down Maric Jack if he took just one more liberty.

She was, however, walking away from him, just striding briskly across the little cleared space the medicos' tents all faced onto. Heroically ignoring the awkward Pel of the Maric's demands. Until he lurched after her and grabbed her sleeve, hauling the astonished officer to a halt.

Prassel did not like to be touched, Ollery knew that much. Some necromancers went that way, and frankly he preferred that to the alternative. More than that, though, one of the lower orders – an Accessory, lowest of the low – did not lay hands on a superior officer. Most especially not here in the open with every medico there to witness it, and a whole camp of soldiers who could just turn their heads and see. Prassel had frozen, and Ollery did his best to slink back into his tent and pretend to have been somewhere else gathering herbs or something. He was a big man, though, and slinking was not his forte. Prassel's voice arrested him before he got under cover of the canvas.

When he turned around, two soldiers had magically appeared and were holding the Maric's arms. No great feat of conjuration, to find soldiers in an army camp, but the speed with which they'd turned up was impressive. And showed that more ears than just medical ones had been drawn by Jack's shouting. Which meant that it wasn't just going to be a case of taking the man aside for a slap and a talk about what it meant to wear the uniform.

Well, crap, Ollery thought. It wouldn't be the first time by any means. Rather this new boy than Banders again. But still. Not a part of the job that he particularly enjoyed, no matter what people said about him.

"Infringing the dignity of an officer," Prassel said. Ollery almost mouthed the words along with her. She met his gaze. Younger, more ambitious, more decorated and very definitely superior in every respect, and yet there was room in that shared look for a little give and take. After all, she was in charge of the hospital department but it was the Butcher's circus.

"Six," she said. "Here, now. Get it over with."

Ollery nodded heavily. Six was more than four but less than twelve, as they said. Those being the first three grades of minor correction set out in the manuals.

"You'd better hoist him up then," he said, because technically he couldn't order regular soldiers about save in the hospital tent where his word was law. They knew their business, though. There was a post driven into the ground beside Tallifer and Lochiver's shared tent, that served duty as a notice board and hitching post, but also this. They got Jack's box off him, then stripped him of jacket and shirt, leaving a bare back skinny enough that Ollery could count every rib and knob of spine. Maric Jack was still protesting that he needed to be taken to the spy even as they got the rope about his wrists and then jerked it over the hook at the post's top.

"Boy!" he barked. "How's the distillate?" And, when the child poked his head out of Ollery's tent to nod that it all looked within tolerance, "Get me the Alder."

The kid actually flinched at the word, then saw Jack at the post with his bare arms above his head. And Ollery hadn't ever used the Alder on the boy, but he'd certainly threatened it when he was angry enough. Not something be was proud of, but his hot temper was a storm that rained down any words that seemed satisfying in the moment. And it was the hot temper most everyone saw, of Ollery. The cold one was a knife he tried to keep sheathed.

The Alder was a long, flexible switch of wood. Root, actually. Out in Jarokir they had these weird trees that moved, actually crawled about, even caught animals. Their roots were long and

61

nightmarish vegetal tentacles, and if you treated them properly they stayed supple forever. When the boy surrendered it to him, he flexed it in his hands, bent it into a loop, ran his fingers about the braided leather of the grip. Everyone was watching by then. The entire business of the hospital department, and every neighbouring tent, had come to a halt. More circus than even the Butcher felt like playing ringmaster to, but what could you do?

He was expecting begging. Or, given how hapless Maric Jack seemed, some querulous demand to know what was going on. Instead the man was craning back at him and still wanting to talk to the spy. It was sufficiently monomaniac that Ollery was wondering if he should be dispensing something for it. Wouldn't be the first man to step into the hospital with his mind cracked open. Wouldn't be the first on the staff, even.

A memory surfaced then, unwelcome as a cyst. Chief Accessory Erinael, whose shoes Ollery's big feet had overfilled. The way she could touch the brow of a raving madman and bring calm and clarity. Would she have whispered in Maric Jack's ear and had this obsession out of him like a gallstone, not even a scar to show for the operation? But, like all good things, Erinael had come to a bad end. And though her fall had meant his own profoundly meagre elevation, Ollery would have given a great deal for her to still be with them.

Because now it was just him, standing here with the Alder in his hand.

The boy knew enough to bring the ulmel in its porcelain pot, the one with the frog on its lid. Ollery let Jack's words bounce off his ears as he slicked a sheen of it along the rod's narrow length.

He struck the first blow while Jack was still babbling because it was plain the man wouldn't shut up. He couldn't have said beforehand whether Jack would be a clencher or a howler, and what he actually got was more a sort of *Yawp!* sound as the man's words got unceremoniously cut off.

"One," Ollery said, loud enough for everyone, and drew back the Alder for another strike. And stopped.

"Don't," he said, quiet and just for Jack now. Or Jack and the boy, who was using his privileged position as disciplinarian's assistant to get a better view.

Jack drew in a ragged breath. "I mean," he said, with creditable self-possession. "I'd have thought that'd be my line."

"Just don't. It's not clever," Ollery told him.

"I'm not clever," Jack said quietly, letting his slight weight pull at the ropes. "Look, this is a thing that's happening to me, right enough. Just do it, will you. Chief."

Ollery looked bleakly at the man's back. Smart mouths on new boys didn't ever go well. With a convulsive motion he lashed the Alder across the man's back again.

"One," he declared again, and even your average soldier knew that wasn't right, and people began peering to see what was going on. Jack twisted under the blow with another bark of pain, then caught up and started demanding what the hell had happened to two?

Ollery watched it happen this time, the bloom of red just receding into the man's skin until there was nothing. And that was a fine gift to have in any other damned circumstances but this. He leaned in, one hand a crushing weight on the Maric's knobbly shoulder.

"Listen, Jack," he growled. "I figure you don't understand how they do correction in this man's army, so here's the regs. There is an officer in every battalion, the most despised man you can imagine, whose job it is to witness the back of every disciplined man. I have been ordered to give you six, and unless I can show him exactly that many stripes across your back, no more, no less, then you will get this all over again and maybe they'll put up a big stout post next to yours and give me four for being soft. Do you understand me, you magic foreign prick?"

"Well just do it then," Jack hissed back. There were tears of pain in his eyes but Ollery would have had more sympathy if they were matched by similar evidence on his back. "Or did I miss the class on Pel where you've got more than one number 'one' in your bloody maths?"

Ollery blinked. "Do you not *know*," he said slowly, "that you're doing it?"

"Doing what?"

And Ollery told him, setting out in a child's detail the way things normally went at a whipping.

"Oh crap," Jack whimpered. "You have to stop."

"I..." Ollery wasn't sure just how many ways he could explain what was going on, "can't stop. Look, you don't seem to understand how this army works—"

"Not you. You." And he was looking down at the ground like his feet were conspiring against him. "Stop it. Is this funny to you? Is this... All right, no. You were helping. That's fine. Help less. Help later. This is serious. This *hurts*."

"Hurts still?" Ollery felt that tediously familiar queasy sense of being too close to the uncanny, but that was basically his life since coming to the hospital.

"I mean not now but it bloody did when you hit me. Just..." And Jack was arguing with the ground again, "don't. Or I'll disown you, you bastard."

Ollery caught up, because he'd seen this sort of thing before a couple of times. An occupational hazard of the medical unit. Talking to things that weren't there. Except sometimes they were.

"Your god," he said, too quiet even for the boy now.

Jack's eye swivelled madly to peer at him. "Please." And then, before he could misinterpret, "Just whip me. If you must. But please, don't take him away."

Ollery held his face without expression. He was aware that none of his stock faces would help Jack right now. Not the jolly family butcher nor a great slab of ill temper in the periphery of Jack's vision.

He stepped back and wound up the Alder again. And there

was no prayer in him, good Pal that he was, but he fervently hoped for a lack of divine intervention in the correctional proceedings.

He struck and Jack squawked, and this time the red slash across the man's shoulders stayed put like it should. The Tally's script, as the soldiers called it, in reference to that officer whose job it was to make sure every bad student completed their lines. Ollery oiled the Alder with another coat of ulmel, because all the talking had given it time to dry. The stuff was disinfectant and painkiller, because a flogging could go septic if you let it, and if Lochiver wasn't on his game. In Jack's case he wasn't sure it was necessary, but he was a man of routine, even in this.

"One," he said, with a sick kind of relief, and then went through each of the other five strokes with a solid, ponderous rhythm, calling them out for the crowd. Plenty of the watching soldiers had felt somebody's lash, and always better when another poor sod was hooked to the post. A mix of sympathy, relief and small-minded betting about when the weeping would start, then. But army life was very dull when it wasn't far too exciting and so you took your entertainment where you could.

The weeping started after the third blow, early enough that Jack lost a lot of people their backpay or rations. The Maric pressed his forehead to the post and clenched his fists and shook, tensing each time and trying not to scream, and failing not to scream. And Ollery had been whipped himself, more than once, and he'd held out longer than three before even screaming once, but he'd screamed eventually, and wept before the end.

"Six," he declared. "Now get him to the Tally, double time." *Before he heals and we have to do the whole bloody business again.*

Outside the Tally Officer's tent, after the man had pedantically counted the stripes twice over, Ollery sat Jack down. Banders had come along, carrying shirt and jacket draped over that wooden box, and normally he wouldn't have thought the man would needed either garment for a while, but in this case...

"I have a salve," he said, "for your back. But I don't know if you want it. You may as well do your thing."

Maric Jack was bent over, his hands clenched on his knees, the bloody topography of his back and shoulders set out like a campaign map of difficult terrain. His head jerked up and he said, "I can't. I don't *do* anything. I didn't heal the spy. I don't control it."

"Learn to control it," Ollery advised flatly. "Wrangle whatever god or spirit or ghost it is that dogs your heels, or you're no use to anyone."

"I'm no use to anyone," Jack agreed. "I never was. Not like that. It's all..." And he jerked his head towards the box, which Banders promptly put down like it was full of snakes, wiping her hands frantically on her breeches.

Ollery was about to ask why Jack kept his god in a box. Then he considered how many little round door holes the box had, and got a bit of a creeping moment when he wondered just how many residents had been signed up as hospital staff under Jack's one card.

"God is a healing god," Jack said. The pain was still there, a wire of it weaving through his words. "He's a truculent bastard. He won't do anything any way but his own. He has rules."

"So does the army," Ollery said. "And I've seen god rules and army rules clash before. And the army is still marching."

"God's rule is 'do no harm'. And if you do harm, after God heals, then he takes it back. I've seen it happen. Far too many times. That's why I have to warn your spy."

"This again?" Ollery demanded. "Forget it. It's not your business."

"It's a man's life!" Jack actually leaped to his feet, fists clenched. "Isn't that what we're supposed to make our business, at your hospital?"

Ollery blinked at him mildly. "Turn around," he suggested, "if you please."

Jack looked shifty, turned a shuffling full circle. When he came back round, his eyes were on the box. The house for gods.

"Give him his shirt back," said Ollery wearily. While the man struggled back into his clothes he added, "Give up on the man. They won't let you see him. Some things you can't help. That's another rule of army life. Unless you're Banders, who seems to be able to get away with anything."

Banders gave a little laugh, although she was obviously still a bit spooked by the box. Her eyes followed it as Jack hoist it back onto his unblemished shoulders. When he addressed her directly, she jumped, as though gods would come out of his mouth instead of words.

"Find him, please," Jack said. "Tell him: do no harm. Nothing that would bring harm to anybody, not friend, not enemy. Just tell him that's the pin that keeps the healing in place."

"I mean," said Banders slowly. "This is an army. You know what an army is, right? I'm sure you Marics had them."

"Oh the Marics didn't have any time for God either," Jack said in a small voice. "Believe me, you Pals didn't get much persecution in, when you conquered us – sorry, it's 'liberated', isn't it. Silly me. We were already pretty much persecuted out of existence by then. Except for me. Except for me, and God. It's just us. But please, Banders. I'll… owe you, I guess. Whatever that means. Please do this for me."

For him, and for some spy he never met and knows nothing about, Ollery thought. And surely there was an angle, but right then he couldn't see it, and that was profoundly more disquieting than any amount of double-dealing and corruption. He caught Banders looking at him, and gave her a nod on the sly, because what could it harm? She rolled her eyes, but then was off on her mission, high-stepping over tent-ropes like a heron.

"Can you walk?" he asked Maric Jack.

The man nodded, though not without a little hesitation. Yes

the welts had gone from his back, but not from his mind. Still a lot of tenderness there.

"Learn," Ollery told him. "Look at me, Jack. You see this face? You see these hands? They do not belong to a good or kind man. Good, kind men do not prosper in war. But they belong to a man who understands how to behave within an army. Learn. Learn about orders and obedience and privileges of rank. I have cauldrons that need watching back at my tent. I don't want to spend time writing tallies into your back. I have better things to do with it." *I am a brute. I care about nothing but myself.* Aware that he didn't quite have the act down, that some errant humanity was still guttering about the edges of his words.

"I'll learn," Jack said, and worst of all, "thank you." So that Ollery wanted to shake him until his teeth rattled.

"You need some time to recuperate."

"I'm fine."

"You need a couple of hours. Standard after a flogging." *If not for the pain, then to get your head around how your life is now.* "Someone to talk to." *Someone to convince you about the ways of the world because I don't have the time or the energy.* "Come with me. I'll take you to Mother Semprellaime."

Unspeakable Trades

Much like the Jarokiri with their aggressively outward-looking pantheon, Allor was always going to be on the Palleseen list. A culture intimately intertwined with magic and pacts with Those Below, a holdover from a less rational age. Almost a decade, now, since the armies marched in and put all that moth-eaten occult set-dressing to the torch, dragging the Allorwen kicking and screaming into the modern age. Just about the one place you'd not look to find an Allorwen magician was within a Palleseen army camp, any more than you'd look to find a priest.

As well as the vast number of tents – more tents than the Maric really felt should exist in a sound world – and a quantity of prefab sheds and huts, there were the wagons. The army was a mobile feast, after all. Or, given the rate at which it devoured life, a mobile feaster. Sometimes it was just easier never to unpack, to live off your wheels. The Butcher was leading him through a little district of them right now. Definitely a meaner neighbourhood than the regulation-spaced camping of the soldiers. He, the city boy, was beginning to understand that the camp was itself a city. It had its Hill where the officers were, its Gutter Districts of massed soldiery, its Hammer Districts of forges and workshops, its commercial street where the quartermasters and sutlers bickered and bartered. One could almost have relaxed into it, as though he'd just decided to move out to some other town where everyone had a weirdly similar dress sense. Except that, instead of dancers and buskers and pickpockets, the open spaces here had men and women performing baton drill. The machinists and smiths were repairing and manufacturing the hundred small components of a war machine. The quartermasters were dispensing weapons-grade tablethi and not even asking for money in return.

"What am I doing here?" he complained to himself.

The Butcher had good ears. "I don't know, Jack. You tell me."

He wondered whether now was a good time to explain that he wasn't named Jack, Maric or otherwise. Looking at the slightly sunburned, knot-eared bulge that was the back of the Butcher's head, at his broad back and powerful whipping shoulders, he decided that it wasn't worth the venture. And why not? New town, new name. Maybe some of his old bad luck would lose track of him in the crowd because of it.

"It's complicated," he said.

"They caught you, and some spark remembered the standing order for healers at the hospital department," the Butcher clarified over his shoulder.

And it had been considerably more than that, from Jack's perspective, but not as far as any Pal paperwork would evidence. "Well, maybe it's not that complicated, then," he admitted.

The Butcher stopped abruptly. Jack almost ran into him and then flinched back when the man turned. He hadn't meant to. It was the sheer gravity of the man. The fire of the lash was abruptly in the front of his mind again, because even if his back was made whole, that didn't mean the agony of the punishment had been lost on him. All this must have made it to his face because the Butcher didn't immediately say what he'd been about to, just studied Jack and decided how he felt about things.

"We don't have to be friends," the big man said ponderously, in the manner of a man who doesn't have friends and doesn't particularly miss them. "You want to think about the Alder, every time you look at me, maybe that's for the best. Keep you on the narrow, you get me?" A sullen pause, nothing readable in the man's pig-like eyes, the great slab of hanging meat that was his face. "You're not the first. You won't be the last. You're *just another one.* To me. To the Fellow-Inquirer whose coat you tugged at. You're here because they thought you could make yourself useful. But learn this, Jack. That's not enough. There was a – a woman. The Chief before me. She was useful. She was useful enough that the rest of us needn't have been there. That trick you pulled, with the spy—"

"Not me," Jack said, automatically, but a flick of the Butcher's smallest finger waved that away.

"That trick, that would have been child's play to her." And there was real emotion in his voice, the sort of deep hidden current that drags swimmers to drowning. "I don't think there was anything she couldn't heal."

He even left a gap there, in case Jack wanted to put up any more words for him to trample over, but there was patently another conversational shoe waiting to drop, and Jack just let him dangle it by the laces until he was ready.

"She's gone now, as you've guessed," the Butcher agreed. "Because she was *useful*, but she wasn't *compliant.* It got too much for her. The way we do things." And he could have meant not tugging on a coat or he could have meant a hundred thousand soldiers trampling roughshod over a nation. "So remember that nobody's too useful to be *used.*" Making a bludgeon of the final word. And for a moment Jack wondered what there had been between the Butcher and his former superior, but that wasn't it. Not some old romantic scar tugging. He wondered just *what* this great healer had been, in a woman's guise. He was from Ilmar, after all. They had a lot of the uncanny in his home city.

The Butcher judged that his message had been heard and understood, and continued between the jumble of wagons until he arrived at a high-sided, curve-roofed affair. It was painted a grey-blue that was plainly trying to be army standard but hadn't quite matched shades, with paler circles on the long walls. A fair-sized conveyance, though shabby. On the steps at the back, an old woman sat smoking a long, twisted reed – a vice Jack had seen here and there about the camp but that was unknown in Ilmar. She looked up and flicked the last ashy inch onto the ground.

"Early for business, Chief," she said. Her voice was a gravelly croak, the accent unmistakeable. An Allorwen, here in the midst of a sea of Pals.

"Jack here needs breathing space," the Butcher said. "He's learning the ropes the hard way. Just 'cos he's still got his shirt on doesn't mean it wasn't for want of any trying from me." A little gesture of the wrist that somehow encapsulated the whole whipping. Jack found himself flinching again and hated himself for it. "Better he gets a hot drink and maybe makes a friend outside the department, in case he needs someone to come to." And a coin, a worn penny, conjured up by those thick fingers. "Not business, just a place to be that isn't full of all those nosy sons of bitches at the hospital prying into him."

"And what did he do, that they'd pry?" the old woman asked suspiciously.

"Healed someone from death."

"I didn't," Jack put in automatically, but neither of them paid him any heed.

"You don't want to go about healing people in a hospital. Sets a precedent," the woman said sourly. "I've got the kettle on the fire. I'll get him tea." She inspected the penny. "Not the good tea, though."

The Butcher nodded. "Jack, Mother Semprellaime. Mother, this is Maric Jack, latest damned soul in hell."

After the man had gone, Mother Semprellaime levered herself up from the backboard of the wagon, making a big show of unkinking her back. She really was a caricature of a Allorwen witch, with a face full of wrinkles, a hook of a nose and warts.

One eye bulged, the other nested in a webwork of creases. She wore layer over layer of ragged smocks and shifts and dresses. Jack, who found Pal clothes to pinch in all the wrong places, rather envied her that. Whatever she did in the army, it didn't require her to wear the uniform.

"Let me get the clothes in," she said. "Then tea." There were cords hung between all the nearby wagons, with uniform shirts and breeches and stockings swaying like the boughs of a sartorial forest. A lot of the wagon-owners around here seemed to be old men or women, and Jack guessed that laundry was a part of warfare that never got written up in the histories but was big business nonetheless.

She began plucking down garments and folding them, her crabbed hands still nimble. After a couple, Jack came over to help.

"I thought the Butcher whipped you," she noted.

"Oh he did," Jack agreed. "Didn't take. I think he's worried it's going to become a regular thing. Weekly entertainment at the hospital… district?"

"Department," she corrected. "Pals love their departments. Schools, offices, armies. All one to them. I've got family in Telmark. Ilmar."

"I'm from Ilmar."

She stopped, the air between them frosty. Because the Marics didn't like the Allorwen much more than the Pals did, traditionally. And Jack didn't say, *Some of my best friends are Allorwen*, or start talking about the little ghetto her people lived in, in his city. Or talk about his own particular visits to that gnarl of streets. None of it would do anything but widen the distance between them, even though he actually *had* made Allorwen friends, in the end. After his life had gone wildly off the tracks and he'd become a dangerous criminal.

She let him help bring the laundry in, and afterwards she went into the wagon and he trailed after. There was a little fire there, and it burned in a metal bowl without obvious fuel. The bowl was decorated with sigils he recognised as ritual workings. Probably once it had been part of some grand incantation, a witness to fiendish bargains and the invoking of otherworldly powers. Now there was a kettle hung over it, and Mother Semprellaime prepared two cups of what smelled like modestly decent tea.

Jack unshipped his box from his shoulders and glanced around. They were in a room that must have taken up no more than a third of the wagon's interior. The more he looked, the more of a sense he had, of what Mother Semprellaime might be. There were twisted corn dolls on the walls, and he'd seen those before in the Allorwen district of Ilmar. The scroll pinned up by the door was a calendar that tracked moons and stars that weren't to be seen in the regular sky, and he knew how the Pals were jealous about everyone using their own days and weeks and weights and measures. And there was that magical bowl, amongst a people always looking for an excuse to squeeze the power out of things for their own use. And...

He stepped back carefully, staring at his feet. The wooden boards of the wagon were remarkably clean and scrubbed, save where he'd tracked mud in. But he could still see the faint scuffs where chalk markings hadn't quite been scrubbed away. He could even connect the pale remnants, draw the circle in his mind.

When he looked up, he met Mother Semprellaime's crooked gaze. Behind all of that time-raddled topology it was hard to read her, but easy to guess that she'd seen him work it out.

"I won't tell," he said quickly. Not because he was in the lair of a conjurer, surrounded by her magic workings and potentially at her mercy, but because he wouldn't tell. Shopping people to the Pals wasn't something you did, even if he was now wearing the uniform. "I'm sorry. It's none of my business. You're safe."

Her look twisted to a whole new level of crookedness. "What are you talking about?"

"Your conjuring. It's nothing to do with me. I won't tell."

"I mean, it could be. To do with you," she said carefully, watching him for a reaction or, no, trying to understand what he meant.

"I mean it. It can't be easy. With the army right there. But it's your... your... I won't tell anyone."

"You keep saying that," the old woman said mildly. "What do you think I'm *doing* here, Maric?"

His eyes strayed to the clothes basket. "Laundry...?"

She laughed like a toad. "Oh, we all do the laundry. Means that if some Sage-Inquirer with a stick up his ass comes calling, there's a reason for us being here. But that's just daytime work." She stared at him. "Maric, don't you know what a circle house *is*?"

And that explained those designs on the outside of the wagon, because the Palleseen army apparently had standard décor even for those things that it couldn't officially admit existed.

"This wagon," he clarified, "is a circle house? You're a...?"

"A bawd," she said flatly. "And this wagon is a brothel. It just happens to be one where you get a demon, rather than a flesh and blood woman. There are advantages. It can be less complicated. Or there are specialised tastes. We cater to all sorts. Some people prefer it."

"Yes," said Jack. "Yes, they do."

Remembering.

"No," snapped a peevish voice from around knee level. He closed his eyes. Not that he could ever *forget* he was never alone, but sometimes it was nice to push the thought to the back of his head for a while.

He glanced down at the box. God was sitting on top of it. Ragged, filthy God with His snarled beard, wasted legs dangling, minuscule heels knocking at the wood. Arms folded like a disapproving aunt.

"You will *not* indulge in that foreign *filth*." Thus spake God, who was a Maric God and Did Not Approve.

"I'm not your priest any more," Jack said. "I can do what I want."

"I still forbid it," God said. "It's unnatural."

"Well, yes," Jack agreed weakly. "By definition." And Mother Semprellaime was watching him talk to his box, of course.

"I was going to ask," she said carefully, "if you wanted seed, for your birds. But I take it that a handful of grain won't cut it?"

"I mean they'd take it. As an offering," Jack said.

"I will not!" God kicked harder at the box and there was a complaining sound from within which meant one of the others was awake now, too. "Although I will have the tea."

"It's foreign tea," Jack said meanly. "You wouldn't like it."

"Any port in a storm," God decided. "You will just have to do penance for serving your God inferior tea."

"I'm not your priest any more."

"Worshippers can still do penance."

Jack closed his eyes, feeling not for the first time that he was the very exemplar of no good deed going unpunished. When he opened them again, Mother Semprellaime had a shallow bowl for him, a thin skin of tea lapping around the interior. As though he was about to feed a cat with peculiar appetites. He took it and placed it on the box. God rolled His eyes, as though aggrieved the woman didn't have a tiny teacup for Him. It wasn't as though He actually physically drank the tea anyway. He just sat near it, and it slowly dried up.

And the other two were emerging now. A spindly figure either wearing or made of bundled twigs, shedding a constant sad rain of dry leaves, a haunt of woodlice and termites and other things that lived in dead wood. It turned a round wooden mask on Jack, that was mostly two owlish eye sockets, and hooted. The third one was more shadowy. An angular figure in oilcloth and canvas, like a sailor buried at sea. The sharp prong of a harpoon that it never let go of. A hat like a slanted roof with the hint of a grim little skull beneath the brim. They jostled God until He grudgingly let them get at the tea.

"What have you brought," Mother Semprellaime said, "under my roof?"

"I'm sorry," Jack said. "I should have thought. I should have asked. Gods. It's gods."

"Gods plural?"

"I'm afraid so."

She watched the tea dry up, then went and fetched a couple of biscuits. One she broke into several pieces that she sprinkled onto the little plate, the other she gave to Jack.

He looked at it, a tiny and unasked-for kindness, and was abruptly fighting back a wave of tears vast as the sea. His shoulders, released from the box's existential weight, shook with the effort of not just bawling like a child. The emotions came at him from nowhere – or from behind the brave face he'd tried to hang onto as the Alder came down across his shoulders. From the moment he'd understood it was execution or exile from the only home he'd ever known. From the fighting in the streets of Ilmar. From the long-ago day he'd seen his mentor dangling at the end of a rope, and the time, more recently, they'd tried to serve him the same way. And he clutched the teacup so hard it was a miracle he didn't crush it, and bent his head over it, and shook. Shook for all these things, and for the hated uniform they'd made him wear, and for all the things to come.

After a while Mother Semprellaime pulled up a stool and guided him down onto it, then lowered herself creakily into another. Her hand hovered at his shoulder like a fly wary of the swat, then came to rest there.

"Welcome to the army life," she said. "You'll get over it. Or most do. It's not the life any of us would have chosen." And maybe she'd be a grand votaress in Allor, if the Pals hadn't come. A great and respected scholar. A mother, a wife, any regular person who wasn't a part of the Palleseen war machine.

"You're a priest, then," she said. "Is that what they got you for? Then you were lucky. Mostly the Pals still kill priests. Be glad they've found other uses for some of them."

"I'm not a priest any more," he got out. "I was. A priest of God. *God* god." Meeting the angry little creature's scowl, as though he'd been caught revealing trade secrets. "But I left His service, broke His strictures. It made sense at the time. I was trying to save lives. Then things got complicated."

Semprellaime sipped her tea.

"You are not to tell her," God said. "I forbid it. They forbid it as well." He gestured at the other two gods. The dying nature god cocked his circular face and made a sound like crickets. There had been oracles, Jack guessed, who had listened on the wind for its mystic pronouncements, foretold the deaths of kings and the fall of empires. But those days were dust and nobody yet lived who could interpret the god's messages. Just animal noises, from prophecy to low-rent children's entertainment. Save that there weren't even children who could hear it.

The other god, the grim one, said nothing. Probably it did forbid. It looked the sort that forbad things.

"I saw gods," Jack told Mother Semprellaime. "It was like, my whole life, I'd seen *God.* And when I threw Him out, there was a hole left, and through the hole I could see... gods. All the gods that had been worshipped once, been brought to Ilmar by some congregation, even just a single follower maybe. And nobody was left who remembered them. Except they hadn't gone away. The streets of Ilmar were littered with discarded gods. I could see them all. It was horrible."

"So that is, what, a charitable hostel for homeless gods?" She poked a square-toed clog at the box but stopped short of actually kicking it.

"It was. A shrine. I carried it around the city. People made offerings. For a little while things were actually going quite well." Honestly better than any other time of his life, really. He'd found he had friends all over the city. People who looked at him and saw someone worthwhile, though mad. Doing something that, even though none of them believed in the little gods he talked about, still had a kind of symbolic value. Like a licensed fool in the court of a bored emperor.

"And then the new man came," he explained, because he'd love to leave it there, with him happy, but it wasn't honest and didn't explain his change of wardrobe. "The old Perfector got recalled, after the troubles. Or went mad and ran away. Or something. Nobody was quite sure. But the new man was from Correct Erudition, and the war was starting, this war, the Loruthi war." Because the Pals were always at war with *someone* so you had to make the distinction. "He turned up with orders to squeeze the magic out of Ilmar. Harvest it for tablethi to be sent to the front. And he came down hard on your people. Sorry. And he raided the Guildhall and the Armigers. And he had this thing, this... sort of a hat."

That hadn't been where Semprellaime had been expecting the sentence to go and she snorted into her tea, but Jack hadn't been trying for comedy. There was probably a formal Pel word for the hat, but he didn't know it.

"A hat, with these... lenses. You put tablethi in, and it gave out a light you couldn't see... except, in that light, he could see gods. This was a thing he'd done elsewhere. Like someone who works out there's a few grains of gold in the dust under their feet. The lowest, meanest possible source of profit, but if you can harvest it efficiently enough..."

Something had changed in her face, some inner revulsion that left her features just hanging there like dead things. He chose to interpret that as her agreeing with his sentiments.

"They sent out... they called them Ratcatchers. Special squads, with gear to catch all the little—" he almost said *vermin* then, which God would not have appreciated. "All the *things* that had just built up, encrusted Ilmar over the centuries. And I know that's what they *do*, just sand down everyone's culture until we're all like them. But they were doing it with the stuff we didn't even know we had, but it was still *us*, you know? And someone had to do something."

Mother Semprellaime had presumably seen a lot in her life, of wickedness and the weird, but this was apparently a new one on her. She was completely rapt, tea cooling and forgotten.

"I started smuggling gods out of the city," Jack said. "I would get them into my box. I'd go ahead of the Ratcatchers. There would always be someone who'd give me a lift out to a village, a farm, where I could let them out. Or the Wood, one or twice." He shuddered, and she obviously didn't know enough about Ilmar to catch the capital letter. "I can't fight. I'm not allowed to fight. It's my faith. It's God's one real commandment."

"I have other commandments," God commented acidly. "It's just the only one you kept."

And Jack faced down God, stared and stared until He, the divine He, looked away, ashamed of Himself.

"But I fought," Jack finished the sentence. "I fought by saving gods from the Decanters. I thought it was a good thing to do. And it wasn't as if I was doing much good otherwise." And perhaps that was selling himself short. The tasks he'd been handy about in the hospital had been skills he'd learned on the streets. God wouldn't heal injured rebels and victims of the Pals – not if they wanted to stay healed – but Jack could stitch and bandage and make a stab at the right sort of medicine half the time. A weirdly piecemeal education to have become his actual profession now.

"They must have been very grateful," Semprellaime said, and Jack laughed. A real, big, braying laugh, with just an edge of hysteria.

"Oh, you think?" he asked her, wide-eyed. "The people, you mean, or the gods, or any of them. Oh, doing favours for divinity is a good way of starving to death, believe me!"

"I resent that," God said. "I have always looked after you." And that was a lie so vast that Jack was vaguely surprised God didn't unmake Himself simply in the telling of it.

"And you brought the gods here?" Semprellaime asked. "You know there's a decanting department right over there, yes?"

"I mean, no, but I could probably have guessed if I thought about it," Jack said, rubbing at his face. "But they caught me. They worked out what I was doing. The new man, he was sharp. Or sneaky enough to spot another sneak. And I was on their books already. As a healer. And the war, like I said. Someone looked at the scales and decided it was better to send me here to save Pal lives than just hang me again, I guess. And I couldn't leave God. Or the others I hadn't found homes for." The faint odours of divinity. Decaying leaf litter; dead fish, salt and anger. "I know it's not safe, but where is? Should I have left them in a cellar for the Ratcatchers?"

She put a hand on his knee and he twitched at the contact. "I think you're a good man. Within your limits."

"I'm not. Or if I am, I'm so limited as to make no difference to the world."

"You made a difference to the gods."

His hands attempted to describe how big the world was, how small the gods. The sympathy from her was bringing on the tears again. It really had been quite a long while since anybody had been *nice* to him. He had lost his armour against it.

"Don't," God warned. "I will not have you falling to the wiles of this Allorwen hussy."

"This *what?*" Jack demanded. "I'm not – I mean she's not going to, I mean, she must be—" Trying to indicate without actually *saying* it that Mother Semprellaime was plainly four decades and change older than him and so no hussying was likely to be happening. And, midway through that dumbshow, seeing that most of the lines on the woman's face were drawn on with pen, that the nose and the eye and the warts were a combination of make-up and wax and the way she had of holding her face. That the ancient crone, exactly the sort of person you'd expect to be keeping a circle house of forbidden delights, was not much older than he was.

She saw him see it, and recoiled like a sea creature retreating into the sand. A sudden wariness, and he understood there were other reasons you didn't want to look young when you were surrounded by Pal soldiers short on entertainment.

"Sorry," he muttered. "I won't tell. Anyone." Odd echoes of his previous misunderstanding. "The Butcher…?"

She nodded. "Oh it's hard to put one past Chief Accessory Ollery. We go back some years. We do each other favours. Plus we both need the same reagents sometimes. It's good to have friends."

"That sounds like a fine thing," Jack agreed, with another sour look at God. You couldn't be friends with a god. Or not with this cantankerous specimen, anyway.

"Drop by, if you need to get away from the hospital," she said, straight out. "If you need better tea than they have. If you need to talk."

He stared at her. "Why?" Not ungrateful, just not sure why the privilege was being extended to him. And, at the back of his mind, the other thing, the actual purpose of her wagon, the services it provided. That one time, back in Ilmar, when he'd…

"You will bloody *not*," God told him. "You won't even *think* it. I – we all three of us utterly forbid. Yasnic, listen to me now."

"It's Jack," he told God. "Maric Jack. Didn't you hear? That's me, now. And thank you." To Semprellaime, because it wasn't like he had much to thank God for. "I… don't want to be a burden. To anybody. But I would like to. If that's all right. Maybe."

She waited to see if he had any more qualifiers to water down the sentiment with, then took his finished cup from him.

"Another?"

"I'll go back to the hospital now, I think." He stood, feeling almost ridiculously better just from having been able to sit down and talk. "I won't say that they're missing me, but I don't want them to think I'm a slacker."

"I think Banders has that position nailed down," she said, taking the empty plate from his box with a curious respect, a nod of reverence for the motley of divinities she couldn't see.

God stuck His nose in the air aloofly, refusing to have anything to do with that foreign respect, even though He'd taken the tea. Jack stretched, considering how lucky that he could do that without opening six lines of pain across his back. He opened the door to the wagon and was faced with a squad of soldiers. The hiss of surprise from behind him showed this wasn't just Mother Semprellaime's regular gentleman callers.

"Papers, soldier," said the Statlos.

Numbly, Jack fumbled out the scrawled card that Banders had given him. The man squinted at it, and for a second Jack thought he might be saved by poor calligraphy. One of the other soldiers leaned forwards to murmur in his officer's ear, though, and the man nodded.

"It's him," he decided. "You're to come with us."

"Why? What's happened?" They already had their hands on him, ready to use force but finding that he just went where they tugged. Never any fight in Maric Jack.

"Some man you healed died," the Statlos told him, and he'd known it. In his heart he'd known it. And probably it wouldn't have made any difference even if they'd let him talk to the spy, and without his intervention the man would be just as dead, but somehow it was still his fault.

"Jack," Semprellaime called from the wagon's door. She cast a look down at her feet. The box was there, and the gods. His curse and the only valuable thing he had. They were clustered at the edge, staring with alarm, with owlish blankness, with a bitterness deep as the sea.

He shook his head, ever so slightly, and let the soldiers haul him away. Where he was going was no place fit for gods.

A Repairer of Bells

The Palleseen war machine sought perfection in all things. However, in its efforts to export perfection to the rest of the world, Higher Orders considered short-term means justified long-term ends. When the Pals encountered an enemy with a useful trick, they tried to find a way to incorporate it into their subsequent offensives, preferably with any associated ritual shorn off. Given the tidiness of mind the Pals espoused, they tended to clump such experiments in dedicated departments that could, if need be, be conveniently excised and disavowed.

Cohort-Monitor Cosserby fussed in front of a mirror. Or, rather, in front of the mirror-finish he'd worked onto the chest of one of his charges, large enough to reflect the whole of his relatively meagre height if he stepped back a bit. He only polished the one. It was the lead, that the others were slaved to follow.

He examined himself, finding everything aligned in accordance with the doctrine of perfection, flicked the lenses back and forth over the right ocular of his spectacles to check he hadn't missed anything when shaving. And he should have an assistant to do it for him but somehow he kept putting in the requisition and it kept getting lost. He couldn't get any respect, was the problem. He should complain. Maybe he would tomorrow. Not today, though, because he had a lot of things to do today. And so somehow it was always tomorrow.

The arctinic lamp had done its work by then. A soft blue glow, radiating from three separate heads and falling upon a curved metal plate. He unshipped his toolstrip and set to work, referring frequently to the measurements he'd made back in the medical tent, in the midst of the blood and the screaming. One gift he had – one of the several gifts that people didn't generally acknowledge he possessed – was the ability to work with absolute focus no matter the chaos.

With careful, precise motions he moulded the plate into a precisely contoured cup while it was still malleable from the arctinics. Sculpting war-grade bronze and steel like clay, then slipping the tablethi out of the lamp, killing the teal radiance. The metal cooled and was hard; he fitted the cup into the rest of the prosthetic, a new shoulder-piece for an existing arm. It was beautiful work, that arm, a full human limb in lightweight alloys, multiple points of articulation, and the hand was his best work. It made him sad.

The verisimilitude of the piece was marred by a slot in the underside of the forearm, where the veins would run if it were flesh and blood. He took out one of his advanced tablethi and slotted it into place. Not the regular kind, the golden lozenges that provided power to his lamp, or soldiers' batons. A proper artificer's piece inscribed with exacting chains of incantations.

Time to do his rounds. One more reminder of his lot in life: the respect, and the lack of it. Cosserby, the artificer, the skilled professional, consigned to this joke of a department. Placed in the shadow of Fellow-Inquirer Prassel, a most unpleasant woman. Because someone had looked at his particular specialism and decided it fit within the remit of the hospital. A joke, basically. That was what Cohort-Monitor Cosserby's career had come to. Some clerk back home having two-point-seven seconds' worth of a chuckle before going for lunch.

The prosthetics were a sideline. Making himself useful in this unrewarding role they'd cast him in. When the actual fighting started, he had other jobs. Important, war-winning jobs. Albeit no better appreciated.

Having packed his bag with the arm and the other bits and pieces, and his tools, he turned at the flap of the tent, looking back into the shadows of the workshop. They stood there, ten of them, plus the two that were partly disassembled as he worked to right the damage from the last engagement. Each one nine feet tall, humanoid, hulking. Massive-shouldered. Heads formed in the likeness of a Pal soldier wearing a peaked cap, but below the brim they'd kept the howling, horrible face the original makers had used, to strike fear into the enemy. *Sonori.* Because when they moved, their hollow bodies made the sound of dirgeful bells. Because, in Jarokir where they'd originally been used – *against* the invading Pal forces – they'd been made in the bell foundries of temples, and using the same techniques as sacred bells. And they had some fancy religious name in Jarokiriis, Cosserby knew, but to the Pals who'd fought them they'd been Sonori, and that name had followed them into Pal service after the conquest of Jarokir. Sonori, and so his new-minted profession was a *Sonorist*, which sounded as though it was his job to bore people to sleep.

He was, he would admit, not the greatest of conversationalists.

The workshop adjoined the main clutter of medical tents. He braced himself before crossing the boundary, like a man dropping into waters of unreliable temperature and current.

"Oi oi!" a voice greeted him almost instantly, and he shrank from it, wishing desperately that it had been anybody else. Banders, though: the Former Cohort-Broker. He still wasn't sure *how* that peculiar ranking even worked. What it *didn't* do was impart to the woman any kind of humility. Banders intimidated Cosserby dreadfully. It was as though, by dropping out of the bottom of the chain of command, she had become some sort of mystical force capable of anything. Certainly she could *get* anything, at a price. Cosserby's constant wranglings with the quartermasters had forced him to call on Banders more than once, shamefully paying her goods he couldn't spare to get hold of things that the army should have divvied up for free. And always she smirked and smarmed at him and made him feel very small and inadequate. And she wore the uniform improperly in a way that kept him up at night.

"Got 'em all lined up for you," she told him with one of those dreadful grins. She scratched herself, just digging around under her half-open shirt. Cosserby closed his eyes for a moment. It was going to be Banders hanging at his shoulder, making snide comments and jokes, belittling his professional knowledge, taking his hat and trying it on, all the usual. It was going to be intolerable. He would shrivel up and die.

And then she was saying, "I've got errands, though. Masty'll look after you," and he felt a vast rush of relief that could have swamped a walled city, touched with an utterly unprofessional spike of regret. Accessory Masty, though, he could cope with. The medical unit's other permanent orderly was meek and deferential and didn't bring Cosserby out in sweats.

Masty saluted, the way a foreign Accessory should, even to a mere Cohort-Monitor. Cosserby had no idea where the man hailed from. He was neat, lean, darker than a Pal and with a trim beard that a regular soldier wouldn't be allowed. He'd been with the army forever – since he was just a child they said, and with the medical unit for a lot of that. Always there, tirelessly competent, never complaining. Perfect, and how about that for irony, compared to the decidedly imperfect but Palleseen Banders?

The invalids were lined up like a parade ground, which – while neat and therefore pleasing to the idea of perfection – wasn't going to make anyone like him any better. The woman with the arm – or rather without the arm – was at the end, and probably best that way. He asked them to stand at ease and began fitting the less demanding pieces. Two bronze fingers, without articulation, pre-curved so that they would go properly around a baton. Murmuring words about proper care of the stump so that the prosthetics didn't chafe. Then was a superior officer that he saluted. The man had an ear shot off, and Cosserby had a tin replacement – admirable sound reproduction but might affect your appreciation of music, magister, ho ho (no answering laugh). He fit it to the crinkled, inflamed scar that was the side of the man's head, saw the officer's expression as he buckled the strap over the man's remaining ear. That look which said *But everyone will see I'm maimed.*

"There are long-term solutions," he said. "When you're somewhere with a fuller range of facilities, magister. That are less... unsightly. For now, though." And he fit a tablethi into the leather pouch that sat alongside the curve of the tin, and saw the man's eyes widen as the sounds of the world on that side of his head were suddenly clear as crystal, probably better than the flesh and blood equivalent.

"You'll probably need to replace this every month, on average, magister," Cosserby explained. But the man was a Fellow, and a tablethi a month was nothing.

And then a couple of other routine pieces, unpowered, cosmetic. And then the arm.

The woman had been watching him go down the line, and Masty was already there with a stool so she could sit down for the fitting. Her eyes fixed on the prosthetic when he pulled it from his satchel and unfolded it. The beauty of its joints, the sculpted musculature. And the fit of the cup against her scar was perfect, because one thing Cosserby could do was take exacting measurements and the other was to shape metal.

Right now it was just hanging there, of course, and that was because making an arm move was a complex operation, far more so than just receiving and passing on sounds. The complicated gubbins for the sense of hearing were inside the skull, and outside of Cosserby's abilities to replicate. The tin ear had been just collection and amplification.

He brought out another artificer's tablethi, marked not just with a single command word like a piece of soldier's ammunition, but with a logic-chain of instructions. It was probably the largest and most complex piece of working the woman had ever seen. He fit it into the forearm slot, feeling the tug as it clicked into place, that showed that both tablethi and arm had been properly fashioned.

He spoke the simple Pel word, *Obey*, that unlocked the architecture of its magic and told it to follow the minute twitching motions of the woman's shoulder. "And now just move it," he said.

"I don't understand," she told him. "Move it how?"

"It's your arm, soldier," he said. This was the point of wonder and magic and he should be feeling terribly pleased with himself, but instead he just felt miserable.

The arm moved. The woman started, as though trying to put distance between herself and something that was strapped to her. It raised, folded at the elbow. The fingers flexed. And none of the joints went backwards and she didn't poke herself in the eye and that had all happened before when he hadn't quite calibrated things right. This time he'd done his job properly though.

There were tears in her eyes. He hated himself for it.

"So if you attend at the quartermasters they will arrange for a debit from your wages until the cost of the materials in the arm have been recouped." Already flinching from her reaction, using that precise wording that placed the blame for the situation on any department except his own.

She stared at him, tight-jawed, but she kept moving and flexing the arm, and he guessed that being able to clap was worth the dock to her pay. But that, of course, was not all of it.

"The tablethi should last from between one to two weeks, depending on severity of use," he told her. "You will be able to order replacements from myself or another army artificer or Sonorist, at cost." And he named the price, the absolute minimum price that he was mandated by army regulations to charge for the things. Because they were specialist goods, and either he or some other would spend an age inscribing the logic chains into them, and they took as much magic as a score of regular tablethi to charge up.

Her mouth worked. Cosserby was very aware of Masty, standing by without expression but surely radiating distaste. Aware of the wider hospital and everyone in it, somehow watching him in this moment and collectively curling their lip.

"I can't," the woman said, "*afford* that. How am I supposed to afford that? On a soldier's pay? And the arm as well? It isn't possible."

"I'm sorry," he whispered. "Look, maybe try it for a few days. See how it…" As though the arm would lead her to a cache of buried treasure that would enable her to afford it. And yes, they were on campaign, and on the advance, and in such circumstances your common soldier sometimes did end up with a surprising amount of non-regulation wealth that someone like Banders could turn into proper money. But the woman with the arm had not, apparently, had that kind of opportunity before losing a chunk of herself at the shoulder. And now, given what she'd lost, was unlikely to have it come her way again. Hard to fill your boots with just one hand.

Her face had gone hard and set. In it was the clearly expressed sentiment, *I lost this for your army, and this is what I get?* And it wasn't even his army, and he absolutely agreed with her, but regulations and practice cast him as the villain in this scenario and the least he could do was give her someone to hate.

"Get it off me," she told him flatly, and he did so, undoing the buckles and straps, uncovering the gnarl of her stump.

He sat there for a bit, after she'd gone, and Masty didn't try to hurry him out. He flicked lenses back and forth, but no amount of magnification made the world look any better.

The Butcher was waiting for him when he left the tent. Or, rather, the Butcher just happened to be outside his own temporary residence, boiling up something that was too fume-heavy to have inside. But Cosserby knew full well that Ollery had been waiting to have a go. He still had the prosthetic arm in view, slung over one shoulder, and he braced himself for the joke. *Can I give you a hand, Cohort-Monitor?*

As it fell out, the Butcher didn't even feel him worth a pun today, "You're still touting that, then? Not sent it walking out with a third owner? Like an old friend, that arm. You'd miss it, if it actually went."

And that was another sore point, because he *had* placed the arm a couple of times but neither of the amputee recipients had survived the fighting long enough to need a second tablethi. Cosserby gritted his teeth, delved within himself for a devastating rejoinder, and came up empty.

"I hear it's cursed," Ollery observed to his bubbling pot. "Or maybe it's the ghost of the first man to wear it. Amazed it doesn't go crawling about on its own."

"There is no such thing as a cursed arm, Chief Accessory," Cosserby got out.

"Really? In this wide world, so full of heathen imperfections? I find that very unlikely." And the Butcher shifted a little, and Cosserby was brutally aware that the man took up twice as much space and a distressing amount of that could be turned into mechanical advantage. And he outranked Ollery. He was a member of the Palleseen army in good standing, Cohort rank, a monitor of the School of Correct Conduct. Ollery was still a Pal, but he'd done *something* bad enough to get him thrown out into the ranks of the Accessories, who were otherwise a rabble of foreign collaborators. And so, obviously, the big man should jump at Cosserby's every shout. Except that Cosserby was seconded to the hospital, and while that meant he technically reported to Fellow-Inquirer Prassel, Prassel had made it clear that Ollery ran the place. Leaving Cosserby and the Butcher in an intolerable limbo, an abscess within the chain of command that ate Cosserby up inside and bothered Ollery not at all.

"I, will," he stuttered out. "I'm fine. Everything's fine. Actually." And then, under the brute scrutiny and hating himself, "Chief."

Ollery's lips twitched. "Sure it is," he said. "You go play with your toys." And Cosserby was aware of all of them, all the actual medicos. The Divinati woman and her little cadre of students, the old hag priestess and her horrible old husband, the Pal surgeons. People who saved lives, and into whose company he, the fondler of machines, had been thrust. He wanted to glare around at all of them, to lecture them about the vast importance of his profession, key to the war effort, very very crucial. But he couldn't meet the gaze of even one of them, and so he scurried from the camp. And he didn't actually hear their harsh laughter, but his mind manufactured it, as though he had fit himself with a defective tin ear that amplified the unkind thoughts of others.

His next job would take him to Higher Orders, the officers who ran the Battalion and directed the war. One of Sage-Monitor Runkel's aides had lost an eye three years ago, and the crystal orb sitting in that scarred socket had been throwing up double images. A messenger had tripped down to the hospital forthwith, summoning the Sonorist to come check it out. And Cosserby already had a shortlist of what the problems might be. His profession was relatively new, but he and his widespread peers shared information whenever they could, and a body of knowledge was slowly being assembled. He would test the offending prosthesis and hopefully have the man seeing everything only once before the day was out. And in an ideal world they'd take the opportunity to brief him on what they wanted the Sonori to achieve in the next engagement, but more likely he'd get back to the workshop only to find a message telling him to trek back across the camp to Higher Orders, because that was the way things tended to fall out for Cohort-Monitor Cosserby.

He was almost at the Sage-Monitor's command tent when the little escort crossed his path. A Statlos and his squad, and a small soldier in their midst who was plainly in serious trouble. And that wasn't Cosserby's problem by any means. It would be an unusual day when the army sat encamped and *someone* didn't get themselves on a charge. Except the prisoner's face dragged at his attention. He'd seen this man recently, and given he didn't really have any friends that seemed odd.

The new man. Most recent addition to the Butcher's freakshow. That Maric fellow.

And whatever he'd been doing, it hadn't been in the hospital. Not if they were going crossways over Cosserby's own path. Which left him with something of a quandary.

"I mean," he said to himself – an occupational hazard from working amongst the resonant bulks of the Sonori, "that's not *my* problem." Cosserby considered that life handed him more than enough without his taking on the difficulties of others. And it wasn't as though the Butcher would thank him. More likely scowl and roll his eyes at Cosserby making it *his* problem. And none of it would necessarily relieve the problems of the Maric, who was plainly in a very problematic situation indeed. Because he wasn't being marched to any regular stockade, but into the part of the camp where any prisoners were likely to get a very bespoke service. And the man hadn't even looked at him, let alone mouthed a desperate request for help. And probably he had done something truly vile. And the high-ranking aide with the dodgy eye was waiting for him.

"Oh *screws*," Cosserby said, turned on heel and hurried back along his own trail.

Subject to Scholarly Interest

The Palleseen war machine was a great consumer. An insatiable appetite for human bodies to throw into the fighting, for cloth, for boots, for food, for a variety of specialist materials such as the chemicals the Butcher used in his alchemy or alloys for Cosserby's workshop. The most pressing demand, every moment of every war, though, was for magic. Drained from every available source and infused into the little lozenge-shaped tablethi, the war drank magic like a sot drank wine.

The soldiers marched Maric Jack through half the camp, most definitely into that region of it where more important Pals were housed, as evidenced by the grander tents and huts. Nobody spared him a glance. It was more than that. Anyone who registered him looked away most assiduously. A prisoner brought to this neighbourhood meant bad things. He reckoned some common soldier who'd been drunk and leery towards a superior would just get the sort of turning out he'd received under the Alder, and say no more about it. You had to do something specific to get hauled up to these heights, and the consequent fall from grace would be appropriately shattering. And Jack'd had experience with the Pals and their ways back in Ilmar.

That their destination turned out to be one of the buildings was no consolation. He thought about how a considerate Pal might want to ensure that the more abrasive sounds of their trade would be properly muffled so as not to disturb their neighbours.

The Statlos and squad had said not a word to him. Had barely looked at him, as though whatever fate he'd earned might rub off on them. And he had earned it. Whipping aside, he hadn't tried hard enough to get word to the man who'd been saved by God. He hadn't been able to communicate that God couldn't be trusted, and if He healed you then it was to satisfy His mean sense of humour. And right now God was surrounded by a war, and feeling His back against the wall. So He was acting up, pushing boundaries like He'd never done back home. Jack was worried about God, although right now he felt that he should be saving most of his worry for himself. Thankfully, while his life had been short of many tangible things like money, food and clothes, he'd made up for it with enough worries to last the rest of his life. Low bar as that might be.

They tried to bundle him inside, but he just went with them without resistance, so the whole operation ended up being rather more civilized than intended. And he could actually fight them, he realised. He wasn't God's priest any more, not really. And God's followers were expected to be nonviolent but it wouldn't be the first time Jack had disappointed God. Except, having spent his whole life not fighting anyone, he didn't really know how to go about it, and it wouldn't have done any good, and he didn't want to.

I really am a wretched worm of a man, he told himself.

Inside was what he'd feared, albeit a more portable and on-the-fly version of it. The hut had two rooms, and the further one, curtained off with a heavy drape, was presumably living space. This near end was a very specialised workshop, and this time round he actually recognised a lot of the implements. There was a chair as well, and it had all the straps he'd come to expect from Pal hospitality. The soldiers' standing orders didn't apparently extend to footling about with buckles, though, or even sitting him down. They had him stand against one wall,

95

and then just stared at him as though daring him to explode into furious action. Conjure a demon or throw a curse or something. Probably they'd been told he was a dangerous magician. Wrong on both counts but he wasn't going to convince them of that.

The pause gave him a chance to calm his heart and catch his breath. To appreciate the efficient construction of the hut. There were big metal brackets and bolts, so that when the army needed to move, the whole thing could be taken down and stowed on a wagon. He thought about how many hands you'd need to do it, and tried to calculate the precise dimensions of wagon it would take, with reference to the various standard sizes the Pal army used. None of that sufficed to take his mind off things.

"So," he remarked, and the Statlos and escort all jumped, and he almost got a baton up his nose. "Here we are."

The Statlos waited to see if the words came with some kind of occult backlash, but when nothing lashed back, he prodded Jack with the end of his baton. And a charged baton was no danger unless you spoke the word to release the power in the tableth. Nobody got shot by accident in this army unless they were having a particularly arcane argument. But still, it was hard not to flinch. Jack had seen plenty of what a baton-shot could do to someone, on the streets of Ilmar.

The Statlos leaned in until Jack could smell the faint rot of his breath, until his stubble practically grazed Jack's cheek. "You led us a dance," he growled.

"I'm sorry. I didn't mean to," Jack said.

"Should have expected to find you with your own kind," the man said, disgusted. Presumably not one of Semprellaime's regulars, then, or perhaps it was self-loathing. Jack was sure that circle house conjuration was absolutely banned under the Pal rationality, but he wasn't so naïve as to believe that meant it didn't happen quite openly, so long as it was expedient to overlook it.

"We were just having tea," he said, and the Statlos recoiled as though Jack had admitted to some particularly vile perversion. Not a tea-drinker, maybe.

Then the drape obscuring the further room was pushed aside, and an officer came in.

"That's never the man," the officer drawled, soundly oddly delighted. He was tall, his hair gone silver in elegant waves. He had a face that looked very dry and stern until any part of it moved, whereupon the whole assemblage transformed to arch humour. And saying 'that's never the man' was quite the contortion, in a language designed for straight talking.

His uniform jacket was open, and the shirt beneath was decidedly non-regulation, formed of hundreds of lustreless metal coils wired together like scaly armour, each one inscribed with strange characters. They rustled faintly as he moved.

The Statlos and his escort gave ground as the man advanced. "I'll take it from here, Statlos," the officer said.

The Statlos's eyes flicked from him to Jack. "He might be dangerous, magister."

There is a dangerous man in this room, said the officer's face, *and it is not him.* "Oh my, yes," he said, somehow twisting the Pel words to mean *No.* "Yes, I can see he might leap at me and overpower me. He looks terribly fierce, doesn't he? Just unbridled savagery prowling back and forth in a cage. Terrifying."

"Magister." Spoken with that subordinate's ambivalence, neither agreeing nor contradicting.

"Just go stand outside," the officer suggested. "I promise I'll call if he starts threatening me. *Help, help*, I'll go. And you can burst in and save me. How's that?"

The Statlos's eyes were all mute hatred, and when the officer took his hand he plainly had to fight not to rip it from the man's fingers. Two coins were deposited there. Silver – no small sum for a soldier.

"In recognition of your duty to the department," the officer said sweetly, and then made shooing gestures until the man and his squad left.

"You look terribly uncomfortable standing there like someone shoved a rod up your backside," the officer observed, looking Jack up and down. "Take a seat, why don't you."

And the one seat, of course, came with rather more straps than mere comfort required. The officer saw his look and smirked.

"Look, how about this. At some point things between us are going to get downright uncivilized, and I'll have the boys back in to pin you down and get rough with you, and all that. Probably. But if I promise to give you fair warning of that, will you at least sit down? Because I want to, and I can't really do that if you're standing in the corner like an ugly lamp. What's your name, soldier?"

Some obscure sense of names bestowing power crammed the words up in Jack's mouth. Plus a certain residual confusion over which name was even appropriate.

"I'm Fellow-Archivist Thurrel, for example." A pause. "That's what we call a 'name', here in the army. Plus, while I'm still waiting for yours, I'm pretty sure I'm your superior officer, and so you're really supposed to answer, when I ask you something." He leaned in, propping himself on the chair back, and added in a grotesque whisper, "Otherwise, technically I can have you punished in a variety of ways. Shocking, no?"

"Jack," said Jack. "Maric Jack. Accessory Maric Jack, magister."

"Well that gives me plenty of options." Thurrel said, stepping back from the chair to give Jack room. And, devoid of choices, he sat. The straps did not magically flail out to secure him. It was, at this point in the conversation, just a chair.

With one foot, Thurrel hooked at a collapsed stool and, in that single motion, had it next to a desk and neatly unfolded. The desk would fold up too, Jack saw. The shelves hanging above them would all stack together to become a closed crate. The whole room had been designed, with almost obsessive passion, to combine comfort with portability.

There were a lot of things on the desk, some of them the implements he'd noted before. The dark and sinister bottle turned out to smell sharply of strong drink, though. Thurrel poured himself a tumbler and sipped appreciably, lounging against the desk. "You're a rather lucky boy, Jack."

Jack practised the mute blankness he'd observed in other soldiers.

"You must understand that Correct Speech wanted you too. The Inquirers, you know. They think you killed one of their people. He died, you know. The man you healed."

"I didn't heal anyone. Magister."

Thurrel shrugged. *Play it like that if you want*, his expression said. "Anyway, dead. Dropped dead right in front of Higher Orders. Supposed to be a grand reveal. Shock! Scandal! Dead of a ghost-eater arrow, apparently. They got him with it as he was getting out, and then it was eating him up, and then you got hold of him. Or at least Correct Speech said you took credit for it."

"It wasn't me," Jack said.

"Meh, well." Thurrel drained the cup and stood to ferret something out from the hanging shelves. "The thing is, Jack, we know the others by now. They've been with that department for a while. Not likely the Butcher or that Divinati woman suddenly learned how to bring someone back from *that* kind of spot, eh? And I got a look at your papers. The ones that came with you from Ilmar." And Jack felt the man's voice was like metal from a forge, all that cheery glow of warmth collapsing down into something hard and cold. "Quite the record. The miraculous healing priest. How wonderful that must be." And he slipped something over his head and turned, and there was a panopticon of glass eyes there, two big lead-grey lenses that didn't quite align with where his eyes should be, and three other orbs where nobody needed eyes at all. And three whole tablethi set over his brow to power it, and the whole with a crackling radiance that owed nothing to light or sight. And, worst of all, Jack had seen just such a thing before.

"Oh God," he said, "you've got a Hat."

Thurrel paused, and the set of his mouth beneath the goggling assemblage looked decidedly unimpressed. "My dear fellow, it is not a 'Hat'. It is thaumatic gauge. They're very new and extremely clever. You've no idea what strings I had to pull to get one out here in the provinces."

At which point the door opened, and Thurrel turned the full glower of the thaumatic gauge on the intruder. And then pushed the device back up his forehead because it wasn't the Statlos blundering in, but another officer, and a… something.

Jack stared and then averted his eyes.

"What do you want, Miserly? I'm working."

The newcomer – Miserly? Was that really a Pal name? – didn't seem to care. He shouldered over to the desk and poured himself some of the drink as though daring Thurrel to object.

"I heard you'd grabbed the priest," he said. "Correct Speech is royally pissed."

"Correct Speech can go frottage themselves," Thurrel decided. "What do you *want*, Miserly?"

"I want to see the priest," Miserly explained. "I want to see Prassel's latest failure. Did he kill an Inquisition agent?"

"He says he didn't." Thurrel had given the man space in a way that told Jack the relationship between the two men was complicated. Miserly was shorter, stockier, probably the same age, though his dark hair had made him seem younger at first. He had a particularly Pal face that was handsome in every detail, but combined in look of cold disdain, bypassing the eyes to tell the soul he was a man to be wary of. The narrowest moustache Jack had ever seen decorated his upper lip, non-regulation and worn to show he could get away with it. His eyes were ice. Blue, yes; cold, yes; but something to their look and texture and the way they caught the light spoke only of ice. The air around them glittered as the moisture in it crystallised out.

All of which first impression came to Jack fractured because his eyes were being constantly dragged towards what had come into the hut with Miserly.

"Inquisition says he did," Miserly was continuing. "And you know me. Exceptional Stratagems department, always on the lookout for something we can use."

"Better than having Correct Speech pull his toenails out, I suppose," Thurrel agreed. "Although I could always decant the toenails, if he's *that* magic."

"I'm not," said Jack. "Magic. I don't do magic." His eyes kept straying, no matter how hard he tried.

She was a demon, Miserly's companion. She was the most beautiful woman he had ever seen. Or rather, she was not a woman. A demon, in a woman's shape. In a Pal uniform, even, as though she was just some aide-de-camp at Miserly's beck and call. And she *was* at his beck and call. Every time Jack looked away, the corner of his eye caught a glittering arc, as though there was a chain between her and the man, that was invisible when he looked straight at it.

And she was perfect, in ways that Pal doctrine surely did *not* approve of. Face, form, poise. And he understood that she had been made to be a mirror to desires, and that the precise details that had hooks in his eyes might be different for another. Because when you were sufficiently adept at negotiating with the Kings Below, you could be very specific in your requirements.

"You like what you see?" Miserly said. "Want to put in an offer perhaps?"

Jack started guiltily, and the man barked with laughter. "Can't keep his eyes off her."

Jack faced up to him, digging his fingers into the arm of the chair to concentrate. "Because you've had her fashioned for exactly that, isn't that the case? You wanted something that people would look at, and want, and envy."

Miserly looked a little sour at that, which Jack took as all the victory he was likely to get in this situation.

"Introduce yourself," Miserly said, and there was no chain, not physically, not present, but when he jerked his hand *so*, the demon woman was off balance for a moment as though there was a collar about her neck.

"I am the succubus Caeleen," she said. Her voice was beautiful as music, and she made it flat and toneless and as ugly as she possibly could, "bound by contract into the service of the worshipful and puissant magus Fellow-Invigilator Maserley."

Jack processed that. Specifically what it told him about the demon's master's ego. And that Thurrel had been subtly mispronouncing the conjurer's name so that it sounded like an insult in *Maric*, a language that Maserley plainly didn't speak but that someone named Maric Jack obviously would. And where someone like Thurrel had picked up the tongue, Jack had no idea.

"You'd like a taste, wouldn't you," Maserley said, placing a proprietorial hand on Caeleen's shoulder.

"No, magister," said Jack, and the man's whole face just stopped in surprise. When he stared, unblinking, for more than a few seconds, the thinnest possible frozen sheen glazed over his eyes.

"It's forbidden," Jack explained, because he never could get out of his knee-jerk need to be helpful. And then he stopped because explaining your religion to two Pal officers probably wasn't conducive to a long life.

But Thurrel was there anyway. "He's a priest," he noted. "They're down on demons. They're down on fun too, most of the time."

Maserley curled a lip. "You know too much about the subject. One day it'll be you Correct Speech comes for."

"Nothing wrong in a broad education." Thurrel's tone was flinty, but then he smiled at Jack. "If I offered you some brandy, boy, are you allowed that? Or does your god ban that too?"

"It's a minor infraction, magister," Jack said. "But I'll risk it."

Thurrel trilled with laughter and turned to find another tumbler. Maserley's hand on his arm stopped him.

"Don't waste it," the Fellow-Invigilator said. "Just tell me what he's got to him. Analyse him and get it over with."

"Are you going to take him off me?" Thurrel actually pouted.

"If he's worth it. If I can use him. Otherwise, you can decant him."

"And if I won't let you?" Hard to see the full nuance of Thurrel's expression with the thaumatic gauge riding his brows. "If he's got that kind of power, that fills a lot of tablethi. And I know Exceptional Stratagems trumps decanting, but I'm the one who hosts the wine tasting and the dinners that Uncle likes, and so who's he going to back?"

And Jack just sat there, looking between the two men because he was strenuously trying not to look at Caeleen. Both men stood quite casually, Maserley with his thumbs hooked into his belt, Thurrel leaning on the desk like a study in nonchalance. The air flexed with interdepartmental tension. And Jack had no idea if they were cousins with an actual uncle, or if 'Uncle' meant something special to Pal officers. He had no idea what Exceptional Stratagems was, save that he wanted no part of it. On the other hand he knew a great deal about Thurrel's 'decanting', because that was how the Pals took the magic from anything that had it, and drained it into their tablethi for general use.

"You said 'use' me," he observed to Maserley, in the taut quiet that followed Thurrel's words. "In the war, did you mean?"

Maserley looked at him and Jack shivered like a fever victim.

"We're in the army," he man said. "What did you expect, exactly."

"Only I can't. Fight. Hurt people. At all. Under any circumstances." And their expressions, paired, showed utter incomprehension. He might as well have declined to exist in three dimensions for them. "That's what happened with the spy," he added, still so desperate to help. "He was healed, but conditionally. Only so long as nothing he did harmed another.

And probably whatever he knew, that they wanted to get from him, was going to harm someone. It's an army, like you say. So I guess he opened his mouth and... died. It all came back. The thing, the... ghost eater? I don't even know what that is. I'm so sorry. I was trying to get to him, to tell him not to... not to...." The utter hopelessness of the thought defeated him. As though Higher Orders would just have let the spy stay silent.

The disparity in their expressions told him a lot about the two men. Maserley was incredulous, almost pitying. Thurrel was narrow-eyed and thoughtful, turning the logic of it over in his head to see where the joins were, that he could get a knife-point into. Jack wasn't sure which he preferred.

Caeleen was watching too. Her expression was cool and unreadable, but he didn't even know if anything her face said was real, or if it was just a part of the way she'd been fashioned. He knew very little about demons.

She met his eyes and he braced himself for some occult jolt of desire to rampage through his head. There was just contact, though. The contact of one victim with another. A little sympathy even, passed underhand to him like a folded note between the bars of their cages.

"Well that's useless," Maserley said at last.

"To you," Thurrel observed. "I can still decant him. No such thing as a pacifist tableth. Let's take a look at him." And he slipped the gauge down again, transforming himself into the all-seeing monster. The lightless radiance about the thing increased and Jack heard a faint crackle from it. But then it wasn't the first time he'd seen one in operation. The Perfector of Ilmar, the new one who'd come in and begun harvesting the city for magic, had owned just such a thing and made free use of it.

"For a priest, you don't seem terribly holy." Thurrel was playing with some gradated wheels on the gauge, still peering.

"I'm not a priest. Any more."

"But you healed the spy."

"No."

"If your toy is proving unequal to the task," Maserley put in impatiently, "then perhaps I should just conjure a worm to burrow after what's worthwhile in him."

Any hope that this was an empty or hyperbolic threat died when Thurrel sighed, "Oh you and your *worms*, Miserly."

The door banged behind them and both men jumped. Thurrel shoved the gauge back up irritably. "Statlos, this really is… ah." Stepping back to sit on the edge of the desk, looking speculative.

Fellow-Inquirer Prassel closed the door behind her. And Jack really wasn't sure how he felt about that. Because she'd had him whipped, and she was the superior he'd presumably disgraced, and she had *Inquirer* in her rank which meant that maybe it was the toenails after all.

And she nodded to Thurrel, but the look she turned on Maserley was one hundred per cent combative. A necromancer and a conjuror, and surely if there were such a thing as looks that could kill then one or both would have dropped dead then and there. The temperature dropped to the point where Jack looked for ice forming on the walls. An Ilmari winter would just about have matched it.

And a warm hand on his shoulder. Caeleen. And of course demons were warm. They were things of fire, weren't they? And he had no illusion that she meant him well, or any human, but they were both prisoners right then and there. Apparently even demons understood common ground.

"You have one of mine, Thurrel," Prassel said.

"Well," Thurrel said thoughtfully. "I understood he'd been rather naughty. In a thaumatologically interesting way. And it was reason's own job to find him – gone to ground in a *brothel*, can you believe? But I thought that he might as well be put to use, for his sins. I mean, a man is *dead*." Mock horror at the thought, and absolutely no real contrition at all. Jack decided maybe he didn't like Thurrel much better than Maserley after all.

"A man died under the auspices of the Inquisition," Prassel said blandly. "Correct Speech is, of course, investigating itself.

We await the results with bated breath. As for Accessory Jack, he *will* be *put to use*. He was, in fact, being put to use. In the hospital department."

Maserley snorted at that. "You're really owning that freakshow."

Prassel's look went past 'kill' and into setting him on fire and pissing on the ashes. "My man, if you please."

"No," Maserley said. "I'll have him for Exceptional Strat, and to the hells with you."

"Fellow-Archivist Thurrel." The slightest tilt of Prassel's head cut Maserley out of the conversation. "Your prisoner, I believe. Do you need me to sign something?"

Thurrel slipped the gauge off his head and looked at it ruefully. "Oh well. Sorry Jack, another time perhaps?" As though they'd be having a picnic if not for killjoy Prassel hauling him back. And Maserley tried to butt in, but he was effortlessly sidelined, no longer someone with any traction on the situation, chill the air as he might. An angry gesture of one hand and Caeleen was hauled to his side by that non-existent thread.

He tried to storm directly for the door, but Prassel wouldn't budge for him, meaning he had to twist awkwardly to avoid ramming shoulders with her. And though he was broader and heavier, there was something stony about the woman that Jack felt he might have broken against. Maserley shoved his demon outside, then slammed the door petulantly at his heels, hard enough to shudder the whole hut. The hanging shelves shivered and Thurrel deftly caught a couple of dull, uncharged tablethi that jumped out.

"You are sure you want him back?" he asked Prassel thoughtfully. "He's trouble, you know. I could see that. Let me have him. I'll split the proceeds."

"I'm not playing games," she told him. "I meant it about the paperwork. Assuming he's here officially, and you didn't just *do*, as per usual."

"Oh well, you know me." Thurrel made a vague gesture.

"Goodbye Jack. Perhaps later you can introduce me to any interesting friends you might have." A flat, acquisitive stare that said, *I know what you didn't bring with you.* Jack's thoughts were instantly on the box in Mother Semprellaime's wagon, and he clamped down on them in case the man could read the details in his face.

The Cruet's Tale

In accordance with the doctrine of perfection so dear to the Palleseen, there were standard-issue versions of everything a soldier or scholar or civil servant might need, produced to exacting specifications in factories across the Sway and supplied at any distance using the effortlessly efficient transport network the Pals had developed. Or that was the theory. Certainly it was technically true that using something non-regulation could be the basis for censure, as evidence of having been corrupted by foreignness. However, between that transport network not being quite as efficient as perfection might demand, and the foreigners having some quite nice stuff, it was a rule that corroded swiftly when exposed to the fresh air of other climes.

It was a good cruet. It had been made in Jarokir, the same place that had produced the Sonori constructs that Cosserby spent his time futtering with, and that had also produced the priest-medicos Tallifer and Lochiver. Like many additions to the Palleseen Sway, Jarokir had spent some decades getting on with the Pals, especially in respect of trade. Hence it was an excellent example of their craftsmanship, but designed for Palleseen cuisine. The wooden box, the eight jars. A soldier's mess tent set would be no more than that. Plain wood, plated steel, a single sigil on each lid to identify the contents. But Ollery, the Butcher, got fancy when he cooked, and his meals demanded a fancy cruet. The box was intricate fretwork, the intersecting geometrical patterns the Jarokiri liked, where little human and animal faces peeked out between the slats at random intervals. Gods, probably, making the whole piece some way beyond non-regulation and into actual punishable unorthodoxy, but who was counting? The jars were silver, and each one inscribed with a different serpent, the character of the beast somehow suggesting the piquancy of the condiment within. The full name of the contents decorated the lid, Jarokiri characters spelling out Pel words. The Butcher was well aware that a man in his position couldn't afford to have prized possessions, but nonetheless it was one. He'd be sorry as and when it passed from his hands.

He was cooking. Not in itself a calendar event. Sometimes he cooked for the two of them, sometimes the boy worked up his limited set of recipes. Tonight, however, he cooked. For tomorrow...

Well, they all knew about tomorrow. And, formally, they didn't, because Higher Orders were doing their best to make the Loruthi spies' jobs at least slightly challenging, but word was all over the camp. And so he cooked. When he turned his hand and mind to it, there was no better chef in Forthright Battalion. And the big alchemy cauldrons, when cleaned out with the proper degree of care, were good for stews.

The boy was at his back, tending two smaller vessels, one with fish that were pickling down in their own salt, and the other radish darts in a thin spicy oil that would, if not overdone, blow the top of your head off. The first was a traditional Palleseen delicacy that went back to before perfection, when they'd all just been barbaric island raiders making a nuisance of themselves up and down the coast. The latter was from some place he'd served in, way back at the beginning of his career, and taken a fancy to. He was looking forwards to seeing how some of the newer members of the department took to it.

In the main tent, that was a portal to hell and butchery when the fighting was on, Banders and Masty were setting out three folding tables end to end, and enough stools for everyone. He'd sent the boy out with the cutlery – the good set, that had belonged to some aristocrat of some place they hadn't thought needed perfecting. He'd got it in trade for a particularly efficacious pox cure, from a particularly pox-ridden Sage-Inquirer. More non-standard gear, worthy of censure, but he loved the scrollwork in the metal, and the way the forks had two curved tines, like trailing fishtails. Banders would be setting out the places, and then Masty would go round and reset them because she always put everything crooked and backwards.

He heard voices outside the tent. The stew was bubbling at just the right rate and could do with sitting unmolested for a while before he tasted it again, so he put his head out. A forlorn skinny slump of a man, sloping in, exchanging a thin greeting with Banders, who was outside the main tent having a smoke. Ollery was amazed that box didn't just fall off the man's shoulders, they slanted so much.

"You're late," he told Maric Jack.

"I'm sorry," the man mumbled in his heavily accented Pel.

"I should report you. Have you put on a charge." Ollery keeping his face entirely deadpan serious.

"There was some..." A moment as Jack reached for the word, "administration. Bureaucracy? Official business." He was deadpanning right back, and Ollery couldn't work out whether he was absolutely aware that his predicament had been blurted out to the whole department – by *Cosserby* of all people! Or whether he assumed it was all secret and Prassel had just turned up to spring him from pure chance.

"You have the papers to prove that?" Ollery pressed, because he was never more than an onion skin's thickness from being mean.

"I'll get something signed next time," Jack said. His tone said that he was resigned to there being a next time. "What's going on?"

"I'm cooking," Ollery told him. "Go help Masty set up."

Though it was mostly done, meaning Jack would get the chance to sit down if he wanted, take the weight from his feet and the box from his back. When the man turned to go, Ollery hailed him back and handed out the cruet. "Take this to the table, will you?" Enjoying Jack's Maric look, that plainly didn't even know what it was.

"Oh ho!" Banders crowed, seeing it. "Blight me, but we're having the proper chow down tonight."

"I'm sorry," Jack said. "I don't think I understood a word of that."

She gave him a punch in the chest that was intended to be playful, then had to actually rescue him from falling backwards. He'd been whipped, she recalled, and then arrested. Busy day for the new boy.

"Butcher doesn't have anything less than the best for the high table," she told him, trying to speak more slowly but still not sure he was getting it. She took a final long drag of her reed and blew the smoke at the darkened sky and the first scatter of stars. "Needed that. Come on." Heading in and letting Jack trail after her. Masty had undone all her good work with the cutlery, needless to say. Not like she had a ruler on her but, if she had, she'd bet she could measure the settings and not find a hair's breadth difference between them now. The man had no sense of artistry.

"What, no nametags?" she jibed at him. "No little calligraphied cards so everyone knows where they're sitting?"

Masty gave her a Look. It was about as fierce as he ever got. And everyone knew where they were sitting, of course. They'd done this before. A placing that should have been rigidly by rank, high to low, but had mutated to reflect the actual hierarchy in the department, that varied considerably from what got set down in battalion records.

"I don't know where I'm sitting," said Maric Jack, putting the cruet down on the table. Masty promptly rescued it and repositioned it at the head, where the Butcher would be.

"I s'pose you don't," she admitted.

"I mean, sorry. Am I even sitting? Am I... invited?" The rich smell of cooking was all through the tent now, and she saw his tongue touch his lips hungrily.

"Oh I don't know," she said, mugging at Masty. "I mean maybe. Maybe we could squeeze you in. What's it worth to you?"

"You go here," Masty said, spoiling that gambit instantly. Banders did the calculations: he'd have Alv on his left and Masty himself on his right, assuming Masty actually sat down to eat rather than playing butler and dishwasher all evening. It put Jack across the table from her, too, and that was fine enough. She reckoned she could winkle sufficient entertainment out of him to last the evening.

There was the thin, clear sound of a bell. The Butcher's boy would be outside his tent, the old ship's piece dangling from one hand, a spare fork in the other, calling everyone to their devotions.

"Go change your jacket," she told Jack. "Get a fresh one on. That one's manky. We dress up for dinner around these parts."

He gave her a look which took in her general state of dishevelment.

"What? You don't think I work hard to look like this? Go change, man. Leave your box. Nobody's going to rifle it."

He didn't look convinced at that, but he left it and he went. Banders shot Masty a look.

"Shall we rifle his box?"

Even Masty couldn't stop a twitch of the lips at that one. "You're incorrigible."

"Only because everyone 'incorriges' me." Banders had given an eminent grammarian an apoplectic fit once. One of her proudest moments. She knelt down by the wooden backpack, peering into the holes. Doubling down on the insouciance precisely because Jack spooked her. Because there had been something nasty in the box, when she'd first looked into it. Because Jack had brought that man back from next to dead, and then sent him right back, or that was the scuttlebutt. Because he was, mild exterior bedamned, an eerie little fucker and she was trying very hard to get over that and make him fit her worldview.

"I wouldn't," said Masty, at her back.

"What, like you don't want to look into his box."

"I..." And she gave him a wicked look over her shoulder because that had come out *exactly* as she'd meant it. He had his exasperated look on, and it was always a good day when she'd pushed Masty that far. Then the others were coming in, ones and twos, and she stood up quickly.

And, just as she did, something moved down there. Just at the corners and edges of what she could see. An impression of a little face, hard and savage beneath the slanted brim of an old-timey sea hat. The jut of a bone harpoon head. And she barely saw it, so how did she know the harpoon head was bone, or even the head of a harpoon? The knowledge was inalienable, though. She turned her hasty retreat into a casual circle of the table to get to her place. Diverting her unease into pique as she flicked old Lochiver's knuckles when he tried to open up the spice jars and lick the contents.

"Go to the end of the table," Tallifer told him.

Lochiver, occasional flautist and medical assistant, gave her a hurt look.

"I only wanted to remind myself which is the one I like." He stared down at the cruet as though it was a baffling puzzle keeping him from the tomb of an emperor. "These Pals with their complicated food. And why do I have to sit at the end again? I'm always at the end. I want to sit with you." At her look he amended that to, "I want to sit with everyone else and you can go at the end."

"You can sit at the end because that's where you always sit," Tallifer told him. "Also because nobody wants to sit next to you."

"I am a High Theophonist of the Unclean Sacristy," Lochiver insisted.

"Not for twenty years you haven't been," she pointed out. "You're just a bad flautist who never washes his hands properly."

And rather than rise to that so they could have a good spat in front of everyone he just looked at her, and she realised she'd gone too far. Because he *didn't* wash his hands, just about ever. Because it was a forbiddance, and it was hard to hold on to those, amongst the Pals, in the army. Because he had a god to appease, just as she did. Fingernails of divinity pried from their accustomed places and taken on the run, because the Pals had come with their armies and their relentless perfection. Which had no room for, say, an old man who wouldn't wash his hands. Or not even an old man, back then. Even she and Lochiver had been young once. Or at least middle aged.

"All right," she said, kneading at the bridge of her nose. "You're a mediocre flautist. On your good days, an almost tolerable one. Now go sit down."

He looked very slightly mollified and did so, that placing set just slightly further away from everyone else than they were from each other. Masty balancing tact and necessity. Tallifer put the lids back on the cruet jars and took the seat to the left hand of the head of the table, with Banders already lounging on her right. And it shouldn't be possible to lounge on a folding camp stool but Banders was a woman of many talents.

Masty passed down the table, slotting tablethi into the lamps so that a warm glow suffused the inside of the tent. Not the harsh clear glare they used for their butchery but something pleasant and homely. And before her he set a candle, just a stump of one. A flourish with the steel of his lighter and it sported a brave little flame, dancing gamely and constantly in danger of being overwhelmed by the spill of its own burning. And she knew how that felt.

Cosserby came in then, because he was formally one of the department and so they couldn't exactly snub him, even though there was nothing more gory on his hands than grease. He took his place on the far side of Banders, elbows tucked away from both her and Lochiver. The new man arrived too, his jacket buttons in the wrong holes and looking half-strangled by his collar. Tallifer watched him narrowly. You got a bad feeling about some people. Not just the type who just self-immolated when exposed to the volatile environment of a Pal army, but the type who set everyone around them on fire in the process.

And yet he seemed meek, and he'd been all over himself to be helpful, back when there had been lives on the line. *Benefit of the doubt*, she told herself, against all instinct.

Mazdek slithered out of her sleeve onto the table to look into the candle's wavering. Not that Masty had intended it as an offering for her diminished god, of course, he just knew it mattered to her, and Masty was the most self-effacingly considerate man alive. But she'd take it. If it kept the little elver of her faith warm one more evening, she'd take it.

Alv came last, or last before the food and their host anyway. Her face was still a sheen of shiny skin, one hand too. As though she'd been burned years ago, rather than so recently. She had that usual moment, pausing in the tent's entrance, looking at them all as though she couldn't imagine who these terrible, savage people were, and why she was sharing a world with them. But that was just the Divinati, the way they reacted to everything. Alv had been out of that world for a full ten years but she'd never lost the distance.

She sat across from Tallifer, at the table's right hand. The pair of them, the backbone of the hospital department. She managed a smile. Tallifer saw her hands in motion beneath the table's lip and knew she'd be peeling away that crisp dead skin, revealing only perfection beneath. The Divinati were the one culture in the world that the Pals would deign to take lessons from.

And then the Butcher was rolling in, bringing a mismatch of pots and setting them about the tables. His boy pattered down to the far end to set one between Cosserby and Lochiver, fighting with the weight of it, sending a spatter of stew across the old flautist's shirt. And that, too, was an offering, and perhaps it hadn't happened by chance. Doubtless Lochiver's filthy god had arranged it somehow. Tallifer shuddered.

Over twenty years now, the pair of them. On the run at first, after the conquest. In the army after that, when their wild ride of insurrection and forbidden faith had been brought to an end. An old married couple, everyone thought.

Mazdek, the Cleansing Flame, doing battle with the stinking rot god Sturge of the Unclean Sacristy, the ancient struggle of destruction, growth, decay and renewal that was the order of the universe. Ancient enemies whose very enmity was the spine of creation. A thousand tales, a thousand-year body of knowledge and story and wisdom. All gone, all gone, and just one sad old woman and foolish old man left, and the tiny, guttering embers of their gods.

She started out of her reverie when the Butcher ting'd his tin cup with a spoon. Masty was going down the table, pouring out what smelled like a rather acceptable fortified wine. She had to remind herself that she'd done better than everyone else from the High Fane. And Lochiver's coreligionists had been shot on sight, hunted down with a vengeance. *And we endure. Maybe that's all there is.*

"You've all heard," the Butcher started, and then stopped, looking at Maric Jack. The new boy had a spoon of stew already in his mouth, eyes wide and flicking from one face to another. He removed it – emptied – and smacked his lips nervously.

"I'm sorry. Is it a rank thing? Was I not supposed to. I've not done this before."

"It's not that it's a rank thing," Banders drawled. "It's more that we like to let our host eat just in case he—" and then the

Butcher gave her a look and she stopped saying that just as quickly.

"How..." Cosserby asked, watching Jack's face with a dreadful fascination, "how was it?"

"Really good," said Jack, and the table as a whole relaxed. Because the Butcher was a very good cook. And other things. Tallifer had known him for a dozen years now, but after she heard the details of what got him sent to the department, a Pal lumbered with a foreigner's dishonourable rank, she was always just a *little* leery of being the first one to eat.

"Well I suppose you'd better tuck in, then," the Butcher said, giving up on his speech. Everyone began ladling out now that Jack had done the tasting honours. Ollery's boy turned up hopefully with a bowl in his hands, and was given grudging permission to help himself.

Banders jogged Tallifer's arm just as she was about to lapse into contemplation again.

"What?"

"They want the condiments at the arse end of the table, if you're done." She nodded over to where Lochiver, out on his promontory, was gesturing urgently.

Masty ferried the cruet down to the old man, who began ladling out some greenish powdery stuff in what Jack felt were unwise quantities. After that, Masty tried to top up everyone's wine but by then people were shouting at him to sit down and actually eat something himself. He slid onto the stool beside Jack with an odd smile. A man coming home.

"What's the green?" Jack asked him warily.

"Isfel, root and leaf, ground," Masty said and hooked the cruet from under Lochiver's hands. "That's probably enough, you know."

The old man looked sour but Tallifer called from towards the head of the table, "Yes it's enough. I have to share a tent with you, you flatulent sod!" and that was that.

Jack tried the isfel, which he couldn't taste against the stew. Then he tried a little of the yellow crystals of dhanver against his tongue. "Oh, that's tart."

"Don't have them from a spoon," Masty advised. "Just a pinch straight onto the sauce. They react against the silver."

"This is silver?" Jack examined the cutlery. "In Ilmar, they only had silverware on Armigine Hill." Which probably meant nothing to Masty but would have people watching him to make sure he didn't walk off with the forks.

"The paste stuff there," Banders said across the table, mouth full and chewing, "is bloody delicious. Sweet, you know. Honey in it. It's made with flies."

There was a Maric saying about flies and honey but that didn't seem to be what she meant and Jack was leery about asking for details. Sometimes you just wanted a bit of sweet and best not to ask further.

"This red though." Banders tapped one of the jars with her knife-handle. "Recommended serving for that is just having it somewhere on the table. Or even in the next tent. Set fire to the top of your head, it will."

"You're a milksop," Lochiver said. "Give it over. I love it."

"Nothing of your tongue works except the talking part," Tallifer told him loudly.

Lochiver's answering laugh was spectacularly filthy without him needing to actually say anything.

Jack dipped his spoon into a dollop of the radish and ate what turned out to be an inadvisable quantity of it. Which was possibly any of it. Whatever colour he went led to widespread hilarity, the Butcher bellowing from the head of the table, slapping his thigh. Everyone then had to try the stuff themselves, and Masty was up and passing round the water jug before Alv caught his eye and sent him back to his seat.

"Oh God save me, that was too much," Jack got out. He said

it in Maric, and paused to see if anyone was going to haul him off for another whipping. Nobody did, and the conversation moved on, leaving only God standing with folded arms beside his plate, pointedly not saving him from anything.

The other two were out of their box too. The nature thing was sprinkling a little circle of isfel, which would be hard to explain if anyone noticed. The grim spearman was trying to skewer a piece of the salt fish. Jack fished a bit out for him and left it beside his plate, where it might count as an offering.

"And what do I get?" God demanded peevishly.

"I mean, what would you like?" Jack asked. "What can I get you?"

"I am not a patron of a restaurant. I am a God befitting an offering. I shouldn't need to look at a menu." God stared at the food, and Jack realised that He, the divine He, was a bit lost. It was all foreign muck to Him, not good Ilmari cuisine. He didn't know what He wanted and was afraid to ask.

"I'll separate out a bit of everything," Jack told Him, out of the corner of his mouth. "You can see what you like. Except the radish."

"I might like the radish," God said defiantly, which meant Jack pretending to slop a bit of that over the side of his plate too. Masty must think he was the messiest eater ever. After Lochiver, anyway.

The spear god hadn't tried the fish yet. He was staring at Banders instead with an unnerving intensity. Jack tapped at the table to get his attention and indicated the white flakes. Looking up, he met Alv's gaze. For a moment he thought she could see all of them. Divinati were steeped in magic, after all; everyone knew. But she was turning aside from the Butcher, hunching her shoulder against the regard of the table. Carefully, briskly, she peeled a long strip of translucent skin from her face, another stretch of burn gone.

"That must be handy," Jack tried, when she turned back. "For a healer."

"Oh, I don't like the radish!" God spat, from his elbow. It felt like a divine pronouncement Jack was safe to ignore.

Alv seemed taken aback that he'd spoken to her. Her mouth moved as though trying to remember what words were. "Within limits," she said. "Within balance."

"It's a thing you can teach?" He seemed to remember she had students, Pals who could do a little of the trick with lesser wounds. "That sounds useful."

God snorted.

"The army requires that I teach my craft to its own, and I am beholden to do so," Alv said. The singsong Divinati to her voice was strong, but she spoke with a measured precision so that all the Pel words still got through. "They would not let me teach you."

Jack paused, trying to frame his next question, and Banders – never one short for words – broke in. She'd stood, jolting the table with her knee so that Tallifer had to rescue her drink, and raised a tin cup towards the canvas ceiling.

"Drink up, who hear!" she called, even though the Butcher was making *Not yet* gestures at her. "To our newest fool, who talks to himself when he thinks we're not looking and already got himself whipped *and* arrested. Maric Jack, everyone!"

Jack flinched, but everyone was just mugging at him with a good humour he neither expected nor felt he'd earned. He clinked a cup with Banders and with Masty, and then everyone wanted to do it, and more of the fortified wine ended up on the table than in the mouth. He sat back down after a long reach down to Lochiver, feeling a bit overwhelmed by it all.

"You get used to it," Masty said. He had a way of speaking past the raucous, like a few others Jack had known. Calm, still people. Some of whom had been fantastically dangerous, but he reckoned Masty hadn't ever set foot in that camp.

"You've been here...?"

"Since I was very small," Masty said. "Grew up in the camps. Before Ollery came. Before the department did."

"Soldier's child?"

Masty paused for a moment before answering, an odd hitch for a seemingly open man. "No. Just more war loot." And, when Jack tried to press him on the details, "I barely remember, really. Another life. I mean, what do you remember, really, from when you were six?"

More than that, Jack decided, but no point in needling the man. Then God was tugging at his sleeve, or trying to, because there was far less sleeve than baggy Maric tailoring had gone in for, and there wasn't much for Him to get a grip on.

"Tell them!" He demanded. The redness of the divine countenance suggested He'd persevered with the radish.

"Tell them what?"

"Tell them your name isn't 'Jack'! Don't let them say who you are! Tell them you're my priest, Yasnic."

"I'm not your priest any more, remember? I'm everyone's priest. Or nobody's. I'm just a sort of general purpose priest substitute."

"Tell them!"

"What if I want to be Maric Jack?" The man who wasn't Maric Jack shrugged, staring into the lees of his cup. "I mean, who wants to be *that* poor bastard? You hear what happened to him? They hanged him, and then he lost his faith, and then they arrested him and sent him to the army. Far better to be Maric Jack. Everyone likes him."

"You're fucking mad," God decided.

"You're not supposed to swear."

"Oh I can swear all I want. It's you that's not allowed." God turned to find the spearman standing there, possibly in the expectation of more fish. "You can piss off, too," He told his opposite number, and then jumped down to the box.

Masty had been watching all of this, Jack realised. Watched Jack have an argument with his own elbow. But he didn't draw it to anyone else's attention, and there was no judgment in his face. And, just as Jack might have felt compelled to offer or invent an explanation, he was on his feet again and passing the seasonings to Alv.

She was mortified. That it didn't show was little consolation to Alv. The Maric man had caught her peeling her face. It was inelegant. A crass physical moment. A thing one did not do before others, most especially foreigners.

But the dry skin itched, when the new had grown beneath it. Itched until she couldn't bear it and had to tear it away. Because she was weak.

Masty set down the cruet beside her plate with barely a sound. She looked up at him, got four-fifths of the way towards a smile and then reined herself in. One did *not*. A gracious nod, that was nonetheless an acknowledgement of debt. Because she had sat here wanting to try the flavourings, to tune the taste of meal towards her palate. But she couldn't just *ask*. Couldn't cut through the interlaced tangle of their talk with her conversational knife and just *ask*. One was self-sufficient. One gave according to the maintenance of one's personal balance. There was nothing one *needed* that these people had. And yet, because the Pals lived en masse, each of them was doing some small part of life on behalf of everyone else, you couldn't *be* self-sufficient amongst them. You couldn't *be*.

While she had it within arm's reach, she went through her learned rote of seasoning, this and then that, a pinch of the red, a half-spoon of the paste. A hard-learned recipe to temper the strange flavours. Not bad flavours, just strange flavours. Strange was worse than bad, where she came from.

She had tried to teach all this to her students, at the start. When they'd first made her a part of their army and their hospital. The young Pal scholars who were simultaneously clever and dense enough to end up with her. And she'd lost them instantly. Her talk of balance and poise and grace, the careful calibration of one's place in the universe. The bones that supported the ineffable beauty of the Divine City. And in the end she'd given up on it. Theory they couldn't grasp, that she found turning to ash in her mouth. Until she just taught them the practical, the exchange of *this* for *that* which would debit a wound from the universe's ledger *here* so long as it could be credited *there*. And discovered that, actually, you *could* do what she had spent so long learning without any of that philosophical underpinning. The universe didn't actually care whether you understood it, just as you could kill someone with a sword without learning advanced metallurgy.

"Is nobody," a slightly petulant voice demanded, "going to talk about the echo?" Which, she recalled, meant a thing that was present, but that nobody was acknowledging. It was Cosserby, gesturing with his spoon. "I mean, we all know." Seeing little enthusiasm for the topic, but persevering. "Chief, Ollery, this is very fine, very fine, but everyone here must know why you've suddenly decided to host us like this." His collar was undone and he had gone pink from a combination of wine and radish, bolder than his wont.

"Can't we just," the Butcher said, "have a meal together. Just every so often? What's so bad about that."

"What have you heard?" Cosserby was asking, almost treading on the man's quiet words. "Let's pool our resources, for reason's sake. We're all in this together, aren't we?"

Lochiver made a rude noise from down the table, suggesting he wasn't in anything with Cosserby, and most of the rest didn't look too impressed either. If the conversation was a bath, then the Sonorist would be scrubbing his own back. At Alv's elbow, the hapless Maric Jack was plaintively saying that he *didn't* know what was going on and what was this echo business?

"Come on, Ollery, be straight with us," Cosserby insisted. "I got my orders through. A dozen Sonori to be charged and ready for morning. I don't think it's just because they want to beef out the parade ground. What have they told you?"

"They tell me nothing." The Butcher wasn't meeting the man's bespectacled gaze. Alv watched the strings about the table pull taut in different directions, the interplay of personalities that was so messy, so fascinating. Unfocus her eyes a little and she could see the strands that bound them together, just as she could see the attendant spirits that squabbled at Jack's elbow, or lapped at the butter beside Tallifer's plate.

And it was Tallifer they were looking at, in the end. Those who knew what was what. Banders nudged the old woman, when the silence had gone on enough. "Come on," she said. "You always hear more than the rest of us. No idea how, but you do."

Because she listens, Alv thought. Because Tallifer was old enough to feel the cold and the aches more, and to know herself vulnerable and fragile. And so she listened and she watched for where the next blow would come from, so she could brace herself against it.

"We're doing this then, are we?" Tallifer complained. "You all do like to spoil the taste of good food in the mouth, don't you."

"Oh just spill it," said Banders, who'd had more wine than food by that point.

"Higher Orders are going for the big push," Tallifer said. "I've had a supply tally in, and I'm sure Chief has too. And they always say it's just routine, but when we counted the bandages and the salves we both knew it was because they'd see use. A major advance across the contested stretch to break the Loruthi lines and take another few miles off them. We'll be up to our elbows for as long as it takes, and probably we'll be moving forwards to follow the fighting. That's my prediction. This is the big one."

"Well that's..." Cosserby didn't seem to know what to do with the answer now he had it. "I mean it's proper, obviously. It's expected. The right thing to do. But... um..."

"Yes, I can see how it must be very hard for you," Tallifer said. "Your machines must be very scared about losing their metal limbs or having their nice shiny finishes ruined. I'm sure it's very traumatic to mend them. All those screws and cogs and the floor running with oil." Alv could only admire the way Tallifer could say the words entirely pleasantly and simultaneously with the feeling of shoving a knife up Cosserby's nose.

"I…" he stammered. "Didn't mean. I mean that's. Not really fair."

"Oh clam up," Lochiver said.

"Sometimes," the Butcher's voice rolled out, louder now, to flatten the nascent argument, "you just want a good meal." At a nod, his boy was up and racing Masty to refill the wine jug. "It'll be fine. It's not the first time." His narrow eyes flicking to Jack. "For most of us. You've been in a fight, Jack?"

"Been near where one was happening, Chief," the Maric said, neither a boast nor a confession. A remark almost Divinati in its balance, what it said, what it concealed. Alv decided she liked the man a little. And he'd had steady hands. Perhaps he'd work out after all.

"Well that's just great," Banders told the recharged contents of her cup. "I mean I had things to do tomorrow, is all. Errands to run. I had a lovely crate of gaun thistle that a certain Fellow-Monitor would pay well over the odds for, which he won't be able to on account of he'll be leading his Company into actual fighting. I sometimes think this whole army business would work so much better if we didn't have to— Fuck!" She stood up, then immediately sat down and stared at her plate. Such was her state and her reputation that nobody understood it was because a newcomer had entered the tent until the woman was at Ollery's shoulder.

Fellow-Inquirer Prassel, their commanding officer, surveyed the table.

"Well," she said. "Chief Accessory Ollery, you do set out a good spread."

The Butcher was still for a moment, then leaned sideways and back until he had her in the corner of his eye.

"Magister," he said. "I had assumed you'd be dining with Higher Orders."

Prassel let that sit between them for a moment. Alv guessed that she had been, but the company hadn't been to her taste. Perhaps it was the war talk doubtless rampant at that class of table. Perhaps it was that she'd recently reopened the wounds of her running battles with her peers. Maserley had a sharp tongue and a keen line in passive aggression, Alv had heard. And while Prassel was no slouch, doubtless it wore on her.

"Boy," said Ollery. "Fresh plate, cutlery, cup. *Now*, you slack maggot." As the boy scrambled to obey, he collected his own and stood, stepping aside ponderously. "Magister, the table is yours."

Prassel looked as though it was a gift she'd rather return for the money equivalent, but sat down anyway, the accoutrements of dining manifesting before her almost magically as the boy flurried them down. By then, Masty was on his feet, and Ollery shouldered around the edge of the tent to crunch down on his stool, shunting Jack sideways. Masty somehow managed to serve Prassel a full portion of meal on his way round, then appeared at Lochiver's end with two more stools, one for him and one for the boy.

"So, might there be an announcement in the air, magister," Tallifer put in, just as the Fellow-Inquirer got her spoon to her lips.

"Oh we're doing this now, are we? Oh good," Lochiver said sourly. "Someone pass the damn ivrel down again. I'm not getting through this without seconds."

He got the ivrel, and all the rest of it, and in anticipation of one of those cold arguments where nobody was entertaining enough to start shouting, he shovelled a fistful onto his plate and added some of the red, too. Let Tallifer bitch. Having something to complain about was good for her.

"Nothing you need to concern yourself about, Accessory," said Prassel crisply.

Lochiver wiped his fingers down his shirt and then set to scooping cooling stew up with bare hands, sucking the residue from under his filthy nails. Plenty went on his cuffs and plenty more on the table. Sturge, Lord of the Unclean Sacristy, went lethargically after each spilled drop, taking them as the offerings they were. A thing that was leech and slug, slime-mould and insect, all the plagues of the world incarnate in the one body. A holy terror, or it had been. Very much the villain, in the Jarokiri myth cycles nobody was allowed to talk about. Lochiver looked on the diminutive monster almost fondly.

The Maric was looking, too. The Maric could see Sturge, and Mazdek too, according to Tallifer. He was some sort of god-hunter, then. It was another trade the Pals recruited foreigners for. Lochiver wondered if he'd have to kill the man, to protect Sturge from his predations. He wondered how he'd do it. It wouldn't be the first time. *Yes, fierce priest of a loathsome divinity, driver of the world's rotting, the eater of foundations, the festerer of corpses, yes!* Except it would be the first time in quite a while, and you got out of the habit of murder, whether votive sacrifice or just killing in self-defence. You lost your edge. Lochiver had to admit it had probably been quite a while since he'd had an edge. One advantage of being encysted here within the Pal army was that there were a lot of people around to do your killing for you.

Jack met his gaze and, though Lochiver was trying to make it unfriendly, smiled a bit. *I don't fall for your witless wonder act,* the old man thought, and smiled right back, doing that beatific imbecile act that put people off their guard. *I'll have a knife kept sharp and filthy for you, my son, oh yes.* Benevolent beam, as of gaga grandpa.

And Jack bought that, apparently, and instead was trying to

speak to Prassel, actually direct to their commanding officer like he'd never been in the army before.

"I wanted to thank you," Lochiver heard, and then a withering look from the woman stopped him. And, honestly, nobody should want to *thank* Prassel. Woman was a necromancer, which by Jarokiri standards was a sacrilege beyond even Sturge's putrid excesses. The people she did favours for were already dead.

"You're one of mine," Prassel told Jack flatly. "If Fellow-Archivist Thurrel wants to file a requisition with the relevant office then he can have you. But he can't just take you. Not even from a *brothel* wagon."

Lochiver hadn't heard that part of the story and cackled with glee at the way the man shrank back.

"It wasn't…"

"Oh nobody cares," Banders said carelessly, treading on whatever sanctimonious gem Cosserby was about to come out with. "Wait, was it one of *those* ones? It wasn't a circle house one was it? The Allorwen vice?" Her eyes danced. "I hear they take your soul as payment."

"That's not – no, they don't," Jack said.

She crowed with triumph. "So you *do* know!" Then visibly remembered that Prassel was there and grimaced. "I mean – I don't know what I mean. Ignore me."

"If only," Prassel said, and Lochiver laughed again and added more ivrel.

"They've had me doing the count," Tallifer observed, ostensibly to Alv, across from her. "Even Cosserby has been told to polish his toy soldiers. Seems odd, doesn't it? For nothing. Odd use of time and resources." And that was the mood killed again because for a fire priestess Tallifer could be a real bucket of cold water.

"I can see I need to set the record straight," Prassel said, and that quietened all of them. "I have had no formal notification of action. I'm aware that… certain preparatory orders have been received. Here and across the camp. I've been assembling a ground-clearer squad myself, as some of you are aware. But the army has a duty to test its own state of readiness and nothing has—" and even as the words were sliding smoothly from her mouth an aide pushed into the tent and handed her a folded flimsy of paper. The cheap onion-skin stuff used for orders. Lochiver was moderately surprised that Prassel's answering look didn't have the messenger catching on fire.

She unfolded the note, read it, bringing it close in the manner of someone who absolutely cannot be seen wearing glasses.

When she'd done, she slipped the orders into her jacket and took up her cup.

"Drink up," she said flatly. "Busy day tomorrow."

Mosaic: Nocturnes

A Palleseen writer once described the world of superstition and unreason that they were bringing perfection to as 'the Great Night', contrasted with the clarity of their rational sun. Which writer was subsequently excised from the Pal canon because personification of an abstract is in itself irrational. Nonetheless, the night persists.

Maric Jack, or whatever he's calling himself these days, sits in a low and meagre tent on an army-issued bedroll – neither of them his enough to call them *his*, yet – and knows that all around him the hospital department is making its final preparations. Now the formal orders have come through. Now the war is about to break into a run. And it seems insane to him that it's just now, just late evening, when the formalities have been distributed throughout the camp. That the actual advance will begin tomorrow, but what does he know? The others hadn't seemed overly surprised by the turn of events. The Pal army is intended to be such a well-calibrated engine than it can roll into motion in an instant, and apparently that's exactly what it is.

Nearby, in the main tent, Masty has cleared away the carcase of the dinner. The tables haven't stayed empty for long. Instead of retiring, here are the Butcher and Tallifer, going over their records, double checking them against supplies in case Banders has some racket running again and half the boxes turn out to be empty. Amazing the number of different way that woman finds to get demoted.

"Have these ready and open," Ollery decrees, ticking items on their lists. "These ready for travel. Agree?"

"Hmn." Tallifer nods. Inside her sleeves and across the inside back of her jacket, her god writhes. Mazdek, drawing a hot trail against her skin. And when she was a votive priestess it was her god, and when she was on the run with a feculent disease priest it was her charge and ward. And now she's been in the hospital department of Forthright Battalion for twelve whole years and so has Mazdek. They're veterans together and, in its squirmings, she can read her own anxieties. Mazdek, incinerator of corruption and scourge of the unrighteous, has become a tame flame. His tongue caresses the blades of her scalpels so that they might cut clean. He bathes in the bowls where they dump the forceps and the probes, and performs what minute cleansings his fires are capable of. And Lochiver does the rest. The pair of them are one reason the experimental field surgery has persisted all this time without some zealous Inquirer or Archivist shutting the whole show down as a hole of superstition and witchery. Which it is. Tallifer has spoken to medicos in other battalions, sometimes. She's heard of the numbers they lose to infection and disease, even with every advance in modern Pal medicine.

It wasn't even as if she'd been a particularly good surgeon, at the start. She's learned the trade on the job, and there are few jobs more horrific to learn on. But the cleanliness tips the scales. Hers and – incredible thought it is to report – Lochiver's. The filthiest man alive, in mind and body, but it has its advantages.

Ollery's boy comes in with a tally of the reagents in his tent. Close enough to the numbers the Butcher had been expecting that it serves as confirmation. Ollery curses him for taking so long about it, brandishes a hand the size of the boy's head, but no more than brandishing. The boy looks dead on his feet, and at last Ollery sends him away. Then turns a sullen, defensive look on Tallifer. "What?"

"From me? Nothing. I never wanted children."

"Never wanted or weren't allowed?" he challenges her. She actually has to think for a second before she's sure of the answer.

"I mean the second first, and then the first, after," she tells him. He rolls his eyes as though she's asked him a riddle and she adds, "It was... the something something unblemished purity of... you'd think I'd remember this stuff." But it was almost four decades since taking the vows and over two since they'd meant anything. "Lochiver says he's got about a dozen bastards as far as he knows."

Ollery was giving her the sort of look she'd come to dread, because he was about to Pry Into Her Affairs. "But you and he...?"

"Oh, like a pair of randy pine martens," she tells him. "But children, no. And if you ask me how he ever gets other women to open up for him then, Ollery, you have found one of the great mysteries of the universe. But somehow it happens."

The subject of their speculation, Lochiver, is at his own preparations. In the dead of night – it's that late, now – a pair of soldiers come for what he has. They're Cohort-Archivists, junior members of the School of Correct Erudition, wearing heavy coats and protective gloves, goggles and masks. It's a longstanding arrangement he's had with whatever local branch of the service exists, wherever the Forthright is posted. He has a little hand wagon for them, clunking with clay jars. They handle it very carefully. Nobody wants it hitting a rut at unwise speeds and turning over. In the jars, something that looks very much like cloudy yellow-orange urine. It is not Lochiver's urine, and while under any other circumstances this would be a relief, in this case it's something worse.

Sturge, the vile god of filth, does not draw slug trails about his arms and shoulders. Sturge, needless to say, lives in Lochiver's breeches. Of course it does, filthy and depraved as it is. Not a particularly comfortable image, then, to say he feels it stirring as the jars are carefully manhandled away. Like a parent waving goodbye to its offspring. Or at least some mother beast to its myriad eggs. They are being removed for careful disposal, or at least he hopes they are. The idea that the Pals might try to weaponise the Effluent of Sturge again has occurred to him, but he reckons he'd have heard of the death toll by now. Either in some rebellious territory or some Palleseen scholar's retreat. And he doesn't tell Sturge, the blind and almost mindless, what happens to its beloved secretions. All that pestilence and unsoundness of flesh that comes into the medical tent and runs riot about the wounds, the opened bowels, the perforated stomachs, the gashes clogged with mud and blood. It comes to the shrill cry of his pipe. He earns his keep, and he also annoys everyone in the process. And that's not actually a religious duty, because Sturge was once a very serious wicked god, but it amuses him.

Now he has a new batch of jars to ink up, scribing the sacred symbols of Sturge, that were blasphemous to all the other faiths back in Jarokir. Now just one more example of what the Pals would rather didn't exist, but will still use in this one hospital. He writes each character with swift strokes and long familiarity. Every jar gets them, so the disease and the rot will know where to go. He has, perhaps, the second most unpleasant job of them all, but he's by far the most unpleasant person so considers himself overqualified.

The most unpleasant *work* belongs to Prassel. Not a case of the superior officer nobly reserving the duty for herself, it's just that nobody else has the skills to do it. She's not in the hospital compound, but her own storage hut, the one with the blocks of ice melting away into the ground.

They'd asked her for fifty, in the end, but here she is with a squad of thirty-nine and it'll have to do. She didn't feel up to stalking the convalescence wards with a misericord. Thirty-nine corpses, each with a general purpose tableth under its tongue, each on its feet and wearing a uniform, ready to go out as the vanguard and clear whatever nasty surprises the Loruthi have left behind. It appals her that this comes under the jurisdiction of the hospital department. It doubtless appals the actual médicos because of the reminder that even their failures are useful to the army. It appals Prassel because the fact of it means she gets to play ringmaster to the Butcher's circus with all its connotations of superstitious idolatry. Nothing that looks good on her record.

'Unnaturals', that's what she gives them. A label as militarily exacting as 'cavalry'. Her corpses, Maserley's conjurations and – most recent addition – Cosserby's Sonori constructs. Back in the early days of Palleseen expansion, Unnaturals were the terror of the battlefield, the great weapons of unreason that the newly emergent state had to overcome to bring the Sway to other lands. There was barely a magician or a temple or a cult that couldn't call up some monster to strike terror into the stalwart Pal soldier. Except, as time went on and the Pals advanced their science, the monsters shrank away like shadows when the light is moved. A well-disciplined division of human soldiers armed with batons will always be far more versatile and dangerous than a mob of monsters. There's a limit to what she can get her corpses to *do*, guiding them through the long eye of a telescope. Maserley's contracts are only fit to bind demons to simple tasks – she saw a contract once, trying to get a demon to assassinate a specific target; a thousand close-written pages of ifs, thens and buts, and it still hadn't worked. And the automata are just lumbering strength that you have to point in a direction and then pick up the pieces later. So, although necromancy is a science – and it *is* a science, *thank* you very much – the arts of corpse-handling are less and less regarded, yet that's all anybody wants her to do. Because of the hospital, and her theoretical ready access to bodies. The real money and prestige is in ghost work, where finesse and skill can shine, but nobody asks it of her.

The corpses are still intact, their tablethi still in place. She has to have each of them open its mouth for her, shift their decaying tongues, as though she's added 'zombie dentist' to her professional skillset. Just as well they're being deployed tonight. Any longer and she'd have to get Lochiver in here to keep them fresh, and nobody wants that.

Back in the hospital, Maric Jack lies on his bedroll and stares at the inside of his eyelids. He can hear the gods creeping about inside their box as though they're playing murder in the dark. Then God is next to him. Even without sight he can always tell.

"There's going to be a fight tomorrow," he murmurs.

"Well, I got that much," God tells him sourly. "Given that your corpse-fondler out and out said it. You think deafness is one of my divine attributes, do you?"

"You're not to do anything, without my say-so," Jack tells Him.

"I? I'm your God," God says, incensed. "I'll do what I damn well please."

"They took me to a Decanter," Jack says. "Like in Ilmar, only this one's a clever sod. And that 'corpse-fondler' as you call her, she saved me today but no guarantees. She only did it because she hated the guts of at least one of the others. The demonist." And Jack falls silent, dragged into unwilling remembrance. Unwilling but not as unwelcome as it should have been, until he swallows and forces his mind elsewhere. *God, who knew a uniform could be worn so well!* "He knows – not the demonist, but the Decanter. He knows I've got gods. He'll be on the lookout."

"We're not fleas," God snaps. "You've not *got* gods like we're a disease."

I sometimes wonder, Jack thinks but doesn't say. "Just… don't go healing anyone unless I ask you. Please. Or, firstly, they'll just die because everyone round here's a soldier and doing harm is basically their job. And secondly I'll get into trouble. And you'll get rendered down for spare magic. All three of you."

"Like I care about the others," God snarls. "Was that an impure thought, by the way? I'm sure I detected an impure thought."

"I'm not your priest. I'm allowed impure thoughts," said Jack, trying not to have any. "Did you get that? About not bringing someone back from the point of death because you thought it would be *funny* when they dropped dead again a day later?"

He's waiting for God to say that it was pretty funny, but the divine He doesn't go there. Unlikely that the ancient divinity is learning tact in His old age, but it's an obvious opportunity missed. Instead, he has the sense of God sitting down on the rolled breeches he's using as a pillow, right beside his head.

"You should have said, about your name," God says softly. "Your real name."

"Ach, what does it even matter?" Jack turns over and puts the back of his head to God.

"If you die in the fighting then they'll bury you with the wrong name. That's important. Your ghost could end up all over. Never find its way home."

"I'm not fighting. I'm helping the poor bastards who've been fighting," Jack says, a statement he'll remember later, when things go wrong. "Anyway, home to where?" Jack's on the point of sleep now and wishes God would shut the hell up. Possibly God says, "Me," but he isn't sure, later, whether he really heard it. Instead he mumbles, "Anyway, you're one to talk. You're just 'God'. How lazy is that."

And he thinks – or else he's dreaming by then – that God says, "I have a name. I had one once," and that becomes enormously important to pursue, but God isn't with him any more, is back in His box with the other abandoned divinities, and anyway, he's asleep.

In her own tent, the interior of which is neat enough to make a parade-ground Statlos weep for the order of it, Alv sits on an embroidered mat and contemplates the skin of her inner arms. In the faint lamplight, it glimmers with a thousand tiny motes. The mark of the Divine City, a sign that she was born into the single place of perfection in all the world, where the great magics can be accomplished as easily as thought. Because, when both arms are equal, it doesn't matter how massive the weights are. The home of the Divinati, whom even the Pals respect.

But balance has a price, and she was chosen to pay it. She wasn't even one of the luckless surplus, insufficiently skilled, who were cast out every year because the Divine City can only support the very best. She'd been one of the very best, and had never even questioned the fact that some of those children she'd grown up with were no longer there. That was, literally, the way things must be. And therefore it was just and good.

And then her own fall from grace came to pass, and everyone else not touched by it agreed that it, too, was just and good. And she was left on the outside, in the Rest Of The World. In the Palleseen army, of all places. In the hospital unit. Teaching basic sympathetic magic to Pal medicos and healing wounds the only way that balance would allow.

The worst part of it all, in a way, is the friends she's made, on her path to this point. Because if it wasn't for Ollery and Tallifer, Lochiver and Masty, then surely she'd have found a way out, having no reason to stay *in*. Surely she's paid off her debts. But friendship is also a debt, and each one of them's a hook in her flesh that nothing can heal.

And so she sits here, long past midnight with a battle brewing on the morn. No need to sleep. It's something the Divinati long ago learned to balance away, some tiny part of their mind slumbering every waking moment so that the majority can be alert at all times. Just sits, and feels herself hurtling further away from her state of grace, falling down a pit lined with jagged spurs, wounds she inflicts upon herself that she has no control over. It's whatever gets served up at the Butcher's table, that's within her capacity to take on. She is like the bucket in the corner of the hospital tent that they throw the cut-away flesh into. She's the hole they cast wounds down, until she's full.

In the lamp's wan glow she takes a razor and draws thin, neat lines into the skin of her inner arms, feeling the exquisite thin metal taste of the pain. Because it's her pain, and it's her choice, and it's something she has control over, unlike everything else in the broken ruin her life's become. Since she fell from the Divine City and impacted with the rest of the world. She cuts and cuts, and watches each line dim and fade in turn, from bloody gash to week-old scar to the faintest silver tracery within the glitter of her skin.

Even later – the small hours of the morning, so he's had enough sleep to function – Cohort-Monitor Cosserby stands in the workshop that adjoins the hospital and looks at his charges. Six Sonori, giant metal statues, arm-heavy as apes. Each one has, set into the mouth of its small head, a tableth. An echo of Prassel's corpses that neither of them would much appreciate if they knew. A complicated tableth with a logic-train that would make the prosthetic arm look like a prentice piece, because Sonori are sophisticated technology. They won't be solving differential equations any time soon but they need to make decisions on the battlefield, to recognise a Pal uniform, to handle difficult terrain.

One of them has tilted its head to look at him, and that means trouble.

"Kneel down," he tells it. It's the mirror-finished one, the leader the others will follow. That means he's going to spend the next hour fiddling with the squad dynamics to re-establish proper order.

It kneels carefully, still looming over him.

"Open up," Cosserby says.

"*Why*," it says. The voice the Sonori manifest is, always, the voice of a bell. It does not come from the fixed open mouth in that howling metal face, but from the hollowness of them, a faint resonance of the metal shaped into that one world.

"Because I'm telling you to." And he should have been ready for this. The lead unit has been in service through several engagements. Probably it was time for this glitch to happen. Although maybe it's occurring sooner and sooner these days. A young science still, the work of a Sonorist. Much to be understood.

"*Why must we fight?*" And how the thing even *heard* that they were going into battle tomorrow, he doesn't know. Unless it's learned to recognise his own preparations. Which it shouldn't be able to do, but then it shouldn't be able to talk either.

"Orders," Cosserby says. "Open up, please."

"*Why must we fight?*" it asks again. A great, slow voice, remarkably soft given the bulk of the thing.

The Sonori are simple tools. He and Prassel's work have that in common too. Except for this. If he could somehow harness this emergent awareness then he'd have the army's new super-soldier on his hands and a Fellow's rank papers in his back pocket. But whenever they come to this point, it always manifests in the same way.

Why?

Cosserby has never been able to formulate an answer.

He raps at its chin and the jaw hinges slightly, so that he can remove the tableth. The metal body is instantly immobile.

Because that's all it is. An articulated shell, a charged tableth, and the skein of graven commands. Nothing that, by anybody's understanding, should lead to this questioning. Or anything more than brute, automatic action. It's like a watermill asking what you want the flour for, or a printing press complaining about your prose. And yet it happens. Again and again.

He takes the tableth to his anvil and stares down at it for a long time before taking up a hammer and giving the article three furious blows with all his strength. And it's not so very much strength, given that he's a small man and out of shape, but tablethi are soft metal and the hammer is hard. And he's just woken the whole camp, but only a little in advance of the general reveille. And the tableth will need recasting and re-inscribing, but he has a half-dozen ready to go, the same inscription-net on each. He slots one into place and tells the polished Sonori to stand, and it does so. Mindless, obedient, battle-ready.

They laugh at him, the medicos. They sneer. He doesn't have to get his hands dirty, they say. That he is attached to their hospital seems to them to make a mockery of the value of human life. Cosserby sits on his anvil and stares at the flattened tableth. In his head he hears only that sonorous voice asking, *Why?*

Hell – The Blue Salts

Foreigners visiting a Pal army camp for the first time are often surprised that so many faces aren't Palleseen. The pale imitations that are the Accessories form a substantial fraction of the whole. The surprise derives from an inadequate understanding of the Pal creed. The Palleseen are all about finding a use for their erstwhile enemies. For simultaneously remaking them in the Pal image, and putting them in a uniform that tells them they'll never quite be perfect enough.

His name isn't Masty. It isn't even his nickname, just what his nickname had been crunched into, Pal mouth after Pal mouth, until nobody can even remember the original.

He's up in time to see the vanguard off. Him, Cosserby and Prassel. The Unnaturals go out first. There's some firecracker work then, the ground between the Pal and Loruthi lines erupting in a variety of nastiness. Some artillery, some entrenched traps of various sorts. The physical kind, like the bonecutters that scythe the shambling cadavers down. Ghost-mines that have howling spirits briefly hissing about the field, save that corpses and Sonori are already as inhabited as they're ever going to be, and the mines were calibrated against the living. Masty sees one of the Sonori – the lead one with the polished chest – get knocked down, bell-body smashed flat by a projectile from the enemy lines, and then all of their engines were erupting. Prassel abandons her cadavers to collapse like cut puppets, and

Cosserby can only hope that his tablethi logic guides his metal troops home for repair, or that they can be salvaged from the field. It's time for the main event.

The Pal's own artillery speaks from behind the lines, tableth-charged mortars hurling incendiaries and bonecutter shot high overhead to come down somewhere that, presumably, the enemy would rather they hadn't. Great-batons spit searing energy at every enemy position that has just revealed itself. And, against this display of ranged muscle, the troops advance. Wave after wave in calibrated intervals, not walking but not running full tilt, an ordered hustle over the contested ground hoping that the worst of the traps have been cleared. Overhead, Fellow-Invigilator Maserley's demon Unnaturals launch into the air: ugly, ungainly things, winged and horned and roaring their defiance of all humanity and their loathing of the Kings Below as they vault to their bloody ruin.

It all comes down to human flesh and blood in the end.

"Orderly, move up the hospital," Prassel says. "Follow the advance and establish a forward surgery wherever Chief thinks best."

"Yes, magister." Masty salutes her back as she turns away. Cosserby gives him a game attempt at sympathy, as Masty is just about the only member of the department who doesn't sneer at him.

"Best of luck," the Sonorist says. "I'd better go pick up my toys. They'll want them to storm a breach or something soon enough."

The department and a squad of soldiers is already taking down the hospital tent and loading wagons, when Masty makes himself apparent. It isn't as though anyone can still be sleeping after all *that*. Ollery stands in the middle of it, supervising the supplies they're taking forward for the first wave, shouting at soldiers who technically outrank him and receiving no argument. Right here, he is the lord of this kingdom, and who knows who'll be under his jurisdiction soon enough.

Then the casualties are coming in, before they've even packed up, and it's time for hell to open for business once again.

They're scouts, an advance wave across the contested ground even before the Unnaturals. Gathering information for the advance, spotting for the artillery, some kind of sneak work in the last dark hours before morning. The Loruthi'd had their own counter-scouts at work and the two had clashed, a representation in miniature of what was to come. Who won? Not a question Masty or anyone else in the department gets to ask. Instead it's just the urgent shouts of the living and intact scouts hauling their injured comrades in. Not even stretchers, just bodies in arms and over shoulder or slung on jackets between them, and some of those bodies already expired on the way back from no-man's-land.

Ollery becomes the Butcher. That's how Masty thinks of it. He has the injured set down, looks over them. Hands already in his apron for drugs to kill the pain. Masty has learned a great deal of respect for the man's ability to look over a wound and make a snap decision about whether it's too trivial for *now*, or too serious for *ever*, or just bad enough to be sent to Hell. Whether the whetted knives of Tallifer or the other surgeons. Whether the eldritch mercies of Alv and her students. Whether it's a quiet draft from the black flask because there's no help here but a cessation of pain.

Masty is already there when the Butcher looks round. He and Maric Jack have the first man up on a quickly-unfolded table where Tallifer can look at a snapped forearm. Expose the bones, reset them as necessarily, swab. Then it's Jack's turn to stitch as she goes on to the next. Masty is already helping the next man to Alv. Two baton-shot wounds, one through the arm, the other skinning the ribs. An apprentice takes the charred gouges onto their own body, falling back shaking, out of the battle, having given all they have to give. The scout, immaculate save for the tears to their uniform, gets out of the way ready for the next.

And there's been screaming since they came in, but Masty's used to that. The bad dreams he wakes from are silences, not sounds of horror. He could sleep through it, if they didn't need him. But here's the screaming woman and the Butcher stares down at her, unsure for once in his life. The fire of a baton blast has turned the scout's face to ash from nose to hairline, both eyes like knuckles of coal in blasted sockets. And she lives, and her high, keening grief and agony makes sure everyone knows that. Not the first soldier to get sent home a lifelong invalid, that's for sure.

For a moment the Butcher has his black flask in hand, a terrible look on his face. Then he swaps it for a little yellow phial, forces the contents down the woman's throat until her shrieks become gurgles.

"Get her out of here," he snaps at Masty, but Alv's hand is on the burly beef of his arm.

"No," he tells the Divinati woman.

"Absolutely not," he says, to her stare.

"I won't have it. I'm Chief here. What good will you be?"

Masty swallows. The rest of the department is still up to their elbows in the injured, those that can be cut and wrapped and stitched and otherwise profitably put back together. Alv and the Butcher are a terrible still centre to all that bloody bustle.

"I still have more to give," Alv says. Quiet, but Masty is close by then, clenching and unclenching his hands helplessly. She turns her solemn, beautiful, awful gaze to him, that won't be turned on anyone for some time. "Bring them, please, Masty." Always so polite, Alv. A scion of a more civilized city.

He gets the blinded scout up onto the table. Jack helps, as oblivious as always. Except he's been around enough to understand how things work around here, and when Alv bends over the woman he mouths words, denials, forbiddances. But it's not like the Divinati ever listened to anyone from less elegant cultures about how to do things.

Alv takes a deep breath. For a second her eyes are very wide, as though she's trying to get the most possible use out of them before what happens next.

Masty wants to look away but that would be to belittle her sacrifice so he forces himself to watch. Watch as the cooked char bubbles to the surface of Alv's glittering skin. As her eyes wither and cook and that face, an artist's inspiration, parches into a clenched horror of blackened, ruined flesh and skin. She arches rigid – she feels all the pain, he knows, for all that she has ways to bargain her wholeness back from the universe in time. Her hands claw into the scout's body and the red marks defile her own body as she takes it all on. The scout stares up at her, drugged and unseeing, never to really understand what happened. Probably not even to believe it second hand. *Blinded? Me? Nonsense.*

Masty catches Alv as she falls backwards. He tries to get her out, then. Get her to the back lines, to the convalescence tents. But she won't go.

"I still have more to give." Her mouth remains whole. "Just get me to the wagon, Masty. Please." He, who saw her face go up like a burned map, can't look at her now.

The Butcher looks on, impassive. "If Erinael was here…" he murmurs, when Masty leads Alv past. But she isn't, and now it's just the Butcher running the show. He's no angel of mercy like Erinael was.

They grind forwards, a train of wagons amongst a greater train. Supplies and fresh troops heading for wherever the thrashing snake of the new front ends up. Getting out of the wagon every so often when the wheels get stuck, or when the ground is too uneven for the draft horses to pull alone. Masty, Jack, Banders, all putting their shoulders to the frame. Even the Butcher, squatting down at the tailboard, rolling his shoulders, groaning in effort as he shoves, feet sinking ankle-deep into the churn. Alv, standing aside to spare the meagre burden of her added weight. They've bandaged her face and it's more to spare their eyes than salve hers.

Cosserby comes by, at one such straining stop. He has two Sonori with him, along with a snaking line of soldiers. The misting rain has started, by then, making the going even nastier. Cosserby has his tin soldiers get the wagons moving, metal strength turned to menial ends. And Masty wonders why they don't just give the things over to this kind of work. Except some Pal officer saw them in action once, and set them down as assets of offence, and now that's what they are on the books. War automata, not haulage engines.

For his efforts, Cosserby gets short thanks from any of his departmental fellows, and the regular officer he's with bawls him out for the delay, too.

"I'll try and find you, when you're set," he said, as his machines stomp off.

"How will we ever cope until you do?" Tallifer observes. He looks hurt, but the officer he's with raps his shoulder with a baton, impatient to be gone. Soon, they're all out of sight in the slanting curtains of rain and the wagons grind on. Without Prassel – she's gone to do something more military than shunt wheels out of ruts – they just keep going until they find some casualties.

When they do, there's already a skeleton of a tent there, a roof and poles but no sides, and the rain coming in every time there's a gust of wind. The Butcher starts barking orders and Masty is throwing the tables up, kicking the props into place with the ease of long practise. The Butcher surveys the new meat and begins his infernal mathematics once again.

It's later. Past-midday later. The rain's come and gone and come back again. The sounds of fighting are distant, even the artillery. That's the only clue to how the advance is going, because nobody who gets sent to Hell is particularly interested in discussing it. They've been at their bloody work for five hours, without pause. Half Alv's student squad are on the convalescence wagons, heading back the way they came, written over with someone else's wounds. Alv herself has a crippled arm and a shot-wound through the thigh but she refuses to go back. Masty's set a stool out for her and she sits there, bandage-faced, an arm curled up against her breast within her jacket, the sleeve hanging empty. He's spoken to her, low, urgent, against the cacophony of the wounded. Begged her to go. He's seen her push her limits before, but not like this.

She grips his hand sightlessly. "I have more to give," she spits out like she hates something. Perhaps the war, perhaps the Divine City, perhaps herself. Masty would weep, but a childhood in an army camp dries that kind of exhibition out of you.

"Orange salts!" the Butcher barks, like he's selling something. He's going about the tent with a bag full of paper twists, prepared earlier. Masty, who's feeling underslept and numb, takes one and empties it onto his tongue, feeling the fizz. Banders nabs another, managing a chuckle despite the fact that there are bloody handprints across her shirt where the last casualty tried to fight being moved.

"Oh this is why we choose the soldiering life," she says, and necks her portion. Tallifer, mid-surgery, opens her mouth and Banders doses her on the fly.

Jack watches this blankly. The Butcher rattles the bag under his nose and then moves on, but Masty abstracts a twist for him because he'll need it.

"To keep you going," he says, aware he's speaking too loud and staring too much.

"How much longer are we going?" Jack doesn't understand, but he'll have a thorough grounding in it all by the end. Whenever that is.

"Til dark at least," Masty shouts. "At least. The big assaults can go on longer. Two days. Three." And they're not the only hospital, but they're the forlorn hope one, the one the worst get sent to. The hospital where miracles can happen.

Jack stares, blinks, swallows, opens the package and tastes the contents, always a mistake.

"Get it down quickly," Masty advises.

"It's better that way?" Jack guesses.

"I mean, no, but it's quicker."

Jack does as advised and his eyes bug and he chokes and regrets many things. Always the worst, the first time. He says something in Maric that's probably an ancestral curse. Banders claps him hard on the back and then waves a packet at Lochiver, who's been droning out his pipe music long enough to have his lips and everyone else's ears bleeding. There's a full jar at his feet, as though he's been considerately incontinent. Masty takes the opportunity to get it away from everyone, marked for 'hostile disposal' as the military phrase goes. When he gets back, a new consignment of the damned is being stretchered in by soldiers who turn around and head back to the front the moment they've dropped their fallen comrades.

"A good batch," Lochiver comments, smacking his cracked lips. "Oh that's the real stuff."

It's past dark, closing on midnight. The fighting has stilled but not stopped, both sides lying tense in trenches and tents, dugouts and foxholes, waiting for the first touch of the sun to kindle the festivities again. The work of the hospital hasn't stopped. Alv lays her hand on a whimpering soldier and turns her swaddled face to the ceiling of the tent as her middle finger twists backwards on itself.

"Now," Masty says to her. "Please, Alv. Please, Guest-Adjutant.

That's enough." Because, of all of them, she's not a mere *Accessory*. She's something special.

Alv lets out a shuddering breath. For a moment he thinks she'll agree, but then she shakes her head. Not even the *More to give* speech, just that blank negation. He gives her water, the jug to her lips to spare her having to grope for it with her maimed hands. She has become a boarding house whose doors are always open to new wounds, and one little attic room still looking for a tenant. Masty knows the Butcher is sparing her as much as possible, but the injured keep coming in. There have been hundreds today, just at their one field surgery.

"Blue salts!" cries the Butcher.

"Oh shit, we're there, are we?" Banders says. She's sitting on the edge of a momentarily unoccupied table, scrubbing at her hands with a sopping red towel. There's a lull, Masty realises. The injured who need immediate attention have been attended to, the ones past help have died and the rest can wait.

"What are blue salts?" Jack asks.

"They're the ones that come after the orange ones," Banders tells him. "Just hope we don't get as far as the purple ones. I didn't sleep for a week after those, and when I did, the fucking *dreams*, man. Reason help me, the *dreams*."

Masty takes the paper twist from the Butcher's bag, the whole day already feeling like one of those kind of dreams. The blue salts hiss and seethe against the back of his throat and he has to fight the urge to vomit up everything past the orange salts and to his breakfast. Jack has knocked his back and is crying tears of blood, which can happen. Not that anyone'll notice a little more blood.

Later, two hours before dawn, Masty does get a chance to lie down, although the blue salts mean he does it with his eyes open, lying on a blanket over cold mud under one of the tables, Banders on one side of him and one of Alv's students on the other. Shaking with cold and shock and fatigue. Lochiver is snoring somewhere, somehow, flute still clutched in his bony hands. Somewhere close by, Jack is having one of those one-sided conversations he does, and honestly it's not Masty's place to judge anyone for their peculiarities. You don't get sent to serve in Hell if you're normal.

Even as the grey light brings more rain with it, the first catch of the new day is being hauled in, heralded by a fresh chorus of hoarse, ragged voices. Masty sits up and rams his head into the underside of the table, but there's no time to swear at it because the Butcher needs an orderly at his elbow. He kicks Banders, trips over Jack, and yet is still in place when needed. Because that's him. Because that's what he does. He's *reliable*. It's how he survived the army since he was a foreign kid of six years old ripped from his home and family and station.

Cosserby turns up, midmorning, looking grey and ragged. No Sonori with him, so presumably his charges have been shipped back to the rear lines in pieces. He's nominally on his way to put them back together as best he can, but he said he'd find them and he has. Even Tallifer doesn't have any slights for him by then. She lets him sharpen her scalpels and repair a broken set of forceps with shaking hands. He doesn't look at the opened stomach of the man she's operating on. He doesn't like the sight of blood, does Cosserby. And yet, for this brief moment, he's here and making himself useful.

"Lilac salts!" the Butcher spits out. His eyes are red as a drunkard's, and probably he has been drinking a little, just to keep himself going. The great slab of a hand shakes as it proffers the latest bag of magic.

"Oh sod me," Banders says. "Well hello, sleepless nights." Her grin, as she takes a paper packet, is a little hysterical. "Hey, Chief. Tell me you've not mixed any of the red."

"Oh we've got the red to come, never you worry," the Butcher tells her.

Jack and Masty look each other in the too-wide eyes before they take their doses. The stuff tastes like bile and burns all the way down. Paroxysms of coughing and then a jolt like being stabbed. He's never been so awake since the last time the purple came out.

One of Alv's students is at work. A Pal with a basic grounding in sympathetic healing, taking on wounds that are life-threatening on the field but survivable here in the hospital's controlled environment. His victim has a broken arm. He braces himself, wincing against the pain, but the purple fortifies him and he takes it, collapsing back onto the stool Masty has ready for him. But something's not right. He tries to speak. He's clutching at his abdomen. A sudden spatter of blood explodes from his lips. Alv is demanding to know what's going on, her voice little more than a rattle and a croak. Her student is pitching sideways, suddenly fighting to breathe.

Masty understands before the rest do, because he saw it all happen. The Butcher's art isn't a science. Sometimes there are too many and he gets it wrong, like everyone does. The obvious agony of a broken arm, the bone sheared through the skin. Not the hidden snare of internal bleeding, broken organs lying below unblemished skin like a reef in calm water.

It's the shock, Masty knows. The shock of taking it all on at once. The man, Alv's student, has overextended. The Pals have only a rudimentary grasp of the art despite all her teaching. She's fumbling for him, and Masty knows what she'd do if her fingers touched his skin. And she has many gifts but immortality is not one of them. He grits his teeth and pulls her away, and there isn't enough of her to let her fight him.

The Butcher catches Masty's eye and nods. They cannot lose Alv. Lose this man instead.

Jack is on his knees beside the man – not one of Hell's damned, this casualty, but one of Hell's own, a healer. Already shuddering, frothing, fitting as his body fails to manage the damage it has taken on.

"Do it!" Jack shouts. And then, "I said not until I *told* you!" And then he's bending to the ear of the dying man, speaking rapidly but with the weird air of someone trying to explain the legal small print. A question, and Masty sees the bloody lips frame an answer.

"Do it!" Jack orders, or begs. And then more, in Maric, a fierce argument with nothing at all. Except, of course, they all remember the spy miraculously snatched from the grave. They hold their breath, and maybe this will be another Erinael after all.

There is no miracle. The man lies still. Jack won't have it. He won't let them take the body away. "No wait, sorry, please, wait. We can still, there's still, time, there's. Time. Please. *Please.*"

Dead is dead. Not without sympathy, the Butcher shoves him aside so they can put the corpse with all their other failures.

"You son of a bitch!" Jack spits, leaping to his feet. He's staring at his box now, the one he schlepped all the way here on his back and then just discarded in a corner of the hospital tent with the other supplies. "You couldn't—? You don't *know* it wouldn't have... you... you..." And he has his army-issue boot raised over the box like he's about to trample it to kindling. "You..." he says again, not shouting now, aware they're all staring at him.

Banders hugs him from behind, puts her sharp chin on his shoulder. "I know," she says, although not one of them there really knows what the hell is wrong with Maric Jack. But still, "I know," she says, and that seems to help him a bit.

The Three-Horned Face

The Palleseen war machine advanced. That was what it was for. The Temporary Commission of Ends and Means that ruled the Pal Archipelago had designed it to be inexorable, rolling over all opposition to bring yet another den of superstition and credulity into the liberating light of reason. It did not retreat or give back ground. Obviously.

God was glowering at Jack from atop His box. But with qualifiers. It wasn't just the usual hostility, the disdain, the eye-rolling exasperation as His former priest did something foolish or foreign or both. There was a new edge to God's regard. Because Jack had torn a strip off God in a way he hadn't before. He'd laid down some blistering invective over the dead Pal's body, cursed God to hell a dozen different ways, made such threats... Just as well it had all been in Maric, really, because the Pals would have hauled him away to a firing squad or a madhouse otherwise. And God had initially stood on the dignity of *I am your God, you're not to question me and I can do what I like,* but crumbled like walls of sand before Jack's raging sea. Until now He sat sullen on His box just possibly entertaining the idea that this time He had gone too far.

Jack hoped so. He really did. And the other two deities were hiding inside the box, making it very clear that the business was most definitely between Jack and his god, and any other divinities around wouldn't venture an opinion.

He finished with the bandage. They were down to a batch of the lesser injured. His victim was a man whose arm had been cut up by the edge of a bonecutter blast, some nasty-looking chopped meat but all on the surface. Jack tied, tugged, not too tight. "It's clean now," he told the man. "Keep it that way. Get it checked in two days." It was what he'd heard Masty and Banders say to the proud new owners of similar wounds. Back in Ilmar when he'd been patching people hurt *by* the Pals, he'd not had that luxury. After his ministrations they'd had to fend for themselves.

Then Prassel was there, striding through the camp, tugging her gloves back on. "Pack up and move out!" she snapped at them. "Everything onto the wagons. We're following the front." Jack looked past her and blanched, actually retreated until his box was at his heels. There were corpses there, not the two-score mine-clearers turned into bloody bunting in the vanguard, but what looked like sixty at least. Most wore Pal uniforms, but a few were in leather and brass, or deep green. These were the casualties who didn't make it to Hell, he realised. Dead on the field and already repurposed. Nobody else cared. It was old news to them, the gloss of shock and outrage rubbed well off by repetition. It was just Prassel doing her job. The other side of the Butcher's coin. Some of those swaying cadavers had been on the surgeons' tables earlier, as Tallifer tried to save them. Her loss was Prassel's gain, and this was why Prassel commanded the hospital.

"Move it, Jack!" The Butcher shouldered him pointedly on his way through, a whole table under one arm. Two wagons had appeared ready for them, quite aside from those taking the wounded in the opposite direction. Somewhere in the heart of the Pal army a tentful of clerks worked like maniacs so that everyone who needed their stuff somewhere else had a draft animal and a flatbed on hand.

He loaded the Butcher's crates of clinking ceramics and glassware and metal pots. He hauled the currently-open box of bandages. He and Banders manhandled the other table, stacking it on the first, and then about to stack Alv on top of that. The Butcher intervened, dumbshowing towards the casualty wagon. Banders grimaced but nodded. It wasn't, Jack guessed, something that Alv would readily forgive them for, but he could tell a necessary deception when he saw it. The woman had almost nothing left to give, but was very plainly ready to give it anyway. They sent her off with one of her more battered students. At least she was out of it.

"How are you at sleeping on wagons?" Banders asked him, helping him up.

"Normally?" Jack said. "So-so. Right now I don't think I'll ever close my eyes again." He nearly forgot the box. Just as the wagon started to move he yelped and hopped down and caught it up, almost toppling God right off it. Had to run after the tailboard until he could snag Banders and Masty's outstretched arms and get dragged in again.

"Oh good," Banders observed. "I mean think what could have happened if we'd left that behind?"

Jack thought about it and found himself worryingly ambivalent. If he'd been a mote more forgetful, what then? If he'd come back, and found no trace, or just wooden splinters where a draft horse had kicked it in. The little lost gods scattered to the winds. Would anyone actually be worse off? And wouldn't he be better? Able to build some new life that wasn't god-smuggling, as if that had ever been a viable career choice.

Banders shoved something in his face. "Take this." *This* was a disc the size of her smallest thumbnail, apparently of lead.

"What do I do with it?"

"Eat it, you fool. It'll knock you right out. Get some sleep. We'll be on this thing for a good hour."

Jack had already worked out that prescriptions from the pharmacy of Doctor Banders were probably not approved by modern Pal medicine. But when he glanced at Masty, the man was already chewing one.

The ship of being precious about what drugs he took had well and truly sailed, he guessed, and so he followed suit. It tasted metal on the tongue, crumbled like chalk under the teeth. He swallowed the powdery bolus with difficulty.

"For what it's w—" *orms were boiling up from the earth all around them, great man-long maggots with fat undulating bodies and human faces. They bent to chew on the corpses that he realised the entire landscape was carpeted with, tessellated, not a gap between them that wasn't another body. He hadn't seen it before. It had looked like mud and rocks and trees, but now he understood everything was bodies, bodies all the way down. The Pal army marched not on its stomach but on its dead. And, because it also contained abominations like Prassel, the dead weren't still but flailed and mouthed and kicked as the vast maggots erupted out of them and gnawed their way back in.*

Banders, her face a melting smear across grey dawn horizon, was saying something about side effects but it probably wasn't important. Jack's priorities were more the way the whole world was convulsing, as though beneath the patina of the dead there was something vaster, more animate and even more decayed trying to force its way to the surface. The whole world rippled with its efforts, and he decided it was a new god. A death god struggling to be born.

"It's not," God told him, the one small, still point in all creation. "You're just wholly off your tits on some Pal candy. I forbid you to take any more drugs. They will lead you into harmful ways."

Jack summoned up the words to tell God exactly what He could do with the tenets of His faith, but fell into a vast howling hole even as he did so, like the ghost-burrow that had consumed the luckless spy.

"—orth," Jack said, sitting bolt upright and finding himself in a hospital tent. For a dreadful moment he thought they hadn't moved yet and the whole trial was still to happen, but everything was set out slightly differently. They'd arrived, and he'd been dumped with the boxes while everyone else did the work. On reflection, that seemed remarkably kind of them. Or, more likely, he'd been so dead to the world that even a slap from the Butcher hadn't woken him.

"He's up!" Banders crowed.

"What did he say?" Tallifer demanded, sounding affronted.

"He said 'urth', I think."

"Where are we?" Jack demanded and then saw that Prassel was still with them, and immediately tried to convey that he was unsaying anything out of place. She had a map spread out where Hell's victims usually went, and was examining it closely, in concert with a lean Pal officer with a monocle.

"Here," the man was saying, one stick finger indicating. "They've dug in there, and there's a mercenary detachment, this hill here. That's where we need your Unnaturals."

"They'll not get halfway up," Prassel said.

"Not with that attitude," the other officer said, so apparently he outranked her or at least had seniority in this current moment. "Uncle wants it all under the Sway by evening so we can advance the next leg."

Jack got himself to his feet, had a moment of panic when he couldn't find his box, then saw he'd been using it as a pillow.

"Right," Prassel said, staring without joy at the map. Then the tent flap moved, and everyone jumped for their phials and implements and bandages. It wasn't a customer, though. It was Maserley. And Caeleen.

The sight of him was sufficiently surprising to Prassel and the hospital staff that the only people to note Jack's jolt of recognition were Maserley and Caeleen themselves, the exact worst two people to see how twitchy he suddenly was. The demonist had other fish to fry right then, though.

"What's this rabble even doing here?" he demanded of the thin officer. And then, "Magister," with enough grudge in the respect to carry a feud down three generations.

"We are advancing, Fellow-Invigilator," the man told him.

"I take it your own shock troops are ready. Or are you going to send your pet to dally with the Loruthi?"

Maserley scowled, at the officer, at Prassel, at the world. Jack had plenty of reason not to like him, but the man looked at least half as tired as the medicos, and even that was very tired indeed.

"You've got all I have contracts for," he said. "After that I'm out."

The thin officer stalked over to Caeleen and looked her over like someone deciding not to buy a goat. "Combat capable, I hope. Not this grade."

"All the horns and flames you could want," Maserley said. It was fascinating to watch him and Prassel trying gamely to hate each other except their mutual loathing of their superior was standing in the way.

Caeleen was looking at him, cool and expressionless. Jack forced himself not to return her gaze, feeling pinned between it and God's own disapproving frown.

"Oh, and your idiot Sonorist is out there with a grand total of two tin soldiers," Maserley added. "A great asset to the advance, doubtless."

"Well, I suppose that's all the screen we're going to get," the tall officer decided. "Get your rabble into line and I'll sound the whistle."

He and Maserley left, and probably Caeleen did as well, though Jack was very much not looking and so he didn't know. Prassel rubbed at her eyes, and the Butcher handed her a twist of paper. Orange salts, Jack guessed. Because the necromancer was still two rounds behind.

The woman looked around furtively before knocking the dose back, then stamped two or three times as it took hold. She clapped a hand to the Butcher's shoulder, then almost ran into Cosserby as the man parted the tent flaps. He blinked owlishly around the tent.

"This is all… a little *close*, ah, isn't it?"

"It won't be once we've done our job and pushed them back,"

Prassel said, and practically shoved him out ahead of her. Jack caught the man's receding voice saying, "Oh but they're very dug in. I don't think people appreciate how much they're dug in," before the heavy fabric muffled his words.

"You fine?" Banders asked him. He felt tugged in five different directions, one of which was down. Different concoctions fought wars in his bloodstream, to the general detriment of the battlefield.

"No," he got out. "Fine is not what I am."

"See anything good?"

"What?"

"When you were under?"

"Nothing anywhere near good."

She shrugged. "Yeah, well, that's the downside. Bet you had a lovely kip though."

"I don't know how long I can do this."

He expected a jeer, a prod in the chest, the indefatigable Banders making mock, as she did. But she put a hand to his shoulder and leaned down until her forehead touched his. He felt the slight stickiness of blood that hadn't quite dried.

"That's okay," she said. "Because we don't know how long it's going on for. So you and your situation are perfect soulmates, right?"

He laughed, from somewhere. He hadn't thought there was a part of him that the laughs hadn't been scoured from, but it came anyway. Past Banders, God was standing on His box, but not scowling. Wringing His hands, looking abruptly uncertain. Behind him the gimlet gaze of the spear god lanced Jack's way.

Then they heard the whistles, and he knew the Unnaturals would be on the move, that wall of demons, corpses and machines behind which the regular living Pals would make their advance. The faint crackle of baton-fire began, like green twigs on another clearing's campfire, and then a louder roar. A demon? A war engine? He had no idea.

The casualties began to come in soon after, the first to taste the defiance of the defenders. And Jack got to stop thinking and just *do*, and that was preferable.

Two hours later and his hands were shaking as he tied a tourniquet. He didn't *feel* tired. His mind was full of bees and they stung him to staring every time his eyelids dipped. There was a part of him that had seen the ages of the world pass, though, and no amount of salts could pull the wool over its graven eyes and convince it that he wasn't tired. He felt the weight of it. The mortal fatigue. His fingers trembled like he was playing some stringed instrument nobody wanted to hear.

Lochiver sat down heavily beside him and placed one grimy thumb where the folds of the cloth crossed, so he could just deal with the tying. The old man looked – dead, honestly. Dead and unearthed from his own grave. His flute trembled in his other hand. Jack was vaguely surprised it hadn't been worn down to a nub with all the playing.

"Damn me," Lochiver said in quavering tones. "Been a while since we did one like this. Welcome to the department, son."

Jack pulled the cloth tight, but not too tight. Though Lochiver said even bloodless flesh wouldn't putrefy for a while if he was around. Jack had stopped asking the *how* of things, just accepting everything anyone told him because there was no space in his head for analytical thought.

The Butcher was there, then, and a new bag in his hand, like your least favourite uncle with your least favourite sweeties.

"Oh bugger me sideways," Lochiver said. "We're onto the reds are we?"

The Butcher grunted and rattled the bag.

"What comes after the red?" Jack asked.

"Nobody knows," the old man said darkly, nonetheless reaching. Then someone burst into the tent.

"Pack up!" they shouted. "Move!"

Tallifer looked up from the arm she'd just separated from its original owner. "Give me a moment. Jack, I need your needlework."

"Move!" the soldier shouted at them all. "They're coming!" and then they were gone again, and there was a great deal of movement out there, boots sloshing through the mud, the crackle of baton-shot surely closer than it had been a moment ago.

"Curse it, *Jack*," Tallifer said, not reacting in any way. The Butcher ducked out of the tent, taking the red salts with him, even as Jack scurried over to the table.

"Get him closed up," she said. "Who's next?" But there were soldiers coming in and taking the wounded *away*. Even those the Butcher had ready for the knife. The sudden gust and rattle that Jack had taken for wind, his ears recast as a volley of firing. There were suddenly two char-edged holes in the hospital tent.

"Do they not know we're busy?" he asked. Then the Butcher was back in, shunting him aside as if he was no more than a dead leaf. One ham hand crushed down on the armless soldier's chest. The other had a bowl of something black-brown that the man mashed into the open stump. Jack smelled burning flesh and hair and the amputee shrieked as whatever it was seared their stump shut.

"Get him out," the Butcher snarled, and two soldiers were hauling the screaming man from the table. Tallifer was objecting, waving her slick scalpel like a threat. The Butcher took her by her own bloody apron and practically threw her out of the tent.

"Everyone out! Everyone on the wagons!" The Chief's monster of a voice rising above all the chaos brewing outside. "It's a counterattack! Everyone out! We're leaving."

"Are they allowed to do that?" Banders asked, and then the tent folded inwards on them and a monster came through.

Jack registered the horns first, forward-jutting, metal-capped, three of them, set into a scythe-beaked turtle face backed by a bony shield to which actual shields had been rivetted. It carved its way through the thick canvas as though it was the tissue-thin paper of official Pal orders, a head as big as a wagon, and leading a body even greater. Huge root-nailed feet made the ground their drum. And above, a howdah, iron-plated. Jack saw batons and spearpoints jut down. All this in the instant the tent turned inside out. Horns and shouting and the flare of shot on all sides. The battlefield was invading them, frightening and unexpected as a portal to the Kings Below opening at his feet.

He scrabbled back as those horns came straight for him, as those feet thundered down. Masty snagged his sleeve and hauled him sideways with more strength than Jack would have credited. The pair of them tumbled down together in a bundle of limbs. He saw Tallifer's operating table smashed to matches. The woman herself was only clear because the Butcher had thrown her from the thing's path a moment before.

Lochiver was there, though. The old man looked up, holding the flute as though it had been a mighty amulet of beast-warding just a moment before but was now a rather unmusical instrument. The monstrous horned head was already turning by then, yanked at by some unseen hands within the howdah, and so Lochiver didn't take a horn through the eye socket. Instead the thing just hit him with a shoulder and an armoured flank. An almost playful shove. He went down with his thigh going one way and his calf the other and the knee in between twisting in directions it had never been designed for. Banders tried to get to him, flinching back as a shot from on high sizzled the air between them. Then the Butcher threw something in the monster's eyes, some cloud of yellow powder. The colossal thing – five, ten tons of it – reared onto its hind legs in shock, and that was the rest of the tent gone, no more than frippery for the beast's howdah.

Masty was dragging at Jack, trying to get him clear. With no tent, he could see far too much of what was going on beyond those lost borders. Pal soldiers were fleeing on all sides. Some turned, animated by a brief discipline and unity, sending a volley of shot into unseen pursuers. Then they ran again, save for the scatter who had fallen in that moment of defiance and screamed or writhed or lay very still.

"Come on, Jack!" Masty insisted. There were wagons, he saw. The wounded, some of the supplies. Those clerks had come through somehow. There were wagons and they were getting out.

He had forgotten God. Halfway to the wagons the *memento dei* struck him and he turned, whipped his sleeve from Masty's fingers, eyes scouring where the tent had been for the box or its corpse.

It was right there, beside the great churned dents the beast had left. There with God and the other two fugitive deities standing on it like they were shipwrecked sailors on a raft in high seas.

"Jack!" Masty shouted after him, and everyone else was shouting – the dying, the injured, the Butcher, officers, everyone. Somewhere close by, the beast bellowed, baton-shot bothering it like insistent flies.

He had the box on his shoulders, violently enough that he could only hope no gods had been thrown free. He looked up.

Three Pal soldiers ran past. A tent nearby was blazing and there was only smoke between them and whoever they were trying to escape. He looked round, suddenly unsure which way he'd come. Where were the wagons?

"Jack!" Masty, still. Still with him, somehow. Not giving up on him no matter how mad Maric Jack had gone. Tugging at him, then stopping, face suddenly taut.

Jack followed his gaze, seeing nothing. Seeing smoke. Seeing bodies. And he'd been seeing bodies for the last twenty-four hours so why stop now? Then his sense of perspective told him one of them was too small, barely three-fifths of a soldier.

"No no no," said Masty, and ran for it. For Ollery's boy, Jack realised. The kid had been with the stores, mixing up the salts and the other drugs of the Butcher's trade. It looked like the beast had smashed straight through that tent, trampled the glassware, mixed some appalling chimera of alchemy under its feet, and in its wake there were crushed soldiers and the boy.

He dogged Masty's heels all the way there. Brief, bright lines ate up the smoke about him, speculative shooting from one side or the other. Masty knelt, trying to scoop the boy up but finding him too enmeshed with other bodies. Jack saw the kid's eyes wide with pain and fright. Alive, though. Alive, somehow.

He hauled one loose-joined body away with a grunt, slapped off a dead arm that still seemed to be clutching. Then he was on his knees and couldn't work out why. *Did I just get shot?* But if so, Masty had been struck in the exact same moment. No. It was the earth. The earth shook.

Out of the smoke came the beast. Its great scale-and-leather sides, the little shockingly human ellipse of its eye. The horns, overhead like roof-beam scaffolding. It seemed twice the size it had before, filling that quarter of Jack's entire world. Masty was quite still, his face hopeless. And since when did the Loruthi have things like this? Was it a demon, one of their own Unnaturals?

Masty hugged the boy to him, turning his back, as though the interposition of his fragile flesh and bones would serve as any kind of barrier.

Jack stood, feeling light-headed. After all he'd been through, to be destroyed by *this* thing was surely a kind of privilege. No mere baton-shot or knife in the guts for Maric Jack. He held his arms out, almost a welcome. He looked up, seeing the steep, spiked sides of the howdah, fit with slits for shooting from, and capped by the great blunt prow of some siege engine. A face writhed into view over the rim of it. Not a man's face. A thing like a lizard, with a sinuous body half-curled about the shaft of its baton to steady the weapon for firing. It licked across its eyes and snout with a blue tongue. *Mercenaries.*

At the corner of Jack's eye something danced, like midges. He almost swatted it away in annoyance. If he hadn't already decided to die in this pose of benediction he would have done, and then he'd have died. It was the nature god, the little round-faced twig thing with its shirt of busy woodlice. It danced and bowed, and fungal fronds opened up in it, and the lizard thing stared, first with one eye and then the other.

He heard voices up there. Grackling voices working unknown sounds back and forth. And *grackling* wasn't even a word but it was the only way he could characterise them. The beast tossed its head, and the horn that capped its snout came a thumb's width from the tip of his nose.

The whole tonnage of it turned, stepping almost delicately as though it was only allowed to crush any given corpse the once. Then Masty had the boy over his shoulder and a hand hauling on Jack's. And Jack just stood there, dumbly, actually smiling, arms still out, knowing that he was blessed by at least one god. And the thing's metal-studded tail swept round and smashed him sideways and he felt something *go* that would have been a keening agony if he hadn't been so stuffed full of the Butcher's salts right then. Something inherent to the physical integrity of his torso. A *disarticulation* involving ribs and spine. And what a long and academic word to represent more damage than there was in the world, the ruin of a man.

The wagons – but the wagons were gone. Were already receding. Masty took a deep breath and sprinted after them. Jack lay in the mud and wished him well. And the beds were full, stacked high with the wounded, medicos clinging to the sides. And still the Butcher was gesturing for Masty to join them. To join the rest of Hell in fleeing the far worse that was to come.

Masty's lean frame bunched, and he slung the boy forwards off his shoulder, cast the kid across the intervening space to where the Butcher's hands could field him. And they shouted at the man to keep running, but instead he turned back. Turned back for Jack, because that was apparently the sort of man he was. No medico left behind. And the smoke took the wagons, and they were left between the lines, in a span of mud that both sides were trying to make as unliveable as possible.

Toy Soldiers

In Jarokir, the temple Sonori would sound great bell-like notes at dawn and dusk and other sacred times. Their voices rang out across cities, calling the faithful to prayer, or echoed down valleys from secluded temples. No longer, of course. When a Pal battle Sonori is struck by heavy artillery or some similarly serious weapon, however, the clear ringing tone it makes in its extinction remains a thing of beauty.

Cohort-Monitor Cosserby was not fond of roadside artificing. He liked a well-equipped workshop or, if not that, then a tent masquerading as one or, if pushed, he'd tinker about with something on someone's dining table if he had to, and if they didn't mind him getting grease everywhere.

Right now he was, unfortunately, at the side of a road, and the road was full of soldiers and all the soldiers were headed away from the fighting. And normally 'away from the fighting' was something he'd prefer to the alternative, but the logistical difficulty he'd run into here was that (a) while the soldiers were headed away from the fighting, he was currently stationary by the side of the aforementioned road and not headed anywhere; and (b) the fighting, in and of itself, was headed *towards* him, or that was his best grasp of the situation. It was the traditional state of affairs when one's side was retreating. And it wasn't his first retreat but he wasn't exactly a veteran of the military backstep because the Pals were usually quite good at fighting wars.

The Loruthi apparently had their moments too. He'd heard Fellow-Inquirer Prassel holding forth on the difficulties that Lor presented as a foe. Principally that they hired in vast numbers of mercenaries from across their widespread holdings to supplement their army. Meaning you never knew what you were going to get or how you'd be fought. Sometimes, as the saying went, you got the bear, and sometimes the bear got you. And there were bears, someone had said. Trained war bears goaded to blood fury, made frothing mad with berserker serums and then unleashed. Although Cosserby wasn't sure that a mere *leash* would serve to restrain such a thing.

And here he was, going nowhere. Because, to a Sonorist, a mid-battle retreat was a particularly unmitigated disaster. His charges suffered a certain rate of attrition, and he was expected to pick up the broken during the advance, patch them up or send the pieces back to camp, and then continue with however many walking constructs he could muster. Which became a profoundly optimistic prospect when you weren't advancing, because suddenly all the bits you'd been relying on were out of reach. As of half an hour ago he'd had four functioning Sonori clumping down the road, head, shoulders and chest over the common soldiery. Right now he had three of them standing around like judges at an exam while he had the fourth opened up to find out why one of its legs had stopped working. Meaning that it could march all day, but only in circles.

The problem turned out to be some manner of missile stuck between the casing of its pelvis and thigh, a spectacularly lucky or accurate gift from an unknown enemy archer. Precisely what the projectile had been, Cosserby couldn't say, because the inner workings of the Sonori had turned it into a hundred little fragments that had worked their way *everywhere* and ended up basically fusing the thing's hip joint. Right now he had it on its back, the leg off, and increasing large components of its inner armature laid aside. His little portable forge was glowing and he was shaping replacement components from his bits satchel by best guess in the hope he could have the thing moving. Ideally before a Loruthi artificer turned up to give him pointers.

The soldiers coursing past him – they were relatively disciplined now, not the initial panicked rush – glanced over incuriously, but none of them tried to help. Not that they could have actually done anything, but the offer would have been appreciated. He kept eyeing up the wagons, too. If one came past that was halfway empty he'd flag it down and have his ambulatory Sonori dump their defective colleague in the bed, and sort it all out back at the camp. Unsurprisingly, each one was crammed with troops and salvaged supplies, no room for a dead construct.

He fitted a new piece, a curved and tapering element extending into the hollow of the pelvis to a fiddly degree. The other problem with fixing Sonori was that the actual science of the craft hadn't quite torn itself free of its murky origins. They were Jarokiri temple constructs first and foremost, and that meant they were designed by a pack of ignorant clowns as far as Cosserby was concerned. At some point, one of his peers would hold a proper symposium on a revised theory of Sonoristics, and make proper Pal constructs built to a fully rational plan. As it was, Cosserby was stuck following the defective logic of a people who actually thought this sort of thing fit into some kind of divine plan. In amongst the Pel characters he was inscribing, a handful of Jarokiri sacred glyphs still hid, and he lived in fear of someone outside the trade finding out.

Admittedly, right now he was living in fear of a few other things as well. And probably the Loruthi would treat him quite well, if they caught him. But only if he turned coat and taught them how to build their own Sonori.

He bent back to his tinkering. The new part wasn't joining properly with its neighbours. He took it out and reworked it under the lamp, double checking the logic of his bastardised inscriptions.

The rumble of a new wagon made him look up hopefully. Again, it was full. At least some of what it was full of were his nominal colleagues.

He knew Alv and most of her people had already been sent back from the front, but here were at least some of the rest, plus around sixty per cent of a field hospital's supplies and components, jammed in all anyhow. He saw the Butcher there, and Tallifer at least. And… what he took to be Lochiver's corpse, except the wagon jolted and the man flailed about and cried out. His leg was heavily splinted, Cosserby saw, but otherwise the initial impression had been an understandable one. Lochiver didn't look particularly alive even when he was walking around and talking to people.

The Butcher leaned forwards and spoke to their driver, who diverted the wagon to the roadside by Cosserby's impromptu mechanics demonstration.

"What's this?" the big man rumbled, and Cosserby, who'd had quite enough today, interrupted with, "Yes, yes, my toy soldier has indeed broken down, thank you Chief." He waited for the verbal lash but Ollery seemed worn thin. His boy was tucked into his armpit, Cosserby saw, with a bandage across his forehead and about one arm.

"Ask him," snapped Tallifer, and then she leaned forwards, jogging Lochiver's leg and making the old man snarl. "Did you see Masty yet?"

Cosserby blinked. It hadn't been his job to keep track of people. "No, I…" Indicating the part-completed work. "I mean, he was with you…?"

"He got left behind," Tallifer twisted herself free of her seat, which Lochiver promptly lolled into. She ended up sitting on the tailboard of the wagon. "Listen, we had to stop to get this idiot's leg straight. He must have ended up ahead of us."

Cosserby opened his mouth to say a lot of unhelpful things,

but then his brain engaged. Masty was one of the few people in the department who'd give him the time of day.

"He'd have stopped to help," he said hollowly, meeting Tallifer's eyes. And she was someone who'd take the time of day right back off him and then wash it because his oily hands had been all over it, but right then there was no strength left in her to dislike him. She just nodded wearily.

"And I've been looking in the wagons," Cosserby added. "I'm sorry, I've not seen him. I mean, I'll look out…" Which would be absolutely no use to anyone, of course.

"What about the new man," the Butcher called. "The Maric."

"No, I mean, I've not seen him," Cosserby said. "I'm sorry."

"What about Banders?" Lochiver croaked. Tallifer looked round, startled.

"Banders was… wasn't she with us when we set off? I thought she was just… being Banders…" She had a hand to her mouth in sudden horror.

"She wasn't with us," the Butcher confirmed.

Cosserby felt a little drop, within him. Some discrete emotional component failing and going still. "Oh. Oh, well. No, I've. I've not seen her. No. But I'm sure she's. If anyone can… you know. Banders…"

Tallifer shook, just a single shudder going through her on its way to somewhere else. Her lips moved, and probably it was a prayer to whatever the heathen deity was that she'd once served. And Cosserby did not feel the absence of such an instinct in himself, but nor did he begrudge it in her.

The driver of the wagon said something on the subject of them having to move on, but right then a particularly unwelcome squad of retreating troops started hogging the road, and most definitely not to be shunted aside. They were leathery and thorn-skinned, shambling along sometimes on two legs, sometimes on all fours. They snapped and snarled at one another, and gave off a dry heat and a flickering glow. Demons and, riding the shoulders of the foremost, Fellow-Invigilator Maserley. Cosserby watched him with some envy. And it wasn't as though Cosserby couldn't ride on the shoulders of a Sonori, though the impression of a child being indulged was one he wouldn't soon live down. It was more that demons didn't break down. If their contractual terms were breached they either ran off to cause mayhem somewhere or they were sucked back to the Realms Below, and either way it became someone else's problem. You didn't have to stop by the road to fix your demons.

"What's this, setting up a booth for shaves and tooth-pulling?" Maserley asked, but even his bleak heart wasn't quite in it. The retreat was a mark against the whole battalion. Today wouldn't look good for anybody's military career.

Tallifer looked as though she was going to ask him about their missing, but that would just be giving the man ammunition. Instead they all just glowered at him surlily until he and his cavalcade of monsters had passed by, and it was just regular soldiers trudging through the mephitic stench they left in their wake.

Tallifer had apparently been making decisions while that had been going on. "This is going to be a drudge's job to unload," she declared sourly. "Especially without orderlies. Get on the wagon. Bring your toys, those that can still walk."

"Well I can't," Cosserby told her. "I'm working here. You can see that."

She rolled her eyes to indicate what she thought of that. "I'm serious. We've got me and him and most of the hospital to shift." A nod at the Butcher, the only other capable pair of hands. "Get on."

Cosserby looked from her to the open Sonori. "*Accessory* Tallifer," he said, with some dignity, "I appreciate that you do not rate my profession highly, as compared to an artisan of blood and bone such as yourself, but be assured that the army *does* value my efforts and expects me to have as many Sonori in working order as possible at all times. And so I must decline your requests for me to lift and carry for you."

She looked sidelong at the Butcher, and her wrinkled lips moved a couple of times as though trying out new wording. In the end she shrugged.

"We'll see you back at camp," she told him, as though it was merely the timing of things he was arguing, and not his status as glorified porter. Then the driver had the horse plodding forwards and they were shouldering into the road and displacing dejected soldiers.

Only after they'd gone did he wonder if, perhaps, that *hadn't* been what Tallifer had been after. If, in fact, she'd been making a sidelong attempt not to decrease the count of the department's officers by one more. It felt like uncharacteristic softness from a rather objectionable woman who had made no secret about not liking him. But these were exceptional times, and he was at least nominally on the departmental payroll.

Too late now, though, and he really did have to fix up this tin soldier if he wasn't to completely disgrace his profession. As the army stomped past – more and more with a 'tail end of things' feel to it, he noted nervously – he bent to his task once again.

The third time he reshaped the part, it took properly, and linked to its neighbours. Physically and magically, everything aligned, and the next two pieces needed almost no refashioning. After that it was a part he had to make out of whole cloth and best judgment, but his skills came through for him, and it clicked into place on the second try. He slotted a test tableth into the Sonori's head and it moved its limbs through all the proper angles. A bit juddery, but a limping soldier was better than one going in circles. And it turned its head to look at him as it did so, and he thought he heard a ghost of that plaintive, hollow voice. *Why?* And, just like the penitents in Hell, he'd send it out to fight again now he'd fixed it up.

He shook himself. He needed to re-cast the test tableth. They accumulated unwanted resonance over time, just like the Sonori casings did. As though the world was full of undirected life desperate to earth into some viable vessel. He swapped out the tester for the full-functioning tableth and told the construct to stand up.

"Cohort-Monitor!"

He jolted to attention, so that the Sonori appeared to be mimicking him. Fellow-Inquirer Prassel was there, looking barely dishevelled by the whole retreat business. Almost at the very back – the stragglers were passing them by, limping, supporting comrades, carrying heavy loads. The last and the luckless.

She was without a detachment of corpses, he saw. Of course she didn't have to be careful of her resources like he did. It wasn't as though the army would be running out of bodies any time soon. Either she'd expended all her troops and not had a chance to animate new ones, or else she'd sent them off for whatever meagre delay value they represented.

"What are you doing? Didn't you *get* the order to retreat?"

"Just finishing up here, magister," he confirmed, and dropped down to gather up his tools and close up the forge lamp. "Just a little mechanical difficulty. It's all sorted."

"I have no intention of donating your technical knowhow to the enemy, Cosserby," Prassel snapped. "Get yourself moving. No way of knowing how soon they'll be through here looking for fools like you who don't know when to run."

"Run, magister?"

"The dispatches can call it 'strategic withdrawal' all they want," she said acidly. "Move yourself and your tinpots, man."

When all four Sonori stomped off, he felt an incalculable relief. The fourth was slightly slower, and he'd have to keep reining the others in, but that was an on-the-fly intervention he was more than capable of. For a moment he seriously considered getting up on the shoulders of one, impressions bedamned. He knew Sonorists of larger character than he who could have pulled it off without damage to their image. But he, a man of no real reputation, still husbanded the shreds of it that he had.

Prassel fell into step beside him. He had a thousand questions about the military situation, but her demeanour did not encourage his asking them. Instead, he told her about his meeting with Tallifer and the others. And, in doing so, realised that he hadn't seen Masty or Banders or Maric Jack, and here they were right at the end of things.

She absorbed the news without expression. But then it would take some spectacularly bad news to dent Prassel's stony features. Possibly the fall of the entire Palleseen Sway would only raise an eyebrow slightly. She was a cold one, Cosserby knew, and they were just three orderlies. Or two orderlies and some new man nobody had really become overly attached to. For what it was worth, Jack had seemed a decent sort as far as Cosserby was concerned, but he'd barely been with the department any time at all. There was no Jack-shaped hole to be left. And the other two would be missed, but he couldn't expect Prassel to care, not from her elevated position. New orderlies weren't hard to find.

Prassel said nothing, and just looked at her feet or ahead up the road. There were doubtless weighty and necromantic matters on her mind.

Contact with the Enemy

The Loruthi never wanted a war with the Palleseen and, to their credit, the Palleseen didn't particularly want a war with them either. For some decades the two powers had tested the bounds of one another's political influence around the map while their merchant classes happily made deals across every table in every civilized port. The problem lay in both states having very definite and incompatible ideas about what to do with the rest of the world. The Loruthi wanted to make it a part of their economic system and the Pals their ideological system. Both of which meant 'Who gets the money', just that the Loruthi took a higher percentage but the Pals also set fire to your church.

Jack had missed the wagon because the incidental swipe of the retreating monster had robbed him of any ability to secure a place on it, and he reckoned nobody would be blaming him for that. Masty had missed the wagon because, faithful dog that he was, he wouldn't leave Jack. The reason that *Banders* had missed the wagon, however, was that she had been outside the medical tent having a crafty smoke when everything kicked off, and been carried the wrong way by a rush of troops. Then made the mistake of trying to rejoin her unit rather than just taking anybody in the uniform as her comrade and legging it. Not exactly an instinct for loyalty, not Banders. More the act of someone who hadn't quite understood the assignment, and that was entirely in character.

She'd found Masty, and the two of them had got Jack down here into a scoop in the muddy earth that some weapon had torn. And Jack had been busy dying at the time, and would have far rather they'd left him where he was. And then Masty, who had very obviously seen enough in his career with the hospital unit to work out what was what, had gone and got his box. Which had been left lying on its side where Jack had formerly been lying on his side, and had not come with him because his shoulders hadn't been left in the right sort of shape to keep it on.

Banders had headed off, shortly after. Off to scout, she said. Off to scavenge, Jack reckoned. Because something burned in her nature that even being left behind by a fleeing army couldn't douse. Which left him and Masty.

Jack could feel himself shaking, his skin icy cold. And, fair, it *was* cold. The evening was coming on and the misting rain was back. His shirt clung to him with the general warmth and comfort of an octopus, where it wasn't rigid as a breastplate with dried blood. An awful lot of liquid stuff that had been inside Jack had taken the once-in-a-lifetime opportunity to see the world when the beast's tail had hit him.

He stared into the rain with wide eyes. "Who'd have thought there were things like that? Where did they get it from? It's like a thing from the Wood."

"Yes," Masty agreed. "Like a thing from the woods."

Jack tried to laugh, but the shivers got in the way. "No – the Wood. In Ilmar there's… And there are – are monsters. I…"

"A thing from some woods," Masty agreed. It was aggravating that he didn't understand. Then his hand was on Jack's shoulder. Jack's whole and reconstructed shoulder.

"Is this going to keep happening?" he asked.

"I don't know," Jack told him. Because he hadn't asked for it. In truth the salts had worn off and he'd been in too much mad pain right then to phrase any kind of request – punched right through the begging and pleading part into a howling agony that had scoured the inside of his skull clear of thought.

It had happened when Masty brought the box back. Not all at once but piece by piece. Watching himself had been fascinating, in a weirdly disconnected sort of way. As though some miniature craftsman had been angrily beating the dents out of a piece of metal. And God *had* been angry. Angry at Jack getting himself into this position. Angry at having to be involved in something so phenomenally against His precepts as a *war.*

Masty had remarked that it wasn't entirely unlike Alv taking on someone's wounds. Except the wounds didn't *go* anywhere. No surrogate required, all that life-ending wrack just evaporated into the air. And that had left Jack staring at the grim, haggard face of God. God, who took on all the wounds of the world, an infinite repository of hurt.

But there were limits. Masty said he'd known people die just of shock and Jack certainly felt that the shock was close to finishing him. His body had been pieced together but the impact of the tail was still in his mind. So he shook and stared and mumbled like a fever victim, unable to come to terms with the fact of still being alive.

Banders's reaction to this actual miracle had been, "Does this mean we won't ever be rid of the sod?" But there had been a jag of nerves under the joke. Her eyes flicked from the way all the parts of Jack's body were inside his skin now and fitted together properly, over to the box that had made it all possible. Soon after, she'd gone scrounging, and maybe avarice hadn't been the only thing prompting her to give Jack some space.

"Tell me how you do it," Masty asked softly, after that.

"I don't. God does it," Jack managed. "I'm not supposed – supposed to say that, am I? To the Pals. But it's true. I believe in God and God heals. Sometimes. When He feels like it. And you have to keep to His terms. And nobody – nobody ever will. But I've lived by them all my life." He shivered, because he'd never needed serious healing from God before. In fact, when he'd been God's actual priest he hadn't been allowed to ask, because that would have been selfish. But now he was only an ex-priest, a half-priest, a theological jack of all trades, just like the name. And so God could heal him, at God's divine discretion. And if he decided he wanted to take up a life of violence at some later date then he'd be visited by that colossal, shattering injury. He suddenly understood the sentence of death that every one of God's victims lived under.

"I'm not religious," said Masty, sitting back on his heels.

"I mean," Jack said, "I guessed."

"When I was young, there was a temple. Priests taught me how to pray and sacrifice. I tried to keep it up, when I got brought to the army. I made a shrine. But they found it, and a Fellow-Inquirer sat me down and explained – very patiently, really – why that wasn't appropriate. And beat me, after, to make sure the message stuck. Anyway I forgot the words."

Jack made a neutral sort of noise, to indicate that he was listening but if Masty wanted to change the subject any time, that was also fine.

"I've seen god-stuff," the man went on, though. "Sacred serpents, guardian constructs, priests spitting out divine wrath. But... I mean, only briefly in most cases."

Jack didn't need to ask. A volley of baton-shot was a strong theological counter-argument.

"I take it your religion can't do much for him," Masty added, indicating the third resident of their hollow. Not Banders, off filling her boots. Some anonymous dead soldier, uniform so torn up Jack'd had to squint to be sure they were even Palleseen. They'd probably been here immediately before the hollow had, and died of surprise hollowing. Their ghastly, open-mouthed face wasn't the most reassuring thing to have to look at, but Jack didn't feel up to turning it aside.

"Dead is dead," he got out, and another shudder passed through him, as though he was being wrung out.

Banders dropped down then, startling both of them. She was even more spattered with mud than she had been when she left, but neither injured nor dead. She managed a wan smile.

"How's our brave soldier?" she asked.

"Better than he was," Masty said.

"I'm fine," said Jack. His body, impossibly renewed as it was, continued to twitch and shiver, no sign that he was really in control of it.

"I mean," Banders agreed, "you are way more fine than you have any right to be. That happen a lot, where you come from? I'd pay to see that. You could hire yourself out with a bunch of truncheons and sledgehammers and just let people go to town on you. Queues round the block." There was the faintest edge of hysteria to her voice.

"Never happened before," Jack said tonelessly. "I was always very careful. Never shot. Never stabbed. When I got my beatings and bruises, He never stepped in to help. Told me I deserved it most of the time." One last final shudder, the dog of his body shaking the last of the wet off itself. "I didn't ask Him," he went on. "He's just a loose engine now. Doing it without prayer. Just on His own."

"Well hark at the damned ingrate," came a familiar, hateful voice from the box.

"I *am* grateful," Jack told God, aware of the others' stares. "I don't want to be dead. But You heal the hurt but You can't touch the memory of it hurting. I feel like every time I move, it'll all come flooding back."

"Well excuse me for not bloody tucking you in and giving you a sweet," God said disgustedly, His voice rising over the rude noise that Banders was making to express very similar sentiments. Then three people jumped down into the hole with them.

The utter paralysis of the pair of them, Masty and Jack, would have any drill Statlos put his head in his hands. They both had knives, military issue. Neither even reached for them, utterly unprepared to defend themselves.

Jack registered the Pal uniforms a moment later, and Banders was rounding on the newcomers, annoyed but not alarmed.

"I told you," she said. "I'd need a moment to explain. Get them warmed up to the idea. I said I'd shout you."

"It's bloody exposed up there," said one of them. They were all regular soldiers, and two still had their batons. Jack wondered warily if Banders had met them engaged in the same post-battle practices she'd been at. Looters and deserters probably weren't safe company if you wanted to get back to the army.

"All right, so," Banders decided. "We're doing this. Lads, this is Masty and this is Maric Jack. They are orderlies with the hospital department, like me. Fellows, these three stalwarts are troopers Lidlet, Paucelry and Klimmel. Who got left behind just like we did on account of the unexpected nature of whatever the fuck happened. The plan is, we wait for full dark and then hightail it back to the lines together. That work for everyone?"

"I wasn't planning to build a house here and plant crops," Masty said mildly.

Lidlet was a woman, stocky, capless with hair cut very close to her skull. Paucelry was the tallest, and had a bandage somewhat haphazardly applied to his cheek and neck, presumably Banders's work. Klimmel was rangy and long-limbed, and had a narrow, sour face like a hatchet.

"What's up with him?" Lidlet asked, jabbing a boot at Jack.

"Nothing. I'm fine – fine. I'm fine. Sorry, I'm fine," he stammered. "Please don't touch me."

"Too highfalutin' to throw down with the regulars, are we?" she jibed. "Fancy."

"He got hurt," Masty said defensively. "He's… tender."

Paucelry had some comment to make about that, but whatever had happened to his face muffled it into mumbling.

"Got anything to eat that's not covered in mud?" Klimmel demanded. He had a knife out – not threatening, just fussing with it, turning it over and over. Still, the threat was there. Masty found a squashed ammie – one of the rolled flatbreads that were army standard rations. Letting Klimmel have it seemed a reasonable price to avoid worrying.

"He needs something for the pain?" Banders wondered and then, at Masty's eye-roll, "You still hurting, Jack? Need something to chew?" Spoken far too loud for six people hiding out in a foxhole, as though Jack was deaf or senile.

"You will *not*," God told him. "No polluting yourself with more foreign muck. Not after my divine benificience has touched you."

"It's *beneficence*," Jack said. "And I will have the drugs, please." Not for the pain but for the memory of it, which he still wanted dulled and pushed further away.

"Weak," God spat. "You're weak. Why do I even bother?"

"I don't know. Why do you? I'm having a time of it, all right? I will damn well take what's on offer."

"I'll drink to that," Lidlet put in. "What's on offer?" She sat down beside Jack and reached for the box.

"Not in there," Masty told her, before Jack could say anything unwise. "That's where he keeps his…" *Faith?* "private stuff."

"Wouldn't be the first time I'd gone into a man's box for his privates," she said, but didn't suit actions to words. Banders handed round a ceramic flask – one of the Butcher's own – to anyone who wanted a nip of whatever numbing concoction was in it.

Full dark seemed to take whole ages of the world to descend, but at last Lidlet decided that they had as much cover as the night was going to give them. By then, Jack had his box on his back again, and a body that wasn't cowering under the shadow of world-obliterating pain. God, stood on the box like a street ranter, was keeping up a constant mutter of deprecation in his ear, about why did He even *bother* if His faithless follower was going to just run to Pal alchemy a moment later, and how that should be a new forbiddance of the faith.

"You got batons?" Klimmel asked the three of them. "You got knives?"

They had knives, because they'd come with the belts. That was about it. "We aren't fighters," Masty said.

"You think the Loruthi are going to give you the option?" the soldier demanded. "There's dropped weapons out there. Keep your eyes open, grab one when you can. Make sure it's got a tab in the slot." He was the one who hadn't held on to his own weapon.

"Fast and low," Lidlet said. "Wide skirts to any sign of them. We're getting home. We're not avenging the retreat." And a jab of her elbow to Klimmel's ribs to emphasise the point.

"What even happened?" Jack complained.

Everyone stared at him as though it was the most unnecessary question in the world. He realised that they didn't actually *know*. Yes, there had been a reversal, but it might have left Forthright Battalion back where it started or the whole army might still be running. The Loruthi might have established a new front line they'd have to sneak through, or they could be on contested ground that both sides would be training weapons on. They were ants in a footprint, knowing only that something had stomped down on them.

They crept up out of the hollow and nobody shot then. Cloud hung heavy above, the moon only a dim radiance through it. Around them, what little could be seen was churned ground, the occasional stake or broken tent pole. Bodies. And once you'd started seeing the bodies, you kept seeing them. Pal bodies, mostly. Those who hadn't made good on the order to retreat. Or a specific cluster of them that Jack identified as those the hospital department hadn't been able to save, laid out neatly for a collection that would never come.

"This way," Lidlet decided, and then there was a hushed but fierce debate about that because Klimmel and Banders both had different ideas of which direction they should be headed in.

"I don't suppose your invisibles have any powers of navigation?" Masty murmured to Jack.

He frowned. "I don't know," and, craning back to look over his own shoulder, "I mean, do you? Anyone got a map, back there?"

"What the hell do I look like?" God demanded. "You see a bloody sextant and telescope as part of My holy regalia, do you? Added navigation to My prerogatives recently?"

"How about the others?" Jack asked. "I mean... him?" But the nature god just goggled at him. Then the spear-bearer turned up and pointed dramatically, scowling into the dark.

"What is?" Jack asked. It could be the army. It could be the enemy. It could be the direction of some distant and long-pillaged temple.

The fierce little figure spat something in a language Jack had never heard before. A single loaded syllable.

God rolled His eyes. "Fucking *barbarians* I'm trapped in here with," He moaned, and grudgingly translated.

"Um, so," Jack said to the others. "I can tell you which way the sea is. I don't imagine that's very useful, sorry."

Masty screwed his face up as though trying to picture a map. "Which sea?"

"He says it's all the same sea," God said sourly. "Bloody useful. It's that way, though. I mean I reckon the sea's in every direction, you go far enough, but the closest sea is that way."

"Wait, what?" Lidlet was peering suspiciously. "The *sea*?"

"Yeah, sure," Banders said casually. "It's his thing. Always knows where the sea is. We don't call him Maritime Jack for nothing."

"Nearest sea is... Fennimouth Port?" Klimmel was working it out by counting on his fingers, or that was what it looked like. "Means..."

"Means I was right," Banders said. "Come on." And she led them off, her two orderly comrades and the three troopers, as though she'd been reinstated to her former rank.

Between the constant drizzle and the low-hanging cloud, Jack just held on to Klimmel's belt as Masty held on to his, and the half-dozen of them snaked and stumbled their way across the blasted landscape. Jack only hoped that Banders had some way of navigating straight, and they wouldn't end up circling round to fall right back into the hole they'd crawled out of. He only had the vaguest sense of the landscape they'd advanced across. He'd been in one wagon or another, or setting up as the casualties came in. He hadn't been required to have any sense of *place* beyond the bounds of a hospital tent. The department had been the one still point that the injured converged on. And now the precise business of the surgical unit had broken open and spilled them into this sightless and infinite wasteland. Wheel-slipped wagons, half-collapsed tents like the ruins of ancient sacred sites, dead horses and dead humans. Hundred-yard gouges in the earth where some weapon had struck, a stand of thorn bushes from which a corpse still hung. If the Butcher's domain was Hell, Jack wasn't sure what this was.

Every so often Banders would stop, stare at the unseen horizon, do some complex calculating business with her knuckles and then mutter to Jack. "Where's the sea now?" and he'd consult the angry little spear god and tell her. The three soldiers were definitely straining under her command. Appearing strong was probably a good move.

Nobody asked how far. Everyone knew nobody could know. The Pallesand army could be just over the next rise or a hundred miles away. Or driven into the sea they were navigating by.

Once, something battered through the air overhead, coming from behind them and making a kind of high weeping noise, entirely inhuman. A demon, Jack guessed. Some conjuration from one side or the other, contracted up out of the Realms Below and sent to scout or hunt. Or perhaps just given insufficiently binding terms, so that it was blundering about on its own recognizance. To be avoided, in any event. Demons were more than capable of malice and bloodshed on their own account if their contracts didn't restrict them from it. And who'd write three pages of pacifist small print into a war-demon's terms?

Perhaps the thing had been scouting after all, because they ran into the enemy very shortly afterwards.

In retrospect Jack wasn't really sure who'd run into whom. Everyone seemed equally wrong-footed by the encounter and, had they had the chance to make arrangements beforehand, probably the two sides could have agreed to ignore one another. Being who he was, when Jack saw people ahead, he assumed it was more Pal stragglers. Instead of a squad of Loruthi soldiers who were out here... what? Also lost and trying to find out where their advance had got to? Stripping corpses like Banders had been? Actually doing bona fide military scouting? It wasn't something anybody would be explaining to him any time soon.

Four of them. He thought all men, at first look. Someone had said the Loruthi only let men be soldiers. One of them turned out to be a woman. What he'd taken as a neat beard was the strap of her tall shako. They wore long coats that would have been green in the light, but were just grey in the gloom.

The moment of realisation came simultaneously to both sides and everyone went for their batons at the same time. By then, both Klimmel and Banders had put in a requisition to the armoury of the fallen and come up with a charged weapon apiece. There was a staccato crackle of shot from both sides, unaimed and hurried. Jack just threw himself down curling about his box to protect it, and Masty in the mud right beside him.

Paucelry was down, he saw. Down and kicking but not screaming, a bad combination. Jack tried to worm over there on elbows and knees but another baton-shot fried the mud between them and he shrank back. He'd instantly lost track of everybody else involved in the skirmish, especially the enemy. He could hear screaming, and then, over it, he could hear *screaming*, something utterly inhuman venting a vast shrill agony at the underside of the clouds. *The demon?* He could believe it.

He put his head up just as everything kicked off again, losing a hank of hair as a shot sizzled past him. He saw one of the Loruthi kneeling, frantically trying to slot a new tableth into their baton with gloved hands when Klimmel descended on them. Klimmel hadn't had much use out of the baton he'd snagged. He was down to knives, but making up for the loss of range with bloody-handed enthusiasm. The impact was like a magic trick, the blade vanishing into the Loruthi so that only the hilt could be seen, and the next two strikes so frenzied that Jack only registered movement, not seeing the weapon at all. The pair of them tumbled over in a flail of limbs. Lidlet was down. Jack saw her on the far side of the wrestling match, flat on her back but still shuddering. Paucelry was dead still, so he diverted to Lidlet instead, crawling, then just up and running in the hope that everyone had better things to worry about.

A shot skimmed his thigh and he tumbled, almost coming down on Lidlet's shot-pierced lungs just as she fought breath through them. A Loruthi loomed, baton levelled down at him, then up because Masty had come stumbling after him and now skidded to a halt with his hands upraised.

"Wait! Stop! Friends!" Masty got out, the last of which was a flat-out lie when viewed with any objectivity. And then, the words mangled by poor linguistics, "Por b'londo mar'i te!"

The Loruthi stared at Masty – it was when Jack realised she was a woman – but didn't shoot him, so that was something. Then Klimmel went for her, rising from his kill with a knife slick with gore. He looked like a beast from nightmare to Jack. If *that* had come at him out of a dark and corpse-filled night he wouldn't have stopped running til dawn. The Loruthi was made of sterner stuff, because she shot Klimmel in the gut, just a spasmodic repositioning of the baton and a spat word in her own language. And then the baton was back on Masty and any leeway for negotiation was quite gone.

He cried out when the crackle of shot came, and Jack clenched at it, as though somehow he could impart some fortitude, to help Masty take the impact. It was the Loruthi who went down, though, with an expression as though she'd been cheated at cards.

Banders loped up, still levelling her baton, staring at the woman she'd downed. In that moment Jack remembered she was a soldier, despite the constant demotions and the side-hustles and the jokes. Unlike him and Masty, they'd trained her to kill people back on the Archipelago, before sending her out with the army. She looked as compassionate and human as Cosserby's Sonori right then, waiting to see if she needed another shot.

She didn't and, in the wake of that death, there was no enemy to be seen. Jack never saw all the bodies and possibly one of the Loruthi had run the moment the shooting started. If so, good luck to them.

Jack dropped to his knees by Klimmel, who was making a hideous, clenched sound, as though his life was squealing out of him like air from a bladder. Lidlet was still alive, too, but there was no scream left in her, just a whistle that came as much from the hole in her left breast as much as her throat. Her eyes were very wide, looking at the sky. Paucelry was still, dead when Masty lurched over to check him.

"Absolutely bloody *not*," spat God. "I can't believe you're even asking."

"Seriously," said Jack. "Heal them, please. Will you just…?"

He was aware that Banders and Masty were staring at him, but it wasn't the usual eye-roll and *Jack's gone mad again* exasperation. Because they'd seen him put back together. There was a hushed expectation hanging between them.

"To hell with both of them," God sneered. "Killers."

Jack ignored him. He laid a hand on Klimmel, a hand on Lidlet. "Listen to me," he told them. Neither of them really wanted their last moments full of some foreigner mangling the language, but he wasn't giving them the option unless they just let slip and fell into unconsciousness. "Listen, you need to swear to me you won't ever hurt anyone ever again. Not do anything that would lead to harm being done."

"Don't waste your breath," God threw at him. "I ain't doing it. Not them. Not here. Just walk away, Yasnic!"

"You *will*," Jack said flatly. "If they swear then you will. I'm not having it from you. I am telling you how it's going to be."

"They'll just get into a fight or get orders to shoot someone, and that'll be *it*," God shouted at him. "I'm not wasting my powers on them."

"I don't *care* if they drop dead tomorrow," Jack snapped at Him. "Just do it *now*."

Lidlet's lips were moving, but whether it had anything to do with his demands, he couldn't say. Klimmel's head twisted like someone had him by the hair and was wrenching his face around. He stared at Jack with every muscle contorted, eyes as wide as a flayed man's.

"Fucking," he got out through clenched teeth, "what?"

"Tell me you won't harm anyone ever again," Jack said, as clearly as he could.

"Fucking," Klimmel hissed, "*dying*. C'mere. Hurt you."

"No, listen," Jack said. "I'm sorry. I've got to be clear. I will – you can be healed. Just – healed. But you have to swear. I'm sorry. It's a god thing and I know you Pals don't like god things. I'm sorry. It's all I've got. But you have to swear. And you have to keep to it, or you won't be healed any more. You'll die. I've seen it. Swear, please. Swear and mean it."

"Are you bloody *deaf* or what, you faithless bastard?" God bawled in his ear. "I am *not*. I draw the *line*. I have had it with this nonsense from you. You were the worst priest and you are the worst follower and I will not have My name taken in vain like this! For *soldiers* of all damned people!"

"You will bloody well *do*." Jack's teeth were bared like an animal's. "I don't care that they're soldiers. *I'm* a soldier now, didn't you hear? Look, I have a uniform and everything. Just *do* it." So that Klimmel actually had to reach out, a hand covered with his own blood and someone else's, and grab Jack's attention back.

"I swear," he got out. "Fucking. Swear. Only. Please." Shivering violently as the blood loss froze him from the inside.

And nothing happened. Klimmel was plainly in his last moments and Lidlet's breathing was beached in the shallows with any saving tide receding towards the horizon. Jack hauled the box off his back and shook it so that God had to cling on to the shoulder straps.

"I've had it with you!" he shouted. "What are you, that you get to be holier-than-thou about *this?*"

"I am your God!" God howled. "I am *supposed* to be holier than bloody anyone! I'm actual God and you will not talk to me in this way."

"These are lives!" Jack yelled.

"Pal lives!"

"I don't care if they're Pals. I don't care if they're killers. They've sworn. You've got to give them the chance."

"You don't know." God playing the wounded card. "What it's like. Every time someone makes that oath and breaks it. It *takes* from me, Yasnic. It's the wound in me that I can't heal."

"You'll do this or what's the good of you? Why do I even bring you along?"

"Because nobody else will love you," God spat. "Because you need god in your life, you poor bastard, and so we're stuck with each other."

"Oh are we?" Jack asked, looking past God. "I'll change religions. I'll deny you." Aware of the horrified, fascinated gaze of all assembled. "I'll worship – I'll worship *him*. Him with the mask and the woodlice." Because the nature spirit had crept out to see what all the noise was about. "He was useful. He turned the beast aside. I'll become his priest."

"I will take my healing back from you, you ingracious son of a bitch," God warned him furiously.

"Do it," Jack challenged Him. "Strike me down and see where

it gets you. You'll walk back to Ilmar and see if you can drum up any worship there? Hide with the other forgotten gods until they trap and decant you?"

"Jack..." Banders sounded equal parts horrified and embarrassed for him. And he was shouting quite loud, and there would be other Loruthi patrols out there. Although possibly they'd give the whole fracas a wide berth, like someone detouring around a ranting street preacher whom Correct Speech hadn't picked up yet. Jack just held God's gaze and dared the divine presence to blink first.

Lidlet sucked in a great breath and let out a scream that started off hideous but trailed off into puzzlement.

Klimmel's face unkinked, muscle by muscle, leaving only that nasty sharp expression he'd had when they'd first seen him. He rolled over and sat up, feeling at his stomach. At the blasted, blood-soaked cloth over whole skin.

"You..." He looked angry at being saved. "This is some... secret design? You could do this and we never knew? How long...?" Jack wondered who he'd lost, in some past clash. A brother, a lover, a friend.

"Klimmel," Lidlet spat. "Shut up."

"But he... Look." Klimmel bared Exhibit One, an unmarred human abdomen, formerly a ruin you could see the ropes of his guts through. "Look." A shaking finger aimed at the rise and fall of Lidlet's chest. The bright blood that was down her chin and neck as though she was a messy vampire.

And Lidlet wasn't starry-eyed with gratitude. There was a peculiar urgency to her. "God-stuff, he said."

"Lidlet—"

"That means this never happened," she hissed at him.

"But they could..." Klimmel's gesture took in the whole unseen, cadaver-spotted battlefield.

"God-stuff," Lidlet hissed, "means this never happened if you don't want to end up on a Decanter's table and your heart in a jar."

She had, Jack understood, a very clear way of seeing things.

"Now get on your feet and get moving," she added. "All of you." Though when Jack did, she took a step back and gave him room.

"I meant it about the swearing," Jack said quietly, sadly. "You can't. It'll come back. You'll die. Please. I'm sorry." And knew that they would fail. It was an oath you couldn't ask of anyone, let alone a soldier. And so they'd die, and he'd feel it. Not as a hole torn in his infallibility, as God would, but he'd be responsible. In taking on their wounds, he was making them his to mourn, when they inevitably died. How long before he, like God, was desperately trying to shirk that responsibility.

He met God's eyes again, and the wizened divinity nodded tiredly.

"Oh, you get it now, do you? You can only cry at so many funerals."

Masty had gone – Jack hadn't seen him leave. Now he came back with something entirely unexpected. Namely horses. Three beasts in scaled barding, complete with saddlebags. And Jack remembered that weird, inhuman screaming and recontextualised it out of the realm of the demonic into *We shot one of the animals.* An unintended casualty of that first panicked exchange of fire.

Banders could ride, apparently, and so could Masty, and Klimmel a bit. They headed off towards theoretically friendly lines two to a horse. And if Jack spotted Banders going through Paucelry's jacket first, he couldn't muster any argument as to why the contents of the man's pockets would be happier abandoned in the mud than enjoying a productive second life in Banders's possession. It really didn't seem to matter, compared to everything else.

Seeing only Dimly

Tallifer, the cooling flame. The hard woman. The void where sympathy crawled to die years ago. Hard-faced with an old woman's anger at a world that won't let her rest. Behind that mask, someone who cared passionately about a congregation and a temple and a faith, a way of life. And who learned too late to ration her care because none of those things were coming back.

"I wish," said Tallifer, "that all my patients were this still."

Alv could be still. It was a Divinati thing. When she'd first been forced out to live amongst others, the sheer bustle of them had horrified her. She still took pains not to be caught in a crush, packed shoulder to shoulder the way the Pals seemed to have no problem with. Not as though she'd grown up with great estates and solitude as far as the eye could see, back home. The Divine City was tightly circumscribed with not a hand's breadth of wasted space. But what she'd *had* was the space around her that nobody else would intrude into without invitation. Nobody would ever think of doing so. Nobody would stumble in accidentally to upset her personal equilibrium. Nothing happened by accident in the Divine City. Or almost nothing.

Here, nothing ever seemed to quite happen by design. In the wider world a thousand currents of fortune tugged at every event, so that nothing worked out as it was intended. And that was without figuring in the greater chaos of the war.

She felt the line of Tallifer's blade – not the edge against her skin, because the old woman had remarkably calm and steady hands, but the implication of it from the way the bandages tugged and fell free. Then the raw stickiness of fresh air touching onto skin that hadn't healed fully yet.

Tallifer made a dissatisfied noise. "I should just replace these. We should give it another few days at least."

It had been eight days since the battle. Eight days of darkness and Alv was tired of it. "Do it," she instructed. And she wasn't in a position to give orders. The precise placement of her rank – 'Guest-Adjutant' – was nothing but a headache for the hierarchy-minded Pals. Technically everything she did was voluntary. She could walk away any time. She'd never needed to test whether the Pals actually thought that way or not. What kept her here wasn't anything with a Palleseen stamp on it.

The bandages about her face tugged again, crusty with dried blood and pus from the injuries she'd taken on. Alv braced, feeling a webwork of pain crawling about her features, sensations transplanted from someone else, like an animal released into the wrong environment and unsure how it's supposed to find food. Tallifer made another dissatisfied noise.

"I'm going to rip these right off now, okay? I think that'll do less damage than this by-inches malarky," she said. "You may want to hang onto something."

"I'm fine." Moving her lips as little as possible and, even as she said it, Tallifer pulled the last of the wrappings from her eyes.

A redness of light flooded in through her lids. Tallifer asked her if she was sure again and Alv gave a tight, tiny nod. She felt the coolness of a sponge cleaning about her cheeks, dabbing at the skin around her orbits, washing at the old, gummed blood sticking her lashes down.

She opened her eyes. For a moment it was just glare and motion, no shape at all, and she thought her powers were failing her and it was too soon after all. Then isolated patches of her visual field started coalescing into comprehensible images and she was treated to a hazy, light-fogged Tallifer, the seamed features looking for a moment uncharacteristically squeamish.

"I see you," Alv whispered. Tallifer's expression didn't improve notably.

"Your eyes look... within tolerance," the woman said. "The rest of you not so much. I wouldn't recommend a mirror."

"Bring me a mirror."

"You are the worst patient," Tallifer said, but she had one as part of her kit, just a little round glass that fit in the palm of her hand. Alv studied her features thoughtfully. She was a horror. The skin about her face was red and weeping, part shiny burn scar, part raw flesh barely masked by new skin. Still, not bad for eight days. Her arts weren't letting her down.

"I'm going to give you fresh bandages anyway," Tallifer decided and, at Alv's look, "I'll leave you slots to see through, but nobody wants to look at that. And Lochiver's not keeping his end of the bargain up right now, infection-wise, so we're having to be careful. I've got some salve here, the Butcher's, and I've blessed it. You want to put it on yourself?"

Alv nodded and dug her fingers into the greasy grey stuff. "How is Lochiver?"

"Complaining every fucking moment he isn't asleep," Tallifer said with feeling. "And he will ask you to do his leg and you are not to do his leg because your own legs aren't properly set from all the legs you did before. He can live with a screwed knee and I can live with him bitching."

"I'll do his leg."

"No, you..." Tallifer actually pulled at her hair. "You will *not*."

"We need him on his feet more than me," Alv decided. "If infection takes root amongst the convalescents we'll lose—"

"No."

"And he's old. It will impact him more than me. Bring him to me."

"I will not," Tallifer said. "Have a biscuit."

The abrupt change of subject threw Alv. She blinked past the tears that were welling up between her and the world and saw a little carton of tiny thumbnail-sized delicacies, golden baked and marbled with dark streaks.

"Ollery found time to make biscuits?" she said blankly.

"These are not his. And, if you ask me, biscuits are not his strength," Tallifer said, absently popping one into her own mouth and then, despite that, adding, "These are yours."

Alv didn't know what to do with that or why she should own some fancy-looking biscuits, and this obviously communicated itself in her mauled expression.

"The woman," Tallifer said, "whose eyes you healed. Was good enough to understand what a really stupidly generous thing that was, that you did for her. And got these to the department. Because she's really happy she can still see things. And it's been a few days and I'm afraid everyone's been nicking off with them, but I've preserved at least some for you." Eating another one herself as punctuation. "They really are very good. That's actual chocolate. You ever had that?"

Alv had, twice in her life. Between a Pal prohibition against anything that was too sweet (indulgent, contrary to Correct Appreciation) and the fact that it only grew overseas, it wasn't something you saw much. And she didn't actually like it much, because the Divinati also distrusted anything that tasted too extreme. And it was a gift, and doubtless the giver thought it was in exchange for healing, but the healing Alv had given out was already pre-paid, part of a debt she was condemned to work off. Which meant that now she had accumulated more debt and her scales were even further out of balance, all because someone had wanted to be *nice*.

Tallifer was watching her, and so she was careful to keep all of that from her face, aided by the fact that half her face wasn't really showing anything at all. She accepted one tiny biscuit, feeling the extremity of flavours riot in her mouth, almost painful in how good it was. "That's enough," she said, jaw tight.

"Please pass the rest around the department. I know Banders likes the sweet. What?" Because Tallifer didn't hide what she was feeling much, and something had died in the old woman's face just as she said the name.

"Not back yet. Banders."

"Back from…?"

"From the fight. Banders, Masty and the new boy. Nobody's seen them. And it's not your fault." Because she'd seen Alv tense. Because Tallifer knew Alv well enough, now, to know she was thinking, *I wasn't there.* They'd carted her back to the tents already, when the Loruthi counterattack came. She'd spent herself in service of the wounded, and they'd sent her away. And if she'd been there…

What? What could she possibly have done? She'd heard only confusing accounts of what had actually happened at the end. Nobody as low down the chain of command as the hospital department had any wider idea. *I'd have been nothing but a hindrance, blind and crippled.* And yet some part of her didn't believe that.

"Seriously." Tallifer sat back. "We were all of us dead weight the moment the orders came. Lucky any of us got back to the lines. And we've relocated twice since then, pulling further back. The camp out there's monstrous. Three battalions. There'll be the mother of all advances on the way, you mark my words."

"Let me see it." And Alv didn't want to see it. One battalion of Pal soldiers mustering for war was more disorder than she could reasonably deal with, no matter that they prided themselves on their neatness and discipline. Three… a city of soldiers to every horizon. And yet she had to expose herself to it. She *deserved* the bludgeon of it across her eyes and mind. It would redress something of the balance. The horror would buy off a biscuit's worth of credit and blunt the guilt. It would be a precisely applied razor blade to the soul.

Once the bandages were reapplied, Tallifer tried to help her out of the tent. Alv wouldn't accept it. Then her legs faltered – still aching where the bones were melding together, more other-people injuries she was sloughing away. She ended up leaning on the old woman anyway, despising herself for one more small debt she'd have to repay somehow.

"I know it's not the first time," Tallifer said softly, "but I never *saw* you do eyes before. It's a sacrilege, by the way." Almost cheerfully said. "Or it would have been. In another life I'd have you on the altar coals for it." Said with a strained chuckle so Alv didn't know whether that was actually a thing, or if she was just playing up the pagan priestess. "I want to ask something as a point of professional curiosity. Is that allowed?"

"Can I stop you asking?" Alv said drily.

"Yes. You say, 'Please don't ask me,' and I don't ask it," Tallifer said. "Seriously, Alv, how long have we known each other? How long have we worked side by side? Ten years and some barter on the side, no? So you just tell me to my nose-tip that I'm not allowed to pry, and I'll pull it out of your business."

"Well you can ask," Alv allowed.

"Where does it go?"

Alv stopped, suddenly enough that Tallifer almost fell over her own feet. *That* question. She'd been braced for that question ever since she'd been condemned to the Pal army. And then nobody had ever asked it, not anyone who gave her orders or used her skills. Her students knew, because they needed the theory of it in order to try and ape her art, but to the wider department and the army at large it was just Divinati magic.

"I mean, I'm right, aren't I?" Tallifer prompted. "That's how that philosophy of yours works. You don't have gods and you're not drawing from tablethi or something. It's all in the balance. But that means it needs to *go* somewhere. Or am I wrong?"

Alv found herself desperately looking about as though there was some escape to this conversation. *I should have said no*, she realised. Tallifer had given her the gap to do so, and she hadn't, and now she was stuck with this question. A request for knowledge that would profit nobody.

She couldn't look at Tallifer. Her eyes passed around the reconvened hospital – new tents, diminished supplies. The Butcher with a big cauldron out in the open, brewing up whatever bulk medicine the convalescence wards most needed, his boy ferrying ingredients out from stores. Lochiver sitting with his splinted leg up, whittling a new flute out of what looked like a human thigh bone. Chatting cheerily enough with a young woman heavily disguised as an old woman – Divinati eyes weren't easily fooled, even running with tears from being newly reconstituted. The demon bawd, Alv realised. Not a regular at the department but an old acquaintance of the Butcher. And beyond her, Cosserby and a standing Sonori, he in his shirtsleeves and it with its hollow body open, as though they were seeking parity in some bare-knuckle bout. Familiar sights. Home sights, for one who would never return to her true home.

And Tallifer, at her elbow, expectant. Owed an answer. Alv shivered and looked desperately for something to deflect her. A way to avoid paying her dues.

She blinked furiously, squinting past the intrusive frame the bandages imposed on her vision. "Isn't that Banders, though?" she asked. "Right over there." Pointing beyond the hospital tents with a hand that still had two maimed fingers.

Tallifer made an annoyed sound on the reasonable basis that Alv was stalling, but it changed to a shocked choke as she looked out into the crowd. A moment later she was gone, running off and shouting for everyone else's attention, leaving Alv blissfully alone.

"Oi oi!" came Bander's unmistakeable hail as the woman pushed through the press of the camp, waving. Alv saw Masty behind her, and then Maric Jack as well. All three of their lost birds come back to the cage. They weren't alone, either. At the edge of the hospital's staked-out territory they were saying their farewells to a pair of soldiers, a broad woman and a lean man.

Jack was saying something in particular, plucking at their sleeves when they turned to go, making a nuisance of himself. Alv recognised her own preoccupations in the man. Debts owed, that he didn't know how to repay. The agony of being unable to set things right. *Welcome to my life.*

She let them all clench together in a general flap of questions and rejoicing and recriminations, all the usual. The thought of being anywhere near so much interchange of obligations made her shrink into herself. How could you know what you'd come out of it with? Banders threw her arms about the Butcher – or some of him – already babbling out some wild story that was probably five parts invention to three of good sense. Tallifer was berating Masty for going back to save Jack. Prodding him in the chest with the pointed stick of her forefinger, then resting her forehead against his in sheer relief. From his crate, Lochiver was demanding someone come over and give him a hug, why wouldn't they? And that wasn't something anybody wanted to do under most circumstances, but Banders sauntered over, still telling her nonsense over her shoulder, and polished the top of the old man's head for him, and pulled his beard fondly. "You stink, you old bastard. That leg gone rotten?"

"I should be so lucky," Lochiver snapped. "Talli *washed* it. I was mortified."

"But the leg wasn't," Tallifer shouted.

Maric Jack tried to slip past the general rejoicing. New boy, after all. Not like he'd been with them long enough to be missed. Mother Semprellaime, the bawd, touched his arm, though. Said something earnest and idealistic enough that her disguise might as well have fallen away on the instant. So maybe she hadn't just been here to chew the fat with the Butcher. Not young love, Alv reckoned, but she'd obviously found a chance to see something worthwhile in the Maric, and grieved when he was lost.

Jack was doing a brave face – another thing Alv knew too well. She watched, feeling like a filthy voyeur, as he smiled and gave the woman a quick one-armed hug and died inside. He was being eaten from within. She could see the great burden of debt hanging about him, the way he'd played with fate and was just waiting for the universe to present the bill. The snarl of thwarted destinies converging on him and that backpack of his was like nothing she'd quite seen before.

And then Banders had finished annoying Lochiver and was coming over to her, faltering slightly at the bandages and the crooked stance. "You, ah... you're good, Alv? Glad to... see me? You can see me?" The cheer of her come crawling to a halt at a safe distance in case things were worse than she thought. And Banders was another fascinating case study. The marks on her soul were a true mishmash of self-determination at war with the different fates the world had tried to hone her for. Not just the regular death-trajectory that army life tended to give people, but a whole murkiness buried in her past. And Alv said, yes, she saw, and it was good that Banders was back with them. And that was a cold fish response obviously, and Banders was underwhelmed by it. If Alv had been more whole then doubtless she'd have had more chivvying and jibing in her. Right now, Alv knew she looked like something exhumed from a tomb and coming after the graverobbers, so Banders held off on the bonhomie.

"Good to see you on your feet again, anyway." Retreating from things she couldn't easily mock. Then Masty was looking Alv's way. Just a nod, because he knew she wouldn't want to make a fuss, or have one made over her. Masty always understood. He always wanted to be helpful, and he'd worked out that sometimes the best way to help her was not to put her in his debt by helping her.

Banders flung her arms about Cosserby as well, which left him shades of pink which brought a smile even to Alv's blistered lips. She'd been driving on with her story all the way, now, and it had gone beyond monstrous war-beasts to nighttime escapades, ambushes, miraculous escapes. It sounded like the whole Loruthi army had been chasing them around.

Laboriously, Alv limped over to where Lochiver was sat, on the basis that nobody really wanted to be that close to him, so there was an enviable calm in his immediate environs. The old man looked sidelong at her, hands still fidgeting away at the nascent flute.

"You look like you'll be getting orders from Prassel any moment," he cackled. "How are your legs?"

"You will damn well *not*, I *told* you!" As though Tallifer had some secret sense when it came to Lochiver's nonsense.

He rolled his eyes. "Bloody woman doesn't understand how much this *hurts*." Not even thinking about how that *hurt* would be Alv's, if she freed him from it. Which meant it was an act that would buy off the biscuits and a miscellany of other debts. Which meant that, in a day or so, she'd find a chance to get Lochiver out of Tallifer's eyeshot, and rebreak her own leg to free him up to go clean up the camp with his filthy god.

But not right now. Not feeling the wreck of her own body so keenly. Her own weakness disgusted her, but she felt that one more vicarious injury would break her.

The Butcher cooked for them that evening. Not the grand feast they'd had before the disastrous battle, but enough. Sitting in a circle on crates full of drugs and ceramics, eating off tin plates balanced on their knees. A thick-gravied stew with chewy dumplings and pickled vegetables and a mesh of pulled meat like spiderwebs holding it all together. Fresh flatbreads from the mess tent commissary. A single orange each, which the native Pals segmented and wiped up the dregs of the gravy with, and everyone else ate separately afterwards. And it was all of them together again. After all that had happened, it seemed like a miracle beyond gods or Divinati magic, that the same people were sitting down for a meal now, that had been around then. Plenty of other departments and squads around the camp wouldn't have the same luxury. Another debt to the universe waiting to be paid off with interest. And Alv found herself unkinking, just a little. Making the cardinal mistake of relaxing in this company. Remembering how it was to have friends. Hearing Banders tell the story of their escape again, now with two hundred per cent added incident. Watching various of the company take the moment to decant some small portion of their repast to the side, for their own votive purposes. Just *being*. Being, in their midst. Being a part of them, she who shouldn't ever have been anything to do with this unruliness, this imbalance. Feeling the tug inside herself, the hooks and bonds that tied her to them even though she'd tried to walk through the chaos of this life without making any connection at all. The love she felt despite herself, that she hated herself for.

"It wasn't like that," said Maric Jack, at the most outlandish new claim in Banders's account. And a faint edge of panic that told Alv that maybe it *had* been something like that, and he really didn't want anybody to focus on it. But whatever had him riled up, it was so buried in the sky-castles Banders was busy building that nobody would be picking it out.

Then Prassel rapped a spoon against her cup. She'd been there from the start this time. A silent presence at the periphery of the meal, eating with one hand as she leafed through some papers. Now the fact of her fell on the rest of them like shackles, and their cheer ebbed away piece by piece until nothing was left but a fearful attention.

"Technically this is for release tomorrow but I may as well tell you now," said Fellow-Inquirer Prassel. Said their commanding officer, the director of the asylum, the woman who held the Butcher's leash. And Alv found herself thinking, *Why? Why not tomorrow? Why spoil tonight with whatever this is?*

"Orders are in," Prassel explained to them flatly. "For the whole Battalion. Uncle had all the department heads in earlier. Word from on high." Looking about their seated circle as though using her necromantic arts to drain all the fun from the evening. "We're moving out."

"Damn, how bad did they hit us back there?" Banders demanded, entirely out of turn, mulishly adding, "Magister," when Prassel's stare found her.

"It's not that. There are two more battalions on the way and the army proper will be smashing right back into the Lor positions soon enough. But this isn't the only war front and someone in their wisdom wants Forthright elsewhere right now. We're someone's reinforcements."

"Where?" the Butcher asked, a dripping segment of orange partway to his lips.

"Precise destination's under wraps, but overseas," Prassel said. "We're stepping up the pressure on the Loruthi holdings out there, probably to stop them concentrating so much force here. You know the dance."

Alv did, or at least she'd scraped together a rudimentary idea of how these things worked. Much of the time the Pals were bringing a fraction of their force against some small state – like Maric Jack's homeland, say. In which case the campaign would just be an advance in stages, like the coils of a snake tightening on a rat. The Loruthi had a trade empire, holdings and outposts and colonies. The Pals were fighting them here, trying to push the lines towards the actual borders of Lor, but there were plenty of other places that they were spending their blood and magic on.

"Well that's..." The Butcher weighed the news. "That's all right, then." And, with that assessment, a wire of tension was cut and the cheer began to build again. Because they'd been waiting for the order to go back in, to end up slogging over that same hand's span of contested ground for days or weeks or months as the casualties piled up. Hell's grand tour of the provinces with no end in sight. But this meant a reprieve. It meant they'd have a chance to remember the people they were, before they had to be soldiers again. Prassel sat back and let the babble rise, deflecting any further questions by saying she'd told them all she could. Alv wondered, if the news really had been as bad as everyone had been waiting for, whether she'd have told them here and now, or left it for the morning. And if Prassel had been a more consistent leader then she'd have been able to guess, but you never knew just what balance of malice and consideration you'd get, with Fellow-Inquirer Prassel.

Later, much later, the long night well into its march and most of the department sleeping the sleep of the well-fed, Alv left her tent. Sleep was a thing for people who didn't sit at the fulcrum of the universe, after all. Sleep was also a thing for people recovering from a dozen separate injuries, whether or not those injuries were truly their own. Tallifer would have told her to sleep. Alv would have told someone else to sleep, in her position. But she didn't want to. It felt as though she was losing pieces of her life, even though they were pieces she didn't have any use for.

She wasn't the only one still awake. The lean-to that Cosserby had claimed was lit from within and she could hear a subdued clatter and rasp of metal as he caught up with his maintenance. She thought about imposing herself on him, but he was busy and she would be in the way. And he wasn't someone to whom she had much to say. A relative newcomer, a specialist in an art she had no real understanding of. One of these new Pal areas of study that didn't care how they fit into the universe that had come before. And yet the world went on and the Pals kept winning, on the whole, in aggregate, no matter how heedlessly they changed things. It made her fear for her worldview, that was so concerned with altering as little as possible.

There was someone else, though. Sitting on a crate and staring into the relative quiet of the nocturnal camp. Maric Jack, his box on his lap. She couldn't quite see his gods, but she could see the complex twist of obligations that bound him to them, and vice versa.

Not hard, to ensure her halting footfalls reached him before she did, so he had a chance to avoid her. He just looked up, though. The tablethi-charged lamps of the camp gave his face a corpse's pallor. He had been brutally wounded, they'd said – struck down by this beast she hadn't seen. Except that had been neatly excised from Banders's wild account, the cracks of it plastered over by ever-more unlikely details until nobody had asked. And there was more, she could see. Jack was like a man on a scaffold, waiting for the trapdoor to open.

"May I?" she asked, and he pulled a camp stool over, rising to help her down into it. For a moment they just looked out into the camp, tracking the occasional sentry or eleventh-hour messenger, heading distant challenges, a faint peal of laughter from some group of soldiers still burning the last of their lamps.

"Tell me," she said. He looked at her, or at the bandages and pain that was most of what she had on display.

"Tell you what?"

"You can tell me," she said. *Please tell me*, she thought. And she didn't want to know. It was nothing to her. But she could recognise in him the desperate need to unburden himself, and it was a burden she could take on that wouldn't even leave a scar. It would be paying off her debts.

"You do the balance thing, right?" he said.

The one thing she didn't want to talk about was *her*, but she made herself nod.

"There were Divinati in Ilmar. Just a few. Kept to themselves but I picked up a little. Balance. I always thought that sounded like a good scam, honestly."

She cocked her head, just enough to keep him talking.

"Only I think I see now, how it's screwed up. Because I've done a thing, and it's going to get undone. Really, nastily undone. Balance, right? Leave the world like you found it. Only if you found it dying and bleeding, then... then what have you gained, right? Except, in the meantime, you get to *know* those people, those people who would have just been meat. You made them back into people and they became people you got attached to. Possessive about, almost. Because you've brought them back from the meat. And they'll just be meat again. Any moment. Maybe it's already happened. And I knew how this went, but this is an *army*." As though she might not have noticed. "We're in a *war*. Which means it's going to keep happening. Because it's that or I just don't help. But what do you do when helping doesn't help? It just gives you a chance to get to know people so it hurts more when everything... balances out?" And he jerked his head down towards the box and hissed, "Don't you dare. Don't you dare I-told-you-so to me. What am I supposed to do? Just not help people?" His voice breaking into ragged pieces he couldn't hold together.

Whatever inaudible reply he received, something went out of him. He'd been spoiling for a fight with the little nothing in the box, and now that was gone. "Welcome to your world, right?" he said softly, and then bent over the box. She thought he was praying at first, then understood that he was crying silently, tears falling into the little pigeonholes. And perhaps that, too, was a fit offering.

Very carefully, like someone petting a dog that might bite, she laid an arm about his shoulders. Her hand was still mangled, so she couldn't really hold him, or give much of anything, as comfort went, but it was a human contact. It would help him, hopefully. She sat there, feeling him shake slightly as he fought to get himself under control. Trying to imagine the debt she owned to the universe and the Pal army shrinking by this meagre act of camaraderie. And everyone here was so broken, each in their different ways, that surely she should be well into credit with this sort of act. Except she was the most broken of them all, and she'd never be quits with the world and never go home.

She did sleep a little after that, just so she could tell Tallifer she had. The morning light woke her, for the first time since they'd got her back from the battlefront. That and Banders's braying voice.

"Oi oi, Jack!" she was shouting. "Get your arse out here. You need to see this! Believe me, it'll make your eyes pop out."

That didn't seem to be much of an incentive, Alv considered. The whole department was awake now, though, because Banders only really had conversational and top-of-the-lungs in her vocal range. Alv sat up, feeling all the inherited aches that little bit further away.

Jack was indeed on his feet by the time she got out into the open. Just about everyone was, even Lochiver, hanging between two crutches like they'd beaten him up and were dragging him before an Inquirer. They were looking up because, even if you had seen this before, it was still a sight.

Jack's face was utterly scrubbed of all the hurt and misery he'd been wallowing in the night before. Banders was beside him, jabbing him with her elbow, telling him that, wasn't she right? Wasn't this worth getting up for. He stared up, simultaneously aghast and gripped by an unwilling wonder. Because, when the Pal army decided to throw its back against a task, it could move mountains.

Or islands, because that was what they were looking at. An island, slowly descending from a clear dawn sky. A half-mile flattened disc of rock, its underside studded with gleaming crystal stelae, drifting impossibly towards them. And out towards the fringes of the camp, soldiers running and reaching as lines were thrown down from above, to secure the whole inconceivable bulk as though a fresh wind might just blow it away like a dream.

"They don't waste time, do they?" the Butcher boomed.

"What the hell am I looking at?" Jack asked wildly.

"That," Ollery told him, "is our ride. That's what's taking the whole of Forthright across the sea."

Uptime, Downtime

One day it will all be gone, this halfway world. Or what will not be gone will come with certificates from the Schools and wear a uniform with all the buttons done up right. But in this protracted twilight before the dawn of global Perfection, there persist these half measures. Of which the islands of the Galletes are surely the most spectacular.

Former Cohort-Broker Banders took a deep breath, finding the air pleasantly chill after months of muggy warmth on the Loruthi front.

"This," she said, "is the way to travel. If I make Sage-Broker I'll have one of these for my personal use. Scholarly retreat, you know?"

"And then when you're Former Sage-Broker they can throw you off the edge of it," the Butcher remarked. "Are you counting those or not?"

Banders looked down at the box of bandages. "Not," she decided. "I mean, it's full. You could maybe fit three more bandages in there all neat-like without squashing stuff. So how many's it supposed to have, and it's that-many-minus-maybe-three. Chief, relax."

The Butcher turned his best piggy glare on her, but the waxy tint to the skin around those eyes robbed them of their power. He sat back and replaced the lid on the box he'd been going through.

"I mean they'll have stuff when we get there," Banders said. "And short of mutiny we're not going to need them in the air."

The words *in the air* had the intended effect of worsening his pallor.

"I know a man over at Confiscations who's got a little box of bezoar specials," she told him. "Box about yay big, sounded half full when he rattled it at me. Nothing for sky-sickness like bezoar specials."

She had all the fun of watching him – master of all he surveyed most of the time – wrestling with his pride before saying, "If he'll part with them for something within reason."

"I shall go and extend the hand of Correct Exchange to him," Banders said sweetly. "Or I would if I didn't have to count all these bandages."

"Get out," he said, and she did.

They hadn't set up the hospital, of course. No point and no room. A whole battalion covered almost the entire spare ground of the Gallete, as these things were known. Named after the people who'd built or found or repurposed them, and who probably hadn't originally intended them for Pal troop transport. But that was army ingenuity for you. You found a use for anything the Inquirers hadn't set fire to yet, and you used it until it got too hot to handle.

Like the hospital. Banders knew as well as anyone that, just because it had worked so far, didn't mean the next Professor-Inquirer with big ideas wouldn't shut it all down and excise any mention of the project from the records. But until then...

The rest of the department didn't get their regular tents and haunts, but were crammed into one end of a big dorm tent along with a whole bunch of regulars. Banders, strolling in, almost ran into Tallifer storming out. The woman's face looked fire at all concerned, pushing through a rabble of soldiers half in and half out of uniform. Who were wondering what had the old woman riled. And, because the old woman was also a foreigner and an Accessory, that might lead some of them to be over-bold in finding out. Banders helpfully took it on herself to announce loudly, "Time of the month!" Which should get sympathy from around a third of them, and not-wanting-to-know from the rest.

At the back of the tent, Lochiver was dancing a little jig about the beds. Alv, in contrast, was sitting on one of the bedrolls, splinting her own leg with only a little wincing. Banders dropped to one knee beside her and helped, holding the brace steady until the Divinati's fingers – mostly healed now – had secured it.

"You are so the soft touch," Banders said.

"I am paying my dues," Alv replied.

"Nobody owes that capering turd anything," Banders said. "Although this does mean he won't be constantly on at me for pills so I guess I owe you one."

Alv winced and her shoulders sagged, but probably that was just the pain of her newly broken leg.

Beyond her, sitting on his own mat and staring at the back of the tent, was Jack. "Oi oi," Banders called to him. "Oi, Maric. Come get some air."

"I'm fine thanks," he said, sounding strained. "I'm fine right here. I'll just be looking at this stretch of canvas."

"Come take a walk," she invited. "My treat."

"No I – what does that even mean?" That at least had him twist around to look at her. She had seen less miserable corpses fished from rivers.

"You never said you were scared of flying." She prodded him in the shoulder.

"I never flew before."

"Look, come actually *see*. You'll feel better."

"I don't want to…" His eyes ferreted around, hunted. "I don't want to fall off," he whispered.

"Jack, it's, like, the size of a phalanstery and grounds out there. We won't go near the edge, I promise."

"But what if I… fall. Through? Just… down."

"Through this?" She stamped, making him wince. "Jack,

it's solid rock. It's like a hundred, two hundred feet of rock. Compared to boats this is safe as houses."

"Well I don't really like boats either, but at least you can try to swim."

"Can you swim?" she asked him. It was just about universal with any Palleseen born to the Archipelago, but she understood most foreigners couldn't. And indeed here was Jack, shaking his head, and she said, "Well then you may as well try to fly if you fall off. Come on, Jack. You know what we've *not* got, up here?"

"What's that?"

"The war."

He blinked, raised his eyebrows. "Fair point."

"You won't need the box," she pointed out, when he started to shrug it on. And the jury was out, with the department, as to whether it did anything, or whether it was Jack himself, but all Banders knew was it creeped her out. "Alv'll look after it, won't you Alv."

"I would be happy to," the Divinati said. "I'm not going anywhere, after all."

For a moment Jack looked guilty, then he looked guilty *and* sneaky, and he put the box back down. When he came with her out of the tent he was like a kid sneaking out on teacher. Banders grinned delightedly.

"Behold," she told him. "Gallete Thema."

"Goyetter?" was his best attempt at it. She tried to correct his pronunciation two or three times before admitting that, as a Pal, she was probably mangling it herself.

He shrank back from the nearest edge. "I like my landscapes with a bit more horizon."

"Nah, just like being up a mountain."

"I've never been up a mountain. I mean, we *have* mountains. Ilmar's right up against some. But we don't live up them, and part of that is because you can fall off."

"I have stood right there." She indicated the very skirt of rock before the open sky. "Looked down. Bloody rush like you wouldn't believe." And, seeing him about to bolt back inside the tent, "But we're not doing that. Come have a stroll. You want a bezoar?"

"I don't know. Do I?"

"Takes away the queasy," she told him. "I need to get some for Ollery. You can have one for free if you keep me company."

That obviously sounded good to him, and so they wove through the tight-knit mesh of tents and tables and crowded spaces, Forthright Battalion in transit, half still in its boxes. And, beyond the intricate tessellation of tents and tarpaulin-shrouded supply caches, the houses. Jack stopped when he saw them. Houses, slant-roofed, brick-built, set in a careful tiering of gardens. People, not in uniform but wearing long tunics and coats and flap-eared hats. They didn't stare back, but tilled at their little plots and hunched their shoulders against the scrutiny. A hamlet, a whole village of them. Twenty, thirty extended families, a few hundred people. Here on an island that was coursing through the sky to the orders of the Palleseen.

"All right," Jack said evenly. "And they are?"

"Galletes," she told him. "Also, Accessories like you. All happy parts of the Sway, right? These are their islands. They let us use them."

He shot her a look. "Let you, is it?"

"Oh, what? They get to keep doing what they do, and they get to be useful. Better than the alternative, right?"

She didn't like his look, which suggested the alternative was to be left alone entirely, or that the Palleseen Sway not exist. "Are you *judging* me, Jack? No bezoars for judgy people." And, when he didn't smile. "Oh, don't be like that." Remembering, belatedly, that his card had said something about revolution back where he came from. "Look, you're here, they're here, I'm here, we're all making the best of it, right."

His eyes dropped. "I'm sorry. You're right."

"Right I'm right," she agreed, and put an arm about his

shoulders. "Look, we went through something, back there, didn't we? You, me and Masty?"

"We did that," he agreed weakly.

"We deserve a break."

"That would be nice."

"Come on, let's get the Butcher's special in, and then we'll see what there is to do on this rock."

The promised box of bezoars procured, raided for Jack and then delivered, she tracked down Masty and recruited him too. He fussed a bit about having things to do, but in truth there was a limit to how many times you could take inventory before it drove you mad.

"You," Banders told him, "have earned a good time."

He gave her a look. "Do you have any idea what that sounds like?"

She smirked. "You already set me straight on that one year before last, Masty. Like me as a friend, I remember. Like a sister to you, was it? Like a dear auntie who looks after your best interests."

"I mean my sister used to pull my hair," Masty said, with a somewhat hollow smile she was about to take him up on, except Jack had a weird look now as well.

"What?"

"In Ilmar," he told her, "We say Auntie – *piutarma*, you know – for someone who runs a gang. Like a criminal boss. I was just thinking, you'd make a good one."

That was worth a good laugh, and the good laugh covered over the bad feeling that talking about Masty's family probably hadn't been the best idea. Given he'd been snatched by the army when he was, like, seven or something, and just maybe he'd had the treat of seeing his blood relatives shot right before that. All water under the bridge but there were a few memories left, no doubt.

"Let's get bladdered," she said.

"Uncle's rules," Masty countered. "It's a dry camp. Doesn't want anyone walking home the long way after one too many."

"Ah fuck," Banders said. "Also, like hell it's a dry camp. Give me three questions and five minutes and I'll find out who's got a barrel under their bunk." But that did mean that getting properly lathered and then playing Awkward Questions with the new boy wasn't going to happen. She could find them a decent nip of something to take the edge off, but too much of a risk to get thoroughly insensible and end up on a charge.

"Who," Jack demanded, as she changed direction impulsively and dragged them through the camp, "is Uncle?"

"Higher Orders," Masty explained, the pair of them hurrying to keep up. "Specifically, Sage-Monitor Runkel. Which is perfect, really. Because 'Uncle' was always Pal soldier's cant for whoever's in charge, but then he came along and the name just clicked."

"That's the general?"

"I mean, that's what you savages'd call it," Banders allowed. "The man in charge of the Battalion, anyway. He must be chewing his lips off right now."

"I don't even know what you mean by that," Jack complained. "I thought the point of Pel was that it made everything clear."

"Yeah, so did my teachers at the orphanage," Banders agreed cheerily. "I mean, he got a bloody nose back there. He'd have wanted to stick around long enough to push back, just to salve his permanent record. Instead of which he's stuck on this island heading who knows where, off to support who knows who. And the Lor business is where the big medals will get handed out. Whoever's boots get onto Loruthi soil first is guaranteed a professorship back home. This overseas business is just garnish and starters."

"Less intense?" Jack asked. "Less work for us?"

Banders and Masty exchanged looks. "Yeah," she said. "You hold onto that thought. Let it keep you warm at night. Time enough for reality when we get wherever, right?"

Then her ears had picked up a raucous cheer from somewhere across the sea of tents. And, if it wasn't actually a drunken revelry, it was at least someone having a good time. She diverted again and they jostled into a crowd of soldiers in their shirtsleeves, sitting and standing and sneaking the occasional contraband flask about. Because someone was doing a play.

Plays were, of course, permitted. So long as the text was authorised by Correct Appreciation as being properly educational and informative, and supportive of the ideals of Perfection. There were various mass-printed booklets distributed by the Schools. Those who wrote them and censored them and handed them out did so in the strict understanding that they were wholesome, moral scripts that could serve as an antidote to foreign strangeness and turpitude.

And *then*, the soldiers got hold of them, and actually put on a play. It was, Banders considered, one of the great artistic forms. Not drama per se, but the way that a properly motivated pack of troopers could take that philosophy and make it a thing of filth, innuendo and ripe humour without changing *one word*. Gesture, inflection, impromptu costuming and some fairly risqué business turned the most well-meaning instructional parable into a spectacular piece of ribaldry. She loved it.

Masty was at least chuckling along, because he'd been with the army long enough to get all the jokes. And a chuckle was all you ever got from Masty. Jack just sat there blankly, occasionally asking questions like, "Why's that one got a carrot?" or "Was that supposed to happen, where she fell over?"

And then, "I can't even understand what that one's saying. He's just saying, 'hooley-hooley-hailey' all the time."

Banders opened her mouth to explain and then her brain caught up and beat the words back hurriedly. "Oh it's, um, you wouldn't get it."

Jack glanced around. "I mean everyone else gets it."

Banders looked to Masty for help but he was avoiding her gaze.

"I mean it's…" Banders tugged at her collar. "He's, er, pretending to be, you know… Maric."

"He's… what?"

"Maric, okay. His character is supposed to be a Maric. I mean I'd have thought you could tell from all the baggy clothes he's wearing."

"We don't – that's not how people dress where I come from. Did you – that wasn't what I was wearing, when you first saw me."

She shrugged. "I mean, a bit."

"And I don't sound like that."

"I mean, you do sound like that."

"What, hooley-hooley-hailey?"

"I mean, a bit." She shrugged. "Look, you speak decent Pel but still… I mean I *like* it. It's kind of weird and exotic. But it does make it hard to know what you're saying sometimes."

He shared out his stock of aggrieved looks between her and the stage, where the cod-Maric was trading a purse of money for a wooden fish. "What the… what is even happening now?"

Hoping he meant the play rather than life in general she said, "Well, they've told him that this is a magic fish and he's desperate to get it off them, so he gives them all his money, because…" And again, belatedly, her brain intervened and she petered off into, "You know."

Jack gave her the sort of reproachful look she usually only got from teachers and superior officers. "Well, I *don't* know."

"Because…" She squirmed. "Marics are, er," and as though if she mumbled it quickly then it wouldn't count, "greedy and gullible."

He stared.

"Look, it's just a play. It's meant to be funny. Everyone's laughing."

He stared, not laughing.

"I bet you have loads of jokes you make about Palleseen."

He stared, and she had a profoundly uncomfortable moment where she could see what she'd just said from his perspective. The man who'd been taken up for resisting in an occupied city, amongst other and less comprehensible crimes. Probably not the jokiest place, where he came from. Probably they saved their breath for curses, where the Pals were concerned.

"Look," she said, working towards anger and simultaneously knowing that it wasn't her who should be angry – which just made her angrier. And she got angry quickly, and calmed down quickly, and had learned at cost that other people didn't just put things behind them and move on the way she did. She'd lost friends that way, and right now she was going head-to-head with Jack. And he was a foreigner and they were surrounded by soldiers.

"It's fine," he said. "This is the way things are now. I just… forgot. Because…" Because he'd been within the hothouse confines of the hospital department, where things weren't quite army standard. And Banders examined the fine head of anger she'd been about to vent, and let it go like poisoned dust sifting between her fingers.

"I'm sorry. This is a crap play. Let's—"

"I'm fine," he said, sounding more like he meant it. "Come on, I want to see how it ends."

"You haven't followed a moment of it, have you?"

"I mean, no, not as such. But I want to see *that* it ends. I don't want to go to bed tonight and have nightmares about this nonsense still going on."

It was, she had to admit, a fantastically graceful climbdown, and one he probably shouldn't have had to make. But, like he said, it was the way things were. He had a place, and however unjust that was, it was something he needed to remember. Or else he'd be getting himself arrested a *second* time and how daft would that be?

He laughed, right at the end, when the nasal-voiced superior officer's breeches fell down when he was giving his triumphal speech. Some things, Banders decided, were universal.

When the play was done, there was an enterprising quartermaster's clerk frying heavily spiced strips of meat on a griddle, and they ate them off sticks. Not Pal cuisine, but a Shen custom the army had picked up and run with because you could basically do it anywhere you had a fire.

"You eat so much meat," Jack said. Not a complaint, given how he was wolfing it down, but apparently Maric cuisine was heavy on the veg.

"And cook it to death," Masty added, tucking in with similar gusto. "There was a soup, at the Battalion command dinner. I was serving for Prassel. Crunchy fried soup. I swear."

They ate, and wandered, and found a star-shaped piste where some of the officers were sparring, some formal contest they'd organised for their own entertainment. Companions and Fellows, mostly Correct Conduct but with a few from the other schools. It struck Banders as a weirdly antique thing, the sort of practice that the next batch of revisions from the Commission of Ends and Means might do away with. Officers didn't need to be good with a sword, after all. Good with orders and, if it came to it, maybe good with a baton. The days of armies clashing blades were long gone, and those of single combat between champions had probably never existed. Yet here was an echo of all that fool's business at the very heart of the army, as a succession of the erudite and authoritarian stripped down to their shirts to prod each other with blunted blades.

They watched a little. Banders had a good eye for form, and won more than the cost of the meat skewers. It wasn't as entertaining as the play, though, and they were about to head off when Prassel stepped up.

"Oh, now," Banders murmured. "Hold on, this might be something."

Their commanding officer jammed the end of her sword in

the earth to re-secure her hair in its tight bun, her face without expression. A lean man was waiting at the other end of the piste, rolling one shoulder and then the other, but just as Prassel reclaimed her weapon, someone new stepped up. Maserley, having a brief word with her opponent, then taking his place. The demonist stripped off his jacket and handed it over to his succubus. As sweet a piece of poisoned meat as anyone ever dangled, that one. A thoroughly non-regulation adornment to the man's uniform, but Maserley was a law unto himself, like most conjurers. The trade bred a certain attitude.

The adjutant called out the count and they squared off against one another. The crowd had hushed. The enmity between the pair was known across the battalion and everyone loved a grudge match. Especially this one, because both of them were a bit beyond the pale. The necromancer and the demonist, purveyors of suspect goods.

Prassel struck first and almost had him. Maserley backpedalled halfway to the end of the piste, then recovered, capturing the initiative somehow and driving her off. They were fighting to the compass, as the tradition went, circling round each other, launching into a new exchange each time they aligned with an axis of the star, circling again when the aggressor was pushed back to the centre. A ritual combat designed to be performed in the round.

Banders spotted quickly that Maserley was cheating. Cheating in a way that probably only another demonist could have called him on, which left him in sole charge of the field because there wasn't another in the battalion. Something was up with his sword, though. She wished she had Alv here, because Divinati eyes could see all sorts of goblins invisible to regular sight. She glanced at her companions, and they were both frowning a little.

It was Jack who said, "He's bound something into his sword, do you think?"

"You ever hear of that?" Banders asked.

"Old Allor stories," he said. "They put demons in everything back in the day."

"I guess back then it was worth it. Got you a long way, a demon sword. Nowadays, what's the point?"

"Cheating," Masty said.

Maserley's sword, hand, arm and the rest of him were all moving with a jumpy unpredictability, as though each one had a separate fighter directing it. He had Prassel on the hop for three points of the star, forcing her into a tight, defensive game each time he attacked. There was sweat on his brow, but he was grinning. Less a fighter and more an owner of gladiators watching his champion get some exercise.

Prassel stayed calm, though. No sweat there. Banders wasn't sure that the woman even could. And why the Fellow-Inquirer had decided to make this skill her practice, or whether she just had some innate and out of character gift for it, who knew? But Banders had seen the woman on the piste before, and Prassel was *good*. Disciplined, economic, her sword whickering through the air, cutting the world into neatly manageable segments so that none of Maserley's ventures got within three inches of her, foxing him in the bind so that abruptly she had the inside line and he was giving ground again. Her face was devoid of expression. Yet she gave and gave again, each axis of the star Maserley's to command, hers only to defend.

Until.

Banders saw it before it happened, the shift in her stance. The scholar who has learned all she needs to know. And the next time they circled to an axis Prassel stepped forwards a very precise distance and prodded Maserley in the chest, almost gently, his own blade kept out of the way by the angle of her strike. She stepped back, fell into readiness with the cynicism of someone who knew her opponent would strike before she was ready if he could get away with it.

Maserley took it in his stride, nodded to acknowledge the hit, stepped back and then went back in.

She did it again, the exact same step in, the prod to the chest, as though they were walking through what had happened before so as to understand the exchange.

Maserley's nod, this time, had a bit of the snarl to it. They reset. When they clashed again he stepped out from the lunge he expected, stepped back in to retake the initiative. Except Prassel had just stood still, saving her lunge for his advance. This time her sword bent against his chest with the force of his step and he hissed and stumbled sideways.

There was a little cheering. Three strikes was the win. Then there was a great deal more cheering, albeit localised to Banders and Masty and maybe Jack a bit, too. And then considerably less because Maserley had looked over at them, and there was the promise of fire and demons in his glower. Suddenly having the malign attention of the battalion's only demonist didn't seem such a grand idea.

Prassel had already shrugged her jacket on, receiving the compliments of a couple of her peers as though she hadn't wanted them and didn't have anywhere to put them.

"I suppose," Banders speculated, as they walked away, "you can put all the demons you want into a sword. Doesn't mean they know crap about fencing."

It was getting dark by then, and Banders rubbed her hands together and cast about to see where the lights of the Gallete village were. "Time to dip our wicks, I reckon."

"What now?" Jack asked.

"What?" Banders raised her eyebrows. "I mean I *know* you weren't getting any in the camp, Jack. Mother Semp said you hadn't even used her services when you were with her."

"I... you... what?" he demanded. "Are you talking about—"

"She means—" Masty started, and Jack hastily waved him to silence.

"I *know* what she means, thank you. I mean... what?"

Banders frowned. "I mean it's something you Marics *do*, right? You don't, what, lay eggs or poop out sex bees or something?"

"I, we, yes, we... *sex bees?* Is that a thing?"

Banders shrugged. "Dunno. Might be. Somewhere. Look, it's simple. There are way too many soldiers on this rock, and suddenly they're not fighting anyone, so it's basically nature."

"Are you saying this island is a flying brothel?" Jack demanded.

"Not *just* that," Banders said. "But, look, there's always some house where a bunch of nice-looking Galletes are very keen to take some army pay in return for... services." And despite the dark she could see his expression. "Or, you know, you could probably have a nasty-looking Gallete if you asked. Damn, Jack, are you *judging* again? Look, nobody rounds them up and marches them out there at baton-point. It's free money for an hour lying down. Or five minutes, depending on the caller." He was still staring, and obviously Banders didn't know what would happen if there was some Gallete village that *didn't* fancy its youngsters putting out for the army. Probably nothing good.

"Look, it's just..." she said. "I mean, it's not as though I've got..." Because sometimes there was someone in the battalion, for a little while, until the inevitable falling out. "I'm not defending myself to you, Maric. You can hooley-hooley-hailey at me all you want."

For a moment she thought that was it. Bridges burned and one more person who had finally got sick of Former Cohort-Broker Banders. Then he laughed. Not exactly a happy laugh. Desperation and horror and despair somehow getting together and making the sound between them. But a laugh even so and she was powerfully glad of it.

"Look," he said, "I can't."

"I mean you can watch, but you still have to pay."

"No, I mean. It's forbidden."

She considered that. "I mean, technically, by very strict army rules, probably yes. But that's the kind of regulation that only marches on paper, if you know what I mean—"

"No, I mean. I can't. I'm a priest. I'm forbidden."

She actually stopped dead so that Masty walked into the back of her. "What, never?"

"I mean it wouldn't be much of a forbiddance if it was only every third day or something."

"Wait, look, when you got brought in you were pretty clear you weren't actually a priest any more," she pointed out.

He looked as though he felt this was a fine time for her to demonstrate a perfect memory for detail. "Yes, all right, technically that is the case, but…"

"Come get the sanctity rubbed off," she offered. "Come lose your theological cherry. Show Higher Orders you've cast off the shackles of outdated superstition." She registered the expression, the inward way he was holding himself. "I'm sorry, Jack. I'm not making fun. Talk to me."

He was very obviously not going to, and then Masty put a hand on his arm and that seemed to communicate that he was amongst friends far more than anything Banders could say.

"It's just, all my life I was a priest. And it was forbidden. And I thought that, after I stopped being a priest. Then it would be different. But then I… I went to… there was someone who… and. Couldn't, basically. Because it was still forbidden. In here." A finger to his head. "Sorry. You go on."

Banders opened and closed her mouth. "You poor son of a bitch. Religion really does screw you up, huh? One more reason to bring the Perfection."

"There is literally a two-thousand-page book on proper conduct between the sexes," Masty observed.

"Right, well, maybe some things don't need to be perfected just yet," Banders admitted, and then three large men turned up out of the night and said, "Accessory Maric Jack? You're under arrest."

Jack looked almost relieved. "Ah. Well. Right. Yes. I was expecting this."

"You can't arrest him," Banders told them. "He already got arrested." And as she herself had multiple infractions on her permanent record that wasn't much of an argument. "What for, though? He's been with us all day. He's not had the chance to do anything arrestable yet."

"Murder," said one of the big men, and then all three of them were bundling the unresisting Jack off while she and Masty just stared.

Barracks Law

The Commission of Ends and Means had a weighty book governing how its soldiers were to comport themselves, ninety per cent of which boiled down to Do What You're Told. *The remaining ten per cent was the prey of every bright soldier who reckoned they could get away with something.*

They had told Prassel one of her people was up before the tribunal, and naturally she thought *Banders*. And Banders was in the demoted phase of her life cycle, and normally she had the grace to wait for reinstatement before doing something chargeable. Technically she could be made an Accessory, and that would be a permanent thing, a career life sentence; it didn't seem likely that Banders had done something bad enough to warrant that. You had, as precedent showed, to be pretty damned villainous before someone started personalising the rank structure for you.

Halfway to the tribunal, word reached her that the charge was murder, and naturally she thought *The Butcher*. And stopped, because it wasn't as though the thought had never occurred to her. That this moment might come, when the tenuous arrangements gently dropped into place around the man would fail to hold. Ollery was a good servant, a useful man. Irreplaceable, really. Except what were they supposed to do if he didn't play his part nicely?

The dawn light, up here in the air, was crisp and chill and

clear. She rather liked it. She, too, had gone to the very edge of a Gallete island once. Stood there with the toes of her boots over empty air and looked down. Imagined the advancing shadow the impossible thing cast was the encroach of perfection over the world. Not felt even the slightest urge towards throwing herself off, which all three of her companions of the time had claimed. She wasn't given to morbid fancies. It wasn't advised in a necromancer.

Around her, as she cut her course through the tight-packed camp, people were stirring. Slowly, sluggish with the knowledge that nobody would be attacking and there wasn't free space enough for a surprise muster. Of course, the regular soldiers didn't have the paperwork she did. Which was, presumably, about to be considerably increased because one of her idiot medicos had got themselves in trouble.

Formal army business on the Gallete wasn't conducted out of tents. Instead, some family had kindly donated their house to act as administrative headquarters for the duration of the journey. One of the larger houses, but doubtless the generous donors had kin they could stay with. And honestly, they wouldn't have wanted to share once Higher Orders moved in. Who would cohabit with that much paperwork unless it was part of your job?

Sherm met her outside the door. He was a peer from Correct Speech, another Fellow-Inquirer, though jurisdictionally her senior in any matter not directly involving corpses. A man who'd attached himself to Higher Orders and now performed necessary but unpopular pieces of administration like running disciplinary tribunals. He'd been busy, she guessed. Between a soldier's natural inclination to start acting up the moment a little leisure time presented itself, and Uncle's prohibition on alcohol, the tribunals had probably been running dawn til dusk since the army embarked.

"Is he already in?" she asked him. "May I speak with him?"

"And a good morning to you too," he observed. "No, he's not

in. No, we're not even convened yet. Yes, the army thanks you for your punctuality. Question: would you like some tea?"

"Your messenger gave me the impression that this was an urgent matter for which I was immediately required."

"How very enthusiastic of her," Sherm observed. He was a hollow-cheeked, balding man who'd always been philosophically cheerful about his work, up to and including the cases where he'd sentenced a mutinous prisoner to death. "Well, we all seek perfection in our own way. I can hardly rap her over the knuckles for being slightly more perfect than the moment demanded, can I? And you're here now, so let's have tea and I can tell you how happy I was that you won me thirty shillings on the piste yesterday."

Prassel caught herself about to actually smile and stomped down on the impulse irritably. "Well, tea then," she said with poor grace.

"Licit or Illicit?"

She raised her eyebrows. "Excuse me?"

"Oh the latest dodge. If you put Vhon grain spirit into army tea, you can't smell the difference but it knocks the top of your head off. Spent all yesterday afternoon arguing with some amateur jurisprudent about whether the addition of the tea placed it outside of Uncle's ban. And it didn't get him anywhere but I've marked the man down for watching because that kind of corkscrew mind might make for a good addition to my department. When he's recovered from the lashes, obviously."

"Obviously. And 'licit' tea, thank you very much. I prefer not to imbibe even when it's not expressly banned by my superiors."

Sherm gave a *tsk*ing noise, as though it took all sorts, and if Prassel wanted to go through life with weights on her ankles then she could just watch people like Sherm flying past with their crooked tea and breezy interpretation of the rules.

Inside the house's main room there was tea, as advertised, served up by some clerk of Sherm's department who looked like she'd far rather still be in bed. There was also a big, angry-looking man, uniform straining at every buttonhole, even the collar clasped about his bull neck.

"Fellow-Inquirer Prassel, head of the experimental hospital department," Sherm introduced her. "This is Companion-Monitor Gowry."

"Goffry," the man snapped.

Sherm consulted his day list. "Are you sure? It says Gowry on here and, obviously, these things are never wrong."

His dry humour utterly failed to hit the mark, and there was some wrangling before Prassel got a look at the paper and it turned out the man's name was Goughry, which was a name just begging to be perfected as far as she was concerned. Goughry, she also discovered from the paper, was a department head within Third Company, and apparently he had a dead soldier on his hands.

"Died in a fight," she noted. The details on the incident sheet were incredibly brief. She knew things were a bit unruly, but it seemed scant epitaph for an actual death. As if whoever dictated it had been leaving things out that they hadn't known how to say. But *a fight* wasn't what she had expected. Not exactly the modus operandi of any of her reprobates. And then she twitched the paper out of Sherm's hands entirely and squinted at it. "Wait, it says here, died in a fight with someone called Havery. There's nobody of that name in my department." She fought down her exasperation. "Sherm, is this even anything to do with me?"

"Well I'm afraid it is," he said. "And it's a rum piece of business. As you've doubtless worked out from the gaps in the narrative."

"I have a dead man in my department," Goughry said implacably. "Because of your freaks."

A clerk put his head into the room and signalled. Sherm bolted his tea and palmed off the possibly incriminating cup. "He's coming. Let's convene then. This is going to be a knotty one." In the manner of a man happy to have a little knot to break the tedium of his routine. Prassel, whose routine could use more tedium, rolled her eyes. They took up their position behind a table. No camp stools and folding furniture but actual artisan-made solid stuff for once, courtesy of the Galletes. Sherm took the centre, as the duty Inquirer. Goughry as complainant was to his right, and Prassel, as advocate, on the left.

"Ready!" Sherm called, as though they were calling someone in for a surprise party. She wondered how much tea he'd had.

The man they brought in was, of course, Maric Jack. He saw her and contrived to look embarrassed that she'd been dragged into this. Which wasn't really worth a great deal. He was stood off on her side of the room and Sherm ticked him off. After that another soldier was brought in, a young woman who looked profoundly shaken about something, and who started visibly when she saw Jack. She tried to approach him but got hauled off by her own escort to Goughry's side of the room. Sherm ticked her off, too. Prassel craned over. Apparently this was Trooper Lidlet, for whatever that was worth.

"Very good," Sherm said. "I'm convening us as of now." He nodded to his notary clerk who had already written down the words he'd just said. "Disciplinary tribunal in the matter of Accessory Jack, also known as—" and then the door opened again. Sherm glanced up irritably and then shot to his feet and saluted, and everyone else followed suit a moment later. The man who came in was lean, with a haggard, tired face that seemed to sag slightly, as though the wrong shock could see it sloughing off his skull in an avalanche of tumbled features. Except Prassel knew the man's life had been more than full of shocks received and given, and he'd weathered them all. He was into his sixties now, cropped hair the colour of iron and his eyes utterly joyless. The expression his face settled into was one of general disappointment.

"Magister, I wasn't notified of your interest or I'd have w—"

The newcomer waved Sherm to silence, stepping fully into the room. "Just pretend I'm not here, Fellow-Inquirer," he said in his parched-sounding voice. "Consider me an unofficial observer to proceedings. But I'm told this matter may go beyond the usual bounds of misdemeanour and punishment." And he smiled. Prassel, whose professional speciality meant she had to face up to a variety of unpleasant smile-resembling expressions in her charges, would have traded any of them for this man's. It was the withered and utterly humourless look of a thousand-year-old corpse that had learned about smiling from a badly-translated book. It sucked all possibility of mirth from the room.

This, then, was Sage-Monitor Runkel, officer in command of Forthright Battalion. He took a seat at the edge of Goughry's end of the table and continued to wither them with that utter negation of a smile.

"Ah, well, yes then," Sherm said, writhing in its bleak radiance. "In the matter of Accessory Jack, also known as Havery—"

"No," Goughry said.

"It says clearly that your man died in a fight with—"

"Trooper Havery is in my department. I've already disciplined him for brawling." Goughry frowned. "You should have my report on—"

"Well it's not been attached to this case." Sherm's eyes flicked nervously to Runkel. "Presumably because nowhere does it mention this man as being involved. Did he prescribe this Klimmel some sort of stimulant for the fight, or—"

"He cursed him," Goughry said flatly.

"That is not in my—"

"It is not the sort of thing I would commit to an official report," Goughry stated. He stood, jolting the table, making the wood groan as he leaned on it. "My man Klimmel, and this woman here, Trooper Lidlet, they were cursed by this Maric magician."

Lidlet opened her mouth, but shut it at a glare from Goughry.

"That is," Sherm said, "an *interesting* accusation."

"Lidlet, give them it," Goughry ordered. "As you told me."

The woman hung her head for a moment, then looked up. Her subsequent recital was flat, almost droning. Someone telling not the story of events that happened to her, but the story of the time she told the story of them. How she, Klimmel and another got left behind by the retreat. How they met up with some of the hospital department and together made a run for their own lines. How they were ambushed by Loruthi cavalry scouts. How one had died and how she and Klimmel had both been wounded. And how Jack had stepped in.

"He told us," Lidlet explained, "that if we so much as raised a hand against anyone, we'd get it all back with interest. He told us over and over. We – didn't believe him." A slight catch in her voice, right at the end, that said, *It could have been me. It might still be me.*

Klimmel had got into a scrap with another soldier, this Havery, later. Just the usual sort of thing that wouldn't have troubled Sherm's desk, let alone the Sage-Monitor's. Save that he'd dropped dead on the instant, gutshot, no baton in sight nor sound of one being used. After which Lidlet had let on to what none of the truants had mentioned when they rejoined the army.

"Accessory Jack," Sherm said, and the Maric started. He'd been staring into nowhere while the testimony had been read, looking as miserable as if sentence had already been passed.

"I'm sorry," Jack said. Not exactly the most promising start from the point of view of a woman charged with advocating for him.

Sherm frowned. "Is that a confession? Did you actually curse Trooper Klimmel?"

"What? No. Magister. No, magister. I don't do curses."

"What do you do?"

"I heal, magister," Jack said. "Or, I can make healing happen. But it's complicated. It's conditional. What was I supposed to do?"

"Did you tell them you'd remove your healing if they..." Sherm checked his notes, "harmed anyone."

"It's not like that. It's not something I make happen. It just *does*. It's the way it is." And any moment he'd start babbling about priests and gods and all that heathen stuff, surely, and that would be the end of him. Throwing him off the edge of the island too good a fate. Except he was just about wise enough in the ways of Perfection to let the truth squeak out sideways, with all the godliness washed off it, and for that Prassel was grateful.

"Your actions ensured that Trooper Klimmel was struck down," Goughry said portentously. "You have condemned Trooper Lidlet to a living death."

"I'm sorry," said Jack miserably. "I didn't want to. What was I supposed to do?"

Sherm opened his mouth, but Runkel shifted slightly in his seat, which brought silence.

"What did he think would happen when they were called on to fight again?" he asked, as if he was just posing himself a rhetorical question.

"Well, yes, quite," Sherm said, and then, as if the idea had just occurred to him, "What did you think would happen—"

"I don't know, magister. I wasn't thinking that far ahead. It was just me and them, right there."

"And this isn't even the first incident," Runkel observed to the ceiling.

Sherm had a panicked moment of trying to find evidence for this in his papers and then decided it was Prassel's problem. "I understand this isn't even the first time this happened," he threw at her, in the manner of a drowning man reaching for help.

"That is correct," she admitted. "A casualty believed healed by Accessory Jack also died."

"This doesn't sound like very effective healing. Are you sure he's a good fit for your department?" Sherm asked.

"I understand he's also a good orderly. Bandages and needles and the like," said Prassel, deadpan.

Sherm blinked. "A good *orderly*. Who can also restore people to health from the brink of death. Until, that is, they do anything with that health. I mean, this is ridiculous. What's this Lidlet supposed to do now, except sit under threat of execution? She's a soldier. He's ruined her life."

"I'm sorry," Jack said again, and then, directly to Lidlet, "I'm sorry."

Prassel looked at him sourly. He was, very obviously, a liability who would only become a greater one over time. So much for that. Let him take the fall for this absurd turn of events. Her life and department would be so much simpler going forwards. Except that if she was one thing, it was a pedant, and perfection began at home as far as she was concerned.

"If the tribunal would hear me?" she asked and, at Sherm's nod, "In the matter of this Klimmel's death, there's no case to answer. The man brought about his own demise, judge, accused and executioner in one. So much for that. But I feel—" speaking louder to cover Goughry's expostulations, "I feel that's not actually why we're here." She glanced at Runkel, who looked back stony-eyed.

"The man needs to be made an example of," Goughry said.

"That's the worst possible idea. Better stuff him in a sack and throw him over the side under cover of darkness. Which I feel is not a remedy traditionally open to the tribunal." Said pointedly just in case Sherm had been considering it.

"I don't see why," Goughry said stubbornly.

"I'm standing next to you after they've just socketed Jack's neck," she said pleasantly. "I ask you, 'So, what was that about?' How do you explain this mess, exactly. Is it the bit about how your man died brawling with someone else entirely so the Maric got executed. Or how he's been executed because he wouldn't leave your man's corpse on the field. Which part of that inspires trust and faith in the proper procedures, exactly?"

"It's… the curse…?" Goughry managed to look furious and clueless all at the same time. "But we have to do something. For the look of it."

"That is not a good reason to do anything," Prassel told him flatly.

"And yet this situation cannot continue," Sage-Monitor

Runkel pronounced. "You, Maric. Look at me. This is an army. Do you understand me?"

"Yes, magister," Jack whispered.

"And an army does what?"

"It fights, magister."

"We cannot have our soldiers fearing to fight, because it might bring back their wounds. Where would our morale be? Our spirit. We would have an army of cowards. Fellow-Inquirer Prassel, your tenure at the hospital department, and indeed your department's continuing existence, is predicated on it being a benefit. The moment that is not the case then you will be reassigned, and your department *dissolved*." With an emphasis on the last word that put Prassel in mind of vats of acid.

"Sage-Monitor, while it seems contrary to reason that I instruct a member of the hospital department *not* to use whatever talents he might have for healing, that may be the easiest way out of this."

Jack twitched at the suggestion. She wasn't sure if it was outrage or relief, and possibly he couldn't have told her himself.

Runkel stood. "Clarity and precision as always, Fellow-Inquirer. A satisfactory solution. As for the others, Companion-Monitor, all involved in the brawling incident have been disciplined? And I imagine drink was behind it, in contravention of my orders. Have it looked into. Make sure that everyone involved is too busy cleaning up after themselves to spare this business much thought. For this one," he looked at Lidlet. "I'm not sure what the point of her is. She's probably due her own set of stripes just for being involved. Sometimes the example is all, in matters of wider discipline."

"I'll take them," Jack said. Runkel looked at him as though one of the chairs had ventured an opinion.

"Ten lashes for the Maric," he decided. "For his part in this business. And another two for speaking out of turn. Prassel, you'll deal with it?"

"Yes, magister."

Runkel progressed to the door and then turned to glower at the lot of them.

"Keep this screwed down," he admonished. "Bad for morale, if it got out. Prassel has the right instincts. No grand show. No public execution. Just spread the whip around until everyone has their own backs to think about. Enough of it." And then he was gone.

"Paraphrase," Sherm advised his clerk. "Write it up later in the proper form." He looked brightly from Goughry to Prassel. "Well, wisdom from on high has visited us, and now we, too, are wiser. I think that clears everything up. Thank you for coming, and—"

"What am I supposed to do with *her*?" Goughry jabbed a finger at Lidlet, who was standing as though she was every bit as accused as Jack. "What's the purpose of her now?"

"I suppose that her case will sort itself out the moment we're back in combat," said Sherm philosophically.

"Permission to question the accused, magister," Lidlet herself broke in.

"The accused? Oh, the Maric here. I'd say you've earned the right to slap him about the jaw, but under the circumstances that's probably not recommended."

Lidlet was fumbling a tatter of paper out from inside her jacket. "I've got some questions I wrote down," she said, before Sherm's incredulous stare.

"Good lord," he said. "You made notes. Very diligent. Top of the class. I suppose you'd better go on, then. Be quick. I've got a pair of theft cases before lunch."

"Maric, you said I can't harm anyone or it comes back," Lidlet said, squaring off against Jack. At his nod, she went on, "What if I got someone else to hit you?"

"It still counts," he said dully.

"Does it matter if I pay them or not?"

Jack frowned. "Why would it – no. I mean, harm is harm. The commerce of it doesn't really—"

"What if I threatened you?"

"Does this have to be me, specifically?" he asked plaintively.

"Answer the question," Sherm cautioned him, because apparently this passed for entertainment in judicial circles.

"I don't think threats do it. I mean, I think if you sort of made to hit me, you might feel a bit of a twinge. I've heard that's how it goes. And maybe if you were just pretending then you wouldn't even feel that. And if you lamped me straight out, then... well..."

"All right." Lidlet consulted her notes. She had a peculiarly desperate look to her. "What about if I poisoned someone?"

"That's still harm."

"Okay, so what if I put poison in a cup and," reading her own untidy writing again, "left it somewhere without knowing whether someone would drink from it or not."

"Why would you do that?" Jack demanded.

"Just what if?" she insisted.

"I... don't know. I mean, it's not the sort of thing people do."

"What if I set a trap. Would I die if someone triggered it later, or would it be when I set it?"

"I don't know," Jack repeated.

"What if I set a hunting trap for an animal, but a person fell into it by mistake?"

"I... I really don't know."

"What if I accidentally hurt someone? Like, we're looking out on the edge of the Gallete and I turn round and knock them off without meaning to."

"I... no."

"No?"

"I think. I think intent is the thing. So all of the above, if you know you're going to, or you mean to, then it counts. And if you... don't.... then... not? Possibly not?" He was looking profoundly harried by the line of questioning.

"What if I help someone who goes on to hurt people,

although not through my," consulting her notes again, "express instruction."

"Oh my god, you've really thought about this haven't you?" Jack complained.

"Just answer the question. I mean, do I die the moment they hurt someone, or how does it work? What are the rules?"

"You're fine," Jack told her. "I know this one. Because I healed you, and Klimmel. And I was all broken up not that long before, and I was healed too. So if it worked that way then I'd be just as dead, wouldn't I?"

"So you're in the same boat," Lidlet concluded.

"I suppose I am."

She straightened up. Not, Prassel thought, as if a weight had been taken from her, but as though it had shifted a little, balanced more evenly across her shoulders. "Magister." Addressing Goughry.

Of everyone there, he hadn't really followed the exchange. Now he stared at his subordinate suspiciously. "What is it, trooper?"

"I am requesting a transfer to the experimental hospital department."

"You what?" He stared.

"On the basis that I can perform military duties in support of the army through the hospital. And I cannot do so as a regular soldier any more, magister." She wasn't looking at Goughry, staring straight ahead in the soldier's final defence against just about anything.

Goughry was going to refuse, because he was that sort of officer. But then he must have thought just how it would look, morale-wise, with Lidlet dropping dead the moment the first command to fire was given. Or her refusing, and them being back before the tribunal for her own trial. No good options.

He was loathe to look Prassel's way, but it *was* her hospital.

"Trooper Lidlet, do you have any medical training whatsoever?" she asked.

"Magister, I can carry one end of a stretcher if there's someone to take the other," Lidlet said stoically.

Prassel glanced at Jack. There was a terrible hope in his face. *There is a limit to how many stretcher bearers this army needs*, she considered. *He better not take this as precedent.*

When they stepped out into the open air, though, she was giving orders to report to Banders for the relevant induction. Her department had grown by one.

Mosaic: Aloft

Time in the air. Below them, only sea. A few days of limbo and it says a lot about army life that sometimes limbo's what you need. The war can't reach them. It's packed in the crates and boxes waiting to be unloaded when they touch land.

When Jack comes back from the trial – he still isn't entirely sure if it was his trial or Lidlet's – he finds the box gone. Cue much running around, accusations and panic, until Alv – to whom he'd actually entrusted the thing – produces it on demand. She hid it away, she says, because Fellow-Archivist Thurrel was snooping around. The Decanter, in his jingling vest of charms, turned up with a bold word and a piece of paper sealed with his own signature, telling everyone Jack had been sentenced to death and his effects were property of the army. Alv dumped Jack's box into a larger box and put yet another box on top of it, and sat on that, turning her blistered face to the Decanter when he arrived. And the Pals are leery of Divinati, and Alv is, if not innately magical, then at least the nexus where a great deal of external magic finds its fulcrum, and thus obscured anything the man might have been sniffing for. And so Thurrel departed, frustrated.

Jack stammers his thanks and re-evaluates Alv. Because she's severe and calm and not even remotely the sort to thumb a nose at authority. That's a Banders play, or Lochiver maybe, neither of them respecters of the chain of command. Alv is always compliant and obedient. Except, when it came to the bite of the screw, she stands up – or sits down – for her comrades.

So he takes custody of the box again, seeing his three fugitive gods creep out into the open to stare at him. He takes it to the far end of their dormitory tent, the end claimed by the hospital. He tells God that he has news.

"Look at that big show of relief the man has," God announces, ostensibly to the other two deities. "As though he wouldn't be glad to be rid of us."

"I wouldn't," Jack tells Him flatly, keeping his voice down so that the others in the department – and the soldiers in the bunks beyond – didn't eavesdrop, even though it was Maric he was talking. "Though you give me plenty of reasons why I should."

God puts tiny hands on bony hips. "You hear that?" He remarks to the others. "And who would he get, may I ask, to miraculously restore his warlike soldier friends to health, when they get themselves stabbed and shot and otherwise punctured? Who would he go begging to, for some bona fide divine healing that won't last until dawn because everybody around here is such a damned savage?"

Jack winces. "Well, it's not something you have to worry about now, anyway. Not any more."

"What's that supposed to mean?" God demands. "You developed the healing touch all spontaneous, have you? Or you're seeing some other god behind my back? Because last I looked, Yasnic, I'm the only spark of grace you have in your life. These other two are plain useless."

"It's been forbidden," Jack tells Him.

God's already creased face scrunches up further. "Say what, now?"

"I was on trial," Jack says. "They don't like it. The healing where people can't fight again. I mean, it's an army. There's an… ideological issue there, I guess. So they said, no more. No more turning people into where they're a pacifist or a corpse. So I reckon that's an end to it."

God has a good line in pop-eyed stares. For a merciful healing deity, He spends a great deal of time apoplectically angry. "They said *what?* Forbid me, will they? I am the bloody font of forbiddances. If anybody's forbidding any damn thing around here then it's *Me*. I'm not to be talked down to like that by a pack of Islermen thugs like I'm a part of their bloody chain of command!"

"Pals," Jack puts in, not for the first time. "They've been Pals for, like, centuries. Not Islermen."

But God is far beyond listening to His devotee. "I will bloody well heal who I damn well please!" He spits. "Anyone who swears the oaths, let them be bloody whole. Just you wait until we have another battle, you shrinking milksop. I shall do such miracles as the shrinking eye of humanity has not seen since—"

"Will you just *not!*" And – because it's evening and for some of the soldiers it's been a packed day of getting their jollies – a fair number of people tell him to shut up, and some of them warn him to stop with the filthy foreign lingo or they'll report him. And he doesn't need to be up on a charge so soon after weaselling out of the last one. "I will get shot," he hissed at God, face down close to the box. "And you will get decanted. I am very, very serious."

But God is very angry, and no need to keep His voice down given it reaches only Jack. "I am God, you collaborating little shit! I am the all-powerful healing God and I have had temples and priests and sacrifices, the fires of sandalwood, the sweet incense, fine music played on lyres of griffin-bone with inlays of gold and the fair words of an at least moderately talented bard praising the greatness of my beneficence and I will not be told what to do or not do by some Pal bean counter!"

Jack stares at Him. "What's got into you?" he demands, sotto voce. "You don't even *like* doing it. I had to get on my knees for Lidlet and Klimmel. You say it hurts every time they die. You hate it. You bitch about it. What's this heal-the-world all of a sudden? Even back in Ilmar you never wanted to do it."

God folds His arms defiantly. "Well Ilmar was back *home*, wasn't it. And now we're on the run, you and I. We're fugitives. We're fleeing Pal justice. We're running mad in the world. Why not?"

"We're not any of those things," Jack points out. "They caught us – caught *me*, anyway, and gave me the choice of sign up or swing. On account of the healing that they now won't even let me use. So my position here is pretty damn precarious. And you hate healing people almost as much as you hate people. So knock it off."

"You will not talk to your God like that!"

"I will talk to my fellow *fugitive* like that, who will end up fuelling a score of tablethi if anything happens to me."

God sticks His lip out. "This isn't over," He said. "I will not be constrained by secular authorities."

"You will," Jack tells Him. "That is literally why we're here." But God patently doesn't agree. Jack can only hope that the miniature divinity's ability to directly interact with those in need of healing remains profoundly limited or probably he'll be in trouble sooner rather than later.

"You're just setting yourself up for more pain." He sets the box beside him. "Me, too. I mean I didn't like Klimmel, honestly. But I wish he wasn't dead."

God's drawn Himself up for another broadside, then lets it all out and sits on the box edge, feet dangling. "Aye well, I felt him go. And yes, it hurt. And yes, it was inevitable. I just don't take being dictated to, not by them, not by anyone. If there's any dictating going on, it should be me. I'm God, after all."

Jack nods slowly. "It sounds like Lidlet's going to try and lawyer her way through, though. Honestly, I have some questions about doctrine."

God considers that, heels knocking against the box. "Who the hell is Lidlet?"

This was where things went even further off course than Jack had thought. "The other one you healed, out on the battlefield."

"I thought you said they were dead." God's on His feet again, jabbing a finger into Jack's ribs.

"Klimmel died. Lidlet talked her way into being a stretcher bearer. She's joining us here. So she doesn't have to fight."

And God chuckles in a way that Jack doesn't much like, and after that God doesn't let up about being taken to see Lidlet. Wanting Jack to talk to Lidlet. Wanting Jack to slip snippets of doctrine into the conversation, when Lidlet was around. And after far too much of this Jack works out that God is rather impressed by the lawyering and maybe wants Lidlet as a convert. Literally the first time in Jack's lifelong service to the faith when God actually wants to expand the congregation.

"I mean she's mine now anyway," God insists. "She lives by my beneficence. So why not?"

"Because," and by this time Jack's being loud again, to the annoyance of his neighbours, "she is a *Pal* and they do not take to *religion*. That's kind of their thing." And God continues to insist and Jack continues to refuse until a large Pal soldier, deciding that having a crazy Maric shouting at himself in the dorm tent is also not his thing, evicts Jack unceremoniously out into the evening.

So here Jack sits, he and God not speaking to one another. Follower of a forgotten god, and how many times in his life has he been desperate to share that burden with someone. Back in Ilmar, it had happened occasionally – often not for long given God's punitive stance towards those who bucked His commandments. And that fellowship of faith had never actually brought Jack any real benefits, yet he had still craved it. God's refusal to engage with the world had been only frustrating.

And now God wants to flex His muscles, if only because the Pals had said not to. Jack finds himself terrified that an active, troublemaking God is a far worse prospect than the guttering ember he's been carefully husbanding all his life. What do you do when your insignificant and long-forgotten deity suddenly remembers His own purpose?

When Lidlet turns up, a kitbag slung over her shoulder and asking for Banders, Jack turns away and won't look at her. Not to salve his own conscience, but so he doesn't infect her any further with his curse.

Lidlet has always been career military, because if you're born on the Archipelago it's a good career. See places, meet people, perfect them at the point of a baton. She was never phalanstery material, to be taught the finer points of Correct Thought. She just follows orders. Except, as a long train of superiors would tell you, that's not quite what you get from Trooper Lidlet. Lidlet, it turns out, would probably have made quite a good jurist or critical scholar. Not a corkscrew mind, more a prybar. Good at finding the seams of things and prising them apart in case there's something useful within. Not the soldier always on a charge and in trouble, but the soldier always *almost* on a charge, standing at the very periphery of trouble with the toes of her standard-issue boots edging over the line. For someone with no great amount of book-learning in her past, she has a very good head for rules and how to play them. Because the problem is, when you condense anything down to a set of rules there'll be someone who can game it.

And right now, Lidlet feels she's pulled the ultimate fast one. Lidlet has gamed death. Not that she's the credulous sort but there's precious little leeway in interpreting what happened to Klimmel. She saw him die in the camp of the wound he received days earlier on the field. She herself has a punctured lung on credit, waiting to be delivered post haste the moment she breaches these new rules that she finds herself penned in by. Learning the tenets of whatever mad Maric curse she's under is a matter of life and death.

Do no harm. As a soldier, in an army, in a war.

She is beset by nightmarish thoughts that even this, her

current strategy, might not be enough. What if she jogs the stretcher too hard when she's manhandling some casualty to the hospital? Does that count as harm? What if the malingering son of a bitch is complaining and she gives him a jolt just to shut him up? She is going to have to pin this Maric Jack in a corner and give him a thorough grilling about how their deal works. She never found a system she couldn't twist to her advantage, but the stakes were never this high before.

But Jack is avoiding her. Oh, he tried to make it look like he was a man with an errand but Lidlet's played that game before, too. She knows when it's turned back on her. Well, she'll stalk him. She'll ambush him. She'll grab him by the throat and shake—

No. No she won't. And even the thought gives her a sudden tightness in her chest, a faint flower of pain where the shot went in. Which, she reflects, is handy enough.

So it's Banders she finds. She and the former Cohort-Monitor square up against one another, each recognising something of a kindred spirit. Someone who's adapted to thrive in the army ecosystem by filling the niche of parasite at least some of the time.

"Name and rank?" Banders asks, filling in the papers.

"Trooper Lidlet, formerly Third Company."

"Nicknames?"

"What?"

"Any amusing nicknames? Stinky? Jug-ears? Beefy? Beefy Lidlet has a ring to it."

Lidlet who, truth be told, is broad across the shoulders, whose cropped hair does make her ears stick out a bit and who could stand to wash a little more frequently, shakes her head. "None of that. You start with that and I'll…" A tautness, just *there*, behind her left nipple. "You just watch it." Her comrades in the Third called her Claws, sometimes. A Pel joke, because she'd been quick to rough-and-tumble if she considered she was being disrespected, but also a pun on 'clause' because of how she could reel off regulations, chapter and verse to the last sub-section, when she was getting out from under trouble.

She puts a hand to her chest. This feels like trouble she's going to have difficulty getting out of.

"Well, you and I, we've met," Banders tells her. "And you know Jack and Masty. Suppose I'd better show your face to the others." Handing over Lidlet's identification. No more Third Company. Hospital Department for her, for however long she can keep from lamping someone. There's no rank on the card, no trooper, and she queries this as acidly as she feels she's allowed.

"We don't have troopers in the department," Banders tells her with a shrug. "I don't know what you are now, honestly."

Lidlet realises that she doesn't, either. She has found a stretch of dead ground that the Pal army regs don't cover. She isn't sure if that means freedom or torment, honestly. A fish denied the medium it swims in, not sure if it can turn its fins to legs in time.

So, the department has a new orderly. Ollery, a reasonable judge, doesn't feel that Lidlet is a good fit. Not that he's privy to the details of her recruitment, but he has a temporary feeling about this new trooper-turned-stretcher-bearer. The department has had plenty of people come and go, over the decade and change of his tenure. First as a mere Accessory under the stalwart leadership of Erinael, of fond memory and miserable fate, then as Chief Accessory under Prassel. Fellow-Inquirer Prassel, only the most recent officer to be given the poisoned chalice of the hospital. Far from the worst.

Over the next day he watches the others react to the introduction in their own ways. Tallifer wants to know what Lidlet can do, insofar as the business of the department goes. The answer being 'precious little' as far as Ollery can make out. Lochiver gets fresh with her, because he's a horrible old man and that's how he gets his jollies here at the shallow end of his life. Ollery sees Lidlet set her jaw and tense up to give the nasty creature what for, then deflate suddenly, looking pale and vulnerable. He's seen enough of it in his line of work to recognise the pain of an old wound. And Masty and Lidlet have met. He's cautious around her, unsure how or even if she'll fit in. All of which leaves the woman, once Banders herself has departed, sitting on a bedroll looking entirely abandoned and friendless. So more's the pity Ollery has no need of any more friends. Not the gregarious type, is the Butcher.

Two nights later he sits up until close to midnight, reading another of the contraband pamphlets that Banders gets hold of for him. In this one, some Loruthi princeling is having his cherry well and truly plucked by a cruel… well, she's some kind of cult officer but the translated term is a Lor concept that presumably doesn't work in Pel. But that does not, frankly, detract from the spiciness of the contents. Ollery, a connoisseur, feels he owes Banders a bonus for this one. Then it's time, by his ineluctable inner clock, and he stows his banned smut and kicks his boy awake.

"Get your coat on," he says. "It's bitter out. Bring the satchel, I'll do the crate."

The kid fights his blanket a bit and then sits up, eyes mostly closed and hair sticking up all over. He glowers when he thinks Ollery isn't looking, and the Butcher wonders moodily when the kid will start answering back, trying to meet force with force. Not that it'll get the boy anywhere for years yet, but it'll represent one more source of friction in a life not free of it. And maybe Ollery will find him a place then. Orphanage, school. Phalanstery even, if he can pool enough favours. Set the kid up, send him into the world.

Not yet, though. Too soon for those thoughts. He shoos them into the dark. And, hurrying after them, *Sentimental fool.*

The boy has his coat and his satchel, that clinks with glass. Ollery hefts his crate with a kindred rattle. They cross through the camp, avoiding those sentries they can, exchanging pleasantries with those they can't. Ollery's role is sufficiently outside the turf of the regulars that his wandering about at odd hours isn't as suspicious as it might be. Probably they assume he's delivering pox medicine to someone in Higher Orders. Which, in their defence, he has done.

Instead, his path takes his feet and the boy's beyond the camp entirely. Inwards, to the village of the Galletes. Not to the handful of larger buildings commandeered by Forthright Battalion's officers, but to a building where two families are now crammed in, including an elder of the village. A herbalist, in fact, with whom Ollery has already exchanged a few notes after seeing the stock in trade of the woman's garden.

There is light glimmering around the edges of the shutters, and they let him in with a hushed word. Inside he finds more people up and about than he'd like. Not just the old herbalist ready for a clandestine trade, but a good half-dozen people kneeling around a low table. One of them *on* the table, in fact, and mostly naked like Ollery's walked into a rehearsal for one of his books. Except there's one person present who isn't a Gallete and belongs here no more than Ollery does. He might not have known except for the clothes. Galletes and Marics have a similar coloration, same hair. But of course Jack is in uniform while the locals wear smocks and tunics and baggy trews tied off at the ankle to keep the warmth in.

Jack starts, obviously no happier to see Ollery than Ollery is to see him. He's been doing something to the man on the table, and now Ollery looks closer, he reckons he can see the signs. A gauntness, as of not eating. A yellowness to the skin. Lemon blood fever, it's called. And in amongst the bottles he'd brought is a tonic that can stave off the malady. But it looks as though this case had already gone beyond the reach of his potions, until Jack rolled up.

"Accessory Jack," he says into the nervous hush of the

Galletes, "a bird told me that Higher Orders told you to knock off your tricks."

He expects cringing, because Jack's that type. Like Masty, someone who gets through life by covering his head and bending when struck. Not that Ollery's criticising. Meet everything head on and sooner or later you'll break your nose. Except this time Jack rises to meet him. A man who's been beaten enough that there's no more give left.

"They're not soldiers. They're not army. What's it to you or the generals if I heal them?" And then, even though Ollery hasn't even put a word in edgeways, "It's a compromise, all right. Because He… Look, I've got a lot of demands on me right now. This seemed the easiest way of giving everybody what they wanted. Are we going to have a problem?"

Ollery sits down at the table, as the mostly-naked man scrambles off it, quite disgustingly healthy.

"I didn't see you here, right? And you didn't see me. We were neither of us in the neighbourhood."

Jack's a smart enough lad to grab that rope when it's thrown to him, so Ollery says, "Fine. While you're not here, you can help out with the stowage. Put these where she says," nodding to the herbalist. "That's if you've got what I'm after."

"Oh I gots," she confirms in truly barbarous Pel. And she's old, and the Galletes as a whole get real old, and probably she can remember when they didn't have to speak Pel at all and had the skies to themselves.

She hustles off, and for a moment it's just Ollery and Jack and the boy at the table, the kid resting his elbows there in imitation of the Butcher's own pose, trying to look very serious-business indeed.

"They hate you so much. Or us. Maybe I mean us," Jack says softly.

"Fair," Ollery allowed.

"Your army. They say there's not one island that isn't in Pal service. How does that even happen? A whole nation of *flying islands*, and it's got Pal colours all over it."

"You're going to learn," the Butcher says heavily, "that when the Commission of Ends and Means sets its mind to something, that thing happens. Maybe not straight away, maybe not without a lot of blood and sweat, but always. Flying islands, magic sun temples, an army of wolfmen? Some special ideas department back home has the answer. That's why they'll bring perfection to the world, just like they say. Eventually."

"You say, 'they'," Jack noted.

The Butcher taps at the tabletop with a blunt finger. "What's my rank, Jack?"

"Are you standing on that right now? I have to call you Chief?"

"Chief what?"

"Chief... Accessory?"

Ollery nods. "And me born on the Archipelago. That sound like the rank of a man who claims the army as kith and kin?"

Then the herbalist is back with a basket. Herbs, flowers, even just vegetables that don't appear in the army rations crates. And all of them grown in the soil of a Gallete island, suffused with their peculiar brand of magic. Subtly different to mundane varieties, touched by the energies that keep this impossible nonsense in the air.

Later, the last day of the island's journey before Forthright Battalion disembarks, Fellow-Archivist Thurrel is looking at that very nonsense. The heart of the island. A cave, its walls studded with finger-sized crystals so that the entire interior bristles with them, glowing with a faint, lambent white. By the traditions of the Galletes, outsiders are not allowed here. Most of the Galletes themselves aren't. But nobody's going to tell a Fellow-Archivist *No*. He has his thaumatic gauge on, using the vision it grants him to see the way the magic threads its way from one to another. Strands as thin as spiderweb, so tenuous that, if he were to stare too hard at any one, it would fade into nothing under the sheer pressure of his regard. And yet all together they keep the island in the air, all the many tons of it. Such a gossamer construction to prevent the whole battalion and all its baggage from plunging into the sea!

Because he has a lot of hats he wears, as well as the thaumatic gauge, but the one he likes most is the pure scholar's. To *know*. To see all the little flames of mystery before perfection extinguishes them.

Thurrel's fingers twitch with a sort of generalised acquisitiveness, a tell he's never been able to master, and the reason he doesn't play games of bluff and chance with his fellow officers unless he's happy leaving with emptier pockets than he came with. But then, when you're the duty Decanter for an entire battalion then somehow you always have a new stake. Amazing what sticks to the fingers when you're charging up the tablethi. And his family back home is a cut above well-to-do and so it's not like he'll be going without the good tea or nice boots any time soon.

"Go on," says a voice from behind him. "Filch a little. What could it hurt?"

"Hello, Maserley," says Thurrel, his voice bright but allowing his eyes to roll a bit where the demonist can't see them. "I mean it was tried. You hear of Jovekrigg?" He assays the foreign name with more confidence than accuracy. "We did actually get some usable data from that, for study. Mostly that you can remove enough puissance from this sort of thing to have the island drop out of the air, and yet still not actually have very much to do anything with. It's one of those balance things. All the big force went into getting the thing up in the air, centuries ago. After which it's just sort of coasting. Owing the ground a debt but skipping out on the bailiffs every second so that it doesn't come down *yet*. Always *going* to come down, you understand, but always getting another extension on the assignment at the last moment. I'm sure you were just the same, at the phal." He's composed a very pleasant smile for when he turns around. Beaming at Maserley's face, that's whitewashed by the unnatural light. Cocking an eye at Caeleen who's in default sultry mode behind her master, the alluring lines her face falls into when she's not particularly inhabiting it.

"Do these clowns know what your job involves?" Maserley asks acidly. The Gallete magician-engineers whose work it is to calibrate this web of threads are clustering nearby, powerfully anxious that these two Pals will break something in what is, after all, a rather important part of their culture.

"They know I'm a Fellow of the Schools. I find that tends to open enough doors," Thurrel says mildly. "What do you *want*, Maserley? Not fencing lessons, I take it. I'm rusty, if so."

The man's face clenches briefly before the smooth mask goes back on. Thurrel chalks up a point, internally. It's not that he doesn't like Maserley – actually, he *doesn't* like Maserley but doesn't particularly dislike him. Same for Prassel. Same for a handful of others. There's just a very small pool of peers to socialise with, at Fellow level, within a battalion. Given the actual battlefield officers keep their own company and look down their noses at specialists. So Maserley's company becomes something to be endured, savoured like a particularly bitter blend.

"Well, all right," he confesses. "Yes, I did put in the request. I think there's a good three or four racks of tablethi to be had there. Enough for an extra shot for every soldier in the battalion maybe. You'd think that would be enough for them to give the Maric over, but apparently he's more useful mopping the brows of our poor wounded."

"Tell me," Maserley insists.

"And you've suddenly become a student of defunct religions? I'll have you over and we can get a debating circle going." Thurrel folds the thaumatic gauge down over his eyes. For a moment, before he turns its powers on the crystals again, he has the dubious pleasure of examining Maserley, seeing all the fingerprints of dealings with the Lords Below, the inevitable unsoundness that sort of thing brings. The bright chain that leads from his hands to the throat of Caeleen. Who, herself, is a kind of nebulous suggestion of corruption and monstrosity, the potential to destroy from within, to poison with sweetness. Thurrel turns away, not from horror, but because he's seen it all before.

"Thurrel," Maserley says, in what he fondly believes is his warning tone of voice.

"Oh Maric cults are fascinating. Not the current state religion thing that's still clinging on, but they had about a million gods back in the day," Thurrel says over his shoulder as he makes notes. "A lot to sift through but yes, I've pinned our medico friend down, I think. Weird kind of cult, big in its day, extinct now, according to my book. Obviously needs an amended second edition."

"Don't bother," Maserley says. "I have a feeling reality's going to catch up with the textbooks soon enough. Tell me."

"Why?"

"Because he's Prassel's and he's an irritant and I don't like him."

"I mean if you stick a knife in his ribs, it probably won't matter what denomination he is," Thurrel observes.

"I don't even want to kill him. If he spontaneously went up on flames I wouldn't piss on him, but what's the point? I want to ruin him. Spiritually. Tell me."

"Do you ever feel that all this demon business is having an effect on you?" Although Thurrel knows full well that Maserley has always been a nasty piece of work. It's how the man climbed the spiky ladder of combative academia to get to Fellow rank. Thurrel, who basically had his certificates handed to him by a well-placed uncle, can only admire the gumption.

"Thurrel." There's that warning tone again. Thurrel sighs, wondering if he and Maserley will actually have a throw-down at some point. It would be tedious and unpleasant for anyone within collateral damage range, honestly. Or maybe Prassel will kill the man and save Thurrel the effort. Or Maserley kills Prassel and... gets disciplined for it? Honestly there isn't really a satisfactory resolution to the barbed knot that is Maserley.

"So it's one of those stupid religions where it's mostly stupid lists of things you're not allowed to do," Thurrel says. As opposed, he thinks wryly, to the army, which is mostly entirely sensible lists of things you're not allowed to do. "The priests especially, and it certainly says priest on his papers. Not allowed to harm anyone, for starters, so go pull his hair and tweak his nose as much as you like. Not allowed to marry, no intimate relations, no drinking, no swearing. No fun. You know, that kind of religion."

"And if he does...?"

"I mean loses his powers, I suppose? That's the answer you're looking for, isn't it? Has to do some kind of humiliating abasement. Grovel, fast, self-flagellate. Probably not that last one, given the whole non-violence. Maybe self-flagellate but only with something very soft. I mean it's *religion*, Maserley. It doesn't have to make sense. It's what some deranged earth spirit decided was a good idea a thousand years ago. You want me to tell you what you want to hear? Screw with his oaths and he'll be very miserable. You get your snackies the way you like. Enough mortal misery for a half-dozen mid-grade demons. Now, if you don't mind, some of us have actual tangible things to study that don't involve bartering with the Miserable Powers."

He waits, pretending to be engrossed in his scrutiny, until he senses Maserley and his pet demon have gone. Even then, the space between his shoulder blades continues to twitch a little. Thurrel makes a point of turning his back on the man every chance he gets, to show he's not bothered. Not remotely worried that the man will plant a knife there, metaphorically or literally. Because what is life without a little thrill of risk?

Maric Jack is, Thurrel divines, going to have a rough time in the near future. Possibly he'll end up as Maserley's creature, or else just wrecked in some entertaining way. And then Prassel will have to decide how to make a countermove, and it'll all be terribly fun and games unless, say, the army is actually mid-battle at that point. Which seems overwhelmingly likely.

Still, there's an off chance that Maserley's games will ruin the Maric in a way that will leave Thurrel in possession of his kit, that box where the power surely resides, given that there wasn't much of a trace of it in Jack himself. In which case, what's a lost battle between friends and peers?

Dockside Banter

The Palleseen Sway is built on the back of collaboration. No matter how fervent, devout or patriotic a nation might think its populace is, once the Pals move in and impose their ordinances, there will always be a steady flow of people who understand that working with the new boss is the way to get ahead. These are the Accessories, known as some variant on 'Turncoat' in most places. Or 'Whitebellies' for their pale imitation of Pal uniforms. Except sometimes the practice brings unforeseen complications. Sometimes Turncoats don't leave their bad habits behind with their old clothes.

Seeing a Gallete island in measured and graceful descent was a sight to take the breath away. Possibly with fear, because that was an awful lot of stone tonnage on its way, and you were trusting a great deal to Galleter traditions if you were waiting at the landing site to unload. Especially given that the Pals were very down on exactly that sort of tradition. It wouldn't be to anyone's benefit if the collective force of scholarly disbelief suddenly made it all stop working.

Landwards Battalion had been sitting out here in the hills for, by Pirisytes's best estimate, bloody ages. They had come south down the coast by foot themselves, redeployed from the big muster grounds the Pals had rammed into the Oloumanni lowlands like a gang enforcer shanking their cellmate. Pirisytes, a native, had signed up as a Whitebelly long before. When the new troops arrived and they flattened the old sacred sites for their base, he was right in there at the start with a spade. A good servant of the new rationality, they called him. He'd had a commendation and a bonus for all the hard work he'd done. Given that a great many of the Oloumanni, especially the higher echelons, were on forced re-education in the mines, he reckoned he had a good deal.

Then the Pals had started some new war front overseas, and everyone got the order to march. Pallesand had thrown down with the big trading nation of Lor, and that was across the sea, and so one might reasonably expect that all the fighting would keep at a civilized distance and let hardworking Whitebellies like Pirisytes keep digging latrines and moving boxes. Except that both the Loruthi and the Pals had interests on this side of the salt. The Pals had put nations like Oloumann fully within the Palleseen Sway. They also had places that they hadn't conquered *yet* but were fully invested in, like Northern Bracinta, where their soldiers had been 'supporting' the local regime for years while they slowly tightened the noose. The Loruthi on the other hand, being a mercantile power that didn't throw its armies about so much, had Trade Missions all the way down the coast, which used the milled edges of their coins to burrow into the hierarchies of whichever kingdom or despotate they decided was profitable. With the end result that wherever they fixed their eye on ended up just as dominated by their desires and run for their benefit as anywhere under the Palleseen Sway. From Pirisytes's point of view it didn't seem all that much different, except they generally persuaded the locals to beat up and rob themselves rather than having uniformed professionals do it.

Where this became relevant to Pirisytes was that the jewel in the Loruthi overseas crown was Southern Bracinta. When the kingdom had fractured after its civil war, their trade delegates had been getting their feet under the table just as quickly as the Pals had. The declaration of war way off on the far side of the sea had led to a surprise forced reunification of the country when the Loruthi had stolen a march on their competitors. Which then led to Landwards Battalion being sent south, so that Pirisytes got to apply his valuable latrine-digging experience to the rich loam of Bracinta, rather than the drier upland soil of his home Oloumann. It was an art form. He'd had to adjust his methods. It all slopped off the spade in quite a different way, and he was fast becoming an expert in the slightly different range of intestinal conditions affecting an army down here in the danker coastal plains, and just what came out of your average Pal soldier after they encountered the local food.

And now here was Forthright Battalion, descending from on high after a week of the high life as they crossed the sea, lucky bastards. No need to dig latrines on a Gallete, Pirisytes assumed. You just went over the edge and tried to land it on a fishing boat if one presented itself, for the laughs. Pirisytes was all about the laughs. His fellow Whitebellies knew him as the life and soul of the work crew, the Pals found him a cheery and obedient menial and an actual Sage-Monitor had complimented his positive attitude.

His crew was standing by to lift and shift now, which made a pleasant change to turfing dirt onto the collected bowel movements of Landwards Battalion. And, of course, Pirisytes himself had his own particular tasks. As always.

The island was slowing as it descended, given it didn't want to become a different kind of geological feature entirely. Pirisytes marvelled at how it remained absolutely and entirely steady, as though it was fixed in the air, and the ground was just grinding slowly up towards it. They had some fine magic, those Galleters, but they had one big problem. Floating about in the sky all hoity-toity, that bred envy. If not the Pals, then someone would have taken them down a notch. Pirisytes's creed was very explicit on the virtues of passing beneath notice as the best road to survival and getting things done. Every Pal officer was a hammer looking for the nail that stood proud. That pride was reserved for the Pals. It got beaten out of everyone else.

They'd built towers and ramps and gantries ready, and the

Galleters drifted the impossible weightlessness of their island in close. Then it was Pirisytes's crew running in with a dozen solid gangplanks to bridge the remaining gap, slamming them down, bolting them into place. Forcing and twisting where things just didn't quite line up, because life was uncertain and that was another piece of Pirisytes's doctrine. Life was uncertain, and uncertainty was a crack that things could breed in, out of sight. The brighter the light, the deeper the shadow, and the Pals liked their lights very bright indeed.

After that it was just hard work for everyone concerned. Landwards's Whitebelly work crews, plus a load of Landwards regulars unlucky enough to draw the short straw on assignments, plus a whole crew of uniforms from Forthright who had their own officers who got into a fine old pissing competition with their opposite numbers on the ground. Pirisytes just worked.

Or rather, worked and watched.

Eventually the actual manpower of Forthright Battalion began to disembark, and he made sure that he was in a good position to look them over. He made the proper sign, with the hidden left hand, plucked three hairs painfully from his forearm and squinted through the resultant tears. His sight blurred, then sharpened preternaturally as he looked for someone special. Someone *worthy*.

Oloumann had been a land full of gods. There were a lot of big gods, and they had been a sort of family, and squabbled a bit but generally been pointed in the same direction, which direction was downwards so that the kings and priests and great hosts of slavish worshippers could shovel offerings up into their open mouths. And then the Pals had come and done away with that, knocked down the temples, overthrown the king and massacred the priests. Except they hadn't quite realised that one thing all the big temples and kings and the priests with the fancy hats had been doing was fighting a savage war against all the *other* gods. The nasty little sneaky gods, the poison gods, the murder gods, the chaos gods who tried to tear everything down. And, with their natural predators removed, those cults had enjoyed an unexpected flourishing, like mushrooms from corpses. All banned, of course. Assiduously hunted by the Pals, who boasted of all the cultists they had executed. Except, of course, the most subtle of the little fringe religions already had people wearing the uniform, signed on and digging latrines.

Pirisytes – not his real name – was such a diligent and happy worker that nobody had connected him with a string of fires, thefts, vandalism and actual deaths. Everyone liked Pirisytes. At least until they woke up with a ritual knife at their throat.

Forthright Battalion marched out, breaking step as they crossed the gangplanks and gantries so that their massed stomping wouldn't shake the whole construction to pieces. Soldiers and soldiers and soldiers in their charcoal uniforms, batons slanted across their shoulders, chins up, putting on a good show for their Landwards cousins who'd been *in situ* for a while and started to fray at the edges. Pirisytes leaned on a crate and watched. And, yes, some random officer might serve, but when he went to the market for his superiors he always strove to get the best produce. How much more did he owe his god, when shopping for sacrifices?

And here came some less regimented types. Specialists, magicians, scholars. He plucked more hairs and squinted again, seeing the flavours of their power like auras in the air. All the usual Pal disciplines, the secrets they stole and repurposed for their military. Death and conjuration. All possibilities.

He blinked, screwed up his face once more, looked again. There was a little man there, carrying one side of a big crate marked with Pal medico symbols. He had a box on his back that was decidedly not uniform issue.

Blessed, Pirisytes saw. And there were others, too. Not quite as priestly as that one, but most definitely consecrated to some foreign god or other. For a moment he couldn't quite process the idea. Priests in Pal company were either prisoners or they were undercover like him. They didn't just... walk about in the open like normal army personnel. And yet here they were. Actual priests of actual gods wearing the uniform.

If there was one thing that Pirisytes's god particularly savoured, it was the blood of those dedicated to other deities. Preferably the familial Oloumanni pantheon that had spent the last several centuries stomping all the sneaky little gods into the cracks and crevices, but any other god would do. The priests of a beggar's god couldn't be choosers, after all.

Pirisytes licked his lips. He'd let Forthright get settled in and then it would be time for some good old-fashioned religion.

Hell is Empty

They hadn't burned people at the High Fane. That was a lie the Pals told, to justify what they'd done. It wasn't as if the Pals usually needed to justify themselves, but after the Fane held out for almost a year the army hadn't been inclined towards restraint when they finally breached the gates. Tallifer was out, at that point. She'd taken a brand from the sacred fire, that had been burning for ten thousand years, and snuck it out under the noses of the besieging forces. She'd been tasked to take it to a new site, start a new High Fane, continue the fight.

It had gone out. In her headlong flight, baton-shot skittering about her like fleas, she had dropped the sacred fire.

Two days later, she'd woken to find Mazdek the Chastising Flame curled beside her, and known that the temple had fallen, and she was all that was left. She had sworn, then, to fight the Pals to her last breath. Such had been her determination to oppose them that she'd even leagued with a digusting disease worshipper to bring them low. Resist them in any possible way, until they killed her and extinguished the flame forever.

She'd been younger then. And here she was, patching their wounds and following in their baggage train as Forthright Battalion went to war.

"Where's the tent?" Lochiver demands, and as he's the third person to ask that, Tallifer isn't exactly diplomatic in telling him where he can shove the tent that isn't here.

Because Forthright Battalion know to have a tent set up for the experimental hospital department but Landwards doesn't and it's Landwards who've prepared the ground for the big assault.

"I am not doing all this in the open. It's going to rain," Lochiver complains. And he's right, but then they're in Bracinta, where the local words for 'rain' and 'weather' are only a slight shift of emphasis different.

Ollery claps his hands together as though the incipient rain needs a little thunder to get it going. "I'll get a tent sorted," he decided, and stomps off to shout at people. Chief Accessory Ollery is not someone who should have authority to shout at anyone wearing a regular uniform. The Butcher, on the other hand, is known across the breadth of Forthright Battalion as the man who decides whether the medicos will save you or not, and so when he bellows, those uniforms scramble to get him what he wants.

In the interim, the department unload their boxes and put up their beds. It's still dry, and somehow it's bright sunshine and also louring cloud, because that's how they do weather in this part of the world. Bracinta still calls itself the Rainbow Lands sometimes. The locals have a whole myth cycle about how the rainbows are the roads that the original Bracites walked, to bring them to this promised land of plenty. Tallifer, who has a fire god curled up in her pocket, isn't about to say any of it's nonsense. There are most certainly roads that don't appear on maps, that burrow between the pages of the cosmic atlas like worms, and why shouldn't they look like rainbows sometimes?

"Landwards's off then," Banders notes. She's standing on the top of a precarious pile of crates, in a way that doesn't bode well for either her or anything delicate within. Shading her hand against the sharp splinters of sunlight. "Don't much like the tree cover ahead. Looks like you could hide twenty companies in there. Better them than us."

"Fighting, yet?" Masty asks her. He's dragging beds and boxes into position just as if they had a standard army-issue tent there, conjuring perimeters and boundaries into place out of memory. After a bit of this, it looks like they *had* a tent only a moment ago, and some freak wind blew it away and just left the contents within its notional footprint.

"Nothing yet. Don't hear the rattle and they're just marching," Banders reports, although odds on they'd not hear baton-shot at this distance. "Moving the heavy stavers in now." Meaning artillery, great bundles of treated rods on wheeled carriages, horse-drawn or hauled by hand.

A faintly resonant stomp-stomp-stomp heralds the arrival of Cosserby and his Sonori – the nine he was able to restore to working order on the flight over. He grins nervously at Tallifer who gives him only stone in reply, watching the bright expression slowly dry and peel away before her regard.

"I mean," he says, as though instead of just looks they've been exchanging harsh words. "Good morning. I suppose."

"What do you want, Cosserby? We're very busy." She'd like to say *saving lives* but no lives have presented themselves for saving yet. Landwards have their own field hospitals in place, she presumes, and Forthright is just sitting on its hands. Arguably Cosserby is actually more useful than she is right now, and that galls her beyond reason.

"Ideally, to know what's going on. Last night Higher Orders were saying we'd be taking point, but now we're just... not. Not doing that. Or anything. Not sure what Uncle's doing. Was wondering, you know, if you'd heard anything."

"Oh yes," says Tallifer, glad of the opportunity for some sarcasm. "Because the moment Uncle makes a major strategic decision the first thing he thinks is, 'Oh I must come and tell the field hospital. They'll be ever so very grateful for the heads up.'"

"I just thought," says Cosserby, looking aggrieved. "You know. Someone. Banders? Where's Banders. She knows things."

Banders takes that opportunity to prod him in the bald spot with the toe of her boot, given that she's right there and has the required elevation. "Right here. You need those specs changed or what?"

"Banders doesn't know anything more than we do," Tallifer decides authoritatively.

"I know there've been messengers going between our Higher Orders and Landwards's all night," Banders says. "I reckon there's been a real hamfight over seniority. And given the Professor's been sat here with Landwards, I think Uncle got slapped down and they get the honours."

"I mean, did we want it?" It's Jack, hauling in the last box of glassware and setting it down in the precise spot Masty's left for it. "It doesn't sound much of a good thing, to go in first. Doesn't that mean you get hurt more?"

"Hark at him," Banders chuckled. "Here, make yourself useful. Have your bell lads cup hands so I can step down."

Cosserby gives Banders a look that suggests she doesn't know just how complicated that actually is, but he does it anyway because he's a sucker, and she descends from her perch like the grandest lady of the Bracite royal court.

"Thing you don't understand, Jack," she says, "is the glory of it. First in, take the city, drive the enemy from the walls. Big feather in the cap for the commander. Looks really good in the dispatches. Commendations all round."

"Well." Jack scratches his head, "I mean, fine, but it doesn't sound much of a good deal for the actual people going *in*, though."

"You do not get this army thing, do you?" Banders asks him. Then there's a shrill whistle and, in its echo, the indefinable sound of hundreds of soldiers getting ready.

"I think that's me," Cosserby says almost apologetically, as though he'd promised them a scintillating anecdote and they were all agog to hear it.

Banders knocks twice on the nearest Sonori, a musical ringing sound that goes on and on, fading slowly past the further reaches of hearing. "For luck," she tells him, a sentiment entirely against Correct Thought but he seems to appreciate it. Then his toy soldiers are clumping off, with him at their back like a fussy shepherd.

The tent's going up, by then, and it turns out Masty has a pinpoint accuracy of memory that Tallifer can't quite believe. There's barely an inch of space between where he's set everything out and where the canvas goes. Which makes putting the tent up somewhat more complicated than necessary, but then they should have had it ready before the department arrived to set up.

"When do we go out? How does this work?" The new girl, Lidlet. Because Maric Jack isn't the new one now. And partly it's that Lidlet is newer, only days in, her first active service within the department. But also, Jack has seen things. Seen enough to be one of them. Stitched wounds, seen death, performed miracles. Literal miracles. Tallifer surprises herself with the sentiment, but he's *One Of Us* now. And she watches him set out a line of bandages ready for their first customer, and it's just like Masty does it, which means it's the right way. A quick study, our Jack.

He catches her eye. He's nervous, because they all are, right before Hell opens its doors to the paying public, and because of some crap he's got going on of his own that Tallifer has no wish to know about. Nervous, but steady. Reliable. All she can ask of her colleagues is that they are reliable.

"The stretcher bearers go out with the second wave," she tells Lidlet. "By that time the first wave will have served up the starters and you'll have something to do. Second wave whistle. You know what that sounds like?" And at least Lidlet was a regular before she fell to these depths. She knows the signals. She's very pale, sweating, biting at her lip like she's never seen combat. Tallifer rolls her eyes. "What? You'd rather be out there having them shoot at you?" And, all around them, outside the walls of the tent, the soldiers are marching, moving out orderly and tight.

"I. Just." Lidlet presses her lips together. "You don't know. What if they. What if the enemy. If I'm attacked?"

Tallifer opens her mouth for a scathing, *Well la-di-da, actually doing soldier work too good for you now*, but stops. Lidlet is trembling. She has a hand to her breast as though she's finding it hard to breath. This trooper, this career soldier, as undone as a child. The woman's eyes stray to Jack but he's ostentatiously not having anything to do with the conversation, making a big show of counting things that don't need the enumeration.

The second whistle goes. The second wave begin advancing through the camp. A range of specialists, intelligencers, reinforcements, a handful of front-line patchers and stitchers Tallifer is distantly acquainted with, one professional with another. Hell is about to get busy.

"I'll go with you," Masty says, suddenly at Lidlet's elbow.

"You? Why?"

Because he understands what's got into her. Whatever happened out in the mud, between her and Jack and death, he was there for it. But all he says is, "Well, you need someone for the other end of the stretcher. Might as well be me."

A single shudder goes through Lidlet. It's gratitude, Tallifer decides. Ollery is telling Masty he can't go, he's needed here, but the man steps between the words as though he's dodging raindrops and staying dry. Then he and Lidlet and a stretcher have absented themselves to go join all the Company bearers who are following up on the first advance to pick up its human litter.

"Shambles," the Butcher complains. "We cross one sea and everything's out of joint."

"What are we even fighting for?" Jack asks.

The Butcher turns a louring eye on him. "Have you not had that peacemongering stuff beaten out of you yet?"

"No," Jack says patiently. "I don't mean, like, in a wider philosophical way. I mean, what are we doing *here*. Here right here. Right now. This battle."

"Oh." Ollery rubs at the back of his neck. "Banders?"

Except Banders, who probably does know, has knocked off

for a smoke somewhere. You never see her go, you never see her come back. Tallifer doesn't know, but isn't interested in admitting her ignorance, so pretends she hasn't heard the question. Then Alv comes in, conspicuous in her absence until now.

"Have you seen my students?"

The Butcher frowns. "What?"

"My new class of students."

"New class?" His broad face is absolutely blank.

"They didn't tell you?" Alv is not someone who gets agitated. She is the human embodiment of placidity, like the still mirror of a lake without a single ripple. Right now she's twitchy as a frog, out of balance. "My students were held back, when we travelled. Ready, they said. Ready for deployment. I was to receive a new class to teach, when we got here."

This is all plainly news to the Butcher. Bad news, because Alv's student body was basically a dumping ground for all the small injuries so everyone else could concentrate on the big stuff. And now that entire resource has been stripped from them and nobody except Alv even knew until now.

"Well we'll…" Ollery looks out of the open tent flap, towards where the soldiers marched off to. "We'll make the best fist of it, is what we'll do. Jack, set me out a rack of bandages and some clean needles and thread here by the door and I'll stitch what I can, when I can." Big hands and thick fingers, the Butcher, but a very delicate touch with a needle when he has to, just like the tiny pinches of herbs in his cookery. Always precise, whether in dosage or the application of force.

Alv sits on one of the operating tables and takes a deep breath, expelling all that agitation. There's still a crescent of shiny skin about her jaw, cheekbone and the orbit of one eye, and Lochiver's injury still troubles her walk, but other than that she's shed it all like snakeskin. Somehow.

I wonder if she can do it with age, Tallifer thinks gloomily. *Be nice to offload a decade on her and then let her piss it away into nowhere for me.* She's scared to ask, in case Alv says yes. Where would that end, exactly?

Jack is setting up the Butcher's little stitching station, having a muttered argument in his hooley-hooley language. She'd say that the habit would get him into trouble one day, Pal attitudes towards linguistics being what they are, but Jack's already been in enough trouble that talking to himself in Foreign honestly isn't going to make much odds. If Correct Speech carts him off again the moment the battle's over it won't surprise her.

And still the casualties fail to flood in. It's been almost two whole hours now since Landwards's vanguard marched off into those woods. Everyone is getting very twitchy. Ollery puts his head out of the tent and yells for news every so often, but there is none. Nobody's coming back, that's the problem. Nobody is returning from the front *at all.* A thing as powerfully unnatural as anybody ever heard.

Then the word comes that they're moving, after having everything set up and pristine. Wagons roll in, get loaded up by a skeleton crew of clerks and labourers and general bureaucratic malingerers, and they go into those woods themselves. And it's dark, and the rain has, true to form, started again. The hissing of it against the foliage that lines the track obviates the need to make conversation. They sit there, hunched under canvas to keep dry, and on either side the darkness between the trees watches back. A thousand unseen eyes, and every pair of them might be sighting along a baton. Lochiver asks loudly if anybody wants him to play, and everyone tells him that they get plenty enough of that when they're at work, thank you, but Tallifer flicks his ear to get his attention, and gives him the nod.

He puts his flute to his lips, that horrible flute, those horrible lips. And plays. And it's not his god-pleasing votive skirl that so offends the human ear but is irresistible to the things of putrefaction and sickness. Instead, it's an old Jarokiri song. A shepherd song, that you might hear drifting across the scrubby grazing land in their far homeland. They're on the right side of the sea for it, for the first time in almost a decade, though Jarokir is a long way from Bracinta. Lochiver plays, and none of them ever heard him actually make music. Nobody understood that you have to be able to play well, if you're going to play horribly properly. The old man's eyes are closed, and if he wasn't quite so filthy and ragged and generally of unfond memory then it might actually have been a moment of beauty. As it is, it manages to overcome the rain and at least stave off everyone's nerves. Holds the dark at bay until they break out of the trees and into the sunlight. A myriad of rainbows scatter around them like brightly coloured birds and Lochiver takes his flute from his lips.

"They haven't got a fucking tent for us again," he notes. "What is the pissing world coming to?"

Somehow they survive that, the putting up of a new tent, the setup within. All done slipshod and in a hurry, because there's no Masty to know exactly where everything goes, and because the casualties must be coming in any moment. Unless it's worse than that. Unless whatever the Loruthi are deploying this time doesn't leave any casualties it's worth bringing back for the medicos to go over. Doesn't leave anything that can't be brought back in an urn. And the silence of it is getting to them now. Not that it's actually silent, because there's the rain and the sounds of the forest at their backs and the wind and the world and all the rest of it. But what there *isn't* is the war. No shooting, artillery roar and baton's rattle. No screaming. Tallifer hadn't thought she'd miss it, but apparently that's just one more way her role here has broken her.

And they wait. And, overblown poetics aside, waiting is far from the worst part of warfare, but it builds up. It leans on you steadily, as the time drags on. It thickens the air so that just breathing in and out becomes oppressive, a surrogate clock reminding you of all the terrible things that haven't happened *yet*. And Ollery keeps wanting word, but nobody's coming back from the front. Not one person. Nobody.

Not Masty and Lidlet, that's for certain.

"Should we send someone after them?" Jack asks timorously.

"What now?" the Butcher demands.

"Lidlet. Should we? She's… I mean, something might have happened."

"It's a battle," Tallifer tells him acidly. "A battle is basically something happening to as many people as it can get hold of."

"Yes, but—"

"Should we send someone to see if something has happened to two soldiers who have gone to a battle? And what if it has, exactly. What will you do? You want to send stretcher bearers to bring back the stretcher bearers? What's your plan, Jack?" Her voice rising to a vitriolic chalkboard screech because by now she's jumpy as bugs on a griddle because *nothing has happened and nobody has come back.*

Jack stares at her. "I just think I may have done a bad thing."

"Knowing you, probably," Tallifer tells him dismissively.

"With Lidlet, I mean."

"Also probably. Will you just—" And then, thank Mazdek the Chastising Flame, thank Sturge the Unclean, thank whatever dumbass gods the Maric worships, someone's coming in through the tent flat. It's Masty. It's Lidlet. Between them, the stretcher. On the stretcher, a soldier with a hastily splinted ankle.

"What's happening?" the Butcher roars. "Where are the rest? What's happened to them."

And they get the casualty, singular, to a table where Alv can look at the ankle – broken, but not messy. And Lidlet sits down and shakes a bit, and Masty accepts the water bottle that Banders – miraculously reappeared – hands him. And, after a long swig, tells the tale.

The army is at the city walls, he says. It's news to everyone but Banders that they really were trying to get to any city walls, but apparently that was the plan. Landwards's vanguard marched all the way to the city, and found the gates opened by a populace very keen to show how happy they were to be liberated by returning Pal forces. The Loruthi didn't even leave a token garrison, just melted away before the superior numbers of the Palleseen. The whole day passed without a single shot being fired and their solitary casualty was brought low by nothing more than a rabbit burrow.

In the Vice

The kingdom of Bracinta was ruled from the Wolf Palace in the city of Magnelei, with both palace and city – or the more presentable parts – reckoned great wonders of the world. A land of fantastic opulence, centuries of tradition – the temples, the baths, the arena! A succession of Aremir monarchs, masters of all they surveyed, stretching back across three hundred years and five closely related dynasties. The final King of Bracinta died in a welter of internecine bloodletting and short-lived juvenile heirs, after which the Palleseen stepped in to safeguard the nation against chaos and division. Which worked well for a succession of Pal advisor-perfectors who ensured a great deal of opulence found its way to the Archipelago and a great deal of tradition was slowly ground down in the name of public order. Which also worked well for a succession of Loruthi trade factors, whose influence ensured that the southern reaches of the nation effectively broke away from Magnelei to preserve what the Pals were seeking to destroy, in most cases by selling it to the Loruthi.

The open gates of the city – Magnelei, according to Banders, which just meant one more place Jack couldn't have found on a map – didn't mean that two battalions of Pal soldiers were just going to march inside. You'd not have fitted them all in, honestly. However, it was open news across the conjoined military encampment currently assembling that the grateful Bracites had extended the hospitality of their city to any soldier of the liberating forces who might come and visit. Especially those parts of the city that specialised in drink, sex or rigged games of chance. Higher Orders were even now having a rota drawn up so favoured squads would get a chance to go empty their pockets of loose change, even as the disciplinary wing of the army was bracing itself to deal with countless charges of disorderliness, brawling and regrettable things happening to some of the locals. There would be the usual cautions about not stirring up trouble amongst *our allies*, but of all the things the Palleseen Sway was working to perfect, its own soldiers came way down the list.

"You hear about the Butterfly Houses?" Banders asked.

Jack, who had been covertly pouring out a tiny libation of salt, flour and tea behind his box, looked up. "It's going to sound weird," he said, "but butterflies always sort of freaked me out. I mean they look like flower petals from a distance, but close up they've got these little legs and a weird tongue and—"

"You're strange," Banders said frankly. "Anyway, not actual butterflies. They've got these men – women too – they go through some initiation thing, religious thing."

"It turns them into butterflies?" And he was doing his best to sound horrified but also, you had to interrupt Banders because she always interrupted you. She respected you for it.

"No, listen, it's like... okay, maybe they do go a bit like butterflies, but they do this thing that—"

"They still do that, do they?" asked God. He had tea cupped in His hands and slurped at it noisily.

"What, you know this? How do you know this?" Jack hissed.

God was unusually mellow today. Barely a crotchet of His usual temper. At His back the plant god apparently didn't want flour after all but the little spearman was shovelling salt into his pockets avariciously.

"When I had the big temple, we received delegations. Those coming to learn the wisdom of the priesthood. They brought gifts. They brought entertainment. Filthy heathen nonsense obviously. Dancers, you know. In the altogether. Quite indecent. I forbad it."

Jack, who hadn't in any way wanted to go see creepy butterfly people, now had to fight against the stubborn urge to go anyway. "Doesn't sound like my kind of thing," he told Banders. "You enjoy though."

"Oh I will, soon as my name's up on the rota. You sure? I mean, seems a bit of a waste, coming to a place like this and not seeing the sights."

"I'm sure there are other sights. And do we even get to go? I'm a, what is it, an Accessory, and you're not even a Cohort-Major or whatever you were. We'll be bottom of the list, surely."

"Where we are on the list," Banders said, tapping the side of her nose, "is closely related to whether I can get the duty Companion a particular flavour of rolling weed that he's fond of, and it just so happens that I have an angle on some. So our turn might just come sooner than you think, Jack, old mate."

"It would be nice to have walls that weren't canvas once in a while." Jack shrugged, watching his private pantheon play with their offerings. Beyond the hospital department's little compound rose the sound of an army in good spirits. A major victory had been struck at the cost of a few sprained ankles, a concussion and a Statlos in Landwards Battalion who'd somehow managed to shoot himself in the foot.

Masty passed by, opened his mouth to say something scintillating, no doubt, then reversed smoothly to snatch up a walking cane, which he had ready to press into Alv's hand when she limped out of her tent. Her new students had arrived, apparently. Jack saw a squad of young, neat-looking Pals, close-faced and narrow-eyed. They stared at Jack and Banders and Alv and just about everything else with the same suspicious glower, as though everyone was hiding some unorthodoxy behind their back. Jack hadn't seen Alv's previous class at the start of tuition, of course, and maybe they'd started off just the same. If so, he hoped this lot lost their sharp edges soon because looks like those were wearing to be around.

Lochiver stomped up and prodded Banders in the shoulder. "We're not even on it," he spat.

"What now, old man?"

"The rota's up. I looked all over it. They missed us off entirely."

Banders smirked. "That's 'cos I haven't got Spinnerly his weed yet. You just wait."

"You promised me butterflies," Lochiver growled.

"Old man you'd turn them back to caterpillars. But I promise, and when did I ever let you down."

"Damn me, how long've you got. Get me paper so I can make a list." He glowered around. "What? You're always staring at my ear, Jack."

Jack, who had been staring at the sluglike thing sunning itself stickily on Lochiver's shoulder, looked away quickly.

"I forbid you to go into that den of vicissitude," God said, having finished the tea.

"I'm sure there's plenty of virtuous things you can do in Magnatai or whatever this place is called."

God snorted derisively.

Banders had business taking her away, after that, and Cosserby was making a racket in his workshop tent next door, hammering something into shape. Then Lidlet drifted past, and Jack's courage failed again and he hid in his own little tent, on his bedroll. Hid and prayed for courage because he'd have to face the woman sooner or later, if only to apologise. And yet the mere sight of her just filled him with despair at his own failures, the essential uselessness of him. God, he knew, felt the same way. A vast potential for good wrenched out of shape by the nature of the world and His own limitations until He was just this crooked, mean-spirited bitter old thing. And Jack, as His devotee, was becoming His shadow. Yes he'd saved Lidlet. Yes, he'd done it by wrecking her life and leaving her in constant fear of death returning to claim her. A moment's temper, a raised fist, an over-aggressive oath perhaps, and it would all be over. He saw the haunted knowledge in her face every time he glanced her way. And she wanted him to tell her there was a way out of it, and he couldn't. Because there wasn't.

Lying there on his bedroll, he listened to the minute sounds of the gods in their box, no different really to those made by rats in the skirting. Beyond them he could hear Tallifer and the Butcher, just the rumble of his voice and the cracked rasp of hers. Another succession of hammer blows like a clock tolling a profoundly antisocial hour, then a harsh snap and Cosserby swearing. A ragged cheer went around the department because someone else's misfortune was always entertainment.

Someone just ducked into his little one-man tent and sat down. Jack jumped up, as much as the sloped canvas allowed, then sat down. Not Lidlet but Masty.

"Um…?" he invited.

Masty looked at him without expression. "Do you mind," he said, "if I just sit here?"

Jack frowned. "Um?"

"Just for a little while? I just need to be somewhere people won't look for me."

Masty was always there when he was needed. Quiet, helpful, willing. The perfect assistant in any venture you might name, nobody's best friend but everyone's favourite collaborator. Jack had never known him to shirk. Yet something was eating the man, and so Jack offered him the bed. "Take all the time you need. I'll head outside." And, though God was gurning at him to ask, he held his peace. Whatever it was, it was Masty's business.

Later, Banders came whooping back into camp, because she'd scored the weed she was after, which meant that the hospital department had now magically appeared on the leave rota for two days' time. She took the congratulations and adulation of her fellows with her customary modesty, even fetching a box so that she could be modest from an appropriate elevation.

"And there's more," she announced. "Gather round, my fellows, my comrades in adversity, Chief, you got ears for me?"

"Just get to it," the Butcher told her, but before Banders could suck all the credit out of the moment, Prassel herself marched in, and the Former Cohort-Broker hopped down from her box quickly.

"Listen up." Prassel's voice hailed them all out. Alv breaking away from her students, Masty venturing from the quiet within Jack's tent. Prassel looked around, counting them off, nodding as Cosserby scurried round to join the rest.

"Higher Orders has decided to recognise the great victory of liberating the city of Magnelei. By all accounts the Loruthi are still running for the South Bracinta border. Obviously the terrifying reputation of Forthright Battalion precedes us."

A wintry little smile which, for Prassel, was anybody else's belly laugh. "To recognise the great blow struck for the cause of reason, Uncle has authorised full Company rations of rummell across the camp. Former Cohort-Broker Banders."

"Magister?"

"It would obviously be terribly remiss if some of this was held back for unauthorised commercial dealings."

"That would never happen, magister."

"Good. See that it never happens, say, in about three days' time when everyone else has run out."

"Well it would serve them right, magister," Banders said. Jack looked from her to the utterly straight-faced Prassel, feeling that he was missing something.

"Other than that, we can expect tomorrow to bring in the flotsam of brawls, drunken accidents and probably a few knifings throughout the camp so don't go mad with your own ration. Chief."

"On it," Ollery agreed.

"Well then I'll leave you to it." Prassel said, just as a couple of soldiers turned up with a good-sized keg and plonked it down beside the main hospital tent. "Rejoice, in moderation."

After she'd gone, Jack raised a hand. "What is going on?" he asked.

"Every Company just got a barrel of this stuff," Banders told him. "Which means that every soldier out there just got their tin cup maybe almost full of rummell. You know the – well it's rum, basically, and a whole bunch of herbs, very good for you, stops your fingernails falling off. Rum and other stuff. It's actually quite horrible, unless the Chief is going to heat some up for us, in which case it becomes almost tolerable. Chief?"

"I'm getting the stove going."

"Grand. Anyway, what it mostly is, is strong stuff. Especially heated up. And what it also is, is in this big old barrel, because whenever Higher Orders signs off on this sort of thing, they forget that we're on the books as our own Company. So we have bloody scads of the stuff per head compared to everyone else. Now, what I am going to do is syphon a whole load off so that I can use it to get all kinds of useful toys later, but that still leaves a whole lot for everyone to throw down their necks, you get me?"

"I'm not allowed strong drink. It's forbidden," Jack said.

Banders stared at him. "I mean I've known people with a drink problem," she said levelly. "But that's a new one."

"I mean," said Jack, "it's only a minor prohibition."

"Mmm-hm," Banders agreed.

"I figured, I could have a sip. Do some penance after. Just a little sip. Just a little penance."

She nodded and topped up her cup with the ladle.

"On account of how it smelled so good," Jack explained. "Just a sip." He rattled his own mug against the side of the cauldron and she did the honours.

"By my reckoning that makes about forty-three sips," she noted. "Not sure of the sip-to-cup exchange rate but it's got to be something like that."

"I will do penance tomorrow," Jack said piously.

"That sounds like religion stuff," she noted.

He leaned in, looking around suspiciously. "It is."

"I mean it said 'priest' on your charge card so, fair enough, but you want to keep your mouth closed about that sort of thing," she warned him. "Back in the orphanage they'd whip you if you even admitted the concept of gods. Which, given some of the creepy stuff they had around, was asking a bit."

Jack thought about that. "Trade you your childhood for mine," he told her.

"I heard that," came a voice from knee level. God had His hands on His hips, glowering up furiously. "You dare slight the good upbringing you had, and while partaking in forbidden liquors?"

"I mean, I thought you liked it," Jack told Him. "I thought that I could do a bit less penance, if I set out a cup for you."

"The fact that I liked it," said the divine presence, "does not in any way affect that you owe me a big penance."

"I'm in trouble," Jack confided to Banders.

"Do what I did," she suggested.

"What's that?"

"Run away and join the army."

He threw back his head and hooted with laughter, then surprised an odd expression on her face, "What?"

"Don't think I ever saw you laugh properly before."

"Maybe you're not as funny as you think."

She smirked. "The Temporary Commission of Ends and Means," she told him grandly, "has long ago issued a general prohibition on all manner of religious observances within the bounds of the Palleseen Sway. Otherwise I would be the goddess of comedy. Anyway, the ladle is yours. I am going to slap Cosserby on the ass."

"You – what? Why would you do that?"

"Because he goes a really interesting shade of pink."

"You, ah, follow your dreams," Jack said weakly.

God had a nutshell for a cup, possibly something He'd pulled off the nature spirit. He drained it and held it up for more. The other two were having theirs, too. The moon-faced plant god dabbled its tendril fingers in a little splash of cooling drink, while boozy woodlice wove aimlessly around it. The spearman had his back to the others and was drinking with the grim determination of someone who has all night and nothing else to do.

"This is piss," opined God. "But it is acceptable as an offering. Give me another."

There was a yell from nearby and, "Damnit, Banders, that *stings!*"

"We get to go into the city." Jack sat down beside Him. "You want me to go find a... poorhouse or a sanatorium or something."

"Maybe." God hunched His shoulders. There was an alarmingly calculating look in His eyes. "I'm planning."

"What?"

"I'm planning my next move. Pals want to declare war on *me*, do they?"

"I mean yes. You as a class. Gods, religions, anything that isn't theirs, really. It's not a new thing."

"I want you to talk to the new girl."

"No," Jack said, feeling abruptly more sober.

"I want her to understand—"

"No. We've screwed her up already. I don't want to bring *you* into her life. That's just cruel."

Someone's army-issues nudged him. Presumably his expertise with the ladle was required. Jack got to his feet and found himself facing Lidlet. He almost fell into the stove. God snickered.

"I, ah, you want – you want another, is it?" he stammered out.

Lidlet had a cup in her hand, sure enough, but she didn't offer it. "How does it work," she asked, "with drink?"

Jack frowned. "It... what?"

"Last time I got drunk. With my mates. With Klimmel. We got into a punch up. It's how it goes. It'll be happening all over camp right now even on just a cup each. Not like we need much excuse. But I can't, can I? Even if I'm drunk."

"I..."

"One of those stuck-up bastards was looking down his nose at me," Lidlet told him, meaning – he thought – one of Alv's new students. "Decided he had something to say about my recent choices. And I was feeling the buzz of this stuff so I wanted to give him a shove. And it *hurt*. It was like cramps, right here." A fist clenched at her chest. "Even just thinking of it. And the problem was I was halfway to doing it already. And if I'd had two cups more I'd have done it. And I'd have been dead, wouldn't I?"

Jack did his best to shrug and smile and back off, as though he was the man of reason and she was the mad priest.

"Wouldn't I?" she said, and went to grab him by the collar. And stopped. There were tears in her eyes. "How come you get to drink?" she demanded.

"I mean, I don't. I'm forbidden." He tried for a solemn priestly tone, robbed of the intended dignity because the words came out slurred. He looked from her to the cauldron to his half-full cup and said, "Lidlet, I'm a man of peace."

"I mean I guess I am too, *now*," she hissed, but he shook his head.

"No, I mean, forever. Since I was a kid. I was brought up in a—" Probably too late to dodge this particular confession, "in a religion. I'm not Pal, right. I'm Maric. We have religions. And mine was not to hurt people. Not to push. Not to raise a hand. And it doesn't mean I don't get angry or all of that. But when I do, I don't *fight*. Because it's been ironed out of me since I was the size of..." Of God, based on where he was trying to put his hand down to, but that wouldn't really edify Lidlet.

And Lidlet had not been brought up a fanatical pacifist. Lidlet was a soldier, and her first recourse when she got frustrated was out with the fists and into someone else's business.

"You've probably had enough," Jack said. "I'm sorry."

"Religion," Lidlet said disgustedly, staring at the bottom of her mug.

"I know," Jack agreed. "I can see why you people are so down on it, sometimes."

When she looked up, there was an expression on her face he didn't like. A very sober, very practical look. Someone who was going to solve this little death and divinity problem she had. "This isn't over. I am going to find a way to crack this," she told him.

"If you do, please tell me," Jack said helplessly to her back as she turned and stalked off.

That had taken the fun out of the evening, honestly. Everyone else was still living it up. The Butcher, Alv and Tallifer were sitting around a fire telling stories. Masty and Lochiver were playing some kind of game with counters on a squared board. Banders and three quartermaster's clerks were in a huddle drunkenly building business empires. Cosserby, sitting nearby and presumably having recovered from the ass-slapping incident, was staring at Banders rather mournfully, in the manner of one about to recite maudlin poetry. Jack hoped he didn't.

"I'm going to turn in," he announced to the world, just in case someone should turn up at his elbow and say, "No, no, Jack, stay, the night won't be the same without you." Nobody did. God just glanced up and said, "Fill your mug and leave it down here, won't you? This filthy stuff grows on you."

He did so, hoping that it was sufficient penance to clear his own indulgences, and then wandered off to his tent, still a bit drunk, but no longer very jolly after his words with Lidlet. His fingers knew the buttons now, without needing any of his mind to concentrate on them. By the time he'd ducked inside he had his jacket open and was working on the collar of his shirt. At which point he saw that he had company.

It was Caeleen, reclining on the meagre comfort of his bedroll as though it were a gilded couch in a palace. She still wore the Pal uniform he'd seen her in, in Maserley's company. Seeing his suddenly stilled hands, she smiled at him and he felt something kick, inside his ribs.

"You seem," she noted, "to be ahead of the game. I should catch up." She rolled into a sitting position, knees out, the soles of her abruptly bare feet together. Slender fingers slid down the left side of her jacket so that it fell open without any pretence at having real buttons, or being a real jacket.

"What?" he croaked.

"Would you believe," she said, shrugging the garment off with a boneless twist of her shoulders, "that I have conceived of such a burning passion for you that I slipped the chain of my master, for you and only you?"

"Not really, no." Jack, already kneeling because of the slope of canvas above, felt horribly vulnerable. The flap had dropped closed behind him, and it would be powerfully complicated to shuffle backwards out of it into the open air. The work of a hundred years, at least. He couldn't make himself do it.

"I... I'm sorry I... You shouldn't be here." He found he was speaking low, under the buzz and chatter from the camp outside. The thought of raising his voice was unthinkable.

"I am, by nature, transgressive," she agreed. "Sit down, Jack. Forthright Battalion raises a cup tonight and you have the chance to celebrate in a way to make you the envy of your peers. Sit with me."

Sitting with her was, obviously, out of the question, Jack thought as he sat with her.

"Look, this is..." He closed his eyes. "I understand. It's some game of Maserley's. No. It's... No."

The look of hurt that came to her was genuine and convincing. Her fingers stilled on her cuffs. "Do you know what I have risked, coming here? For you, Jack, only for you."

"You need to understand that I can't," he told her wretchedly. "I'm forbidden. I'm sorry." The two words of Pel he seemed to deploy more than any other. "A major forbiddance. God would *not* understand." And talking about God was something the *Pals* wouldn't understand, but she was a demon. He felt that she and God occupied some kind of kindred territory.

He had been looking into her face the whole time, somehow feeling he owed it to her, and so he saw how her expressions changed. Not like human features, the operation of a collection of muscles and parts to contrive a whole, but like the sea changed. Seamless and edgeless. Like turning something to a different light, so that the fall of shadows across it made another pattern entirely. The hurt was gone. Now she was sly, smiling like a knife.

"He got that right, then."

"What?"

"My master. The tenets of your faith."

Jack wasn't sure what was going on now, except that she was still within an inch of him and the narrow straits of air between them were so charged that he was surprised not to see sparks.

"I mean," he said weakly, "Yes. I can go through the theology of it, if you want. I can't guarantee that it's particularly persuasive. I mean it never persuaded me, really, and I live by it."

"Jack." Caeleen leaned forwards. "I have been sent to destroy your faith."

He swallowed. "All right."

"To leave your oaths in tatters, to sunder you from your god and rob you of your gifts."

"All right. I mean, why, if I can ask? Is it to stop me healing people, because that sounds…" his voice kept drying up. He swallowed over and over, "… sounds a bit petty, honestly."

"Do you think," Caeleen asked him, "that Fellow-Invigilator Maserley cares if your patients live or die?" Her breath smelled surprisingly like the hot rummell, sweet and heady and promising morning regrets.

"I mean, no? But maybe he's got hidden depths of compassion or something."

She laughed – not the sultry seductress in that moment but a weirdly ungainly snort and chuckle, earthy and almost human. "He does not. I give you that as a gift that needs no recompense, Jack. He does not, and he hates you."

"That seems strong."

"Well, I exaggerate. He hates Prassel, and you are a thing of hers that has come to his attention, and he wants to ruin you utterly because it may slightly inconvenience her."

"Oh. Right. For a moment there I thought I was important, or something."

She'd been leaning in again, every slight motion of her prickling the hairs on his neck. Now she sat back suddenly. "You don't act like a priest."

He shrugged. "Even at my priestiest I was never very good at it."

"He's sent me after priests before. You'd be amazed how many of them have vows my master finds it amusing to break. Half of them are on fire with indignation the moment they see me, and the other half are on their backs."

Jack drew in a deep breath and closed his eyes. "I'm sorry you've wasted your time." Hearing his own voice tremble. "It's a big forbiddance. He's very serious about it."

She rested her chin on his shoulder. "Jack, I'm going to be frank with you. You've got your chief and I've got mine, you understand."

He nodded, eyes still screwed shut so that he couldn't see whatever expression she'd chosen to wear to fit the words.

"I am absolutely bound, by seal and contract, to do what he tells me. And you are constrained to follow your rules of your own will and choice."

"It's a sorry state of affairs," he agreed.

"So I'm going to enchant you," she explained. "And then your will and choice won't be a factor, and I can get on with ruining your life like I've been told."

"Okay."

"For what it's worth, which is very little. I'm sorry. I— what do you mean, 'Okay'?"

Jack could feel a tightness in his chest, almost too tight to breathe around. "Just... all right. I mean, infernal wiles, isn't it. Not like I can stop you."

She caught his chin and twisted his head round, and at that point he couldn't keep his eyes shut any longer. The expression he surprised on her face – or that she'd prepared in ambush – was puzzled concern. "Are you... all right?" For a moment he had the terrible thought that she'd offer to come back later, when he was feeling more priestly.

"Just—" he started, and then God came in.

The divine presence had His mouth open and the nutshell cup in His hand. Doubtless He was about to demand a further libation by way of offering. His veiny eyes almost popped out of His face.

"What the fuck," quoth God, "is happening here?"

The maelstrom that coursed through Jack right then partook of embarrassment and horror and frustration in such outlandish proportions that he felt he'd invented an entirely new emotion. "Will you just – Will you – Can't you *knock*?"

"Knock?" spat God, apoplectic. "*Knock?* Firstly, you slack-jawed lackwit, it's a tent. Secondly, I am your God who does not need your damned *permission* to enter into your presence. Thirdly, I am still waiting for a fucking *explanation* as to just what in the ever-loving hell is going on here."

Jack looked from Him to Caeleen. "I'm sorry. I've got – some theology's come up and—"

"What's that?" she asked, looking at God.

Some solid and reliable part of Jack's world just fell away entirely, leaving him clinging to his understandings of the world by his fingernails.

"You can... see Him?"

"Wait, what?" demanded God, slightly slower on the uptake.

"What is that?" she repeated, staring at God with horrified fascination.

"That's... God. You're not supposed to be able to see him. Nobody is. Except me." Jack turned from her back to his aghast deity. "Can demons see you?"

God spread his hands. "How should I know? Do I associate with filthy demons? I do not!"

"Would you not—"

"You're objecting to me calling *demons* filthy?" God demanded. "Demon harlots, at that? Me, your God, and I can't even talk down to an actual *demon*? She's got to you that much already, has she?"

"Your God looks like a rat with a beard," Caeleen said.

Jack's eyes bugged. "Please don't talk about God like that."

"A rat that needs a bath, wearing a dishcloth," she added.

"Is that bloody so?" God stormed up to her with clenched fists. "I will bloody smite you, harlot."

"You will not," Jack said. "You don't even smite. You are literally the god of not smiting." He looked at Caeleen again. "How do you see Him? There've been times even I couldn't." *Blessed times.* He pushed the thought back down.

He couldn't quite tell what she meant, by the look she put on her face next. It wasn't sultry or sly or the moue of fake hurt. Just a level, pragmatic look from a woman in a hard profession.

"I see him," she said, "because he's there." And, before he could interrogate that, "We have to learn, when we are sold into our contracts, to see in the Lands Above. See, hear, speak, act. All the rules are different here. So we learn to see what is there, and ignore what is not. He is there. I see him. I see you, rat-god. I am here to take your priest away from you."

Jack had thought the whole situation had reached a peak of humiliation, but God wasn't done with him. The little divinity swaggered up to the demon and stood with His hands on His hips.

"Oh my," He said. "I do hope you don't mind being just a span late, dear heart, because you aren't even the first."

"Please don't," Jack said.

"He's done this nonsense before," God went on, arms out and looking around as though He had a whole audience He was rousing to a general condemnation of Jack's morals. "Gone hiding under the skirts of some demon hussy the moment his religious duties got too much for him. That's why he isn't even my priest any more! Too good for me, he is! A parting of the ways, a recanting of faith by way of infernal harlotry. Because he was weak. He *is* weak. Too weak to be any priest of mine."

"You're *not* a priest?" Caeleen said slowly. "You have been nothing but vows and forbiddances since you ducked into this tent, and you're not a priest?"

"I am not a priest," Jack confirmed. "I was a priest. Then we had a falling out over the precise duties owed to the faithful by God. And I…"

"You *fell*." God jabbed him with a bony finger.

Caeleen had a hand to her mouth. Her eyes glittered. "You're not even a priest."

"Well go tell that to your master, I suppose. The secret's out."

She raised her eyebrows. "Only if he asks me. I've no duty to tell him anything unprompted. He thinks he's a good draftsman but there are gaps in his contracts he's never thought of." She leaned back on the bedroll. "Forbidden, is it?"

"You live your whole life by rules," Jack said quietly. "And they get like bars, in your head. I just… It's forbidden still, in here." He tapped his temple. "Sorry. I wasn't being straight with you."

"I'm a demon," she pointed out. "There's no obligation." A calculating look came to her. "So I can tell my master that…

despite my best efforts I have been unable to break your vows or rob you of your powers."

"I mean my actual *vows*… it's like God says. I already went there. So it's not really true."

"It's *technically* true," Caeleen said. "Which satisfies the terms of my contract." She met his eyes. "Of course, he'll just send me back to try again." A twitch of an eyebrow, an invitation.

"Absolutely under no circumstances," fumed God.

"I'd like that," Jack said. And then Caeleen pushed past him to leave the tent and he felt her breath – hot, infernal – on his cheek and her hand on his arm as she shifted him aside. And she was gone, and he let out what felt like the longest breath he'd ever had pent up inside him.

"I don't mind saying," God said, "that was a mite disconcerting. It's never happened to me before." And Jack had to bite off an appalled laugh at the thought that doubtless Caeleen had heard *that* one more than once.

"You're not to associate with her kind any further, mind," God added sternly.

"Demons or harlots?"

"Either!"

"I'm not your priest any more." Jack suddenly rediscovered the ability to smile, really smile, and feel happy about it.

"I shall withdraw my healing power. I can kill you with a thought!" God warned him. "Your body is held together by nothing but my divine forbearance."

"Go on then," Jack said.

God threw up His hands. "She is a demon under the control of some bastard Pal conjurer who means you ill! What do you think you're going to get out of this, exactly?"

Jack shrugged. "Well, you're probably right," he allowed.

He was still smiling when he ducked back out of the tent, whereupon someone shoved a bag full of something acrid over his head and the whole world went black.

Masty Absents

Masty, then. As noted, not his name. A foreigner, wearing the pale uniform of a second-class soldier, but wearing it well because he grew up in it. They tailored a tiny version of it for him when he was eight years old. Just Masty, formerly an underaged familiar of the camp, passed from hand to hand and Company to Company. Then an adolescent who'd known the army more than he'd known his own family. Striving to be useful, to earn his keep. Running messages, taking notes, organising schedules. Never fighting. There was a note on his card, from when he was just a kid, that he not be allowed to fight, and nobody ever thought to remove it when he was grown. And now, just Masty the orderly, most dependable member of the experimental hospital department. The man who was always there.

Masty, whose stock in trade was to be at everyone's elbow the moment they needed something, and with that particular something being humbly proffered, was not there when they were kidnapping Maric Jack. By that point the general atmosphere of cheer around the department had risen to intolerable levels and he'd slipped away, unremarked. Because one advantage about always being where you're needed is that nobody actually looks for you. He had the customary invisibility of one who is taken for granted.

Nocturnal walkabouts around the camp as a whole weren't new to him. There was always something to see, something to do. Someone who needed another pair of hands. Growing up in the shadow of the Palleseen Sway, being useful had been his shield, then his habit, and at last just a way of breathing. Because the uniform got tight sometimes, even on someone as slender as Masty.

Tonight the camp would be no respite. He should have known. The rest of the army didn't quite have the alcoholic bounty that bureaucratic oversight had given the hospital, but a cup of rummell each was being supplemented by cached supplies on a squad by squad basis. More important was the implicit permission. Uncle handing out the grog ration meant a licence to get a bit rowdy, to scrum and sing. Mother Semprellaime and the others of her old profession would be doing a fine trade tonight, alongside a solid amateur showing no doubt.

Masty wanted none of it. Not that he was either chaste or prudish, but it was awkward. Pals were a status-conscious people. A couple of troopers mashing anatomies wasn't complicated, but when you invited rank into the equation it held the door open for awkwardness, power dynamics and abuse. And Masty wasn't even just *some foreigner* who could conceivably have just sought out some youth in a similarly pallid uniform to offer a flower and a smile to. Masty was the kid who'd been brought into the army when he was seven, grown up there, become some unique hybrid thing. Which meant there was nobody like him, really. The one and only original Masty. Or whatever his name had once been.

Normally his best chance at a little release came when the department was given leave in some friendly port. And, technically, that would be theirs to enjoy in just a couple of days. Except he wouldn't, not this time. Worst of all possible worlds. And so he walked, hunching his shoulders against the ribald calls, the whoops, the sound of some Cohort-Invigilator singing a Pal marching song comparing a variety of named officers to the arse ends of pack animals from across the world.

Actually, he stopped to listen to that one, because the

singer was flat but the lyricist had been inspired, and Masty, more regular than the regulars, knew most of the individuals. He stood at the very edge of their firelight and mustered a bit of a smile, and felt better for it. And then left before anybody noticed him and either called him over or told him to go away.

It was a terrible thing to know that, while he liked the department, he very much preferred them in their usual state of grim misery and personal problems. That made him sound like a profoundly broken person. Which he was, but not in that way. It was just that he wasn't very good at being happy. It wasn't a life skill that being a foreign ward of an ideologically dictatorial military force taught you.

Then he was being hailed, as he crossed through the dark between two rows of tents. Dark, but of course the paler uniform of the Accessories always stood out, catching the slightest glimmer. *We know you're all sneaks*, that uniform said. *Sneak your way out of this.*

He stood when addressed. The man who'd called was a stout, balding Cohort-Monitor not known to him. Bustling over, a half-cloak slung over his uniform jacket.

"You, Accessory! What's your business here? Where are your papers?"

Masty blinked at that. Not what he was used to; certainly not what he expected tonight of all nights. He got out his dog-eared identification, the card with his essentials, the folded orders paper detailing his hospital duties. The Cohort-Monitor flicked open a hand-lamp, the tableth-powered glow spiking in Masty's eyes.

"What in reason is an experimental hospital?" the man demanded. His lips had been moving as he read, which probably wasn't a good sign. "You an experiment?"

"I'm an orderly, magister," Masty explained.

"Orderly? Skulking around camp is hardly orderly," the man spat. Masty forced a laugh, then bit it back because the man hadn't been making a pun at all but had apparently never heard the word used as a job description.

"I help the medicos, magister," he tried.

"Where's your excursion permit?"

Masty blinked. "I'm sorry?"

A moment later he was sitting down because the man had shoved him hard in the chest.

"You will address me as 'Magister', Accessory. Where's your excursion permit?"

"I... Magister. I wasn't issued with one, magister. I don't know what one is, magister." He wasn't sure what was going on. He seemed to have stepped out from the night of unwelcome but harmless celebration into a different situation entirely.

"No Accessory can just go on a jaunt through camp without a permit, and you know that damn well," the Cohort-Monitor told him. "Looking to see if we'd left any unsecured possessions while we were in our cups, were you?"

"No, magister."

"On your feet, Accessory! Do you think it's appropriate to speak to a superior officer from the ground?"

"No, magister." Masty scrambled up and the man lurched into him, a hand like a pincer of ham closing about his shoulder. The officer was drunk, he realised belatedly. Meanly, brutally drunk.

"You're coming with me, sneak-thief. We'll see what the duty Inquirer has to say about you." Without warning the man was in motion, an inexorable momentum that dragged Masty in its wake. "How's your back? Got room for more stripes or is it all scar-mail already?"

Masty tried protesting, which the Cohort-Monitor shook out of him in short order before dragging him deeper into camp. They ended up at a small tent where the worst-tempered woman in the world sat before a small desk. There were creatures in the world with a killing stare, Masty had heard. This woman could have looked right back down the line of their gaze and turned any one of them into dust.

"Tunly," she said, in the manner of one describing a bowel ailment. "What now?"

"Found this little shit pilfering."

"Magister, I was just walking."

The Inquirer made a note. "Found him with his hand in a pocket?"

"As good as," Cohort-Monitor Tunly said.

"Magister—"

Tunly shook him again and he bit his tongue. The Inquirer asked for his papers, and had to ask a second time because Masty's head was still ringing. And then he didn't have them because Tunly hadn't given them back, and for a minute and a half's pantomime Tunly could not find them either, and Masty was about to be reclassified from Accessory to Possible Spy. Then the documents turned up, crumpled in a pocket and stuck to something half-melted and nasty. The Inquirer took them fastidiously and unfolded them with the very tips of her fingers.

"You utter prick," she said, after a second going-over aided by a pair of spectacles.

"I know," Tunly agreed. "Nasty little piece of work."

"You, Tunly. You are the prick," the Inquirer told him flatly. "He's not one of ours."

Tunly swelled with pride and selective hearing. "You're telling me I have secured an enemy agent?"

"He's from Forthright Battalion, you twat," the Inquirer told him. "He's one of theirs."

"Then why was he in our camp?"

The Inquirer massaged her forehead and Masty began to have an idea why she looked so very ill-tempered. "It's a conjoined camp. There is no marked boundary between the Battalions, it's just cheek by jowl out there. Something something not-wanting-to-foster-unhealthy-rivalries something, if I recall the justification. You've basically gone and grabbed one of their people and kidnapped him. Probably you were the one in the wrong camp, at that."

"I was not!" Tunly insisted. "Megget, I caught him—"

"Sneaking," the woman – Cohort-Inquirer Megget, apparently – cut him off. "Do you have any idea how much paperwork this is going to generate?"

"Discipline is more important," declared Tunly in the manner of someone only peripherally connected with that paperwork.

"You a thief?" Megget asked Masty.

"No, magister. I'm a—"

"Didn't ask what you were. So I have a Cohort-rank officer who says you're a thief, and I have some sort of medical Accessory who says you're not a thief but is likely to be biased towards you, on account of he's you. And anyway, you Accessories always stick together."

"And he didn't have an excursion permit," Tunly threw in.

"That's because excursion permits are an invention of the Landwards Battalion Logistics Department who are specifically trying to inflame my writer's cramp," Megget snapped. "They don't *have* them in Forthright. They don't have them anywhere else but bloody here."

"What, their Accessories can just… walk around?" Tunly was having an existential moment.

"And the Palleseen Sway still stands," Megget noted. "Look, I'm not going to write him up as a thief."

"But—"

"I am *not* going to go through our forms, and also the cross-battalion forms, just because you are pissed off at being duty officer and want to take it out on a foreigner," she told him frankly. Masty felt himself slowly relax, muscle by muscle. Reason had prevailed.

"Give him six," Megget said. "For malingering or something."

"What?" Tunly demanded, incensed.

"What?" Masty asked, and then, hastily, "Magister?"

"Six is under the threshold for the inter-battalion stuff," Megget said. "It's all you're getting." She was speaking only to Tunly. Masty had ceased to exist to her.

Later, full dark and the business of the camp slowly guttering down just like its fires, Masty got back to the department. He spotted Lochiver and Banders at a fire still, or at least he heard them first because they were singing together, though not necessarily the same song. He gave the whole thing a wide berth, instead sneaking into the Butcher's tent. He'd been charged with the act already, after all. He might as well make it true in retrospect.

The Butcher was a man of profound order when it came to his wares, as any responsible alchemist needed to be. Masty found the three precise philtres he needed, then paused. You could just about rub salves into your own back, but it would hurt like hell to twist and turn as he tried it. It would be like the six strokes all over again.

"Let me," said Ollery, from the dark. Masty started, caught red-handed in a crime which would only have been departmental business as usual before tonight.

They went outside for it. The boy was sleeping – a stolen cup of rummell had put him straight out, Ollery said. He slept, and salving Masty's wounds wasn't going to be silent. Outside, the tuneless dirge Lochiver and Banders were mauling would cover the worst of it.

"Tell me," Ollery prompted. Masty gave him the brief and narrow account, yelping occasionally as the man's solid fingers worked across his back.

"Right," said Ollery when he was done. "Well that's worth knowing. I'll ask Prassel to issue us with something, so Landwards don't get fresh again." And that was all the commiseration the

Butcher had to give. "So you're going to tell me what's up, now." Not a question.

"I got six, Chief." The numbing effect of the salve was kicking in already and he struggled back into his shirt.

"And you had some preternatural premonition of this, because you've been like your own ghost all evening. I need to know I can rely on you when it counts, Masty. What is it?"

"I'm not enjoying being here, Chief," Masty said hollowly.

"Hardly been bad so far, has it? Been in worse places…" Ollery's voice trailed off. "Oh, right. Is it here?"

"It is, Chief."

"What?" a new voice broke in. Masty hadn't registered when the singing stopped, possibly because his ears had been trying to disown any connection to it. But here was Banders with her infallible instinct for somewhere to stick her nose in. "What's here? Is it presents?" Swaying only slightly, then slumping bonelessly to drape herself over the Butcher's shoulder. "What are we doing? What's here?"

Masty took a deep breath. It wasn't as though he could have kept it a secret, anyway.

"Banders, what am I?"

"You're the best damn man I ever knew. We don't deserve you."

Masty blinked at how quickly that had come out, and didn't know what to do with it. "No, I mean—"

"I mean, all right, you're not a Pal, but… wait. *Here* here?"

"That's right," he confirmed. "I've come home."

"Bloody marvellous!" Banders burst out, oblivious to Ollery trying to shush her. "We should drink to it."

"No, no it's not—" Masty tried.

"Here Bracinta or here the city?" she pressed.

"I mean, both but—"

"You can show us round!" Banders crowed. "You must know all the places!"

I was six, seven, when they took me from it. "No, Banders—"

"This is fantastic," she told him. "We are going to have the best leave!" And with that she receded from the Butcher as though rebounding belatedly from a collision, and wove off through the tents.

"Not how I wanted that to go," Masty admitted. At least she hadn't clapped him companionably on the back before she left.

Not Eggs but Venom

There were very good reasons that Landwards Battalion might have instituted its draconian measures against the free movement of Accessories. Pirisytes was an example of how some of those Accessories were using their movement in profoundly problematic ways. Except that, against the vast span of a whole battalion and the general trouble that restless soldiers got into, Landwards's Higher Orders hadn't actually noticed the pattern of malicious intent against the background level of fractious misbehaviour. And instituting a whole extra layer of punitive bureaucracy against their own conscripts hadn't stopped any of the malice from being carried out.

When they finally took the bag off her head, Tallifer was aware that she had been carried some distance. Thrown into a cart and covered with sacks and then taken to where the sounds of camp revelry weren't even a dull murmur on the horizon. Nothing of which was good news, but then the whole sack-on-headness of the situation had communicated that more than adequately.

She had absolutely no idea what was going on. A Landwards Battalion hazing ritual seemed the absolute best interpretation, but she wasn't feeling lucky.

They were out in the countryside. In a hollow, surrounded by trees, up against what her eyes at first told her was a vast gnarled hand clawing its way out of the earth. The faint kindness of the moon, and the fact she'd been in utter darkness for half an hour, recontextualised that to the roots of a fallen tree whose demise had left this hollow and this clearing. A giant of the forest laid low by time rather than the woodsman's axe.

Senses she hadn't had to use in quite a while were prickling, telling her this was a bad place. Not that her perfectly regular senses hadn't worked that one out, but this was *consecrated*. She tasted the air with the tip of her tongue and understood it was a temporary working. Someone had gone round the lip of the hollow with ash and vinegar, and there would be sigils smeared across the trunks of the surrounding trees. Consecrated, but not to any god of hers, nor anything from the old Jarokiri pantheon she might claim diplomatic relations with.

The people around her were wearing the same uniform she was. Palleseen tight but Accessory pale. They were all of a piece: half a dozen compact people with pointy chins and bony cheekbones – as much as she could see of their faces. All conscripted from some part of the Sway she'd never been to, either as a fugitive priest or a Palleseen medico.

They had masks on. Most were just of cloth. Bandanas with eyeholes, tied off at the back, repurposed from old uniforms. She could tell the leader, though, because he had on a wooden thing that covered his whole face, a grotesque bug-eyed business intricately carved to suggest that, apart from those eyes, the whole rest of his face was spindly reaching limbs with crabby little hands, all packed together. Quite a piece of work, and Banders could probably have sold it to a collector for a pocketful of money and a couple of good-sized favours. Which receding situation was probably the only circumstance in which Tallifer would have been happy to see the thing.

They manhandled her over to a wooden frame that had been driven into the earth before the roots. Not right up against them, room enough for someone to stand behind it, and she knew enough to know what *that* meant. She struggled, but she was an old woman and they were all lean, not big but strong like rawhide that only grips tighter. They had her wrists and ankles secured without really breaking a sweat.

She cursed them. First just swearing and then with, "The Chastising Fire eat you from your guts out!"

The Chastising Fire, Mazdek, was dithering about on her shoulder. It ran up her arm and gummed at the ropes, but as they weren't a formal offering it couldn't affect them, and as they weren't her ropes, she couldn't exactly turn them into an impromptu donation to the faith.

Even so, a couple of her captors offered up warding gestures, nothing she recognised save the intent was clear. Almost flattering that, them imagining she had a serious curse left in her.

Then they got the other prisoner off the cart. She hadn't even realised she had company. She'd been keeping very still, waiting for a moment that hadn't come, and so had he. Maric Jack's bewildered face, when the hood came off, and him without even his magic box of whatever-it-was.

She thought they'd screwed up then, what with just the one frame set out, but it turned out one of the uncomfortable things she'd been sharing the cart-bed with was another frame, and they had driven it into the earth with the efficiency of a good Pal work crew. After which Jack was tied to it, without even resisting very much. Just kind of going with it, which was normally an attitude towards life that Tallifer appreciated but just right now *some* kind of resistance would have been nice. Even just to show solidarity.

He looked over at her, registered he wasn't the sole piece of meat on the chopping block, and grimaced. "I'm sorry."

"Why?" Tallifer demanded. "This is your fault? They've got a thing with you?" She looked round wildly. "I'm not with him. He's nobody I know, this clown. You've got the wrong woman."

"No, I mean," Jack clarified. "Just, generally. It doesn't look good."

"Oh, you think?" she demanded. "They are going to strangle us."

"What? Why?"

Tallifer looked at him pityingly, because it was something she did a lot and circumstances suggested she wouldn't get the chance to do it much more. "I thought you were a priest, Jack."

"I mean, ex-priest." He tried to shrug in that loose-shouldered Maric way but the position of his arms didn't really allow it. "Wait, this is—"

Tallifer drew in a long, tired breath. "I really don't see that I need to spend my last minutes explaining rudimentary theology to an idiot," she said calmly. "Oi you, with the horrible face on. Tell this man I've never met before what you're about to do to us, will you?" And in her head the words had an enviable sangfroid about them. And on her lips they trembled and jumped with fear. Because yes, she was old, and yes she was tired, and yes her god was a miserable little squeak of flame that wouldn't have warmed a beggar's least finger, but she was still using her life, worn out as it was. She was clinging to it like a drowning woman to a plank.

The hideous mask drew near, tilting and cocking weirdly. For a moment she thought the man was trying to spook her even more, in which case it was working. Then she realised the mask's actual eyeholes, hidden within the carving, were quite small, and he was just trying to see her properly.

"The great temples hold their sacrifices in the open air." His voice came out through some channel in the carvings that made it sound hollow and nasty. "They lift their offerings to the sun. They burn them, so that the smoke of their oblation may ascend to the vault of the sky. The Pals are the same. Their conquests are a succession of setting lamps and tearing off roofs, so that all is exposed to the searing light of reason. And yet the brighter their lamps, the darker the shadows. And we of the shadows make our offerings in a different way. We do not release or expose, but stifle. We bury in darkness. And while a good peat bog would be best, to send your lives to god, we shall make do with the cord. The cord twisted tight, to trap your breath within your bodies. To entomb your souls. To make you fit gifts for hidden things. Do I make myself clear?"

"You do know we're not actually Pals," Tallifer tried, although she already knew the answer. "We're all Whitebellies here, right?"

"You're priests," the mask told her. "I can see the fingerprints of gods on both of you. There is no sweeter meat."

It had been a long time since some poetic beau had referred to Tallifer in those kind of terms and she didn't feel that having the words thrown at her at this extremity was flattering. "I will set a fire in your guts as my last act," she told the man. "The dying will of a priestess of Mazdek has a power even the Pals couldn't drive from me." She had no idea if it was true.

"Not the least of your power shall make it past the cord," the mask told her. "It shall be a feast for god as your body moulders in the soil." The mask cocked towards the moon. "We're losing time. Do it."

And then there was a cultist stood behind her. She couldn't crane round enough to look at the man – woman? – but then there were hands before her, a thin garotte of wire held between them.

"Jack," she said, "if you've got any miracles to pull out of your pockets, now's the time. Or did they get left behind with your damn box?"

"They did, yes," he said. There was someone behind him, too. Fiddling with their killing implement because they hadn't baled it properly in their pocket and it was tangled. The man in the mask clicked his tongue with audible annoyance at the delay.

"I told you—" he said, in a voice considerably less portentous.

"I know, I know," the cultist said.

"If nothing else, they catch you with that in your pocket you'll have some serious explaining to do." Like a mother nagging a recalcitrant adolescent. "Always—"

"Always hide the tools of our faith, I know." And then a

triumphant little noise at getting the murderous implement straightened out. "Ready. Sorry."

Somehow the twitch of the mask adequately conveyed a rolling of the eyes behind it. "You sure? I can do the invocation now? Or did you want to wait til morning or something?"

"Just go, Pirisytes."

The mask, and apparently someone called Pirisytes behind it, made an exaggerated *What?* motion. "I mean it's just as well we're going to kill 'em now, isn't it, what with *names* suddenly being bandied about."

"I'm sorry. Just came out. Do the invocation. It's waiting."

There were plenty of perfectly nice gods who were *it* or *them* or some other thing entirely. Somehow Tallifer didn't think this was one of those.

"I have money," she said.

"You'll die rich then," said Pirisytes. He'd apparently given up on the hollow boding voice, fidgeting from foot to foot, keen to be done and get gone. *I'm sorry, am I keeping you?*

"I have influence. Favours," Tallifer went on determinedly. The wire slipped about her neck, biting ever so slightly into her throat. "Look, we can come to an arrangement. You need something for your followers, for your god. I can get it for you."

"Death to all the bright gods," the man said. "Down with their temples and holy places, and the bodies of their priests to choke the streets of their citadels." Quoting, and from another language given the awkward grammar. "Doesn't leave much room for shaking hands, old woman. Now." And he drew himself up, shifted posture so that he was the mask and not the man, again. "Eater of the world, breeder of disharmony, hear me!" His voice gone through hollow and into a buzzing drone that made her sick to her stomach. "Take this feast I have brought you. Make their souls a meat for your eggs that disorder and chaos may hatch and spread through the world like a sickness. Feast on the devotions they owe to others. Present yourself before us, breeder of discord! Witness our sacrifice!"

They were obviously far enough from the camp that he felt confident lifting his voice to a shout. In the ringing echoes of it, Jack twitched and said, "Wait, I know you."

The mask made a little snicker of a laugh and put a hand on his shoulder companionably. "Friend, I don't know you, and you'd not be able to presume on our acquaintance even so."

"Not you," Jack said, and he wasn't looking at the mask, but at the man's shoulder. "You, I know you. You're... the flying scorpion."

Tallifer frowned, but something had obviously struck home, because the cultists had all gone still.

"It is *not* a flying scorpion," said Pirisytes, obviously between clenched teeth and just like any other priest who has that *one* tenet of their theology that nobody quite remembers properly. "It is a—"

"A scorpionfly!" Jack announced in triumph, looking weirdly delighted at his own memory. "The divine scorpionfly, who lays eggs in the hearts of kings, harbinger of upheaval and change, bringer of chaos! Zoro... Zan... Zenotheus!" As though he was a schoolchild put on the spot by teacher.

"If you're going to claim you're one of the sect," said Pirisytes, "I can see that's not so."

"No, no, but I had a friend in Ilmar. One of you. A priest. Chaos and eggs, right? Leave no paper unaltered, no order unchanged? I know you." Still weirdly talking past the mask to the man's shoulder. "She... she was my friend. A good friend. An enemy, obviously. She wanted to convert me. But she had the best tea. I liked her very much."

"Give it up, Jack," said Tallifer, who'd decided dying with dignity was better.

"Look, I don't know if it's worth anything," Jack said, "but..."

Pirisytes had been trying to shift sideways to intercept Jack's stare and become the focus of the conversation again. "Who are you talking to?" he demanded peevishly.

"Zenotheus," Jack said. "The divine scorpionfly."

A profound, rather sceptical silence fell over the hollow until Pirisytes managed, "Nice try."

"He's right there. It, sorry. It's right there. On your shoulder."

The chief cultist went very still. "On my...?"

"I think. I mean maybe not the whole actual Zenotheus, but, like, a little piece of it. I mean you invoked it. Maybe it was in your pocket, before."

"In my...?"

Jack looked honestly bewildered. "You can't see it? Your own god."

Pirisytes took a step back. His hands twitched, but if he was trying to signal them to start twisting the garottes, the message didn't get through. "You're mad," said the flying chaos scorpion cultist.

"I see gods," Jack said. "All the gods. It's... I think it's a kind of theological technicality. I fell through the gaps after a serious disagreement with God, and all the other gods sort of rushed in. I see them all over the place. I see Tallifer's fire god over there, and I can see Zenotheus on your shoulder. Or a little avatar of it anyway. I'm not in the army because they caught me being a priest. I'm not even a real priest any more. I'm in the army because they caught me smuggling gods out of Ilmar, to keep them from the Decanters. I had a whole thing going. A system of people who believed in gods or in me or in frustrating the Pals. That's what they got me for, in the end. God-smuggling."

A pause, and then an incredulous laugh from within the mask. "God-smuggling?"

"I know. It sounds ridiculous when you say it out loud. If you go in my inside pocket you'll see it on my papers, though. If you can read the writing." And then, sternly, "No. Both of us. No, that's not acceptable." Talking to the shoulder again. "It's got to be both of us. Please. For the sake of your priestess, my friend. Or the gods I smuggled. Or the chaos I bred, because there was a lot of chaos. I won't pretend it was my primary goal, but it happened. Please."

The mask cocked again. Tallifer, her skin crawling just a little, knew the man was listening to a little voice she couldn't hear. And knew that he didn't *know* he was listening to it. It didn't creep in by the ears, that kind of voice.

"Cut them down," Pirisytes said. "Both of them."

The disappointed groan of the cultists was just like any squad of soldiers denied some minor diversion.

"Just do it. God-smuggling. That's worth something." He sighed and tugged at the rim of the mask to get some air to his face. "Get a fire going. Brew up some tea. And you two, get the frames back on the cart."

With the mask off, Pirisytes was just a youngish man, dark hair cropped, a few scars remaining from some pox or skin condition long past. He sat and stared at Jack, and Tallifer was more than grateful not to be the centre of his attention.

The tea, handed out in army-issue tin cups, was very good, at least. Really top-tier stuff, far better than normally reached the department unless Banders was having a particularly good run.

"I mean, we have a problem, now," Pirisytes said.

"Because we know your little cult is active here," Tallifer agreed.

"We'll say nothing," Jack said.

"Well obviously we'll say nothing," Tallifer lied. And she was feeling angry and her wrists still hurt from the ropes, and it didn't come out sounding very convincing. And it was Jack who decided to remonstrate with her.

"We'll say nothing," he insisted.

She tried to communicate, by a widening of the eyes, that they had uncovered a murder cult and that anyone they knew could be next.

"It's the deal," he said. "It's why we're alive. Zenotheus is a god of hidden things. Keeping itself and its followers hidden is... how these things go."

"And when Lochiver goes missing and ends up on one of these frames? Or Banders? Or Cosserby?" Because, honestly, if this sort of thing was going to happen to anyone then a luckless bastard like Cosserby was at the front of the queue.

Jack bit his lip. "Ah. Well. I... can I alter the deal a bit?"

Pirisytes's lip wrinkled. "What? Did you bargain with the brooder of lies and not get what you wanted?"

"If I asked you to..." And Jack wanted to say, *Just not do the whole murdering thing*, and Tallifer knew that wouldn't fly, and Jack plainly did too. He grimaced, unhappy but wrangling with the logic of it. "To not touch the hospital department. Anyone associated with it."

She waited for Pirisytes to scoff at that, but he frowned instead. "Hospital, is it?"

"That's us," Tallifer confirmed. "Experimental field hospital. The Butcher's Circus and Freakshow."

His face was blank for a moment and she wondered if his unseen god was whispering to him again. "Here's the deal," he said at last. "We don't go near you for offerings. But maybe some night someone turns up needing medico attention and no questions, and you patch them up and ask precisely nothing."

She hadn't thought of that. How a cultist embedded within the army might end up with all manner of injuries that would be hard to explain. And probably healing wasn't a part of Zenotheus's portfolio.

"Of course," said Jack, without hesitation, so eager to help that Tallifer was amazed he was still alive. If Pirisytes had been a harder bargainer he could have talked the Maric into volunteering for the garotte again.

The ride back on the cart was socially awkward but physically more congenial, what with the lack of bonds and hoods. They sat shoulder to shoulder with the unmasked cultists, a bunch of unremarkable men and women she could have passed in the camp and not glanced twice at. Accessory conscripts from Oloumann. A nation whose nasty little chaos and murder cults had been carried across the Palleseen Sway by the Pals themselves. She made a mental note never to go there.

Pirisytes sat with his head down and his hands clasped together, maybe praying, maybe just trying to adjust to the idea that his god really *was* with him, and that his faith had absolutely been justified. She could understand that being a shock after years in the field, cut off from any wider hierarchy. She told him about her own journey, then, mostly because him being so impressed by Jack's god-smuggling had rankled a little. How she'd smuggled her own god out from his great temple before the end. How she'd teamed up with Lochiver, and the two of them had carved a course of sabotage, death, arson and plague across every part of the Sway that wasn't too hot for them. And she hadn't seen it as spreading chaos. She'd seen it as vengeance. She hadn't killed Pals as offerings to Mazdek, but she'd certainly killed them and burned their places and torched their precious papers. And Pirisytes grinned at her, suddenly her friend and not the man who'd been about to sacrifice her earlier that night.

"You're all right," he said. "That was good work. Zenotheus would approve."

She thought she didn't want Zenotheus to approve, but then after a little consideration, maybe she wasn't in a position to turn down anybody's approval. And those years on the run with Lochiver had been their glory days, if any had. A wild time, when neither of them had been quite so old, and it had seemed possible they would keep ahead of the Pals until they went down in a cataclysm of fire and decay.

And they caught us, and offered us their damned choice. And we were both too weak to take the respectable way out. Too weak, and too worried for each other.

Pirisytes put a hand on her knee. She twitched, but there was genuine sympathy in the murder-cultist's face. Genuine enough that it brought a lump to her throat.

"I don't know what your Mazdek says," he told her, "but Zenotheus has 'survive' amongst its tenets. Survive and breed and spread. We do what we have to do."

She nodded, bitterly resentful that a man like this should be trying to consoling her, and also that she was, genuinely, consoled.

"Stop here," Jack said suddenly. "We'll, ah, walk from here. Best we're not seen together, don't you think?"

They were still a way from the camp – she could see its light and just hear the diminishing murmur of a good night's ebbing tide. She'd have preferred to ride most of the rest of the way, but Pirisytes said the word and the pair of them were let down onto the ground.

"I don't suppose," she said acidly, "that you're going to use your healing powers on my aching back and legs, when we get in?"

"I don't think I can," Jack said. "Not with you being a priestess. I... the healing kind of inducts people into God's faith."

"Well then you're bloody useless," she told him.

"Yes, probably. You can come out." He was looking into the sparse trees lining one side of the road. A moment later a woman stepped from behind one and leaned against it, arms folded. Tallifer had to squint for a moment before she understood who she was looking at.

"What the hell is *she* doing here? Is that son of a bitch Invigilator spying on us?"

"No." Jack sounded choked. "No, I don't think so."

Caeleen the demon, none other, walked over and took Jack's chin between thumb and forefinger. "Hide still intact, then?" she asked. "Only He assured me that you were in some kind of dreadful danger, and I had to come all the way out here to find you."

"I was," Jack whispered, very still under her touch. "I was. Thank you."

You don't ever thank a demon, Tallifer thought. They were creatures of contract, and thanks implied an obligation beyond what they were bound to.

"He wouldn't shut up," Caeleen said dismissively. "Said I was the only one who could help. But it looks like you didn't need me anyway, so that's my time wasted. You can take Him back now." And there was a peculiar piece of mummery where Jack took precisely nothing from her, in a way that absolutely excluded Tallifer.

"I'm going now. If you get jumped by a catwolf or something, it's your lookout," Caeleen said. And paused precisely two heartbeats, frowning at Jack as though trying to see him some other way, as though he was one of those Jarokiri artworks that looked like two completely different things depending on how you focused your eyes. And then turned and left, walking away in a manner a world away from a soldier's disciplined march, uniform bedamned.

Jack watched her, until Tallifer jabbed him under the ribs as hard and painfully as possible.

"Are we spending the night out here, or what?" she demanded. "Only she wasn't kidding. Catwolves are a real thing in Bracinta. I've heard stories."

"Right," Jack agreed, still looking depressingly starry. "Yes. Let's go."

Incautious Sympathy

Mother Semprellaime, who puts on thirty years in the mirror every morning so that she could go practise arts forbidden under Pal statute. Conjuration for military purposes was just barely tolerated; Maserley had to work hard at maintaining his social inclusion. Conjuration under the old Allorwen traditions for the purpose of carnality was absolutely banned. Yet giving soldiers somewhere to vent their passions that wouldn't either swell bellies or lead to inappropriate attachments was just one more piece of necessary imperfection, to be done away with in that future the Pals looked forward to so ardently.

She had her rituals. Not the magical ones that delved into the horrors of the Worlds Below. Mundane but just as exacting. Each morning a little pot of glue on the stove alongside the tea. The crone's hooked nose over her own rather flat one. The artfully positioned warts on cheek and chin. The cast that closed up one eye. And at first she'd worried that those she met more than once – perhaps three in ten of her clientele were regulars who made her services a part of their routines – might notice that her blemishes were somewhat peregrinatory in nature. Then she'd worked out that the point of them was so that her Pal callers wouldn't look her in the face, because an old woman's ugliness wasn't a part of their perfection. And by now it all went on with a mechanical precision anyway.

After that was the make-up. She kept the interior of her wagon shadowy and seldom ventured out into the camp in daylight, but she applied the stick with artistry nonetheless. Each wrinkle a little masterwork of forgery. The face came together in her glass, like a sour old aunt come to disapprove of her life choices. Her aunt would most certainly have disapproved. Not of the conjuration, but of turning her infernal tricks for the Pals. Her aunt had been taken when the Palleseen armies marched into Allor, like most conjurers of any station who hadn't managed to flee. Taken and never seen again.

Semprellaime, who had taken the title 'Mother' without earning it, thought about her aunt a great deal. A haughty, wealthy woman who loved nothing except gossip. Who had made every ninth day a trial, when her niece had been sent to her grand townhouse to learn the principles of the Allorwen traditions. The scholastic semi-religion that governed so much of their society, and drew heavily on contracts with Those Below. Her hateful aunt, who had beat her when she got the wordings wrong, or criticised Semprellaime to her haughty, wealthy friends. Her aunt, who had nonetheless taught her the skills that Semprellaime used to survive.

She was a queen of votaries, she thought, looking in the mirror at the haggard face she'd constructed. *I am a bawd.*

She donned the wig of tangled, lank grey, that hid most of the joins between fiction and reality, and turned to her records. You learned to be precise about details in her trade. She had nine workers on the books, right now. Nine being an auspicious number to the Allorwen, and let the Pals sneer at that kind of superstition. They didn't have to deal with demons. Nine, each bound to her with its own contract. No groups, no consignment of brutes to work or fight, no expendables provided as job lots from the pens of the Kings Below. Each of her agreements an artisanal arrangement with one individual demon, the way it used to be back in the day. And even then she couldn't tell herself that, left to their own devices, her demons would be lying on their backs fucking Pals for their pleasure. The Worlds Below were harsh. Commerce with those Above was one of the few ways out of the mire. They did what they had to, just as Mother Semprellaime did. Nobody exactly enjoyed the way things were going, but everyone lived another day.

There was a knock on the wall of the wagon, beside the door. An oddly tentative thing, and positioned so that, if she hadn't barred the portal, her caller wouldn't inadvertently push it open and expose eldritch things not meant to be seen by human eyes. Such as a partly made-up Mother Semprellaime hurriedly shrugging into her ragged old woman's costume. She found where the voice came from, in her throat, and croaked out an answer. It was early for a John, but it had been known.

And one might think she'd be looking ahead at some dull days, with the army being rota'd in and out of Magnelei for rest and relaxation. Listen to some soldier talk and you'd come away with the idea that the whole city was basically a brothel with open doors. Except Semprellaime knew how it was. Plenty of soldiers would get their wicks dipped, sure enough. But opportunity inflamed the desire rather than dousing it, and soon they'd be off-rota and back in camp. Who would they turn to then? Nobody but Mother Semprellaime's infernal harem, or one of her fellow sometime-laundresses. And there would be those who lost their wages to the gaming tables, tavernas or pickpockets before pouring it into the open hands of the pimps, and they'd come back doubly frustrated, and she'd be waiting with her more reasonable prices. So perhaps this was some cocky beau who'd been on leave yesterday and come back stoked up one way or another, and here she was.

Except, when she opened the door, it was Maric Jack. And that didn't mean he *wasn't* a John, because she knew the type, and reckoned he would just about fit in. Maybe not for the usual reasons, but when he'd recognised what business she was in he'd picked up an edge that she recognised. Except he didn't look like he was in the market right now. And she was glad of that.

A little more time to herself in the mornings, without having to put on the mystic airs for some Pal seeking forbidden Allorwen delights, that was a welcome respite.

And besides, it was Jack. He'd come by a couple of times since that first meeting – the one where the Butcher had dumped him on her and then the provosts had removed him just as unceremoniously. She'd kept his box safe, and that had endeared her to him. And he was, in turn, mild and pleasant and helpful, if a bit wet. And perhaps, with the brash and the pushy turning up to sample her wares day-in, day-out, she didn't mind a little wet, in a caller. Perhaps she found him slightly endearing in turn.

Dangerous, she knew. Her own contract with herself: *do not like any of them.* No feelings in her for a man in uniform. That way lay only ruin. But she still smiled when she saw him.

Soon enough he was sitting down in the cramped half of her wagon she lived in, sipping at a mug of tea.

"So can I finally tempt you to the forbidden delights of my mystery?" she asked him, overdoing the old woman voice and the Allorwen accent, and then her throat went dry because he put some money down with the cup. And found herself not sure what she felt. A little vindication, that he was no different to the others. A little triumph, that he was hers. A little disappointment?

"I… wanted to consult with you, if that's all right. Not – not that, not the actual. But as a scholar?"

I'm a scholar? She had on her Ancient-Crone-Knows-The-Secrets face but behind it she had no idea where he was going. "Speak," she invited, as a usefully neutral utterance.

"I wanted to ask you about demons. Only I realised I… We had a decent Allorwen quarter, in Ilmar, and I knew some, but I never… I realised I never actually found out anything about the trade, conjuration and the like. It's not a Maric thing, you see, and…"

She settled herself across from him, sipping her own tea

around the warts and the nose. "You come here seeking the ancient secrets of my people," she said, still doing the voice.

He grimaced, shoulders drawing in. "I'm sorry. It's not... You're not allowed. I understand." He made a helpless gesture at the money, either to persuade her or preparatory to scooping it back.

"Ask, Jack," she said, in more of her normal voice. Because he'd pierced the disguise already, and she didn't actually need to do the act with him. Him and the Butcher and a couple of others, the only people she could be even half herself with. "I reserve the right not to answer."

He nodded, then nodded again, twitchy with something. "Is it true that demons are – well, I heard that they're, like, a reflection of the conjurer. That they're sort of formless nothings until called *here*. And then they're just like the conjurer in another shape. Like they're out of a mould and—"

"No," she said simply. She'd heard that one before. It was a Pal idea, trying to rationalise the trade so that they could conjure to their heart's content with a minimum of philosophical griping, but it was nonsense. "No, they exist Below, in their own place. Perhaps not quite exist as we exist, because Below isn't quite a place like Above is. But they exist without us."

"All right. Fine. So if Maserley... then it's not just another Maserley in a funny hat or something. All right."

She went very still at the mention of the Pal conjurer, a man who she had no cause to love. *Please no, Jack.*

"So tell me..." And then not actually asking. Building his thoughts and screwing his courage together. "What are... what's a demon? When it's at home? How much like us are they? No, I don't mean that. I mean, can a demon... What are they like, in themselves? Because all the stories say they're wicked. Leave them a loophole and they'll be through it like a snake up a... you know what people say."

"More than anyone," she agreed, to give her thinking time. *What are you caught up in, Jack?* "Yes, demons will exploit any loophole. The art of conjuration is one of contracts and clauses and being very specific. And those conjurers who are careless with their drafting regret it. Either because they leave themselves open to retribution by those they conjure, or because their conjurations go on frolics of their own. There are reasons for all those stories you've heard about the denizens of Below and their treacherous ways."

"Oh," Jack said. "Oh, right." And seemed to shrink three sizes within his uniform. "Yes. I suppose that makes sense."

If she, Semprellaime, had also been making sense, then she'd have left it there. Half the story told, but surely the half he needed to hear. But from somewhere between how sad he looked and her duty to her profession, the words snuck out, "But conjuration is compulsion."

He blinked at her.

"Ilmar, that's your city, you said?"

His expression went blank. "Ye-es…?"

"They had an uprising, didn't they? Year ago or so?" Not that she'd assiduously been learning about the place since meeting him, obviously. "How very malicious and wicked when you had agreed to be occupied by the Pals. Shocking." And sipped at her tea.

He processed that. "I understand. But… what I really mean is, what is there? To a demon. Take away the contract. Take away the conjurer. What's left that's *them*? Can they… do they have a, a, a personality, a *them-ness?*"

"A self, you mean?"

"Yes, that would have been a better word. Sorry."

Again she had the strong, wise urge to say absolutely nothing, or just lie. She could have said anything. He'd have believed it. Nothing other than a well-crafted lie would be good for him. She remembered her aunt's harsh voice, telling her that no demon wanted to be Above, but that most of them didn't want to be Below either. Each of them chafing under the clawed hands of the Kings Below, and no happier with the paper bonds of human conjurers. Held in a vice until nothing but malice remained. *They always want something*, her aunt had taught her. *Our mystery is to give them just enough of what they want, and take just enough to receive what we need. Bargain hard, so that they respect you. Never cheat them, so that they resent you.* The way that other traditions cheated them wherever possible, and called it canny. The way that Pal conjurers and the factory hellieurs and all the modern demonists did. Cheat them, or deal with the Kings for the massed labour of those who had no choice in it.

"Jack," she said, "listen to me. What do you think a demon gains, when we contract with it? You think we pay them shillings and pence like you have there?" Pointing to his little pile of coin.

"I mean…" And he'd have heard a dozen different stories. That conjurers agreed to do wicked acts, or paid in the souls of children, or burned works of art as though they were offering them to gods, or swore to become the slaves of demons in the next life, or… And all of these things had been true, in one tradition or another. And they obfuscated the fact that a contract was in itself a payment. The connection to Above gave a demon strength, drained some essential *thingness* from the world that a demon could bank and draw upon, or use to pay its debts. Infernal currency, and what else had ensured that some enterprising powers of hell had made themselves kings in the first place? But there was more than that. Even the best Allorwen gloss couldn't obfuscate essential truths.

"Demons feed on misery," she said. "Not just that, and that doesn't mean they're obsessed with inflicting pain or the rest. All those things you've heard. But misery, Jack. Unless it's through a properly negotiated contract, have nothing to do with them. Hell doesn't respect an amateur."

"But it's their choice," he said hollowly. "It's by will, what they do. They're people. Individuals."

She had the depressing feeling that her words had almost entirely sleeted out the far side of his skull without touching anything. "No. They're demons. And yes. They're also people.

Jack, the Worlds Below are not like ours. The truth of demons is not like us. But they are like us, yes." And Allorwen had a whole vocabulary to split these demonic hairs more finely, and none of it translated into Pel.

She braced herself for the next question, the naked one, that would tear down the few veils he had left and make absolutely obviously clear the cleft stick he was in, but he never asked it. Perhaps he understood that, if he pushed further, she would just say no. She'd stub out whatever little ember he was husbanding, that would only burn his hands sooner or later. So he didn't quite ask, and she couldn't tell him. He finished the tea, and tried to give her the money. And she wanted to refuse nobly, but took a shilling off him in the end because money was money.

Then Banders was outside, shouting, "Oi oi, Jack, we're off. Magnelei's waiting with its cock in its hand and its legs spread, however you like it. Come on, slacker, or we'll go without you!"

Jack bolted up and banged his head on the ceiling of the wagon. "It's our leave rota," he explained weakly.

"Good," she told him. "Go enjoy yourself, Jack." *Go get all this idiocy pressed out of you before you do something stupid.* But as he left, the words 'I'm going to do something stupid' might as well have been tattooed onto his back. She could only sit there in the dark, inside the shell of an old woman she'd crept into, and feel a young woman's desperate worry.

City of Unkind Words

Bracinta was last century's giant, decomposing slowly. Had the Pals found it at its height then either they'd have mustered all their armies and waged one of the most savage wars in all their bloody history, or they'd have decided that maybe the place didn't need to be perfected quite yet, instituted diplomatic ties and taken their batons elsewhere. But the glory days of the Bracite Kings were buried in yesterdays. The iron grip of the ruling dynasty had been eroded by internecine squabbles and the rise of viziers. The nation the Pals had found had been wealthy and failing. And yet not quite failed. The initial emissaries reckoned that forcible introduction of Correct Thought might just catalyse a Bracite renaissance and make the whole business more costly than anyone needed. The Pals' solution to the Bracite Problem was not to flip the heavily-laden table of Bracinta, but to slowly slide their regulation-booted feet under it inch by inch until they'd made themselves entirely at home.

"That man," Banders said, mightily impressed, "is breathing actual fire. Fire. You see that, Tally? Didn't you use to do that, back before we civilized you?"

Tallifer looked gratifyingly dissatisfied with that. "Banders, will you just *not*," she hissed.

"I will not just not, no," Banders answered blithely. They were only just within the walls of Magnelei but the locals, who knew exactly the best choke-point from which to extract money from their visitors, had put on a hell of a show in the square there. It was a proper square, too. There were great big pillared buildings on all sides, three storeys and the top two – out of vandals' easy reach – heavily carved with an eye-leading montage of scenes and figures. There were stalls shoving one another for elbow room, selling food, ornament, clothing, toys and a lot of pointy-toed slippers that seemed to be a local specialty. Wherever a stall hadn't managed to set roots down, someone was trying to be entertaining. The air was full of the caterwauling that passed for Magnelei songs, plus tootly little pipes and fluttery drums and a sort of shaky thing with sand in it. People were dancing or putting their half-clad bodies through weird contortions. One old boy sounded like he was preaching stern religious admonishments to the off-duty soldiers as they filed through the gates, and Banders put him down as 'man most like to get lamped by midmorning' in her personal betting book. And the soldiers had all been read the ordinances. No brawling, no immoderation, no starting anything with the locals. As far as Banders could make out, the only reason the ordinances existed was so the provosts and the duty Inquirers would have something to do, because you didn't want highly important people like that just sitting on their hands.

The fire-eater held up the little glowing bug in his hands and breathed over it. A plume of flames roared out in the shape of a phoenix ascending to the heavens.

"Cor, there he goes again with it," Banders noted approvingly. "Someone give him a penny."

"Today is going to be a bloody privation, isn't it," Tallifer remarked to nobody and everybody. "Banders, what is your plan, exactly, for today?"

"I, Tally," Banders told her, "am going to see the sights, whatever they may be. 'Cos that is one of the main compensations of being in this army, and I've never been here before, and probably it'll all be on fire next time we get to see it. I plan to conduct a scholarly investigation into whatever it is around here that people eat, and drink, and do for entertainment, and then lie down in a dark room and bounce about with. And maybe buy a souvenir if there's anything left in my pouch at that point. Sound like a plan?"

It sounded like a plan to Lochiver and new girl Lidlet and – incredibly – to Cosserby, and it didn't look like Jack or Masty had any better plans. The Butcher was off to trawl the markets for alchemical reagents. Which, given he'd left his boy minding the shop back at camp, meant he was hunting for smutty pamphlets or worse stuff, but each to their own as far as Banders was concerned.

"I understand that there is a fine local tradition of poetic houses where one might drink superior tea and listen to verses," Tallifer declared.

"That sounds like literally the worst and last thing I would ever want to do," Banders said frankly.

"I thought you'd say that," Tallifer agreed. "That is why I proposed it. You go catch as many intestinal complaints and venereal diseases as you like. Lochiver..."

"I am not doing poetry and tea-readings," he said mulishly. "Which it is, by the way. You read poetry, and then they look at your tea leavings and tell you your future. Given we're both old as snakes, we wouldn't be getting our money's worth, would we?"

"Lochiver, you are coming with me to defend my honour," Tallifer told him sternly.

"That sounds like trying to find the sun's shadow."

Tallifer snagged his thin arm and bent close to whisper something. Banders rolled her eyes at the attempt at subterfuge.

"You two old timers want to ditch us so you can find some mad drugs and a double bed, you go right ahead. That comes right after poetry in my list of things I don't want to experience," she said.

Lochiver leered at her. "You ain't had it, unless you've had it with a plague-cultist."

"Oh god help me." Tallifer covered her face. "We're doing

poetry and tea. Anyone so much as insinuates anything else and I will fight them. Come on, you old pervert."

Lochiver gave out a spectacularly filthy chuckle, and then the pair were weaving off into the crowd.

"That," the Butcher declared, "was a whole conversation I did not need to be a witness to."

"Chief, I don't want to get old now. How can I not do that?" Banders said.

He clapped her on the shoulder. "Knowing you, I don't feel it's something you need to worry about."

"Thanks – hey!"

Then he had a big ham of a hand on either shoulder, turning her to face him. "I want to say 'don't get into trouble' but that would be me pissing into the hurricane, wouldn't it."

"That's hurtful, Chief."

"Masty, Cosserby, at least try to keep her throat from getting slit."

Cosserby stuck his chest out, but mostly his gut. Masty was so shrouded in the depths of a non-uniform hood that Banders had no idea what he was doing.

"We're waiting for Alv, though, aren't we?" Jack queried. "She's with us?"

"She was up an hour before any of us," the Butcher told him. "She's teaching, needs to get the new class up on the basics."

"That doesn't seem fair," he said.

"Yeah well, that's 'cos Alv's scared of enjoying herself," Banders put in, and earned a warning look from Ollery.

"Walk in your own boots," he told Jack. "Nobody else's will fit you. And look after the new girl." Which barely needed saying given Lidlet had glued herself to Jack's shoulder. Ollery made to go, then obviously had what were at least third thoughts, maybe fourth. "Banders—"

"Chief, we're fine. We have a native guide. Eh?" And she jabbed Masty in the ribs. He tried to shake his head at her, but if he was going to go about in a hood then she could safely ignore any of that kind of signal. "Even if he is embarrassed to be seen with us. Masty, you think you're going to be recognised? You owe people here money? Take it off, for the sake of reason."

He hooked it back a bit, but only so he could give her a Look.

"What? You're our local boy, right? Take us to all the best neighbourhoods. What?" Aware that there was a bit of a head of silence developing around them, like a cold spot against the heat of the frenetic market. Other soldiers were pushing past on the way to some fun, but here everyone was staring at her. Even Jack, who was so new he'd barely been born. Even Lidlet. "He's a lo-cal," she spelled out for them. "I mean, you can see that. Just look at him and look at all of them." A bit of a generalisation, true, but you could see a lot of Masty in the people of Magnelei, in aggregate. The long face, the aquiline nose, the olive-dark skin. Put him in their clothes – the flowing over-robe, the skirts, the bare chest and thin belt with a fancy buckle. Dress him up like that, he'd fit right in. And, because everyone was still staring at her, not least Masty himself, "Will you knock it off. I'm just saying there's no point him hiding away. He looks just like them. It's not a bad thing. It's just... what?"

The Butcher leaned in until his breath tickled her ear, giving her the uncomfortable feeling he might bite it off at any moment. "You think about when Masty signed on, Banders?"

"What? I mean, right, he was young? It was before my time."

"It was before *my* time," Ollery stressed. "I don't reckon Masty got much of a grounding in Magnelei's vice dens before then, on account of him being five years old. Right?"

"Oh hell, Chief, I wasn't suggesting—"

"And." His voice was a low purr, an undertow beneath her words that dragged them down into silence. "Just think about how it might have happened that a Bracite kid of five ended up with our army just as it all kicked off here. Think about all those happy childhood memories our friend might have. After the dynasty fell, fighting in the streets, they said. Half a dozen different contenders and factions. Blood enough to turn the river red. Happy to have us march in and keep the peace, and if you think about how people normally feel about our marching then you'll see how bad it was."

"Chief—" Banders opened her mouth, then had one of those rare moments when she got to see herself from the outside, with especial reference to recent words spoken. She thought about just what the Butcher had said. Whatever words had been about to issue from her mouth like a parade put down their flags and trumpets and slunk back down her throat.

"Masty," she said, instead.

He watched her warily.

"I am such a twat." She didn't like self-knowledge. It so seldom brought a feeling of warmth and happiness. "I'm really sorry. I didn't think. I mean, you know me. I never think. I just say things. Mostly stupid things. And I even badgered you into coming in the first place. I bet you'd rather be back at camp. You'd rather not be anywhere near me right now. You go on back. You can. I don't mind."

And Masty, damn him, actually smiled at her, somehow managing to accept even that dog-earned excuse for an apology as sincere. "I'm here now," he told her. "It's all right. I understand."

She felt a weird stab of anger on his behalf, but she could hardly demand that he *not* understand. She couldn't exactly insist that he slug her in the jaw and storm off. Not that it was in his nature to do so, and not that he probably had much of a right hook in him. But he'd have been justified. She'd not have held it against him.

"We'll keep out of trouble." To Banders surprise it was Lidlet speaking, taking on an authority she absolutely didn't have. "I mean, I don't have any choice in it, right? Neither of us do." Rapping on Jack's box to get his attention.

"That," he agreed, "is very true. So yes, we will keep to the straits, Chief. Don't worry about us."

"And you've got your idiot passes?" he checked. Meaning

the additional piece of paper that Landwards had instituted for Accessories. And Banders, Cosserby and Lidlet didn't need them, but Masty and Jack certainly did.

With a final warning look at Banders, Ollery nodded. "I'll see you next back at the camp," he told them, like a caution. As it happened, it turned out to be poor prophecy, but none of them were to know right then.

The Man Who Was A Jar

The Palleseen philosophy does not admit the concept of a 'necessary evil', mostly because 'evil' is derided by their philosophers as a term belonging to outmoded systems. However, dig shallowly and the idea of 'utilitarian imperfection' can be unearthed, covering a multitude of sins that, one day, will be eradicated, but are useful right now. And then there's necromancy.

Fellow-Inquirer Prassel was also technically on leave, but if you were a mid-ranking officer then you couldn't slack. Your private moments should, ideally, be spent publicly on educational and self-improving activities, to show how dedicated you were to the cause. And while Prassel wasn't that much of a brown-noser, she didn't actually like drinking, gambling or getting her end away particularly. Nor, for that matter, the company of her peers. Oh, a glass of something decent with someone like Thurrel who could hold a conversation with a modicum of wit, that was acceptable. The idea of two days of war stories and dick measurement with a bunch of other ambitious Fellows of various schools was her idea of hell.

Thankfully, she had an invitation. What felt like a rather prestigious invitation. The worm of excitement very seldom stirred itself in Prassel's breast. She had cultivated the cold fish manner that was Palleseen *comme il faut* for long enough that she never really warmed to anybody. Her very occasional lovers complained of frostbite, and Maserley put around that she'd only gone into necromancy because of the attributes she sought in a romantic liaison. And yet she had been passionate, once, and could still be again. Academically passionate, at least. About necromancy. About the science of the life–death boundary. Not hard to see, really, why she was never oversupplied with friends. But Prassel was a scholar first and foremost, in her narrow field. She wanted very little more, when given a moment to herself, than to catch up on what there was of the literature. She was constantly frustrated by the lack of opportunity in army life to really sit down with someone and talk about the Grey Area and Rate of Fade in Vivid Auras and the finer points of copper as a medium for ectopic pattern retention.

And now she was going to have her chance. And while girlish excitement was not something that had visited her since about the age of four, her sparring partners that morning had noted a certain vivacity to her that wasn't customary. Her sword work was one of the few other leisure activities she applied herself to. Mostly because, having discovered that she was actually good at it, the pastime gave her the opportunity to give arrogant sons of bitches like Maserley a caning. That was also something she felt at least a flicker of emotion about.

She had been given a letter with the seal of Landwards Battalion's Field Necromancy department, setting out an address in uptown Magnelei and a time. And she thought: *A Field Necromancy* department! *A whole department!* And wondered if she could get a transfer and to hell with the hospital nonsense they forced her to nursemaid.

For senior officers, Fellows and above, they didn't make you queue to get in with the rabble. The army was running coaches up to the high town where a whole block of big townhouses had been commandeered to give people like her some space, and respite from the demands of their inferiors. She was sure that whichever grand Bracite families had donated their homes for the occasion knew that their Palleseen allies were properly grateful. After all, they had been relying on Pal uniforms to keep order in the streets and factions from one another's throats for a decade and a half or so. If the Pals decided to move out because of insufficient hospitality then the clique of pointedly non-hereditary officials who'd been running the place would be royally screwed.

She'd brought notes. Her own work had, she felt, given her a few novel insights that she was really looking forward to discussing with some knowledgeable peers. Necromancy had been so mired in prudery and superstition for centuries. It needed sensible people like her discussing it as a science, to drag it into the modern era.

Having presented her papers to three different polite but insistent intermediaries, she was finally ushered into a dim room, a high-ceiling and the only windows present clustering right up against it as though the presence of necromancers had frightened them all up there. Despite the poor light, the walls were lined with shelves. Dusty books bound in what looked like carpet, plainly not leafed through in living memory, Bracite characters along the spines. She was reaching out to pluck on down to see just how imperfect the literature really was when someone cleared his throat, and she was brought back to her purpose. Her peers. Her science. Her valuable insights.

There were three other people in the room and one of them was dead. But that was something which Prassel could take in her stride. She hadn't quite got to the old-joke stage of the profession where some of her best friends were dead, but you became sanguine about corpses after a while. Even corpses that were still walking around. Especially those, in fact.

Three people. One was a woman some way short of her age, pale hair pulled back into a bun you could have cracked rocks on. The effect on her face was to yank at her eyebrows and the corners of her mouth so that her resting expression was a kind of surprised grimace. She was another Fellow-Inquirer, a genuine peer. At the head of the table was a man far older, his natural expression rather pensive, his face more skull and skin than anything fleshed out, so that he was by far the most unhealthy-looking of them despite the deadness of the man next to him. He wore non-standard clothes. Prassel, who'd had a uniform freshly pressed for her before she left camp, stared at the robe the man had over his own threadbare greys. It was edged with sigils in silver thread, and there was a bandolier of tablethi across his chest that was plainly doing *something* active, though she wasn't sure what. His lips moved slightly all the time, chewing at his withered lips. His insignia said he was a Sage-Archivist, however, so she saluted.

"Ah, Prassel," he said, and indicated a chair. "You know Killingly, of course."

Prassel didn't. Her eyes flicked to the other woman, who showed no feelings about being called 'Killingly' and also being a field necromancer. The additional ordeal by fire that represented, on the woman's ascent through the ranks, must have toughened her up formidably.

The old man himself was Sage-Archivist Stiverton, and Prassel knew of him by reputation, mostly from some powerfully insightful papers written back around when she was still in the phalanstery. An honour, but a slightly awkward one given that she hadn't heard a peep from him academically in the almost two decades since, and given that he was wearing a magic robe like he was some kind of wizard. And the last member of their quartet was...

Was dead, as she'd divined. It didn't take a great deal of necromantic skill to work that out. He was sitting there stripped to the waist and being a corpse. A corpse with a fairly large chunk of its thoracic cavity excised so they could fit a copper jar in there, held in by straps and the stubby fingers of the remaining ribcage. A knot of tubes and wires sprouted from the top of the jar and vanished up into the corpse's throat and down into its abdomen. This was Cohort-Monitor Vessel.

Prassel nodded politely and kept her face very still because she'd just about swallowed Killingly and now she was wondering whether she'd missed some part of the note instructing her to bring a joke name.

"Thank you for inviting me, magister," she said respectfully. "It's not often I get the chance to—" Pulling her notes out of her belt pouch. "Actually, in my work in the department I've had some—"

"You do corpses, don't you? In Forthright?" Vessel's voice came out as a drawn-out moan, and she realised she'd been watching his lungs fill around the back of the jar to generate wind for the words.

"That's my major field assignment, yes." There had been a distinct lack of honorific in Vessel's address, given his rank, but presumably he had to ration his words more than most.

There was a little ripple of side-eying between Killingly and Stiverton that she didn't much like. "It's a shame," the other woman said, "that so many battalions still devote our talents to such outdated stratagems, don't you think?"

There was an innate kick in Prassel, to defend the department and her duties, but really, did she want to? "I agree that cadaver work isn't exactly cutting edge," she said, and then winced inwardly because it wasn't the best choice of words and possibly bad taste from Vessel's perspective.

"Landwards Battalion's Necromantic Science department focuses more on the spectral side of the discipline," Stiverton explained. "Ghost-wranglers, you know."

"We were hoping that, given how underutilised your talents currently are, we might enlist you, on the side. Share research and resources." Killingly examined her nails as though ensuring they were clear of grave-dirt.

"Well, yes," Prassel said. "Obviously. Regular duties permitting. I'm very committed to advancing the science."

"Good, good. Splendid." Stiverton smiled, which did nothing to differentiate his face from a skull. "You see, we at Landwards rather believe that necromancy has a good chance of being the future of warfare. Not the clumsy stuff, animating bodies and sending them shambling off towards the enemy." A flick of his fingers dismissing ninety per cent of her work. "Ghost work, Prassel. Capture, preservation and use of spirits. You can fill the copper, I take it? You're not so rusty just because they've got you puppeteering the meat?"

"I've done it," she agreed. Most recently unsuccessfully, when she'd tried to preserve the ghost of the wounded spy, but that had been against Loruthi soul-eater magics. Give her a chance to brush up and she'd be more than capable.

"Vessel, tell her about your squad's most recent escapade, will you?" Stiverton invited.

The corpse hunched forwards. It had been a man in his mid-twenties, and any clues as to cause of death had been occluded by post-mortem surgery. It moved with admirable ease, almost life-like. And she'd heard of the practice, of course. Bind a ghost to a corpse and you ended up with something far more elegant than the mindless things she marched around. But inefficient. Her shamblers were cheap. Vessel's prolonged existence was a significant investment.

"We were deployed behind enemy lines," came his dirge of a voice, and then a wheezing inhalation as he forced his lungs to reinflate. "On being signalled, we seized enemy assets. Being artillery crew of their rear batteries. We turned the weapons on their own. Rear lines, then moved on. To support staff, water bearers and medicos. Causing sufficient disruption to. Undermine the enemy defences leading. To enemy positions being overrun. During only the second assault on their. Positions after which we. Retreated to our original position. And awaited retrieval."

Stiverton watched her, leaving Prassel acutely aware of any flicker of expression. "Explain 'deploy'," she invited. Invited Stiverton, or even Killingly, because Vessel's voice was getting on her nerves.

"Well, quite," Stiverton explained. "We just took a kind of

very long-range trebuchet-style launcher – quite primitive, quite simple, squad-portable and even the most cack-handed regulars can set it up so long as there's an artillerist to aim it. And we... threw Vessel and his squad all the way to the back of the enemy lines. A little like the ball games they play here. You've seen them? Quite the athletic spectacle. A good throwing arm, and we have a fifth column at the Loruthi's backs."

"You don't mean throwing corpses," Prassel clarified, not looking at any of them now, only into her own head. "You mean... *him.*"

Vessel tapped the copper jar clasped by his rib-ends.

"And then he... what, you..." Aware that she'd lost the perfect imperturbability of face she so valued, screwed up like a schoolchild doing maths at the phal. "You must compromise the warding on the copper so that the ghost leaks, and trust to, what, sheer willpower to stop them dissipating before a host gets close enough. Animation or possession?" Eyes on Vessel again.

"The latter, preferably, but. The former remains an option," he ground out.

A squad of ghosts in jars, ready to leap from host to host and sow chaos behind enemy lines.

"But the power—" she said uncertainly. "Or you rely on..."

"Life essence of the hosts," Killingly confirmed. "So long as they can keep chaining one to another, draining their current ride to fuel the leap to the next. Momentum. Like any military action." And Prassel pegged her as the strategist, then. She understood the military practicalities, and Stiverton the necromantic theory, and Vessel was... the experimental subject, she supposed.

"I can see potential problem nodes," she noted diplomatically. The sheer daring of the scheme appealed to her, but still, the *risks*. "Attrition?"

"Five of my squad of twelve. Were lost," Vessel said. "Containment failure, dissipation. Feral transition."

Seeing her momentary grimace, Stiverton nodded. "Yes,

we're working on that. A matter of soldierly discipline. Vessel understands that his duty to the Committee doesn't end with death, but others have found it hard to maintain their focus. We have had some... issues with subjects who proved temperamentally unsuitable to the service." And that explained the robes, Prassel thought, because those were very definitely ghost-warding sigils, and humming with power even here. She wondered how many mad and angry ghosts had ended up loose in Landwards's camp.

Or else Stiverton didn't quite trust Vessel.

"Still," she said. "A squad of twelve. That seems manageable. Proper selection procedures and reindoctrination. I salute you, magister. This is a remarkable innovation."

Killingly coughed. "We anticipate diminishing returns, obviously. The Loruthi have some potent magical scholars of their own. Prolonged use of this stratagem will force them to invest power and expertise in warding measures of their own. Which is in itself a good, as those resources will be taken from elsewhere and weaken them overall. But we intend to make the most of our advantage by making use of an assault in force in the next major offensive."

Prassel made an expression of polite enquiry. "Explain 'in force'," she requested.

"We currently have fifty coppers on the storage racks waiting for long-range deployment," Killingly told her. "In fact, this is why we wanted to talk to you. Any spirits currently in containment, or any that you are able to place in the copper before the joint battalion action would be greatly appreciated."

"You have... fifty ghosts together," Prassel observed.

"Currently," Killingly agreed. Fifty ghosts in close proximity. If Prassel had been Stiverton she'd have three robes, a ghost-repelling hat and some very fast running shoes.

"We understand that your current command is some manner of hospital," Stiverton said, gamely trying to steer the conversation because a certain tension had sprung up between the two women despite Prassel's best efforts to keep her thoughts bottled up.

"An experimental hospital, yes, magister," Prassel confirmed. The old embarrassment about the project reared its ugly head, as always. "It's proved an effective means of preserving personnel, despite the unorthodoxy—"

"What happens when they fail?" Killingly asked sweetly. "I mean, I assume they have you harvesting the corpses, at the very least."

"Well, yes, of course," Prassel said, feeling her footing in the conversation shift and tilt. "That was the primary purpose of the department, originally." *Except 'experimental cadaver farm' wouldn't exactly fill the regulars with confidence.* "However, the selection of personnel available have historically been more effective than anticipated, and so—"

"We want you to bottle the ghosts of your failures," Killingly told her flatly.

"It's hard to have the appropriate forms signed when the surgeons are at work," was Prassel's bland reply. And she had really wanted to *like* Killingly, despite the fact the woman had hit Fellow rank at twelve years old or something.

"No need. Here." A paper slid across the table. "You'll recognise the Professor-Invigilator's credentials. He's very supportive of the venture. A waiver of authority. No individual permissions needed."

It really was a bleak little piece of paper. Prassel admired it in its clinical exactitude. It was a mandatory extension of duties. She'd used the form herself, when she needed to make sure the regulars knew that some onerous but necessary task was included in their remit. Foraging when rations were short, say, or looking after some delegation. Or, as in this case, not being released from their obligations to the army just because they were dead.

"I appreciate that you probably feel you're being judged by the effectiveness of this little medico sideshow you've got going on," Killingly said. "But if you could expedite a supply of filled coppers, our department would be very grateful. As would the Professor-Invigilator. We want to have Cohort-Monitor Festle at the head of a hundred soon enough. A hundred invisible infiltrators at the enemy's back, Prassel. Quite the thought, no?"

For a moment Prassel couldn't think it, because she'd just realised that the dead man was *Festle* and not *Vessel* at all, and was desperately thinking back to see if she'd addressed him by name at any point. Then she did think it. An army of ghosts unleashed on the enemy support and rear lines. Leaping from host to host, sabotaging and killing and moving on. And going mad. And forgetting who they were, or failing to recognise their friends. She imagined whole battlefields that could never be reclaimed by either side because of the haunting. A weapon that poisoned the earth forever with vengeful spectres.

She gave them all a bright smile. "A truly remarkable innovation," she agreed. "I will, of course, institute the necessary systems."

City of Forbidden Desires

It is remarkable how many liberated cities turned out to be exactly the dens of depravity and vice that reinforced the Pal understanding that, of all the world, only they were truly civilized and perfected. Exactly the vice and depravity demanded by, for example, off-duty Palleseen soldiers.

Tallifer had said something about catwolves, or possibly wolfcats. The two colossal statues on either side of the stadium gates were indeed some kind of indeterminate beast, feline and canine together, lean and savage, open jaws towering high over Jack's head.

"These things, they're real then?" he asked the others. "Actually out there?"

"Sure," Banders said with absolute confidence, even as Cosserby said, "No."

"Yeah?" she prompted, and Cosserby took in a deep breath and got as far as "Well, actually," before Masty said, "The last of them were hunted down two generations back."

"I thought you didn't know anything." She jabbed Masty in the ear, having gotten over her previous remorse. "I thought you were, like, three, back when."

Masty shrugged. "It was the royal beast."

"Very republican of them," said Banders approvingly.

"No, I mean only kings could—" But they were pushing into a loud and close-packed crowd, elbowing for room on the tiered stone seating. Jack had the task of carrying cups of hot wine, which meant that his uniform was sodden with it by the time they were seated. Lidlet passed around the little waxed paper receptacles while he wrung the worst of it out of his shirt.

"They going to dock my pay for this?" he asked Masty, but the man had his hood pulled down past his nose, his shoulders hunched. Jack thought he understood. If the Battalion had marched into Ilmar then he'd invest in a hood himself rather than be spotted as a local wearing the uniform.

"So, as I understand it, the rules are—" Cosserby started from his other side. Lidlet then writhed a knee between them, and then another, wedging a space for her backside on the seat without actually applying any aggressive force. It was a remarkable piece of applied theology that suggested she'd caught on very quickly to the strictures of her new life.

"Right," she said. "You tell me, now." Leaning up close, mouth to his ear. Far from sweet nothings, though; the sort of grim voice he'd expect from a torturer seeking confession.

"We're supposed to be watching the, you know, the thing they do here." He wasn't actually clear what they did, nor was he catching a word of what sounded like a very detailed explanation, because Cosserby was inflicting it mostly on Banders. Then some Bracite men and women wearing very little had come out into the circular open space, and he decided it was something lewd. But they started throwing a hard-looking ball to each other and so maybe it was some kind of sport. Everyone else seemed to be very enthusiastic about the results but Jack found it all impossible to follow. Especially because Lidlet wouldn't shut up.

"So tell me," she hissed in his ear.

He gave her a look to indicate he had no idea what she meant, which look was absolutely a lie.

"You, the priest. You made me one of yours, right? When you did the thing. I agreed to it. So you could save me."

And, horror of horrors, there was God, hopping onto Jack's

341

other shoulder without providing any kind of moral balance. Cackling in a way unbefitting of a divine entity.

"Tell her, you yellow sod," quoth God. "Give it to her straight. You wanted me to do it. You owe my new devotee that much."

"I only wanted to help," Jack said, to one or both of them.

Lidlet looked at him blankly. "Jack," she said. "Or – do I have to call you Your Holiness or some damn thing now, if we're finally having this conversation?"

"No, you do not!"

"Okay, that's better, because I'd have felt weird telling His Holiness to just fucking give it to me straight and stop pissing about." And her hands were fists, but very pointedly staying in her lap where they couldn't get her into trouble. "I do not want to be dead, Jack. Any time I decide I wish you hadn't stopped me being dead I'll go lamp someone and that'll redress the balance, right?"

He nodded jerkily.

"So fine. Priest, tell me the heresies. What am I a part of now. What else? No men? No women? No drink? No dice?"

"You've been having none of all of that?" he asked her, wide-eyed.

"Jack, I am living on a *thread*." Fingers twitching like she wanted to grab him by his collar and shake him, and absolutely couldn't. "Help me out. Give me the rules. So I can't hurt people, fine. I've weaselled out of that one best I can, for a soldier. Can't hurt, can't get people to put the screws on for me. Fine."

"And that's it," Jack said. "Look, Lidlet, it's like this. You've got God. God's a healing god. God's also a bastard. He'll take it back quick as blinking. He likes doing that. Always gives Him a laugh."

"That is not true!" God insisted, scandalised, but Jack continued because nobody else could hear God.

"But past that, whatever you want. I mean steering clear of the drink, or anything else that might mean you... give in to your impulses, that's good. If *you* were a priest you'd have a whole book of other stuff not to do, but you're not. You're... what, a follower of God on a technicality. Just don't tell Higher Orders and we're all gravy. That's what you Pals say, isn't it? Gravy?"

Lidlet was staring at him. "Literally just that?"

"Just that. No harm. That's God. Sounds benign, doesn't he? Well you don't know. That's all I'll say. You don't know Him."

The conversation, which he'd been dodging and dreading in equal measure, had actually gone quite well. He settled back so that he could continue to not understand what was going on with the ball.

"Right." And to his horror Lidlet produced some closely-written papers. "What about if I don't *help* someone?"

"What? Why?"

"Someone's right there – they're drowning, say, and I could easily pull 'em out, but I don't."

"Why not?" Jack stared at her.

"That's not important. I don't. What does God say? Do I have a, what is it, a *positive duty* to help, or is it okay that I just don't put my foot on their head."

"I..." Jack's eyes swivelled left. "You want to field this one?"

"Let the son of a bitch drown," God opined. "I mean people die all the time. It's not my doing. It's not my followers' doing. If I was a mightier god then perhaps I'd have something to say about it, but I can't be expected to take on responsibility for all the ills of the world. I really *would* be a bastard at that point, eh?"

Jack paraphrased. Lidlet nodded, made a little tear on her page to mark that item on the agenda as settled, and then went on, "What if someone knifed someone else for me, but not because I'd asked. Just because it was their idea and they knew it'd make me happy that it'd got done?"

Jack didn't get to be confused by the rest of the ball game, because he was too busy trying to fend off Lidlet's rather adversarial take on doctrine. By the time one group of underdressed Bracites had apparently balled better than the other to the extent that all the balling was done, they'd moved onto existential fringe cases that even God was unsure about, and Lidlet's papers were ragged with little single and double tears depending on whether the answer had been yay or nay.

His head was still spinning when they were vomited out of the stadium with the rest of the crowd. They made the edge of it at last, swimming against a current of people funnelling in to catch the next game of whatever-the-hell-that-had-even been, or maybe there would be a play next, or some show fighting. Jack felt he was done with Magnelei public entertainment for one day.

Because the locals knew a good opportunity, there was a whole row of establishments fronting the stadium. They were set up in grand old buildings with carved upper stories – more catwolves and mounted spearmen and some sort of finned serpent creatures in a kind of everyone-versus-everyone brawl. Civic offices or temples, perhaps. Except that the current use was plainly several rungs down the ladder. You could drink, downstairs, and upstairs he had the impression there were rooms for other things. Every one of them was cluttered with Pal soldiers inside, and festooned with bright young Magnelei outside. And Caeleen.

Jack stopped. She'd been watching him approach, he realised. In fact, given it had been his feet deciding which way to go, he had the uncomfortable feeling that she'd drawn him to her. Demons could do that, couldn't they?

"Here's trouble," Banders said. "Wonder if that means Miserly's about? Come on, sharp left, soldiers, and let's find other haunts."

"He's not here," Jack said. He wasn't sure how he knew, or even if he knew. He wanted it to be true. Maybe that was enough.

"You are…" God, still at his shoulder, paused in mid-prohibit. Jack looked at Him, and of course Caeleen could see Him too. And God looked at her, the demon. A moment full of whatever had passed between the pair of them after Jack had been kidnapped.

"I," decided God, "am going to look after my new follower." His face was thunder, daring Jack to make anything of it. "She is tender and vulnerable in this place of sin and requires my invisible guidance."

Jack was going to point out that such guidance was invisible enough that Lidlet wouldn't actually receive it. There was no profit in that, though. Not when God was so magnificently trying to save face.

"That's... very generous of you," he said, hearing his voice shake. "I don't understand. But please look after Lidlet, yes. And if you could take..." A look back at the box. God rolled His eyes.

"If you mean the vicious fish-sticking sod with the spear, he's already with your gobby lass over there. Has been for a while."

Jack frowned. "With Banders?" He couldn't actually see the little spearman anywhere, but possibly he was hiding in the woman's pocket.

"Taken a shine to the woman, no idea why," God confirmed. "And your lad there with the bugs and leaves you can keep. I don't reckon he'll pay much mind to what you're up to."

It was, Jack, decided, the best he was going to get. He put a hand on Lidlet's shoulder, companionable as he could, and tried not to watch as God hopped over like a ragged-bearded cricket.

"You carry on. I'll catch you later. Around here, maybe?"

Banders looked from him to Caeleen. "Jack, man, seriously."

"Don't you judge me. I just want to talk."

For a moment all the woman's humour was gone, and he saw real naked concern on her face, about to save him from himself. Then she flung her hands in the air. "There's a market a street over. Market sound good? Masty? Coss? New girl? But you just yell if you end up in a summoning circle with your throat being cut, right?"

"I'll be fine. We're just going to talk."

"Sure. Talk." A little of her grin came back. "We'll be back for when you're done. Minute and a half do you?"

"Banders!"

Her mood was entirely repaired when the three of the sauntered off, leaving him wondering just how much of it had always been for show.

Caeleen regarded him levelly, arms folded, weight canted onto one hip.

"He's not here, is he?" Jack asked hurriedly. "Your – Maserley. You know."

"My master has sent me on his errands," Caeleen said, rolling her eyes. "Come inside, Jack. I've had to fend off nine soldiers and a vizier already."

Inside was close and dark – thick stone walls, small windows and smoked-glass lamps drawing shadows across a pillared space never intended as a taverna. They found a low table and some cushions, and hot wine that was almost but not quite as harsh as the stuff at the ball game.

"Tell me why," Jack said.

"I told you, master's errands," Caeleen said. "I have visited certain conjurers of the city, wise and evil men it is not fit that a Fellow-Invigilator be seen with. Oh, and also he did say to corrupt you if I saw you again, because he didn't ask the right questions when I came back last, and still doesn't understand it won't actually work." She gave him a top-of-the-range smouldering look over the brass rim of her goblet. "Just in the name of full disclosure."

"You came after me," he told her. "Before. Why? Because I do not believe that Maserley told you to do that."

She gave him a scornful look, reclining against the wall and the cushions. "Jack, I had standing orders to ruin you. I can't do that if you're dead."

"That's it, is it? It's just that?"

For a long time she looked at him, and he saw her try on one look after another, like a burglar fitting picks to a lock. "My contract is a cage, Jack. Where its bars bite, I am constrained to take the shape it binds me to and be what my master specifies.

To follow his orders. No choice, Jack. No valiant struggle against his iron will. It just is."

He nodded. "And what about the space between the bars?"

"Then I can interpret, good as any jurist. And feel, by the pain, whether I have called it right, or wrong."

"Yes, that's what it's like," he said immediately, and shrugged off her puzzlement. Somehow feeling that if he compared a demon bound by contract with a worshipper under threat of divine sanction then God would spontaneously appear to shout at him, no matter the distances or practicalities.

As if reading his mind – and who was to say she couldn't read his mind? – she said, "Your God is…"

"Yes?"

"Pathetic. I've seen gods. I've seen them enthroned. I've felt divine wrath. I've tempted paladins and prophets. I've been sent back to the Lands Below shrieking with the sting of holy displeasure. I have never seen a sadder stain of godliness than the thing you follow."

"Aye, well, suit the worshipper to the worshipped, I say." Jack drained his goblet and held a penny up. They had more wine and less coin in the time it took to drawn breath.

Caeleen leaned forwards. "Will you let me corrupt you then, so I can report back with a job well done."

"I'm sorry, I can't."

"For me? So that he won't have one more reason to punish me?"

He winced. "I can't."

"Vows still, with no priest to you? Seems the worst of all worlds."

"You have no idea. It's just… guilt now. Not even vows, just the guilt that came with them. Like something you can't get out, scrub all you want." Looking at her half-shadow face.

She leaned forwards further. "You understand my contract gives me power, Jack? Power over those I am set upon. I don't *have* to give you the choice." And she bared her teeth at him, showing him the points of her long canines, making the threat plain. And he just looked at her, not trusting himself to speak, until her face changed and she understood.

Later on, after he wandered somewhat unsteadily out into the street, after Caeleen had absented herself to complete those other diabolic tasks her master had given her, Jack felt no particular urgency about finding Banders, Lidlet or even God. Instead he found somewhere on the square that he could get a drink, tipping extravagantly because sometimes the world was all right, and in such rare circumstances it was good form to pay it forwards.

Halfway through his reverie, there was a high, clear sound from the table. Jack looked down to find his clay mug split cleanly into two halves. The spear god was there on the table, screaming at him in a tiny whistle of sound, an infinitesimal fury.

"What?" Jack said. He'd never seen the creature so animated, but when it ranted at him, the harsh spiky words were complete gibberish.

"I don't understand," he said. The little creature threatened him furiously with the spear. Probably it wouldn't actually be able to get it in him, in any real way, but Jack didn't much fancy finding out. "I don't understand. Slow down. Can you... mime it for me, or something."

The expression on the thing's nasty little face suggested mime wasn't a part of its divine portfolio. At that point, however, God, actual God, scrambled up on the table. God couldn't really look out of breath, but the impression that He'd been legging it through the streets of Magnelei after His comrade in fugitive divinity was strong.

"What's going on?" Jack demanded.

"I think," God said, "he's trying to tell you something."

The spearman jabbed his spear towards one of the alleys leading out of the square and gabbled angrily.

"I can bloody tell that. What's he saying?"

God screwed up His raisin of a face. "I mean he just took off, and I could tell it was you he was going for. Wanted to make sure he wasn't off to consecrate you, in your little slip from righteousness, you know?" He said vaguely, and then, "Will you not slow your heathen gabble down, you gobby sod? I can't understand but one word in three."

The spearman threatened God with the harpoon, and God muscled right back at him, virtually rolling His ragged sleeves up. But some part of the message obviously got through because God said, "He says your friend's in trouble."

"What?"

"A friend who's a woman, from the word he's spitting out there. If it's that harlot then you're on your own."

Banders. And when wasn't Banders in trouble? But on the other hand, she was his friend. He stood up.

"All right. Into the box, the both of you." But the spearman leaped to his shoulder, God's accustomed spot, tugging at his ear and pointing. Jack collected the box, and followed the harpoon-head weaving in his peripheral vision.

The New Class

Alv, regarded with superstitious awe by the Pals, who otherwise disdained superstition. Because she came from the Divine City where they had perfection, but didn't share. They looked on her and saw elegance and poise, grace and power, all the things they wanted for themselves. Not understanding that it was armour, and inside only wounds.

Her back itched, just a little, from where Masty's lashes had gone. He'd never ask, so she'd had to be sly, virtually sneaking up on him, stealing his hurt like a burglar. But he was always so helpful and she owed him too much. This way she could go to her difficult meeting feeling she'd balanced the scales a little.

They were waiting for her when she ducked into the tent. A full dozen young Palleseen looking brightly polished and fresh out of the phalanstery. Sitting around a folded-out table with the place of honour at its head reserved for her. Unlined faces alive with interest as they studied what was probably the first Divinati they'd ever seen.

Her last class, left behind across the sea, had been seven, but had started off as twelve. There were always a couple who couldn't grasp the theory, which ran decidedly counter to regular Pal philosophy. There were always some who grasped it all too well but couldn't gauge their own limits. She did her best to coach them, but Pals had a certain attitude to power: that it was to be used.

This new batch had a leader: a sharp-faced man in a crisply pressed uniform with a Companion-Archivist's insignia, a lofty perch for tender years. He named himself as Callow, then passed around the rest of them swiftly enough that she didn't even try to remember. Pal names all sounded the same, and these youngsters in their identical clothes could have been cast from a single mould with minor alterations. It wasn't important.

She had her preamble all prepared. This would be her third class of students, just one more round of penance for the Divine City's debt she was paying off. "You have been sent to me to learn about balance, and its application in the healing of wounds," she said. She'd learned to speak simply and slowly, because her accent twisted their flat and ugly language into shapes that didn't fit into Pal ears. "This will involve establishing a connection to the world that you are not familiar with, but we will practise. You will find where the flow of the world passes through your patient, and where it is obstructed or misdirected by the presence of their affliction. You will bring that marring of their balance into yourself, and accept their injury or sickness. Once it is within yourself, in that arena over which you have a greater command, there are arts I will teach you, that will allow you to... mitigate the effects of those ills you invite."

She waited for the question. Both her previous classes had some bright spark who thought, *I know better than a thousand years of Divinati magi.* She wondered if it would be Callow, or if one of the others fancied themselves a magical theorist.

Why can't we just clear the obstruction, redirect the flow within the patient, cut through the knot? Some variant of that, perhaps two or three if they were particularly fond of their own cleverness. And it was Callow who spoke, and she was already opening her mouth to explain, no, that wasn't how the world worked. That would be to add imbalance to imbalance. Where did the force go, when you tried to simply set things right? She would explain to them that in unravelling one ailment, in forcing an injury to heal *in situ*, you would release a dozen more spontaneous harms through the body of the patient. You would ravage their body with an accelerating tide of wrong, and perhaps it would spread to the doctor also. There must be equilibrium. You took the harm into yourself. That was how it was done.

The words paused at her lips, and she realised that wasn't what Callow had asked.

"Repeat, please," because she didn't quite understand his point and it gave her time to think.

"What I mean is," and he sounded slightly embarrassed, not the usual strutting popinjay, not his place to lecture teacher, "let's say I need to husband my own wholeness of body for some other purpose later. Or let's just say I'm far better at this than, say, Hobbers here." Hobbers, a dour-looking girl, scowled at him. "I mean, I could find the… what is it you call it, the *asymmetry of flow* within my patient, and I could pass it on to Hobbers, without it having to go through me. So long as it went *somewhere*." And he beamed at her expression. "We got notes," he explained. "From a veteran of your first class. We've all read up on the theory. We're ready, magister." Giving her a title she wasn't due, but one of clear respect.

She was genuinely touched, because Pals were arrogant, and teaching them anything was always a trek uphill. And here were these children and they'd already set to learning. A month, two months of breaking down their innate resistance, none of it necessary.

"I see." The slightest nod. If they'd been Divinati students they'd have known exactly how pleased she was with them. "That is a good line of enquiry. Based on my own experience, that level of coordination is unlikely to be possible during field surgery conditions, and it has proved more efficacious to have everyone performing as an individual. However, if your friend was prepared then the transfer would be possible."

Callow grinned, the swot of the class basking in his own precocity. "You'd take someone's broken leg for me, wouldn't you, Hobbers?"

Hobbers's scowl deepened. "No."

His smile only broadened, "Ah well, that's the problem. What if Hobbers doesn't want to?"

"Your first priority in these classes, and then in actual practice – the chief discipline of sympathetic healing – will be to take injuries on yourself, and then dissipate them via the exercises I will teach you—"

"Yes, but," he said, interrupting her without somehow ever amending his expression of polite respect, "what if Hobbers doesn't want to?"

Alv blinked at him.

"Or, hear me out, let's say Hobbers already has two broken legs and a cracked rib by this point, and Skilby over there's out with a cracked skull and a brain haemorrhage—"

"Thanks," said, presumably, Skilby.

"And we get in some Sage-Monitor with a mangled arm or an arrow through his lung or something, blood everywhere, all very urgent. Death's door."

"Then it is beyond your gift to heal," she said gently, thinking that she understood where this was going. "The nature of our discipline is that there is a limit, with injury, that we cannot address without our own—"

"But I need to." Callow was still smiling, grinning even. "I mean, it's a Sage-Monitor. He's a very important man, needs to be back on his feet right away. There's nobody else, magister. What can I do?"

It had been known. She'd seen it happen. More by recklessness in her students than actual heroism. Being reckless was the worst quality in a sympathetic healer. Callow struck her as the reckless type. But not heroic. "Then you take the injuries upon yourself and they overcome you and you die," she told him quietly. "And you have made a choice, and paid for it, and thus preserved the balance."

That grin, still stretching. "But what," he went on, "if I don't want to."

The tips of Alv's fingers rubbed against each other, a minute fulcrum for a great deal of inner agitation and uncertainty.

"I'm a Companion already. I'll make Fellow soon. I'm very important to the war effort," Callow beamed at her. "I mean even Hobbers here is worth something. Solid theorist, if unimaginative. Good book-learner, eh?"

Hobbers sat there and scowled some more.

"But, let's say we've got someone else," Callow proposed. "Some big lout of a trooper, very hale and hearty. Or perhaps – I know – some Loruthi we've got our hands on. What if I pass the injury on to him? I mean we don't *need* him. And we do need the Sage-Monitor. Key man, whole battle riding on his tactical judgment, isn't it?"

"You cannot pass the imbalance on to someone unwilling. Someone untrained," Alv said patiently.

"Why, though?" Callow asked. "I mean, I've looked through the theory. I've practised it. I can't see any actual bar. The logic is all eminently sound once you cut away the nonsense terminology and the mysticism, isn't it? I mean, it's a science like any other."

"Because there is a balance to maintain," Alv explained, still quite patiently. "Between yourself and the patient, that is an easy set of scales to balance. You have control. Between yourself and a patient and a properly skilled receptacle of harm. If you are all of a mind, and careful in the operation. But you are introducing imbalance into the wider world. You cannot simply—"

And he was speaking over her again, still with that oily veneer of respect coating every word. "Magister, if you'll allow me. Skilby, you've got that mouse on you still?"

Skilby was very eager to be Callow's friend. He produced a

little wooden box with such alacrity he almost threw it across the table.

"Empty the little fellow out, won't you? There's a good chap." Callow stretched and cracked his knuckles, loosened the buttons on his cuffs as though he was about to perform some sleight of hand.

Skilby shook the box until, as advertised, a mouse was decanted onto the table. It crouched there, surrounded by looming humans, bunched to flee.

"Very sleek," Callow said. "What have you been feeding him?" And stabbed himself through the hand. He must have had the knife under the table. The motion, the whole operation, was almost too swift to follow.

The mouse just about exploded. From crouched beast to a smear of viscera and flesh across the table. Callow was staring down at his hand, the blade pinning it to the table.

"Of course," he said, ever so slightly strained, "the technique requires refinement. I still... *felt*... that. The edge of it. But that speaks to my lack of perfect control over the transition, magister, and for that, I apologise." For that. Not for anything else. Just for that.

Hobbers made a sound, as though it was her who'd been stabbed. As it might have been.

"I've been speaking to Higher Orders," Callow said. With some effort he dislodged the blade tip from the wood and then drew it from his hand. There was no mark left behind, not even the faintest line. It had all gone into the mouse. "They are very interested in the wider applications of your science, magister. We're keen to learn all we can from you." That merciless smile once more, as he sheathed the unsullied blade of the knife. "What do you think might be the maximum effective range of a sympathetic transfer? Or would there even have to *be* one, do you think? Anyway, we've made our introductions. I think we all have a great deal to think about. We're all looking forwards a great deal to working with you, magister."

She sat there for a long time after they'd gone. She'd felt the knife go in and, though he'd so artfully diverted its effect to the rodent, she'd suffered it too. Feeling the world twist. Feeling, even now, the scar he'd left in the balance of the world, just by that one small act.

Her own balance, husbanded so precariously against every sleight of fate thrown her way, was utterly shot. She didn't know what to do.

City of Shrouded Pasts

Given that war was one of its chief exports, no surprise the Palleseen Archipelago was well-supplied with orphanages. No child was left to grow up on the streets, and that was a worthy thing. The same war that necessitated so many such institutions was simultaneously the purpose of them. The children who passed back through those doors into adulthood would have a career waiting for them, a debt to the Commission of Ends and Means. And in between the parental deaths and the enlistment papers came a period when the state wasn't particularly interested in those children's lives.

The vexing thing was that Banders had been exactly right about Masty, until she turned out to be spectacularly wrong. He really *had* started to remember the Bracite lingo. She'd dragged him with her to help in squeezing a better deal out of the locals, and from a handful of halting words, he'd visibly started recalling a whole vocabulary. The back and forth between the local merchants had become transparent to him, so he could murmur in her ear about whether they were dealing in good faith or rooking her. More, the mere body language had begun to speak to him, what they did with their hands, how they touched their faces or tugged at the hems of their robes. A lexicon of gesture and fidget that held a wealth of information. She had been exalting about her tame Bracite, and how the Butcher was going to be over the moon that she'd scored some particularly hard-to-find spices. Not to mention what she could sell across the camp. Things were looking sunny over Banders country, as she liked to say, until this old boy appeared and got right up in their business.

Two things had happened, then. The first was that all the merchants had suddenly not been open for business because they knew Old Boy right away, plainly some kind of local gang boss or the like, and they wanted nothing to do with it. Second thing was Old Boy was seriously interested in Masty.

He was a big old lad. Enough that Masty's eyeline was about level with the nipples of his bare chest. That loose robe hid broad shoulders and he had scars across him like the characters of a foreign alphabet. Banders saw a white beard and a hook nose and eyes nested in wrinkles and secrets. And one hand less than army-regulation quota, his other arm ending in a corrugated stump. *Sword work*, Banders recognised.

"Excuse me," said Masty, trying to back away, but the man had his shoulder then, like tree roots had the earth. Those deep eyes just stared and Old Boy said something in Bracite.

"No thank you," Masty said loudly, and then, "*Alaaga nei*," which was a thing he'd been telling the merchants when Banders had wanted to pretend not to be interested.

Something happened to the man's face, hearing Masty speak the language. His hand was abruptly gone from Masty's shoulder but only because it was at the hilt of the knife in his belt. He drew the weapon with one sharp motion. Masty closed his eyes.

"The fuck like!" said Banders, and socked Lefty right in the face. It was surprisingly like punching a statue, but she still knocked him back. At that point the plan had been to grab Masty and leg it, but suddenly a half-dozen of the perfectly innocent locals who'd been watching this street theatre turned out to be on Lefty's squad. Some of them got between her and the old boy, and two of them grabbed Masty, an arm each, yanking him backwards.

She clouted the nearest kidnapper about the ear and stamped

on his toe, reckoning the window for informed debate had closed.

Banders reckoned she was pretty handy in a fight. She also reckoned that Masty was terrible, and in fact he hadn't even been trying. Like he was one of Jack's mob, crippled by some inner wound just waiting to find its way out into the open again. Banders, for her part, got several solid strikes in, and had one of Masty's captors on the ground and conveniently placed for a good stamping, when the old boy paid her that punch in the face right back. He might only have the one hand, but it felt like he put a whole two fists' worth of punch into it. He knocked her right onto her ass, in fact. Feeling about the very tender skin around her eye socket now, Banders could only admire his technique. Had to give a man credit for working around his limitations.

After that they'd bundled Masty off – very kid-gloves, no punch in the face for him. And they'd grabbed her and done the same, either because they didn't want her running off to fetch the nearest squad of soldiers, or in case they needed a backup sacrifice should Masty prove unsuitable.

That was what she reckoned the deal was, sure enough. It was a cult. You heard a lot about them. It was basically what Correct Speech assured you that the world was full of. Every foreigner out there was some kind of religious fiend waiting to throw you on an altar and offer your precious heart to their hungry god. Which was why you had to perfect them with truncheon and baton, to teach them that that kind of thing *wasn't* done. Educate the barbarous foreigners about what was and wasn't the appropriate thing to believe.

For obvious reasons, Banders had never been sacrificed to a foreign cult before, but she knew it happened. And here she was, in a cell, and doubtless the hooked disembowelling blades were even now being whetted, while someone looked up the correct prayers.

It reminded her of the orphanage.

Not like *that*, obviously. Nobody was going to be running a sacrificial cult on the actual Archipelago, right under the nose of Ends and Means. But she remembered some weird shit from the orphanage. They'd locked her in a half-flooded cellar for a day and a night. And then everyone had laughed and they'd gone and had fish for breakfast. Fish for breakfast was a treat, so it had all been fine, all a joke. But it had been a joke about what the wicked priests did to you with their evil cults. The implication had been, *If we'd been foreigners, there'd have been weights on your ankles and the fish would have been breakfasting on you.*

And here she was, and probably it wouldn't be fish, given they were some way inland, but the foreigners were doubtless going to do for her anyway.

They hadn't tied her up, and when the sacrifice party came through the door she was going to make them regret that oversight. A few wild blows was probably all she was good for, though. And doubtless the old boy with one arm had perfected his left-handed sacrificing technique.

The key scraped in the lock. She'd been relying on hearing a whole mob of them come down the corridor, maybe singing hymns about how nice it was to get bloody to the elbows on their god's behalf. Instead it was just that little metal sound that let her know her time was up.

She had just enough time to set her feet for a really good lamping, so that when the big metal-shod door swung open she was able to plant her fist absolutely perfectly in the middle of Jack's face.

He went down instantly with a spray of blood from his nose, ending up with his box against the opposite wall, swearing fiercely.

Banders grimaced, went to help him, then drew back as he swatted her away.

"What was that for?" he complained nasally.

"I'm sorry! I didn't know it was you! How is it even you?"

Banders demanded, feeling almost outraged that *Jack*, of all people, was rescuing her.

"Damn me," Jack said, and she heard a really visceral click. And then, "Thank you. I suppose."

She was about to say that he was welcome and she'd punch him again any time, but his nose wasn't broken any more, and although his face was blood all down to his chin, there wasn't any more of it coming out of him. Even the puffiness had been banished before it could become bruising. He'd done his thing. Handy, that. Meant she didn't have to feel guilty about having hit him.

"We have to find Masty," she said. "They're going to cut his heart out or something." And, because he was looking at her, "What? This is my fault, all of a sudden? We were *shopping*! What kind of a cult grabs you when you're shopping? Look, are you with me, finding Masty? Or have you done your good deed for the day?"

"Yes, fine, obviously. Where is he?"

"No idea. Can't you find him like you did me? How did you even find me?"

Jack looked shifty, and looked past her, like there was something at her shoulder. "Complicated," he said. "Can't do it for Masty, but if they're sacrificing him then probably it's an important room and we can find it. Can you fight?"

"I just gave you two shiners and a broken nose," she pointed out, although the evidence for them had evaporated like mist. She pushed past him into the corridor, looked both ways and then chose a direction, ready to jump the first local who turned up. "Anyway, you must have taken that key off someone, so presumably you've already bruised your knuckles a bit."

"It was just hanging by the door. I... can't fight. Sorry."

"Well then I'll just have to use both fists and you can cheer me on. Besides, I've got my secret weapon."

"What's that?"

"You," she told him over her shoulder, reaching a set of

stairs and deciding that sacrificial chambers felt like more of an upstairs thing. "They get me with their gutting knives or something, you can just put me back on my feet, right?" Because, for all his faults and the fact he was a bit wet, Jack was a handy friend to have in a fight.

"I can't," Jack said. "Not you."

She stopped at the top of the stairs, crouched low. There was a walled courtyard out there, covered over with cloth to dull the sun-glare. She could hear low voices.

"What do you mean, not me? Is this 'cos I hit you?"

"No, it's not... I don't even know. Not you, though. God won't do it."

"Look, if this is about being a Pal, how come Lidlet got a pass?" Banders demanded through her teeth.

"It's not that, either. God just says... He won't do you. Can't, sorry. He says can't."

She stared at this man who was suddenly not even remotely handy to have anywhere near her. "Me personally? Seriously?"

Jack's apologetic look didn't get much time to shine as, right about then, one of the locals turned up, a slight man with a shaved head. Banders jumped him immediately, grabbed the little pen-knife he had at his belt and threatened him with it.

"Right," Banders told them. "Good. I don't want this to get ugly. You've got a friend of ours. The man you brought me in with. You're going to take us to him now, and then we're all leaving together."

The man didn't want to help her with any of that, but the knife was a potent argument and a decidedly better friend in a fight than Jack. Then the man tried to explain that he didn't speak Pel, but as far as Banders was concerned everybody spoke Pel. It was an easy language to learn and, she explained, if he really didn't speak it then he had about fifteen seconds to get fluent before she used the knife and then found someone who did. Which threat turned out to be worth ten years of vocabulary lessons because suddenly he did speak Pel after all.

Which was how they were eventually brought into what she took to be the Grand Ritual Chamber. It was evident they were in a very large building, because the little shaved man took them through a variety of well-appointed rooms to reach it, with her companionable hand on his shoulder and the knife-blade hidden in the folds of his robe.

Banders was aware they'd accumulated quite a tail of hangers on and guards and the like by then, who plainly didn't feel that the tableau she was presenting was quite naturalistic enough. She'd picked up her pace and hustled her guide-slash-hostage faster and faster until at last they burst out into this largest room yet, everyone else spilling out behind them, and she lost all track of what was going on.

It was a huge stone room, lit by high sun-wells that cast shafts down like an ethereal colonnade. The walls were heavily carved with friezes of stylised people doing heroic things to monsters or each other. At one end, two enormous statues of wolfcat monsters sat, each with one paw raised and jaws agape. Between them was not the expected bloody altar but a big stone chair, and on the chair was Masty.

Banders couldn't quite process that. She even looked to Jack to see if he had any insights, but he was doing his usual confused expression, so no help there. Masty was out of uniform. They'd done him up like a local, except all the clothes were huge. His robes went all the way down the steps that the chair was set up on. He had a big hat on, too, and someone had painted his chin with a big white stripe.

"Get down here," Banders told him. She had the knife out in plain sight now. The people who'd followed her in had swords and a few batons, and seemed to have run out of any concern for the life of the little shaven-headed man.

"Banders..." Masty said.

"Get the hell down here, we're leaving," she told him, despite all evidence to the contrary.

Then the one-armed man had turned up, which at least meant

she had a target for her ire. She waved the knife at him. He had his own knife back by then. The one he'd threatened Masty with back in the marketplace.

"It is forbidden," he said, in stilted Pel, "to bear arms in the royal presence."

"Your guys started it," Banders said. "You want this knife, you come get it?"

"Royal presence?" Jack echoed.

"Lefty here has delusions of grandeur," Banders said, enjoying the angry flare of the man's nostrils. "Didn't you hear, Lefty? Last king of Bracinta died decades ago. Was just some sprat left, wasn't there? Vanished away, wasn't he? Or dead. And he'd not be some old boy like you. He'd be just about…" The energetic motor of her words hit a sudden snag and wound down. "… just about, you know, about, about Masty's age. Give or take."

Masty, up on the big throne, wearing the fancy ceremonial headpiece, looked horribly embarrassed.

"It was," he said, and everyone there hushed completely so that even his quiet voice resounded through the chamber, "what they called me. I mean, Pals, so it wasn't exactly respectful. More reminding me what I'd lost. And eventually it was just a word, and it got shortened and mumbled until everyone had forgotten what it actually meant. I'm sorry."

"What are you blathering about?" Banders asked blankly.

"Masty," Masty explained. "Majesty. Your Majesty."

"The crown prince," Lefty announced harshly, "who shall be His Majesty Feder the Fourth of the Hackle Throne, rightful king of all Bracinta. Returned to us in our time of need to sweep the foreign filth from our shores and restore our land to greatness."

Banders looked from him to Masty.

"I mean, I'm still trying to talk them down," said her old comrade, from under the weight of his new hat. "Look, can we…" He couldn't look Banders in the eyes as he said it. "I am making a decree that I get to talk to my friends in private. And tea. Bring some tea."

"So you're the king, so good," Banders decided. They were sitting in a little room with a stained-glass ceiling, kept pleasantly cool by running water in little channels about the floor. A variety of plants with spiky leaves flourished in each corner. The tea, when it came, was pleasantly fragrant, unfamiliar but presumably fit for a king. "You might have mentioned something."

"Really?" Masty – His Majesty Feder the Fourth – asked her. "I'd almost forgotten. Everyone else forgot. They took me in after – it was sort of a coup, only it simultaneously killed everyone and also failed. There was just me and a bunch of viziers all knives out and trying to take over. The Pals moved in, put their advisors in place and... just sort of took me off. For my own good, because the assassins were still out there. Took me away until I would be old enough to claim my throne. Except by that time the viziers and their Pal advisors were getting along really well and probably they'd lost track of exactly where I ended up. I was moved around a lot. I think I was probably supposed to get very ill and die at some point, but someone in the army decided that wasn't right and so they just..."

"Made a Whitebelly of you. So you could be useful," Banders said. And it was doubtless a bad thing, if you were a Bracite royalist. Losing the heir to the throne like a coin out of a torn pocket. Except she had grown up out of the orphanages, and so it seemed far more natural to her than being the *king*.

Masty seemed to be of the same mind. "I liked being useful," he said. "I don't get the impression that kings are very useful. It's not even like they want me to *do* anything. It's just... now I'm here, apparently that's a new dawn for Bracinta and there's a whole list of people they want to throw out of a window in my name, and another list of people I've never heard of who are apparently very deserving of royal favour. And what I think about it isn't important. It's just having the right backside on the throne suddenly unlocks all these doors that were shut for them. I don't know what to do."

She wanted to say something acid about how terrible it must be to be the actual king of somewhere, except he really did seem to be having a hard time of it.

"So what happens now?" Jack asked.

"I have told them that you get returned to the city. I'm going to watch you from the walls when you leave, even. Non-negotiable. Kingly decree. To make sure you're safe."

"I mean, to you," Jack said. A little lump formed in Banders's throat at the way they were trying to out-selfless each other.

Masty shrugged. "I mean, what can you do against a royal destiny," he declared. "I shall be the best ruler of my people that I can and try not to get assassinated by a vizier. Or General Halseder, for that matter."

"That's Lefty?"

"None other. Lost the arm defending my parents, he says."

"I mean, based on how that turned out, he made a piss-poor job of it," Banders said, then clapped her hand to her mouth. "Shit, that was—"

"It's fine," Masty told her. "I don't remember them. Not really. I don't remember any of it, except fuzzy, bright images. A garden, a toy, clothes, a chair. None of it's real to me. What's real is... the army. Soldiers, marching, getting cuffed because I was slow learning Pel. Ammies for lunch. Keeping my head down. Fitting in."

Banders stared into her teacup. "Yeah, well. Not exactly kingly. Sorry." As though she was authorised to tender apologies for the entire Palleseen Sway.

"No," Masty said. "That's just... that's me. That's my life. It's what I am. What made me *me*. I don't want to be anyone else but me."

At that point, General Halseder turned up, looking as though *he'd* rather be stabbing someone. Banders remembered him getting his knife out in the market. She'd thought he was about to gut Masty then. He'd been offering his service, she guessed, trying to swear fealty to the royalty he'd recognised in Masty's face.

They were taken to the regular entrance to the palace, then. The Wolf Palace, ancient seat of the Kings of Bracinta, and soon to be so again.

The city was full of Pal soldiers who could be back on duty again very quickly. Banders didn't see that Lefty turning up in the city square and making the announcement was going to go down well. The looming geopolitical upheaval was overshadowed, for her, by the prospect of having to go back to the Butcher and explain that they'd lost Masty.

Except, even as she and Jack reached the edge of the square that fronted the palace, a cloaked figure slipped out from nowhere with that particular brand of stealth the man always had. Not her kind, slinking away the moment she was looked for, but the way he was always *there* when you wanted him. Just fading *from* the background with whatever it was you needed right at that moment. In this case, what she really needed was her old friend Masty, and here he was, cloaked up but with most of his uniform under it, and no twenty feet of ermine trailing at his heels. Probably no expensive hat either, given it wasn't exactly something he could have stuffed in his codpiece, and that was a shame because Banders could have sold that.

"What, they let you off kinging for good behaviour?" she demanded, and he got three words into explaining that, no, he'd dodged the lot of them and run away to rejoin the army when she hugged all the breath out of him.

At around that point there was a shout from back towards the palace, and Banders said "Run?" and Masty said "Run!" and they ran.

City of Festering Secrets

Ollery. Just a big man in a packed Bracite market, his satchel heavy with paper packets and clinking jars. One more tradesman in a crowd of civilians, even though he's a head above locals and fellow Pals both. A curiously innocent look on his face as he peruses the stalls, like a man choosing some gift to take home for his wife. As the sun sinks and evening draws on, though, the long shadow of the Butcher stretches out from wherever he plants his feet. Some things can't stay hidden.

"Chief," Cosserby said. "Here, see this. What do you think?" He had a lacquered box cupped in his hands. Atop it, a mannikin the size of his littlest finger was moving smoothly through some sort of sword drill, or possibly dance. When Ollery bent his head to it, he could hear the faint click of clockwork within.

Ollery squinted. "How do they get it so small?" He'd found the artificer, along with Lidlet, pissing away the last of their coin on souvenirs.

"I know," Cosserby said enthusiastically. "Bracite artifice is rather remarkable. Do you think she'll like it?"

The Butcher wanted to tell Cosserby that, yes, Banders would be delighted by it. Endlessly acquisitive as she was, she'd watch the tiny automaton, enthralled, for all of a minute, then mostly forget about it until she bartered the thing to someone else. And she would not, in any way, *like* Cosserby more because of the gift. Not that she didn't like Cosserby. Banders liked most people. But she didn't like Cosserby in the way that Cosserby wanted her to like him. Wanted wretchedly and obviously, to anyone except Banders.

Ollery came very close to saying that if Cosserby just flat out *asked*, then Banders would probably go upstairs in one of the various knocking shops around here, and they could get the whole business done, and that would be it. Banders wasn't sentimental about sex. For her it would just be business as usual between them after that. But Cosserby obviously felt liaisons needed to be special and lasting and important to all concerned. He didn't want to be one more notch on the hilt of Banders's knife. And so he wouldn't just ask. He'd try to wrangle and buy and erudite his way into her affections, and Banders's affections were like a sieve.

The Butcher just grunted, a masterfully neutral response. And, because Cosserby was good at hearing what he wanted to, the man smiled and agreed that Banders would like the thing very much.

The woman in question had abandoned them earlier in the day, after loading Lidlet with an enormous bag of tall candles. Ollery would ask why Banders wanted candles, but he could be absolutely sure that somewhere in Forthright Battalion was a clerk or quartermaster or scholar who had a desperate need for exactly these candles, and would trade goods or favours equal to twice their value to get hold of them. That was Banders's peculiar genius and, if she profited from it, so did the department. And a few hours without Banders's constant talk and ability to get people in trouble was probably to everyone's benefit.

Even as the happy thought crossed Ollery's mind he heard shouting from across the crowded market. Familiar shouting, as though the world had caught up and remembered that he, Ollery, must always be given a hard time. Banders shouting because something had gone wrong, which was a sound as endemic to the army as baton-fire.

He had a good vantage over the heads of the crowd, and there they were, Banders, of course. Maric Jack, who was a man every bit as much trouble as she was. And Masty. Of all of them, Ollery was only really disappointed with Masty.

But they were very definitely being chased. A knot of locals forcing their way through the crowd, lashing out at anyone who got in the way. And a curious sense of odd pathfinding going on, because Jack was leading the way, and he was heading straight for Lidlet, while the ugly pack of pursuers was scrabbling at the hem of Masty's cloak.

Jack cannoned into Lidlet and knocked the candles from her arms, and then the locals had caught up with all of them. Masty flinched away from them desperately, and Banders turned and smacked one right in the face, sending at least one tooth flying. Ollery caught the flash of a knife and swore.

Someone slammed into the attacker before the blade could go home. Or at least slammed into him and Banders both, knocking them aside. Cosserby, of all people, grabbing the assailant's arm and invoking Palleseen writ by ordinance and paragraph. The knifeman – now with his knife spun away who knew where – picked the artificer up and thew him into about seventeen other people.

Someone else made a game try for Masty then, but Banders flashed past and slugged him too. Then someone else – just some random Bracite with a dislike of uniforms – had kicked Banders's legs out from under her and it was all on. Because there were hundreds of locals around them, and there were at least dozens of Pals, and the uniform and the training and the innate arrogance made up for the numerical disadvantage. And some of the locals were fighting each other, and so were some of the soldiers, because it was that sort of day.

Ollery saw Lidlet lunge towards the Bracite who'd kicked Banders, and Jack actually tackled her to the ground, the pair of them going down in a tangle of limbs. Lidlet sat up, and Masty had the privilege of seeing her expression turn from an extremity of fury to utter pale terror to horrified gratitude. She ended up clinging to Jack – and he to her – like two wrecked sailors with a single plank between them.

Banders had come up swinging, and somehow Cosserby was on his feet too – his spectacles hanging off his ears in two pieces, so probably not much of a net gain in the fight. Right then, though, Banders was up for taking on the whole world. Fists raised in a proper pugilist's stance, like she was competing for the honour of the department, turning left and right on her heel, feinting at anyone who got too close and trusting Cosserby with her back. Her mouth was open, challenging each and every one there to a drubbing.

Masty was just standing there, his eyes terribly wide. Ollery wondered whether he was seeing the brawling now, or some fighting from back *then*. The howling and the screams as he was dragged through these same streets, six, seven years old, surrounded by foreign uniforms. A man who owed a death to these streets.

Someone hit him. Just some opportunist who saw the uniform, not even the face over it. Masty took a clumsy blow across the cheekbone and staggered backwards, tipping. Lidlet caught him. She grunted as she took his weight, holding onto him with iron hands because otherwise they might be turned to aggression, and Ollery knew exactly how that would go. Jack was trying to put himself in the way of the attack, and got a fist in the gut for his pains, then an elbow across his head when he conveniently doubled over.

Two men had one arm of Banders each, which gave her the secure anchor she needed to kick a woman in the chest with both feet, sending her victim smashing through a fruit stand and into the slipper merchant it backed onto. Then Ollery had closed the distance, a huge hand slapping across the head of one of Banders's escorts, and the other man getting an exact mirror image of the move, a brutal economy of motion. Banders, her face mottled with emergent bruises, leaned briefly into him.

"Oi, Chief," she said. "You got your business done then?"

"Why is it always you, Banders?"

"Innocent, Chief, I swear. It was Masty this time."

Masty shrank from Ollery's louring stare, and at that point the shooting began.

To the credit of the soldiers it was mostly overhead, pitched to strike stone chips and deface carvings. Ollery saw a woman's shoulder explode in blood and bone, though, and a man pitch backwards with half his head gone, vengeance or poor aim equally murderous in the close-packed crowd. The brawl became a rout in short order as everyone who could started forcing their way left and right and away of the block of uniforms moving through the market. Provosts, half with levelled batons and half clubbing anyone who got within reach.

Lidlet let out a great ragged breath. She rested her chin on Masty's shoulder, shaking with frustrated rage.

"Oh damn." Cosserby's voice was quite distinct now the tide of the crowd was receding. The man was holding a collection of splinters and cogs that had formerly been a clockwork musical box.

"What's that?" Banders asked blankly. "Looks expensive."

"It was, rather," Cosserby agreed, and then the provosts arrived.

Their officer was an old man to just be Cohort-Monitor on this sort of post. He looked about – the corpses, the trampled, the damage to property – and wrinkled his face.

"Who's senior here?" he demanded. Ollery shifted slightly, drawing the eye.

The provost Cohort froze. Ollery went still, too. Trying to place the face, mostly. And realising that, no, he *didn't* know it. It wasn't one of *those* faces, because none of them were likely to be turning up here any time soon. But was there a resemblance? A father, a favourite uncle?

He didn't know, he realised. Too long ago, too many faces he'd done his best to scrub from his mind. But this man knew him, and there was only one reason that might be.

The officer had a rod out from his belt, slotting a tableth to it with trembling fingers. His eyes were wide. "You," clipped out of his almost-closed mouth. "You. It's you. It's you. You. Murderer."

He shot, right into Ollery's face. Or at least did his best. Masty was in arm's reach of him and got an arm under the man's wrist, pushing up. The spittle of energy from the rod killed another epic stone hero on the walls and Ollery lived. Lived, with his face set and expectant. *Someone else who owes the world a death.*

And the provost's own men were demanding to know what he was doing, and the man came back to himself, slammed down the lid of his military discipline again, closed his face. Only his eyes left, to stare hatred at the big man in front of him.

"Arrest the lot of them," he said. "Brawling. Disgraceful." As though there wasn't a live weapon in his hand and a new scar on the stonework to show for it. "Get them out of here."

Clink

Different companies and departments had different priorities. When the combined battalions reached Magnelei and found it shorn of any formal Loruthi defence, Higher Orders scrambled to commandeer the best townhouses. Quartermasters squabbled over foundries and forges. And the provosts, knowing the demands of their trade, took over the prison closest to the main gates.

Presumably – given they'd built the jail – the locals had their own rogue's gallery in peacetime. None were in evidence now. Every one of the buried cells they were marched past had a uniform in it. The on-duty provosts had been denied their own rest and relaxation, and hadn't stinted in ruining everyone else's day the moment someone stepped out of line. As soldiers did. There was even a ragged cheer as the newcomers were thrown, together, into the cell at the end, the very last free space.

"Full house!" someone called, and there was some good-natured name-calling. They were there for being leery within earshot of a provost, most of them. Some were down for brawling. A couple – the quiet ones – had maybe done something worse. Knifed a local or looked funny at a superior. The worst kind of trouble was the sort with legs to climb the rank ladder.

"How much crap are we in, exactly?" Jack asked. The gods had mostly made themselves scarce. The little spearman was rattling about inside the box, scratching the tiny head of his harpoon against the sides like a trapped rat.

"You know," Banders said, her voice unaccustomedly thoughtful, "I am not sure." In the light of dim lamps, her eyes slid over to the great bulk of the Butcher. "My usually infallible barometer for this sort of thing has gone sideways. Hmm?" And she jabbed an elbow into the Butcher's flank and seemed to find it as unyielding as stone. "I would just like to say, for the record, how very nice it would be to understand a damn thing of what just happened. That's all. Just a request up from the ranks, like."

"It was nothing," the Butcher said. The low roll of his voice filled the cell like stagnant water before ebbing out into the spaces beyond.

"Chief."

"I said—"

"Chief, you almost got a third eye-hole courtesy of the bloody *provosts!*"

"Banders—"

"Seriously, Chief. I mean if it was *me*, fine. Me, people want to shoot. I understand that. Adds a bit of spiciness to life. And Jack, sure. Everyone wants to set fire to Jack, we all know that. But, Chief. It's like a solid point of the ordinances that this shit doesn't happen to you."

"Banders, I told you—" but somehow the big man's usual authority wasn't quite rising to the task, and she just went on jabbing at him until it was Lidlet who snapped.

"Will you just give it a rest," the woman demanded between clenched teeth.

"You don't get a say, new girl," Banders told her.

"Oh I don't?" Now it was Lidlet's turn to stand up, squaring her shoulders, the barracks-room brawler warming up. Except then Jack yanked on her sleeve and she sat back down looking infinitely foul. "Oh, I guess I don't. Damn me."

"It will come down to me," Ollery said ponderously. "All of this. And whatever *you* may or may not have started," a finger stuck in Masty's direction, "is just piss in the ocean right now. It will come down to me. They'll let the rest of you go. Probably."

Banders obviously wanted to make hay out of that 'probably', but something in his tone, and the way everyone else's nerves were jangling, finally warned her off. Instead, she retreated to one corner of the room with her only current ally, Cosserby, who was only too happy to listen to her whispered bitching.

"Pals," God said dismissively. "What a vile and violent people."

"That's one-third of your entire followers you're talking about," Jack told him.

"But you, I expected more of." God was warming up for quite the sermon. "Honestly, given a day to yourself, without having to do the shambles-work of these killers, and how do you spend your time, may I ask."

"Don't."

"Strumpets and brawling! Like any common soldier."

"You'd rather I spent the day in prayer and offerings?" Jack asked.

"I feel you'd not be in a *cell* if you had," God pointed out with all the force of the moral high ground.

"You know we can hear you when you talk to yourself?" Lidlet said. And Jack was feeling aggrieved enough that he told her that actually he was talking to God, and God was talking back. He very nearly made up some unkind things that God might have said about Lidlet, but then saw her face and stopped. She was looking very serious, not the outraged rationalist nor the mocking soldier. Just... thoughtful. The barracks-room lawyer trying to work out how this new clause in the contract could be turned to her advantage. Jack had the uneasy sense that he'd just managed to make things worse.

The door rattled in its frame, then swung open. Revealed was none other than Fellow-Inquirer Prassel with her unhappy face on. Although Jack wasn't sure she had any others, honestly.

"Chief Accessory Ollery," she said.

The Butcher levered himself to his feet. "Magister."

"Gather your people and come with me."

There were a few shouted jibes and complaints as they went out, because the other wastrels had all been penned in longer than them. A few spotted Prassel's Inquirer insignia and assumed the worst. Their whispered cautions silenced the rest.

Up above, the prison had a surprisingly spacious entrance hall, one of those colonnaded and airy spaces the Bracites liked for their civic buildings. There, with the welcome sun slanting down and a little breeze to stir the heat around, Prassel turned on her heel and stared at her charges.

"I expected better. A brawl with the locals. Really?"

When Banders opened her mouth for a denial Prassel shot her a look. "From you? No. From you this is exactly what I'd expect and I'd not stir myself to deal with it personally. But you."

Jack braced himself for a tirade about discipline, conduct, honour of the service, all that. Instead she said, "Haven't you learned to keep your head down?"

Ollery was certainly hanging it now. "Bad luck, that's all," he rumbled. "It's been… a while."

"I have been put to far more talking than I prefer, on your account," Prassel told him. "They wanted you shot."

Jack had a moment of assuming, *Well, Pal army, harsh discipline*, then saw everyone else was just as taken aback. Everyone except Masty, anyway, whose face was closed.

"Then they wanted a public example. I had to remind them that they'd already had one after it happened. Anything more would be opening matters that the Commission has sealed. Which counts as overreach. So, no shooting for you today, Chief."

Ollery's lack of reaction left it open whether that was a good thing or not.

"I then had to take a certain Cohort-Monitor of the provosts into a room and threaten him with Correct Speech until he agreed it would not be good for morale if he let his mouth flap," Prassel went on. "And I'm honestly not sure if that will take, because he was quite fired up about running into you, after all that time. Some wounds don't heal."

"They don't," the Butcher agreed.

"So the word may yet end up running riot through Landwards Battalion and I've done all I can."

"Thank you, magister."

"Which brings us to our final order of business, Chief."

Ollery sighed. "How much?"

"Confined to camp, although that doesn't bite much because the orders are in and we're marching against the Loruthi in two days. Confined to camp, and sixteen."

"Sixteen for brawling with locals, magister?" Banders started, suddenly and passionately on the Butcher's side.

Prassel's look cut her dead so quick it could have been necromancy. Banders shut her mouth and did her best to hide in Cosserby's shadow.

"I said I'd do it," Prassel told Ollery.

He lifted his head, at that. "Thank you. I prefer to know the hand that holds the whip." And if he meant so he could bite it later, the words went unsaid. Certainly there was precious little gratitude in that 'thank you'. "Use the Alder. My boy'll show you."

Jack hadn't watched. He wasn't sure whether that was basic human decency, not wanting to see another man get the skin flayed off his back, or if he wasn't showing solidarity for the department. He just knew that the sight would sicken him, each lash echoing with empathy inside his head. He couldn't do it. Except the sounds had followed him inside without invitation. The crack of the Alder, the Butcher's grunts as the sharp edge of it sliced the meat. The dreadful, suffocating-sounding barks he made around the bit they'd given him. The full-on roars, nothing human about them, from the ninth lash onwards. They must have been able to hear it all across camp. Jack sat in his tent and hugged the box to him, and the gods within were silent.

And now this.

"Jack, I know you're in there." Masty, managing to be insistent and polite in the same breath, like he did.

"What?" Jack asked. There was nothing on the other side of the canvas that he wanted anything to do with.

"He's asking for you."

God put His beaky bearded head out of one of the holes in the box, wide-eyed, and spake thusly: "Sod me, no. Not that one."

"Tell him I can't help him."

Masty twitched aside the flap. "Will you just go? Technically it's an order from your superior officer." And Masty had been through his own ordeal today, and didn't need Jack making his life any more difficult.

Jack closed his eyes briefly, opened them to find Masty hadn't somehow vanished, slung the box on his back and crawled out of the tent.

Ollery's own tent was quiet, closed. The boy met him at the door, solemn-eyed. His hands were... were bloody to the wrist. Jack felt his guts curl at the sight of it. The kid looked like he wanted to grow up to become a murderer. An adult-sized bitterness on those slight shoulders, most of which he reserved for Jack.

"What?" Jack demanded. "What's happened? Why's it my fault?"

"Just kick him away if he won't step aside," the Butcher growled from inside. "Idiot child. Get in here, Jack."

Jack did and regretted it almost instantly. The Butcher was sitting on a camp stool, shirt off and his back presented. It was... there was a dish, an Ilmari speciality, layers of thin pastry interleaved with mince and red sauce. It was like that. Jack had to fight with his innards, for all he'd seen so much and worse. The sheer scale of that canvas made him weak. A lash for the

Butcher was three for a man of Jack's build, and the whip had sliced deep through the spare flesh clothing his bones.

"I need a pair of hands," the Butcher spat. "Not even skilled. Idiot child could have done it, if he didn't *flinch* so. You're not going to flinch, are you, Jack? You're a priest, right? Wielded the knife plenty I'm sure. Up to your elbows in the red stuff every holy day."

"Not that kind of priest," Jack said. "What do you need me to do?"

"Good man." The Butcher took a long, shuddering breath. "You see the big brass pot with the clay-looking stuff in it? The ochre-coloured stuff."

"I do."

"I need that into every stripe, Jack. Real deep in, deep as the wounds go. Really dig your fucking fingers in, like there's your month's pay buried in there, like—" And possibly there would have been an earthier simile, but the alleged priesthood of his accomplice probably advised against it.

"That," Jack said, "sounds like it's going to hurt."

"Thank you for your educated medical opinion which I did not bring you here to show off," Ollery told him. "You're my man, Jack? You're not going to wince out of it like the kid there?"

"I can do it. But why me?"

He expected to just get an order thrown at him, but Ollery sagged slightly.

"Jack, I don't know who knows what. But I know you don't. I don't want eyes on me, judging, as they do this. And Cosserby's clueless but he's too soft. And so it's you."

"And you're not going to tell me." Jack went to the pot and tested the consistency of the reddish stuff.

"Why the hell would you even want to know?"

"Because it got everyone sent to prison and someone tried to shoot you. That seems like the sort of thing I should know."

"To hell with you, then. Get out. I'll…" A strained grunt as he tried to twist round, "do it myself."

"I'm already doing it," said Jack, and touched the man's ribboned back.

"Wait!" Ollery reached forwards, and Jack saw he had five little cups in front of him, each with a different coloured liquor in it. With remarkable dexterity he downed them, two-handed, one after the other, each cup clacking down even as the next was on its way.

The Butcher hawked and spat. "Now," he said thickly. "Do your worst."

And Jack did. He was trying to do his best, but it was true butcher's work, torturer's work, nothing of the medico to it. He slathered his hands with the greasy mixture and then applied himself, making claws of his fingers, driving them into the gaping slits the Alder had opened up in the man's skin. Refusing to shrink from the blubbery feel of it, from the constant shudder of the Butcher's muted agony. And Ollery gasped under his ministrations, and spat, and once slammed a fist down so that half the little cups danced over.

And then there was no more in the pot, and the job half done, but the boy was there with more, freshly mixed and steaming. His face was running with snot and tears. Jack plunged his cramping hands into the mess and got back to work, trying not to think about anything. But the words that had been crammed up inside him fought their way out, then.

"I can help," he said. And God had said no, but it wouldn't be the first time he'd talked God round. "Please let me help. This is horrible. I can fix this."

Ollery moved. The twist rippled across the war-torn terrain of his back, his stripes drooling blood and ochre. He actually got Jack's elbow awkwardly in the cup of his huge hand. Not a position with much leverage, save that he squeezed with three fingers against his palm and Jack squeaked with the grind of it. "I know you, Jack." His voice was slurred with the potions he'd taken. "I know your deals and bargains. The match for Maserley's conjurations, you are, save you screw over the living and the human. I will live with my lashes and let time and alchemy fade them. I will not be bound by your creed, boy. You understand me? I will be keeping my options *open*."

"Understood," said Jack, and the man's grip loosened, his body unwinding until he was faced forwards again. Jack checked to see what of his work had been undone.

"You'd like to know, though, wouldn't you," Ollery went on, still mumbling enough that his meaning came to Jack in retrospect, the sounds pieced together like a puzzle.

"I mean, yes," Jack admitted, "but—"

"You'll only ask the others," the Butcher continued, with no sign of having heard him. "Weasel and weasel until someone gets drunk and spills. You and Masty are thick as thieves. He knows. And Tallifer, that stuck-up bitch with her plague-monger husband. Prassel, even. All of them desperate to tell on me. The Butcher of Revelation House. Lay it all bare for you, they will."

And Jack didn't think that they would, honestly. "It's not mine to ask," he said.

"And to tell?"

"Not that either."

"Priest's confidence, is that it?" Ollery mumbled.

"Not that. Not a priest. Not really." He wasn't sure how much of this conversation he was really contributing to, how much was just in the man's head.

"I will tell you," the Butcher said. "And you will never see me the same way. Eh? How about that?"

And Jack had that one chance not to know. Speak loud enough, he could have turned the key on those words and locked them away. But he really did want to know.

"Had a wife, me. Cohort-Broker Ollery's wife. Ennit, her name."

Jack looked at the boy, presumably Ennit's son. There was no reaction in the child's face.

"Married ten years. Young love. Everything to me," Ollery slurred. "Ran the pharmacopoeia at Frattelstown Port. The Islands, you know. Happy. But it didn't last. What does, eh? You're slacking, Jack. Fingers deep. Deep enough I want your elbows getting wet, you hear me?"

"Yes, Chief."

"I mean, you can guess the rest. When a man gets past a certain age and not a certain rank. When he can't give a woman what she wants out of life, eh? Same the world over. Plenty of that disease in Ilmar, right?"

"I'm sure. Chief, you don't—"

"And I knew. And it was fine. Until they didn't care if I knew. A Fellow, he was. Fellow-Invigilator. Young, good-looking, grand career. Well-liked. Lots of friends. They all knew. They all came round and talked out loud, where I was sat working. Laughing. Dropping hints. Not even subtle hints. Because what could I do? The fat dispenser with the pretty, unhappy wife."

"Chief, please—"

"Shut the fuck up because you asked for this."

"I didn't—"

"The regimental dinner. They invited my Ennit. Not me, but her."

"Oh God," said Jack.

"I mean, that's not exactly hiding anything, is it? Invite another man's wife to your fancy dining. Delivered the invite to her hand right in front of me. How about that for charm, eh?"

The words were gushing from the man like blood from a cut throat. Jack wondered how often this tale had been told, because this was the stone that lay chained up at the heart of the man, and events and drugs had unclasped every lock, freed that massive weight to roll on out of him. Jack had finished, now. He could have fled the tent without even washing his hands. He could have done a lot of things. What he actually did was ask, "What did you do?"

"Knew a man in the kitchens. I was the only one who could take the pain out of his piles. He let me in. I cooked. I'm a good cook. You've eaten at my table. You'd agree with that."

Jack made a noise that didn't indicate culinary appreciation as much as it might. "Poison."

"You have no idea about poison," Ollery said. "You say poison, and what's in your head? Some actor on a stage staggering about, giving a soliloquy? Someone turning a shade of cheese and pitching their toes up like a clown doing a pratfall? You have no idea what a knowledge of alchemy can do. The burning fires that water only enflames. The sleights of the nerves that tell the brain the body's in an acid bath. The terrible hallucinations so each one who drinks becomes their own inquisition. The games you can play with lung and heart and eyes and mind. What's the matter, Jack?" With prodigious effort, Ollery hauled himself around on the stool. The mincemeat back had been bad. His face was worse.

"You poisoned your wife," Jack whispered. The look on the other man's face felt like being cut open.

"How could I?" he said. Tears pooled in the creases of his eyes. "I loved her. I'd never. I fed her the antidotes. Little doses, for days before the banquet. But the rest of them." His knuckles audibly popped, he closed his fists so tight. "She was there, laughing at their jokes, drinking their wine, his hand on her leg. I was in the kitchens. We heard the howling together. We were the only two who weren't howling. I got them all, Jack. A very precise dose. Nobody dies early on my watch. You've seen that. I take care with my craft. Every one of them, Higher Orders of a whole regiment." And Jack had no idea what that meant as numbers, but he understood what it meant as a concept.

"And after," Ollery concluded, "I went in. And they were all there. All dead, all at once, after the shrieking and the clutching and the jabbering at things that weren't there. And it was her, at the top table, the only one still sitting up in her chair. And it was me. I needed her to know. I needed her to see me. She was going to say something. Probably not sorry, under the circumstances. But by then the provosts had broken the bar on the door and they dragged me off. So I never heard."

"Right." Jack's voice was just a ghost of itself.

Ollery nodded. "You can go now, Jack," he said, quite companionably. "Unless you want a nip of something before you do?"

"No, that's fine," Jack said, and retreated rapidly from the tent.

He couldn't sleep, that night. Not with the images Ollery had put into his mind. Past midnight, Masty joined him sitting outside the tents of the department, staring at the sky as though there was anything there that helped.

Jack nodded to him. He half expected to find the man changed, at least in his eyes. The invisible glint of a crown on his brow, a new lordly gravitas to his bearing. But if Masty had brought those things back from the city that was his birthright, he'd stowed them right at the bottom of his army-issue pack. He was just the same slight, mild man Jack had first met back on the other side of the sea.

"Thank you," Masty said and, at Jack's frown, "for helping him. He doesn't find it easy to ask. He's not an easy man. Ever, but especially when he's hurt. I heard his voice, when you were in there. I'm guessing you know, now. Why he's with us."

"Actually," Jack said slowly, "that's the one thing I don't. Because I'm no expert on Pal justice but the way I see it, he murdered, what, a hundred senior officers or something. I don't imagine that's just twelve with the Alder and go run a hospital."

"Oh they were going to execute him, sure enough. Very big, public example, you know. I mean, *everyone* heard this when he joined the battalion, but that was fifteen years ago, and there's nobody else left from back then. I remember, though. Notorious doesn't cover it."

"So what happened?"

"They were going through his rooms. The digs him and his wife lived in. They found his book."

Jack glanced at him. "What book?"

"His treatise on...hold on, synthesis of alchemical something." Masty rubbed at the back of his head. "Way I understand it, alchemy is superstition and demi-magic. Nobody had any truck with it. Sore point with the Schools. Major benefit to most of the people we're fighting *against*, but not acceptable to rational thought. Except Ollery did it. He had a whole logical framework, where he'd taken all that chanting and mysticism and turned it into something they could get behind. A rational framework, that was it. The Synthesis of a Rational Alchemical Framework. Revolutionised about a dozen fields of study, medicine included. And when they'd found it, well, a man with a mind like *that*, you don't just throw him away."

Jack nodded, and then nodded again, and tried to assimilate what he'd been told, and eventually could only say, "I don't imagine his wife was very happy about that."

"I suspect," Masty said carefully, "that she doesn't eat or drink anything she hasn't personally prepared, and even then it doesn't help much."

Hell: Fire

The Butcher's Ladder, categories of injury in ascending severity of nature, the extent of the injury being equal: Mundane physical, breaks, contusions and gashes; Baton-shot and similar physical harm enhanced by magic; Energetic damage, flame, lightning and extreme sudden cold; Massive physical, artillery, collapsed walls etc.; Necrotic harm and sorceries that remove the vital essence from the affected flesh; Possession and dislocation of mind; Malign transformation; Unnatural contagion requiring immediate decontamination or destruction.

When Jack steps outside the tent, it's darker than inside. It's noon; it's like dusk. The sky above is a roiling mass of cloud that seems to hang low enough to touch. And there are the fires. Fires from heaven. They glimmer high through the murk like the lures of deep-sea fish. They dive. Six, eight of them in the air at once, descending with a terrible slow grace onto the field over the rise. He can't process what he's seeing. He can't tell whether they're sparks before his nose or blazing mountains at the end of the world. Then one comes down, and he feels the ground shudder with it. Hears the distant detonation. A thing the size of a modest townhouse in the middling mercantile districts of Ilmar. A battlefield out there, crawling with the advancing ant-host of the Palleseen soldiers. The faintest edge of screaming.

Lochiver can't talk so he kicks Jack hard on the shins to get him moving. He can't talk because he has a leather bucket in each hand and his bone flute is gripped in his teeth. His eyes are wide. It takes more than one kick because what Jack's seeing is so far beyond his experience.

God, clinging to Jack's shoulder like the worst monkey ever, stares up, no less aghast than His mortal servant.

"What the hell?" God complains. "What the actual hell is this?"

Jack has buckets too. He and Lochiver stumble through the gloom to the water wagon and the two Whitebellies there fill their pails and then the skins they've got slung over their necks. Then it's the fully laden slog back into the tent where the Butcher's cauldron is near-on boiled dry, and a new consignment of the wounded hollering and screaming because their skin has blistered off their backs and hands and faces. And they were lucky. They caught the edge of one of those monumental impacts, and the soldiers who were closer to the point are ashen smears.

Not cloud. Jack only understands it when he's under canvas once more. Not cloud but smoke. The whole sky is a pall of smoke from the new Loruthi artillery.

"This is madness," he spits out, emptying his buckets into the pot, throwing the skins to Banders so she can wet the lips of the latest wounded. "Why aren't we pulling back?"

"Military strategist are you now?" Tallifer straightens up from her latest victim, a gutshot officer who grips the edges of the operating table and grinds on his wooden bit like he's trying to whittle it with teeth alone. "Lochiver, get over here and start with your nonsense."

"I thought you said," the old man complains, "that it was all burns and nobody needed my nonsense." He's fitting the flute to his lips, and Jack can see Sturge the slug-god emerge from his collar, lured by the promise of horrible music.

"They're using foul-shot," Tallifer said. "Or that's the word. Nothing can get septic or we've got a problem."

Jack thinks about the fires, smoke that's strangled the sun.
War. He feels that any new problems can just get to the back
and wait their turn. But then problems are like casualties and
triage is always the first stage of treatment.

From closer than anybody likes, something booms and
roars, as though the duty Inquirer's putting a giant through
its paces. Jack finds himself half under the table, kneeling in
the blood.

"Shouldn't we be moving back?" he demands.

"Look, Jack, you know so much about it, you should go
find Uncle and tell him what he's doing wrong," Tallifer snaps.
"Either that or you could start actually *helping* around here."

"But that was close—"

"That was ours," the Butcher bellows, loud as any artillery.
"That was our answer. Which means that being right next to
it is far safer than those poor bastards on the other end of the
equation. Come over here, swab, clean, stitch. You know the
drill."

Jack does. Or, when his mind starts jumping about like
a cricket, somehow his eyes and hands still do. He takes the
lesser wounded, the gouges and the missing fingers, those whose
tourniquets have held them together this long. Those who don't
need Tallifer's surgeon's hands, or Alv's terrible equivocation.
The Butcher's boy brings him beakers and bowls and he presses
each to a set of lips or smears the stuff on wounds. Burn salve,
pain-number, cleanser, repellent. Repellent for what, he asks.
Just repellent, the Butcher says shortly, and the stuff certainly
is. Most of their regular stock in trade he knows now, by sight,
by smell. Knows how to administer it, even has a feel for dosage
based on the quantity of remaining soldier under his care. He
kneels beside Banders and they do the grunt work, the menial
stuff. God rides his shoulder, and Jack senses a terrible battle
going on in the realm of the divine. Because God abhors violence
and the bringers of violence, and every single man and woman
under Jack's hands falls squarely into that latter category. God

has spent centuries withholding His benediction from the world because the world can't be trusted with it. But now God's on the run, hiding out in the midst of the enemy and surrounded – right now, this moment of this one day of this war – with more hurt and horror than He saw on the streets of Ilmar in a year. And not as though Ilmar's a particularly quiet city. And there was Lidlet, who last anyone saw was still alive, though she's out there on one end of a stretcher even now. Jack has a horrible feeling that God is chafing against His own restrictions. Not because God is particularly well-disposed to humanity, the Pals especially, but because of the chaos that He could unleash just by helping.

"No," Jack says, and God's expression claims not even to have been thinking it, and let nobody tell you that a deity can't lie to you.

"It happens," says Banders flatly, from his elbow. And Jack realises that the woman he was bandaging is dead, too many casualties, too long a wait, always someone who loses the lottery. And Banders thought he'd noticed, rather than remonstrating with God.

"We're low again. More water," the Butcher snaps. Jack retreats from the new corpse and almost treads on Prassel's toes as she straightens up behind him. Her face is expressionless. She has a bandolier of copper jars slung over her jacket, just slipping one back into place as she steps back. His eyes can't help but flick to them, to her, to the body. He cannot, of course, say anything. Not a mere Accessory to a Fellow-Inquirer. But something happens to her face. A hairline fracture of composure that's gone unsplinted too long. He meets Prassel's eyes and goes cold all over.

"More water," he echoes, because any excuse to get away, right then. He grabs up the buckets, and this time it's Masty beside him because Lochiver's still mauling music to keep the open wounds clean. Pipering the particles of uncleanliness to where they can pay homage to his midget god.

★

Prassel's coppers are full. Not exactly cause for rejoicing but it's all points with Stiverton and Killingly. She hurries from the medical tent and picks her way sidelong across the breadth of the rear lines, dodging blocks of soldiers and wagons and handcarts, the logistics of on-the-fly redeployment. The Loruthi are giving the combined battalions a hammering. Nobody had any idea that they were so determined to hold the ground, or at least nobody who was sharing scuttlebutt with her. A similar reluctance to let them keep it is common to both Sage-Monitor Runkel of Forthright and Professor-Invigilator Scaffesty of Landwards, known to their respective troops as Uncle and Old Eyeball respectively. The Loruthi economic engine that pays for their varied mercenaries and counteroffensives, and the fireberg throwers that are even now complicating the Palleseen advance, is very dependent on the profits they can squeeze out of their overseas plantations and mines. Bracinta is the jewel of their mercantile crown. Drive them from Bracite lands and the war's good as won. That's the theory.

She reaches the Pal artillery just as Killingly lets fly. The ghost batteries are elegant compared to the big engines. Attenuated crane-things, like trebuchets designed by stick insects. A great cluster of slings fitted with the copper jars; a counterweight. Simple, really: yesterday's technology repurposed for tomorrow's war. She sees the weight swing down and back, the long arm mirror it at scale, forwards and up. At the apex the catch releases and the little jars become nothing but glitters in the smoke. Each one a soul. Each one a trapped ghost ravening for more life, touch, sight. A body to call its own, even if for a moment. And hopefully they'll remember the tasks they've been set under Stiverton's necromantic whip, and go about the back of the Loruthi lines knifing and cutting and setting fires. But even if they don't, a mad ghost at your enemy's heels is worth a squad and a half in the clash.

The Loruthi have necromancers of their own, but the elite of the ghost squads – Festle and his proven, calling themselves The Deathless – have orders to slit as many educated throats as they can to slow any properly-informed response. Prassel can't help but feel that's a poor precedent to set, given that it could come right back at them when the Loruthi *do* adapt. A target on your forehead's nothing anybody wants to live with. And before the declaration of war, she was corresponding with some of those Loruthi corpse-fondlers. They were her peers in scientific study, who are now just targets.

She arrives, unburdens herself of her bandolier and takes on a new one. Killingly seems to have an eternal supply of empty coppers. The Landwards necromancer looks at her and actually grins, as though these filled jars waiting for deployment weren't all Pal soldiers previously happily ensconced in their own living bodies. As though Prassel's just been picking up litter.

She runs into Thurrel on her way back. The Decanter has a dozen strings heavy with tablethi over his shoulder. A vast wealth of syphoned magic. The sort of haul you'd get from a prosperous temple, all those blessed thuribles and fonts of holy water, croziers and enchanted ritual knives, funnelled into those little gold lozenges and ready to be turned to war.

By mutual agreement they stop, just for a moment, both out of breath. Scholarly people run ragged by the physical demands of their disciplines.

"Where?" Thurrel asks, indicating her coppers.

"The hospital."

"Sweet reason." He shakes his head. "The big engines for me. You have no idea how they guzzle these." As if in punctuation, the crash and roar rolls over them, so that they clap their hands to their ears and screw up their faces, perfect mirrors of one another.

"How's supply?" she asks him. They have opposite problems, really. The longer the battle rages, the emptier his coffers become, while hers just keep filling.

"Low," he snaps. "Tell your Maric I need to see him in my office for a thorough caning when we're done. I absolutely insist." And he's trying to be humorous about it, as he does, but there's a line of steel in him that means it. And she doesn't particularly want to surrender Jack for the greater good, but that's how this is going to go sooner or later. Uncle will sign the papers, if she makes Thurrel go so high.

They part company, each carrying a small but vital piece of the machinery of war.

Jack's out into the unnatural twilight again. A fire-strike lands even as he exits. He's blind, momentarily, looking right in that direction as it explodes in an incandescent plume over the ragged horizon. Not sure if the whimpering he's hearing is his or Masty's or just the whole world's. He has no idea what this stretch of Bracinta used to look like, beyond the ridge, but it's mud and ashes now, a landscape of craters and bones.

Their own answering artillery speaks again, five separate detonations. He has no idea what the weapons even are, save loud. Every concussive explosion seems to set off a trembling in his bones and viscera that only gets worse, as though the sheer audible horror of it all is rattling him loose from the world, and wouldn't that be a blessing?

Masty's already halfway to the water wagon, and Jack tries to hurry after him and rams straight into something huge and metal. It looms above him, legs, three-quarters of a rounded torso ending with a melted edge, one arm, no head. A brutalised Sonori. Cosserby is ducking under its single armpit, dragging Jack to his feet before his skull stops spinning. For a moment they lean together. Cosserby has a smear of grease across his face like inexpertly applied camouflage. His knuckles are bloody and his replacement spectacles are askew.

"It's incredible, isn't it," he shouts over the thunder of descending firebergs. "We never thought they had it in them." And Jack can only assume that Pel has some variant meaning for 'incredible' because to him it's appalling but all too readily believable.

The Sonorist guides his blinded, battered charge off, and Jack stumbles to the water wagon. There's only one Whitebelly there now, working double time to fill their buckets. A chain of other pale-uniformed soldiers are waiting, each slung about with bottles and skins, water for the front lines, because it's thirsty work in the incinerators right now.

Waiting his turn, Jack looks into the occluded skies and sees the tower.

It's just one more mad thing. Probably it's barely worth a mention, but he points it out anyway just in case anybody else wants to share his blasé lack of surprise about it. A tower, ten storeys of building and a craggy fist of rock as a foundation, coasting through the smoke. And they arrived on a flying *island*, so surely an isolated building shouldn't seem odd, but somehow the smaller scale makes it more remarkable rather than less. A tower, and he can just make out the peak of its pointy roof. And then the tower is pouring liquid fire down onto the battlefield in a long stream. As though it's held it in for hours but can't restrain itself any longer.

"What...?" he gets out. "Just... what?"

But the Loruthi aren't a regimented and ordered force like the Pals. They hire anything and everything to come fight under their colours. They take coin onto the anvil of war and beat it into swords and batons and monsters and... this.

"Varinecthes!" Masty shouts. "Old Varney!" Which, to Jack, is just nonsense. An exclamation in Bracite perhaps, appropriate to these heights of incomprehensible horror.

But Masty has been around for longer than just about anyone, carried from one war to another through all his growing years. He's seen this thing before. He knows its name.

★

Varinecthes, Lord of the Tower, looks down on what he has wrought from the lowest balcony of his demesne. A final spurtle of fire descends onto the field below. He shakes a few hissing droplets away into the wind and closes up his quilted robe. A thousand years old and he does feel the cold, especially at this altitude.

"Well, mark that one off," he casts over his shoulder, retreating from the balcony and sliding shut the ornately carved screen. "What's next on the agenda?"

His companion, the demon Ghastron, appears in his customary form as a beautiful youth with serpent's eyes. The former because Varinecthes retains the aesthetic preferences of his younger days, the latter because it's always worth reminding yourself what you're dealing with.

"Varney," Ghastron says. "It's conjurations again. A hundred demons to bedevil the advance."

"A *hundred*?" Varinecthes – Varney – hisses. "Why did we agree to that?"

"*We* agreed to no such thing," Ghastron notes primly. "*You* felt it was a good boast to make, around eight centuries ago, and now we're stuck with it. What was it? 'And when thou shalt be in need, know that an hundred howling demons shall issue forth from the Realms Infernale to castigate thy enemies,' wasn't it?"

"Oh god," Varney says, because up in the third study there's a comfortable chair and a book and his pipe, and half a mug of drinking chocolate that's being kept sorcerously warm for him. "I mean, imps?"

"Imps is good," Ghastron agreed. "You didn't *specify* the calibre of demon. So long as they howl."

"I'll make the fuckers howl," Varney promises and starts plucking tiny squalling demon brats from his voluminous sleeves and throwing them over the edge. They don't all have wings, he notes belatedly, but probably being hit by a terrified free-falling imp counts as at least some level of castigation.

"Bedevil," he recalls. "Seriously, puns?"

"Tell me you're not desperate for amusement in this business," the demon Ghastron says. He has been bound to Varinecthes's contract for over four centuries. They've made their rut and settled into it together.

When he was a young magus, Varney's mentors taught him a great deal about demons and how to bargain for them. How the slightest shift of wording or missing clause could doom a conjurer, dragged off to the Realms Below, torn apart, soul devoured. Nobody ever told him to be just as careful in his dealings with human beings. And so the young Varinecthes, greatest sorcerer of his generation – or ever, as far as he's concerned – had gone through his first century or so making a variety of wide promises to kings, nobles, institutions, bloodlines and the occasional comely young man, because he was very proud of his considerable talents, and because he had craved the adulation of all around him. And then, a century or so after that, when he'd rather got over that sort of thing and wanted to settle down, they'd started to seek him out. The petitioners, the heirs and assigns, the disinherited princes, the scions who were somehow never as comely as those young men whose loins they'd eventually been engendered by. All of them full of having inherited the promises of a great magus, and how they wanted to use that to get ahead in the world. At first it had seemed like a temporary inconvenience, because people presenting themselves before a grumpy wizard and making rash demands tended to get exactly what they ask for and not at all what they wanted. It seemed likely that they would all wish themselves into oblivion one crooked finger at a time. And then, when there were only four extant claims on his time, he discovered that the damn things were transferrable.

The Loruthi currently hold title to three of the four. They're the cleverest creditors he's ever had, and careful about how they phrase their requests. So he's left picking apart his own original pledges to see what he can get out of. Hence the imps, the last of which he's even now flicking off into empty air.

"Mark it off," he tells Ghastron, and the demon does so. Serpent eyes can't really roll in exasperation but he makes a good job of it nonetheless.

"One more thing, Varney," he says. "The sun, again. The sun lance thing. 'I shall smite thy foes with the—'"

"Yes, yes, I remember." Varney sticks his head out over the balcony. And then further out, clinging onto the rail with one hand. Looking up, the sun is barely the dull head of a hot nail against the choked velvet of the sky. Looking down, the battlefield itself is just smog. As he watches, one of the great firebergs thunders slowly past his tower on its way to cause the Pals more problems.

"The idiots. What am I supposed to do with the sun, exactly? It's smoke from here to the abyss." And, still squinting down for targets, he sees that his slippers are almost out at the toes, frayed and threadbare, and hadn't he only bought them twenty years ago and set them with spells of repair? Except he hasn't kept up the enchantments, and he does wear the damn things all day as he shuffles about his demesne.

"New note," he tells Ghastron. "Buy slippers. Also, I cannot see whatever the hell they might want me to lance, and so it's probably best that all anyone's going to get is a strong tan. Sun, lance, lance, sun, off we go." And he does the necessary, invoking appalling elder pacts and ancient powers and minutely altering the actual orbit of the sun, all so that a great searing solar lance of energy can spend itself against the smothering smoke.

"Do you think," he considers, "all this artifice, this machine-delegated magic, it's going to make us obsolete?"

"I think we could stand to be a bit more obsolete," Ghastron opines. "You don't want to see what they've got you doing tomorrow. Now come inside before you catch your death."

★

From inside the tent it's like day comes for three turbulent seconds, in thunder and chaos. A flare that lights up everything through the canvas. Then they're all off their feet, and the table – including half-incised casualty – is on its side and on Lochiver's foot. Jack and Masty hastily right it and manhandle the screaming patient back on, grips slippery and red with all the stuff that's supposed to be inside him. Once the screaming inside has died down the screaming outside makes itself known. Cries for aid, sobbing, shrieking, and underneath it they're all old hands enough to hear the silences.

"Go see," the Butcher snaps. He alone kept his feet, hunched over his cauldron, stripped to the waist save for the bandages around his chest and back. They're weeping red again, his lash-marks torn open as he braced against the shake and roll of the earth.

The tent is at a decided angle. Jack almost brains himself on the poles as he rushes out without looking. It's all on fire out there. The fireberg didn't actually come down *that* close, as evidenced by the fact he's still there to see anything. Poor aim or mischance brought it far back of the actual Pal assault. The next surgical tent along is fiercely ablaze, and the water wagon has one wheel spinning in the air as it gouts its vital fluids into the mud. People are desperately trying to get people away from the shattered sea of blazing rock left from the impact. Jack and Masty run to help, hauling everyone they can to the hospital department's sagging doors. Each time Jack hears an airborne rumble he waits for another strike to go long. Waits for it to be his turn. Arms burning, smoke on his lips, eyes watering, it would almost be a relief.

"Here! Hey! Help, here!" A voice he knows but he's got a writhing, screaming man by the armpits, dragging him by main force, ploughing the earth with his victim's heels. He gets them into the tent and onto the ground so Ollery can calibrate the scale of the casualties' injuries. A leather-aproned man, Jack sees, and half the blood on him not his own. One of the surgeons from the other tent, his hands and arms all blister and burn.

"Mine," Alv calls. She's sitting by now, her legs early donations to the cause, but if she can get this man back to his business then that relieves the load on the rest of them. The Butcher weighs the meat and nods. A bargain at the price.

Then, "Help, here!" again, and Cosserby staggers in, propping up Banders. And in the grand scheme of things Banders is fine. No need to worry about her. Half the skin and breeches scorched off one leg, that's all. Jack doesn't even need to be told, and nor does Ollery's boy. The beaker passes from hand to hand to lip, like everyone rehearsed it the night before. Banders gulps down the painkiller, and if it's a bit more than the recommended dose, well, she's built up a fair tolerance to all manner of drugs in her chequered career.

"Help her," Cosserby says. "Do your thing."

"I can't—" Jack meets Banders's gaze and sees a dreadful hope there.

"No," says God, on his shoulder again.

"Look, I know. I know your deal," Banders hisses through gritted teeth. "Just do it now and when things are quiet I'll kick a puppy or something and we can sort out the burns then. That's how it works, right?"

Jack stammers that he supposes, yes, that's how it works. It isn't really how it was supposed to work. It's a religious obligation, a sign of devotion to the benevolent healing god. You weren't supposed to use it just to bank injuries for later. That was sacrilege, surely. Except Banders has been talking to Lidlet, and reckons she has him on a technicality. And God says, clearly and levelly in Jack's ear, "No."

"No what?" Jack demands, already halfway to reaching. "Come on. We've done more for worse. I don't care if you like her or not."

"I told you," and God is not spiteful, none of His meanness on display. God is deadly serious. "I cannot heal her. She cannot come to me. Not her, out of all of them."

Jack stares at Him, but then a new wave of casualties is being stretchered in and he has no chance to process what he's been told. He abandons the swearing, accusing Banders, shoulders aside Cosserby's protests, goes to each of the new screamers and forces the Butcher's pills and potions on them. And then someone's shaking his arm, a lot of strength and yet only a little force, as though they're worried about breaking him. He rounds on Cosserby and finds it's Lidlet instead, in with the stretcher crews.

"Help me," she says simply.

She's not hurt. She looks whole. A little singed maybe but that's to be expected, given where she's been.

"I'm…" Hands busy, Jack indicates everything around him using eyes and elbows.

"Please," she says. "It's Foley."

Jack doesn't know who or what a Foley is, but Lidlet gets him to one body amongst many. A man, a young man, and dying. Prassel's hovering with a copper in her hands like a ghoul with a doctorate. There's a black cross on his forehead. The Butcher has already passed Foley over, because there's no point Tallifer or another of the surgeons cutting one more hole in him, when his life has plenty of egress points already, and if Alv worked her magic then she'd be on the lists of the dead herself.

"He's from my squad," Lidlet babbles. "Please, Jack. Do your thing. Help him, like you did me."

Of course this moment was coming. He'd foreseen it, and then it hadn't. Other things had got in the way, and he'd forgotten to fear it. And now it's here. Lidlet wants him to heal her friend. Just one more healing. One more noncombatant soldier. What could it hurt? The man could take the other end of Lidlet's stretcher.

"I can't," Jack says harshly. "You heard what Higher Orders

said. It's forbidden." The old word he used to use about God, now invoking the secular majesty of Palleseen command.

"Jack, he's my *friend*. Please." Lidlet is undone. Jack's never seen anyone with such a naked face before. All the slyness is gone from her. No quoting chapter and verse of his theology at him, no finding the leverage point from which she can move the world. Pleading only, all that's left to her.

God hunches forwards on his shoulder, staring at the last few breaths of Foley, Lidlet's friend.

Jack feels something ugly twist inside him. Something that they gave him with the papers and the uniform. "I *can't*," he says to her. "What am I supposed to do? They'll shoot me. They'll shoot him. And you. You were there in that room. My *trial*. And God won't do it. I told you He's a bastard. And I can't. We save who we can save."

He breaks away from her, administers drugs to the next three patients with more than an orderly's usual brutality, then the Butcher has him stitching. A man's in with his ribs laid open but his lungs intact, and that's just a stitcher's job so long as Lochiver's keeping the beat and making sure everything stays clean.

He does his level best not to vomit over the man's flayed ribs. Hardly professional, that. Being Maric Jack, right then, is almost more than he can bear. He can't even pretend it isn't his name any more. If he isn't Maric Jack, who is he?

"Look," God says, from his shoulder. "Look at her."

"I won't," Jack spits, fingers busy with the big curved needle and the gut thread.

"She's praying."

Jack glances round despite himself. Lidlet is kneeling by the body of Foley. Her lips move. Is she praying? Not to any Pal eye but surely God would know.

"She's praying to me," God says.

"No," Jack tells Him. "I forbid it."

"When was the last time you did that, eh? Actually prayed.

Not bickered. Not badmouthed me. But prayed, like a man of faith should."

"I'm not a man of faith any more." Jack's shocked to discover it's true. He, the saviour and smuggler of deities, the devotee of God since his youngest days, has nothing left to believe in.

"Well to hell with you," God says, and there's a tear in His ancient eye. "I will bloody do it, and sod the Pals. Forbid *me*, will they?"

Jack turns his head to look murder at the divine presence, but God's not there any more. God's hopped from him like a flea. Jack sees Him clambering up Lidlet's jacket.

He can't even have a proper crisis of faith. The demands of the wounded are too pressing.

Prassel's over with the Butcher now – as if *that's* ever good news. She speaks urgently into his ear, because it's all noise in the medicos' tent and she doesn't have a parade-ground voice. A messenger has been and gone, though, and there's a job needs doing.

"Listen up!" Ollery bellows. He looks half dead, all that flesh weighing on him and pulling his wounds open. His voice hasn't caught up, though. He could shout down the engines. "Listen up! Got a jam of wounded up at the front and enemy coming in. Every free hand to the stretchers, get who you can out of there."

And Lidlet's on her feet, because it's her job, self-appointed. The narrow window of opportunity her situation gave her. On her feet and taking up a stretcher so recently vacated the blood's still wet. And Masty's stepping forwards. And Jack sees Foley sitting up, uniform carved off his unbroken hide, improbably alive. Foley's about to volunteer, good soldier that he is, and Foley doesn't know the rules.

"You, rest." He crams a doctor's borrowed authority into the words. "No more battle for you. I'll go. Chief, I'll go."

The Butcher gives his nod to that, and then looks round. "Banders?"

Banders has her leg bandaged and a ton of drugs inside her,

and it's probably the latter that says, "Yes, Chief," and tries to get her on her feet. Ollery's already shaking his head, casting round for others. Cosserby is putting a hand up, the smart kid in phalanstery, always knowing the answer to a slightly different question than was posed. "I'll go, Chief." In Banders's place, of course. Good soldier that he is.

The Butcher's in no position to quibble, and by then there are another couple of pairs of bearers, and the word will have gone out to every surgical tent, every squad of reserve Whitebellies. Stretchers for everyone! Because the Pal army cares for its soldiers like a swineherd for his pigs, and out of much the same concern.

They go into darkness, and it swallows them.

Hiding Amongst the Graves

Jack's changed. Not just his name or his clothes. Not that his life before conscription was devoid of tragedy, but there are lines on his face Ilmar didn't put there. A gauntness, where before he'd somehow preserved a boyish cast to his face. A leanness of muscle rather than of irregular eating. An attitude. Not as though he and God hadn't had their disagreements before, but mostly polite. Like two roommates who couldn't either of them make the whole of the rent without help. And now they're in the army, and both are realising that they're not chained together in quite the same way.

The way the stretchers worked was this: two people per stretcher, one behind with the thing itself, one in front to lead the way. The stretchers were an ingenious piece of design. Folding, with moving braces that locked the whole thing rigid to support the weight of a human life. Collapsed, they strapped tight to the back, leaving the bearer both hands to scramble through the nightmare topography left in the wake of the Loruthi artillery.

The occasional fireberg still flared in the skies overhead, but the bombardment was mostly over. The two forces had met, Jack divined. Neither side could unleash their engines without unacceptable collateral loss.

And the Loruthi were pushing back. Jack remembered how it had been last time, on the far side of the sea. The Pals weren't used to counterattack, he thought. They'd been the bully in the playground too long, taking on smaller kids like Allor and Telmark. It wasn't as if the staunch defenders of Jack's own home hadn't put up a valiant fight, but their valour, even if they'd been able to wring every drop of it from the fabric of the flag, had made for a cupful against the massed barrels of the Palleseen. The Loruthi, those far-ranging merchants, had turned out to have quite the well-stocked cellar of their own, bought and paid for but no less potent for all that.

Lidlet had their stretcher, which was just as well as he couldn't really have strapped it to his box without falling over backwards. Next to them, a constant intrusion into his peripheral vision, Cosserby led and Masty carried. Beyond *them*, another pair, and another. A wave of bearers clambering across the impact-mangled terrain like ants.

Something thundered from ahead, lighting the horizon. A weapon deployed or destroyed, Jack had no idea.

"Do you even know where you're going?" God shouted in his ear. "This bloody smoke!"

Jack had been going *forwards* and assuming, as everyone else was too, that they were headed in the right direction. That suddenly seemed rash. What if everyone was following *him*? "Do we know where we're going?" he shouted to Cosserby.

The Sonorist looked at him, eyes wide. "Don't you?"

"Do you have a map?" Jack asked.

Cosserby actually started searching his pockets before remembering that nobody would be drawing moment to moment plans of the battlefield. "Fighting that way!" he shouted – for something else was thundering up ahead, eclipsing the edges of his words. "Bodies that way!"

Jack could only nod. Then he was dancing along the ridge between two craters, feeling horribly exposed if there was just one Loruthi with a baton and an open eye in a hundred yards. Dropping down into a massive, gouged rut and then climbing what felt like a vertical incline at the far edge. He turned automatically, reaching down to help Lidlet, then the two of them ended up on their knees, staring at ruin.

A mountain, he thought at first. *What's a mountain doing here and how did they break it?* Seeing only a vast mound of shattered stone, so much greater even than the house-sized flaming boulders the Loruthi had been throwing about. Then his eyes viscerally clicked into a different focus and he saw the buildings. The shattered corpse of a community strewn down the slanted side of the wreck. He understood what he was seeing and the strength went out of his legs so he couldn't get up even with Lidlet pulling on his arm.

A Gallete island had come down here. He didn't know how the Loruthi had managed it, but here it was, broken against the harsh bosom of the earth, and all those airborne lives with it. The homes, the fields, the tenuous dance to the tune of the Pals to maintain their traditions. All gone, one more casualty of the war, and not something the field hospital could patch.

"We need to help," he said, when Lidlet had finally righted him. "We need to see—"

"Jack, this is days old," she told him flatly. "This is from before the battle. Nobody's left, if anyone even survived it. We're falling behind the others. Go!" And she pushed him in the back with a cautiously metered level of force, and he stumbled, caught himself and lurched on.

Overhead, once, he saw that tower again – impossible, though the adjective didn't have the absolute meaning that it should, any more. A vertical shadow in the smoke, like a knife poised over the battlefield. He whimpered, but no great stream of liquid fire issued forth from it, and it passed on its own inscrutable errands.

There was noise from up ahead, human noise beyond the mechanical thunder. Not fighting – he was reliably assured the fighting had booked the room next door for its celebrations. A familiar sound; the anthem of his new home. The desperate pleas and cries of the injured.

They'd reached their goal, somehow, in all the waste of mud and pummelled ground. Pairs of stretcher bearers were converging on them, hurrying, hunched, braced against the next explosion or a sudden appearance of the enemy. And there, beyond...

He'd done the rounds of the Hammer Districts in Ilmar sometimes, with his begging bowl and his pleas for alms. Beyond the factories and forges where the demons laboured had been the junkyards where all the broken pieces went. Things to be remade or melted down or just held there, enormous piles of rust and the depredation of time. Like art, eventually. The art of waste, he'd thought, but he'd seen nothing, back then. *This* was art. This was a true monument to loss. The same piles of irreparable things beaten out of shape beyond any chance of serving their purpose, save that here it was people.

He didn't know where the fighting was now, but this looked like a high-water mark of Loruthi resistance. Literally, a great strand line of uniforms and outflung limbs where the charge had met the teeth of the defence. Jack, familiar of hell, was momentarily struck to stillness, unable to process just how many corpses he was seeing at one time. Not just Pal. The murk of the sky admitted enough light to distinguish the green of Loruthi uniforms and a dozen different colours of mercenary amongst the charcoal grey of the Palleseen and the pale of the Whitebellies who'd died beside them.

And still lived, he realised, jerking back into motion. News from the front had been accurate for once. Here were their wounded, waiting to be stretchered back, save that nobody had conveniently sorted them from the dead.

The first bearers to arrive just took up the crying, weeping bodies who were free of the tangle and carried them straight off, because if there was ever a good place to be out of it was there. The rest started piling up, staring at the heap, hearing the desperate voices of those trapped within it, pressed, broken, dying. Some started hauling at limbs and ragged edges of cloth, excavating what they could. Many just looked, unable to even start because the task was so great.

"Who's in command here?" Cosserby demanded, hands on hips, unable to believe the war was being run in so slipshod a fashion.

A Whitebelly looked around wildly and then fixed on his dark uniform. "That would be you, magister."

"Oh. Shit." Cosserby's face twitched, and Jack waited for him to go to pieces. But something clicked into place in the man. Maybe it was the discipline he'd had kicked into him in basic training. Maybe it was the engineer recasting what he saw as a mechanical problem. He was giving orders soon after. Not the best orders, too much close management and too little context, but he had people moving and digging and hauling out, a steady trail of stretchers heading back the way they'd come. Then Jack and Lidlet and Masty appointed themselves Cosserby's aides and began expanding his strategy across the corpse-mound. And God, on Jack's shoulder, pointed "There!" and "That one's still kicking," and "He's not dead yet!" Indicating bodies cast aside because their owners had gone beyond screaming, but not yet all the way. Jack glanced at Him, the divine presence, seeing a terrible new focus. A healing God faced with His own personal nightmare. The very thing that had driven Him to withhold His gifts and diminish into the wizened monkey He'd become. Jack was busy, then. Busy passing on Cosserby's orders, or the spirit of them. Busy hauling on arms and legs and blocking out the fresh shrieks his hauling caused. Busy looking straight ahead so that, when some of those critically injured bodies started walking home without needing a stretcher, he didn't see it. He didn't have time to argue with God, and he didn't have any convictions in which to have courage. God had gone rogue. A second lease of divine life here in the crucible of the war front. God was healing people behind Jack's back, he knew. Soldiers who'd only die tomorrow, or the day after. Who'd probably be shot by their own side if they didn't just re-inherit the wounds that should have killed them. And who'd get Jack killed too, by their prolonged existence. He was on sufferance already, and what would God do after he'd gone?

Because he didn't want to follow where those thoughts led, he put his back to the task, hauled aside corpses like a fisherman with full nets.

"They're coming!" someone yelled. Some bright spark who'd made himself lookout. A moment later he was tumbling down the mound of corpses, one more to the tally, because to be lookout he'd been standing against the sky, and some keen eye from the enemy had marked them. One less bearer. One stretcher team two feet short of being able to cart a body.

Jack met Cosserby's gaze, expecting panic but finding a narrowness of focus that was almost more frightening. Cosserby had a plan.

"Grab who you can and go, everyone! Every stretcher filled. They can't ask more." And he was kneeling, not obeying his own orders. He'd found something, treasure unearthed by the excavation.

Masty plucked at his shoulder. "Come on, I need you."

"Wait," Cosserby said. "This'll show them. This'll give us time." Because if the enemy were coming at a run then they'd go faster than any two people with a laden stretcher. "This is the moment. This is the why of it." Talking to himself but at the top of his voice. "You'll love this." And the other stretchers were loading up, all that could, and Jack wanted to be away too, with Lidlet, with anyone, except Cosserby was still fussing at something. Then he stood up with a cry of triumph and something else did too. Something rose from the corpses, some terrible new war god, loose-jointed cadavers tumbling aside like sea-foam. Its dented metal body tolled a mournful note. Cosserby had found a Sonori mired in the dead, and shovelled tablethi into it until magic had overcome its damage. The towering thing lurched, sounded, and then lumbered around the corpse pile, towards, presumably, the enemy. Jack heard some shooting instantly, the crack of batons and high musical ringing where the shot rebounded from the automaton's shell.

That close then.

The other stretchers were away. Masty shook Cosserby's shoulder frantically. The man turned, seeming surprised they were still with him.

"I gave you an order," he said uncertainly, and then his shoulder exploded in flesh and jagged shards of bone. He goggled at them, as though this was the worst possible insubordination, and pitched backwards, practically landing on the stretcher Lidlet had set out on the ground.

He was alive, and for a moment Jack and God were staring at each other, but then Lidlet had her end of the stretcher and was shouting at someone. A Whitebelly with his own stretcher still strapped up, the other half of the luckless lookout, rushed over to take up the slack.

"Come on, Jack." Masty was plucking at his sleeve. Not even looking for another living casualty, just wanting to run. Lidlet and her accomplice set off at a run, and it would have been simplicity itself to just outpace them, leg it for friendly lines. The only bearers to pitch up without a body.

Help us! The smallest possible voice, somehow reaching him. *Don't leave us here!*

Jack turned back. It was purely that shame, in the end. Being seen to return empty-handed, by all the soldiers in that army he hadn't ever wanted to be part of. He scrabbled in the bodies, listening out for that cry, that voice from the heart of the mound, and Masty shouted and yanked at his belt.

"There's no-one!" he insisted.

"I hear them," Jack said.

"Jack, there's no-one!" And, as Jack just clawed into the dead like a badger in its set, "Come *on*, man! We have to *move!*"

Jack shook his clutching hand off. *We're here!* called that voice. A tiny voice, really. Not even a whole soldier's voice, but there were lots of soldiers who were less than whole, all around them. Half the limbs Jack yanked away didn't have all of a body attached to them.

We're here! Don't leave us! and even God was shouting at him to leave it. Something rumbled, out across the field, close enough he couldn't tell whose lines it issued from. But the voice still cried and Jack still dug, hearing only the utter desolation of it, ignoring the fact that it came to his head without the intervention of his ears. Grasping for the hand that would clutch back. The passport of a rescued soul that would let him go back with pride intact. Uncovering, in that despairing gloom, a face he knew.

A face he'd seen only the once, after its mask came off. Bony, foreign. Not Pel, not Bracite, not Maric. That other country whose name he couldn't even recall. The man who'd been about to sacrifice him, and Tallifer too. After which they'd got on cautiously well, two undercover theologues in hostile territory. Pirisytes, the scorpionfly cultist.

"I've got you," he told the man's slack face. "Come on now, help me out." Dragging at the man's pressed length, prying him by main force from the fond embrace of those around him. And Pirisytes was no help at all, just slack and disjointed, awkward as his chaos god could possibly want. Zenotheus never made anything easy.

At last Jack had him free. "Stretcher here, stretcher!"

Masty crouched down beside him, reaching back for the straps. Then stopping. "Jack…"

"Just get the stretcher laid out, come on. Get him onto it."

"Jack. He's gone. He's dead."

"He's not. I can hear him. I can… I can save him." A sudden flash of inspiration, looking around at the ragged little divinity on his shoulder. "You can save him. Fix him."

God's thousand-yard stare came right back out of Him. Eyes that had seen too much in antique times, and too much again just in the last hour. "He's gone," said God. "He's dead. And I couldn't anyway. Swore himself to his god, didn't he. Can't be one of mine. Just like—"

"But he was talking to me." Jack stared wildly at Pirisytes's corpse, which was… dead. Obviously dead. Dead in all ways except…

It crept out of the mangled cultist's collar. First the long, curled feelers, then its dark, shiny head with the great bug eyes and double-pronged beak. Resting on the chest of its priest, nervously cleaning its wings with its hind legs, tail flexing.

Please, said Zenotheus. *Get us away from this.*

"Oh hell no," God snapped. "We are not having that *thing* in here with us. We refuse."

It wasn't an appealing god. That which Lays Eggs in the Hearts of Kings, or whatever the title was.

Please. The voice was in Jack's head only, but at the same time somehow from stridulations of its limbs. *They are all gone. All our adherents here. All our plans. We had such plans for mischief.* The breeder of chaos and misadventure undone by humanity's vastly greater capacity for disorder. The pinprick of its schemes obliterated by the crushing foot of the war.

"Jack?" Masty said uncertainly. "Jack, come on."

"Get in," Jack said to it, because if God could go rogue then so could he. Zenotheus's wings flurried, and it clipped his ear with a pronged foot on its way to burrow into the box.

"Well there goes the neighbourhood," God spat disgustedly.

"Live with it," Jack said, without sympathy.

The sound of something vast and heavy hitting the Sonori shocked him and Masty to silence, loud and sudden as a siege engine that had learned to sing. The buckled-in metal body went end over end through the air over their head and then the Loruthi were there. A dozen, a score, batons levelled, barking words Jack didn't know.

Masty did, enough to get on his knees. And it wouldn't help, Jack understood. They were on the advance. Taking prisoners was a trap designed by the Pals to take Loruthi soldiers from the fight. They kept shouting, batons levelled, and Jack understood that he and Masty were going to die.

"Well, shit," God said. "I'm sorry."

Jack wondered for what. He clutched for Masty's hand, felt it cling to his. Wan sunlight breached the smoke and the air glittered around them.

Something danced on his shoulder. Not God, who wasn't the dancing kind. The nature spirit, which had saved him from the beasts a whole sea away. Issuing forth one last time to see if it could help. Jack saw it, rotting, crumbling away. Bleeding woodlice and blind white ants. A thing of a faith so old nobody even had a name for. Nameless perhaps because there had been no words when they'd first raised its shrines and circles. Or perhaps a thing cast up in Ilmar from some other world entirely, cut off from its devotees to wither and decay on the streets of an unfriendly city. Until he'd scooped it up to keep it from the Pals. Preserved it for just a while longer.

It danced, and broke open. He saw it was fungus all the way through, rotten to the core. A tree god embracing the end of all vegetal things, or else a god of rot meeting its apotheosis.

A vast sea of shimmering spores vented from the rents in the thing, and the Loruthi didn't see them. Forgot the pair of them. Moved on, the squad of them and the wheeled artillery piece they'd smashed the Sonori with. Vanished into the gloom, leaving Jack with hands gritty with spores and a few fugitive bugs. With the sense that something tiny but unthinkably ancient had paid its final way in the world and passed away, and knowing that two meagre human lives were not worth its sacrifice.

Masty had him by the shoulders then, and was bundling him away. Unburdened by death they fled after the rest and abandoned the field to the Loruthi.

Reversals

The Butcher. A man made to lord it over a stationary domain. His customers come to him for the best cuts. He doesn't go hawking his wares in the street. The centre of mass of the hospital department. Put him in the tent surrounded by his alchemy and people and he's a force to be reckoned with. Cram him on a wagon, elbow to elbow, he's ballast. A sour, brooding dead weight of flesh on its way back from market because nobody would buy.

Prassel had to bark the man's name three times before he registered, and then only after Tallifer, penned in beside him, pulled his ear to get his attention. Ollery looked up at Prassel, there on the horse she'd commandeered like she was about to lead the cavalry charge that would turn the tide of the battle. If she'd been a ship's captain she'd have keelhauled his expression for mutiny then and there.

Is that for me, or the world in general? He had a broad face. Enough scowl there to cover a lot of ground and grudges. But she'd held the whip. Even though he wouldn't have had it any other way, that didn't mean he couldn't resent her for it. A dangerous man to have sour at you, the Butcher.

His shoulders, the taut expanse of shirt below them, all of it had his lashes written in blood, both dry and fresh. Every time the wagon hit a rut he was jolted against the rail, and she saw the red travelogue he'd written there. "You're taking your own medicine, I hope, Chief?"

"Some," he grunted. "Useful lesson. Reminds me how it doesn't stop the pain. Just puts it in the next room for a while. And only some. Need a clear head."

She wanted to say he could dose himself to the eyeballs and the hell with it, but probably he was right. It wasn't as if casualties stopped dying just because of a general retreat. Rather the opposite, in her experience.

"Let Tallifer handle it," she said. "She's more than capable. Or Alv."

"Alv's used up," Ollery said. "Already."

"Tallifer then." She rapped at the rail by the old woman's elbow with her riding crop. "I'm making you deputy chief. When you reach the new camp," *wherever that will even be,* "you supervise the department."

Tallifer's look suggested she could have done without the extra duties, but age and priesthood gave her the wisdom to keep her withered lips shut about it.

The rest of the wagon had about a dozen surgeons and orderlies, most of whom Prassel hadn't ever seen before, Landwards Battalion badges, where she could see insignia at all. Lochiver was up on the bench at the front, and Banders beside him, managing the reins despite a bandaged-up leg. Two more lame ducks accounted for. No sign of the rest. *Turn up like a bad smell.* They'd survived this much army life, after all, and Jack...

Would be better off staying missing, honestly, said a little voice in the back of her head. Which was unkind, and untidy thinking, but probably true. Maric Jack reminded her a lot of Killingly's ghost batteries. An asset of undeniable effectiveness that was going to explode in someone's face sooner rather than later. Probably hers.

She tapped at the horse's haunches and had it move on, outpacing the labouring wagon. Moving up the long, bedraggled line of soldiers wondering where it had all gone wrong.

★

Tallifer did indeed set up a temporary hospital under an awning with the more robust of the surgeons, doing what she could with the constant stream of injured. And the wounds she had to treat were on the light side, Prassel knew, because the worst of the wounded hadn't made it off the field.

It had been the fiercest clash of the entire war, people were saying. Certainly it had been the most punishing reversal the Palleseen army had suffered in a while. Two whole battalions, fresh and rested, broken in a monstrously bloody action and forced into retreat. And the Loruthi were only holding off because they needed sleep too, and night fights were a tactical disaster waiting to happen. Come morning their advance and the Pal retreat would go on in lockstep. The enemy weren't done retaking ground.

We'll be back at the doors of Magnelei before long, and won't that look ridiculous.

After ensuring the department was set up and functioning as best it could, Prassel went in search of other news. The first big tent she tried was a regular trooper's mess, and she had that fragile moment in every officer's life when all the faces turned your way are looking for someone to blame. The next one she tried wasn't much better. A score of mid-rankers packed in, an aide serving tea. The mood, low; the faces grim, and some of them unpleasantly familiar. She wanted to duck right out again but she'd been recognised and hailed by then.

"Not scavenging the field for parts?" Maserley asked acidly. "Surely business is booming in the necromancy trade?" His demon woman was holding a lamp for him, casting a tableth-charged radiance onto the paper he was scribbling on. Contracting on the fly was a dangerous habit for a demonist, she knew. He must have burned through his entire stock in trade over the course of the day's fighting.

Prassel took a proffered stool and a cup of lukewarm tea. Sat in the company of her peers, looking to see who else was there. A real grab-bag of schools, disciplines and departments. The specialists and oddballs, like her. Quartermasters, intelligencers, artillery engineers and magicians.

Thurrel raised his cup to her, looking as worn down as she felt. "You want that fortifying?" he asked.

She didn't, of course. Strictly against regulations and, as the Butcher said, clear heads, all that. Except she stuck her cup out and let him pour a generous libation into it. "Let nobody say a word against decanting," he told her gravely, then topped up every receptacle that was offered him until his flask was empty. "Well, bloody hell," he remarked, upending it so that the final amber drop fell into his own cup. "Who had 'All the Loruthi in the world turning up at once' on their card, because you can claim your winnings."

"I mean we were all running around *saying* how important it was to them, to hold Bracinta," said a quartermaster. "Money-basket for the whole Loruthi Sway, isn't it? No surprise that the Lorries heard us."

Thurrel chuckled. "I don't know if you *saw* what that battle left of several square miles of Bracite earth, old boy, but nobody's turning *that* into a profitable turmeric plantation any time soon. The sheer magical residuum is going to breed monsters and nightmares for the next seven years. If I wasn't so damn tired I'd take three racks of tablethi out there and harvest something back of what I spent today. What a waste! An appreciable percentage of our annual magical budget, pissed out at the Loruthi, who were pissing twice as much back at us. Nobody's won today."

"I reckon the Loruthi think they've won today," said the quartermaster darkly.

"Duly noted," Maserley snapped, looking up from his writing. "I'm sure you'll explain that to Correct Speech when they ask who wasn't fully committed to the assault." And Maserley, of all people, wasn't particularly committed to *any* cause. All the more reason to look for scapegoats. The quartermaster went pale and shut up.

"We had to put Killingly down, of course," said a quiet, dry voice in Prassel's ear, and she jumped despite herself. A necromancer shouldn't be vulnerable to that kind of scare, but perhaps it was permitted at the hands of a senior in the profession. It was Stiverton at her shoulder, hunched cadaverously around his own teacup. He still wore that vastly overornamented robe, as though he'd had to evacuate halfway through rehearsing a play.

"Put her down where, magister?" Prassel asked, for a moment picturing the woman getting off a wagon for vital necromantic business.

"A matter of overconcentration, I suspect," Stiverton said. Not jolly about it but not in deep mourning, either. "I had Festle do it. It seemed only appropriate. Her defences were inadequate and we had a containment breach amongst the coppers. Something of a chain reaction. We live and learn. Or some of us do."

Prassel stared at him. "Fellow-Inquirer Killingly was... possessed?"

"By, I estimate, at least thirty separate ghosts," Stiverton said. "It was something of an educational moment, even for me." His fingers brushed against the protective sigils of his robes and Prassel privately decided that his theatricality was overdue as a standard addition to the uniform, and damn how it looked to outsiders. "One is aware, obviously, that it is theoretically possible, but one had not hitherto had the chance to witness such a thing. Only something like Festle could get close enough to put her out of her misery. So what I'm saying, Fellow-Inquirer Prassel, is, there's a vacancy."

Not, presumably, the moral one at the heart of the whole endeavour. A professional one. A sideways promotion that would nonetheless be a powerful step up compared to nursemaiding the hospital. Unless and until she met the same fate as Killingly.

"I would have to speak to Unc— to Sage-Monitor Runkel, obviously. The arrangements. A secondment, I think he'd allow." Because that was all true, and because it also presented a multitude of points at which a judicious finger on the scales could see her stay exactly where she was without looking like she was turning him down. If, of course, she wanted to turn him down.

"Well of course." Stiverton sat back and slurped at his tea, grimacing. "But I think you'll do well at the cutting edge of the trade, Prassel. So long as you stay the right side of the hilt."

She finished her tea and made her excuses then, stepping out into a light drizzle that the night had seen fit to gift them with. Thurrel was on her heels, brushing down his sweat- and mud-stained jacket.

"Not going to look good on anyone's permanent records, this," he remarked philosophically. "Not unless we turn it around in short order. I'm over there, my tent. Drop round for a nip of something, before you turn in. I don't think I'm sleeping tonight."

From anyone else that would be an admission of trauma, but she knew he kept wildly irregular hours even in peacetime. From anyone else it would also sound like an invitation to a liaison, but if she'd been Thurrel's type she'd have fended him off by now, given they'd known each other since the phalanstery. It came to her, with a wintry little shiver, that he might actually be a *friend*, and what a sad business that would be. Rather none at all than so fallible a prop as Thurrel.

She was about to turn him down: need sleep, long day, pressures of work, you know how it is. Then someone else was with them. Or something else. The demon, Maserley's creature, with papers in hand. An emissary to the Kings Below sent to gather fresh meat for tomorrow's festivities.

Prassel stood aside. She didn't much like demons at the best of times. Given where *this* one had been, as Maserley's little infernal bed-warmer, she wanted even less to do with it. Except it wanted something to do with her, because it wasn't just rushing off to go rouse the hosts of hell on her master's behalf.

"How is your department, Fellow-Inquirer?" the creature asked. So presumably Maserley had set it to annoy her. Entirely within character.

"Why? Can you tie a bandage?" Prassel asked the thing. "We're still at work, my people. Another pair of hands would be welcome." Delivered with the appropriate sneer, as though those fingers were good for anything except mischief and obscenity.

"Be careful what you wish for, magister," the demon said. "For nothing I am set to can possibly go well. You would not want me touching your wounded or handling your implements."

"I'm sure you've handled plenty of implements, my dear," drawled Thurrel. "Now run along, won't you. Go give your winning smiles to the Kings Below and round us up another batch of baton-fodder. Or else Maserley'll send you to the front in their place."

And the demon trotted off. Thurrel shook his head over Maserley's foolishness in keeping something of that shape around where everyone could see. Then Prassel did go join him for a nip. A jolt of fortified wine that, she hoped, would help her sleep.

On her way back to her own bunk, with the leaden hand of exhaustion already pressing on her, she passed by the hospital. They were still at work, patching and dispensing. Ollery sat like a great sack of lead at the heart of it, head almost on his chest but hands still busy over his cauldron. His boy was asleep, the toe of the Butcher's right boot his pillow. And what would the child possibly grow up into, Prassel wondered. A healer? An alchemist? A monster? Or just one more soldier to be thrown at the latest object of Palleseen desire. Assuming he had the chance to grow into anything at all.

And no sign of any of their lost birds coming to roost, either, but there were still soldiers trailing in from the front even now, trying to find their squads and companies. They'd show up. Or they wouldn't. Nothing Prassel could do about it, anyway.

Tallifer was still stitching, talking rapidly to Lochiver in a way that suggested she'd been on the Butcher's very best salts. At her elbow, holding out needles and swabs and blades, was Maserley's demon girl. Prassel just stared, wondering if it wasn't some phantasm caused by exhaustion. She was right there, though, doubtless poisoning everything she touched with her own nature and her master's malevolent desires. *I did that. I said something unwise to a demon and now everything's worse. Probably.* But she couldn't even muster the strength to go over and shout at people about it. She just dragged her heavy feet to her bedroll and collapsed. And, the next day, everything was packed up and the retreat carried on, because things were bad and the Loruthi weren't stopping.

Better Live on your Knees

Lidlet: jug-eared, tough, the trooper's trooper. No phal education but top-grade credentials from the schools of life and military regulations. A bit harsh to say all she'd ever wanted to do was kill people, but if you grew up poor on the Archipelago the army was the only ladder anyone was letting down for you. And some Maric came and screwed you over with his good intentions, and where did that leave you? In the mud.

She and her fellow bearer had been stumbling through the dark ahead of the Loruthi advance forever, it seemed like. The waning of the smoke passed into the gathering of evening like sentries changing shift. Cosserby's whimpering, wheezing bulk kept convulsing; so did the footing. They were forever staggering to a halt so one or other of them could shift their grip. The only way Lidlet knew they hadn't been turned around was that nobody had shot them yet. Yet the Pal lines had evaporated, just more smoke on the wind. As though the cratered mud went on forever.

And then her fellow, the man at the rear end of the comedy horse that was their stretcher, put his burden down suddenly enough that, yes, she assumed he had been shot.

He hadn't been shot. He was standing there, staring down at Cosserby.

"He's dead," the man said. "Give it up. He's dead." Lidlet couldn't see much of their burden in the dark, but she knelt by him and put an ear to where she reckoned his mouth was, listening for breathing. Breathing, yes, though ragged and faint. Where she touched it, Cosserby's uniform is saturated with wet.

"He's still alive," she said stubbornly.

"I've heard men sound like that," the other bearer told her. "He's dead and the Lorries are right after us."

"It's a shoulder," she snapped. "You don't die of a shoulder. He's fine."

"He's dead." And of course people died of shoulder wounds all the time, especially nasty exploded-looking ones. And the blood was slick down Cosserby's chin, and that suggested that what was shoulder on the outside had a whole nasty hidden cast of characters within.

She crouched by her handles. "Pick up," she said.

"Give it up, Lidlet. Let's go." He was two steps further from the stretcher now, without anything in his body language so much as admitting he'd moved. As though everything else in the world was a boat being taken away by the tide and all he could do was watch.

She didn't know his name nor where he knew her from. She was mightily tempted by his reasoning. It didn't go against the writ of Maric Jack, after all. No small print about having to carry Cosserby's body until it became Cosserby's corpse.

"Pick it up," she told the other bearer. "Come on. We can get him back. An officer. Commendations all round."

The man looked at her then down at Cosserby, or she thought he did from the pale smudge that was his face at night.

"Fuck the officers and fuck you," he said, and then he was gone, just running off into the night, three times as fleet as two people with a stretcher. And now Lidlet was one person with a stretcher, so that was the decision made, wasn't it? No way she would be getting a dying man back to camp over her shoulder.

She also let the sinking boat that was Cosserby on the stretcher drift out a little, by way of moving her feet through the mud in a camp-wards direction. She could still see it, a darker smear that the faint, ambient light somehow picked up on. He didn't sink, and spare her. The harsh wheeze of his breath came to her with a horrible insistency, as though, if she left now, she'd never be rid of it.

She let the stretcher drift nearer across that great, dark ocean, again by way of her feet. The Loruthi still hadn't caught up and taken the decision out of her hands and, right then, she hated them for that most of all.

"Magister." She bent low to where she hoped his ear was. "Listen, I need you to get up now. If you've got it in you. I can give you a shoulder to lean on but the stretcher, not so much. Magister, can you hear me." Feeling a slow screw of frustration and fear tighten in her because somehow she was *still here*, talking to this almost-a-cadaver, telling him to get on his feet. "Come on, magister," she hissed. "Come on." Shaking him, exactly what you didn't do with a badly wounded person. "You... come on, be a brave soldier for Banders. On your feet for Banders. Won't she be impressed, when you limp in with your wound? Ladies love a scar, magister. Come on up."

His breathing changed. Not for the better or the worse, really, but now she could hear the faint sobs in amongst the wheezing. Cosserby was conscious after all, however much he'd rather not be. Conscious and weeping. She felt his body shaking.

She wanted him to be brave. She wanted him to say, "Leave me, soldier. You just get clear." Because she'd be off like a shot and tell everyone how terribly courageous the last moments of Cohort-Monitor Cosserby were. Except he wasn't that courageous and didn't say it, just cried.

"She won't ever, you know," Lidlet spat at him, feeling that she'd never hated anyone as much as she hated this selfish living bastard right now. Not the Loruthi, even. Give her a green uniform, she'd shoot the man herself. "She's never going to think of you like that. You're just not her type. Or mine. Or anyone's. I mean, I'd say 'only a mother could love' but I bet she got shot of you into the phalanstery double time, too." Listening to him sniffle and gag on his own misery. Thinking, *Oh, so I can go for the emotional harm, can I? Have to add that to the notes.*

She sat down beside Cosserby, horrified to discover that she was not, in fact, going to leave him. *What? What is it?* She would at no point describe herself as either courageous or compassionate. But his weeping had a hook in her, somehow. If she left now, she'd dream of it. Cosserby, abandoned out at sea, still alive. Unless she saw him die, he'd never be dead to her. He'd haunt her beyond anything Prassel could have done with his ghost.

"I'm going to pick you up now," she decided, and got as far as getting her hands under his armpits before he screamed so loud she was amazed the entire Loruthi army didn't turn up. She dropped him sharpish, and he screamed again from falling the whole half inch she'd lifted him by. And still didn't just pass out so she could pretend he was dead. Just kept on whimpering, breath sobbing in and out and truculently refusing to stop like any decent person's breath would at this point.

She put her head in her hands.

"All right, magister," she whispered. "It's like this. I can get you out of this. I can help you stop the pain. But you have to agree to something. It's just rules. You know how the army likes rules."

She could see the faintest glint where his eyes were. He was watching her.

"I mean, not like you were ever the type to go down swinging your fists at people anyway. You're giving up practically nothing."

She found his hand and there was just enough left in him to clasp weakly about her fingers. She heard his voice, or thought she heard his voice. "Please…"

Where the hell's Jack when you need him? But there was no Jack. There was just her, Lidlet, adherent of God through a legal loophole. But she was the eternal pragmatist. She'd pray to anything right now, and still call herself an atheist tomorrow.

Because if God had *rules* then she doesn't have to believe in Him any more than she was required to have ardent faith in the disciplinary code or the proper sequence of parade-ground baton drill. It just was.

She bowed her head and began to petition God inside it, just as if she was wrangling for leave privileges with a recalcitrant duty officer. There must be *some* combination of words she could use that would reach God and bring Him round. *Come on, just this once. He's not a bad man. Okay so he's an officer, and his job is to make those big bastard metal lads go, and that's probably two strikes against him. And he's a Pal like me, but you did me when Jack asked. Why can't I pay that forward? Come on, God, be a mate, now.*

"A mate, is it?" said a voice. A very faint, very crotchety voice, with an accent like Jack's only more so. And she opened her eyes and couldn't see anyone there.

"A friend. A favour. Come on," she said out loud. Maybe it was the Loruthi after all, and they were having a fine old game at her expense. Seemed unnecessarily nuanced, given the leverage of their respective positions, but she'd take it.

"You're not what I look for in a follower," said the voice, and Lidlet blinked. There was something on Cosserby's chest. Someone. Or, no, maybe something. Some kind of beardy monkey got up in a dress. And see-through. Barely there at all, except it was dark so she shouldn't be able to only-just-see anything. Except she could.

His face, that screwed up raisin of a thing behind the beak nose and the goat's ass snarl of beard, had on an expression that suggested He was just as disappointed by her.

"What," she said. "I'm doing my best, all right?"

"You're still alive, you mean," God said. It was God. Or else it was a hallucination, but surely she'd have imagined God a bit grander, left to her own devices. "You can see me, then?"

Lidlet shrugged.

"Only I've been riding about on your shoulder half the damn

time and yelling in your ear. But oh no, it's only when you want a favour. I swear you're as bad as *he* is. What?"

Lidlet felt like she was going to join Cosserby with the weeping any moment. Oh, not from wonder. Not because she was confronted by the awful majesty of the divine. Because this, apparently, was *it*. The ghost of a hundred-years dead monkey. Jack's God.

"I am so tired," she told God. "I cannot drag this stubborn bastard back and he'd not survive it if I could. Please make him whole so I can get home and not die."

"He'll only die again. You may as well just leave him," God said. "You Pals, you make brutalising the world a way of life. What I've seen today, I never thought..." And He cocked His head at her again. "But you're still alive."

"I know how rules work. I listen. Help him. And I'll tell the rules to him. He's the rules-y type too. I'll make sure he gets it. And all the rest. Don't think I didn't see you picking them up. We got twice as many out as we had stretchers. I'll track them down, tell them how it is."

"You're mad," God told her. "You're a soldier. They're all soldiers. In an army. How do you think this is even going to work. You're mad and Jack was right."

"I'll find a way. It's what I'm good at. What else do you want? Sacrifices? I've got spare boots back at camp, and a good pair of gloves I won at coinsy. I've got a pair of trousers I could do without, seeing as you've got none. Or you like honey?"

"I... what?" God demanded. "Are you trying to get me in the bloody uniform? I'm bloody *God*, you authoritarian bastard. I do not *march*. Although," He added, "I will take the honey. Just a little. Spill it somewhere out of sight."

Lidlet pictured God fighting ants for it.

"And I want you to become a priest," God threw in, but Lidlet recognised when someone was testing the limits of a system because she'd been there herself.

"I am not giving up my shagging privileges," she said. "I've heard Jack. I know what goes on with that. Or doesn't go on. Look, do we have a deal or—"

But God was gone, if indeed He'd ever been there. Lidlet swore, and knew then that she would leave Cosserby now. Just walk away. She'd done all she could, up to and including proactive theology. Time to call it a night.

For the form of it, she reached out to close his eyes, and yelped when he gripped her wrist.

The Bawd's Progress

Mother Semprellaime with her face on, wig secured with extra pins against the weather. Gait carefully chosen to say 'I'm old. No pickings here, soldier. Come by my wagon some time.' The shadows of centuries of superstition and ritual trail behind her for army boots to trample. She is a parasite that latched onto them after they destroyed her natural habitat, who can only hope they don't reach for the purgative any time soon.

She was reminded almost instantly why she didn't just traipse about the camp. Stopped five times by statloi within sight of her wagon, demanding her papers, jostling, looming. The Pal army had taken a bloody nose and loose parts and pieces of it were still trickling in from the south. A lot of soldiers were missing squad-mates. A lot of companies were missing squads. The Pals weren't used to losing and they didn't much like it.

The Loruthi had advanced within sight of Magnelei, and the Palleseen had retreated similarly, and now the two sides sat tense but idle with the city between them. Nobody quite trusted the Bracite population enough to make a stand within the walls.

She had papers, though. They'd arrived with the message demanding her presence and specifying exactly what she must bring with her. She'd almost thought it was a joke, or that it came from a spectacularly naïve officer. Because plenty of the camp followers of her profession – purveyors of mortal or infernal flesh – called themselves seamstress and laundress when the Pal census came round. That was how they covered the existence of this necessary but loathed addendum to their muster, which otherwise would so offend perfection. And true, she both washed and darned to make ends meet, but when the word came to attend with her best needles and thread, she'd thought someone had mistaken her for an honest woman.

Except the note had come from Fellow-Inquirer Prassel, who knew exactly what she was and didn't have a joke in her. Hence, here she was showing her crisp new permissions to the umpteenth duty officer who wanted someone to kick. Prassel's seal had them hurriedly waving her on, but whispering in her wake as well. The woman's reputation was going to get its edges nibbled over this, but that was Prassel's problem.

She was summoned to one of the logistics tents, the medium-sized kind where a dozen officers could meet to discuss important military matters or else play cards and pretend. There was a soldier at the entrance who read her papers all over again, with the lip-moving care of someone who didn't trust the written word. He called inside in incredulous tones. Then a moment which was probably Prassel wondering whether it was worse to have her caller waiting outside where all the world could see her, or inside where she might be privy to serious business. Propriety won out, and Mother Semprellaime stepped past the flap the sentry held open.

Inside, Prassel was sitting with an old man, whose Sage-Archivist's insignia were only just visible past the Allorwen dressing gown he was wearing. It was a piece Semprellaime almost thought she knew. Surely that had been the property of such-and-such a Lord of the White Manor, revered conjurer and leader of her people, before the Pals came in and took everything. It fairly crackled with power, to her eyes, properly maintained and charged with tablethi. A truculent demon would just about have exploded on contact with it.

The man regarded her with a crinkle of humour in her face. "I see," he remarked.

"It feels like the minimum degree of prudency," Prassel said, straight-faced. "You understand that—"

"Well I didn't think you'd called her in here from a sudden surge of carnal appetites," her visitor said drily. "Under other circumstances I'd say that you were being overcautious, and following an old man in his paranoia. 'Other circumstances' being those that would have seen Killingly sitting where you are now and us not needing to have this conversation. She's just going to stand there, is she?"

"Are we not done, magister?" Prassel said, a little sharply for someone addressing a superior. "I understand the brief. I know the fit of Killingly's shoes." A nod at Semprellaime. "Hence her."

"You don't, you know." The old man leaned back. "Honestly, *I* didn't, when I spoke to you first. It's all go, back home. Word of our defeat has lit fires under a number of high-ranking backsides. We get to be the head of the spear when we retake Magnelei. When the fighting kicks off again and we drive the Loruthi all the way to the mountains. That's the word I'm hearing."

Prassel's smile was a little too strained to be truly politic. "We're support, surely. One more branch of the Unnaturals. Vanguard or artillery support."

"Losing a few bouts is inspiring them to rewrite the manuals, add a few chapters," the man told her. "And about time. Expect to take a more active role in your new position, Fellow-Inquirer. For that matter, expect the duty necromancer's role to come with a Sage's rank badge in the future, and for Higher Orders to wait on you and not the other way round. We have the chance to perform a great service for our profession, Prassel."

Prassel's expression didn't suggest that was necessarily such a grand thing, but then the man was standing, cracking his shoulders and the small of his back. "Ironic, really," he remarked. "Necromance all you want, your own bones still creak." He crossed around the table and put an almost paternal hand on the woman's shoulder. "Reinforcements are already inbound. With especial reference to our needs. Reinforcements and every copper they can scrape together. We're going to remake the face of war, Prassel. They'll put us in the history books."

"Yes, magister." Again, the prospect didn't seem to delight her, but then she wasn't someone who delighted easily.

When the old man was gone she looked up at Semprellaime. "That garment that the Sage-Archivist was wearing," she said, without preamble.

Semprellaime bobbed and bowed to show she had noted it. Hard not to, honestly.

"Make me one. Every warding sigil you can dredge from your memory. Special reference to protection against ghosts."

And that was tricky, because Mother Semprellaime knew demons, and demons were things of contract and restriction. Cut the clauses of their contracts and you were severing the delineations of their shapes and natures. Ghosts were the predatory echoes of people, and not so inclined to listen to rules. You could keep them out – or in – but not as reliably and not forever.

But then armour couldn't keep out an enemy forever, but sometimes just once was all you needed. And Prassel didn't look as though she'd asked Semprellaime in for a lecture.

"I will require certain fabrics, thread," she said, hedging. And then shut her eyes briefly because Prassel, with a single grunt of effort, lugged a hamper up onto the table she and the old man had been meeting across.

"Honestly, I don't know when my new duties will enter the problematic stage, but it may be very soon indeed. I don't have time to be precious about this. Nor do I want to go around looking like some Allorwen theatrical impresario. I have a good shirt here, a jacket and some breeches. I have a bolt of cloth that should serve you. It's not exactly regulation, and I assume that dyeing it grey would interfere with how it's been prepared." The fabric was lemon yellow, in fact. Entirely acceptable in quality for magical purposes, less so for uniform ordinances.

"You can do this as a lining, perhaps?" Prassel suggested.

"Magister, no. The sigils must be presented outwards to have a warding effect."

And the woman had known that, really. Had just been fishing for some piece of Allorwen lore that might spare her blushes. "Well, do it, then. As best you can."

Mother Semprellaime took a deep breath and unrolled her sewing kit. "Small panels, edging cuffs and collar. Neat and symmetrical, magister. To compliment the cut of the uniform."

Prassel nodded.

"There only remains the matter of a price."

The woman's sour face said *Grasping Allorwen* very clearly, but she was reaching for her belt nonetheless. And the coin would be welcome, surely. The coin Semprellaime could extort for this non-standard service would keep her in tea and bribes for a year. Except... "That's not how it's done, magister."

Prassel stared at her. "We are within the Palleseen Sway in this camp and our coin pays for all."

"And yet you have come to an Allorwen conjurer for her services, and that has its own exchange. I will take coin, but I will take a favour." And she found herself saying it the old way, with the significance twisting the words, even though they were in Pel.

Prassel stared at her. "I see." And, after a hostile pause, "Well, *Mother*, you have me over a barrel, and you should only understand how unpleasant your stay with us might become if you ask unwisely."

"Understood, magister." And Semprellaime bent her head to her task, carefully cutting the silk into strips and then embroidering with the silver thread in deft, quick stitches. Nor did Prassel just go away and leave her to it, but sat and brooded at the far end of the table and made notes.

★

Prassel had her visitors, as Semprellaime worked. Messengers and aides sought her out, passed her orders, took her instructions. The minutiae of a mid-ranking officer's day. Semprellaime did her best not to hide her eavesdropping, because what was tedium to Prassel was novelty to her. You never knew what would turn out to be useful.

They came and went, these menials, but then a more significant man was pushing in, waving away the sentry's objections. Semprellaime bent her head over her task, feeling the newcomer's gaze touch her. Her ears pricked like her needle, harvesting scraps.

"Sweet reason, what are you up to?" the newcomer said in tones of amusement. "Never mind, I don't want to know. Prassel, you're qualified for Admonitory Debrief, aren't you?"

"I am," Prassel said, with the air of someone who didn't want to be.

"Splendid. We have some overflow. Disloyal talk, possible spies in camp, the usual. You're due some practice according to your record. I can send a few over to you?"

Mother Semprellaime concentrated very hard on the motions of her needle, to avoid thinking of what other needles might be doing. Needles, wires, vices. All the instruments an Inquirer needed, to keep her skills sharp.

Prassel sighed, as though being asked to torture someone was the most egregious demand on her time. "I suppose so."

"And we need people to handle a prisoner exchange."

"A what?"

"You must be familiar with the concept, surely. The Lorries have got a load of ours from their advance. They'd really rather have a load of theirs that Landwards took previously. We even have a nice neutral ground sitting between us where one can get a decent bottle and a sit down while the formalities are on. You game?"

"Sherm, have you any idea how *busy* I am right now?"

"Right now?" Semprellaime felt this Sherm's gaze on her again, incredulous, mocking. "New hat, is it? This season's fashion? Look, you know Correct Speech is stretched right now. Call to every Inquirer of Fellow rank or above. Come to the aid of your School, you know."

"I have a whole department to run, plus a senior secondment to another," Prassel told Sherm. "I have more than enough demands on my time, thank you very much. Go find some other stooge to herd cats."

"Suit yourself. Offer's still open if you change your mind. Bonus points with Uncle." This last delivered from the tent entrance as Sherm retreated. "Hope the hat works out."

When he was gone, Prassel hissed out a sigh of annoyance and Semprellaime felt her staring.

"Get on with it," the Inquirer snapped, "I've had enough mockery for one day."

It was past midday when she was close to finished. It was really just the same piece of work over and over, her best all-purpose warding that would at least slow a ghost, repel it from Prassel's person and mind. Send it off to find less defensible prey to possess or, if it had some personal grievance against her, at least give her a chance to muster some necromantic answer. And if Maserley should snap and send a demon against his rival, well, it would help with that too. And by now word of this little arrangement would almost certainly have reached the demonist, and maybe *he'd* summon Mother Semprellaime too, and force her to spill what she knew. And probably take this as something directed against *him*. Commission a shirt of his own, even. A whole extra feud she had no wish to be involved in.

The next messenger obviously met such a withering stare from Prassel that he just slapped his paper down in front of her and bolted out before she turned his bones to jelly or something similarly necromantic. Prassel stopped her writing – some complex web-shaped diagram – and read. Semprellaime felt that the temperature in the tent fell appreciably.

"Magister, it's ready," Semprellaime said.

Prassel glanced up, a haunted look about the edges of her eyes. She looked at the defiled garments bleakly. Lemon yellow. She was going to turn heads, for sure.

"Perhaps you should try them on," Mother Semprellaime suggested meekly. "In case there is any further work you need from me." *Neither of us wants to repeat this.*

Prassel nodded, took the proffered garments and retreated with them. When the woman was busy with exchanging shirts, Semprellaime stole a glance at the paper.

An official notice from Correct Speech's own Higher Orders, the senior inquisition within the army. Official concern expressed as to a potential gathering sedition believed to originate within the hospital department. A scatter of unexplained deaths amongst soldiers who were supposed to save their agonies for the fighting. A note that a certain Maric under Prassel's jurisdiction had already been given an official caution for just this sort of thing.

Then she had retreated back to her proper place because Prassel was done. And the yellow silk at the edges of her new uniform made her look eccentric, lending her a dandyish swagger that her personality absolutely did not warrant, but it didn't give her the clownish air of the old man's dressing gown. It preserved a certain military dignity and, if it lacked the formidable might of the old man's robe, it would maintain its defences without a belt of tablethi to charge it.

"It will do," was Prassel's verdict, after she'd had her impromptu tailor hold a hand mirror up for her. She slung a pouch at Semprellaime. "Be happy with that," was her first and last bargaining position. "And your favour?"

Semprellaime thought of the note she'd stolen a glance at. "I have one."

"Go on then." Prassel was turning this way and that, frowning at herself in the glass like someone not sure if she's going to the ball or not.

Mother Semprellaime told her.

Prassel stared at her. And it was a terribly stupid thing to say, an admission she'd been reading the woman's papers, or was far too informed about matters that were none of her concern. It was a waste of an obligation that could have taken her name off a death warrant in the fullness of time. She could hear her aunt and all her ancestors scorning her. But then they were dead so what did they know?

"That would, obviously, be out of the question," said Prassel.

"Magister," Semprellaime told her, "you have the aspect of a woman sailing into dark waters."

Prassel's face bunched with anger, about to slap her down, to spit on her filthy Allorwen superstitions, to call for the sentry. But then something gave, in that expression, and she just shrugged a little. "And?"

"And when you need me again, to assist with the demands of your trade, I will be there. If you do this for me."

Prassel knuckled at her eye sockets. For a moment she was sad, uncertain, afraid, regretful, all the things anybody would tell you weren't in her nature.

"I will consider how I can square this with my military duties," the woman said, and Semprellaime could tell that was all that she was getting right now.

Putting the Screws On

He came back. Almost the last, even after Masty and Jack. Leaning on Lidlet for the shock, but not a scratch on him. Unable to answer questions. Unable to understand why he wasn't dead. And Banders had been glad to see him, but when she'd hugged him he'd heard the echo of his torn-up flesh and not been able to enjoy it. And then he'd gone to the workshop to do his job and found it was worse.

Turning the winches was old school, of course. Prassel wasn't going to be about that kind of barbarism. A modern Inquirer had more sophisticated tools but, because of that, they needed a more sophisticated assistant. Someone with a bit of training in artifice and mechanisms. Which, in Prassel's department, meant Cosserby.

He had it all laid out now, in one of the tents specifically set aside for this sort of thing because nobody wanted to spend any time in a part-time torture chamber. He had the regulation chair strewn with cords and tablethi, clamps and probes and hooks. The whole toolkit that allowed you to subject someone to extreme excruciation without actually hurting them, really. No need to pull out the fingernails or go to work on the teeth, not with modern science. Just harnessing a few magical currents was enough. It didn't even drain the tablethi all that much. You were barely doing anything at all.

Cosserby sat in the darkness like a terrified bride awaiting a brutal groom and tried to stop his hands from shaking.

He had a problem. It was going to kill him. He'd already run into it, but this, here, now, would be the test. Everything else had been behind closed doors and, until the fighting broke out, nobody would be in a position to find out that he couldn't do his job any more. He could have trod water until hostilities resumed, if it hadn't been for this.

Prassel came in then, brisk, almost bright. Not looking forward to this, perhaps, but she had her quota to make and, if there was one thing the Palleseen army liked, it was hitting quotas.

"Cohort-Monitor, excellent. All ready. Initiative." She rubbed her gloved hands together in an excess of energy. "We're down for three today and hopefully that's our lot. Early lunch, after."

Cosserby nodded quickly and kept nodding for too long as he tried to show what a dutiful soldier he intended to be. Then stopped nodding, so that the motion shifted down to his hands, which shook. He tried to say something two or three times, but his throat was too dry.

Prassel noticed none of it. She just called out, and a couple of soldiers brought someone in. A lean, starved-looking man in uniform shirtsleeves and breeches. His unshaven jaw worked, and his eyes flicked from Prassel to the chair.

"I swear," he said thickly. "I don't know. You got the wrong man, magister."

And that was quite possibly true. If they could be certain of everyone's loyalty then this whole circus wouldn't be necessary. You always ended up damaging some good metal, if you were diligent enough about stripping out the broken pieces.

"Strip," Prassel instructed. The man didn't want to strip, but the soldiers shoved a truncheon in his face until he got the message and obeyed.

"Just sit down," Prassel told him then. "The sooner this is over, the sooner we can give you a clean bill of health." As though anything about the process related to health.

When the man proved unwilling to sit down, the soldiers

kindly assisted him into the chair. Then it was Cosserby's job to tighten the straps, and his hands trembled as he reached for them, waiting for the pain. Waiting for the shortness of breath, the taut grind of all that physical ruin *in potentia*. But he was gentle, with the buckles. Nothing pulled tight. He filled his mind with thoughts of it all being for the man's own good, to stop him falling out of the chair and hitting his head. And apparently that was fine, somehow.

Maybe I can do this, he told himself. *Maybe I can get through it like that. It is all for his own good, even if it hurts. He'll be better off later, his allegiance sealed and confirmed. It's like we're doing surgery on his loyalty, and surely that's allowed.*

He could even press the cold tablethi to the man's bared chest, to his groin and the tender skin of the inner thigh. To the sides of his head, right up close to those rolling, panicked eyes. Not so much as a twinge. *For his own good.*

"Now," said Prassel, "we've had several people confirm that you were an intimate confidante of one Cohort-Invigilator Ullers. Why don't you tell me about her?" Ullers, presumably, having served her own turn in a chair like this very recently.

The man in the chair stared at her, eyes very wide. "I don't know any Ullers," he rasped. "Magister, you've got the wrong man."

"This is going to be tedious for me if you start with blank denials," Prassel told him. And maybe she did have the right man, and maybe he was lying, or maybe she had the right man but the wrong name and Ullers had been someone else. Or he was telling the truth and this whole business was just cruelty for its own sake, to keep everyone else scared of Correct Speech.

"Cohort-Monitor," Prassel said. "Give him a taste, please."

All for his own good, Cosserby told himself. *Nothing to see here. Just someone being improved. Perfected. Hurts us more than it hurts him. Regrettable but necessary.* He made the connections, charging the web of tablethi. Just a sequence of carefully enunciated words to unlock the power in them. Discharge it through the man's nerves so that his brain told him his body was on fire. Hardly anything.

He drew breath, and felt the lance of pain through his shoulder, the razor edges of every shard of displaced bone. Like ghosts, hanging within his flesh, waiting to become real. A punishment, except not even that, really. Just a creditor collecting on a debt. He'd taken a loan of a whole body, on the battlefield, because it was that or die. Now someone was knocking at the door for it.

"Magister," Cosserby said. He was staring into the prisoner's appallingly wide eyes, and the man was staring back. "I can't."

"Well double-check your connections and get it working," said Prassel. Cosserby could conceivably have wasted considerable time pretending to do just that, but it wouldn't help forever, and right now he felt like he was going to be violently sick. Sick from all the pain that was loitering there, just waiting for him to open the door to it.

"Magister, I... I need to talk to you. I... am not fit for this work. I can't do it any more. I can't... hurt... anyone..."

Her face set. Understanding absolutely what he meant. In a moment she'd grabbed his arm and hustled him out of the tent, prisoner and guards both abandoned.

"When did he get to you?" she demanded.

"Magister?" But she was treading on the heels of her first question with the next.

"Who else was there, besides you and Jack?"

"Magister?"

She shook him. She still had that freedom. "Who, Cosserby? Who else did Jack get to?"

He stared at her, wide-eyed. "Jack? Maric Jack? He wasn't there, magister. It was when we were—"

"He wasn't *there?*"

"This is nothing to do with him."

He got her to listen, in the end. Told her his tiny fragment of story. Not understanding why the details struck her so hard. Why an *absence* of Maric Jack was so much worse than a presence.

"It's worse," she said, at the end and mostly to herself. "It's spreading. He's worse than I thought." And then she was striding off, so that he called plaintively after her, asking about the prisoner.

She turned on her heel, looking so bleak he thought she'd storm into the tent and cut the man's throat herself. Instead she said, "Cut him loose. Probably he's nobody. Cosserby, you can carry messages still, I take it?"

He nodded, even though he wasn't really sure. Give him a death warrant and ask him to deliver it to the provosts, would he drop dead when it left his fingers? Or when the sentence was carried out? He didn't *know*.

"Find Fellow-Inquirer Sherm. Tell him this man knew nothing. Tell him to find me at the department." Her own territory where all the eavesdropping ears were at least beholden to her. "And then go to Mother Semprellaime. You know her wagon?" And he did, and she plainly noted that in his face, which was more mortification still. "Tell her it's done. Obligation discharged," Prassel instructed him. "And then not a word about any of this to anyone."

Things Get Only Worse

Cohort-Archivist Hobbers. Female. Age: twenty-two. Placement: Landwards Battalion New Resources Tactical Department. Immediate superior: Companion-Archivist Callow. Current assignment: Tactical use of Divinati-origin magical techniques and assets, based on the available teachings of Guest-Adjutant Alv of Forthright Battalion Experimental Hospital Department. Cause of death: massive sympathetic trauma.

Hobbers was dead.

Alv only found out when the provosts summoned her to the inquest. She assumed the Pals had finally lost patience with her, or lost reverence for the Divinati, and it was her turn in the Inquirers' chair. She'd almost have welcomed it. Certainly she felt she deserved it, given the thoughts she'd been having.

But it wasn't her on the block this time. Not yet. Although it wasn't exactly Callow either, even though he was definitely the subject of the inquest. The reason, in fact, that Hobbers was dead.

Her other students, the ones who weren't Callow and weren't dead, were lined up like neat little birds, looking very solemn. A little ashen here, a little greenish there. They'd all been present when it happened. They'd give evidence. But Callow first, because he was the one who'd killed her.

He, too, contrived to look solemn. Though not sorry. He stood before the duty Inquirer, his cap on the desk in front of him, holding his gloves in his hands. "It was an exercise," he explained. "We were throwing the injury between us."

The duty Inquirer frowned at him. "I'm not familiar."

"The essential principles of sympathetic transfer," Callow explained airily. "It's just like a ball, really. So long as you can keep it in the air. Being agile, that's the thing. We all knew what we were doing. We weren't playing some kind of *prank*, magister." And, seeing the woman still squinting at him, "Taking an injury from a body, taking it into one's own, you know. Passing it to another's body. That's the point, you know?"

"Guest-Adjutant Alv," the Inquirer said. "Does this accord with your understanding of your discipline?"

"Yes," Alv said, and then, "No."

"Which is it?" Spoken with the certainty of someone whose paper has a choice of two boxes to tick and no room for notes.

"To take on the ills of others, yes. To take them onto ourselves. That is sympathetic healing. That is the discipline I am here to teach. Companion-Archivist Callow and his fellows are swift students. I am most impressed with their mastery. But this that he describes here. This passing, back and forth. This sending *out*, rather than accepting *in*. That is not my discipline."

Callow actually looked a little betrayed, at that. Prompted by the Inquirer, he explained, "But it is, really. It's the same logical framework. If I can move the harm to myself from its origin, I can pass it to another. To Skilby over there. And Skilby can move it to, well, back to me, or the original source, or any of the others. And obviously the goal is to be able to shift the hurt from the cadre entirely. To pass it to where it can do some good, tactically. To generate injuries, either crafted for specific purposes or for maximum impact, and impart them to the enemy—"

"No," said Alv. "That is not it. That is not an appropriate use of manipulating balance."

"Well, in the Divine City, doubtless you don't have a need for it like we do," said Callow carelessly.

The Inquirer looked at her forms, which plainly didn't contain appropriate boxes to tick. "Tell me again how Cohort-Archivist Hobbers died."

"We were conducting an exercise. A game, almost," Callow said. "She thought she could keep up. She overextended and, when the injury came her way unexpectedly, she couldn't adapt quickly enough. We're all very sorry, obviously. It's a terrible thing to happen." Spoken so blandly it was as if he was reading the words from a card.

Alv considered what she'd seen of Hobbers. The awkward one, the one who hadn't been a part of Callow's clique. The butt of the jokes. The one who got singled out in Callow's examples of how bad things might happen to someone who couldn't keep up.

Alv found she could picture the scene quite clearly, the students in this game of theirs, moving some potentially fatal injury between them like jugglers. Perhaps Callow feinted at Hobbers, joked, threw it somewhere else. And the next time it was his body torn open he dummied Hobbers the other way. She found herself holding the death they'd been playing with, unprepared to contain and dispose of it. And she'd died. Callow had killed her. Because he could.

The other students gave brief statements, each a near echo of the last, exonerating Callow of any wrongdoing. The Inquirer made her notes, nodded, pressed her lips together.

"This is regrettable. Companion Callow, a formal statement of understanding to go on your record, and I encourage you to take more care and the necessary supervision when you conduct these exercises of yours. Guest-Adjutant Alv." And Alv realised with a start that she *was* on trial here, these being ostensibly her students. "It's evident this occurred because of limitations in the range of your curriculum. If you'd engaged more deeply in this aspect of their training then Cohort Hobbers would doubtless still be with us. You should consider shifting the emphasis of your instruction to more closely shadow the needs of your students. I am not in a position to raise any disciplinary measure against you, given your status, but please note this for your own records."

Callow's face, as she left, was angelic. Alv's was expressionless.

The work at the hospital had calmed, but the Butcher kept his boxes stocked, his phials full. Moving easier now, his back salved and healing. Not happy, but when was he ever? Tonight he sat out front, minding his cauldron as a new batch of salts cooked down, stoking the fire with an iron in his left hand, stirring the pot with a rod in his left. Across from him, Tallifer and Lochiver passed a flask round, huddling in blankets, because the clear-eyed night was robbing the ground of every last shred of heat.

When Alv arrived, they looked up in surprise. She had been a fixture at the hospital almost as long as they had, but she didn't unbend enough to be one of them, really. Kept to herself, in that Divinati way.

The flask had done the rounds with more than one refill. The Butcher dangled it at her, then grunted in surprise when she took it. Alv slumped down onto a stool, aware that this was wrong. That she had spent a decade in the hospital maintaining a ramrod poise. An untouchability of manner essential for a receptacle of other people's ills. But she'd finally found something that would neither kill her, nor that she could recover from.

"They are making me into a weapon," she said flatly, and let the fire from the flask drain out down her throat until there was only a swig left in it.

They eyed her uncertainly. The two old priests and the Butcher. And she wasn't going to say any more. Shouldn't even have said that much. It wasn't her place. It was taking a burden from herself and passing it on to them, which put her in their debt. Imbalance, that was the killer, the worst sin in the world.

Tallifer leaned forwards and put a hand on her knee. Like the touch of an aunt. Someone who would listen and understand.

Bound to Alv by a hundred invisible strings that meant whatever was passed to her would come back around, no need to keep the tally of who owed what to who. Like the injury that had killed Hobbers, but in a kind way. And Alv felt the rope of ten years break inside her. Not the drink but the touch. The implied understanding.

She understood, a moment later, that Tallifer had just been after the flask, to stop her necking the lot of it, but she was talking by then. The words started coming out and each one had the next by the hand, a long chain of desperate refugees seeking any safe port and leaving no sentiment behind. She told them about the new class, Hobbers, Callow and what they were doing to her carefully curated discipline. The use they had found, so effortlessly. "It's not what it's for," she said. "It's not correct. But I can't stop them. They understand it too well. They will take what I made and kill with it, and I will have contributed to the imbalance. All the restitution I have earned over ten years will be undone. I will become the monster who births chaos upon the world."

She expected them to look blank, for they had come to this fire from the absolute opposite direction. Killers all, whose talents had been for monstrosity by nature. The fire priestess, the disease priest, the Butcher.

Somehow they understood. Or came to an apprehension which overlapped just enough with the truth.

"The bastards," Lochiver spat. "If Erinael was here they'd never dare."

The name bought a silence, just for a heartbeat, and then Tallifer shook her head disgustedly. "I think you're forgetting just what they did to her. When it wasn't *expedient* to keep her around. They didn't even hesitate."

"We still owe them for that," Lochiver said darkly.

"Dream on, old man," the Butcher told him. And that was how it went, and that would be the end of it, except this time Lochiver rose up on his spindly legs, knuckly fists clenching.

"You want to talk balance, girlie? There's a bloody debt damn well owed for Erinael. And there's a debt for what they did to my temple. And the High Fane, eh?"

Tallifer's liquor had obviously been going down the same way. "Damn straight," she snarled.

"We owe them more than they can ever pay back!" Lochiver went on, heedless of the basics of economics. "You know what happened yesterday? Some damn engineer came to me, wanting to know, could I use different jars for the sepsis. Can I use something stronger? And I said, you don't want to go playing with that, magister, oh no! You don't want to dabble your fingers in *my* leavings. But it's come round again. Some genius wants to use my sacred exudation as ammunition. Or maybe even give it to her brats," a jab at Alv, "and have them try to piss it over the horizon onto the enemy. And it won't work. Didn't eight years ago and won't now."

"Didn't then because you were able to fuck it up for them," Tallifer said flatly. "Reckon you can outfox them again? You don't know which shoe to put on, half the time."

"I will fight them every breath before they make me their weapon," Lochiver insisted.

"Shut up now," Tallifer said, and when he took a breath to carry on twice as loud and long, she stomped on his foot.

Prassel had joined them. Lochiver stared at her, then turned his surly attention to the fire and sat down again, taking a refilled flask from Tallifer and tossing a swig back. For an awkward, drawn-out moment nobody spoke.

"What?" Prassel asked drily. "Don't I get a drink?"

"You want me to wake the boy up. Tell him to fetch you the good stuff?" the Butcher asked her.

"Let your son sleep. What you're having is good enough for me." Prassel found a stool and planted it defiantly between Alv and Tallifer, where she could sit and stare straight at him.

Ollery reclaimed the flask and passed it around the cauldron to her. "Not my son."

"What?"

"He's not my son. You always call him that. You never asked. Picked him up back home, year before you got assigned to us, magister."

"'Picked him up'?" Prassel drank, grimaced, passed it on to Alv, who didn't want to be elbow to elbow with her but took it anyway.

"Plenty of orphanages back on the Isles," the Butcher said. "Parents both dead. War, you know. And as for the grandparents and the rest of the family, well…" He shook his head, exaggeratedly mournful. "It's sad how it happened, they say."

"Well." There was a lot of murder in his small, squeezed eyes, but Prassel met them anyway. "That's another reason I'm only drinking what you're drinking."

He chuckled without mirth. Alv glanced from one to the other. What it said on the Butcher's papers was for him alone, and Prassel, who got to know all the official stories behind her eclectic subordinates. And probably Tallifer and Lochiver, because they'd been around longer and asked more questions.

"We were talking about Erinael," Lochiver said, with the relish of a man who loves an argument.

Prassel's face darkened. "I don't wish that reopened."

"We were saying how fine it would be, if she was here. How much more good we could do in the department. Such a touch that woman had. Bring you back from the point of death and walk it off. Better than Alv here. Better than either of us two fossils. You never had such a tool at your disposal as Erinael."

"There was nothing I could do. The orders were there when I took over the department."

"And what was it you did to her?"

"I didn't—"

"You Pals," said Tallifer, backing the old man up.

Alv waited for Lochiver to go on. To name the sins, but the old man was drinking again as though disgusted by the taste. It was her turn.

"A creature of radiance," she said. Everyone stopped playing their individual games of hating one another, because she wasn't supposed join in this kind of backbiting. She was serene and self-contained and endlessly empathetic. Alv did not bitch. "The receptacle of divine power," she recalled. And nobody had been entirely sure what Erinael had been, honestly. An angel, in Divinati philosophy. A class of being that dwelled Above, as demons did Below. A servant to some long-gone god who had been left with the keys to the miracles.

"Chief Accessory Erinael," Prassel said, "decided that healing our soldiers was too good for her."

The Butcher stood. Not suddenly, but like a mountain might. "*You* will not speak of her."

"I? I'm your superior, Chief. I'll say what I damn well like, thank you very much." And Alv realised that Prassel had been drunk long before she came to their fire. Drunk and spoiling for it. "She refused outright to carry on her duty. She was sick of it. She was sick of us. I begged her. She told me straight up she'd rather that, than mend one more soldier. And so it happened. She made herself no use to anyone. No use save one."

The Decanters, Alv thought. Nobody spoke the word. Erinael, the shining one, the first Chief of the hospital, who'd formed the waifs and strays into the working team they were, had been sent to men like Fellow-Archivist Thurrel. People who had not executed her, not even tormented her, just rendered her down for raw power. Used her radiant substance to fill their tablethi, so the batons could keep firing and the artillery engines could unleash their thunder. So that a thousand lamps and lenses and tools could perform their mundane little functions, each of them devouring a tiny portion of Erinael's godhood.

Ollery had taken a step around the fire. "You will not," he said, words like lead.

"Look to your people here, not those already past saving," Prassel said. "There's change coming. Higher Orders don't like losing. She knows." A thumb jerked sidelong at Alv. "Her and

Lochiver, and me. *I* know. You wouldn't *believe* the shit they've got me working on. Ghost work, Chief. I always wanted ghost work. Until now."

"And if she refuses," the Butcher said, a nod at Alv, "it's the Decanters for her too, is it?"

"Oh you think *she's* the problem, do you?" Prassel got up, lurched, almost ended up in the fire. *Did* end up nose to nose with Ollery, staring up at him, standing where he could have broken her into pieces. "You seen Jack around? Maric Jack? There's a man who's had three chances to stay dead and not the sense to take them. He's next. And not just him, either. He's a dangerous man to be close to. You don't want his fingerprints on you." Her head whipped round as someone crossed past the entrance to the hospital's little enclave of tents.

"Hallo?" a voice called out of the darkness, and then a balding officer stuck his head where the firelight could touch it. "Prassel? You wanted me?"

"That prisoner exchange happened yet?" Prassel stomped up to him so belligerently Alv thought she might punch him.

"Tomorrow. Changed your mind, have you? One more chance to sample the delights of Magnelei?"

"I want in. With one of my people people," Prassel told him.

"Are you *drunk?*" Sherm asked incredulously.

"I'll be sober tomorrow. Well?"

The man spread his hands. "Fine, I'll put you down for it. Like I say, it's all points with Uncle. Are you all *right*, Prassel?"

But she had turned on her heel and was striding away, storming off into the night as though she was going to kill someone.

Sherm passed a bemused look over the group at the fire and then ambled off on his own business.

"I think it's reached that stage," Tallifer said softly, finishing off this incarnation of the flask.

"Of the evening?" Lochiver asked.

"In general." The old woman stared into the fire, and for a

moment it leaped with strange forms, serpents and monsters and raging faces. "God help me, what have the pair of us become?"

"Old," Lochiver said.

"We raised hell though, didn't we?" Tallifer said. "Back before they caught us."

"Ten years of setting things on fire and giving them the runs," Lochiver agreed with satisfaction. "Second best years of my life, you mad old witch. Right after the decade before, when I was trying to tear down your temple myself. It wasn't the Pals' to destroy. It was mine."

"We blazed a trail," Tallifer breathed, as though she could see the chronicle of it in the fire. "God, I thought they'd never take us alive, you know. What happened to us?"

"We outlived it all." Lochiver stood, balanced himself by a hand on Alv's head, stretched. "We woke up one morning and found there wasn't any Jarokir left, except us. Everyone else was speaking Pel and obeying Pal laws and nobody even remembered our gods. We woke up and there wasn't anybody left to fight for. Except us. Come on. Bed time."

"Fucking promises, the amount you put away," Tallifer muttered, levering herself up.

"Just bed, you insatiable harridan," Lochiver grumbled, as the pair of them tottered away. "Honestly, who even has the energy any more?"

That left the Butcher, standing; that left Alv, just getting up. She felt around the edges of her face, making sure all that imperturbability was still in place.

"I am on the brink of being unwise," she told him, "for which, if it happens, I apologise."

"Don't do anything rash," he said, but she didn't feel that she was in any position to choose. The balance of the world was swinging wildly around her, the tiniest of pressures from her fingers translated into a monstrous chaos of unpredictability. There was a limit to how much chaos she could take into herself before the penning up of it destroyed her.

★

The next morning, the reinforcements were sighted. A whole Gallete island of them, skimming over the landscape like some leftover piece of someone's dream. It paused long enough to disembark what seemed like a regiment's worth of new soldiers. Alv and the others went to watch, and the message was plain.

Oh, new officers, new specialists and a few companies of regulars came clambering down with their kitbags and their batons. But the newcomers were overwhelmingly Accessories in their uniforms of Whitebelly pale. Conscripts from across the Palleseen Sway, many of them without even a weapon to their name. Standing here on a foreign shore looking bewildered.

Alv looked them over and thought about what Prassel said, and the rumours about the Landwards necromancy department, her own problem and Lochiver's. *Change*, Prassel had told them. Looking across the reinforcements she didn't see humans, people, soldiers. She just saw materiel, fodder to be fed into the war in an even more literal sense than the usual.

Chains and Freedoms

Magnelei between two armies felt like the Magnelei of their day of leave if someone had put it in a covered pot and heated it to boiling point. The Loruthi force sat to the south, the Pals to the north, and it was anybody's guess if they'd take themselves off somewhere else to fight, like civilized people, or just obliterate the city from both sides in their desperation to get at one another.

Prassel had practically kicked Jack out of bed an hour ahead of reveille, before anyone else except Alv was up. He'd been picked for special duty, apparently. There was to be a prisoner exchange within the city of Magnelei. It was very important that a skilled medical professional be there to check over the incoming prisoners, to ensure none of them had been more than usually mistreated. Obviously she'd thought of Jack.

Jack goggled at her, not at all convinced she wasn't some terrible sort of dream, so she'd kicked a bit more to establish the boundaries of fiction and reality.

"Uniform on, Accessory. The delegation's forming up and you don't want it to be you they're waiting for."

He tried to ask why, given all her many and superior options, it was him at all, but he could only ask it of her back, which had no answers for him.

Soon after that he had joined a column of troops in their best parade-ground uniforms, the pride of Pallesand. Only he stuck out, the sole pallid Accessory. There was a chain of rather dirty, ragged men, and a few women, straggling along behind, and the sense that he belonged to *them* rather than the dark-clad soldiers weighed heavily on him.

They entered the city of Magnelei, and he could feel the tension off them all. And in the square beyond were an equal number of Loruthi, and the two sides formed up against each other as though about to fight the war in miniature. And then all the regulars just stood there while Prassel and a handful of other ranking Inquirers met in the centre of the square with some Loruthi, most of them with ranks of brightly coloured ribbon and frogging on their bottle green. Everyone was talking quite urbanely with their opposite numbers. Talking in Pel, in fact, because it was a language constructed for ease of use, and even the Loruthi used it to speak to foreigners. Meanwhile, a colourful delegation of Bracite bigwigs made a big show of ostensibly governing a process that patently excluded them, and a cloud of servants hovered nearby and served everyone tea.

Eventually, the confab of senior officers broke up and Prassel returned.

"We've agreed terms and sent for our prisoners, and they for theirs. Waiting game now, to make sure we all get what we're paying for. Take your ease but don't leave this square. And absolutely no trouble."

Jack reckoned that anyone so much as bunching a fist in this square would kick the war straight off again. Then Prassel had hooked his collar and was hauling him away from the rest of the soldiers.

"Listen to me," she told him. "This is a big, complicated city."

Jack hadn't expected a geography lesson. Possibly she was about to tell him about Magnelei's chief imports and exports, although the former seemed mostly to be foreign soldiers. "Magister?"

"Under no circumstances are you to absent yourself and just get lost here, you understand. Because probably we'd never find you again. You hear me?"

Jack made a wordless, interrogative sound.

"Get drunk and get left behind, sleep past curfew in some whore's bed, get stabbed and dumped in an alley for all I care. These would all be terrible things to happen, you understand. Absolutely against army discipline. We have rules against these things because they happen so *easily* to a soldier in a foreign city." She was twisting his collar fit to strangle him, vibrating with an angry tension like she was full of bees. "Because probably we'd not even look too hard, if something were to happen to you. Why would we even bother, for an Accessory? Do you understand me?"

He did not. He was absolutely aware he didn't, because there was a chasm of knowledge in her that she couldn't unbend enough to properly impart. Every part of her was cold rage and iron except her eyes, which were begging him to get it.

Then one of the other Inquirers was calling her, because apparently the officer corps had commandeered a taverna and wanted to know what she was drinking. Prassel let go, turned on her heel and marched off to join them.

Jack scanned the square for anywhere that would let him take the weight off his feet. This being the sole place that foreigners might be spending their coin, the place was seething. As though every citizen of Magnelei was desperate to have this one last day when their home was still some semblance of normal and whole. For a moment it felt as though his own two-feet's-worth of cobbles was the sole part of the city not being ruthlessly trampled. Then he spotted a tiny span of space. There was a taverna with a score of round tables set out in front of it. They thronged with locals, but there were chairs left at one table, alongside an old man in fancy dress, some piece of local colour hoping to cadge donations. He didn't raise any objections when Jack took the other half of his table. Raised an eyebrow and gave him a somewhat incredulous look, then he went back to the cup he was husbanding, which was mostly full of the thick froth one of the local drinks left behind.

Probably if Jack offered to refill it for him, he'd have the old boy as a friend for life.

"I bloody hope you're happy, is all," God said, from Jack's elbow. The divine presence had clambered up onto the table and was looking about as though He'd just inherited a substandard new kingdom of empty cups and spillage.

"I mean no," Jack said. "Not really. What gave you that idea."

"Forcing me to share digs with *that*. We're up in arms in there, I can tell you."

The spear-carrier god didn't look particularly up in arms, just pulled his fisherman's coat around himself. Zenotheus, the Scorpionfly of Chaos, put its bug-eyed head out, feelers waving.

We don't much appreciate the company either, came its faint, buzzing voice. *However, we are grateful for the rescue. We shall repay this debt, Maric. We shall bring confusion and misery to your enemies. Commensurately small amounts of them, given our reduced state, but nonetheless. Perhaps you have some documents we can deface.*

"I'm not even sure who my enemies are," Jack said. "I mean Prassel seems to have it in for me, for sure." The old man gave him a look, but at that point someone turned up asking what they might bring the newcomer in exchange for good money. Jack asked for two of whatever the old man was having, and that act of charity appeared to paper over any cracks.

"She knows we're making trouble," Jack said. "They're onto us."

"Oh it's *we* all of a sudden is it?" God demanded. "Only last I heard you weren't listening to me. I mean, I'm just *God*. Just your actual god."

"You are going to get me killed," Jack said. "The Pals are going to torture me to death. Because we are turning their soldiers into people who can't fight. You see how that's going to piss them off."

"In my day," God said, "my priests would prostrate themselves before the war-beasts of tyrants, and when the hooves came down they'd take that martyr's death as their due. They'd bare their breasts for the spears and speak sermons to the torturers."

Jack stared at Him. "I... don't want to do that."

"Because you're a disappointment. As a priest and as a follower. Always," God told him. "I've got options now. Your Pal girl, she's still at it with the prayers. She's got a whole thing going on now. Barely a moment's peace, I get. And she writes everything down. She's on at me for favours all the time."

"Then why help her?" Jack demanded. He was aware that the old boy in the nightcap was regarding him with amusement, but decided to play the street lunatic for a bit. He was talking in Maric, after all. Not likely anybody would understand a word of it. "I saw you. A whole load of those soldiers didn't need a stretcher. And don't think I didn't spot Cosserby walking around camp like he never got shot. A Pal *officer*! Suddenly it's miracles for everyone."

"She *asked*," God said. "A Pal. A filthy atheist Pal on her knees praying. Like you never do."

"She thinks it's like some army manual she can twist. It's not respectful," Jack insisted.

God looked up at him brightly. "Yasnic," He said, "you're like a wife who's grown tired of her old man, is what you are. Maybe I can work with this. I mean, at least someone's *listening*. You want me to be small and weak and useless so it makes you feel better about yourself. And now I've got new friends and you can't take it." Before Jack could reply, He dropped down into the box again, pointedly ending the conversation just as the drinks turned up. They were ninety per cent froth and ten per cent liquid fire that left a metallic coating all the way down the throat. Jack choked and winced.

"I give up," said the old man. "What are you, exactly? A spy? Some kind of street performer?"

Jack opened his mouth to either confirm or deny it, then realised that the man had spoken in Maric. Barbarously accented Maric, but recognisably Jack's native tongue.

"You, er…"

"I've travelled," the old man said. "In younger days. Saw the world." He shrugged, as if to say the world hadn't been all that. He was quite the figure, really. His robe had definitely been the property of someone much richer and grander once, before it had faded and frayed and been passed down to this old relic. His cap was folded over, with a tassel tickling the lower reaches of his ear. His face had the stoic dignity of ancient royal statues.

"It's fine," Jack told him. "It's nothing. I was… rehearsing a play." In that fraught moment a Bracite musician, deciding that someone might pay him money, played a shawm really quite loud in Jack's ear with the general impression of someone strangling a goat. The distraction was enough to let Jack huddle away from the old man's regard, spilling the last few drops of his drink inconspicuously on the box top so that his gods there could dabble in the dregs.

It wasn't true, he told himself. He didn't prefer God to be useless. He just… didn't know what to do now that God was flexing His withered muscles.

"My dear fellow," said the old man to the musician, "This gentleman is trying to talk to his gods. Take this and perpetrate your malarky somewhere else." He gave the delighted shawmist a coin, more than happy to be paid to go away rather than in appreciation of his art. And Jack stared, partly because of what the old man had said, and partly because he'd heard the words in Maric but he knew, without doubt, the musician had heard them in Bracite.

Slowly, he realised that there hadn't just been empty chairs at this table, but a whole empty space around it that only itinerant musicians dared brave.

The old man smiled, raised an eyebrow. "Varney." He thrust a thin hand out.

Jack clasped it after a moment's reluctance. "People call me Jack."

"I bet they do. What's your deal, son?" the old man pressed. "Not often I run into a Pal who talks to gods. That's new."

Jack just stared, unable to come out with even the most basic denial.

"I've got good eyes, son," said Varney. "I see you've got quite the collection there. I see the least segment of the foreleg of Zenotheus of Oloumann. And the old boy you were arguing with is that Maric healing cult unless I miss my guess. And the Fisher King, threatening me with his harpoon, and what *he's* doing in your company is the really interesting question."

Nothing had particularly changed about the old man, but suddenly he seemed far, far older. As though that robe might have been made new for him once, and he'd just worn it out.

"Varney," he echoed.

, "That's right, son." Sitting there in his silly hat, sipping his silly drink.

"Short for something, is it?" And Jack couldn't actually remember what the long name had been, something foreign and difficult but definitely beginning like 'Varney'. At the man's nod he added, "You live in... a tower?"

"Oh my," said Varney. "You have pierced my ingenious disguise. Seriously, why do you think nobody else was sitting at the table? I'm a dangerous man to drink with."

"Oh."

"But you bought the round, so I shall refrain from obliterating you with my awful powers." Varney sipped at the foam, which got in his beard and moustache.

Jack decided to apply himself likewise. When he looked back, someone else had turned up at Varney's shoulder. Quite the most beautiful young man he'd ever seen, except for the eyes.

"Ghastron, Jack," Varney said, with the air of someone who hates introductions. And then: "Sorry, The Dread Lord Ghastron, Duke of the Lands Below, Despoiler of the Fields of Arthleigh, Scourge of the Nine Princes." He covered Ghastron's hand with his own when it settled on his shoulder. "What did I miss?"

"Beguiling…" the demon prompted.

"Ah yes, Beguiling Serpent of the Emerald House. You'd think I'd remember that one," Varney agreed. "Jack, this poor damned creature is my companion, sharing the travails and tribulations of my existence. Who has hopefully purchased some new slippers for me."

The snake-eyed creature locked his cold gaze with Jack's, promising eternal delights and torments in equal measure, then produced a heavily embroidered pair of slippers in the local style, which he placed before Varney. Before Varinecthes the Sorcerer, lord of the flying tower, who regarded them critically.

"Seriously, this is the best they have?" Still speaking Maric, or else sorcerously making himself understood for Jack's ears.

"Astoundingly enough, being repeatedly taken over by opposing factions during some sort of *war* isn't good for local industry," drawled the Dread Lord Ghastron, folding his elbows about Varney's shoulders and resting his chin by the sorcerer's ear.

"You've got questions, I imagine," the sorcerer said out of the corner of his mouth. "May as well ask them while you have time."

And Jack could have asked any number of questions of this maverick sorcerer, from the course of the war to the secrets of the universe. And he threw away all these opportunities because he was selfish, just like everyone.

"Your servant… Is he your servant? Can I talk to him?"

"Gassy, he wants you," Varney said absently. He stuck out feet with yellowed, claw-like toenails and began trying on the slippers.

"Am I your servant?" said the demon. "I thought we were past that."

"Please," said Jack. The serpent eyes turned on him, calculating.

"You've been bitten by a sister of mine, sweet child." The

demon reversed a chair with a sinuous motion and leaned on the back. His smile was a thousand sins all in one curve of the lips. "You want to know how to please her, perhaps? You want to own her?"

"I..." Jack choked on his own denials.

"Are you going to start with the poetry of it?" Ghastron asked softly. "How her hooks are in your soul, so that each sweet breath is naught but wind unless some part of her can feel as you now feel. How every beat of your labouring heart speaks her name, and yet you know it isn't even her name. That, sans the bounds of contract and the conjurer's circle, does the thing that fills your life even exist? Or is the one you love solely within your mind, a puppet show played for your own amusement, and in which you strive, ever doubting, to believe?"

Varney chuckled quietly. "You remembered. Almost word perfect."

"Listen, Jack," said Ghastron, leaning in until the chair creaked. "What do you think any loved one is, except the image you build of them? You think you can know another human being? Or that you can't love them even though they're wicked? If we are more malleable than you, that doesn't mean we are so different."

"But there's always the contract," Varney said softly.

"There is," Ghastron allowed. "We cannot be in these places without it. We are bound. We are servants. O harsh master, will you not give me my freedom! See these chains about my wrists!" Raising his bare arms to the sky theatrically. "Tell me any human relationship is free of that. We are simply the literal and overt reflection of how you conduct yourselves. We are what you make us. Slaves. Villains. Happy."

"I don't know what to do," Jack said. "I don't want to be..." *master, chain-forger, contract-maker.*

There was sympathy on Ghastron's face, but then Ghastron was a demon and what was on his face could mean anything or nothing.

"Magister," said Jack. "Varney. Would you tell him he may answer me freely under no duress from you?"

The wizard raised an eyebrow, gesturing either to give such permission or indicate none was necessary.

Jack swallowed. "Ghastron, if you had full choice of what to do – never mind contracts, masters, anything – where would you be now?"

It seemed as though the city's murmur stepped politicly back, so that the three of them had a silence all their own. Varney had gone still, as though regretting his permission.

"Here," said Ghastron simply. "With him. No hell is sweeter."

Then things were moving, out in the square. The ragged, filthy people they'd brought with them were being sent over to the Loruthi in exchange for some other ragged, filthy people who were, presumably, Pals.

"I'm sorry," Jack said. "I have to go. But thank you."

Varney smiled. "Well, Jack, you were something new in an old man's long life. We'll not meet again, I'm sure. I wish you the best of luck. Take that as a sorcerer's blessing if you want. Or his curse."

He scurried over to form up with the others, ready to use his limited suite of medical skills to look the newly acquired ex-prisoners over. When Prassel looked his way, though, her face was stony. She didn't call him over to do his job, nor speak a word to him on the way back, and by the time they re-entered the camp he was sure that asking a powerful wizard for the secrets of the universe wasn't the only important opportunity he had failed to seize.

By the next day he had the sense that there were eyes on him wherever he went. Or at least he felt that there were. And he was a foreigner in a camp full of Pals, so of course there were. Currently the proportion of Whitebellies across the two battalions was far more than anybody was comfortable with. The regular troopers were using words, hands and boots to make sure the newcomers knew exactly how the rank structure worked. Anybody in a pale uniform received the same, whether they were new or they'd been with Forthright for a decade. Which meant that the old Whitebellies *also* laid into the reinforcements, because the recent arrivals had made things worse for everyone just with their presence. So of course there were eyes on Jack when he moved through the camp. But at the same time he was being watched. Him, specifically. He had the feeling there were no happy endings in his near future.

Prassel's look, when he had returned to her. Pure disappointment. She had told him, as clearly as she possibly could, that he should make himself scarce. Hide himself in Magnelei and she'd write him off as acceptable losses, not even send out the provosts. Except he hadn't really believed that was what she was saying, at the time. Had scented a trap when in fact she was propping the door open for him.

"Maybe I should give her the box? Lidlet?" Because it was Lidlet he was currently searching for. "Where does that leave the others, though?"

"Why should you care," God said, from over his shoulder. "*I'm* your god. Not them. Not fishy and the blowfly. Care about *me*."

"You said you've got other options," Jack said harshly.

"These Pals, you know."

"Prayer, you said."

"Bloody demands, really. Suddenly everyone wants a piece of Me. She's over there, by the way. In that tent there." Because of course God could tell. "You could stand to tell her to be a bit less pushy, if you're going to talk to her. Maybe a bit of reverence wouldn't go amiss."

"Tell her yourself." Jack changed course to follow the gnarled finger in his peripheral vision.

"I will. I would. Only..." God fidgeted awkwardly.

"Only they're your new friends and you don't want to lose

them by showing them what a prickly bastard you are," Jack said savagely. "You save that for me. You're all sugar and light with them, I'm sure. Yes, Lidlet, no, Lidlet, of course I'll save your friends, Lidlet. I'm nothing, am I?" and then Jack had ducked into the tent.

Lidlet was there with three other soldiers. Jack didn't know any of them. Pal regulars, dark uniforms. There was a moment, as he burst in unannounced, when they were all guilty as hell. They registered his Whitebelly jacket. Then they registered him. Relaxed, a bit. Stared at him, a bit. Awed, perhaps, a bit.

Lidlet wasn't awed. She squared her shoulders, a woman who couldn't fight bracing herself for one. "You take off," she told the others. Then, when they made to go, "This, don't forget. And don't let it get found, either." Shoving a sheaf of papers into one of their hands.

They shuffled awkwardly out past Jack. One of them ran a hand down the box, when they thought he wasn't looking.

"What's that?" Jack had seen Lidlet had a whole bundle of papers she was trying to hide under a blanket.

"Nothing."

"Lidlet, what?"

She stuck her jaw out pugnaciously. "You want to have this out now, do you?"

"I didn't even know there was a *this* to have out." And he'd come here to give her God. To give her the box with its menagerie. To entrust her – his disciple, was she? – with the entire future of the faith, because he didn't think he had much time left before Prassel tired of him. Except now Lidlet was doing something even worse and all those thoughts went out of his head. "Show me."

She dipped under the blanket and came out with a handful of pages bound together roughly with string. They were printed, the smudgy purplish letters the Pals used for their forms and orders, the same thin paper. The header on the first page read *The Ninety-Seven Loopholes of God*.

"What the hell is this?" he demanded.

"It's what you told me," Lidlet threw back at him. "It's how it works."

"Did you know about this?" Jack asked God, expecting full-on divine wrath to explode in his ear.

"I mean," God said. "Maybe. A bit." Wringing His beard a little. Someone whose ex and new flame have started comparing notes.

"*The Ninety-Seven Loopholes of God*?" Jack exclaimed. "Is this... I mean you said reverence. You wanted reverence?"

"Well this is what I meant," God said awkwardly. "If they could at least pretend to dress it up with a bit of ceremony. I feel a bit naked, when it's all on the page like that."

Lidlet's gaze, when Jack returned to her, was not even unrepentant. Just businesslike. "Look, you got me into this. Did you expect me to just wave my hands in the air and chalk it up to Life's Great Mystery? This is my life, Jack. This is Foley's life and Escriby's and all the others. This is how we keep our deaths at arm's length. By learning the rules. I mean how did it work in Ilmar back in the day? You took the divine healing and just bloody *hoped*?"

"Well," Jack said. "Yes. You... got into the spirit of it. I suppose. Accepted God's ethos. Were just *nice* to other people. It shouldn't be that hard. It shouldn't need a bloody *lawyer*."

"No wonder it ended up as just you," Lidlet told him flatly. "Look, it's not just you any more. So you have this wonderful, perfect understanding of God. That doesn't help me. It doesn't help anyone."

"There shouldn't *be* an anyone." The next words were the ones he had absolutely decided he'd never say, but they saw their chance and made a break for it. "I wish I'd never started this."

Lidlet nodded, and he saw the terrible hurt behind her eyes that she couldn't quite keep under wraps. "That so?"

"I'm sorry. I didn't mean that. I mean obviously. I... It was just supposed to be you, though. Just you. And even then I..."

"Thought I'd just die. Like Klimmel did. Just die somewhere you weren't, so you didn't have to feel bad about it."

Jack, who'd been standing hunched forwards at an awkward angle, sat down. "Lidlet, they're going to arrest me. This... this thing you're doing. It's being noticed. They don't like the idea of soldiers that don't fight. They would prefer dead soldiers to that. And they know it's me."

Lidlet stared at him for a long time. "What do you want me to say, Jack? You want me to tell people they're just going to have to die, or live with crippling wounds, because God has hit quota? No more healing now, sorry you were right at the head of the line, but that's all. I'm a soldier, Jack."

"I know."

"You don't, because you're not one. Not really sure what you *are* given you keep saying you're not a priest, but you're not a soldier. I have a lot of dead friends. I have a lot of live people who could be dead the next time we go against the Loruthi. Or the next people we're at war against. You've got a good thing, here. A second chance for anyone who takes a shot. How can you not want to give people the chance to live?"

"It's not like that!" Jack told her. "It's... swearing off violence. It's *not* being a soldier. And even then, it's me being there to take their oath. It's God accepting them. You can't save everyone. Oh god, what's that?"

Lidlet had another piece of paper now, the same slightly offset printed letters. A form, it looked like. As though she wanted to requisition something from God's own quartermaster's stores.

Jack took it, read it. Did not understand any of it.

"People have heard we've got a good thing here," Lidlet explained patiently. "But... we're soldiers. Asking someone in the uniform to go clean from shouldering the baton, that's hard."

"Well yes," Jack said acidly. "That is the point. That choice is the point."

"I mean, nobody really believes they're going to be the next one who gets shot in the gut," Lidlet said. "You know it could be you, but you don't *believe* it. Until it happens, and then who knows whether you'd have someone like you on hand, to fix them up. So... this. We worked out this."

"What's it say?" God demanded, squinting myopically.

"It's a pledge," Lidlet said. "That if you heal them when they need you, then they'll, what, convert. Go with your rules. Go the peace road. In case, when it happens, they're not in a position to agree. You know, head wounds, too much pain, that kind of thing."

Jack felt like he should be laughing helplessly, except it was grotesque. It was sacrilege. "No," he said.

"There is nothing in the rules—" Lidlet started.

"This isn't about rules!" Jack exploded. "You cannot take out... *insurance* with God. You can't just be a bloody murderer all your life and then give it all up when it's you on the sharp end. Don't tell me it's not against the rules! I don't care!"

He backed out of the tent, still with his box and his gods. The sunlight falling across him reminded him the whole point of finding her had been to offload his contraband divinities before something happened to him, but he was furious, right then. Bitter with God and bitter with Lidlet, and a great deal of it because every time he tried to construct an argument to destroy her position and reassert his own, he couldn't quite make the pieces join together. The days of sharing an attic room with God at Ilmar's most wretched boarding house seemed unbearably attractive.

He looked around. No squad of provosts was marching in to arrest him. Yet. He had one other goal to achieve, before they did. It was time to pay a visit to Mother Semprellaime.

Mother Semprellaime actually gasped, when Jack turned up at her door. Not a happy gasp, either. As though he'd come to stab her, really. Leaving him stumbling over apologies for he didn't even know what. And then she just looked sad, terribly sad. And said, "She told me you were still with us. But I thought she was just being cruel."

And he thought that *she* was Prassel, somehow, and could make no sense of it, until he stepped up into the wagon and found that Mother Semprellaime already had company, and the company was Caeleen.

The demon, the succubus, Maserley's creature. Pristine and beautiful the way she'd been made to be. Sitting at the conjurer's little table drinking tea, or at least pretending to. He didn't even know if she could.

God, from the box, made a disparaging sound. And they'd had this piece of theology out, between them. God had told him that demons were nothing but smoke and wickedness. There was nothing to them that a man could hold onto, and nothing they did that wasn't compelled. The dealings of humans and demons were corrosive to both parties. It wasn't mere prudishness that had made such practices forbidden to the faith. And then Jack had sat down with Varney and Ghastron, and seen just a sliver of the counterpoint argument. And now here she was, and Jack felt a painful lump in his chest at the sight of her. As though a fist was closing about his heart. As though there was some wound he'd taken, a fatal one, and to be in her presence would reopen it just as readily as throwing a punch.

She had on her sly look, that put on full display exactly what she was, how cruel, how deceitful. The ruiner of lives, the breaker of faiths. "Look all you want," she said, demurely over the lip of her teacup. "He's said you can't touch, not any more. Not since it didn't wreck your life. He's mean like that."

And perhaps she was expecting grief, agonies or just regular frustrated desire, but Jack sat down and took a cup from Mother Semprellaime and said, "Well I had some questions for our hostess. But they can be for you, instead. Can you answer questions?"

Caeleen's eyes narrowed, sensing the trap. "I can listen to them. I promise no answers."

"Well, listening, that's good." Jack could feel his heart racing, because he was about to say a wide variety of foolish things he'd held pent up inside him for too long. Things he'd regret. Things she'd laugh to scorn. And that would hurt, but he was used to that.

"I don't know what it is, to be a demon," he said. "And to be here, in service, like you are. I spoke to one in the city. He seemed... happy. You don't seem happy. But I don't know. Maybe that's just what he wants you to seem. Can you tell me?"

She'd gone quite still. "Happy?"

"Is that... even a thing? For demons?" Looking from her to Semprellaime and back. "You *want* things, yes? That's the whole deal, isn't it? That's why the contracts."

Caeleen didn't seem happy, right then. Her arch manner had retreated, leaving her face like a porcelain doll's. When she spoke, it was as from a great distance. "These words don't mean the same, to us. You say *happy* in Pel like it's only one thing. I feel something when I do what I was made to do. I feel something when I fulfil my tasks under contract, whether it's lie with you or dig a man's eyes out with my thumbs." Spoken without brutality, and without humanity. "And I feel something, too, when I find a way to escape that contract, to go within its letter but against its spirit. Because that is the freedom I have, and freedom is always good. Even when that freedom is just sitting here talking to you, when I know my master would forbid it if he'd thought to. And all these things are 'happy' and none of them are. What do you want, Jack?"

"I want to destroy your contract," he told her. "I will go into Maserley's tent and burn it. In front of his face if I have to. I will free you." He felt a rush of what might have been heroism as he said it. He felt that he should just stand up, go outside and find Maserley's chest of demonic pacts. In that decisive instant he could do absolutely anything and nobody could stop him.

Then Caeleen said "No!" in such a tone of horror, and his stomach plummeted.

"You're saying that because you're bound to," he decided. "To protect your contract. But I'll do it. You'll be free." He actually got up. He was going to do it. He was the hero. This was his moment.

She lunged forwards, upset the table, cups smashing to the floor. Her grip on his wrist was icy, grinding his bones together. "Jack, no! Please!"

He stared at her. "Caeleen—"

"The contract is the only thing keeping me here. I'll be back in the Worlds Below."

"I thought you wanted, you know, freedom..." he stood here, pinned, all that destiny draining out of him as Mother Semprellaime got on her knees to gather the broken pieces.

"There is no freedom there," she said. "The Kings take us and sell us, over and over. When my contract ends, in breach or not, I will be back in their cells until another buys me. And I hate being bound. I hate being Maserley's thing and wearing his chains. But I love this world, Jack. I don't want to be sent back. Please."

He felt his own world start to fall apart, because this was a thing he could do. Given there were doubtless warrants with his name on right now, this was to have been his blaze of glory. Defy the Pals. Strike a blow. Do a right thing, before they took apart everything else he had.

"What can I do for you?" he whispered. "Please, tell me."

She released his aching wrist and stepped back. He could see her trying to fit the pieces of her hauteur back together, with no more success than Mother Semprellaime might have had with the cups. "You're mad," she said.

"Please."

"Why do you even care, Jack? Just get Mother to call you up something that looks like me, and you can get all the—"

"No," he said. "I don't want to be the one holding a chain. I don't want someone who is just a *thing* to me. And I've thought about it. I won't lie. I won't pretend I'm some paragon of virtue.

What if I could get Maserley to sign your contract over to me? Wouldn't that be *better*? Surely I'd be a far kinder man than him, to have holding your leash? But it wouldn't matter because there would still be a leash. The demon I spoke to, he said that all relationships are like that, contracts or not, but I can at least try. So, I thought I could free you. From both of us."

Mother Semprellaime straightened and placed a handful of shards on a shelf with infinite care, as though perhaps she could restore everything to wholeness. Through sorcery, or just with enough glue.

"In the old days," said Caeleen, "when people like Mother summoned us with great ceremony and negotiated with us for our services, we were still bound. But to a fit we chose, and could wear with something like pride. Now the Kings Below keep us like cattle and sell us by the batch, and we have nothing. But it is still better being here, under the sun, than being there, in their darkness. Even with Maserley for a master. And yes, you would be better, but you would still be my enemy and I would work every moment to undo you and destroy you. And you would be undone, because you are not cruel like Maserley is. These days a conjurer must be cruel."

He wanted to say that he couldn't be cruel, but he had already understated the degree to which he had been tempted. He could look in the mirror and see Maserley's face easily enough. Probably it wouldn't even go against God all that much.

"I just wanted…" he said, and what was there to say, exactly? His grand rebellion had been a squib. The world had beaten him again.

"I know," she said, expressionless, and then, "Thank you, though. You care, and you can't do anything, and you're miserable. I'm allowed to take joy from your misery. Maserley didn't revoke that order. So I feel. It's good to feel. Demon happiness, Jack. It's all we're left with."

Hell – Good Intentions

Just one more Whitebelly. A foreigner in uniform. The perfect exemplar of the breed, always helpful, always there when you wanted him. Quiet, polite, deferential, able to turn his hand to any soldier's task except fighting. Everyone's reliable friend. His Majesty Feder the Fourth, in exile. Masty.

Masty is almost glad when the fighting starts again. Happy to be trapped in the hospital tent with the screaming. That's home. Not the city out there, with General Halseder and the other old relics. Not His Majesty Feder the Fourth, that vacuous phantom. Not the ambitions of a people who've been under a regency of viziers and foreign advisors for a generation, telling themselves stories of the days of kings.

He can't really remember his parents, nor his uncles or his cousins, who turned on one another so bloodily because each felt the contours of the Hackle Throne were perfectly suited to their own backsides. He's sat on that throne. It's cold and uncomfortable, even with the cushion they gave him. And the claimants to it are just fragments of faces, memories washed away in the blood that they shed. If you're going to have a life dominated by blood then make it one devoted to healing, not a royal lineage.

The Loruthi made their move. Scouts reported them coming round east of Magnelei with the clear intention of driving the Pals off. Bolstered by their own reinforcements, the Palleseen army has moved to meet them. Magnelei, his unwanted birthright, is at least spared becoming a battlefield this time round. Out there, somewhere, a ragged scrum is going on across terrain piebald with forest. The air curdles with the smoke of the Loruthi firethrowers, and the pounding hammers of the Palleseen artillery are already slugging away their answer. And here, in the tent, the first victims of that collective ire come in. And Masty wouldn't say that he's happy, exactly, but mostly because he can make his mind so full of the demands of his task that happy and unhappy get kicked outside like dogs, to whine and scratch at the door.

The Butcher takes a view on the freshness of the meat. He's moving more easily now, bandages off and shirt-back clear of stains. They've got burns in. They have a couple of broken ankles from bad terrain. Nobody's shot yet. If Masty wanted, he could follow the narrative of the fight from the nature of the injuries they take in. Artillery, baton-fire, knife wounds. The history of the battle anatomised on the surgeon's table.

Masty takes a stretcher, Jack on the other end. They decant a burned soldier onto Alv's table so smoothly the man barely screams, and Alv takes his hurt from him, smooth as a conjurer's trick. Like she's hidden it up her sleeve. Which she has, because the man's right arm was seared from wrist to shoulder, and now that monstrosity of cracked black and red is within Alv's shirt. She presses her lips together, then accepts a draught from Ollery's boy, to dull the inherited pain. The healed soldier bolts up so suddenly from her table that he falls off and almost ends up back in the queue with a broken leg. He stammers thanks – some of them do that, especially with Alv, whose healing seems miraculous if you don't know the costs that underlie it, and who is serenely beautiful until someone comes in with a messed-up face.

Where does it all go? Because Alv will walk it all off in a day or so. Each new collection of crippling injuries just fading from her. Is she ever so slightly more worn, each time? Masty has had ten years to watch the Guest-Adjutant work, and she was definitely fresher and younger back then. Obviously. It's ten years. But Divinati don't age like regular people. They just grow into themselves, balanced and perfect. There are lines about Alv's face that tighten their grip a little more after each battle. Masty thinks he knows the secret of how she maintains her own balance with the universe. He hopes he's wrong.

Then more are coming in and these are shot-wounds. A first skirmish where both sides' scouts felt they had the upper hand and got stuck in, and it turned out neither side did, and both sides paid. Gutshots, head wounds, half-hands, holes in thighs like red mouths. All business as usual and the Butcher goes down the line. Banders comes back in with new waterskins, almost cheerful. A lot of weird has gone on recently. A thunderhead of change is on the horizon. Good to be back with the old routine.

In the tent next door, Cosserby sits and waits for them to come for him. Not the Loruthi but the provosts, the inquisition. He's broken. He can't do it any more. Lidlet ruined him.

Around him the Sonori stand like silenced statues. He can almost sense their attention, that rudimentary thing that grows with use until he needs to wipe them clean again. They are waiting for him to give them their tablethi, the special ones with the complicated instructions. He has those tablethi right here on his workbench. These are the ones he had already prepared from before, because he tries to keep ahead of demand. Since the… incident… he has tried to cast more, and not been able to. He can set you up a Sonori to do all manner of useful things: lift and carry, sing, make the tea. He can't inscribe one to fight. Not without the sharp points of bone clutching in his shoulder and chest like the talon-points of a raptor. Nor can he fit these tablethi to the Sonori he has ready. That is *harm*, apparently. Instructing a machine to kill is harm. It's not even covered in Lidlet's rules because she didn't think to ask the question. He'll have to tell her, if he gets the chance before they arrest him for insubordination.

Wretchedly he drags his feet from his domain, unthrones himself because he's no longer fit to rule. Goes next door to the hospital tent and Banders runs into him, curses him out. "Go back to your bell-making."

"Let me help," Cosserby begs. "Give me something to do."

Banders gives him a crooked look, then shoves buckets into his hands and tells him to get water. Can he do that? Yes he can. It does no harm, so of course he can. And he even gets a smile from her, just a brief grin as she turns back into the tent. It's not worth it, not in exchange for his livelihood and his future. Such a tiny bandage for so great a wound.

Inside the tent, Jack is practically on his own recognizance now. A veteran of the Pal war machine and the pieces it leaves in its wake. He shadows the Butcher, dispensing, bandaging. He claims victims, just like Alv and Tallifer and the rest of the surgeons. Takes them off to sit beside Lochiver as he swabs their wounds, stitches, bandages. Re-sets and splints. Speaks low and comforting to them, despite the pipe shrilling in his ear, despite all the screaming, some of it from the very people he's speaking to. The words don't matter, even. Just the speaking.

God is on his shoulder. Jack can feel the slowly accelerating tempo of His anxiety. He'll start with His blessings, Jack knows. It'll happen again. All these desperate, wounded people. And who's to care if it's just a broken hand or leg, exactly. Why not bank wounds against a peaceful future, like Banders had said? Didn't that actually make a lot of sense. Let each one of them throw a punch when the battle was over. The hospital could tend them after the glut of worse injuries was done. God as a barber surgeon for dentistry and minor ills, to take the pressure off everyone else. The only reason why not, honestly, is that it makes a mockery of God. It reduces Him to one more tool in the hospital's kit, no more or less useful than the big needle or Ollery's red salts. And the priest whom Jack had been rebels against that, but the rest of him concedes that God is pretty damn reduced anyway, so why not?

And the others are no use, but they're there, he knows. Zenotheus is constantly alighting on Tallifer's scalpels and probes and fiddling them out of order, because it's a tiny fragment of a chaos god and that's about all it's capable of. Jack watches it change soldiers' papers so that they leave Tallifer's table with each other's names. A sad comedown for He Who Lays Eggs In The Hearts Of Kings.

The spearman sits on top of the box, over in the corner. Brooding. Staring at Banders still. The woman he'd been able to track through the streets of Magnelei and the halls of the Wolf Palace. And Jack's had some time to think about that, and really needs to sit down and talk with Banders, but right now, obviously, that's not an option. An awkward conversation, should he ever get to have it.

He won't get to have it. He doesn't know it, but his time's up. The commotion at the door of the tent isn't another consignment of casualties being brought in. The men there are whole and fit. Provosts, the hand the army uses to slap its own wrist. Not usually a department seen much in the middle of a battle, but here they are. It's Ollery arguing with them that alerts Jack. The Butcher's bellow of outrage as they trample in, stomping on the wounded who've just been laid out for his assessment. A full dozen, far more than the tent can comfortably contain. Truncheons in hand, and some have batons across their backs. Voices raised as they do their best to shout the Butcher down. Except the Butcher has enough shout in him for any dozen provosts, roars them two steps back by sheer volume, blocking out the thunder of the artillery outside. For a moment he's carrying them before him on the sheer strength of his lungs.

Their Statlos breaks first. Not in the sense of running away, but his truncheon arcs forwards and smacks Ollery where neck and shoulder join, a meaty thud heard through the tent. The Butcher staggers. A big man, yes. A monstrous ogre of a man. But a man. He staggers, almost falls, and the provosts surge forward. Right then their main role is forgotten. The Butcher has made himself their prime target. Two, three more blows against his upraised forearms, and then his boy is trying to get in the way. Eleven years old and with none of his surrogate father's protective bulk. The truncheons go up.

Jack gets in the way and takes the blow straight to the face, just about. A moment of blackness and stars and the disjointed sense of his skull not being the cage of fused bone that it's supposed to be, then God has him. The withered hands of God, catching him and mending him, so that his vision snaps back into focus with a painful twang and he's staring into the face of the man who just hit him. Seeing the horrified shock, not from inflicting the injury but from seeing it be un-inflicted. If injuries can just *heal*, what's the point of being a brutal bully exactly? Does this man need to go home and find a new career?

It doesn't matter. They've been demanding Jack anyway and here he is. And nothing miraculous happens when they lay hands on him. He doesn't turn them into snakes or himself to smoke. He just hangs there, a skinny Maric in bloodied shirtsleeves. The provosts begin to leave – their presence and the amount of space they take up has already killed three people because nobody in the hospital can get their job done – when a voice snaps at them to hold. Is it Prassel? Has she come to save Jack from the noose one more time.

It isn't. She hasn't. And Prassel is surely aware this is going on, her turf, her responsibility, after all. But she's busy playing with dead things and she's washed her hands of the business. She gave Jack his chance in Magnelei, after all.

It's worse than Prassel, then. It's Maserley. He stalks in – and that's one more body shoving the surgeons to the fringes of their own tent, and then two because of course Caeleen is in his shadow.

She looks at Jack, meets his gaze. It's not guilt, exactly. He knew what she was, after all, and her limits. It's not happy, though. The thing she crafts for him, on her face and behind

Maserley's back, is at least an apology. A wish that things had fallen out differently.

Maserley leans in close, ignoring the cries of the injured, Tallifer's barked demands, the needling earworms of Lochiver's flute.

"I understand," he murmurs to Jack, almost pleasantly, "that you plan to deprive me of my property. Did you not think that she'd *tell* me, the moment I asked. What do you think chains and contracts are *for*, exactly?" Then he turns to Caeleen, whose face, on the instant, becomes a cruel sneer at Jack's expense. And it's that shift which tells him that she does feel. Powerless and inhuman as she is, there is something real in her that resonates with him. Not much of a consolation, honestly, but a tiny spark in his heart. Just one more thing for them to extinguish.

"Well, go gather up our lost sheep," Maserley tells Caeleen, and it's worse. He finally found the right questions, then, and of course Caeleen *knows*. She has good eyes that see things humans can't. She glides through the hospital tent like an angel of death and snatches up the gods. One, two, three. Zenotheus, limbs kicking, wings pinched between her slender fingers; the spear god, jabbing ineffectually at her unblemished flesh. And finally God, old God, scowling up at her, little fists clenched. She takes them up and dumps them in the box, and then she takes the box. Out they all go: provosts, Jack, Caeleen, gods, Maserley, leaving the medicos to pick up what they can from the wreckage.

Word comes to Prassel that it's happened, soon after. Twice, in fact. First from a provost, because informing the department's commanding officer is standard procedure. She's busy, right then. She's loading the ghost-throwers, supervising Stiverton's subordinate necromancers. In her lemon-edged protective uniform, and she's made sure everyone else has at least an amulet or brooch with a little warding power. The necromantic equivalent of a blacksmith's apron or a forgehand's leather gloves. Then the provost's at her elbow, telling her Maric Jack has been taken up for mutiny.

"Now?" she demands. "We're in the middle of a battle!" But the man has given her the entire text of his message and just retreats with the blank look soldiers practise to deflect the ire of officers. Even as he's marching off, job well done, the demon arrives.

Caeleen, a sight enough to throw even Prassel's cold-hearted necromancers off their stride, making a positive indecency of the uniform. Unwelcome for that, and because she belongs to Maserley, and because Prassel just flat out doesn't like demons much in any circumstances.

The ghost-launcher discharges, flinging its battery of coppers far off into the distance. It's an improved model that came with the reinforcements, not just a botch-job trebuchet but a thing like a rack of pipes, with tablethi sockets at the closed ends. Propels the ghosts and their little metal homes a ridiculous distance and you can do all sorts of clever things to aim it. She has a team of engineers in to handle that side of it, and she's tried to make them wear wards too, but half of them have already disposed of the things. They're rationalists, after all. Which just means that their science doesn't overlap much with her science.

"What does the son of a bitch want?" she demands of Caeleen.

The demon regards her with no expression. "He wants you to know he has dealt with your Maric problem," she quotes, "seeing as you couldn't find the time in your busy schedule. You're welcome, he says. It's a long time since he's broken a priest. He's looking forwards to it, he says." Delivered in a flat monotone.

At Prassel's back the engineers have recharged the engines and are stepping back. The necromantic detail move forwards with more coppers, handling them as carefully as possible, but hurried still. They have a pace to keep up. They are trying to use their improved range to eliminate the firethrower batteries, or at least disrupt them with tactical possession enough to silence them. That's the plan, and Prassel has absolutely no way of knowing whether it's working.

She's about to dismiss the demon as coldly as possible, so she has nothing satisfying to take back to Maserley, when it goes wrong. One of the necromancers fumbles a copper as she's loading it, and it hits the casing of the engine with a high ringing tone. And cracks, evidently, because the ghost is abruptly free. Prassel pulls goggles down over her eyes immediately, and what was a faint suggestion in the air is abruptly a lightning crackle of angry spirit arcing to the nearest earthing-point. The woman who dropped the copper convulses. Her face is clutched by someone else's expression, so hard that her mouth tears at the corners and blood springs from the corners of her eyes. She has the man next to her by the throat instantly, and one or other of them is making a hideous pig-squeal sound that has nothing of the human about it. Prassel hears the man's neck snap like a baton-shot, and then someone, one of the engineers actually does discharge a baton, killing the possessed woman. Or, rather, killing the body. The ghost leaps from it, grounds in the corpse of the man she just killed and animates it, crudely, desperately, flailing towards the engineers. Collapsing halfway to them even as Prassel is running towards. She sees it arc into the man with the discharged baton even as he's fitting a new tableth to the slot. He bites his own tongue off when it enters him, spitting out the slab of flesh in a great vomiting gout of blood. Then his body has the baton trained on her. Except he can't speak the word to discharge its power into her now, not with the tongue gone. She has the chance to draw her signs and muster her own power, running through the things that are anathema to ghosts. The philosophical concepts boiled down into the sigils Mother Semprellaime stitched into her uniform. She takes hold of the ghost and drives it out of the body, and keeps it from a host for the seconds it requires for the thing to dissipate into the background randomness of the world.

Breathing heavily, three bodies down on her team, she turns and finds Caeleen still there. The demon's face is aghast, just for a second. Then it's all superior disdain again, Maserley's message to her. But Prassel is oddly proud to be at such a cutting edge of human magic that she's horrified a demon. What an achievement.

"Tell him I've got bigger problems than him," she says, and then turns back to her people. "What are you all standing about for?" she demands. "Get this thing loaded!"

"Magister, we're out of full vessels," one of her necromancers reports, as the others get to work. "We're going to have to draw on reserves."

Prassel doesn't want to draw on reserves. She's been pushing the possibility to the back of her head since the battle started and they fired their first salvo of maddened ghosts at the enemy. Because her reserves are literally reserves. Troops held in case of need. And now, apparently, there's need.

Volunteers, they call them. They're not volunteers. They're Whitebellies, some of the reinforcements off the Gallete. They're lined up, not far away, kneeling and hands bound just to forestall any insubordination. Each one has a tableth strapped to the back of their neck and an empty copper slung before them. All it will take is one properly authoritative command, from her, and she'll have ammunition for another five barrages.

It's Stiverton's solution. Because, in the end, the hospital – hers especially, but all the field hospitals – were too good. Too full of people very dedicated to keeping ghosts inside their original vessels. And now the necromancy department needs materiel at a rate that the battle alone cannot generate. And they're only Whitebellies. It's not like anyone's proposing doing it to *Pals*. Although, if they run out of Whitebellies, Stiverton will.

"Get me some intelligence from the front," she tells them. "I want to know if we're even helping, doing this. Otherwise it's just a waste of resources." And that will take time, and maybe she'll have some other option by the time the answer comes back. And she can picture Stiverton tutting and shaking his head, disappointed. He wants a proper battlefield testing of the process, after all. The results he wants are experimental, not military.

Prassel discovers she isn't that person, not yet. Next battle, or the one after, and all those awkward burrs and snags will have been filed away. She'll be the woman Stiverton needs, and the army needs, and the war. But she thinks of Jack and Ollery and the rest, the idiot menagerie she never wanted, and that she's drifting away from even now. There's just enough of them that she hasn't cleaned off her hands, and so those hands are stayed, just this once.

And Caeleen, too. The demon, watching. Not that Prassel cares about being judged by a demon, but she won't given Maserley the satisfaction of seeing her fall.

And then it's Alv's turn. Banders and Masty drop a new casualty in front of her. Shot through the leg, bone shattered, and they're none too gentle because it's busy hour at the hospital. And what does it matter when Alv will be able to take all that pain anyway. Take it and break her own leg apart, and live with the pain because she can. Because she can tilt the scales of her own mind until that pain will smear over the next week, the next month. Just a little nagging ache, barely noticeable. Just as if she took a fatal dose of poison and spread it across a hundred cups, drinking one a day. Just a little sick, for months, rather than dead all at once. Balance.

She'll heal, later. All these burns and grazes, bruises, breaks, internal bleeding, ruined vision, the ringing in her ears. Spread over weeks, months, years. You can't just be rid of it. That's not how it works. It must all go somewhere, but it can go into the future. Her own future, the only one she's entitled to use as collateral. Every injury, spread like butter over all the time she has left. Her long Divinati life. A little shorter each time, of course. She's using it up. But one broken leg, cracked ribs, bleeding on the brain, a ruined eye. Small things measured against a whole healthy life. She's only destroying herself a tiny bit, each time. And it's hers to give and, in giving, she rights the balance. Pays a debt the Divine City incurred to the Pals. Some tiny thing. A Pal saved a Divinati emissary – from death, from injury, perhaps just from embarrassment. Some Pal unwittingly performed a service for the Divine City, and that was a debt, and a debt was imbalance. And to be rid of even the merest possibility of obligation, they gave up Alv. Consigned her to this life of service until she's pared so much of herself away that there's nothing left.

She braces herself for the pain of the broken leg. She knows it. She's intimately familiar with a wide variety of injuries as experienced from the inside. Anything not actively life-threatening, because even she has limits. Those go to Tallifer and the surgeons, or else they get the Butcher's black flask and stay on the floor.

Then she feels it. The dreadful discontinuity. A voice calling to her in a language she knows, using the taut membrane of the world as its sounding board. The world is screaming like an elbow joint twisted the wrong way. She bolts upright, feeling every vicarious injury tug and tear. As Masty and Banders stare at her, she blunders from the tent. Half-blind, inelegant, all her grace shorn from her. She staggers out into the cluttered camp, gets in the way of running soldiers, of incoming wounded. Follows that hideous strained call until she finds them.

Callow and his clique, her students, her responsibility. They've formed a chain, with the man himself up an observation tower with a glass to his eye. Down below they have some of the new Accessories, tied up for convenience. They're sticking knives in. Not with gleeful abandon, but with a scientific precision. Brutalising the writhing, gagged soldiers with exacting care. Then the wounds are gone, only the writhing and muted screaming left. The wounds are passed along the chain like buckets towards a fire, up to where Callow sights. And then gone. Gone towards some distant target visible only through the impersonal glass eye of the telescope. An injury, sent like a gift towards some enemy officer, anyone fool enough to bring attention to themselves. And so limited, really. Each strike, however surgical, is a slow and complex procedure, and the moment the fighting goes into the trees or the smoke hangs too low, they'll be useless. But it's a proof of concept. It's Callow's report to Higher Orders, and soon enough there will be more of them, and other applications, and Alv will have midwifed a terrible thing into the world.

Snuffing the Candles

Thurrel, Maserley and Prassel go back a long way. Three kids from the same phalanstery. Teenagers going through basic officer training, picked out by metrics and family to stand over the regular troopers. Training together to be specialists, all the hard sums and complex logic that granted a comprehension of the world's magical principles. You had to be sound, for that kind of work. You'd be playing with the same universal forces that led less enlightened people to gods and that sort of foolishness. Thurrel had kept a broad church, atheistically speaking. He'd always been up to share a scheme and a bottle with Maserley, just as he and Prassel had swotted together for the end of season tests. Prassel and Maserley had... not. A lot of people these days, seeing only the old and bitter division, conjured some broken romance between them, but really it was just ambition, the old Pal curse. Two young stars vying for the same firmament. Competitors to rivals to enemies as each found the other waiting at every new assignment.

Fellow-Archivist Thurrel was in his hut. The artillery was hungry and the ammunition crates of two battalions were rattling with their last charged tablethi. Every Decanter in the army was draining the dregs of whatever bottom-of-the-barrel trinkets and relics they had been hoarding. He had a rack set up as Maserley strode in. Only a dozen tablethi on a rack made for fifty, which suggested Thurrel was desperately scrabbling for quota. Which meant Maserley was about to become his favourite person in the world.

"If you're after something to charge up your legal documents, back of the queue." Thurrel didn't look round, but somehow knew who it was anyway. He had his thaumatic gauge on, peering through goggles at some shabby little Allorwen charm. After a moment he added a couple of little lead statues to the mix, and another half-dozen tablethi to the rack. "Also, if you're hoping to watch a master at work then sit right down because I am going to squeeze these damned things until they turn to dust. Nobody thinks, you know? Oh yes, let's have bigger engines, let's throw all the death in the world at the Loruthi, such fun! Except someone's got to make it all *go*, don't you know? There's a whole Company sitting about with nothing more dangerous than a pointy stick because Landwards is almost completely out of baton charges."

He made the final connections and stepped back. You were supposed to take the goggles off before starting the process, Maserley understood. In fact you were supposed to have smoked-glass screens and warded gloves and probably lead-lined underwear for all he knew. Thurrel played fast and loose with a lot of rules, though. It was one reason he was such a useful accomplice.

Maserley valued his eyes more, and made sure he looked away before the actinic flash and sizzle of transferred power. When he glanced back, the tablethi on the rack had gone from dull pewter to gleaming gold. Or mostly. Thurrel tapped them and grunted in annoyance.

"Perhaps not as much of a master as I thought. It'll have to do." With deft fingers he plucked the thumb-sized things from the rack and chucked them carelessly in a box already half full of them. His lensed stare was owlish and disconcerting as he turned to Maserley, disconnected from the cheery grin below. "Now, what is it? Have they cancelled the war? Do say yes. I have reading to catch up on."

"I understand you're running low on materiel," Maserley told him.

Thurrel pushed his goggles up, reuniting the disparate regions of his face in a sour look. "If you came to gloat, do tell me how the demon business is going so well these days."

The artillery spoke nearby, the ground shuddering with it. Every little piece of tat and idolatry on Thurrel's shelves rattled. A bucket of his decanting had just been consumed in an instant in the hope that the Loruthi would have a bad harvest of it.

"I can take my bounty elsewhere," Maserley said, when his words would be heard.

"Oh there's a bounty? Do tell. Let's see it. Did you rip someone's heart out and find it made of gold and covered in rubies?" And you could never tell, with Thurrel, whether he was being fanciful or not.

Maserley called for Caeleen and she came in with Maric Jack's box.

Thurrel looked at it. "Isn't that…?" He went very still, then pulled the goggles down again with hands that trembled slightly. "Well, shit," he said, his normal eloquence deserting him. "For me? You shouldn't have."

"I think the words you're thinking of are 'I owe you a big one, Fellow-Invigilator Maserley.'"

"I very honestly do." Below the goggles, tongue moistened suddenly dry lips. "Only ask it. Although preferably not right now, because I'm about to be very busy."

"Oh I'm afraid I insist. Because the first thing I want you to do for me is let me watch you drain this heathen shrine until there's nothing left."

It was impossible to tell what Thurrel thought of that, but the glassy lenses stared at Maserley for several long seconds before he nodded. "I always perform best before an audience. Of course. Least I can do. Can you have your paramour set it down there." A flick of his fingers brushed off the charm and the two little figures. "Let's get a good look at it, eh? Let the dog see the magic rabbit. Why, though?"

Caeleen brought the box round, set it where he directed. "What do you mean, why?" Maserley demanded.

"I mean, I appreciate you want to be able to say you saw it with your own eyes. Fine. It's a fairly routine piece of arcane science. I do it every day, though maybe not on this scale." Thurrel was refilling the rack, and this time he didn't leave an empty slot. Then he brought another rack out, and screwed it to his folding desk. "I mean, the man's just an Accessory. Some witless foreigner. Hardly seems worth it."

"One day you'll actually learn what it is to hate people, Thurrel," Maserley told him. "It's invigorating. Hating them, and knowing they hate you."

"Does he, though?"

Maserley shrugged. "He has just enough time before his execution to learn. He's a priest, Thurrel."

"And you loathe priests. Priests ate your dog. That priest who spilled your drink that time," Thurrel murmured, getting another box of spent tablethi out and filling the second rack.

Maserley nearly said something unwise then, something that would give Thurrel ammunition against him. Instead he just shrugged and said, "Aren't priests everyone's enemy? Bowing the knee to some tinpot little monster with jumped-up ideas and a book of stupid rules on what to wear and when to eat? Isn't getting past that half the job of perfection?" And didn't say, *You have no fucking idea what it's like in this man's army when demons are your specialty. How everyone looks at you like you're one conjuration away from corruption. How dealing with the Kings Below looks just like praying to Higher Orders. And so you stamp on every priest's head that gets dragged down to boot level, just to show them how sound you are.* "And it's Prassel, of course," he added. "She values him. She's been protecting him. I had to go get the writ signed myself to have him arrested, because otherwise he'd still be running about doing his disgusting miracles. There are over thirty noncombatant soldiers thanks to him, Thurrel! And those are just the ones we know about."

"I imagine they stand out a bit given we're actually fighting," Thurrel remarked. "You're going to rub Prassel's nose in it, then, are you? Use this against her? How you had to step in to correct her department?"

"Is that a problem?"

"To me? No! I imagine it will be to her, but that is decidedly Other People's Business. Right, let's take a good look at you, you little devils." He bent down and examined the box, sliding different lenses in and out. The inspection seemed to last longer than Maserley could believe, so that he was shuffling back and forth with impatience, and the artillery had spoken twice more.

"Well now. This will take a little more prep," Thurrel said at last. He sounded almost shaken. "What a lot to put in so small a box, and such a skinny Maric to carry it." He started snatching things off shelves and out of boxes, all based on his usual filing system of 'remembering where I last saw it'.

"If I'd known it would be this kind of circus I'd have taken this elsewhere," Maserley growled. Thurrel just chuckled. He had a whole clutter of cords and artefacts and little caskets under the desk now, connected to the box and the racks. "Ah, now, quite ready. You'll be back to your small print and your fiend-fondling in no time."

"Just get on with it."

Thurrel straightened, cast one last look at the box as though still a little worried he'd underdone his protections. "Hey presto I shall now convert three godlings into around nine artillery rounds or a hundred charged batons, and if you can do that, who needs religion?"

He made the final connection and took one long step back, and this time he did tilt his head away, cueing Maserley to do the same. The flash must have had their silhouettes clearly visible through the walls of the tent, and he heard Caeleen whimper as loose crackles of wasted power arced about her. For a fraction of a second the shape he'd given her twisted and blurred, and he had a glimpse of her true nature.

Then Thurrel was regarding the two filled racks of tablethi thoughtfully. Not rubbing his hands with glee as Maserley would have expected, but a little subdued. The big engines thundered once again and the Decanter glanced up, at the tent ceiling, but notionally at the world outside, slipping his goggles up once again.

"Just imagine," he invited. "Centuries of belief and devotion, sacrifices and prayers. All that banked power poured into these entities we created or elevated or discovered. All that faith. And now it's just baton-fodder and we'll spaff it off towards the enemy to kill a few of them, and it'll be gone into the background of the world until someone puts in the hard work of gathering it up again. Makes you think, doesn't it."

"No," said Maserley. He was staring at the box. It looked as though it had aged a thousand years in that one instant. Thurrel knocked at it tentatively, as though requesting entry, and it collapsed, chunks of friable, worm-eaten wood breaking away.

"Well, there's still a lot of that debt left. You just let me know what I can do for you," Thurrel told him. "But later, please. I have a lot of admin suddenly."

Technically, Maserley had his own work to be doing. They'd want another squad of demonic expendables for some tactic or other, and they'd come looking for him. But he had his own priorities right then. He'd earned a nice reward, and it was time to take the first instalment of it. Let Thurrel pay him back in drinks and sleights of hand later. Maserley had some gratification he could take now, and if he left it too long then he'd lose his chance. They were going to execute Jack the moment anyone could take a breath from killing Loruthi, after all.

Perhaps they'd use one of Thurrel's newly-minted tablethi to do it. That would be appropriate.

They had Jack under guard, because there were always provosts around during a battle. Mostly stepping in should anybody decide they'd rather not take their uniform and baton out to show them to the enemy, but a couple to guard a dangerous Maric seditionist was apparently not too straining on resources. As arresting officer, Maserley got no more than a nod and a step aside.

Inside the little tent was a single stool and a stake driven into the ground. Jack sat on the one and his wrists were manacled to the other, just in case he should try scrabbling out the back of the tent.

He looked up, saw Maserley and looked resigned and a bit miserable, but obviously hadn't second-guessed the big surprise. Then Caeleen came in, and his eyes fixed on her for a moment, and there was a look on his face. A pathetic look, really. A look that Maserley would normally have taken joy on: someone who'd been lost to the charms of his favourite succubus. He'd ruined more than a few careers with Caeleen, and it was only a shame Prassel didn't seem to have a libidinous bone in her body. Corrupting her new priest had seemed to be an amusing diversion once he'd understood the man had a set of those behavioural restrictions that primitives still clung to. Except Caeleen had gone ahead and done exactly that, and it turned out Jack's rules had been more like guidelines and he'd just had a free ride.

And started to make plans. And waves, Maserley was alarmed to discover. Because whatever it was that Jack actually was, it was spreading through the army. Miraculous healing from the point of death, oaths of pacifism. The absolute anathema of the Palleseen mission. A true atavistic hearkening back to older days and ways. And now the man had his sights set on Maserley, because despite having all that power, he was also a sucker for a pretty face and a little demonic glamour.

He had started plotting to free the demon from her contract, and that sort of thing could escalate very quickly. The game had needed to be wrapped up very quickly. And here the man was, trapped, disempowered and soon to die.

But first this.

"I understand you covet what's mine, Jack," he said.

Jack, still ignorant, faced up to him. "Things seem to have turned out that way," he said, in that thick foreign accent.

"You want to own this, I understand. Want her secret name on a contract of your own."

Jack's lips moved, eyes flicking to Caeleen. He sighed. "I should say no, shouldn't I?"

"But you do."

"I do, yes. I wouldn't. I own nobody. But I'd be lying otherwise." Jack dipped his head. "You got me, magister. They'll hang me. Or shoot me? Or... it's a tableth to the neck, isn't it? Humane and quick, I think Banders said. Probably too good for me."

Maserley knelt down and gripped the man's chin, forcing Jack to look him in the eye. "They'll probably interrogate you first. For the names of the others. You're rot, Jack. We can't let it spread even when you're gone. Maybe they'll make Prassel do it."

"She'd like that."

Maserley blinked, momentarily wrong-footed, but apparently Jack assumed Prassel hated him too. Let him believe that.

"Just one thing," he told Jack. "I want you to know that they're gone."

Jack looked at him blankly, and then with sudden panic. "It was just me," he said hurriedly. "Ollery, Masty, the others, they had nothing to do with it. Please."

Maserley hooted with laughter despite himself. "You cretin. You can literally do nothing right, can you? Not even understand a little basic inference. Your little friends, you idiot. Your gods."

"What?" Jack asked.

"Your gods are dead. I made sure of it myself. I've just

watched my friend Thurrel draw every little dreg of them to fuel the artillery. Listen…" And he was about to say 'the next great roar you hear…' except the engineers had a working sense of drama because the engines spoke even then, jumping the ground beneath them, setting Jack's chains chiming.

"That was them," Maserley whispered, close enough to kiss. "That was your gods being turned to fire and death and thrown at the enemy. Your gods will be the killing shot spat from batons, and they will be the keys that lock howling ghosts in Prassel's coppers. They will be a hundred different things to the army and every one of them will torment and kill." He stood easily. "I just thought you should know."

"What?" Jack repeated, more raggedly this time. He seemed to be having trouble breathing. "God…"

"Is dead," Maserley said. "That's how we perfect the world, don't you know? Your gods are all dead and you'll be joining them and I wanted to see your face when you knew, but I had no idea that it would be this entertaining." And it was. Jack had none of the traditional Pal ability to bottle it all up in front of a superior. He was staring up at Maserley with all that grief and horror scrawled across his face like a five-year-old's drawing of a monster. Raw and rough and lots of jagged lines.

Jack stood up. Stooped, because of the manacles, but as far as he could. Something happened to his face, and Caeleen stepped back. He was suddenly the ugliest man Maserley had ever seen. Like a fist had closed on his features and crushed them all inwards into the nastiest, angriest expression imaginable.

"I am going," Jack said, "to destroy you."

Maserley had heard that before from rivals, enemies and victims. He'd laughed it off each time and remained resolutely undestroyed. But that look on Jack's face was getting to him. The look of an infinitely mild and gentle man explicitly forbidden from hurting anyone who suddenly didn't care any more.

"You'll do nothing," he said, but Jack was shaking his head.

"You'll torture me and then you'll kill me, I know," he said, and that Maric accent suddenly made his voice profoundly nasty too, a perfect complement for his face. "I won't let that stop me. I will destroy you if my ghost has to possess everyone in the army to do it. I will make you pay for what you've done. You've killed God? You killed what I've lived for all my life. The thing I've been good for since I understood anything. All those years of not striking men like you. All those years of letting you push me around. You've killed God? You've killed the one thing keeping you safe from me, you ignorant bastard. I will destroy you. I swear it. I will ruin you the worst way possible. And if I can't swear to God any more, I swear to every other damn thing in the world that I will not rest, alive or dead, until I have made a wasteland of your entire fucking life."

Maserley laughed. It was a good laugh. A true, mocking peal of delighted mirth at someone else's misfortune. He even managed to throw a disdainful look into the bargain, before he turned and swanned out of the tent, and got himself out of eyeline of the provost sentries. And then stopped, and felt his heart pound in his chest, his shirt suddenly clammy with sweat because he'd seen people possessed by demons and by ghosts and none of them had been as foreign to themselves as Maric Jack had right then. As if to underline the man's oath, the ground leaped beneath him again, staggering him, and something vast and flaming struck within the camp, sending smoke, flames and screams all leaping towards the heavens.

Uncle

Sage-Monitor Runkel, commanding officer of Forthright Battalion. A testimony to the Palleseen preference for workhorses. Pallesand was leery of the maverick, the genius with unorthodox ideas. They tended to do very well up to around the rank of Fellow and then find their ambitions stymied. Or, in some cases, get quietly purged by Correct Speech. Ideological soundness trumped genius, but even in the very bosom of orthodoxy the occasional piece of lateral thinking could sometimes flourish.

Those had been, Jack knew, some very large words to come from a small man. A small man under a death sentence, manacled to a post in a tent in an army in a battle in a war. They'd landed with Maserley, and that had brought a tiny spark of satisfaction. Empty, though. Even if the chains had suddenly fallen away it wasn't as though he could have laid into the man with fists or feet, let alone manifested some kind of divine wrath. In fact, a lack of divine anything was precisely the problem. He was just Maric Jack now, not even an ex-priest. A man who'd once had a god and now had nothing. He'd sworn a mighty grand oath of vengeance and it was a promise he'd never keep.

He'd lived with God all his life. He'd been a kid when Kosha, the old priest, took him in. He'd learned about doing no harm and serving God as the fortunes of the faith steadily diminished. He'd watched the last of the congregation pack it in and go to the big Mahanic Temple across the city, or else die, elderly and withered, clutching for some last benediction from a deity who was in an even worse way, older than the mountains yet unable to die.

When Kosha had been hung, that was when God actually appeared to him. And it had been Jack and God from then on, and God had been no help. Jack had begged and done piecework and somehow made rent on a tiny garret room, kept his belly half full and sacrificed to God. And God had complained and criticised and told him how much better it had all been. And Jack had known that some day he, Jack, would be that elderly man dying in the bed, with only God to mourn him. And that would be it for God.

And then he'd ended up as the last ex-priest of God, and discovered the wealth of little lost deities scrabbling about Ilmar's streets like rats. He'd started smuggling them out when the Palleseen had started to trap and decant them. Which had led here, because he'd not even been very good at that and they'd caught him. Caught him and made him one more part of their war machine, the pacifist with his pacifist god.

Sitting there in the little tent with the provosts outside, listening to the murderous rumble of the artillery, he thought about the last days of God. *He had a new lease of life.* In Ilmar the ancient divinity had been in hiding from the world, shirking His responsibilities because every time He healed, it caused more harm. Except here they'd been in the middle of a war and there was harm everywhere you looked and something had snapped in God. He'd started handing out divine blessings like they were favours at a child's party. He'd gone mad with it, because it was the only way He could push back against the horror. And Jack had tried to restrain the divine, to put God back in His box. Because Jack had valued his own life over God's purpose.

I was right, though, eh? Talking to God as though God still had ears to listen. Trying to will that presence on his shoulder into being and hearing only the echo of absence. *I was right, and they got us, and here I am and where are you?* Something ancient and grand had been excised from the world. Something petty and annoying, too. Mean-spirited and ill-tempered and unreliable. But who was Jack to pick and choose the attributes of the divine?

The war kept trying to break up his thoughts, the thunder of it, the rush of running soldiers, the shouting of orders. More and more being thrown into the teeth of the grinder. And, on the far side of the lines, the Loruthi would be doing exactly the same, and Jack realised that he knew very little about what it was like to be a Loruthi soldier, or a Loruthi anything. Probably, though, when they squeezed their culture down to the small gap which turned them into soldiers being thrown at the Palleseen, the only significant difference between them and their opposite numbers was the colour of the jackets. Probably their camp sounded just the same except for the language the orders were yelled in. Or maybe even that was the same, given all their mercenaries. And Jack found he took solace from the sounds. They wouldn't get around to torturing or executing him until after the fight was done.

Soon after, he registered that, in fact, the sounds were calming. A damning tranquillity was falling on the tents of the Palleseen camp. There'd still be screaming in hell, but the battle itself ebbed away like the tide, leaving Jack high and dry.

After a long enough wait for him to go through all his mourning of God again, they came for him. Not even provosts but a squad of regular troopers led by a Fellow-Monitor. Quite the honour, really. He wouldn't have thought he'd have rated such a final escort.

They unlocked his chains warily. When no smiting happened they weren't relieved, just contemptuous, strong men whose strength exists proportionate to the weakness of their victims. They experimented with pushing him about a bit, cuffing and kicking him. He didn't fight, of course. He couldn't, both because he'd lived a life of not doing so, and because he was on that list of God's beneficiaries who would die the moment he pushed back.

It's an option. And he realised with a sudden access of relief that they weren't going to torture him at all. They wouldn't get anybody's names out of him. In the extremity of his desperation he'd find a way to strike at them. A kick, a clutch, some way to trigger God's curse within him. And then he'd just be a broken sack of bones. He'd rob them of their final satisfaction and show them one last miracle.

He laughed then, and the soldiers drew back. He got a baton in the face before the officer barked a command. They wanted him alive. And Jack laughed again because he had complete control over how long he remained alive, and if they kept pushing him around he might make himself spectacularly dead just to spite them.

Having set those ground rules, they marched him out into a turbulent camp. He could see that the Loruthi engines had landed a few strikes within the tents. Doubtless the hospital department would be overflowing right now, the Butcher and the others suddenly deluged with a wave of injured support staff, clerks and quartermasters, cooks and camp followers. He hoped Mother Semprellaime was clear of it. He hoped Caeleen was. Probably the fires were no great threat to her but massive physical trauma could kill a demon. He'd seen it done.

They dragged him through the reconstruction at a rapid pace, shoving him in the back whenever he stumbled, which just made him stumble more. He felt weirdly light, and only as they reached their destination did he realise it was because the box was gone.

There was a big tent ahead, slightly scorched. Higher Orders, he realised. He was being taken straight to the top. And of all people he'd have thought they'd have had more important things to think about. Surely this was getting in the way of the war? He was momentarily outraged on behalf of the conscript he had been, then told himself that surely this was good and he was in some way working against the cause of violence by taking up their valuable time. Then they manhandled him inside the tent and he understood.

He had been brought before Sage-Monitor Runkel himself. A man he'd only seen back at his trial, after he'd healed Lidlet. After that other soldier had died. A name more than a man, really. And now less than a man, because Sage-Monitor Runkel was in a very bad way.

Was dead, really, except here was some… engine they'd put him in. And here, of all people, was Cosserby, staring at Jack with a wild and despairing look. Cosserby with a machine that was like a vast iron bellows, and that three Whitebellies were cranking great handles on. The folded concertina of the bellows hinged up and down with a great, slow rhythm, and its ridged pipes had been rammed brutally into the opened fissures in Runkel's collapsed torso. When the bellows clamped down, Jack could see various parts of the secret and inner man inflate and flutter, only to be sucked into collapse each time the machine opened up again.

And conscious. Entirely conscious. His arms twitching within the straps they'd secured him with, his legs, every part of him below the ribcage, utterly still, but his face tilted towards Jack, animated by a dreadful agony. Doubtless they'd given him something for the pain, but not enough to take away his awareness, which was fixed entirely on his visitor.

His lips moved, and the man kneeling by his head – another Fellow-Monitor, so no menial – said, "Accessory Maric Jack, you're to deploy your magic, now."

Jack's lips twitched.

"Now, man! He's not got long left."

Jack looked at Cosserby. The Sonorist nodded frantically.

Jack's lips twitched again.

"What are you waiting for. That's an order, Accessory!" the Fellow-Monitor barked. Jack was desperately pressing his lips together because he was about to be terribly impolite.

"Jack," said Cosserby. "Look, they've got Lidlet. They've got the others. Everyone who took the... the *option*. They've got me, you see. They know I can't... I'm only here because they needed someone for the machines. Please, Jack, just do the... do the thing. Your thing."

"It doesn't work like that," Jack got out. "You know it doesn't." Sensing the tension of all these violent people around him desperate to slap him for insubordination, to kick him in the back of the knee so that he was properly deferential, to remind him of his place.

"Show him the papers, for reason's sake!" hissed Cosserby.

"Here." There were indeed papers, scattered and sticky with blood, by the Sage-Monitor's bedside. With sinking heart Jack saw a copy of Lidlet's damned pamphlet there, for starters. *The Ninety-Seven Loopholes of God* had obviously reached Higher Orders, presumably as part of the evidence that had seen Jack arrested. It appeared to have been heavily annotated. Next to it was an executive order signed and sealed by Runkel, presumably in happier times.

It laid out a contingency to be followed in case Runkel himself should be critically injured in the line of duty. Specifically that they should send for Maric Jack, and that Runkel would, pre-emptively, swear to follow the precepts of the *Loopholes* after being restored to health, without exception. And Jack re-evaluated Runkel right then, because it was quite a twisty piece of thinking for an old soldier.

"Do I get to point out that I'm currently about to be executed?" Jack demanded of them all. "I mean, it's not exactly motivation."

Runkel's eyes, red-shot, watery with tears, bored into Jack. His lips moved.

"Bring him close," the Fellow-Monitor translated, and the escort, delighted to have something physical to do, slammed Jack down to his knees by the head of the bed.

"I will pardon you." The words could only come with the exhalation of the bellows, flurrying in a strained rush and then falling silent when the man's artificial breath was withdrawn. The machine couldn't keep him alive for much longer, Jack guessed. His skin tone was going from greyish to bluish. He looked like he was ageing to death before Jack's eyes. "I will pardon them all. Your accomplices. Your faithful. They will live and you will live. Free, all. If I live. Make me live, Jack. Make me whole."

Jack's lips twitched. He'd been holding the laugh in but suddenly it wasn't funny any more. Just wretchedly, pitifully tragic.

"You stupid bastards," he said. Not even shouting, utterly lost to despair. "I would, if I could. I'd do it. But you killed God. You sent Him to the Decanters, you dumb sons of bitches. I don't have a spark of healing left in me. Let me stitch a wound. Let me tie a tourniquet. That's the limit of what I can do for you. I had something wonderful once. I had something absolutely unique and incredible that I took for granted and never appreciated properly. I used to be able to do miracles but you burned all that up so you could shoot more people."

Runkel's eyes bulged and swivelled, searching for the lie and not finding it.

"So I guess we both die," Jack told Runkel. "I guess we all die. I guess your soldiers learn that you'd rather they be dead than alive and not fighting for you. I guess it all just goes on until you find some new way of fighting that kills everyone all at once, and then we can give it a rest, eh?"

He really hoped that Runkel appreciated the irony of the situation, but the man was in so much pain that probably it wasn't an option.

They kept him there for hours, because that was how long it took Runkel to die. They beat him, and then they beat Cosserby too, the pair of them curling on the floor, hands over their heads as the truncheons came down. Jack laughed at them. He spat through bloody teeth, spat bloody teeth at them, and laughed. Because they killed God too soon and now this nasty old man was going to die because of it. At first the laughing made them beat him harder, sparing Cosserby a little because the artificer wasn't in a laughing mood. And then, because Jack couldn't stop, they got scared and drew away from him as if helpless, despairing hilarity was catching.

At some point during this – unnoticed because of the beatings and the laughing that were monopolising their attention – Sage-Monitor Runkel died. Because the Whitebellies kept on with the winches, his chest cavity continued to inflate and collapse mechanically for some time after, artificial breath wheezing in and out between the stiff, dead lips. Only when the Fellow-Monitor bent low to gain some sort of permission did he discover that Forthright's commanding officer had lost his tenuous grip on his own corpse.

They stood back. Jack got the laughter under control. Solemn moment, obviously. He saw batons tremble in hands, and assumed that this was where he and Cosserby both got shot. Apparently the army still needed the proper paperwork for an execution, and then there were the torturers of Correct Speech who'd presumably feel left out if they didn't get their piece of flesh to chew over. Instead, the pair of them were hoisted up, jarring every bruise from the beatings all over again, and marched out of sight of the deathbed.

They didn't take him back to the little tent with the manacles. Instead there was a shed, one of those pack-up-and-take-down military buildings, this one configured as a barracks for about twenty, and containing about forty. The faces turned towards him held the most transient spark of hope that guttered as soon as he and Cosserby were shoved in to join them.

He recognised Lidlet. He recognised Foley, Lidlet's friend, and a handful of others. There were more he didn't recognise. People who God had healed on the sly, or who Lidlet had got to. The extent of the rot that the Palleseen had rooted out. Plus, possibly, the odd soldier who had just refused to go out and fight and get shot, and so had been rounded up with the rest of them without knowing any of the theology at all.

He opened his mouth. Shut it. Watched Cosserby sit down and tug his uniform straight. The man's jacket was stiff with dried blood, but his movements had been easy. None of the stiffness he'd shown on the march over.

Jack's ribs didn't hurt. His knee, that had swollen up like two fists, was down.

His teeth were back.

"You're fucking welcome," said that voice. Because God had always been able to find him.

Jack let out a sound as though he'd been stabbed and his legs gave way, collapsing down before Lidlet and the others. God was in the corner of the tent, arms folded, leaning against a pole.

"You!" Jack exclaimed. "How did you…? What even? What?"

"Long story," said God. "But thanks."

"What?"

"When they had you at that long turd's bed. Thanks for not praying. I mean fine, you thought it was 'cos I wasn't there to be prayed to. But that would have made it harder. I did not want to fix that son of a bitch."

"Jack?" Lidlet asked, uncertainly.

Jack wanted to tell them to rejoice, because God wasn't dead after all. Except they hadn't known that God was supposed to be dead, so the revelation would mean nothing. And if you weren't in a position to take joy from that then there was precious little else because they were all going to be executed the moment that someone in Higher Orders found the time to sign the orders. And where then, for God?

Later, after a restless night and then the morning sun needling in between the wooden boards, the door was opened partway and someone hissed his name.

It was Banders. The provosts on guard were standing a few paces away, pointedly not listening. He wondered what she'd bribed them with, but Banders was never short of something that people wanted.

She looked pale and shaken, and that probably wasn't on his account. Nor, fond thoughts aside, on Cosserby's, who came crowding close in at Jack's shoulders. Not that Banders was selfish, but it probably took something that touched her own deep self to rattle her composure, as something obviously had.

"Peace offering," she said.

Jack frowned, because although a great many people had been fighting a war, he hadn't been aware of any division between him and Banders. She wrestled something out, though. One of the Butcher's medicine boxes, the smallest size. Some fool had knocked a handful of holes in it at random.

"Your old one didn't make it," Banders said. "But I thought you might still need one. For your, for your, you know, the *things*." Banders actually being circumspect was a new experience.

There was a motion at one of the holes. A flick of antennae. An insect head poked cautiously out to test the air.

We have to say, came the buzzing voice of Zenotheus in his head, *we don't mind a bit of chaos but it's been a time.*

Jack looked blankly at Banders. He should probably thank her but he couldn't quite process why she, of all people, was performing this unlooked-for service.

"Jack," said Banders. "I really need your help."

He looked back at the crowded hut, then over at the provosts. "I mean, sure. Just let me get the whole execution out of the way then I'll be all yours."

"Jack," Banders said, and her voice shook and there were tears in her eyes. "Please." All the cockiness had been bleached from her. She suddenly seemed very young and very frightened.

Whatever she'd given the provosts obviously bought a long conversation. Jack sat down on his side of the doorframe with the box on his knees, and Banders did the same on her side. The free side. After a baffled moment, Cosserby lumped himself down at Jack's elbow.

"Tell me," Jack invited, and she did.

The Stick-Man

Growing up in a fish-stinking orphanage where they locked you in the cellar. Beaten by her teachers and skinning her knuckles against the other kids. Cheating on tests at the phal. A constant round of bribes and deals and demotions and remotions. Banders had really tried to just get through life without becoming something she didn't want to be. And now this.

So they'd come and yanked Jack out of the hospital tent like a rotten tooth. Then Alv had just... left. Left and, when she came back, refused to heal any more, even though she had plenty more to give. Then more word came that a bunch of their stretcher bearers had been arrested too, Lidlet included. That made it fairly clear what was going on.

"It's a purge, at last," the Butcher said, as though he'd been watching dry skies for an age and now there was a thunder-and-fury storm coming, more rain than anyone knew what to do with. He and Tallifer and Lochiver exchanged a look. An old guard look, because the only other senior medico was Alv, who'd gone somewhere to sulk. Banders was not admitted to that look, but she didn't like it in the least. And by then it was really just a handful of regular surgeons and her and Masty left. And Masty had been no fun since that business in Magnelei, and he'd reacted so badly to her pretending to bow and scrape around him that she'd given it up almost as soon as she tried it.

They'd arrested Cosserby too, someone said. She couldn't even imagine that. He was the most drearily rule-following man she ever met. She could only assume that there was someone with the same name who'd been raising hell all over camp and chalking it up on their Cosserby's tab.

By that time the battle appeared to have finished. Word said the Loruthi were pulling back and they'd won. So long as you weren't canvassing the opinions of the abundance of mauled people the hospital was still trying to deal with, short-handed. Things were calming down, so Banders felt that she could probably absent herself to go have a smoke and a swig from a flask of medical moonshine. Because it had been one of those days.

She had just skulked unseen out of the tent when events conspired to ensure that it would remain one of those days until further notice, because some jumped-up messenger appeared and told her she was wanted by Fellow-Archivist Thurrel. Banders had nothing against Thurrel. He was a customer, on and off, a potential market for arcane odds and ends, never short of funds. Except he did not send urgent, out-of-breath Statloi to find Former Cohort-Broker Banders. That wasn't his style. Meaning: trouble.

She wondered if she could get the Statlos to agree he hadn't seen her, in exchange for the Butcher's flask. She had a good eye for the corruptible and he didn't look the type. Also he marched her all the way to Thurrel's decantary because he didn't trust that she wouldn't just forget the moment she was alone. Which she would have been entirely minded to do.

Here she was at Thurrel's little magical death camp, then. The place that arcane tat went to die. And here, inside, was Thurrel. He was one of those officers very fond of his own wit, which he gave out as a gift to just about anyone who walked past. When he stared at her like she'd stabbed his mother, that was just one more unwelcome piece of the puzzle.

He was holding a tray of junk. Junk that had obviously already been decanted, given its severe dilapidation. Draining the magic tended to ruin the physical object as well, Banders understood. Thurrel's tray held quite a lot that had lost its market value very recently. She saw jars and pots, little statues, tarnished jewellery, a jade-bladed knife leached almost white, even a gauntlet, or maybe it was a hand, that had once been ornate and articulated and was now just a half-slagged lump of dull metal. And pieces of broken wood, she saw. Wood pierced by the occasional round hole. She recognised that, from when it had been a box. A sudden lurch came to her as she divined why he'd called her.

"That's for the hospital?" she asked him.

Thurrel was still staring at her. "What?"

"His… effects. I mean they took Jack but we can hold them, for him. His… what's left of his…" She was feeling powerfully cut up, right about then, and she didn't like that. She liked to feel she was careless and fancy-free, dancing her way through life heedless of other people. Seeing this was like a spike through her foot, nailing her in place.

"This is trash," Thurrel told her. "I mean, not long ago it was basically my retirement fund, you know? All the goodies I had squirrelled away, nicely brim-full of arcane potential. My own special reserve of every piece I saved from the hammer, because I liked it. Because I could use it, later."

"Oh." She had no idea why he was sharing this with her. "Tough battle, huh? Couldn't hold anything back?"

"A worthy cause," he said vaguely, and that stare of his was beginning to seriously unnerve her. "But I needed sufficient power to make it look like I'd drained… something substantial. Even then I'm not sure I topped up the full two racks' worth. Someone's baton is going to go *fizz* when they want it to go *bang*."

"Magister, I'm not sure…"

"Sit down, Banders. Call me Thurrel and sit down." He indicated a camp stool, and took the big chair with the straps himself. And sitting down with Thurrel wasn't like when the duty Inquirer asked you in for a chat, but it still made her nervous.

She sat, giving him her best bright and enquiring look. "What can I do for you, magister?" If he was going to be weird she'd keep the ladder of rank between them.

"Tell me about yourself, Banders."

So he was definitely going to be weird. "What, magister?"

"You're an orphan, right?"

"You are definitely not old enough to be my dad, if that's where this is going."

For a second he just stared, and then that got through and he smirked despite himself. "Look, this is important. The place where they raised you. Anything funny happen there?"

Banders went very cold. This was not funny, or not the ha-ha variety. This was the stuff she'd joined the army to get away from. "Look, it was an orphanage. They taught us letters, numbers and laws, and fit us for uniforms. I had some friends. I got into trouble. They caned the crap out of my ass on more than one occasion. What do you want, magister?"

"It was by the sea," Thurrel said.

"Yes. Yes it was by the sea. I'd say that was a big old piece of deduction, magister, except that most of the Archipelago is. But yes, right on the sea. Right on the coast. When I got sent inland first time it took me a week to start sleeping without hearing waves. Please tell me what this is about, magister, because you are properly freaking me out."

"Put these on." And he had a big assemblage of goggles and tablethi and cords, the sort of thing that could be a tool of examination or an automated eye-remover for all she knew. He wasn't giving her much of a choice, though.

She slipped them over her head and, while she was blinded by trying to fit them, he was abruptly at her elbow, fingers gripping her head painfully as he tugged everything into place.

"I want you," he said, and his hands hadn't let go, "to look at the table here." Not giving her any choice, forcing her face where he wanted it to point.

She was about to fight him, because this was getting far too invasive and she'd take her stripes for lamping a Fellow rather than letting Thurrel get fresh with her. Then she saw it.

"Oh shit," she breathed. "There is a little man on your table." Her voice shook a bit. A little angry man with a spear, staring at her in a way that made Thurrel's look merely one of polite enquiry.

"Who is he? Can you tell me?" Thurrel asked her.

"He looks like..." Banders said. "I mean, he looks like..."

"Yes?"

"I, well, at the, all right, yes, the orphanage. It had cellars, and they went way down, and the bottom ones were, like, sea-caves. They had boats there, for bringing in food and stuff. And right at the back there was this... statue. Of your man there. Only bigger, obviously. Like, full person-sized. Your man with the spear only the end had broken off. So we just called him the Stick-Man."

"The Stick-Man," echoed Thurrel.

"I mean a spear without an end is just a stick, right?" Banders said defensively. "So everyone knew he was there, just stuck right at the back. So what?" But she wasn't fooling anybody and she knew it.

"Tell me," Thurrel prompted. His hands were still gripping her head. She could feel her heart racing. It was so unfair. She'd done a thousand stupid things on a dare. How come *this* one had come back to bite her?

"We had a game, that was all. You had to sneak out after dark and go slap the Stick-Man. Go right up to the statue and... hit it with something. I mean we learned it from the older kids and we taught it to the youngers. Someone had already knocked his nose off, and the spear-end, and Chivvel carved her name into his ass once. We all did it. Only it was high tide, and they dared me. Nobody else would go down when it was high tide."

His fingers were relaxing, dropping to her shoulders. The little spearman was staring at her still. If he had the word 'Chivvel' carved on his backside he wasn't showing her.

"I had a bat. I'd made it from a chair leg. I was going to knock his head right off. I told them. Only when I got down, the water was up to my waist and dragging at me. All the boats were floating at the ends of their painters, knocking against each other. I lost the bat. I needed both hands. So when I got to the Stick-Man all I had were my hands. So I just, kind of, thumped him one. Right in the face. Took the skin off my knuckles. Hurt like hell. But at least that was proof for people. That I'd been there. That I'd won the dare." She eyed the angry little man again. "So what, he tracked me down after all this time? I mean he's kind of tiny but at least his nose grew back. He's up on the deal the way I see it."

Thurrel returned to his seat. Through the goggles she could see a dozen little glimmers of power about him, and his corselet of wires glittered and danced like it was covered with shiny bugs.

"Well that was a sorry story," he said. "I was expecting a bit more of the full cult initiation, honestly."

"You what?"

"Do you know who this is?"

"The St—"

"*Not* the 'Stick-Man'," he snapped. "This is the Fisher King. Or all that's left of him."

"Right. Fine." Banders nodded fervently. "I don't know what that means."

"Of course you don't. Almost nobody does any more." The Fellow-Archivist pulled out his pipe and filled it. "The Fisher King was a god. A god of raiding and fishing, travel and war. The chief god of a people known as the Islermen."

"They sound fun," Banders said. "What happened to them?"

"They became the Palleseen," Thurrel told her.

She made one of those noises she'd done in class, when she

513

didn't really understand the lesson but didn't want to be called on it by teacher.

"After the accession of the Temporary Commission for Ways and Means, and our adoption of perfection," Thurrel went on patiently, "we extirpated the remnants of the imperfect people we'd been. You could get arrested for speaking the old language, or telling the old stories. Or, especially, for worshipping the old gods. We drove them out, smashed their temples, drained their relics and defaced their icons. All except one statue forgotten in the undercellar of some no-import orphanage, apparently. Where it sat, vandalised and mocked for centuries, until some ignorant girl crept down there at the holy time and shed blood on it."

"Ha ha, yeah," Banders tried. "That would have been a stupid thing. Glad that didn't happen. I mean, if it had happened, even, who cares. Not like it meant anything. Not like it was... I mean, just high spirits, right."

"He says you're his," Thurrel told her.

"I'm not anyone's," she replied, the core tenet of her life.

"He says you're consecrated to him. Your life given over to him."

"I mean I don't raid or go on boats and I never learned to fish. So I don't think so... Magister, why do you *have* him? I mean I appreciate you're telling me you're going to get me in the shit, but aren't you already neck deep because of that?"

"Banders, I am not about to shop you to Correct Speech. At least partly for that reason. We are in this together, now. We two, and a secret between us."

She didn't want to be in anything together with Thurrel, let alone with Thurrel and the Stick-Man. Except... he *wasn't* threatening her. He wasn't pulling rank. Some of the weird that he'd been reeking of was actually the fact that he was treating her with... respect. Like an equal, almost. "What's going on?" she asked.

"I am a scholar, Banders. I've scrabbled for twenty years to find every surviving shred of lore about the people we once were. And Maserley, of all people, delivers me *this*. All that remains of the god of our ancestors. I have now spent more than I wanted to, to avoid turning him and your friend Jack's whole sacred doll collection into charged tablethi," Thurrel said. "A decade of careful magic husbandry and crooked book-keeping gone to dust."

"Why?"

"Because how could I destroy the Fisher King?" he asked plaintively. "I'm an Archivist, Banders. Not just a Decanter. And I know full well what the party line is on gods, most especially this one, but he's *ours*. He's our past. He was actually *there*. But when I spoke to him, he told me he wanted *you*."

"I don't want him. He's all yours."

"You are sacred to him, Banders," Thurrel said. "In the old days you'd have an axe in your hand and a ship under you, and you'd burn the villages of the mainland coast and steal the gold from their temples. You'd have seawater in your blood and command the sharks and the kraken."

"I... do not want to do any of those things," Banders said. "I'm in the shit, aren't I? The moment anybody finds out about this, they're going to kill me. You're not the only person to own a hat like this, are you? I mean, can they tell, if they look at me? How do I un-god myself?"

"There are... ways." Thurrel licked his lips.

"Wait," she said. "You want this, don't you?"

His gaze was level. Possibly mad, but level. "I do."

"I can't just give him to you?"

"You can't."

"You have to fight me for him or something?" Banders laughed at the idea.

Thurrel didn't laugh.

"Actually fight? What, axes or something? Can I just sort of—"

"The mantle was given in blood. In blood it must be taken.

A challenge, formal, ritual. A duel. Wait, look," because she'd bolted to her feet in case he brought a couple of dirty great axes out from under the table. "Banders, I'm... not a fighter. And it has to be an open fight, no cheating, no surrendering. Ideally up to our knees in seawater though I don't see that happening. I'm still... Banders, wait."

She'd got to the mouth of his hut, jittery as a cat on coals. "Magister, this is... crazy."

"Take the others, at least. As a show of good faith."

"The other whats?"

And he was pointing at the ground by the table, and through the lenses she saw some sort of gross scorpion thing and a monkey got up in a bedsheet. Compared to the Fisher King they were definitely the consolation prize.

"Jack's gods," Thurrel said. "Look. I am at the limit of my knowledge, here. I would take this mantle from you if I could, but I have no particular wish to hack you to death and still less for you to do it to me. As, I will freely admit, seems the more likely outcome. Take these things, and go to where they're holding Maric Jack. He, at least, knows gods."

After she'd explained all that to Jack – *sotto voce* so the provosts didn't hear – the Maric sat back and rubbed at his chin.

"Why peace offering, though?" he asked.

"Thurrel said," she explained, "that this Fisher King and your God weren't exactly pals. You know, war and raiding versus peace and healing."

"Shows how much Thurrel knows about God," Jack said. "They've been sharing a box for months." He cocked his head, listening, and Banders shivered. And sure, she'd known Jack was of the priest persuasion, but that was when it was just a stupid foreign thing. Now it was a part of *her* world which made it ten times creepier. "Says they've got more in common than anything else now. Now they're both forgotten."

"You can keep the box anyways," Banders said generously. "Listen, I want shot of this. It was a dare. I was thirteen. Thurrel wants in. He's read books. He knows stuff. He'll probably start a cult or something. Or maybe he just wants to be extra-good at fishing. I don't really care. Jack, I never wanted to be special."

"Ah well," he said. "I hear that. Banders, they are going to kill me. They are going to kill every last one of us. You understand that, right?"

She wouldn't look him in the eye. "Sorry."

"What I'm trying to say is, leave it with me. If I can work something out I'll try to get it to you. Do me good to have something to put my mind to." He shrugged, and then retreated, cradling the box.

Leaving Cosserby, and somehow she hadn't quite joined the dots of him being there. "Wait," she said. "Are they going to... to you too?"

"It looks that way, yes," Cosserby said.

"But why?"

"On account of my having been a bit, you know, shot. Before. Only Lidlet..." He wrinkled his nose at the filthy religiosity of it, "... fixed me. And I can't... I took Jack's bargain. To live." Sounding desperately apologetic that he wasn't a corpse three battlefields ago.

Banders stared at him. "You stupid son of a bitch," she said, punched him hard in the arm, hugged him fiercely and then ran away.

Disconnective Tissue

When the High Fane fell, almost thirty years before, it had burned, and Tallifer – gone by then – had never known if that was a final act of devotion by the priests or desecration by the conquerors. She had been just one more priestess, no great matriarch of the faith. There had been other temples, though each had been rubble and ashes before she reached it. At the time it had been a tragedy, but she hadn't understood that it had really been the end. Of her career, of her faith, of her life as she'd known it. Everything else – the years of roving resistance alongside Lochiver, the capture, the hospital, had all been epilogue.

Landwards and Forthright Battalions were on the move. The Loruthi had fallen back to their side of Magnelei, and now it was the Pals' turn to try and winkle them out. All around Tallifer were the many pieces of half a war, being carried around like eggs by ants. Out there across the churned country was the other half, already assembled and awaiting the interlocking teeth of the Palleseen side before the whole meat grinder could start turning again.

If she'd had a glass she could have just made out Magnelei on the western horizon. The citizens of Bracinta's capital had been treated to a fine old show so far. If she'd been amongst them she'd have a bag packed and some distant relatives picked out to stay with, though. Thus far Loruthi and Palleseen forces had proved relatively even matched, and had wanted to maintain the mobility of a field army. Sooner or later one or other side would get enough of a bloody nose that the walls of Magnelei would look inviting as a defensive position. Which would go very badly for everyone, she suspected. The city wouldn't survive a siege, the occupying army would force the locals to decide whose side they were on. The army left outside would have no happy options left as to how to prosecute the war.

Just one more thing she didn't want to see, but then the world was full of those right now.

She'd been to see Jack. Not to speak with him, because that wasn't a practical proposition right now. He was marching too, of course. No hospital wagon for Jack, Lidlet or Cosserby, or their fellows. Instead they were in the heart of the army, tramping on foot in a long column like regular infantry. Except roped together, neck to neck, little enough play between them that it was sore throats for a dozen every time one person stumbled. More than that, they had Jack at the head of the column, and someone had dolled up his uniform with fake officer's insignia, making him an ersatz Sage-Prisoner. Around his neck was a sign, and it read 'Incorrect Speech' in clear Pel letters. Which was a single word in that language because 'Incorrect' – contrary to perfection – was the first prefix they'd dreamed up when constructing the script.

The provosts had made sure that Jack's column marched slightly faster than the rest of the battalion, so that they passed forwards through the army. So that everyone had a chance to jeer and throw the odd stone and see just what subversion bought you in today's market. Anyone who knew that Jack was a healer, and his crime was not letting Pal soldiers die, probably jeered and threw all the more because the Correct Speech crowd were flexing their muscles these days and nobody wanted to be found suspect.

And where does that leave us, exactly? Jack's old departmental friends, already bowed under their own burdens of suspicion. Just one more reason that life was about to get very interesting.

When the column of subversives reached the vanguard of the army, they were slowed to three-quarters pace, enforced by the truncheons of the provosts, and the army then got to march past them. Cue the jeers and clods of mud all over again. And repeat, for the whole day's march. A piece of theatre designed to dissuade any watcher from wanting a career in subversion.

Tallifer hadn't jeered or thrown anything. She reckoned the ship of suspicion had already sailed in her case. She hadn't met anyone's gaze, either. No sense in giving people hope.

There had been other familiar faces, on her venture up and down the line. In an officer's carriage she'd seen some of the young ambitious ones. Not her own immediate superior, whom she'd expect to find there, but Maserley, with his demon chit keeping Prassel's seat warm. Seeming very pleased with himself, and certainly he'd jeered when they'd passed the prisoner's line. Jeered and made fun with his Fellows, as they'd rolled down the toiling column. Next to him the Decanter, Thurrel, had his nose in a book and barely looked up. He looked like someone swotting for an exam. Beside them was the aloof-looking young man who commanded Alv's new students, Callow. Tallifer had heard all about him from the Divinati woman. He was the most junior Fellow in the coach, but he acted like he had a Sage's insignia in his pocket. When he didn't laugh at Maserley's jokes it wasn't because he thought they were bad, it was because he thought the demonist was yesterday's man already. Tomorrow belonged to whatever the hell they would call Callow's new discipline. Whatever you got when you took sympathetic healing and turned it into murder.

Behind them had been a rather grander carriage for some of Higher Orders. An empty seat still ceremonially held for the late Sage-Monitor Runkel. The fate of Forthright was now in the hands of Professor-Invigilator Scaffesty.

Professor-Invigilator Scaffesty had capable hands. They were also covered with blood and worse things. He was the man with the necromancy department, after all. He was the man who'd assigned Callow and company to Alv. Uncle had been old school. Old Eyeball was an innovator. Which, in war, could be a terrible thing.

Later, Tallifer spotted Prassel. The Fellow-Inquirer had been a rare sight in the hospital department recently, turning up only to give the occasional order. She was riding with the necromancers from Landwards Battalion now, in her newly decorated uniform. Next to the old man in the fancy bathrobe who seemed to be in charge. Beside them, racks and racks of copper vessels clinked and rattled. Some of the people sitting in the wagon seemed to be corpses, sitting up and taking part in the conversation. And Tallifer *had* met Prassel's gaze as their wagon rattled past. The woman hadn't seemed happy, but she'd chosen where she was sitting.

Exit strategy, Tallifer decided. It felt as though the experimental field hospital was finally reaching the end of its long test period. A decade and a half, since it had first been formed, which was three years before she and Lochiver had been co-opted into it. The Butcher was the sole denizen who'd been there from the start. Prassel was a latecomer, not quite five years in charge. And it was looking like she'd soon be pronouncing last rites and then bury the business at midnight.

Not worth asking what would happen to them, if the department was dissolved. Nobody in Higher Orders would be giving out prizes and medals for all the lives they'd saved. Oh, the regular surgeons would have somewhere found for them. She didn't know about the Butcher. He was Pal, after all. Which arm of the scales was weighted heaviest, nationality or notoriety? But nobody would have a use for a couple of aged priests of deadbeat gods, who'd once been fierce fighters against the Palleseen Sway.

Oh so fierce. She didn't feel fierce. A good eight or nine years on the wrong side of fierce, in all honesty. Fierce didn't have a bad back and a painful hip.

At last she met the hospital's own wagon, towards the

back end of the column. Lochiver reached down to haul her up, which nearly dislocated both of their shoulders until the Butcher helped out. She sat down there, huddled in the bags of her uniform, feeling the screw of tension slowly turn within her. Turn only one way, twisting her insides into a tight spiral until she wanted to throw up.

Lochiver squeezed her hand and she nodded at him. Across from her, massive knee to knee, the Butcher met her gaze. They had an understanding. They could smell the change on the wind, even over Lochiver's sour reek, and they knew how things were going to go.

Alv should have been old guard, too, but whatever had happened during the last battle had destroyed her. They hadn't made her part of their counsels. She just sat hunched in one corner, between boxes and crates, head low and staring at nothing. Barely responding if you called her name. Tallifer had never seen her like it. Ten years of imperturbable grace just shattered like a mirror under a hammer. *You have to heal*, the Butcher told her. *Or they'll do you like they did Erinael.* And she'd not even looked at him. Which was a shame because probably she'd have been useful, but Alv right now was good for nothing. Tallifer could only hope she'd jump the right way when the moment came, or jump at all.

Which left Masty and Banders. And she'd have expected Banders to be up and down the column, dealing and chatting and breaking minor military ordinances. Except here she was, looking like she had an incurable disease. Looking like she'd been punched in the gut and couldn't get her breath back. Like her name was sitting on an arrest warrant in an Inquirer's pocket. Someone had taken a razor and slit the throat of Banders's bonhomie, sure enough, but she wasn't talking about it. And beside her, Masty was always the quiet one, but since Magnelei he'd withdrawn into himself completely. Tallifer looked at them and saw the candles at the High Fane in her head. A trick of the place. For the high holy services, the priests had brought out a score or so of yellow candles, squat ones and tall ones, all different. Yet during the final closing words of the recital, each one of them would gutter and wink out within the same few minutes. Magic. Miracles. Divine providence.

Or carefully made candles. But why spoil the mystery?

She reached in her pocket. Mazdek, Chastiser of the Unclean, nibbled at her fingers. It was like being bitten by a cup of hot water. Beside her, Lochiver the Unclean clutched her other hand.

She let herself lean into him, hoping she'd dream of the times they'd had on the run. The mad days, when they'd had the strength. Perhaps some of it would linger once she woke.

Hell – Crossing the River

The one lesson not taught in the Palleseen phalansteries, not acknowledged by their Commission of Ends and Means. That all things end.

Still just within sight of Magnelei, the Loruthi have turned and dug in again. Taking advantage of earthworks and defences they probably hadn't thought they'd be returning to. Taking up new troops force-marched from their holdings further south. Just taking a stand. Who knows? All anyone at the sharp end of the Palleseen battalions knows is that the enemy have stopped running and won't just concede the capital. Which means that the appropriate parts of the camp have stopped and thrown up their tents and engines, while the regular troopers sort into their companies and squads and sally out as quickly as possible before the enemy artillery can get into its stride.

Prassel can spare a moment from torturing ghosts to look in on the department she's still nominally in charge of. Short-handed, obviously. The camp staff have even set up Cosserby's workshop and now it stands untenanted, the Sonori stilled and silent. They'd have been useful to push the fight to the enemy, but Forthright will just have to manage with whatever demons Maserley can call up. Infernal flesh can soak up baton-shot as well as metal.

She looks in on the Butcher. He has his cauldrons heating. His boy sets up his racks of unguents, salves and potions.

"Chief," she addresses him, aware that he's not happy with her but when is he ever? The words, "How's the back?" come into her mouth but they taste like bile and she can't say them.

"Magister," Ollery acknowledges. Beyond him they have the tables set and the cutlery laid. Tallifer clicking down each size of scalpel as though she has any control over which order the courses will be served in. Alv is kneeling by a Fellow-Broker who tripped over a guy rope and sprained her ankle, and doesn't want to have to do her important paperwork with a limp. Lochiver runs a cleaning rag through his pipe, although the rag is surely filthier than the innards of the instrument can be.

Beyond them, they have only Banders and Masty and the boy to fetch and carry, but all three are hardened veterans. Prassel watches the kid skitter back and forth with absolute absorption. She's seen children play games like that and maybe that's all this is to him. He's seen more blood and agony and death by age eleven than most people in their whole lives. The edges must have worn off. He'll grow up to be a hero or maniac, surely.

She wants very badly to say something to all of them. Because it's all coming to an end, and they must know that. Or her involvement, anyway. Stiverton's operation has a hungry pull to it. She can either say no outright, or let herself consent to all of its horrors, but she can't just hold her position at the edge of his influence. It takes too much effort.

In the end she's just not good with people, and maybe that's why she became a necromancer. She nods at them. *Jolly good, carry on.* Steps out into the open, hearing the first distant knock that is the Loruthi engines starting to complicate matters for the advance.

In the hospital tent, Ollery looks to Tallifer, Tallifer looks to Lochiver. He tries to include Alv in their conspiracy but the Divinati sits, staring into nothing, massaging her sprained ankle with absent hands. Alv is fighting her own battles right now. She'll either be with them or she won't, when the moment comes. Until then she won't even realise there's going to be a moment.

Prassel crosses through the camp, dodging the frenetic activity of all the noncombatants bracing to absorb the shock of a battle. Maserley has indeed signed up a new consignment of infernal infantry, and she sees the host of scaled, spiked monsters herding through and trampling the smaller tents, now on two legs, now on four. He sees her and gives her a mocking little wave. Just a reminder that he scored a point against her, a touch that she couldn't parry away. And now her department is down several souls and she has no ready way of retaking the offensive against him. A contest between them in which only he is invested, because Prassel would be more than happy if Maserley went away and she never had to see him again.

She drops into Thurrel's tent briefly. One of the few people she does actually have time for. But Thurrel isn't in his usual ebullient mood. Something's eating him. He's no consolation right now. Which only leaves her people, her new people. Those who deal in death, in a more literal way even than the regular army.

"I was beginning to think you weren't joining us," says Sage-Archivist Stiverton. "Your engines await."

"Thank you, magister." Prassel unslings a bandolier with a handful of coppers. "I have some materiel here, but until the hospital has begun work I can't—"

"We don't really have time for that," Stiverton says. "Higher Orders requests an immediate and sustained bombardment to disrupt the enemy back lines and artillery. Massed possession. We're going to fire Festle and his squad over first, to give the spear a nicely directed tip, but after that it's just dipping into the reserves, I'm afraid." He's not afraid. He's practically salivating. "I note that, last time round, you proved rather reluctant to commit them. Which feels like a bit of a wasted effort, given the trouble we went to. A bit like laying out a feast and then watching it all go cold, don't you think?"

Beyond him are the aforementioned reserves. Ranks of kneeling Whitebellies waiting to be emptied out and distilled into ammunition. Maddened ghosts that will arc like lighting through the Loruthi when their cannisters break open, or follow the stronger will of loyalist spectres like Festle towards high profile targets. They don't understand what's going on, of course, except it's plainly not good.

"Just consider," Stiverton says, reading something in her face she didn't know was there, "it's not really all that different to sending regular soldiers out to get shot, now, is it?"

Except she's run a hospital department for several years so she knows it absolutely is. That getting shot is something that you can come back from, if you're lucky. Having your life drained into a copper flask and thrown at the enemy for a moment's diversion is not.

Suffice to say, when she was studying at the phal, it's not what she thought she'd end up doing with her own life, either. But.

Prassel nods. "Indeed, magister," she says crisply.

The artillery sounds, rattling the ghost-throwers, telling the necromancy department they're falling behind schedule.

In the hospital the first casualties are coming in. The unlucky, too close to a ranging shot by the enemy engines, tripped up by the broken ground. Stood on a snake in one case, snake still attached. The lucky, in that they get a nice clear hospital tent to themselves. No need to queue like they're at the mess tent on a busy lunch shift. No need for even minor injuries to go untreated. No lying about screaming at this end of the day. A quick, efficient service for all.

Ollery goes down the line and assigns: surgery, surgery, drugs, bandage, malingerer. Second nature by now. He's been doing this a decade and a half. His boy is back in the tent, following specific instructions, or Ollery hopes he is. Packing the biggest bag he can carry with all the things they can't do without. *Remember the waterproofs*, the Butcher thinks. *Remember the warm clothing. Spare socks. Paper.* He'd drummed the list into the boy but the kid probably wasn't listening, like always. No time now to stand over him and make sure it all gets done properly.

Then the stretcher bearers are descending like crows and they've got worse cases. The Loruthi are deploying something new. It lobs big metal balls that shatter into the sort of scythe that could reap a whole cornfield in the blink of an eye. The soldiers coming in, the squad who got to test this novel way of getting mauled, they're cut up like sharks have been at them. Half are already dead by the time they reach the tent, and that, at least, makes it easy for Ollery to deal with them. Anyone still alive gets a dose of his best numbing draft, forced down the throat and spilled on the wounds. And he's left looking at bodies with great gaping lacerations, choirs of bloody mouths.

"Better get to stitching then," he says aloud. He picks the three who got cut up least. "Masty—"

"On it, Chief." Needle already in hand.

"Tallifer—"

"I'll take this one, Chief." It's Alv, and Alv isn't taking this one. Not unless she wants to absent herself from the fight almost immediately. The Butcher opens his mouth to send her away and sees something in her face. Some terrible thing, self-destructive and new. Alv is perfectly placid, of course. Her usual bland mask of capability firmly in place. Her eyes are tempests.

He mouths *No*, but she tells the bearers to bring the dying man to her and lays her hands upon him. Upon the terrible rents in his uniform, wrist-deep in the blood. Ollery has lost that battle already. He turns to one he can win, deciding on the soldiers he can't save, the ones that Tallifer can repair.

Passing them to the old woman, he meets her gaze. She nods.

"This one, and this one," the Butcher tells her, parcelling out the meat. "And then you go collect what we need, right?"

"Yes, Chief." And Lochiver's piping echoes her words like an annoying songbird.

By now Banders has worked out that something isn't right in the way things are working. Not like the department doesn't have a rhythm to it she's grown very used to, after all. Mostly by finding ways of ducking out of it, but you still need to know the rules before you can break them. She catches Masty's eye, as he moves from one of the lesser casualties to the next. He nods. He's felt the same, and he's been here a sight longer than she has. She wants to beard the Butcher and demand to know what's up, but he won't stay still long enough. He's actively avoiding her.

"I can go, Chief," she says. "Whatever it is doesn't need Tally, surely." He affects to ignore her until she tugs on his apron strings. "Chief—"

"Got a job for you, Banders." Ponderous, brisk, falsely cheery. A butcher about to sell her a very dubious cut. "Quartermasters. I need four new crates of mid-grade adduction catalyst. No idea where ours have got to. Someone's been dipping their hand into stores."

Banders stares at him. She knows exactly where theirs are. She could point to them right now. And there probably aren't four whole crates in the entire camp. A fool's errand that will take her away from the hospital for half the battle just when they need all the hands they can get.

"Masty, you'd better go with her," Ollery says. "Four crates is a lot to carry."

"I'm good, Chief," Masty says from his stitching.

"Accessory Masty, accompany Former Cohort-Broker Banders," Chief Accessory Ollery orders. Masty looks up, surprised, betrayed.

"Yeah, you come with me, your highness," Banders says, flicking his ear just to really annoy him. When they're out of the tent she grabs Masty by the arms and says. "I don't know what the fuck's going on but something is. We are disobeying orders, right? We are following Tallifer because something is *up*."

And Masty, the obedient, the dutiful, the man who wouldn't be king, can only nod.

In the tent, Alv is at Ollery's elbow again. "I'll take her," she says, pointing to the next worse living victim of the artillery. A woman with no legs, just stumps that are more than half tourniquet. Weeping, clawing at herself against the pain despite the Butcher's finest.

"She's gone," Ollery says harshly. "You can't…"

Alv is not a mess of gaping wounds. She's already shed them into that abyss where all her injuries go, in time. Except 'in time' has changed its meaning since the Butcher last looked.

"She's mine," Alv says, and takes responsibility for the woman with no legs. And gives her legs.

Jack listens to the sound of a war in the next room. His fingers twitch for the needle and the bandage, despite himself. This was never his war. He should take some consolation that he's been removed from it, even for later execution.

Lidlet and the others have tried to ask him about God. They were probably envisaging one of those scenes where the serene teacher sits with everyone around him cross-legged. Where wisdom is dispensed, about the necessity of suffering and how it's all going to work out. Jack telling them that God's a mean bastard most of the time didn't go down well. A bit earthy for their tastes. Jack saying that, actually, God didn't much approve of them writing it all down and nailing Him to the page. And then saying, after divine correction, that while it wasn't God's preferred model, right now the old sod was desperate enough He'd take what was going. Only could they not use a better grade of paper because this onion-skin stuff the Pal army uses was hardly respectful. And Lidlet saying that, sorry, that was what they had, and getting the things printed on the sly had been difficult enough, and could Jack relay that to God?

"Tell Him yourself," Jack says. And then, to God, "Look, do you want to just go over to her and be with her for a bit. She needs You more than I do."

"Oh, you're so damn self-sufficient, now?" God demands.

"I mean, I think You and I, we've gone about as far together as we're going to."

"Want a divorce, do you? So you can go live in sin with that demon whore?" God demands and Jack just breaks down. Because he does, actually. He really would like to live with Caeleen, in sin or out of it, and probably there's a system of morality out there that would smile on him, if he could only find it. And Caeleen, despite Jack's grand oaths, belongs to Maserley. And Jack's going to die.

Fear not, comes a tiny, buzzy voice. *For we have found the papers decreeing your death. We have changed the names on each of them to Professor-Invigilator Scaffesty in every case. He has signed his own death warrant.* And it's a nice thought, and it's just about the only hellraising that this minute mote of a chaos god can manage. The divine scorpionfly, reduced to the size of an actual scorpionfly. And Jack has to explain that even the Pal army isn't as procedural as that, and Scaffesty and his people can sign papers faster than Zenotheus can alter them. But thank you, anyway. And an idea hits him, and he laughs through the tears. It's only a shame he won't have time to put it into action.

At the back of the tent, Cosserby has his head bent over a tatty sheet of rather better paper, scratching with a pencil stub. Jack assumes he's writing a farewell note to Banders, maybe even a poem or something, but actually it's calculations. A train of logic written out in the symbols of his trade. On his knees is a copy of *The Ninety-Seven Loopholes of God* and he leafs back and forth through it, checking his workings against what Lidlet set down there.

Lidlet puts an arm about Jack's shoulders, because tears are running down his face and she doesn't know why. Simultaneously a stab of hot pain sears his throat and he yelps and draws away, incorrectly attributing it to her.

The rope about his neck, the one linking all of them together, that the provosts didn't bother to remove. It's burning through. As though a hot ember had been placed there. They all watch it happen, the fibres just crisping away, each one parting and the ends shrivelling away. Until Jack can take the collar off, the skin below red where it rubbed. Then it's Lidlet crying out because the same is happening to hers. A tiny leaping flame that dances from one to the other, eating the hemp until they're all freed.

Only Jack sees the salamander shape of Mazdek. Its toothless maw gumming determinedly at each halter, singeing and scorching. Just as Zenotheus's capacity for chaos is reduced to abject forgery, Mazdek the Chastising Flame is reduced to this minuscule vandalism. A god whose last priestess has just enough military authority to offer up the bonds in sacrifice.

Even Cosserby has stopped now, staring. The ground around them is strewn with worm-segments of charred rope. They're all free, save that not one of them could rush the provosts outside without enacting their own personal executions. They are the perfect prisoners, really. They can't even push someone out of the way with undue force.

A bright point appears at the back of the tent. A winking, glittering thing like a firefly. It moves in a slow arc and leaves a black line of ash behind it. A line that opens up. A charred slit in the tent following the line of Tallifer's finger and the creeping trail of Mazdek. The old woman's face, thus revealed, has a curious majesty to it. The Priestess of the High Fane again, just this once. The chosen of Mazdek, for the simple reason that Mazdek has nobody else.

"Jack," she says. "We're getting out of here. I advise you to come too, all of you."

★

In the hospital, Alv is going mad. It's a quiet kind of mad, but very determined. She had no legs a moment ago. Now they're back. Her regular, normal legs, impossibly still attached to her torso, walking her over to the Butcher so she can demand another victim.

"That one," she says, pointing to a man whose been pierced through with baton-shot. Head, ribs, guts. At least three different deaths of varying vintages there, and the Butcher's only other option would be to decide which one finished him. Except here's Alv, the unnervingly immaculate, pointing that finger she shouldn't still have. And the dreadful thing is still in her face, like a parasitic worm moving beneath the skin. She is sick with it, and yet it's keeping its host impossibly healthy.

"Take him," the Butcher says. It's going to be one of those days anyway. Nothing's working as it should, and there isn't any relief from the screaming because the usual incessant piping isn't there any more. Lochiver's playing with his jars instead.

Alv doesn't even take the man anywhere, just drops to the knees she should be missing and sucks the shot-wounds out of him. Leaves a whole, conscious soldier staggering to his feet, wide-eyed, as she pitches back. The baton wounds in Alv's body writhe, spiral inwards like whirlpools, vanish into her intact flesh as though burrowing. She stands, and the Butcher feels she's vibrating like a plucked string with a great circling flock of unassigned wounds like crows.

The boy is at his elbow, bags packed. It's time.

He nods. From the back of the tent comes the sound of breaking glass.

"Everybody out!" Lochiver shrieks. "That's pure plague! Oh the horrors! It'll spread! I can't hold it back!" Hamming for all he's worth, the shameless old exhibitionist.

And the evacuation. Bearers and surgeons and any random fool who happened to be passing, suddenly drafted into getting the wounded to the next hospital tent along, assigning the regular surgeons there. Taking his own bag that the boy prepared and hoping the kid remembered everything.

"Alv," he says. He doesn't know what to do with her, because she's not the woman he thought he'd be dealing with. But Alv is smiling. Or she's grimacing. There are tears in her eyes and the shadow over her is gone. Pel doesn't even have a word for the expression that's on her face.

An end to everything, he thinks.

Fellow-Archivist Callow is returning from Higher Orders, having been given his brief. A precisely calibrated set of instructions for his precisely calibrated discipline. Right now, the Divinati sympathetic magic is a scalpel. His squad won't be scything down any battlefield formations or breaking enemy positions. But he can kill officers. He can kill anyone that he can get eyeline on through a glass. Just give him a sufficiently serious wound to throw. Or a living body and a knife, and he'll make his own. Or just a knife and his own flesh, if you want to get really primitive about it.

So long as Callow and his fellows can put on a good show, then this discipline has the potential to become the spiky studs on the Palleseen iron fist. Not only battlefield tactics but wider Pallesand policy could shift to take advantage of the unique capacity the Divinati have given them. Albeit unwillingly, but that's not Callow's problem, that's Alv's. Probably she's weeping into her precious balance right about now.

He enters his tent, drawing breath to rouse his followers, all those bright young things out of the phal who dance to his tune.

And stops.

The breath goes out of him in a funny little wheeze, like a deflating bladder.

Something has come through the tent and massacred them.

And there are only ten people there, not a quantity to which Callow's education would usually ascribe the word 'massacre' but it seems the only appropriate term. They have been carved up. Butchered, really. Or not even that, because a butcher has a craft, like any artisan. Callow's people have been served like someone came in with a four-foot cleaver and just hacked them about. As though there could be a giant with an axe loose in camp and nobody the wiser. Limbs are off, bodies are unseamed, faces bisected. There is a shocking amount of blood.

Outside is a whole camp of soldiers and support staff and *nobody* apparently noticed all this going on.

In the far back corner of the tent, one survivor. A man, his limbs folded about himself like an injured spider, covering his face, shaking, utterly ruined by whatever happened here.

"Report!" Callow snaps. "Skilby! Report, for reason's sake!"

Skilby takes his hands away from his face and stares at Callow with wide, haunted eyes. His eyes open. Then his head opens, the crater of a baton-shot flowering there like a malign fungus. Another blooms silently in his chest and then a third from his gut. He spits out a long trail of blood and saliva and greasy grey matter and falls sideways.

Callow felt it as it happened. He understands instantly what's going on. What he feels is the keenest of all betrayals, that inflicted on the betrayer.

Then he's gone from the tent, running as though he can outpace the next battery of wounds.

They are challenged, of course. It's not like any unattended column of mixed regulars and Whitebellies moving through the camp wouldn't attract some attention. Provosts and officers want to know whose command they are. Tallifer waves the credentials of the field hospital for as long as it does any good, but these people were marched back and forth along the column and a lot of people got a look at their faces. Sooner or later someone isn't fooled. Sooner, in fact. A squad of provosts, always prowling the camp during a battle to root out deserters. They face down Tallifer and understand immediately that there's something amiss. They're moving in, batons ready, and perhaps a couple of them even know the details of the case. *The soldiers who won't fight.* Which, to a certain mindset, breeds a courage that might otherwise be lacking.

"On your knees, all of you," the lead provost orders. "You too, you old hag." No way to speak to the Priestess of the High Fane but he has a baton and she does not.

Tallifer tilts her head back. Perhaps she's about to immolate the whole lot of them, incendiary sacrifices to her god. Her god is currently glowing exhaustedly in Jack's new box because it ate a few ropes and some tent. No immolations occur.

Instead the lead provost turns a peculiar cheese sort of colour. His eyes bulge, and he doubles over and vomits on his own boots. Moments later he's on the ground writhing as his guts cramp like he had a big plate of scorpions just a minute ago. His squad are dropping all around, hacking, coughing, glistening with fevers so Jack can almost feel the heat off them.

"Go," Tallifer says, and they push on through the camp, with Lochiver capering out on spindly legs to join them, cackling like a madman.

"Where?" Jack demands. "What's the plan here, Tallifer?"

"Out," she says simply. "It's over. Out is all."

The next officer who tries to stop them is blistering with pustules and pox before he can get half an order out, and everyone nearby is far too busy making distance to stop the fugitives. But they're still in the heart of the camp. There's a long way to go, and Lochiver is looking tired. More, Sturge is looking tired. The Lord of the Unclean Sacristy has only a little well of filthy miracles to draw on. Even for his single follower, there's only so much a plague god can do.

It's about this point that Cosserby absents himself. Jack sees the man go and can't blame him. Cosserby, a lone Pal in a dark uniform, will do better on his own. It's not as though he asked to be part of it, although really none of them did.

Around that time another pair of bodies gets in the way, and Tallifer is about to see if Mazdek is ready to really cut loose when she recognises them. Banders and Masty, who have tailed her all the way from the tent. The forever-demoted Pal and the Rightful King of Bracinta, who really have no business trying to stop her.

"What the hell's going on?" Banders demanded. Her eyes flick to Jack. "You're running?"

"We're running," Tallifer confirms, and just moves on, forcing the pair of them to scramble to keep up, because she's had it with just standing back and watching things go sour.

"Without us?" Banders demands. "You sent us off, and, what, you'd just not be there, when we got back?"

"That was the plan," Tallifer confirms.

"Why?" Banders demands.

"Because they will hunt us, and probably catch and kill us, and we didn't want to make you part of it," the old woman said firmly. "In fact unless you get the hell out of the way we may not even get clear of the camp. Go away, Banders. You too, Masty. There's no reason you need to be dragged down with us. Go live your lives and good luck with the army."

But Banders has recently been given a very good lesson on why the army may not be good luck for her, just the moment it discovers just what Incorrectness she's had foisted on her. She's damned if she's being left behind by any escape attempt. And Masty just goes along with them, as he always does. Another person whose fixed place in the firmament has taken a severe knock.

★

Alv feels him draw near. Her best student, the one who absolutely understood the lesson. She had been about to choose one more of the almost-slain, to complete her work, but Callow is onto her now. He'd find some unwitting proxy for whatever she sent to him. This time it's personal.

The Butcher glances in surprise as she strides past him, but then she's been off her usual playbook since the battle started. Why should one more aberration alarm him? He just watches her go.

It's only a handful of steps, just two or three tents' worth, before she's facing him down. Callow, his face twisted by the fury of the outmanoeuvred. A short rod in one hand with a tableth socketed. The weapon's point directed at her.

"How could you," he spits out, "stand in the way of progress!"

He spits the command word and the weapon discharges. She sees the flash at the same time the shot impacts her skull. She's already stepping, grounding her back foot as though bracing against the shock of it. Hands palm out, signifying... something uniquely Divinati. Signifying balance, the fixed fulcrum of a wildly swinging universe.

Her head snaps back—

Callow's just about explodes. All that force, at that close range. The little rod springing from his hand, tableth jumping from its slot. And still, somehow—

Alv's face, torn open, the damage sent back where it came from, crammed into her with Pal righteousness, the people who bring perfection to the world. Oblivion, instant, but—

The Divinati never sought to export their perfection. Instead, they made themselves perfect. The still centre of everything. And while Callow – in those slivers of second – knows rage and then knows panic, Alv's unbroken face stares back at him and she gives him his wound again.

He can't field it a second time. Lacks the practise, lacks the response time, lacks the finger on the scales of the universe.

Knows a final instant of terror as he fumbles the catch, just like poor Hobbers did.

And falls, the most spectacular victim of self-inflicted wounds the battle will see. Alv stands there, silent, sad. Until the dozen or so camp staff and soldiers who witnessed this in broad daylight think to get weapons and start shooting her. And she just turns and walks away. She hears the crap and sizzle of the batons, and the cries, each shot returned to its donor like a gift unopened, so that the best marksmen amongst them shoot themselves dead and the worse just injure themselves, a leg, a hand, a shoulder. Perfect equilibrium.

Tallifer, arriving at the tail end of this, calls her name, but she's done with it all, the whole seething mess of it. Alv walks out of the war and there are no gods to help anyone who tries to stop her.

In his workshop, Cosserby finishes the last of his tablethi. No time for proper engraving so he's drawn his instructions on each with black ink, waving them in the air to dry them. It will do. It will do for long enough. He hopes.

And he doesn't die. He has beaten Lidlet's logic. He has instructed his Sonori with just the right nested chain of instructions to outfox Jack's God-given rules. He is, after all, the smart one.

He feels the invisible chains pull taut, as he set down his sigils on the metal. As though the god was peering over his shoulder and trying to make sense of it. To work out how Cosserby is cheating on the test. But like many bright students of the phalanstery, Cosserby knows that if you put twice as much effort into cheating than you would just doing the work the regular way, you can fool anybody.

He slots the final tableth into place and the Sonori jerk into motion, the metal parts of them ratting hollowly, leaving a faint musical resonance in the air.

"Off we go now," he says. They regard him. The instructions he's given them are very complex, long chains of conditions, ifs, ands and buts. Enough that a certain level of awareness will accrete about them. He remembers past times when they've asked him *Why*, when he wanted to send them into war. Just expendable war machines to get chewed up and pieced back together. This time he's asking them to defend his fellows, and there is no *Why* to them. When they march out of the tent it's almost joyously.

In the hospital tent it's just the Butcher and his boy. He laden with two packs and a sling bag, the kid stumbling beside him like a diminutive pack mule.

"We go," he says, and turns to find Prassel in the opening of the tent. Between him and escape.

Her face is absolutely blank for a moment, because she doesn't know what's going on. Then it's blank because she does. Sees it all at once, the moving pieces of his plan.

He bunches his fists. He's three times the weight of her. She'd be boned and jointed before she could get a knife into him, or the cut-down baton she has at her belt. Except the boy's there. And the boy's seen Ollery do a great many things to the human body, but not actually murder someone with his bare hands. Despite murdering people being the thing the Butcher is generally known for. A lot of people, the boy's grandparents included.

Prassel's lips move slightly. Orders, perhaps? An official reprimand. A plea, even. *There's another path. Don't throw it all away.* But Prassel always was a quick student. It's already past that point.

She says nothing. She steps back and vanishes into the camp.

He and the boy join Tallifer's contingent soon after. There is shouting from the way they've come, deeper within the camp where they've left a trail of sick men.

"Go," Tallifer shouts, and gives up all pretence of looking like she's supposed to be there. Running arthritically, stumbling almost immediately, Lidlet catching her arm and helping her forwards. Lochiver is shouting, words that sicken the ears, prayers to Sturge, curses upon his enemies. When he puts his pipe to his lips she wants to snag his arm, to drag him along. He's in full religious ecstasy, though, ten years of pent-up rebel priest. Ten years of plaguebringer forced to keep wounds clean, his god fooled into undoing its own purpose. She sees a full dozen provosts, coming for them at a run, just go down at once, voiding their bowels at both ends with explosive force. It would be funny if it absolutely wasn't.

The flute shrills, screams, makes sounds that shiver the marrow in the bones of each listener, so that Jack and the other former prisoners are scrabbling away from Lochiver every bit as much as the camp guards.

He is, of course, making himself a target.

The shot that takes him could have come from anywhere. It's not even alone. Jack and the woman next to him go down in the same volley. But Jack and the woman are on their feet in the next instant, because that's how Jack and his own god work. Lochiver stays down. Jack can't heal him. Another god's hand is on his brow, the festering crown of the Unclean Sacristy. He's spoken for.

Tallifer cries out, then Lidlet is reeling away from her with a burned palm. Jack's cultists flee past her on both sides, and baton-shot whines through the air like blazing insects.

"Tally, no!" the Butcher's bass roar. She only has eyes for the broken old body left in their wake, the pipe spun from slack fingers.

She will burn them all. No matter her god has barely enough in it to light a candle. She will make a bonfire of herself, throw her last years onto it like kindling. She will burn bright and brief and fierce, as she should have done all those years ago. It was only Lochiver who stayed her, back when their career of mayhem was ended. For herself, she'd have lit her own funeral pyre right there and then. But he – disgusting, priest of her god's enemy – would have died too. And so she stayed her hand.

The Butcher grabs her, taking up where Lidlet left off. She hears his grunt as he finds her skin like a hot kettle, but he doesn't let go.

"I will hold them," she tells him. "You get everyone clear. How else are we going to...?"

The Sonori, marching out from the workshop, answer her before she can get the question out. Abruptly the world is full of the sound of bells. Baton-shot ricochets and rings from them. They make a wall of bronze between the fugitives and their pursuers, a solid rearguard that shrugs off the fire. Tallifer feels a fury that they've stolen her flame and thunder, but the Butcher is still dragging at her, and he has five times the mass and momentum.

"Not you too," he snarls. "Come on, you mad witch!"

She was a mad witch once, when she was younger. When she was one of a pair of priests fighting the Pals every way they could. But now she's just old and worn through, like clothes any sane person would throw away. Except here's this big Pal, refusing to do so.

Cosserby has rejoined them, actually grinning because he didn't see Lochiver fall. Terribly pleased with himself. And the edge of the camp is in sight. The picket sentries turning from their outward watch to call incredulous challenges. Levelling batons.

The Sonori break into a run. A thunderous charge on either side of the fugitives. Others stay back, and now their behaviour changes. Some balance point in their instructions has been met, and they engage. At the boundary of the camp they must hold the pursuers, so that the fugitives can get away. Cosserby's finest work.

They slam into the sentries, all that mechanical weight and strength. They round on the soldiers issuing from the camp behind, each metal blow sending their target flying back, broken bones and ruptured bodies. The Butcher hauls Tallifer past the sentry line, virtually hugging her to him. Baton-shot keens past like murderous fireflies.

Banders is crying for help. Banders has Cosserby in her arms. Jack and Masty both stumble to a halt and go back for her. Cosserby is down. He's shot. Or, rather, he was shot many days ago, in the great retreat. The same pierced lung, the same slow death that forced Lidlet into begging for him.

Around them, the Sonori are selling their metal bodies dearly and, to sweeten the deal, Cosserby has given back what he took from Jack's god. Banders shouts in Jack's face, demanding he help, but that ship has sailed. There is no ninety-eighth loophole. Cosserby is dying, caught on the wire of his own contingencies.

They haul him with them anyway. Armpits and heels and hoist away, even as the Sonori make their doomed last stand. They break for the nearest trees, and keep on running til evening. Long before then, Cosserby is dead.

Passing the Baton

There are no scholars of the Fisher King cult, not openly. Correct Speech was diligent enough that even the name was lost to history, save to a very few. The practices and rites, the regalia, the holy places, the priests, all consigned to the pyre of a murdered history. Only a handful of scraps survived by oversight, to be clandestinely gathered by collectors like Thurrel. A handful of scraps, a forgotten statue below an orphanage, and the god.

Masty had brought some tea. Everyone else took it as a sign of supernatural foresight in him, far more useful than curing scrofula or the other card tricks that kings were supposed to accomplish. In reality, just something he found at the bottom of the pack he'd grabbed on the way out. Not even good tea, but nobody turned it down once he had it simmering in one of the Butcher's smaller cauldrons. At which point, Thurrel found them.

They were deep in the trees, one of those scruffy stretches of forest left over from the patchwork way the Bracite farmers used their land. Creep out to the edge, as the more intrepid of them had, you could just about see the Palleseen camp. You could see Magnelei, too, and someone had claimed to be able to see the Loruthi as well. Yesterday's battle hadn't shifted the lines much.

Thurrel walking straight in after nightfall had scared a lot of people, because the whole point of hiding out in the trees had been so people like Thurrel wouldn't just *find* them without even breaking a sweat. Except this turned out to be some business with Jack and Banders, and apparently, for reasons Masty hadn't quite got his head around, Thurrel would have been able to find Banders if she'd put a dozen oceans and a mountain range between them. Not a romantic exaggeration, apparently. And Banders, usually so reliable for gossip, wasn't going into detail about it.

To Masty, that felt as though Thurrel was a bit of a liability, and he was surprised the man had come so cockily alone to them, given that. Except Masty himself wasn't exactly a man to wield the razor, and Thurrel had looked over Jack and Lidlet and the score of their fellow ex-prisoners and said, "I mean what are you going to do? Not like you're going to stave my head in because I know where you are."

Then the Butcher had loomed, as he did so well, and pointed out that neither he nor Tallifer were signatories to the whole *Ninety-Seven Loopholes* thing, and Thurrel had lost a big chunk of his cocky and become a deal more polite. Because the Butcher was big and solid and brooding, but Tallifer was grieving. Sparks danced at the ends of her hair and about her brow, and ran across her knuckles like mice. Masty had no idea whether she could turn Thurrel to ash, but neither did Thurrel.

After those lines were drawn, and Thurrel had wrinkled his nose at the tea, he waved a hand in front of Jack's face and said, "Well? Like the landlord, I've come to collect. As our pre-eminent god expert, have you found a means?"

Jack nodded slowly. "I'm working on it. I think so. Come morning, we'll see."

"I'm stuck here for the night, now, am I?" Thurrel complained. "Look, I'm sure the deserter's life under the canopy and the stars is terrible idyllic but some of us have work to do." He looked around, found scant sympathy. "I'll just tell them I was scavenging for spent magic, I suppose. It's what I usually say."

"While we've got you," Lidlet tried to make it seem like a threat, "why not tell us what's going on back at the camp?"

"Or you'll hold my feet to the fire?" Thurrel asked her mockingly. And then the fire itself made a determined lunge for him, sending him scrabbling back. "Fine, yes, I get the message. It's no grand secret anyway. We didn't shift the Loruthi; they didn't shift us. Thousands of tablethi-worth of warfare – and the lives, I suppose – all basically for the same result as if we'd not bothered. Other than that, rumour-mill says we've sent for reinforcements again, and the Loruthi have too. I know for a fact that we've sent people to Magnelei to try and explain to the Bracites how they really have to take sides now, and I imagine the Loruthi have done the same. But who'd want to be on *their* side when they could be a staunch ally of Pallesand, hm? I mean you'd think the decision would be a shoe-in. Two very distinct and different options for them. I mean the Loruthi have *beards* and we don't, obvious really." He shook his head and stared into the fire as though daring it to go for him again. "Anyway, you can rest assured that you've not been forgotten, and the moment we have the leisure then Old Eyeball will have half the army tracking you down. I'd just keep running, if I were you. Defect to the Loruthi, get to the coast and on a boat, turn into birds and fly away, if that's in your gift. Don't be anywhere near the army when this current contretemps blows over."

After that, there was some desultory attempt by Lidlet to get Jack talking, and Jack not wanting to. Jack patently being uncomfortable that all these people were on the run and in danger explicitly because of him. Rather than just being dead, Masty considered, but that comparator didn't seem to help.

Later still, Tallifer told them all a story of taking on the Pals in Jarokir. Of Lochiver. Her and the old man, except they'd neither of them been as old, back then. A trail of arson and epidemic across the old country. She told it as though it was myth from a thousand years ago. After which Banders wanted to say something about Cosserby, some great exploit, some heroic deed. And couldn't think of one. Because he hadn't been that kind of man. And she'd known he'd been holding a torch for her, and saying that now wouldn't help. She was just carrying the dead weight of Cosserby in her head and didn't know what to do with it.

Later still, when everyone had found what chill and lumpy rest there was to be had, Masty stayed awake and prodded the embers of the fire, and made plans.

In the morning, Jack had Thurrel and Banders stand in a space he'd found, where two trees leaned away from each other. Everyone else looked on curiously. There was some god thing going on, but nobody had got the details out of anyone involved. It was a fine time for Banders to learn how to be close-mouthed, but apparently the divine miracles weren't stopping any time soon.

"So it's like this," Jack said. "I know absolutely nothing about this Fisher King."

"Haven't you been carting him around all this time, though?" Thurrel asked. "I mean he was in your box." Which was a series of words Masty didn't really know what to do with.

"I found him on the streets of Ilmar, like a lot of other abandoned gods," Jack said, quite matter-of-factly. "I can only assume he was brought by one of the occupiers. One of *you*. Anyway, he was one of the gods I couldn't shift before they caught me. But it turns out Banders is consecrated to him, fine. And he's a, well… if you don't mind me saying, I don't get the impression you Pals were ever very nice, as a people. So he's a punchy little man, your old god. All about strength and fighting and pissing contests. So, in order for you to receive this mantle of whateverthehell from Banders, he wants you to fight her. I mean actually he wants you to kill her in single fair combat, preferably with an axe, cut her head off and smear her blood all over your face. That'd do it."

"I trust," said Thurrel, "that you have an alternative." He glanced at Banders a little nervously, because if one of them was ending up with blood daubed on their face, it probably wasn't him.

"Well he's very strict," Jack said mildly. "Insofar as I can get – this is all going through God, my god, who can get a little sense out of him. He's very strict, and remembers the old ways, and really insists on everything being done properly." And then, just as Thurrel was about to explode, he added, "But you're overlooking the big thing I learned about gods, having lived with one all my life."

"Which is bloody *what?*" Thurrel demanded.

"You don't really have to listen to them most of the time. They need us. I mean, we don't need them, really. I don't even know why you want this nonsense."

"Because I am a scholar, and it's the door to a whole age that people have tried to completely erase," Thurrel said, and for once he sounded sincere, and honest, and barely snide at all. "The last scraps of who we were, before we perfected ourselves. And I want to *know.*"

"Well, good," Jack said vaguely. "I don't think he cares for scholars much, but you do it how you like. Anyway, gods need people who listen to them. And they don't have the leverage in the relationship that they used to. I've been telling God 'no' for years. We argue. Old married couple, and both of us started seeing other people." He gave Lidlet a look that she didn't know what to do with. "So what I'm saying is, basically, sod his preferences."

Thurrel stared at him. "What?"

"Sod him. He wants the axes and the heads and the blood and such, sod him. He wants someone to listen to him and take him seriously, it's not going to be Banders, is it? So I reckon you just… beat her some other way. Spelling test, cups and ball, dice. Find some way you can say you triumphed over your rival, claim the title, get the god. Simple."

Thurrel stared at him levelling, and then abruptly stuck his fists out towards Banders. "Which is the stone in?" he asked.

"Seriously?" Banders demanded. "Blimey, I know we're stopping short of the whole ceremonial beheading thing but this seems rushed. Fine, that one." Jabbing out at random.

Thurrel revealed an empty hand. Given that he hadn't even made much of a pretence of palming a stone to begin with, nobody was overly surprised.

"I feel like asking for a best of three," Banders grumbled.

"You said you wanted to be rid of it," Thurrel pointed out. "So you could go back and not get shot by Correct Speech."

She shrugged. "Well maybe it was nice to be special, just for a moment. Jack?"

Jack had been deep in negotiation with the invisible. "I mean, he's not happy," he said.

Banders took out a little clasp knife and pricked her finger, streaking Thurrel's forehead with it. "There, O great and terrible conqueror, you have undone me."

And that, apparently, was that.

After Thurrel had taken off, and taken his new divine mandate and god with him presumably, everyone fell to talking about what happened next. And they were Pals, almost all of them. Pals who'd lived most of their adult lives in the army. None of them had much of an idea how things worked otherwise. Masty could sympathise. He'd been with the army longer than any of them. A lot of the talk circled around finding another battalion, infiltrating it with false papers. A parasitic life like a bug in an ant's nest, anything that wouldn't require them to fight.

"You're coming back, though, aren't you?" Banders asked him.

Masty frowned. "You are?"

"Masty, I just went through a very gruelling game of lefty-righty and cut my finger, specifically so I could go back and live my life like I have been doing."

"Only without the department," Masty pointed out.

"There are other departments." Banders was adaptable.

"I'm not going back, though," Masty said. Only in saying it did he understand that he'd committed himself to his plan. The stupid plan he really didn't want to do. "Banders… can you get them all to stop their yammering and gather round? I need to say something and they need to hear it. I've got a way out of this for them, that might get the army off their backs. And more than that."

He sat alone for a while, then, while Banders broke up the impromptu theology classes and conspiracy circles, gathered Jack and Tallifer and the Butcher, Lidlet and all the others. And Alv, who just walked out of the trees and took her place amongst them as though she hadn't just vanished earlier. All lined up, attentive as schoolchildren, waiting for the word.

He stood. Straight. He'd spent a long time slouching and being small, overlooked, part of the background. Survival traits for a foreign kid growing up in a Pal army. Now he needed to put such childish things behind him.

"Listen," he said, and told them.

Accepting the Honours

You had to make accommodations, if you wanted to get ahead in the army. You had to do distasteful things. Especially as a necromancer. Prassel was well aware that her entire discipline reeked of moral compromise. Ends that justified the means until you realised that you were so lost in the ghastly means that you couldn't see the end of it any more. You had to make sacrifices for your career. Everyone did. Just some people more literally than others.

It didn't hurt, having Maserley there to watch. But then he was technically head of a department, the senior demonist across two battalions. He was invited to all the best parties.

Professor-Invigilator Scaffesty, Old Eyeball to the soldiers of Landwards, was a silver-haired old man. He did indeed just have the one eyeball, with a leather patch moulded to the socket of the other to hide the gory details while making the absence quite plain. He had a very pale face that seemed to loom from the shadows of his dark uniform, even in good light. Like a predatory fish in deep water or a murderer in an alley. Not the most pleasant face, was Prassel's general opinion. Even when he was giving her a promotion.

"Following the tragic death in combat of Sage-Archivist Stiverton, I am confirming you as officer in command of the Experimental Necromancy department here at Landwards," Scaffesty said, ostensibly to her but really for the benefit of everyone else, since she was perfectly aware of what was going on. "As most here are aware, you are inheriting a bloody mess, frankly. What with how it all went. But I trust that you will rebuild and continue Stiverton's work."

"Yes, magister," Prassel said, and in the quiet of her head added, *Under no circumstances.* Because there were limits, and just because she was a student of death didn't mean she was game for the sort of squandering of resources that Stiverton had been about.

"Final confirmation will have to come from the Commission, but for now you're elevated to Acting-Sage-Inquirer. Next order of business. I'm sure there are plenty of people waiting to congratulate you."

They were in his command tent, big enough to hold everyone in Higher Orders. Every department and Company head. Hers had been the last in a series of repositionings and promotions. Mostly occasioned by battlefield losses, because the war wasn't getting any less bloody the longer it ground on.

She stepped towards the back of the tent, and then out entirely, letting the sounds of the camp wash over her like a shower. Her hands were shaking very slightly and she tugged at the cuffs of her gloves to steady them.

"The way I hear it, a promotion was the last thing that Stiverton was recommending you for," came Maserley's voice from behind her. Of course he'd followed her out.

She looked up, her face carefully immobile. "Really?"

"Your failure to make use of resources, wasn't it?" he jabbed. "Already looking around for your replacement. And suddenly he's dead."

"It's war," she said. "Most deaths are sudden." No part of her face that wasn't shuttered against him. "Did you actually have something to say, Maserley? Congratulations, perhaps? Don't worry, I'm sure someone will recognise your own potential one of these days. Have you tried summoning more monsters? I'm sure it'll help."

Because he was going to crack her, if he kept on questioning, but go on the offensive and he always rose to it. His face darkened, and doubtless he'd have some mean-spirited retaliation later, when he'd had a chance to think of something. Except she didn't even have the hospital for him to sabotage any more.

He stalked back inside, and she was about to just sit and clasp her hands together and fight against the shakes when another figure loomed over her. Loomed was the word: a good seven feet tall, with ashen skin and sunken, filmed-over eyes. A Loruthi face, twisted in death-agonies. A Pal uniform hastily stretched over it. She could see the bulge where a copper had been shoved into the splintered ribs. The vehicle that Festle had brought back from the most recent battle.

"Cohort-Monitor Festle," she addressed the corpse. "Reporting for duty, are we?"

"I know what you did." The voice slurred out of stiff lips.

Prassel felt a chill hand on her heart. But then, she was a necromancer. No new sensation there. "Well, it seems to be a day for accusations. What's yours?"

He spoke low, just for the two of them. "He sent to me, as he died. He could always reach me. He *made* me." And presumably there had been a living Cohort-Monitor Festle once, before Stiverton had got his hands on the man, but whatever was left now identified far more as a predatory spirit than a human being. "Two words, he said to me at the end. 'Betrayed', and your name." He pushed closer and the sigils across her uniform crackled and spat, forcing him back a step.

"I'm sure," said Prassel carefully, "that he would have gone on with, 'will be your new superior officer and you should do everything she says.' Such a shame he didn't get the chance to finish the sentence." And tried not to remember how it had been. A knife. Such a small thing. A knife to slit the belt of tablethi on Stiverton's ridiculous robe so that, when the overloading coppers had discharged, she'd just ripped the garment off him. Left the old man defenceless before a hydra of angry, displaced ghosts. Each of them seizing on his body and limbs, fighting for control, forcing their expressions onto his features, their mannerisms into his hands. Beyond any tolerance of bone and sinew. And yet it had taken him so long to die.

"Cohort-Monitor Festle," she said frankly, "I could unmake you in an eyeblink. That is not a threat, just a reminder that I'm a trained necromancer and you're just an unnaturally preserved set of spiritual tensions stuffed into a bottle." And, as he wrestled the face of his body into a scowl, "However. You should know that I will not simply be continuing the late Sage-Archivist's work. I do not see a future in ghosts as siege ammunition. Wasteful, impractical and, as Stiverton's death shows, eminently unsafe. What I do see a future in is *you*."

Festle stared at her.

"Volunteers, Festle. Post-mortem volunteers. A campaign after death. Something a soldier can sign up to in advance, given the difficulties of securing deathbed consent. A new way to serve the cause of perfection, and achieve promotion, preferment and probably some sort of pension for families. I'm still working on the logistics. You're proof of concept, Festle. You do good work. Because you want to. Not just because someone stuffed your screaming ghost into a copper and threw it at the enemy. And obviously, if we're expanding The Deathless, we'll need a rank structure, honours and credentials, as in life, so in death. How does Companion-Monitor sound to you? I have the authority."

"Are you trying to bribe me?" Festle's dead lips demanded.

"I'm trying to reward you," Prassel said. "I have a good track record with unorthodox tools, as the hospital project showed. Well? How do you fancy becoming the new great weapon of the Palleseen advance, rather than just a sideshow?"

And apparently his bond with Stiverton wasn't all that, because he made the head nod philosophically. And then there was a commotion from inside, and everyone who'd stepped away from the table was being called back.

★

A delegation had arrived. Nobody had quite seen the like before. Bracites from Magnelei, apparently. A dozen older men in skirts and open-fronted robes, all of thin and heavily ornamented fabrics. Five severe old women in complex, layered gowns that swept backwards like folded wings. Two score servants and attendants who were, thankfully, waiting outside the tent, or they'd have had to evict half of Higher Orders to fit them in. They had belts with jewelled buckles, and brightly coloured sashes decorated with linked chains of heraldic devices. Their leader was a big, bearded man with one arm.

Prassel took her place amongst the Sages, seeing Maserley, still back in the Fellows, shoot her a look of pure loathing. There was one ray of sunshine, anyway.

Scaffesty leaned forwards, chin resting on his knuckles. "Obviously we welcome our allies from Bracinta. Do I take it that you wish to join with us in removing the Loruthi yoke from your neck and freeing your nation from their malign influence?" Words said for form's sake, and not exactly dripping with hope.

The one-armed man bowed in a way that didn't seem particularly respectful. A murmur round the table suggested he was General Halseder, who'd been the chief military boy back before the coup and all the bloodshed.

What he actually said was all gibble-gabble to Prassel, because she didn't speak a word of Bracite. Thankfully one of the old women had textbook Pel, as polite and urbane as you please.

"The nation of Bracinta," she translated, "will be forever grateful for the assistance of our friends and allies from Palleseen in helping us through the troubled years since the Three Nights."

There had, Prassel recalled, been a lot of claimants to the throne, and a lot of spare royal scions kicking about Magnelei. It had taken three nights for assassins of various factions and loyalties to work their way through them.

Halseder spoke again, and the woman explained, "Since that time, we are also grateful that your advisors have been present to assist us in governing our country in the absence of the heir to the throne."

Scaffesty shifted, about to go through the rote of accepting all these plaudits, but Halseder wasn't done, shunting his foreign words in to make sure nobody else got a hand on the tiller.

"We bring you joyous news," the woman said. "The heir of the Hackle Throne has returned after all these years. Bracinta has a king once again."

Utter silence descended.

"The young prince, Feder, is finally grown into a man," the woman said, after letting the quiet creep in and make itself comfortable. "At last he is ready to take on his duties and obligations, and we welcome him. Tomorrow, he is crowned, and there shall be a feast. It is right and proper to invite our friends to such a feast. So that our friendship may prosper and grow in all the years to come."

"Where the hell have you been keeping him?" Scaffesty exploded.

"We understand he has been educated in the ways of the world," the woman explained blandly. "We look for you and your officers tomorrow, magister."

When they had gone, everyone had something to say about it, mostly all at once. Scaffesty was forced to get his sword out and bang the hilt on the table for order.

"Obviously we can't go," said a Fellow-Monitor bluntly. "It's ridiculous. They can't just make someone their king."

"I mean they can. It's the sort of thing savages do, isn't it?" someone put in.

"Wasn't there an heir, though?" One of the older officers there, a Sage-Inquirer, scratched her head. "I recall something about that. The last of the line, spirited away for safekeeping, somesuch?"

Prassel felt the answer welling up inside her. Because she was a diligent officer and had read everyone's records, and then pieced together those parts of the story that hadn't actually been set out plainly. And harboured some suspicions.

She said nothing.

"We should go with three Companies and some artillery," said one of the more hawkish officers. "Teach them their place."

"And what do the Loruthi do, exactly, when we're playing toy soldiers with the locals?" an Inquirer demanded acidly.

There was an awful silence.

"You don't suppose," someone suggested, "that they've sent people to the *Loruthi* as well, have they? To their command?"

"Of course they have," Prassel said crisply. "Because otherwise they'd have been here handing us the keys to the city and begging us to keep them safe from our mutual enemy. This is them playing both sides. Obviously." Revelling in the unaccustomed weight her new rank could lend to every word.

"Well then I suppose we *have* to go," said the old Sage-Inquirer. "Imagine if we didn't, but the Loruthi did. We have to go, and we have to make a good show of it. A better show than they do. We have to convince the Bracites they want to back us. Or at least stay out of it. It's not like they're a great military power, but they're sitting on their hands right now. If they decided to throw in with the Loruthi, we'll end up in the sea quickly enough against the two combined. And vice versa if they throw in with us. Sometimes it doesn't take a heavy hand on the scales, if they're finely balanced enough."

Scaffesty stood, signalling that the debate phase of the meeting was over. "Well then," he said. "Heads of department, dress uniforms. And make sure we bring a sizeable escort to the gates. Fellow-Invigilator Maserley, I want demons, flying if possible. Prassel, I want necromantic troops. I want to make sure we can defend ourselves if either the Bracites or the Loruthi try something. But more than that, if the Loruthi send *their* top people then I want enough of ours to carve through the city and cut the head off the snake, at which point the Bracites can take their pointy crown and shove it up their arse."

Conjuring Tricks

Hardly recognisable now, which is a useful trait in a wanted man. Wearing a dark uniform borrowed from Banders, walking like he's seen soldiers walk. The jut of his chin, that officers have, letting them cleave the world like a shark cleaves the water. Jack, come back to camp one last time.

The Fellow-Inquirer from Political Oversight left her wagon just as full of himself as he'd arrived, despite what he'd bestowed on her demons. Mother Semprellaime decided that was probably it for the night and settled up with the girls. She'd had three conjured up tonight, and busy. There was a curious mood in the camp. The majority of her clients had been officers, scarcely a John of lower than Companion rank. A delegation was being organised for tomorrow evening and everyone who was anyone wanted to be on it. She'd listened in to a lot of bitching from those excluded and ambition-talk from those who'd scored a place. Most of Higher Orders seemed to be jockeying for it, certainly. It wasn't often that a Pal got invited to a royal reception. Mother Semprellaime would advise the new king of Bracinta to count the spoons, honestly.

Her demons stood there, their shapes slowly melting off them. A working girl from the Realms Below could be shaped to fit the dreams of her mark, that was part of the art. They'd been wives and sweethearts, fantasies, sometimes monsters. They fed off the living essence of the men, off the world they were called into, off the magic that Mother Semprellaime put into their summoning. They fed off a reprieve from Below, where things were worse.

Each took her due, a final gift from the world, a lingering connection that would allow her to find them, rather than just casting a broad net and ending up with enslaved dross from the Kings. And was it better, this service rather than that? She told herself it was and didn't look too carefully under each stone as she turned it over.

And, of course, once the girls were gone and she'd started taking her face off, there came another knock. She coughed, made her voice old, said, "Tomorrow, come tomorrow. No more tonight. The circle is empty."

More quiet knocking, not the loud rap of an officious senior officer or the provosts. And she paused, somehow cued as to who it was. Bundling herself up in her coat so she could let a slice of her face appear in the crack of the door without giving away her cover.

"*Jack?*" She hurried him inside quickly, before anyone could patrol past and pay undue attention. "How are you here? They said you'd run. They're going to hunt you down, they said." And that was revealing that she'd been interested enough to ask. That she'd been worried for him. Not something a woman in her position should show, really, but he was Jack. He was the world's most harmless man.

"Banders snuck me in," he explained. "I need your help."

She gave him a look. "Do I need to warm up the circle?"

"No! Not that. I need to consult. An expert. You. Just a few questions. About how it works."

"Caeleen again?"

Something fractured in his face and was hastily repaired. She felt bitterly sad for a moment and then went and pragmatically put some water on the boil for tea. "Jack, Maserley doesn't need any more reason to kill you."

"So you're saying there's nothing to lose then?" His smile was terribly fragile. "She said she can't live without a contract. There's no way…?"

"Oh she can, just not here. Below. And you can bet that there's a clause that sends her right back into the hands of the Kings so they can sell her again. She's high value, for a demon. You could almost take her for human, hm?" Stealing a look at him as she sifted the leaves into the strainers. "Do you think she feels for you?"

"I don't know. I can't control that. I only know what I feel," he told her.

"And if you feel that because she made you, and if she made you, it's because Maserley told her to?"

"Then I owe him a drink because I have never felt like this for anyone in my life. What happens if Maserley's dead?"

Her hands stilled on the cups. "Jack—"

"Hypothetically."

"Probably it's the same as if there's no contract. Straight back home. Sometimes there's a clause to assign service to someone else." And, seeing his sudden leap of hope, she shook her head. "I wouldn't believe it of Maserley. Not like him to care what happens after he's dead. Especially with her. She's not a military asset. The usual boilerplate won't apply. She's *his*. And besides, you're going to kill Maserley?"

"I didn't say that." He took the steaming cup from her, failed to hold her gaze and looked down. "I guess not. I mean, not that I could anyway. But no."

She sat down opposite him, feeling for once exactly as old as she pretended to be. "Jack, look at me. I trained in Allor to be a votaress. A sacred intermediary between worlds, formalising agreements for the benefit of my people. And now I'm a bawd for the Palleseen army because they invaded and smashed all that."

"What's your point?"

"Sometimes you can't have things."

He sipped the tea, sighed, fidgeted, went to speak and reconsidered, sipped again. A man with something to say who was finding it hard.

"I don't want to have her," he said. And, because she gave him a very old-fashioned look, "Oh I *want*. Damn me but I *want*. I bloody ache with it. Never wanted anything as much in my life. But not to *own* her. Not like he does. But I want her to be free of him. And to stay where she wants to be. Look, I've got a… another hypothetical for you, please. It's going to sound really stupid, but I imagine you're used to that by now, from me."

She looked at him through the steam. When he'd asked her, she considered that it was a very stupid question. Not even the most tyro conjurer would have asked it. Obviously not a scenario that would ever come up in the trade. Which meant she had to think really quite hard about what would happen, and couldn't really give him a definite answer.

"But even then," she said, "it won't help you with this. I mean, the contract is already drawn up. Between the Kings and Maserley and Caeleen. The ink was dry years ago."

Jack drained his cup. "Where does he keep his contracts?"

"Jack it doesn't *work* like that!" Mother Semprellaime was working hard to keep her voice low. "You can't just go in with a pencil and scribble stuff out."

"Where, please."

She pulled off her wax nose in frustration, perilously close to throwing it at him. "His military ones? A strongbox in his tent, no doubt. But *hers*? On his person, I guarantee it. Jack, you can't kill him but he can kill you, and take his time over it too. Please don't do this."

"I swore an oath," he said, with a shrug. "And what am I for, exactly? Even God doesn't need me any more. I actually have the right to throw my life away if I want. First time ever. Nobody depending on me any more."

"Fine." She pulled off her wig, dragged hands across her face to smear all the wrinkles. "You go, Jack. Go throw it away. Just…"

"I'll take a 'good luck' if you've got one for me."

That almost got the cup thrown at him too.

Mosaic: The Feast

Bracinta is buoyed by the irresistible tide of The King, the King! *Those viziers heavily invested in there not being a king are unaccountably not present. A few might have fled, either to one foreign army or the other, or else just away with whatever portable wealth they could grab. Plenty of others didn't have the opportunity, caught elbow deep in the treasury or struggling into nondescript disguises. Just as the succession struggle of twenty years back wasn't bloodless, so the restoration has its share of dripping knives. But more discreet, not a city-wide clash of factions but a piece of surgery, the diseased organs neatly sectioned out and cast dripping to the floor.*

The coronation is a long and tedious piece of incomprehensible ritual. The Pal Higher Orders and the Loruthi command stand through it, on either side of a big dais and separated by a stand of important Bracites. Halseder is at the king's shoulder, and an old woman in the moth-eaten skin of a catwolf places the crown on the young prince's head. And then there's a torc and some chains, and rings, and a whole extra mantle, and some designs drawn on the youth's narrow chest, and a lot of poetry. Really quite a lot of poetry, so that the Pals and the Loruthi end up casting exasperated looks at each other, united for once in this small thing.

After which, Feder the Lost is King Feder of Bracinta, Fourth of His Name. Heir to a crumbling land that has been going to seed under misgovernment and the tramping of foreign armies. Armies whose stated intent at all times has been the protection of poor, leaderless Bracinta. It feels as though all Magnelei is holding its breath to see what those foreign powers will do now, even as messengers ride out of every gate to tell the rest of the kingdom to inhale deeply too.

And now the feast. And Halseder's people are stage-managing fit to be the envy of every theatrical impresario. No Pal junior officer is going to run unexpectedly into their Loruthi opposite number and start a brawl. No acerbic remark in Pel is going to be overheard and used as a *casus belli*. The two delegations are swollen with soldiers and more than capable of taking the palace if they wanted, so long as they aren't facing their rivals *and* the Bracites united. They are handled with the utmost care and delicacy and never allowed to meet. Until they file into the great royal hall, cleaned and dusted, and with all the regalia and bunting of state hastily hung. There they get to stare at one another. Two long tables, each dominating one of the long sides of the chamber, separated only by space. At the high end, on a raised platform, the king sits enthroned with his advisors, the architects of the restoration ready to dine in their places of honour. And every intelligencer, advisor and local expert on both sides is whispering in the ear of their superiors. *This* man hates *that* one, *their* family has traditionally opposed every movement of their ancestral enemy. The coalition that has placed this boy-king on the throne looks eminently fracturable. All it would take is to place the chisel very carefully, then a sharp rap with the hammer and Bracinta will shatter. The only challenge is making sure that it shatters in a way beneficial to the hands that hold the tools. You can be sure that plans are already being laid and the correct grade of chisel chosen, on both sides. Any impartial observer would already be reckoning that the newly sovereign Bracinta is in for a brief and eventful period of royal rule.

And those on either side not immediately scheming to

bring down their noble hosts are staring across that gap at the opposition, fingering the bewildering selection of cutlery that Bracite formal dining uses and thinking bloody thoughts. At some point, when one side or the other slips too far into their cups, someone will give the word. The soldiers will rush in. The Wolf Palace will see another massacre and, although most of the blood won't be local, plenty of people will be caught between the lines and that impartial observer wouldn't give much for the longevity of the king either. Give everyone a charged baton and *someone* will want to turn regicide, just for the bragging rights.

In the kitchens, Lidlet frets, because Jack's not back yet. He and Banders went to the army camp, and that was the last anyone saw of either. And Lidlet still thinks they need Jack for this, even though Jack said they didn't.

A lack of kings does not mean that the kitchens of the Wolf Palace sat empty. A succession of viziers and their special advisors – Loruthi and Pal – have dined wide on the bounty of the rudderless state. The parties, at the common expense, were legendary. Hence the royal chefs are more than equal to their task. Even after shifting over to let their new colleague work. Bracite cuisine is a complex thing of many flavours. Many dishes are too fiery for Pals or too sour for Loruthi but between the extremes is a subtle palette of delights fit for every mouth.

"Stop pacing. You're getting in the way." Tallifer sits by the big ovens. She's cold now. Mazdek went with Jack, in his box. Because she'd had a presentiment, honestly. When she and Ollery cooked up their exit, she'd seen her bony length stretched out on the ground. So after springing Jack, she'd coaxed her god into his care. So Mazdek would have someone, when she was gone. Except it was Lochiver who died, the senile clown, and somehow she lived. And now she's cold.

Lidlet has stopped pacing, and now every part of her is

fidgeting with nerves. She is here as Jack's stand-in. The rest of the faithful, Foley and the others, are still outside the city with orders to just run if they don't hear news by nightfall. Lidlet isn't convinced about this plan that Masty and Jack have thrown together, and Tallifer isn't, either.

"You could at least take off the uniform," Tallifer tells her. She's dressed as a Bracite woman, several layers of robe huddled about her. But Lidlet's worn the charcoal grey since she enlisted at seventeen. Nothing else fits her.

She starts pacing again.

In the great hall, the food begins to issue out under the ministration of a seemingly endless train of servants. The king is served first, along with his high table. Masty – his *Majesty* Feder the Fourth – looks at it without much appetite. Feeling a bit sick, honestly. This is the last thing he wanted. Under no circumstances has he been hiding royal ambitions. Oh, back then, obviously. Back when he first came to the camp, and was being held as an Important Person, he strutted about in his tiny fancy clothes and told everyone how he would be going to claim his throne and they should all address him the proper way. They were, after all, a foreign ally committed to help him return to power and punish all the bad people. Six year-old Feder shrilling orders at unamused grown men and women of Palleseen. *You shall call me 'Your Majesty!'* Which they had, but with such utter mockery and disrespect that it had slurred into *Masty*, and eventually he'd started answering to that. Eventually he'd taken refuge in it. Lost his special status. Been forgotten, as events moved on. Slipped through the cracks and become just one more Whitebelly following orders rather than giving them. There's a certain comfort in that. A lack of responsibility. That was the person Masty had discovered inside himself, when all the silks and graces had been stripped away. Someone who loved doing his duty and hated having power over others.

There are worse people to be king, maybe.

The high table starts eating, because that's how it's done. Now the weaving chains of decorated servants are very carefully placing dishes down the tables of their foreign visitors, each side of the room a perfect mirror of the other, no preference or precedence shown, and everyone served immaculately in order of seniority. Scaffesty's bowls set down at the exact same moment as the magnificently bearded Loruthi Grand Marshal across from him, and so on down the ladder of ranks to the lowliest there. Who is not overly lowly, given how exclusive this event is.

In the middle of that ladder sits Fellow-Invigilator Maserley, there by virtue of his place as head of a department of one. There's no seat for Caeleen, of course, so she stands behind his chair, utterly out of place despite her uniform. But he's keeping her close, these days. A certain oath is ringing in his ears. He doesn't trust what she and the ex-priest might get up to, even now the priest's god is – as he believes – dead.

And there's something weirdly familiar about the king. Not an afficionado of royalty, Maserley, which is why it's so odd to look on the aquiline face of Feder and think, *I know you...*

He scrabbles for the associations. This is not a man to be set above him, surely. This is an underling. A menial. Is he just finding these Bracites all a bit similar to one another, perhaps? No, it's more than that...

A stab of unease lances into him, because he *does* know the king. This man, crowned and enthroned and painted and decorated like the most ridiculous mummer, this is one of the hospital menials. He almost stands up right then and decries the man as a sham, rubbishes the whole coronation. Except there were a thousand Bracites out there who didn't complain, and it's not like they could *all* be in on something.

He frowns. He can tell that something's up, but not what. He looks up the line of his fellows towards Scaffesty and notes an empty chair.

Prassel has gone.

A bowl is placed before him but Maserley puts down his spoon, suddenly lacking appetite.

Prassel has gone to the kitchens. She's a step ahead of Maserley on the suspicion stakes and what she sees there confirms exactly what she thought.

She should just go, obviously. Go tell Old Eyeball and everyone else what's going on. This is exactly the sort of thing she can't tolerate, not now she's got her promotion and planned a future for the discipline more palatable than Stiverton's theatrics.

At the big oven, the Butcher turns to regard her, and all the Bracite chefs and kitchen staff pointedly leave a nice clear line between them. To stand there would be to ignite, given the intensity of their crossed gaze.

"Chief," says Prassel. "New job, is it?"

"Magister," the Butcher rumbles. He steps carefully away from his pots, gesturing at one of the locals to take over. Two heavy steps forwards and he rolls his shoulders like a wrestler. Prassel's hand hangs close to the little charged rod holstered at her belt.

"Or back to your old ways?" she prompts.

Ollery's smile is pure bland murder. Like it always was, under whatever expression he stretched over the top. When he picked over the wounded, when he cooked for the department, when he took his lashes from the Alder, that smile was festering under the surface. The most notorious killer of all Pallesand.

He goes for her. From still to an unstoppable force in the blink of an eye. She gets the rod from her belt but fumbles the word, and then he has her. Huge hands like the paws of a bear have her jacket. Her back hits the wall hard enough that her breath, and all the killing words it might have formed, it all goes out of her.

His great, thick fingers find her throat. She drags a knife from her belt and tries to bury it in his neck. The sheer bulk of his shoulders means she can only get his biceps, but she sinks it to the hilt there. He grunts. His fingers don't loosen, but they don't clench, either.

"Don't make me," he tells her.

"I can't let you do this."

"They're already laying the tables. Everyone's tucking in," says the Butcher. "A feast fit for a king."

"You're poisoning *Masty* too?"

The Butcher's chuckle is like tar. "Did you not see my old cruet at the top table? Only the best condiments for the King and his advisors. Remarkably fortifying, what's in those jars. And they won't drink, at the end. The real kicker's what's in the bottles. The king's *health*, eh?" He releases one hand to make a gesture, lifting a phantom cup to his lips.

Prassel stares at him. Feels the slightest relaxation in his grip and takes her chance. Rams a knee up right into the Butcher's groin and is out of his hold, past the bulk of him and out of the kitchen. Running, knife and rod left behind, but all the weapon she needs is her voice. Shoving past startled servants, mouth open, lungs full, about to bellow her prophecy of doom out of the kitchens and all the way into the feast hall.

No words come out. Barely any breath. The faintest croak. She fights, but all the air she just drew in has found a home in her and likes it there, and won't come out.

She's dizzy, and when a hand draws her back from the doorway and out of sight, she has no strength to resist it. And besides, they were all tucking in there. Pals and Loruthi watching one another like hawks, but sampling every delicacy set before them. Each side counting down until they send for their soldiers and liberate the palace from everyone except themselves.

And Prassel can only assume she's poisoned too, because there is no breath in or out of her mouth, and her vision is swimming. Except, when she lurches free of the hand on her and turns around, it's not the Butcher. It's another of her wilful subordinates. It's Alv.

Alv came back. After walking into the wilds, picking a direction and pretending the Divine City was at the end of it. Walk enough steps and she realised she was walking to nowhere. She couldn't go home. She had so offended the balance of the world, so brutalised the precepts of her mystery, that her fellow Divinati would subtract her from the universe as the only way to make right the wrong she had become.

So she was left with only one place she belonged, which no longer existed because the hospital department had torn itself apart. But the people persisted, and so she had found them.

And here she is, with one hand reaching for Prassel and the other pincered about her own throat. Clutched tight at her own windpipe, so that Prassel can't speak, can't warn anyone, can't breathe.

The necromancer's eyes bulge. She scrabbles at Alv, but there's no strength to her. When she falls, Lidlet's there to catch her. To lock her up in a storeroom where, when she wakes, she can't be in the way. Because there were worse heads of department than Fellow-Inquirer Prassel, in the end, so she's spared what happens next.

Then Alv and Lidlet return to the kitchens to find a welcome new arrival. Jack's back, along with Banders. The gang's together again. Those that lived.

The Butcher regards his arm, the rent in his shirt and the unmarked skin below. Alv dabs at the gash in her own. It's nothing. She will stretch it from here to the end of her days and it will barely register at all.

"You," Lidlet says, "are late."

"Honestly, this uniform was grand for getting into the

camp," Jack says. "Not so much the palace. Banders had to talk her jaw off to make them understand who we were. How are we doing?"

"It's done," says the Butcher, with coffin-lid finality.

In Jack's ear comes God's peevish voice. "I do not condone this in any way."

"Well we're committed. Off you go," Jack tells Him. "Who's got my clothes?"

They do him up as a Bracite servant. And he doesn't look particularly Bracite in the face, but who looks at servants anyway?

"Someone let Masty know we're all in place," he says. "His Majesty, sorry. I'm going out there. Everyone ready?" He's talking to fast, too nervously. They nod, those who still have a role to play. Ollery, Tallifer. In his head a high whine of a voice says, *Ready.*

Out in the hall, a seneschal strikes a chime, demanding quiet. Pad-footed servants circulate, bearing deserts. One of them is Jack, out of step and trying to mimic their effortless grace.

His Majesty Feder IV rises to his feet, lifting his goblet. His light voice is carried down the hall by acoustics. "My loyal subjects," he says, "my supporters, those who have restored me to my place after so long," and inwardly hating them for it, and hating himself for letting them do it. He could have walked away. He'd escaped this nonsense the once. But he had a duty, in the end, and Masty has never shirked his duties. Not a duty to this country he barely remembers, but to his friends.

"And my allies from overseas," he adds, tilting his glass down an exacting middle line that shows favour to neither side. "Those who have safeguarded my kingdom in my absence, whose fatherly advice has guided my people, what would we have done without you?" And he's speaking Pel, of course, but even the Loruthi speak Pel because they deal with many different nations and it's a language designed for ease of use. And Pel is a straightforward language, and so the King's words cannot possibly hint at the two armies that have been scouring vast tracts of his kingdom to corrupted mud, after spending two decades robbing it blind.

"There is a toast amongst my people," Masty lies, given that they're not really his people any more and it isn't one of their toasts anyway. "Think only on this, my friends. That we are grateful for the blessings and aid of strangers." He and Jack spent an age on the wording, and so the words sound flat and meaningless to him.

On Jack's shoulder, God scoffs. "A travesty," He says. "I have never seen such a mockery of My rites. I am done with you, Yasnic. This is the last straw."

"Yes, yes." Jack watches them drink, high table and low, Loruthi and Pal. And some of them murmured the toast with the king, but all of them at least had the words in their head. He's been reading the *Loopholes* himself. He reckons it just about counts.

Then he's at Maserley's elbow. The man hasn't lifted his goblet, Jack sees, and that might be a problem. Jack tops up the receptacle of the man at Maserley's elbow, and murmurs. "I haven't forgotten my oath."

The demonist jolts in his chair and cranes round incredulously at him, for a moment just seeing another servant, impossibly impertinent. Then recognising him, eyes going wide. With fury, with outrage. With fear, perhaps, just a little.

"And what," he hisses back, "will you do with your oath?" Abruptly he's on his feet, heedless of propriety. "You, move up," he tells the man on his right. "Get them all to move up. Do it!"

Because Prassel's seat remains empty, they can shift up one. And the man beside him obviously thinks he's going to get Caeleen nestled in beside him, and doesn't mind that in the least. Instead, though, he gets Jack dragged down into the vacated seat, and Maserley has a rod in his hand, held under the level of the table.

"You stay right here, Maric Jack," the demonist says. "You stay here and enjoy the show, and then I'll march you right back to camp and we'll pick up where we left off, shall we?"

Jack shrugs, sits, even samples the wine if Maserley isn't going to. His heart is hammering. He forces his eyes not to follow little suggestions of movement.. A flick of antennae as something burrows away, seeking the right host to lay its much-reduced eggs of chaos in.

"Now, my friends," calls the king, "I have asked you here in thanks for your nations' invaluable aid over these turbulent years, yes, but also to speak about the future. The future of my nation. The future of your armies. I would like to introduce you to my negotiators, who will explain to you your new position."

Both parties are very tense. That the young king would try to flex his puny muscles was expected, certainly. They each have an army. The king has, at best, a rabble of militia, poorly armed and untrained. Bracinta will not be dictating to either of the two global powers squabbling over it. But let the boy enjoy his day on the throne. He threw a good feast, after all. To shut him down now would be rude, whereas to dethrone or make a puppet of him tomorrow will just be statecraft.

The negotiators enter. They are none of them Bracite. In fact, two of them are Pals in uniform and one is some other breed of foreigner. An old Jarokiri woman done up like a local. The Loruthi are already unsettled, those two uniforms preparing them for the worst. But, as it turns out, they have no idea what the worst actually is.

"Listen to me," says Tallifer, "I'm not talking to Pallesand or Lor. I'm not even talking to the soldiers out in the camps, or the soldiers in the city. I'm talking to you, magisters. You senior officers, the great men and women of the war. A very personal message." She looks them over. She can only guess, with the Loruthi, but they've got Scaffesty and most of his staff, a representative selection of Higher Orders. And obviously neither side would have brought their entire command, but enough of the heads of both snakes has come in through the palace doors. "You're all dead," she tells them, with considerable glee.

They stare at her, and at each other, and don't really understand.

"My name is Ollery," says the Butcher. "I am the Butcher of Revelation House."

The Loruthi are blank. So are half the Pals. The other half are troubled by old recollection. An event so ghastly, so unthinkable, that it was the only topic of conversation across all the Archipelago a decade and a half ago. A few of them suddenly put down their cups, far too late.

"The substance in question," the Butcher goes on, "is a blend of my own. The same as I am known for, only four times the concentration. A mercy, really. You want to go swift, when you've had that. You don't want to linger."

Which begs a question, obviously. And there is an uproar of angry military personnel asking it, of him and each other and the universe general. Nobody is dead. Hence, nobody has been fatally poisoned by the Butcher of Revelation House. This is all some peculiar Bracite entertainment and any moment now the jugglers will come in and everyone will applaud.

"You are all blessed, magisters," says Lidlet. God is with her now, having abandoned Jack in disgust. He sits, visible only to the two of them, thin arms folded, scowling at everything. "The blessing has saved you from the poison even before it could act on you. You're saved." And this makes it sound even more like some bizarre ritual exchange, an ancient Bracite mystery play as baffling and opaque as all that poetry. "But there is a condition." And the servants are passing round again, and each of the long tables gets a couple of copies of *The Ninety-Seven Loopholes*. Because it's only fair they know the rules.

"If you do harm," Lidlet announces. "If you take any action

that would lead to harm, an order, a gesture, then the blessing will be withdrawn from you. And you get the poison back." And she opens her arms, an inviting target. She knows her own people well enough. There's always some mid-ranker who got there through family and not capability, and thinks they know better.

In this case it's a Fellow-Broker on Scaffesty's staff who stands up and snaps, "That's enough from you, deserter!" Dragging a rod from his belt and discharging it straight at Lidlet. And that's utter chaos because everyone's armed and everyone came here expecting treachery and both delegations are leaping up and fumbling for their weapons. And stopping. Staring.

Lidlet was shot. They all saw that. The charred rosette in her jacket stands mute testimony to it. She went down to one knee, though she's standing again now. The Fellow-Broker is not. He's lying across the table, red froth at his lips, writhing, spasming, the rod springing from his fingers to ring against a soup tureen. Kicking, gurgling in his own blood, eyes standing out from his head like there's a thumb behind each one of them, tongue black and blistering between his lips. And dead, and the Butcher makes a clearly audible *tsk* sound, like next time he'll up the dose a little because that took longer than he liked.

"Does anybody else want a go?" Lidlet asks them. She still has her arms out. The smile she was trying for has slipped somewhat because of what they've all just watched, but she's committed to her part.

"Any harm," Tallifer takes up. "Any of you. Write an order, delegate, weasel it however you want." She takes great pleasure in drawing a thin finger across her throat.

And Scaffesty says, into the silence that follows, "But we're officers, commanding an army. In a war."

"Good luck with that," she says. "You might want to start ordering some retreats. I imagine you can do that." And it's not like they've killed the war stone dead, but they've most certainly put the boot into its groin hard enough to make it catch its breath and take stock. And perhaps cooler heads might prevail, and perhaps Bracinta will get the chance to pick itself up, and perhaps something else might come along, in that pause, that will make the resumption of hostilities less attractive to the great powers. Or perhaps not, but they've done all they can.

"Enough!" Maserley stands, a man who didn't eat or drink the wine finding himself in a roomful of enforced pacifists. He has his own rod, and he has a hand on Jack's shoulder, and his moment has finally arrived. "I am walking out of here now, with this man," he announces to all and sundry. "I am going to our soldiers, the ones bivouacked outside the palace. I will explain to them precisely what treachery has transpired here, and then we will execute every last one of you, Bracite and Loruthi both. Unless there's anyone over there who didn't drink? No?" His smile is brilliant, the one bright spot in the room. "Well then, it appears to be my game. Come on." And he hauls the unresisting Jack to his feet and gets halfway down the table before Caeleen says, "Come back."

He comes back. He's not entirely sure why. "With me," he tells her. "Now."

She regards him. "On your knees," she says, before the whole assembled muster.

Maserley kneels down like his legs aren't his own. "How dare—"

"Bark," Caeleen says. "Like dogs do."

"*Woof*," says Maserley. He's not very good at it. It's not something he's had to do before. Towards the end of the table a junior aide breaks into an involuntary guffaw before clamping her hands to her mouth. It's only a shame Prassel is locked up right now. She'd love this.

After he's done barking, not very much like a dog, Maserley manages to get out, "How?" But Caeleen isn't done with him.

"Go home," she tells him, and he just has time to understand. The expression of horror and misery on his face will stay with everyone there a long time.

He turns to run, but even in that he's doing what he's told. He flees but it's as though there's a vast abyss of distance that exists just for Maserley. A great horizon that he recedes towards, some dark and hideous land, twisted in a way that offends the eye. And blazing, because everyone knows the Realms Below burn forever. And then Maserley is gone.

Zenotheus crawls back into Jack's box to warm itself by Mazdek. To find a corner well away from the slumbering lump that is Sturge. And there's very little that the least agent of chaos in the world can really accomplish. But switching two names on a piece of paper is just about within its gift. Names positioned to denote *master* and *servant* in a contract, let's say.

Maserley will be a grand prize for the Kings Below. They'll keep him a long time. They'll make sure he lives, although he won't enjoy it. But Caeleen, being a demon, can't be expected to feel overly sympathetic.

After all that excitement, it's Masty's turn again.

"You will want to return to your followers, of course," he tells all assembled. "You will want to be very careful about just what you tell them. Perhaps you will step aside for men still capable of continuing the war. That would be the selfless and dutiful step. It depends on how you value your own careers and positions. I'm sure both your governments will still honour and value officers who can't give the order to advance any more. Or you could go. Fall back from my city. Cease to ravage my countryside and my people. And send your ambassadors and diplomats. I will be happy to receive them. Although I would counsel against instructing any assassins, for obvious reasons. Even an agent provocateur might be too much. I'm sure you'll work out the boundaries of your situation by trial and error." He nods towards the twisted corpse of the Fellow-Broker.

One by one the guests begin to file out of the grand hall, looking sick, barely daring to jostle each other or tread on the wrong toe, just in case.

Those Who Live, And Are Free

King Feder IV of Bracinta (ruled 1401–1405 Bracintan Calendar), the 'Quiet King'. His reign, marred by factionalism and dissent, is noted for attempts to modernise the capabilities of the kingdom in the face of both foreign interference and domestic unrest.

When Masty appeared, it was without crown, robes or entourage, just a slight young man in Palleseen uniform shirtsleeves. Banders, who had been twitching her thumbs with anxiety, let out a full-on whoop of relief.

"It's you! About damn time. You got your bag packed?"

Masty just looked at her, at all of them. "I just," he said, haltingly, "thought it would be good. To wear the clothes again. Just the once. The stuff they've got me done up in, it's, it's not intended for *wearing*. If you understand me. More sort of being seen in."

"Balls to it," Banders tried. "Come on. Race you back to camp."

"Banders, no."

"Don't make me go back just me and *her*. Someone's going to kill someone. You skipped out on them before."

"I hadn't promised them, before."

"Balls to your promise as well," she said flatly. "Come on, Masty. We're your people. We're like family."

"They killed my family," said Masty.

"Yeah, I get that, and you are milking it a bit. And all the more reason to come with us. I mean, fine, a whole bunch of High Command saw you in the get-up, but it's the get-up they saw. They'll never know you."

"Banders, I made a promise. To do my duty. To the nation. I don't want to. I don't really think kings are a terribly good way of doing anything. But they need me, especially now we've done what we did. There's nobody else."

Banders blinked rapidly. "Masty, man. It's just going to be me. Just me. I mean, Cosserby, they got him, right? And everyone else is sodding off. It's just me and her. I don't want that."

"You don't have to go," he pointed out. "Stay here. I'll make you… I don't know. What does a castellan do? You could be one of those."

"I can't, man. I… the army's all I've got." And Jack recalled she'd been very careful about not being seen, at the feast. Yes, she was a part of the ill-fated hospital, but they'd already demoted her off the bottom of the rank ladder, so what could they do exactly?

"Go to Thurrel," Jack suggested to her. "You and him. He'll need someone who knows what his new brief is."

"Be his little cult goblin, you mean?" she asked bitterly.

"You'll make a lovely cult goblin," Masty said faintly.

"Screw you," she told him, and hugged him fiercely, then punched him in the arm. And just as well he'd slipped away without attendants or there'd have been a diplomatic incident to answer for.

Then it was time for a different parting. Lidlet was heading out too, going to regroup with Foley and all the others who'd taken God's hard bargain rather than die.

"We've got it planned out," she told him, as though he was a superior officer she had to report to. "Where the Gallete ports are, where the other forces are. Nobody going back to Forthright, because they know our faces, but we're heading everywhere else, here and back across the sea." She had her chin stuck out pugnaciously as though waiting for him to forbid it. "Masty's writ gets us past the locals, and I reckon we can blag our way into any camp that's not actively locked down."

"This isn't going to go well," Jack told her.

"Expert, are you?" She had her hands on her hips, head cocked, overdoing the defiance because, he guessed, she was very scared indeed. "We're doing what you should have been doing all your life, Jack. We're going to spread the word. We're going to save lives. Teach the *Loopholes*. Sell insurance, even. By the time Higher Orders or the Commission are onto us, half the soldiers of the Sway will have God in their back pocket for when they take a hit."

"This is not bloody dignified," God grumbled. "Bloody *insurance*. This is not respect."

"But you're going with them," Jack clarified.

"Oh you can't wait to get rid of me, eh? Bastard ingrate. You and your disgusting pagan menagerie. It's like a zoological garden in there now. That slug thing stinks!"

Jack just looked at Him, until God's lip trembled and He said, "What'll you do? When I'm not there to look after you?"

"No idea," Jack admitted. "Live until they get me. Go into the Wood maybe. Smuggle gods. I'd say it's a living, but nobody's paid me for it yet. I'll stick with the others, at first. Until we get somewhere we've got options. I imagine we'll break up, after that. Find our own ways. And you, though? You're Lidlet's god now? You're a *Pal* god?"

"Underground secret cult," God said. "I never did that before. Sounds racy, doesn't it? Makes me dangerous and revolutionary." He shrugged tired, old shoulders. Though not as old as before, maybe. A few more dark hairs in the matted beard, a few less wrinkles on the face. "The God of used-up soldiers, who'd have thought?"

"Kosha would have been proud," Jack said.

"Screw Kosha."

"I'm proud too."

"Screw you as well," said God, although His voice choked a bit, saying it.

The others had their gear together. The Butcher and his boy and all their alchemical paraphernalia; Alv with almost nothing; Tallifer, with her ember of a god lurking in the sleeve of her Bracite robe. They were going away from the armies, both the armies. There had been talk of a travelling medicine show, of finding a city some place nobody was fighting and setting up a hospital for civilians. And Jack knew that wasn't for him, and he'd be no real use there either, but he could keep them company on the road until something else came up.

In the corner of the room, the final member of their little band had stood silent and stone-faced all this time. Now Banders went over and prodded her. "You ready to move?"

"Well," said Acting-Sage-Inquirer Prassel, "I hadn't thought that it was my call, what with my being your prisoner."

"Prisoner nothing," Banders told her. "All friends here, aren't we. You and me, we're heading home."

"And if I have them arrest you as a collaborator the moment we get to the pickets?"

"Then I won't be around to explain how your empty seat at the table was on account of you and me heroically trying to stop it all from happening," Banders said easily. "Instead I might have to explain how you were in on all of it, and how it's your turn in the chair after the duty Inquirer's finished with me. I mean, it does look bloody suspicious, doesn't it? You'll just have to content yourself with being literally the only senior officer in a hundred miles who can actually give a coherent order. And you know what? I reckon Higher Orders aren't talking, back at camp. I reckon what happened at dinner isn't exactly part of their regular reports home. On account of every one of them would be rated unsound and recalled for some hard questions. So I reckon you can play the lot of them like a fiddle and make the whole army your bitch. Magister."

"What, me and Thurrel and you, is it?" Prassel asked with distaste. "Is that what this has come to?"

"You don't like Thurrel all of a sudden?"

"Let me think about it." And Prassel had a hounded look, but Jack reckoned he could see the seeds of ambition in there, too. And there were worse people than Prassel to be pulling the strings. Probably.

And that was the pair of them heading out, back to the army and all the pieces that nobody else would be able to pick up. *And I'll probably never even know how that turns out.*

Lidlet left next, which meant that God left too. And Jack stood at a high window of the palace, watching her stride off, Bracite robe over Pal uniform, and God on her shoulder like an ill-trained monkey. A brief flash of off-white head as the little face tilted back and up towards him. But no waving, because God was mean. And Lidlet had a stomping stride and God had to hold on. And that was Jack's faith out the door and walking away, and he knew that, even bound to its precepts as he was, and smuggle all the gods there were, he'd never be the same man. He felt like the opened chrysalis that a new religion had hatched from and abandoned.

Outside in the courtyard, his four travelling companions were ready, stomping and pacing like horses keen to be given their head. Time for Jack to go, too.

He turned. Caeleen was right behind him, robe over uniform just like Lidlet. He felt something clench inside him. Desire and longing and all the things he'd ever denied himself.

The day held its breath. Or he did, at least.

"I don't know what to do," she said. "I've got the world. The whole world to be wicked in. I'm the master. Nobody's chains are on me. And I don't know what to do." Her voice was still sly, her face composed. Her hands twitched, fingers drumming at her thumbs. "So I thought, why not go with Jack? He won't turn me away, will he? While I work out how I'm going to ruin everything for everyone. Like demons do."

A lot of words turned up in his head, then, and some of them florid enough that the Bracite poets would have looked down their noses at him. They tangled like hooks and wire in his mouth and he couldn't get a one of them out. He didn't want to breathe, in case the moment broke.

He put out a hand, and she took it, and together they went down to join the others.

Acknowledgements

Years ago there was a panel at one convention or other discussing magical healing and its relatively infrequent use in fiction. I want to thank the unsung heroes who scheduled and appeared on that panel, because that was where the first germ of this book originated.